SPECTRUM:
DETOUR OF WRONG

JILL THRUSSELL

ISBN: 1999955307

ISBN-13: 978 1999955304

CONTENTS

The Creation

The basement laboratory was extremely quiet as darkness started to slowly creep into the building through the small rectangular window in one of its concrete walls and as the blackness started to wrap it arms around the room, Leah sat in the semi-darkness as she tinkered around with several technological gadgets and her computer in total silence. Particles of blackness from the night continued to silently seep into every nook and cranny of the basement as Leah worked as she completely ignored the entrance of the night and the darkness it brought along with it which gradually clung to every single corner of the underground space and slipped into every crevice and crack as the final remnants of the day were silently chased away. Some deep internal considerations were thoughtfully engaged in however as Leah performed her technical tasks as to her professional choices as she silently considered the life and profession that she had chosen and then pursued with every ounce of her being.

Throughout Leah's undergraduate years she had opted to follow the passions that she had been drawn in life to as she'd accepted the extremely long hours and dedicated herself tirelessly to her chosen profession but the lack of glamorous attire which mainly composed of white lab coats and plain white tunics certainly weren't what one might consider elegant. Life as a technological scientist was a far cry from some of the other much more glamorous careers, professions and vocations that many of Leah's female friends had sought to pursue and she definitely knew it.

Hopefully however, quite soon Leah hoped, all her sacrifices would be worth it and her goals would be fully realized because a breakthrough was definitely headed her way and although at the moment, she sat quite delicately balanced on the verge of success as she waited for it to manifest itself in reality, it was definitely close by. Achievement and success seemed to tease Leah's mind and body, almost like invisible wisps of wind as she worked and as she made a few adjustments to some codes that sense of achievement even began to tickle the tips of her fingertips and made her skin tingle in eager anticipation but somehow, actual completion kept itself just beyond her reach which slightly irritated her.

Rather frustratingly for Leah, the completion of Spectrum was now situated just a few steps away from where she currently sat and as that completion lurked upon the not too distant horizon of her professional life, it seemed to tease her mind each day as it drove her to work harder and harder and she strove for longer and longer to realize her goal. For the past month Leah had existed in what seemed to be a state of total frustration because Spectrum's completion had lain just outside her grasp and somehow, achievement seemed to gently mock her and tug away at her thoughts each day, just to remind her how near it actually was but rather frustratingly, it could not yet be reached. Incomplete tasks would suddenly come to Leah's attention, mount up and then achievement would be deferred again as it would rather strangely, abruptly disappear from the forefront of her mind, chased away by her increased workload and the vision of perfection that she aspired to realize which rather frustratingly, silently eluded her.

A gentle sigh escaped from Leah's lips as she shook her head in total frustration because although success had danced through her thoughts every day for the past month, success wouldn't it seemed, allow her to join in the actual celebration and imperfection after imperfection had continued to present themselves to her and those professional hurdles had silently taunted her mind. Each imperfection and professional hurdle had challenged Leah to drive forward and strive harder but still Spectrum's completion lay just outside her reach and she had not yet arrived at her intended destination which was technical completion and construction of the Spectrum prototype. Total satisfaction was very frustratingly, a destination that Leah hadn't quite managed to arrive at yet and although she had definitely put in the additional hours for the past month and the extra intellectual effort that had been required, Spectrum's completion still remained, unrealized and her prototype unfinished.

Somehow, it now felt to Leah as if the final work on Spectrum had become an actual contradiction in itself because it seemed that the closer she came to actual completion, the further away she found herself from the realization of her goal because tiny imperfections would be discovered and then niggle away inside her thoughts, until each one had been properly corrected and fully perfected. At times, Leah's progress on Spectrum actually reminded her a bit of a greyhound in pursuit of an elusive electric rabbit at the races that it would never actually catch because her pursuit to complete Spectrum had recently become a major source of frustration to her and every working day, she seemed to take another step backwards as each imperfection was uncovered and discovered.

"At least I have a quiet basement to work in." Leah thoughtfully reminded herself as she released a tired sigh and then glanced around the room which was now almost pitch black due to the entrance of the night. "Things could have been much worse, I might have had to work in a corporate laboratory every day that was littered with people and riddled with lots of distractions and then I'd have been pulled around from project to project and I would have got absolutely nothing done at all."

Essentially, the basement area of Leah's home had pretty much been her home for the past month because it had been converted into a technological, scientific laboratory solely for her use several years ago and inside that space, she could perform the scientific and technology tasks that related to Spectrum in solitude with minimal distractions and absolutely no disturbances. The underground laboratory certainly wasn't huge or very well equipped by any stretch of the imagination but it was definitely accessible to Leah at any time which meant, she could work there day or night which really helped because her current working hours really weren't sociable, or even very consistently structured.

Truthfully, Leah quietly considered as she visually inspected her allocated workspace, the basement laboratory that she worked in each day really wasn't much to look at, in comparison to some larger, far better equipped corporate laboratories but it was definitely all her own and the convenience of its location, inside the couple's home, at times, really helped. Regarding the technical facilities available to Leah inside the basement, her equipment certainly wouldn't be considered state of the art by anyone in Leah's field but Zidane her partner had kindly helped her to renovate the basement and then had assisted to fully equip it so that it would be suitable for the purposes for which she'd intended and it definitely sufficed.

Several glossy white worktops had been adorned with various pieces of scientific and technological equipment and a huge wafer thin television screen clung silently to one of the basement walls and those were some of the features inside Leah's laboratory but none of those objects were actually, the main attraction. Tucked neatly away underneath one of the glossy white worktops there was a small black fridge that usually contained a few liquid and edible necessities and on the worktop directly above it, there was even a hotplate warmer that Leah herself had invented which she could utilize to heat up a meal whenever she wished to but those were not the main highlights of the basement laboratory either, or the main focus of the work that she actually performed there.

Situated upon a small platform in the very center of the basement, there was a body sized, transparent capsule that had been specifically designed to house the Spectrum system and that was the main feature of not only the basement but also the main product of Leah's years of tireless efforts, diligent hard-work and devoted professional dedication. A small microchip in the capsule's smooth surfaces governed how Spectrum actually functioned which allowed it to operate and Leah's first major invention that she had formulated, designed and created herself, was the real highlight of the basement and the product of all her professional efforts from the past few years.

A small window situated in one of the basement walls let in just enough rays of light or shadows of darkness to let Leah know roughly what time of day or night it was and there were also some electric lights which could shine brightly or be dimmed inside the basement itself that she could utilize, if and when required. The laboratory wasn't particularly well equipped but it did accommodate and fully facilitate every aspect of Leah's work and although her surroundings certainly weren't lavish and or what one might consider luxurious, she appreciated that at the very least, the basement was her own professional space and that provided her with a degree of professional freedom.

Despite the fact that the basement was situated directly below the couple's main residence, in recent times, the underground space had almost become as familiar to Leah as the lounge because she had spent the greater part of her days inside it in order to chase her elusive professional goal which was namely, completion of the Spectrum prototype. Ever since Leah had completed her first research post, just a few years ago which she had started straight after she'd graduated, she had worked diligently and tirelessly towards the creation and development of Spectrum, her ground-breaking invention and now, she'd almost reached her goal.

Due to the technical complexities of Spectrum, a tremendous portion of devotion had been required from Leah and it had truly been a labor of love as she had nurtured her creation and attempted to breathe some life into it as she'd sought to combine her scientific and technological knowledge in a manner that would be commercially viable. The potential completion of the Spectrum prototype itself excited Leah immensely because it would be the physical manifestation of her very own research work which was something that many technological scientists and even many scientists in general, often yearned to achieve but rarely managed to realize in reality and that potential achievement had driven Leah towards her goal because that completion, really would be such a huge professional achievement for her.

Usually as Leah was fully aware, most scientists predominantly worked on other people's research projects for either corporate or scientific entities and it was extremely rare that they would ever have the chance, or the resources to actually work on their own creations or inventions. Occasionally, if those in Leah's field were fortunate enough to receive a development grant that financial support would then allow them to pursue their own projects but only a few were lucky enough to be in that actual position and so in many ways, Leah actually felt, quite privileged.

Since Leah's chosen area of specialization was really quite unique because she had chosen to pursue a combination of both science and technology that had meant that research development grants for such specialist areas of work, were even harder to secure and even rarer to come by. A quite moderate grant had however in the end, finally been secured from a prestigious scientific research institute just after Leah's first research post had ended three years ago and although it didn't quite cover all her living expenses or even all the costs of her work, it did contribute positively towards Spectrum's development and her professional goals.

Spectrum was actually Leah's own creation, her baby and what she had striven to achieve, ever since she'd created the initial research paper and designed the prototype model five years ago and so this had very much been her own choice but as Leah now fully appreciated, a choice could at times be much harder to live up to and live with than it had initially been to make. Since Spectrum was now almost complete, for the past month Leah had worked even harder than usual as her ship of aspirations had been firmly steered towards the port of completion but because she had tottered around on the brink of realization for that entire month and had faced several professional hurdles, a tidal wave of frustration had definitely built up inside of her which now sat behind a wall of incompletion, much like a dammed up wave that waits impatiently behind a concrete wall to be released.

Some angry, hunger pangs suddenly started to erupt from the depths of Leah's stomach and as each one growled hungrily away very impatiently, she quickly glanced down at her cellphone to check the time which was situated on top of the white, glossy worktop directly in front of her. A temptation rapidly began to tease Leah's thoughts as she glanced across the room and then looked hungrily at the small black fridge and hotplate warmer inside the basement as she began to internally deliberate as to whether or not she should actually raid the fridge's interior and contents.

"I definitely need to eat something but now it's just a question of where I should eat that something, down here or upstairs." Leah whispered to herself as she gently shook her head. "Well, it is quite late now and Zidane will definitely want to eat dinner with me at some point today, since he has already waited practically all evening to do so." She thoughtfully reminded herself. "I guess I should really pack up for the night now and spend some time with him."

Irrespective of hotplate warmer's convenient location and the extremely flexible features that it offered and currently possessed as it sat on the worktop just above the fridge and silently bragged that it could heat up a meal evenly in less than a minute, another important factor definitely had to be considered by Leah and that she definitely knew. Since that factor was just as important in Leah's mind and life as the incomplete work that still had to be done upon Spectrum, it now actually seemed to obstruct her from the temptation and potential dietary satisfaction that a sudden dash towards the fridge offered to her as she started to internally consider and empathize with Zidane's position. Despite all Leah's internal considerations and deliberations however, the hungry rumbles inside her stomach didn't seem to subside and continued to keep her company as each one became louder and louder and as the noises refused to depart, the angry growls tugged away at her being until she was physically urged to surrender and so she quickly began to pack up for the night because each noisy, internal, thunderous eruption, demanded food, total compliance and immediate satisfaction.

"Time doesn't seem to care about our plans, or our individual ambitions." Leah whispered to herself thoughtfully as she released another tired sigh. "And I just can't seem to negotiate with the hours of the day, no matter how much I want to or need to."

Time as Leah already knew had definitely run out for her that day and since it was now, actually quite late, she felt completely and utterly worn out as she suddenly rose to her feet decisively and then prepared to abandon her work upon Spectrum and vacate the basement until the next morning. Rather frustratingly for Leah, a definite conundrum was indeed currently present in her life because it seemed that the closer she actually came to Spectrum's completion, the harder she had to work to realize her goal but Leah's frustration and all her hard work didn't seem to make the days last any longer and time seemed to mock her every day as it ran out before she wanted it to. Each working day, Leah wished and hoped that the conundrum which had found its way into her world and had it seemed, decided to settle there, would merely be a tourist and a visitor to her life not a permanent fixture and that total completion would one day soon, finally be actually achieved and fully realized.

"Time doesn't negotiate with anyone and time it seems, doesn't want to give me a few more hours each day." Leah acknowledged. "Which right now, I could definitely do with."

Another weary sigh escaped from Leah's lips as she began to cave in and surrender to her physical tiredness in totality as her muscles began to ache because her strive for perfection certainly wasn't easy and the hours really weren't very sociable. Rather frustratingly, every working day for the past month Leah had uncovered various small imperfections that she'd had to address, correct and tweak, some of which up until that point in time she hadn't even noticed at all and those final refinements and adjustments it had transpired had required, even more patience, focus and dedication from her than usual.

When Spectrum was finally released onto the commercial market, Leah wanted her prototype to be absolutely perfect and that was the one thing that she had always been absolutely adamant about. Consumers and commercial buyers simply wouldn't forgive any mistakes or errors in the final product as Leah already knew and they would complain about any purchase that they had made that they felt even slightly dissatisfied with and so she wanted to ensure that she did not present anyone with a less than perfect end product. Customers and consumers were not Leah's friend and they wouldn't simply smile and say, 'it's okay that Spectrum didn't work the way I expected it to because I like you' and that was one thing that Leah felt absolutely certain about.

"Time is a very stubborn companion and perfection is a very demanding friend." Leah advised herself conclusively as she glanced down at the screen of her cellphone again and then picked it up as she started to check the device for any new messages.

Perfection was a very essential component when it came to Spectrum's completion and a highly desirable outcome for Leah because her creation simply couldn't be sold, until that goal had actually been achieved. The strive for perfection had definitely had an impact upon Leah's life however because it had meant longer hours inside the basement, the consumption of meals at sporadic intervals and it had even resulted in significant delays to the actual completion of Spectrum itself. For Leah however, the delays she felt would definitely be worth it in the long run because she had to ensure that Spectrum arrived on the commercial market in the condition that she wanted it to be consumed in, since she wanted consumers to be totally happy and absolutely satisfied with the finished product but in some ways that strive for perfection now felt like it had become an actual hurdle in itself because it had been extremely hard to achieve and realize.

Usually, whenever Leah worked inside the basement, in order to avoid any potential distractions or disturbances, she would keep her cellphone on silent to ensure that no interruptions caused a lapse in her concentration but it was hardly even worth the effort since not many people called her anyway and today, absolutely no one had called her at all. One solitary, lonely unread message envelope did however, flash up on the screen of Leah's phone as it waited to be opened and as she glanced at the message envelope, it silently urged her to read it as a smile rapidly began to spread out across her face.

The single, solitary text message could only really be from one actual person in the entire world and that one person was extremely important to Leah and so she quickly opened the message and then began to read it enthusiastically. Deep down inside Leah already knew who the sender of the message actually was before she even read his name on the screen of her phone or a single word that the text message contained because that one person was totally dedicated to her life and her heart and that romantic dedication could not be faulted, since it had always been absolutely impeccable. Absolutely no introductions to the sender of the text message were required or necessary because the message was of course from Zidane, Leah's long suffering partner and the love of her life and as she read his words, she prepared to joyfully surrender to the loving request that the text message silently contained.

'When are you coming upstairs Sweetie, I miss you? I miss your smile, I miss your lips, I miss your arms and I miss your hips and I've been waiting all evening for you, very impatiently.' Zidane's text asked.

A sudden wave of joy seemed to silently wash over Leah's body as her physicality welcomed Zidane's every word and each drop of love that his message contained as she rejoiced in his positive enthusiasm, admired his tireless devotion and appreciated his total dedication to her because Zidane had been her firm pillar of steadfast support, ever since Spectrum's initial conception. In fact, since Leah had begun her work upon the Spectrum prototype three years ago Zidane seemed to both understand and respect the fact that when Leah was working down in the basement, it was far better just to send her a text message that she could respond to and answer as she wished than to disrupt her concentration with non-urgent phone calls or personal appearances and that respect for her work, encouraged Leah immensely as his message was gladly received.

Fortunately for Leah, over the past three years the couple's relationship had demanded her attention at times and that affectionate requirement had both pleasantly and politely distracted her from the very long hours inside the basement that she could so often easily become lost in as it delicately and discreetly, rebutted and dismissed the temptation to overwork. A tired brain was definitely far less competent than a fresh one and so sleep was an absolute necessity that Leah's body definitely needed, even if at times she felt quite reluctant to adhere to her own body's physical requirements and so for Zidane's devotion to her, she was truly, deeply appreciative.

Due to the nature of Leah's work and her commitment to it, there would quite often be a temptation that lurked silently inside Leah's mind which urged her to work longer hours and her relationship with Zidane not only ensured that she slept at a decent hour each night but also demanded that she maintain a healthy balance in all aspects of her life. Sometimes, the huge temptation that urged Leah to overwork in order to complete Spectrum more quickly would cause her to prolong her return to the ground floor of the couple's home on weekday nights because she was prone to work until she physically dropped, especially as she drew closer to Spectrum's actual completion. The couple's relationship and Zidane however, demanded a balance from Leah with regards to her professional and personal life that was not only healthy but also very consistent and that had perhaps saved Leah for the past few years from physical exhaustion and total burnout.

From the very first day that Leah had met Zidane, approximately six years ago, he had stolen Leah's heart successfully and ever since then he had held it totally captive with his jet black hair, soft dark brown eyes and extremely handsome face and so as far as Leah was concerned, Zidane was definitely a catch and not just in the physical sense. Fortunately for Leah, Zidane's physical attributes were not his only admirable qualities and his interior was also lavishly adorned with equally pleasing characteristics that appealed to her just as much as his physical exterior and those qualities had served their relationship very favorably over the past six years. In terms of Zidane's personality and character, he was caring, patient, devoted, tolerant and understanding and quite frankly, he really had to be for their relationship to even exist and survive at all because Leah's dedication to her work was not easy to tolerate and nor were the long hours that she'd had to invest into Spectrum.

Recently, the late working nights had almost become the norm for Leah and as she had drawn closer to Spectrum's actual completion, an even more frequent occurrence and Zidane had tolerated both the demands of Leah's work and the increase in her hours inside the basement with endless amounts of patience. In terms of Zidane's attitude towards Leah, it had always been supportive, kind and extremely tolerant and he had never complained, not even once and nor had he made any unnecessary demands for her time and attention as he'd allowed Leah to pursue and indulge in her professional desires as she wished to and humored her innovative mind.

Sometimes Leah's hours inside the basement ate very greedily into the potential time every weekday evening that the couple could spend together and so Leah often wondered how much longer Zidane would tolerate the lack of attention that her exploration of science and technology inflicted upon him on a regular basis because Spectrum really did consume so much of her time. A hopeful wish however, lay deep inside Leah's mind and heart that Zidane's patience and support would not run out before Spectrum was complete because in recent times, she really had pushed the boundaries of his love and stretched his heart out as far as it could possibly go and so now, she just hoped that his devotion to her would not break before Spectrum was finally ready to be sold.

When it came to the romantic matter of Zidane's faithfulness to Leah as far as she knew, he had never strayed and cheated on her before and every weekday evening or night, after a long day inside the basement, Leah would find him faithfully plonked on top of the sofa inside the lounge where he usually waited for her. Various television programs and games would usually be watched and played on the entertainment center throughout the weekday evenings as Zidane amused himself and waited for Leah to emerge from the basement and at times, he'd even doze off as he waited for her to resurface so that she could tend to their relationship.

Just how long that tireless devotion would continue on Zidane's part however, Leah was extremely unsure and very uncertain and so she fervently hoped that she would finish Spectrum before the sands of his patience totally ran out and evaporated into absolute nothingness because men like Zidane certainly weren't easy to find and Leah fully appreciated that reality. In every sense of the word, Zidane was the prince of Leah's heart and their land of love was a very peaceful and extremely pleasant place to reside because their kingdom had been built from the bricks of love with the tools of devotion and they had both fully committed themselves to their love, their future and to each other right from the very start.

"I'm on my way now Zidane." Leah whispered to herself as a

warm, affectionate smile spread out across her face. "So, I hope you're still awake."

Since the text message had actually been sent to Leah's phone over an hour ago as she walked towards the steps that led out of the basement and back upstairs, she hoped that Zidane had not yet dozed off because it was highly likely as Leah already knew that he would have surrendered to fatigue and sleep already. The meal that Leah's body now urgently required, she had decided in the end, would definitely have to be eaten upstairs and with Zidane because he really deserved some of her time and attention and goodness knows that day, he had certainly waited around long enough for it.

Usually each working day, Zidane would arrive home from work at around seven or eight in the evening, dependent upon his work schedule on any given day, recently however most days, he'd not seen Leah until at least ten or eleven at night. Sometimes during the past month, Leah's absences had even stretched out as far as midnight and on a couple of occasions, her hours inside the basement as she had worked upon Spectrum had even tumbled into the early hours of the next morning and she'd not come upstairs until around one or two. Despite Leah's much longer working hours in recent times however, Zidane had tolerated those very late nights with huge dollops of patience as he had amused himself and managed to keep himself company but as Leah already knew, his tolerance would not last forever because the generous chunks of Zidane's patience would one day, finally be fully consumed.

Once Leah arrived at the foot of the small flight of stairs that led up towards the ground floor, she quickly commanded Spectrum to switch itself off which happened almost immediately as the system responded swiftly to her voice commands and Leah smiled at the efficiency of the voice control system that she had invented and created for the couple's home. Deep down inside Leah definitely knew as she began to mount the steps that the couple really needed to spend some time together that night which meant, Spectrum would definitely have to wait, at least until the following morning because Zidane really couldn't and their usual weekday evening quality time was now definitely in the red and totally overdue.

Joyful enthusiasm suddenly, rapidly began to fill Leah's core and so she started to bounce up the stairs as a sudden burst of energy spurred her body on and propelled her legs to move forward more quickly towards not only the ground floor of the couple's home but also towards the lounge and even more importantly, towards the love of her life Zidane. Perhaps Zidane would be fast asleep by now, Leah considered quietly as she arrived at the top of the stairs and then stepped out into the hallway that led towards the lounge because after all, he had actually sent her that text over an hour ago and it was now almost half past ten at night.

When Leah arrived outside the entrance of the lounge, just a few seconds later, she immediately noticed that the lights were switched off and that the room actually looked rather dark and as she gingerly entered inside the room on tiptoes, she approached the back of the sofa quietly where Zidane's form was seated. Whether Zidane was still awake or fast asleep was another issue entirely and since he didn't move an inch as Leah approached him, uncertainty rapidly began to fill her mind because if he had already dozed off, she really felt quite reluctant to wake him. Sleep in Leah's mind and as far as she was concerned, was a precious luxury that had to be treasured, appreciated, savored and enjoyed whenever it possibly could be and she definitely appreciated the fact that since Zidane's working days started a lot earlier each weekday morning than her own did, he usually succumbed to tiredness during the weekday evenings far more quickly than she did.

The large, wafer thin screen that clung to one of the walls inside the lounge was still switched on and a car program was clearly displayed upon it which seemed to be all about the capabilities of motor vehicles and their engines, Leah silently observed as she drew close to the back of the sofa and then cast a quick glance towards the screen. Despite Leah's deep love for Zidane, her absolute devotion to him and her profound adoration for him, those affectionate sentiments certainly did not extend to his appreciation for motor vehicles and his love for cars which at times, really bored Leah and so she shook her head as she began to frown. Thankfully however that evening at the very least, the boring car program had managed to fully retain Zidane's attention and it had kept him happily entertained whilst Leah had been busy and absent and quite fortunately that night as she rapidly discovered, Zidane was still very much awake as he suddenly turned round and faced her.

Sometimes working quite late into the night down in the basement on Spectrum it appeared really did have some actual advantages, Leah silently concluded as she flashed Zidane a sweet smile because it meant that she didn't have to watch tedious, boring car programs with him during the weekday evenings. Nevertheless, Leah silently considered, despite the television program's very boring nature it had kept Zidane company throughout her prolonged absence that evening and so in that respect, on this particular occasion, it had been extremely useful and at times it seemed, even yucky car programs actually had their uses.

Upon Zidane's face, Leah observed, there was an affectionate smile as his crystal white teeth flashed through the darkness that surrounded him which it appeared had nearly engulfed his body and swallowed him almost whole. Darkness and the night it seemed waited for no one, Leah thoughtfully concluded because Zidane's handsome face was barely even visible to her through the blanket of blackness that surrounded him which had blanketed the whole interior of the couple's lounge. The darkness from outside had now seeped into and covered the entire lounge as it had fully embraced the couple's home and invited itself into their private abode but Zidane's shiny white teeth had somehow, still managed to shine through the dull blackness and so fortunately, Leah could still see his gorgeous, delicious smile.

For the next few seconds Leah didn't utter a single word as she just stood next to the back of the sofa for a moment and admired Zidane's physicality which really was so very fine and as her eyes grew accustomed to the darkness, the rest of his handsome physique gradually became more visible to her. The very handsome face and the hunky chunk of masculinity that made up Zidane's human form that was now situated directly in front of Leah's eyes, were definitely something to appreciate because as she knew, every part of Zidane was completely and utterly devoted to her, their relationship and to the life that they both shared and in that respect, Leah felt extremely fortunate because as she knew, life could have been so very different for them both.

In comparison to some of the other men that Leah had met and even dated prior to her relationship with Zidane as far as Leah was concerned, he was by far the most decent, truly the most dedicated, absolutely the most faithful and definitely the most handsome and it had been an easy victory on Zidane's part because he had it seemed, given his heart to Leah in all its fullness. Initially, when the two had first met, Zidane had romanced Leah whilst they had both attended the same university and he had wooed her with generous portions of charm, chivalry, generosity and grace which had also been accompanied by his external good looks and as a result, he'd won her heart over completely, almost immediately.

At first the relationship between the two had been slightly frustrated by the fact that Leah had actually been based at another campus situated at least a thirty minute drive away and also by the fact that Zidane had a part time job which had meant, they had only really been able to see each other on alternate weekends and when coursework hadn't been due. Despite the various challenges however that student life had presented to them both, Zidane had been extremely dedicated to his romantic pursuit and it had seemed as if Leah had totally captured his attention because he had persisted in that pursuit extremely faithfully and had then managed to successfully sustain a long term romance between them that even now, still stood head and shoulders above Leah's prior romantic experiences. The enthusiasm, eagerness, devotion and dedication that Zidane had initially displayed towards Leah had deeply impressed her and ever since then their relationship had remained firmly rooted to Leah's heart and as the years had gone by, the two had become virtually, romantically inseparable.

Much like a romantic spore, the couple's love had been nurtured over the years until it had begun to sprout through their devoted attention, consistent commitment and affectionate dedication to it and then their relationship had even managed to flourish, bloom and grow, due to their combined efforts which had fertilized its roots inside their hearts and provided them both with essential romantic nourishment. Somehow and despite all the tricky issues that the couple had faced in life since the start of their initial courtship, their love had not only survived but it had now also fully blossomed into a beautiful flower that adorned their hearts and filled their home with its beautiful scent of love every day and so now, Leah definitely appreciated Zidane's very stable and consistent roots of commitment that truly treasured her heart.

From the very first attempt that Zidane had made to secure Leah's heart, she had been extremely impressed because the usual dating protocols, romantic practices and culture of courtship around her university campus had been totally obliterated by his romantic efforts and so she'd succumbed to his arms willingly as she had accepted him practically straight away, with very open arms indeed. The couple had participated in some highly unusual romantic outings in the early days of their relationship and Zidane had bestowed many generous gifts upon Leah as he had paid that little bit of extra attention to her and she had definitely appreciated his very sincere, romantic efforts.

Every romantic effort that Zidane had made had been welcomed by Leah's heart because his approach and his positive attitude towards romance had differed so greatly in comparison to the usual, often very grubby, seedy drinking dates that so many of his peers had offered to the women around them that they had pursued. Usually as Leah had been fully aware at the time, those seedy, grubby drinking dates would be undertaken with any willing females that those young men had been able to lay their hands on and dates of that kind had been situated a million miles away from the kind of romance that Leah had wished for, hoped for and that she had truly wanted.

The grubby, seedy dates embarked upon by most of Zidane's male peers around that time, would usually have occurred inside the various student bars situated close to each campus where cheap alcohol would often be utilized as a lubricant to enable casual, tacky, sexual flings which would result in tears, regrets, heartbreaks and sometimes even, unplanned pregnancies but Zidane had offered

Leah a far superior alternative to those very unromantic, hopeless disasters. Unlike those awful, unromantic catastrophes that had been so prevalent among the couple's peers at the educational institute which they had both attended, Leah had been extremely relieved when Zidane had offered her not only something completely different but also something so beautifully, deliciously and joyfully, romantically superior. Although Zidane hadn't been Leah's first romance in life, or even her first romantic partner whilst in attendance at the university that they had both attended, he had definitely always been Leah's first real true love and so for six truly delightful and romantically pleasant years now, her heart had remained united with his as they had journeyed through life together.

"Are you finished in the basement now Sweetie?" Zidane suddenly asked.

Leah nodded. "For tonight yes." She replied.

"Thank goodness." Zidane said as he breathed a sigh of relief. "I thought I was going to have to move our bed down there."

"Seriously Zidane?" Leah asked.

"Yes." He replied. "Very seriously."

Leah leant over the plush cream and black leather sofa and then wrapped her arms gently around Zidane's neck as she began to whisper softly in his ear. “Are you hungry?” She asked.

“I might be. What are you offering?" Zidane teased playfully as he smiled. "Are you on the menu tonight?”

“Definitely, I'm the desert.” Leah replied flirtatiously.

"Then I'll have a double helping." Zidane joked. "No in fact, make that a triple helping."

"No problem Zidane. I can definitely provide enough portions of desert tonight to fill you right up." Leah quickly confirmed as she enthusiastically nodded her head.

Zidane smiled.

Despite the couple's playfulness and jokes however, there was one thing about which Leah could always be absolutely certain and that one very consistent factor was that Zidane's romantic intentions towards her were absolutely sincere because over the years, he had earnt not only her appreciation but also her deep respect. The very strong physical attraction that Leah felt towards Zidane had always been an additional bonus as far as she was concerned because it was so very rare to find someone that you liked physically, emotionally and psychologically but for Leah, Zidane had ticked all of those boxes and more. Usually as Leah was fully aware, a romantic partner might tick one box out of the three required areas of compatibility but to meet someone that ticked all three so naturally, was almost virtually impossible yet she had found that romantic perfection with Zidane.

Approximately six years ago, when the couple had first met, Zidane's attentiveness, serious attitude and Leah's physical attraction to him had quickly lubricated and then rapidly ushered in a romantic union between them both and Leah had never, not even once, looked back or regretted their romantic partnership because for her, it had always been and still was absolute romantic bliss. When it came to the issues of romance and passionate matters of the heart, Leah wasn't usually particularly great at making romantic choices and decisions but there was one thing that she now knew with absolute certainty, Zidane had been the one romantic choice and passionate decision that she had definitely got completely right.

Several other potential suitors had attempted to romance Leah at around the same time as Zidane and they had tried to entice her to dabble in romantic affairs with them but he had completely blown them away with his attentive efforts and his total dedication to her. Due to Zidane's absolute devotion and his positive romantic attitude towards Leah, she had therefore given Zidane the greenlight almost immediately as she'd allowed him not only to occupy her life but also to fully occupy her heart. When the two had initially met although Zidane hadn't been the only man in pursuit of Leah's heart, he had always been and still definitely was the only man that had truly managed to capture her attention and then he'd actually, fully retained it. The unusual nature of Zidane's approach to love, life and Leah had not only titillated and excited her but also totally captivated her and Zidane had managed to hold her interest firmly by the hand in the long term and so six years later, they still remained by each other's side and as much in love as they had been when they'd first met.

Irrespective of the difficulties and challenges that life had presented to the couple during their six years together, their relationship was quite simply the best romantic relationship that Leah had ever experienced in her entire life and now, much to her total delight, it was in its sixth year and still going strong. The solid rock of commitment that the couple had built their home of love upon had not only been amazingly sweet for Leah but that rock and their love filled abode had also managed to stand the test of time because Zidane had displayed a tireless amount of loyalty, commitment and devotion towards Leah that in terms of her past romantic experiences had been second to none.

A smile was present upon Leah's face as she suddenly released Zidane from her affectionate embrace and then began to walk towards the door of the lounge as she started to make her way towards the kitchen because the couple's evening meal which Leah had already prepared and cooked earlier that day had been stored inside the refrigerator and so now, it was almost ready to be consumed. Inside the couple's home the kitchen was situated in another room directly opposite the lounge which meant, Leah had to actually leave the lounge in order to access dinner and then return to the lounge to eat it because the lounge also served as a dining room since a large area at one end of it accommodated a dining table and chairs and that was where the couple usually ate their evening meal together most evenings.

Earlier that day Leah had actually prepared the couple's evening meal which meant, there really wasn't much left for her to do now because all she had to do was heat the food up inside the hotplate warmers in the kitchen and so her visit to the kitchen that night fortunately for Leah, would not require any laborious effort on her part. In order to make the couple's life slightly easier Leah had designed and then built some hotplate warmers for their home and although the contraptions were another one of her scientific creations, in terms of their size and structure each contraption was far smaller and had been much simpler to make than Spectrum and so that task hadn't taken Leah several laborious years to achieve.

Once Leah stepped inside the kitchen, she immediately approached the refrigerator and then she began to serve up two generous helpings of the sweet potato chips, cobs of sweetcorn and the two racks of sweet, smoked, sticky barbeque ribs that she had prepared earlier that day which she placed quite clumsily upon two plates. When Leah felt that each plate had been sufficiently populated with enough morsels of food, she then approached the two hotplate warmers situated upon one of the kitchen worktops and placed the two now full plates inside the contraptions.

The responsibility of cooking each day was generally something that the couple had always shared, along with the duties of shopping and cleaning the house each week because Zidane was very much in tune with the needs of the household and his positive attitude towards their home had always pleased Leah but that day, since it was a weekday, she had assumed the culinary responsibility. Ever since Leah had been at home throughout the week as she had worked on Spectrum full time, she'd taken on a lot more of the household duties on weekdays, not because she had to but simply because she'd wanted to due to Zidane's external work commitments.

Usually throughout the weekends and even sometimes during the week, Zidane would enthusiastically contribute to the household chores and culinary duties because he was very much a modern man in terms of his mindset and fortunately for Leah, he wasn't scared of the kitchen or the cooker in any way, shape or form. In fact that was one thing that had always absolutely delighted Leah about Zidane, because not only was he very much in tune with the actual needs of their household but also with her own needs as a woman which not every man was and that Leah already knew, for absolute certain.

From Leah's point of view, Zidane's positive attitude towards their home had really refreshed her when they had initially moved in together five years ago because he absolutely never ever shirked, or tried to avoid any domestic household related duties, much to Leah's relief. Routine tasks that the couple both knew, definitely had to be performed every day or each week were tended to and contributed to on a regular basis by Zidane voluntarily and Leah never ever had to ask him or plead with him to do anything around the house which made her life slightly easier. Every single weekend Zidane would attempt to cook the couple at least one evening meal and at least one lunch and he actively sought to keep their home tidy, organized and clean which pleased Leah no end because his responsible attitude was like a breath of fresh air.

Prior to the couple's relationship and romantic partnership Leah had often feared and dreaded the possibility of being in a serious committed relationship with a man that might be totally chauvinistic who might see household duties as purely Leah's responsibility but Zidane had absolutely squashed those fears with his positive attitude and his willing hands. Some deep seeded fears had definitely lurked in the corners of Leah's mind about men and their lack of interest in the home which had originated from some of the negative things that her mother had warned her about in her youth which had related to men's attitudes towards women but fortunately for Leah, Zidane had always rebutted any possible manifestations of negativity directly through his positive actions which had not only challenged each fear head on but also laid them to rest.

When it came to the actual issue of the daily maintenance of the couple's home Zidane had always approached such matters with joyful enthusiasm and a very willing spirit which had been a total relief to Leah because that meant, he didn't see her purely as a live-in house maid and that he truly saw their relationship as a romantic partnership. Despite those initial negative reservations that had lain buried deep inside Leah's mind, Zidane had immediately expelled every single negative possibility when the couple had moved in together because he had mucked in voluntarily and so Leah had rapidly discovered that not all the negative things that her mother had told her about men were true and that some men did cook and clean and that some men even, actually washed the dishes.

Due to the shifts that Zidane worked every weekday which started very early in the morning, by the time he normally arrived home each weekday evening he would be completely worn out and physically exhausted from his long day at work and so Leah always tried to support him as best she could. Since Zidane had supported Leah's professional aspirations financially for the past three years which had allowed her to stay at home in order to focus and work upon her creation Spectrum full time, Leah had therefore decided to take full responsibility for the preparation of the couple's evening meal each day during the week and also that she would perform any required household chores, so that Zidane would not have to physically exert himself any further when he returned home from work. Life for Leah during the week was generally much more relaxed than it was for Zidane in that she didn't have to wake up very early every weekday morning to go anywhere important, or even to go anywhere at all and so she had taken his external work commitments into consideration and had attempted to accommodate his employment responsibilities.

The weekday household commitments which involved the preparation of the couple's evening meal each day and the assumption of responsibility for the performance of any required household chores had been easy commitments for Leah to make because she simply worked inside her makeshift laboratory in the basement every weekday and both tasks rarely took her more than a couple of hours. Essentially as far as Leah was concerned, the weekday routine that she had committed to not only suited the couple's schedules but also made perfect sense to them both and so it was a commitment she had made easily and a responsibility that she felt totally at peace with.

A satisfied smile crossed Leah's face as she glanced at the two hotplate warmers that sat upon the black kitchen worktop directly in front of her as the contraptions heated up the plates of food that had been placed inside each one and as the warmers nestled gently against one of the kitchen walls, the contraptions began to invoke some fond memories inside Leah's mind. Just after graduation the hotplate contraptions had been Leah's very first invention and they could be described as a cross between a microwave, grill and oven but the major difference was that each warmer heated up every item of food placed inside it perfectly and evenly, without any kind of human intervention at all. Once a plate of food had been placed inside one of the contraptions, only the actual food upon it would be heated up not the actual plate itself and not even a single crumb of food would ever be burnt, raw, undercooked or overcooked. No huge laborious effort was required to utilize the culinary contraptions that Leah had invented and any food placed inside them could be cooked to absolute perfection in a matter of minutes but she only really utilized them to reheat food, rather than to actually cook an entire meal from scratch because she liked food to be seasoned, marinated and slow cooked properly, since it felt a little bit more natural.

The hotplate warmers were however to Leah, a perfect example of the fact that sometimes Leah's chosen profession could actually save the couple some money because her first independent creation was not only extremely useful but it had also reduced the couple's energy bills due to the microchip inside each hotplate contraption which made each one super-efficient. Whenever an item of food was placed inside one of the hotplate warmers the microchip inside each contraption would automatically calculate how hot the temperature needed to be, how long the food should be heated up for and how that heat should be dispersed because the sensors inside each one scanned the weight, texture and composite structure of anything placed inside it.

Rather satisfyingly for Leah, despite the lack of glamorous attire and long unsociable hours, one of the positive advantages that accompanied her chosen profession was that she now possessed the knowledge, skills and ability that enabled and allowed her to design, invent and create gadgets which made life slightly easier and that were ultra-convenient and those capabilities had definitely helped the couple over the years. The hotplate warmers were an extremely fast way to heat up food and could even be utilized to cook meals from scratch and so Leah had called them Zappers because they were ultra-handy and over the past five years, the contraptions had literally saved her tons of effort.

According to Leah's now very well established weekday routine, she usually prepared the couple's evening meal first thing in the morning and then she would store the food inside the fridge until the couple wanted to eat dinner later that day and so that day had been no exception to the couple's usual weekday routine. When Zidane returned from work each weekday evening all Leah then had to do, once her tasks down in the basement were complete, was reheat the food as required which allowed the couple to spend more time together and that ensured that the couple actually ate an evening meal together every single weekday.

Recently however, due to Leah's increased working hours and since she had dedicated more time than ever to the completion of Spectrum, the couple hadn't actually eaten their evening weekday meals until quite late at night and so the frequency of late meal consumption inside their home had definitely increased dramatically. The couple's routine and lives had definitely adjusted in order to accommodate Leah's increased workload and tighter professional goals but in the short term as Leah fully appreciated, there was very little that could actually be done about that until her work on Spectrum was actually complete.

Usually during the weekends, when the couple's routine differed vastly, if they had decided to stay at home Zidane would often explore his culinary skills and attempt to cook both a lunch and a dinner and sometimes, he even attempted to cook two lunches and two dinners in the same weekend. In recent times, because Leah had increased her working hours upon Spectrum, she would even spend some of her weekend mornings and sometimes, part of her weekend afternoons inside the basement and so Zidane would at times, saunter down at lunchtime armed with a tray filled with food that he had prepared which he would carefully balance inside his hands. More often than not however, fortunately for Leah, during the weekend evenings the couple would usually spend some time outside their home as they visited restaurants and eateries and enjoyed date nights which at times saved Leah's palate because although Zidane could prepare some basic eatables, he certainly wasn't a chef by any stretch of the imagination.

Much to Leah's amusement, several times over the past five years Zidane had actually tried to make some very elaborate, extremely complex dishes during his weekend explorations of the kitchen but they were usually a total disaster and barely even edible. Seasonings and marinades definitely existed in Zidane's mind but he had absolutely no idea how to actually utilize them properly in order to make food taste nicer and whenever he did make any attempts to do so, the results were usually, completely disastrous. On several occasions in the past, Leah had even had to beg Zidane to stop trying to make anything that required too much seasoning or a very complicated marinade as she'd appealed to his sense of reason because such culinary efforts on his part, usually tasted absolutely awful.

"Just make simple things Zidane." Leah had advised him several times. "Simple things taste good."

So nowadays most of the food that Zidane usually prepared actually tasted quite bland because he really didn't understand seasonings or marinades, or how to use them properly but Leah definitely appreciated all his very sincere, heartfelt efforts. Irrespective of Zidane's lack of competence when it came to his culinary efforts however, there was definitely one thing that Leah certainly couldn't fault him on and that was his total dedication to her because during the past month when she had been down in the basement on the weekends, he would usually bring down a tray of freshly prepared sandwiches for lunch and she would immediately stop working on Spectrum just to eat lunch with him.

The interruptions to Leah's work when Zidane visited the basement could at times be slightly inconvenient, especially if she was in the middle of an important task because it definitely distracted her but she appreciated his efforts and his attempts to not only prepare some lunch but also to spend some time with her. In terms of Zidane's attitude towards Leah and the couple's relationship, his dedication absolutely never ever faltered and that was something that she really could not ignore or reject, regardless of how bland or awful his culinary efforts actually tasted.

When it came to romantic matters like devotion and effort, Zidane's heart had always been and definitely was in the right place and his affectionate actions, regardless of his hopeless culinary skills, Leah truly recognized were an attempt to hold on to a relationship that he desperately wanted to protect from any possible deterioration due to lack of care. Irrespective of the wonderful discoveries and inventions that Leah could or could not make that might or might not potentially change the couple's financial future, their relationship was definitely important to Zidane and that made Leah feel loved, appreciated and valued because he consistently demonstrated this to her on a very regular basis.

At some point in the future Leah hoped that Spectrum would provide the couple with a substantial capital lump sum, when the prototype was actually sold but as she already knew that income was dependent on a lot of other factors and therefore it wasn't totally guaranteed. No actual financial pressure existed however that urged and pushed Leah to generate a huge profit because Zidane had always accepted that a return on the couple's investment might not be definite and since he earned a decent amount that could adequately cover their outgoings with a few treats thrown in, no heavy financial expectations had ever been placed upon Leah's shoulders, much to her utter relief.

Several short sharp beeps suddenly alerted Leah to the fact that the food she had placed inside the hotplate warmers was now actually ready to be consumed and so she quickly opened up the contraptions and then began to lift the individual plates out of each one. Both plates of food were carefully placed upon a tray as a delightful aroma silently greeted Leah's nostrils and as the delicious smell gently wafted through the air and awakened her senses, it seemed to arouse her hunger even more as she hungrily plucked a sweet potato chip from one of the plates and then bit into it enthusiastically. The mouthful of food quickly confirmed to Leah that the sweet potato chip was crispy on the outside and soft on the inside just as it should be and she smiled as for a moment as she quietly appreciated how effective her Zapper contraptions really were.

Two large lumps of butter were quickly scooped out of the butter tub and then dabbed onto the cobs of sweetcorn that sat on the side of each plate as Leah generously adorned each cob with fat and although she knew it wasn't very healthy, the butter sure tasted dam good and that mouthwatering taste as far as Leah was concerned, was far too good to resist. Each lump of fat glistened as it began to silently melt and as Leah watched the butter dribble and slither down the sides of the corn, each drop slipped silently into the grooves and gave the cobs of corn a salted overcoat and oily dress that in Leah's sight, looked totally irresistible.

A jar of spicy tomato relish sat upon the kitchen worktop right next to the two plates and as it stood to attention on active duty, since Leah had just retrieved it from the fridge, she felt as if it seemed to silently await its distribution by her hands as she cheerfully picked it up and then prepared to oblige. Upon Leah's face there was a very satisfied smile as she quickly opened up the jar and then spooned out two generous helpings of the spicy, sweet sauce which she then rather clumsily plonked down onto the side of each plate because this meal really was one of her absolute favorites. Irrespective of how well prepared the food actually was and how delicious it smelt however, the two plates in the end didn't seem to look very tidy at all, Leah observed as she quickly glanced at each one and then grinned but the contents of the two plates which included the two racks of sweet, smoked, sticky barbeque ribs, sure smelt absolutely delicious.

Some cutlery and a few napkins were quickly placed upon the tray beside the two plates and then Leah left the kitchen as she began to make her way back towards the lounge and back towards a very hungry Zidane with the tray balanced carefully inside her hands. In terms of the food that Leah had prepared for the couple's evening meal that day, her culinary efforts certainly weren't a three course meal by any stretch of the imagination but the smoked, spicy, sweet, sticky ribs, crispy sweet potato fries and buttered sweetcorn sure smelt and looked dam good and so now, Leah's stomach was hungrily eager to digest the actual contents of her plate.

The tray which Leah had placed the two filled plates of food upon was carefully and slowly carried towards the lounge as Leah walked because she was anxious not to drop even a single grain of food since it all smelt very delicious and her stomach was by now, extremely empty. Some thoughts about the work that still remained on Spectrum and the time it would take to complete that work, occupied Leah's mind as she stepped back inside the lounge because recently, her work goals had driven her to work later each evening and even now during the day on the weekends which had definitely had an impact upon the couple's usual quality time each week. A definite decrease in the attention that Leah usually paid to Zidane had occurred because her working hours had increased, not only during the weekdays but now also on the weekends and in some ways that worried her.

Deep down inside herself, Leah knew that she really had to be mindful not to take Zidane's presence in her life for granted because to find another life partner like Zidane would be difficult, if not virtually impossible, if he ever chose to leave her side. Men like Zidane only came along once in a lifetime, if they ever actually came along at all and that reality was definitely something that Leah had to not only respect but also appreciate and due to that reality, she had absolutely no desire whatsoever to jeopardize the relationship between them both through her lack of attention to it.

Scientific and technological creations could as Leah fully appreciated, be very time consuming and her work demanded both intense levels of concentration and heaps of attention and for the past few years, Spectrum had already consumed vast amounts of her time. Essentially, Leah's whole life had almost been totally dedicated to and greedily consumed by Spectrum for the last three years and the demands of her work as she now fully appreciated, could very easily put a strain upon her relationship, if she allowed Spectrum to take over her entire life.

Until recently, Leah's weekends had always been kept totally free and fully reserved for Zidane but as Spectrum's potential completion had drawn closer and closer, she had committed more time and effort to her work as she'd attempted to wrap things up more quickly so that she could sell the Spectrum prototype to a commercial buyer. For the past month that had therefore meant that Leah's work inside the basement had actually spilled over into the couple's weekends and so for Zidane as Leah fully appreciated, it had been a very lonely month because he'd had to not only tolerate but also cope with the reallocation of her time and her attention.

Long gone were the weekday evenings when Leah would adorn her curvy, voluptuous frame with scanty outfits that oozed sexual allure and then greet Zidane seductively at the front door when he returned from work and now, such romantic delicacies had almost been totally forgotten. At one time Leah had made the effort to provide those sexual delicacies to Zidane regularly and she had frequently applied those personal touches to their relationship but now such actions sat at the very bottom of her priority list as she sought to finish her work on Spectrum as quickly as she possibly could.

Marriage and children were definitely things that Leah wanted to experience and things that she had planned to do with Zidane and so she hoped that the sale of Spectrum would usher in those events more quickly because it would provide the couple with a much needed, potentially large, capital lump sum. The couple had planned to move home before they married and started a family but since Zidane hadn't been promoted at work for at least two years now and there were virtually no opportunities for progression, Spectrum was their only real, current hope when it came to the realization and achievement of both those goals due to the financial hurdles that stood in their way. In order to secure the financial resources that the couple needed to enjoy the future that they had planned to have and wanted to spend together, Leah not only had to complete Spectrum but then also sell the prototype and rights for a decent amount and so Spectrum absolutely had to be in perfect working order when the prototype was sold, to ensure that it could be sold for the amount that she had hoped for.

One thing Leah did try to maintain however, no matter how much the pressure mounted, how hard she worked or how many hours she spent inside the basement as she labored upon Spectrum, was her conscious commitment to ensure that she always ate at least one meal with Zidane every single day. Sometimes, now and again, Leah felt tempted to continue her work inside the basement and skip the odd evening meal but so far she had managed to resist the temptation to do so as she'd forced herself to be disciplined about her commitment to not only Zidane but also to the time that the couple spent together.

Fortunately for the couple as Leah already knew, Spectrum was now almost complete which meant, the strain that her work had placed upon their relationship would soon be over and then she would have not only more time for Zidane but also for herself. When it came to the issue of the couple's actual relationship although Leah had never physically cheated on Zidane with another man, her creation Spectrum had in some respects, become a very greedy lover and the seductive grip of her work had literally devoured hundreds perhaps even thousands of hours of her life which would never ever be returned to her irrespective of any potential capital gains that may or may not finally be realized from all those hours of devoted professional effort. In fact, the final refinements, problems and tweaks as Leah was well aware had virtually swallowed her life whole as she had sought completion with every available moment, almost every ounce of her being, every possible single breath and every available second.

Romantically speaking, the couple both knew, those hours of additional professional devotion that Leah had given to Spectrum in recent times, should have been spent together and upon their relationship but she just couldn't complete Spectrum any quicker because she was physically going as fast as she could go. The pressure had now definitely mounted inside Leah's mind because the couple's future required more financial resources than they currently possessed and had access to and so she wanted to contribute financially towards that future and help to overcome those financial hurdles because their future essentially at some point as Leah already knew, would be restricted by biological factors and her own biological clock which would not wait for anything or anyone.

Due to Leah's additional hours inside the basement that past month the impact of her work upon Zidane's life had definitely been more severe and although Zidane had never complained, Leah had noticed that recently, he had become slightly frustrated and that he'd expressed that frustration to her several times, albeit in a very polite and jovial manner. Despite the very human factors at play however,

Leah had continued to work tirelessly towards the achievement of her goal because the sooner Spectrum was actually complete, the sooner the prototype could be sold and then the couple's future could actually begin.

Once Leah arrived next to the coffee table which sat directly in front of the sofa, she carefully placed the tray of food down on top of the shiny, black, glass surface as she flashed a smile at Zidane. A heavenly aroma emanated from the sweet, sticky, smoked barbecue ribs upon Leah's plate and so her mouth immediately started to water as she enthusiastically sat down beside Zidane and then prepared to consume the delicious food that now sat directly in front of her.

Usually, the couple ate their evening meals together seated around the large, black glass dining room table situated at one end of their large lounge but that day, Leah had deliberately steered their evening meal away from such formalities and had totally avoided the additional effort that would entail because she felt, absolutely famished and completely worn out. Hunger had by now already totally hijacked and fully gripped Leah's stomach and since time was definitely in short supply that day, or what was left of it, such formalities for once had been totally excused.

“Thanks Leah. Dinner looks and smells absolutely amazing." Zidane mentioned appreciatively as he glanced at her face, smiled and then cheerfully plucked some cutlery from the tray and a plate filled with hot food. "How’s your work coming along?” He asked.

“Fine I guess. Hopefully, I should have a final breakthrough soon.” Leah replied as she enthusiastically nodded her head. “I can feel it coming now and it's definitely on its way but it'll probably be a couple more weeks before I'm finished and then you'll have me all to yourself in the weekday evenings again."

"I can't wait." Zidane announced happily as he began to eagerly load his fork up with food.

"I know, it'll be a nice change won't it because then we won't have to squeeze our evenings together into the end of each day?" Leah agreed.

"Don't worry Leah that final breakthrough will turn up soon, you're a very intelligent person, so it can't hide from you forever." Zidane encouraged.

For Zidane, although he was definitely interested in everything about Leah their conversation about Spectrum was very intentionally, kept extremely brief as he prepared to consume the food situated on the plate directly in front of him that waited eagerly and deliciously to be eaten. Intricate, involved, complex questions and discussions were deliberately avoided on Zidane's part as he began to tuck into his evening meal as he internally appreciated the fact that at least now, Spectrum was almost completely finished.

Some small lumps of corn drenched in butter eagerly slipped down the back of Zidane's throat as he began to devour the morsels of food on the plate directly in front of him and not a single word was uttered as he focused solely upon his now, very hungry, empty stomach. At times Zidane did feel slightly curious about Leah's work but on the few occasions in the past when he had attempted to delve more deeply into the issue of Spectrum, he'd felt a bit lost in the mass of complex information that Leah had heaped onto his brain in response. Despite Leah's best efforts to provide Zidane with some thorough explanations, her regurgitation of facts, details and information about Spectrum had simply flown over his head like a bird that migrates in the fall, desperate to avoid the harsh cruel claws of winter and he had actually been none the wiser as a result and so the topic that evening was intentionally left unexplored and for the most part undiscussed.

Over a year ago Zidane had made a very conscious decision that to understand the more prescriptive, complex elements of Spectrum and Leah's work would require time, energy and patience, three things that were in very short supply by the time he'd arrived home from work each weekday evening and even more so by the time Leah had resurfaced from the basement. Usually, by the time the couple ate their evening meals together during the week, Zidane was already mentally drained and physically worn out from his own day at work and the later working hours that Leah had recently engaged in, certainly hadn't helped or done anything to reduce his general levels of fatigue and so a complex, technical conversation on that particular topic was usually, completely avoided.

In terms of Zidane's intellectual capacity, he was certainly clever enough to understand Leah's work but since he had chosen to specialize in computer hardware and software maintenance, he'd never intellectually dabbled in a potential crossover between science and technology and so for him that area of expertise was very unfamiliar territory. The areas of knowledge that Leah worked and specialized in were completely alien to Zidane in every way imaginable and they were not something that he had ever been exposed to throughout his studies, or even during his working life and as a result, he knew very little about her chosen field.

Irrespective of the fact that Zidane definitely loved Leah and everything about her, he had decided long ago that the time the couple spent together each weekday evening was definitely far too precious to be spent upon discussions about Spectrum. The collation of very complex, technological and scientific knowledge that Zidane had absolutely no need to know that he would never ever utilize as far as he was concerned, served no actual purpose to either of them and therefore such discussions were deemed as conversations that he really did not want to have and especially not on a weekday evening.

Due to the technical complexities that surrounded Leah's chosen profession as Zidane was fully aware, it would definitely take him time and mental effort to understand anything about Spectrum and his main priority when he spent his recreation time with Leah, was quite simply Leah and their relationship, not her inventions or even Spectrum. Over the past six years Zidane had learnt to accept as the couple's relationship had developed and grown that he didn't actually have to understand everything about Leah's work and that all he really needed to do was be there for her, love her and encourage her and that was definitely enough for him. The love that the couple shared every day and each night meant the world to Zidane and that love as far as he was concerned, was definitely sufficient enough for him and more than satisfied his mind and heart and so he had both realized and accepted long ago that he did not actually, have to love Spectrum too.

"Sometimes Zidane, I just feel so frustrated because perfection really is very hard work." Leah acknowledged as she turned to face him.

"I know and you've worked so hard on Spectrum Leah, you really deserve to succeed and for Spectrum to be a tremendous success." Zidane said in-between mouthfuls of food as he nodded his head in agreement.

"We deserve to succeed." Leah immediately replied as she smiled at him and then picked up her cutlery. "Isn't that what it's all about us? We're a romantic team that is united by love and our happy future together is our romantic goal."

Zidane nodded. "Definitely." He agreed.

"How's dinner?" Leah asked as she began to dive into her meal.

"Lovely. Absolutely delicious. Thank goodness one of us can cook." Zidane joked. "Or we'd probably live on baked beans on toast."

"Well, there are always microwave meals and there is such a thing as takeaway food." Leah teased. "I know what you mean though, sometimes it's nice to eat a proper home cooked meal and this dish is my absolute favorite"

"Is your food still hot?" Zidane asked.

Leah nodded. "It sure is." She replied.

Several forkfuls of food were rapidly and eagerly shoveled into Leah's mouth as she hungrily attempted to soothe the angry rumbles that continued to growl away inside her stomach as her body urged her to fill it. A thoughtful glance was cast towards Zidane's face as Leah ate as she silently reassured herself that once Spectrum was fully operational and once her prototype functioned correctly, things would definitely be very different and much better for them both because then their current rushed minutes of quality time each day would no longer be in such short supply.

Since Leah had only just started to consume her meal and Zidane had begun the consumption of his evening meal at least a few minutes before she had, Leah noticed that his plate was now almost empty because he had rapidly consumed the dinner that she'd so lovingly prepared for him earlier that day. In many ways, Zidane's eagerness encouraged, satisfied and pleased Leah because it reassured her that at least some of her efforts could be fully enjoyed and appreciated in the same day and without years of delay. Unlike Spectrum the couple's evening meal had been made by Leah and then enthusiastically consumed, all in the same day and the mountain of frustration that she'd had to climb up every day for the past three years inside the basement fortunately, was nowhere to be seen inside the couple's lounge that night.

Once Spectrum was sold Leah hoped that there would be far less late nights, a lot more money and that then perhaps the couple would get married and start the family that they had always dreamed about and discussed but when exactly that would happen as Leah already knew, was for now quite unpredictable. When that change finally occurred however, Leah would then become not just a wife but also a mother and their children would be the couple's own unique, shared biological creation, unlike Spectrum which was just Leah's individual professional creation.

Spectrum itself was an extremely complex system and due to that fact, it had taken a lot out of Leah as she had worked tirelessly upon it for three years non-stop and the past month had been even more labor intensive than usual and so by the time she normally arrived in the lounge each weekday night, she usually felt, mentally drained. Much like Zidane's hungry consumption of his evening meal, Leah's creation had devoured the majority of several years of her life but the financial rewards she expected to be quite large and so she hoped that it would eventually be worth all the sacrifices that the couple and she personally had made.

When it came to the actual issue of Spectrum's operation the system required that a person lie down inside the User Capsule in order for it to function and it would then allow that person to participate in various experiences and emotional journeys within a simulated world as they slept. A wide range of emotional landscapes could be explored and Spectrum provided users with flexible features that allowed them to adjust their own personalities and physicalities whilst they explored those landscapes in order to flex their experiences as they desired and wished to. The various functionalities that Leah had built into Spectrum allowed consumers to not only enjoy a variety of emotional experiences from a range of different perspectives but each flexed aspect could also potentially heighten and intensify the enjoyment, satisfaction and pleasure that each user could actually derive from their participation within the emotional planes that they visited and hence it offered a very wide range of assorted, recreational experiences.

Although the scientific and technological system that Leah had created was deeply rooted in various scientific theories and principles, somehow in the end Leah had actually managed to combine various elements of science and technology in order to produce a recreational product that she hoped would be commercially profitable. Science and technology had been woven together in a constructive but elaborate manner to produce a hybrid product that Leah hoped would deeply engage, emotionally satisfy and captivatingly entertain its consumers and participants and so Leah really felt quite proud of what she had now, almost achieved because Spectrum was definitely, a very unique creation.

For Leah, the main objective when it came to Spectrum was the provision of an enjoyable, recreational experience for consumers that engaged, fulfilled and emotionally satisfied them and that was Spectrum's unique strength and its ultimate selling point. When Spectrum was finally complete, Leah hoped that the overall results would offer consumers more than just a recreational experience because it would actually provide users with a range of emotionally satisfying adventures that they could embark upon as many times as they wished to and absolutely never ever get bored.

Quite frustratingly however, due to the time that it had taken to create Spectrum the completion of the prototype had now almost become like a heavy weight that Leah carried around with her everywhere she went but as she already knew that weight would not be lifted from her being until Spectrum was complete. Once Spectrum was sold, not only would Leah be free but so too would Zidane because that heavyweight was tied to the couple's actual future and since it restricted their mutual enjoyment of the present, at times Leah definitely felt extremely frustrated.

Very unromantically, the practical responsibilities of life now restricted the couple's current enjoyment of their relationship and as Leah was fully aware, her hopeful, professional aspirations had inflicted a shortage of time upon them both that they were now very eager to change but until the Spectrum prototype was complete that would not actually happen. When Spectrum was finally ready to be purchased as Leah knew, the couple would then be free once more to enjoy the companionship that they had treasured from the very first moment that they'd met and they would also be free to love each other more fully once again but Leah just couldn't wait for that change to actually happen because it now felt so frustratingly overdue.

"Let's go to bed now Leah." Zidane suddenly suggested as he watched her consume the last mouthful of food on her plate and then quickly stood up. He stretched out a hand towards her as he offered to pull her to her feet. "We've finished dinner now and I have to get up early tomorrow morning."

“What about the dirty plates?” Leah asked as she took his hand and then allowed him to pull her gently to her feet. She leant her head affectionately upon his shoulder as she joined him. “I should really wash them now, or the scraps of food will get all hard and impossible and then I'll really have to scrub them."

“The dirty dishes can wait until the morning.” Zidane whispered softly in her ear. “I need you now, I can’t wait."

A quick glance was cast towards the coffee table and the two dirty plates that lay upon it as Leah silently prepared to succumb to Zidane's request as she thoughtfully began to consider the suggestion of a compromise.

"Okay but at least let me put them in the sink." Leah suggested. "So that they can soak overnight."

"Sure, we can do that on our way to the bedroom." Zidane agreed as he quickly leant down and then picked up the two plates.

"I'm so proud of you Zidane, you've finally learnt how to multi-task." Leah teased as she giggled.

Very politely, Leah suddenly realized, Zidane had allowed her to eat her evening meal with absolutely no verbal interruptions at all and even though he had wolfed down his own food, he'd then just waited patiently for her to satisfy her hunger in total silence. Possibly, Zidane's politeness had been motivated by his desire not to prolong the consumption of their evening meal and his own tiredness, Leah rapidly concluded, because the more the two conversed, the longer it would have taken her to actually consume her meal. Due to Leah's daydreams about Spectrum and the couple's future, she had been totally lost in her own thoughts and her mind had been somewhere else throughout their entire evening meal and as a result, the couple had hardly exchanged a single word but since they were both quite tired and very hungry that silence Leah felt, had somehow been perfectly acceptable to them both.

In fact, Leah had almost completely forgotten about Zidane's work schedule which dictated that he had to wake up very early the next morning and so she could definitely understand Zidane's desire to immediately abandon the lounge and head towards the bedroom as soon as they had both eaten, since it was now almost quarter past eleven. Essentially, Zidane's attitude could be fully understood and as far as Leah was concerned, was to be expected really because it had been an extremely long day for them both and so now, she felt just as eager to rest her body as he seemed to be and she longed to spend some time wrapped up in his arms because some intimate quality time was definitely, well overdue. The rapid interruption from Zidane at the end of her meal, Leah silently decided as she began to follow him out of the lounge had really been good for her because it had brought her back down to earth with a gentle bump and affectionately reminded her that now was their time and that their time that day had to be appreciated, enjoyed and treasured before it totally vanished, silently evaporated and completely ran out.

Upon Leah's face there was a peaceful smile as she followed Zidane's lead and accepted his request as she silently agreed to leave the dirty dishes until the next morning, since a compromise had now technically, actually been reached. Every single weekday morning without fail as Leah already knew, Zidane would wake up religiously at six on the dot in order to prepare for work and the following morning would certainly be no exception to his strict weekday morning routine and so any further delays that night on her part would not be helpful in any way. Sometimes, Leah considered thoughtfully, it was perfectly acceptable to be a little bit messy, especially when there was an urgent need for the expression of some tender affection and some loving care and so the compromise that the couple had reached had in the end, been an acceptable outcome to their discussion and one that she now felt, totally at peace with.

Just a minute or so later, after a quick stop off at the kitchen en-route, the couple arrived inside their dimly lit bedroom and as they did so, Leah inwardly began to prepare herself to spend the remainder of her night in the comfort of Zidane's arms where she could enjoy his provision of devoted adoration and bask in the sensual companionship that adorned their relationship every single night. Some gentle flames of passion immediately started to smolder and dance around silently inside Leah's body and as sparks of desire flickered away just below the surface of her skin, she drew closer to the king-size bed that the couple usually occupied and shared every single night which was situated in the very center of their quite large bedroom.

The very long day that the couple had just endured was now almost over and so that meant, it was definitely time for bed, passion and all of the affection that the couple could possibly provide to each other and as usual, Leah had saved a little bit of energy that day purely for that purpose. Some small grains of energy did still remain somewhere deep down inside Leah's body and so she began to muster each one up from within as she prepared for the final hour or so that the couple would spend together that day as she quietly accepted that very soon, it would actually be tomorrow and the start of another long working day for them both.

Unlike the cold harsh realities of the world outside the couple's home, Zidane's strong capable arms provided Leah with a protective shelter and an affectionate refuge and so as she snuggled up inside his two physical, masculine shields, she rapidly began to relax and allowed her worries about Spectrum to gently melt away. No matter what difficulties, troubles or problems Leah faced in life, Zidane's arms always seemed to provide a comfort to her whenever she felt worried, stressed or even when she just felt totally worn out due to the demands of her work and his arms were always open to her as they welcomed Leah with bundles of encouragement and heaps of affectionate acceptance. Essentially, for the past six years Zidane's arms had truly been Leah's sanctuary because whenever she lay inside them, they immediately drove away any doubts that niggled away inside her mind and any thoughts that worried her and his arms seemed to somehow, silently provide her with a warm blanket of reassurance with just one simple embrace.

Just outside the couple's bedroom and home as Leah fully appreciated, the world was full of harsh realities but those harsh factors, somehow seemed to become totally irrelevant and even vanished completely as soon as Zidane wrapped his masculine arms around her body. Any obstacles that stood in Leah's path and hurdles that life might present to her, no longer seemed to matter when Zidane held her close because he provided Leah with a warm place to exist where she was immediately accepted and a place that was hurdle and obstacle free. Inside Zidane's arms, Leah knew that she would always be welcomed, wanted, loved and appreciated and for that one firm, stable, consistent, steadfast pillar of love and support, Leah definitely felt, truly grateful.

A smile of total contentment adorned Leah's face as she lay inside Zidane's arms and gazed up at his face as she silently considered that life wasn't always a place filled with acceptance because as she already knew, the world outside the couple's home didn't always welcome everyone with a pleasant reception and open arms. Somehow however, in the midst of all that very human chaos, Leah had finally managed to find a place where she felt that she would always be accepted for who she really was, regardless of how perfect Spectrum was or wasn't and despite her successes and failures in life. The caretaker of Zidane's physical form it seemed, would always allow Leah inside the building and open up the doors of his heart to her own and there would always be a place for Leah inside Zidane's loving arms and that beautiful, truthful, consistent, affectionate reality, now comforted her heart immensely as she lay peacefully inside his arms.

On top of the couple's bed there was a black and gold satin duvet cover that glistened and shone as some particles of dim light bounced silently of it and as the couple snuggled up underneath the duvet, they began to rejoice in the warmth that the material provided and the heat that radiated from each of their bodies as they gazed into each other's eyes in silent adoration. An unspoken silent agreement definitely existed between the two which discreetly stipulated that no matter how tired they usually were, a small remnant of energy would always be saved for bedtime every night and for each other and that was something that they both looked forward to every single day. Quite often that final portion of conserved energy would be utilized simply to spoil each other with physical displays of affection before the couple rested at night but at times that last remnant of energy would be expended to satisfy their sexual desires however that usually depended on exactly how much energy was actually left.

"I love you so much Leah." Zidane whispered softly in her ear as he began to gently caress her earlobe with his tongue and lips seductively. He ran his fingers across her naked skin and his flesh rapidly started to stir with sexual excitement as he was instantly aroused. "I really don't know what I would have done without you."

Each word that Zidane spoke struck a deep chord inside Leah's heart as an opera of romance started to silently play and as his warm breath caressed her skin and delicately tickled her cheek, every seductive note formed by his sensual touch began to vibrate passionately inside of her. Every single breath of warmth that rippled across Leah's skin seemed laden with excited passion, tender affection and sensuous desires and as Zidane stroked her navel, Leah began to silently rejoice in his physical adoration and his overt displays of love as she accepted both his verbal and physical appreciation. Instinctively, deep down inside, Leah already knew that every word that Zidane had uttered, he had actually truly meant because the couple's entire relationship had initially been birthed from tragedy and their love had provided Zidane with a lifeline of hope when he had needed it the most.

Very tragically, just before the couple's first meeting six years ago, three of Zidane's closest family members had been on board a plane that had crashed and they had all actually perished. The tremendous loss that Zidane had suffered had been absolutely monumental and his life had been totally devastated by the disaster and as a result, he had quickly sunk into a deep sea of depression straight afterwards. According to the holiday plans that Zidane's family had initially made, he had been expected to attend that actual family vacation but due to some last minute additional coursework, he'd had to drop out and so he had been absent from the actual trip itself. Despite Zidane's absence the family vacation had still gone ahead without him and he had even suggested at the time that one of his closest cousins Brian should be invited along instead and that Brian should take his place and so Brian had dutifully stepped in and participated but the tragic trip had sealed the three vacationers' fate because they had not returned from it.

Both Zidane's parents and his cousin Brian had been on board the plane when the disaster had occurred and as the aircraft had plunged rapidly down towards the sea, it had headed towards the very bottom of the ocean and once it had sunk onto the watery, sandy bed, it had never resurfaced ever again. The ocean had quickly become the passengers' watery grave and absolutely no one that had been on board the flight had survived because the merciless waves had claimed the entire plane full of human bodies as its own with no regrets and absolutely no remorse and not even a single person had been spared. No passengers that had been on board that plane had managed to survive and none had managed to escape from that flight of death because the doors of the plane had remained tightly shut as the aircraft had sunk extremely quickly and absolutely everyone inside the plane had perished.

A tragic accident had left its mark upon human hearts and its scars upon human lives and there had been no survivors, no human remains and absolutely no human bodies to mourn over and bury at the funeral services held for family members afterwards and as Leah knew that tragedy had almost completely destroyed Zidane. In terms of Zidane's life, it had virtually been torn apart by the traumatic events which Leah knew at the time had totally devastated him and as a result, he had been thrown completely off balance because his main reason to exist had been totally obliterated in one deadly afternoon and there had been absolutely nothing that he could have done about any of it.

After the accident, depression had almost drowned Zidane's mind and thoughts because emotional waves of sadness had consumed and engulfed him and his heart had rapidly plummeted down into the murky depths of an ocean formed from total despair. Somehow, it had almost been as if Zidane's body and emotions had become completely crippled and totally drained due to the nonphysical injury that he had suffered because his life had suddenly become very empty, totally void and completely meaningless in one deadly, foul swoop of fate.

Less than a month after the horrific accident which had almost completely destroyed Zidane's life, he had hit rock bottom and he'd nearly dropped out of his degree course at the beginning of his final year because he had felt unable to continue with his life and actually living and that had been when the couple had met for the very first time. The couple's paths had initially crossed when Zidane had been on his way to the main university administration office which had been based at Leah's campus because he had wanted to hand in his course termination form and she had been the first person to pull him back out of the pit of sadness that he'd almost been completely buried inside. Somehow, Leah had given Zidane a reason to carry on with life because she had encouraged him and reassured him that there was indeed, still something to live for and then she had gently retrieved his broken spirit and brought him back to life.

For the first couple of years the couple's relationship had almost been totally saturated in heartbreak but somehow, Leah had finally managed to breathe life back into Zidane in a manner that healed and he had slowly and surely been restored back to life as she had resuscitated his broken heart and rescued him from the brink of despair. The deep pit of sorrow that Zidane had been buried in had almost fully consumed him but Leah had managed to pluck his heart from the murky depths of that sorrow and she had motivated him to once more return to life and to actually live again, despite the horrors that he had suffered and endured. Total despair had almost drowned Zidane's being from what Leah could see at the time and his spirit had definitely been broken but gradually that despair had begun to dissolve, disintegrate and evaporate as Zidane had been encouraged that life could indeed continue and that he could indeed, actually carry on.

Somehow with Leah by his side, Zidane had managed to reach deep within himself and he had embraced not only her arrival in his life but also her willingness to be a permanent part of it at a time when he'd almost given up on life completely. The hopelessness that had once almost consumed Zidane had then begun to slowly depart because Leah had provided him with a human lifeline of hope that had nursed his broken heart which had not only motivated him but also soothed him, until slowly and surely Zidane had started to not just exist but also to live again.

However, despite Zidane's initial dependency upon Leah as she had provided him with an emotional crutch with which to stand up again which he had then been able to utilize to walk through life that dependency it had now transpired had not been singular because Leah had later discovered that she had actually needed Zidane almost as much as he had initially needed her. The years of the couple's subsequent relationship and Zidane's faultless, tireless devotion to Leah had now shown her very clearly that he was just as much a gift to her heart as she was to his because no other man would have supported Leah's professional ambitions and hopeful aspirations as enthusiastically and faithfully as Zidane had and still did and she definitely knew it. In every way imaginable, Zidane had supported Leah every single day and he had tolerated the lifestyle that such ambitions entailed and endured the long working hours that Leah's work required and that tireless devotion to her as she was fully aware, was a very admirable quality that would be hard, if not virtually impossible to find in any other human vessel that currently occupied the face of the human planet.

Every part of Zidane had invested himself not only into the couple's relationship but also into Leah's professional aspirations because he had given her six solid years of financial, emotional, romantic and physical support very consistently on a daily basis, without any excuses and without any failure on his part. The research that had gone into Leah's work and the subsequent development of the Spectrum prototype had involved years of commitment in order to achieve the results that Leah wished to realize and that commitment it had now transpired had not just been Leah's to make because Zidane's commitment had also proven to be equally as important.

A responsibility had fallen onto Zidane's shoulders and he had carried it with a very willing heart and without any complaints and he'd even tolerated the lack of time and attention that Leah had provided to him for several years without one single act of betrayal. Not even once had Zidane placed any demands upon Leah for more than she could give and he had never once complained and so she definitely now knew, without a shadow of a doubt that no other man would have accepted such romantic terms in a relationship, or tolerated such awkward conditions to keep one alive.

From the midst of heartbreak and against all odds, somehow the couple had managed to find a love that had transcended the various obstacles that life had presented to them both and not only had they found solace in each other arms but also a tremendous amount of comfort and that comfort had shielded them from the harsh realities of the world around them. Somehow, in the midst of tragedy, the couple's relationship had miraculously been formed and then as they had faced difficult, external and internal circumstances and commitments, their relationship had even managed to flourish, been strengthened and had grown over the years and somehow, their love had actually survived.

Rather intriguingly for Leah, although it had initially seemed as if she had actually saved Zidane, in reality Leah now fully appreciated that he had also saved her heart too because he'd stepped into her life and saved Leah from any possible heartbreak that another man might have delivered to her heart, purely due to her dedication to her work. Regarding Leah's professional aspirations, Zidane had actually, really saved Leah in more ways than one because he had provided her with a fully equipped basement laboratory and also some much needed financial support which had then allowed her to pursue the things that she had wanted to achieve in life instead of being stuck for years in a job that was overly laborious and a mind numbing experience and so on his provisions, Leah truly could not fault him. In some highly miraculous, amazingly glorious way, the two had perhaps now become each other's human saviors in various forms and that salvation had created a deep, unspoken human bond between them both and an emotional connection that most other couples simply didn't have and that deep depth of love which had been fully demonstrated over the years by their sacrifices for each other, Leah definitely, truly cherished.

"I love you too Zidane." Leah whispered as warm, gentle waves of sensual passion and erotic desire began to ripple silently across the surface of her skin. "I've loved you since the very first moment we met."

Every inch of the couple's bodies suddenly started to surge with a current of excited, sensual passion as their flesh rapidly became intertwined and as Zidane caressed Leah's naked skin with his tongue and lips, she started to moan with pleasure. Some deep waves of sensual enjoyment rapidly flowed and washed across Leah's body as Zidane began to penetrate her and as she welcomed and accepted his masculine presence inside her being, her body began to arch in absolute ecstasy. The couple's love making that night was tender, delicate and sensual because every touch was meticulously orchestrated to heighten each moment of passion that they wanted to share as the two celebrated their mutual physical appreciation and shared their passionate adoration as they gave themselves fully to each other and to the night.

Sometimes, the couple would make love frantically and they would grab each other's clothes and then hungrily tear them off each other's bodies as they sought to fulfill their unquenched passionate desires but tonight was not such an occasion because tonight was gentle and tender. Enveloped in the dusky, darkness the couple moaned in unison with pleasure as Zidane penetrated Leah more deeply and she gripped onto his naked back as she welcomed him inside her. Between the two, there were no fears, inhibitions, or constraints as they surrendered to their deepest sexual desires and attempted to quench each other's sexual thirst, satisfy their passionate hunger and explore each other's bodies with sensual touches and seductive kisses as the darkness of the night embraced and surrounded them.

For Leah as she surrendered herself completely to Zidane's masculine presence and as he lavished his physical attention upon her, she allowed him to take full control of their ship of passion and for that precise moment in time that was all there was that mattered in the world to them both, each other. No other considerations were allowed to occupy Leah's thoughts as she focused solely upon the sensual interactions that she was currently engaged in and enjoyed each one in its fullness because soft, tender moments with Zidane were a beautiful remedy to a long frustration filled day and so as the night progressed, Leah adoringly allowed Zidane, love and their passionate, sensual romantic harmony to guide her fully into the night.

A Jestful Jaunt in the Joyful Kingdom

When the next morning landed upon the runway of Leah's life, it dawned peacefully enough and as she woke up, she quickly discovered that as usual Zidane had already left home and gone to work. Since Zidane started work and had to leave the house at a set time each morning, according to his agreed contractual shifts, it was usual for him to rise at six before Leah even awoke and then he would prepare for work as quietly as possible and leave the couple's home without her and so there was nothing particularly unusual about Leah's usual weekday morning solitude.

In fact, every weekday for the past five years, Zidane's usual weekday routine had been pretty much the same and very consistent because he had worked for the same company and so he had conformed to the same weekday routine as per his employment commitments. Occasionally, Leah would wake up just before Zidane departed and be given a farewell kiss and hug before he went but more often than not, Leah would usually sleep straight through his departure and so she was very used to his usual weekday morning absences. From what Leah had been told by Zidane, he usually planted a soft kiss on her forehead, cheeks or lips before he left the couple's home each weekday morning but she would usually be none the wiser because she normally slept straight through his departure.

The couple's night had involved several deep dives into their ocean of passion and so Leah had woken up slightly later than usual which also meant, even when she did finally awake, she was in a slightly more sleepy state and not in an actual rush to get up or join the day which had clearly started without her and then marched full steam ahead. On this particular occasion, although Leah had not even stirred and she had slept straight through Zidane's departure as she picked up her cellphone and then glanced at the screen, she could clearly see that Zidane had already sent her his usual, cheerful, affectionate weekday morning text message that he faithfully sent to her every working day, the minute he arrived at work and that morning had certainly been no exception.

At times and on some quite rare occasions, by the time Zidane's usual weekday morning text arrived, Leah would either be in the shower or halfway through breakfast but more often than not, she would still be fast asleep and that day, she had been fast asleep as usual. A peaceful smile crossed Leah's face as she began to read the message and silently absorbed every word that it contained because those affectionate communications would be sent to her cellphone every working day, regardless of whether she was still fast asleep or wide awake and each one reinforced Zidane's very consistent approach to their relationship and their romantic commitment to each other because it reminded Leah how loved she truly was.

Despite Zidane's ability to rise early and his interest in the world before eight each weekday morning, Leah was a firm believer that the world shouldn't even function before nine every day and so her sleeping patterns usually fully aligned with her philosophical beliefs and her slightly more laid-back approach to life. The world did not usually see hide nor hair of Leah until at least nine during the week and usually, it was far closer to ten and sometimes, it could even be around eleven by the time Leah finally crawled out of bed and officially started her day.

Once up and fully awake Leah would venture outside the bedroom that the couple shared each night and then she would spend the rest of her weekday morning, or what remained of it, fully occupied and involved in the performance of various household chores and engaged in the preparation of the couple's evening meal. The couple's evening meals would usually be fully prepared by the time lunchtime arrived and once Leah's daily household tasks were complete and she had eaten lunch, Leah would then wander down to the basement and start her day's work upon Spectrum.

In terms of the couple's usual weekday routine, it was by now pretty well established and although some slight fluctuations and small variances to that pattern of regularity did sometimes occur, either when the couple had indulged in a very late night, or when

Leah had to perform some particularly complex tasks down in the basement, all in all it was pretty predictable. When it came to the actual life that the couple shared as far as Leah was concerned, it wasn't that the couple had become boring, it was just that they were totally dedicated to each other, very disciplined and united in their approach to life because they both had things that they wanted to achieve together which they worked as a romantic team to realize and that romantic continuity and stability had kept Leah very focused over the years.

After Leah's usual morning chores that morning had been performed and once the couple's evening meal had been prepared as lunchtime and twelve noon arrived, Leah prepared a quick lunch, hungrily consumed it and then headed straight down to the basement. The morning had literally flown by and as the early afternoon started to approach, Leah's body began to rapidly fill up with excitement and eager anticipation as she prepared to start work again on Spectrum. Upon Leah's face there was a hopeful smile as she stepped inside her basement laboratory as she internally prepared herself to start work because that day, she fervently hoped that her breakthrough would finally show up since she had been stood up by success every working day for the past month now and achievement had rather frustratingly, silently eluded her.

A flame of hope had however, now been ignited inside Leah's heart and mind due to Zidane's words of encouragement the night before that perhaps that day, she might actually finish her completion work on Spectrum which would then allow and enable her to perform some walk-through tests inside the Spectrum environments that she had created. The prospect of completion had mockingly teased Leah's mind for the past month but now as she was fully aware, it was an actual, real possibility because only one incomplete task really remained for Leah to complete and then she could embark upon her very first Spectrum adventure.

Eager anticipation seemed to bubble away just below the surface of Leah's skin and her body began to tingle with excitement as she walked towards the laptop that she usually utilized to interact with the Spectrum system every working day as a hopeful sigh escaped from her lips. Eight sensational emotional journeys had been created by Leah that lived inside Spectrum which promised to deliver adventures to consumers that would amuse, entertain and excite because she had programmed the system to provide some absolutely phenomenal experiences and so now, she was eager to try each one out herself.

Although a huge question lingered and hung inside Leah's mind as to whether Spectrum could really, actually deliver what she had initially intended it to, Leah at least felt encouraged as she sat down and commanded Spectrum to initialize that throughout that day, she might just actually, really find out. Every single aspect of Spectrum had been diligently fine-tuned, very precisely because Leah had striven for absolute perfection and so now, she just couldn't wait to explore that perfection for the first time ever in a personal capacity herself.

Later that afternoon and just before two, Leah's professional dedication and all her tireless efforts did not go without reward as she finally completed the required formula and system codes and then the Spectrum system immediately began to initialize as it lit up. Much to Leah absolute satisfaction and total delight, the transparent Spectrum capsule in the center of the room had clearly indicated that it was now ready to be occupied and for user interactions and so Leah quickly, enthusiastically jumped to her feet and then eagerly headed towards it. A deep, excited breath was taken as Leah mounted the small steps that led up to the capsule, slipped inside it and then lay down as she prepared for her mind to participate in a Spectrum experience as an actual User for the very first time because it truly was a significant moment and one that Leah had waited to experience now, for several very long years.

Nothing but total silence surrounded Leah inside the basement as she issued a voice command and the capsule lid automatically descended as it closed down over her body and so Leah rapidly closed her eyes as she prepared to wait for her first Spectrum experience to actually begin. For the next eight hours of that day as Leah had planned, she would be whisked away to an unknown fantasy environment by Spectrum, a technology that she herself had created and so now, she just couldn't wait to experience the many wonders that Spectrum actually offered and contained.

Each emotional journey inside Spectrum actually required ten hours exactly to complete but because Leah had already factored in the time that day that Zidane would need to spend with her later that evening, a ten hour experience on that particular occasion was totally out of the question, if Leah wanted to spend any time with Zidane before the couple slept that night. Inside Spectrum there was a timer which had already been set and programmed according to Leah's time constraints that day which would wake her up at exactly ten that night which meant, Zidane would not be particularly alarmed or worried that evening by any prolonged absences which suited Leah right down to the ground because the timer provided her with a degree of control over her interactions with the Spectrum system.

On this occasion Leah had already decided that eight hours would definitely have to suffice and as far as she was concerned, that aspect of her participation that day was totally non-negotiable because Zidane needed to eat dinner later that evening and so too did she. Dinner was an absolute necessity on a daily basis and that Leah had already accepted and factored in to her decision because her body definitely required food and so that time constraint was an easy one to adhere to since it was after all, also in her best physical interests and an evening meal had already been prepared in advance that day for the couple to consume.

For the purposes of Leah's first adventure inside Spectrum, she had decided that no adjustments to her personality or physicality would be made since she wished to experience Spectrum for the very first time in a pure form as herself, even though she could actually make such changes if she wanted to do so because she had built that functionality into the Spectrum system. In order to make Spectrum more interesting for consumers, users could choose from various personality and physical adjustments from a range of choices that they could make at the outset of an emotional journey, even though their initial User Profile was built upon their own physical being and distinct individual personalities. However, since

Leah wanted to experience Spectrum that day in its raw form and it would be her very first visit to an actual Spectrum environment, no personality or physical tweaks would be made that day for the purposes of simplicity because that would allow Leah to fully analyze her first experience inside Spectrum in a much simpler manner.

Once personality and physical changes had been made to a User's Profile inside Spectrum, those changes could then be saved and implemented throughout the rest of a particular emotional journey because Spectrum would save those preferences as each user required and utilize them for the remainder of any ten hour visit, so that changes could last for an entire experience in a seamless manner. If a user wished to utilize any changes for more than one emotional journey, the Spectrum system could also be commanded to be apply those changes as required to future visits and so the Spectrum system itself that Leah had created, invented and built was highly complex and extremely flexible because she had intentionally built all those very precise functionalities into it.

Since it was Leah's very first visit to Spectrum however, she had wanted to explore Spectrum in its pureness as herself so that she could measure her experiences more easily, before any more elaborate experimentation was undertaken and so Leah's basic User Profile that would be applied to her first emotional journey on this occasion, would simply be her natural self. The first emotional journey that Leah was due to explore that day was one that was supposed to be filled with joy which she had intentionally chosen simply because it was to be her first escapade and adventure inside the fantasy world of Spectrum and that particular journey promised to be full of fun and laughter. Quite intentionally that day, Leah had steered away from and totally avoided anything that might be slightly scary and any emotional journey that might involve much more complex, far heavier, or any negative emotions on purpose, purely to ensure that her first experience inside Spectrum would indeed be a pleasant one.

In terms of Spectrum's design the system was extremely elaborate in that it allowed each user's thoughts, choices and decisions to define their subsequent actions and movements which were then interpreted and implemented by Spectrum in a predictive manner which meant, all Leah had to do now, was lie back and enjoy her experience. The small microchip situated inside Spectrum's transparent case contained a brain scanner and neurological wave device that Leah had programmed and installed which allowed Spectrum to function with live user interactions and incorporate their desired actions and reactions into any Spectrum environment. Everything about Spectrum was extremely high tech but as Leah fully appreciated, it really had to be in order to allow the system to function effectively and to ensure that each emotional journey felt as real as possible to the end user because that was Spectrum's unique strength and main selling point.

Fortunately for Leah, she had chosen sleep as the preferred means of entry into Spectrum's fantasy environments and so that meant that no energetic, physical expenditure was required to enjoy the Spectrum system which for Leah was the optimal choice because that also meant, consumers would not be restricted by any mobility issues or any physical challenges. Another huge advantage of Leah's choice regarding Spectrum's complex design was that consumers would not feel totally worn out after they had utilized the system, or at least not in a physical sense because they would sleep all the way through each experience and for Leah that specification held a lot of appeal, since it would allow people to really relax and not physically drain them.

Some particles of sleeping gas rapidly began to circulate inside the capsule and fill its interior as Leah inhaled deeply as she prepared to be transported to another world and essentially, a fantasy world that she had created through a technology that she had built every single day for the past three years. Not a single word was whispered as Leah began to drift off as the sleeping gas rapidly began to fill the interior of the capsule and as it hit her senses, she quickly fell into a deep, peaceful slumber as for the very first time ever, she entered into the world of Spectrum.

Just a minute or so later, when Leah's eyes reopened, she immediately found herself strewn out across the ground upon a lush, emerald green bed of grass in the middle of what looked to be a huge meadow. In every direction that Leah looked, the grass it appeared stretched out as far as her eyes could see and the monotony of the continuous green was only broken by some small delicate flowers that contained all the colors of the rainbow which decorated the blades of grass at sporadic but frequent intervals. From what Leah could see at first glance, her surroundings definitely appeared to be genuine enough and seemed very pleasant as she quietly absorbed her current environment and then smiled a satisfied smile because ultimately, her goal with regards to Spectrum had definitely been achieved, since everything around her looked so very real and so convincingly authentic.

Once Leah had satisfied her mind that she was indeed, definitely inside her first Spectrum environment, she then quickly stood up and brushed some bits off her clothes which it seemed had collated not only some strands of grass but also some particles of dirt amongst the folds. Much to Leah's surprise however, as she glanced down at her body she suddenly noticed that she was now clothed in a long, pretty, golden dress that adorned her frame perfectly which looked slightly regal. A smile crossed Leah's face as she observed that some shiny diamond like jewels appeared to be sprinkled across the dress that decorated and clung to the material which sparkled as rays of sunlight shone down from the sky above her head and bounced playfully of the surface of each small, delicate stone. Gone was the simple pair of rather drab looking black trousers and gone too was the plain white tunic that Leah had worn earlier that day and the very basic attire that she had dressed in that morning was quite intriguingly, no longer actually present or even remotely visible to her.

The golden dress that now adorned Leah's frame inside Spectrum was definitely very pretty but she certainly hadn't been wearing it that afternoon when she'd initially arrived inside the basement and so that amused Leah slightly as she began to appreciate just how spectacular her outfit actually looked. One visit to Spectrum had provided Leah with a better outfit than the current contents of her entire wardrobe in real life which swiftly provoked her to conclude that a shopping trip definitely had to happen sometime soon because that wasn't necessarily a positive thing and that one outfit had just made her whole wardrobe suddenly look, extremely shabby.

Not more than a couple of meters away from Leah's current position, almost hidden amongst the blades of grass, she suddenly spotted a rough dirt path which appeared to lead somewhere and so she began to walk briskly towards it and then started to follow it in the only direction that she possibly could. Really and truly as Leah thoughtfully observed, there appeared to be no other direction that she could walk-in that seemed to lead anywhere because the path had started just a meter or so away from her initial position and so it seemed to be the only logical thing to do, the only real choice that she actually had and the only direction that she could walk-in that appeared to lead to somewhere. Unlike the usual cement street walkways that Leah was accustomed to in the real world, she rapidly noticed as she started to fully cooperate with the path's presence and follow it that this path wasn't clearly defined or even very smooth and it certainly wasn't straight and it looked as if it just been formed from the dirt below the grass which had been trampled into non-existence, purely to steer people in a particular direction.

For about the next eight hundred meters or so, Leah did nothing else but walk as the dirt path twisted and turned in various directions but as she walked, she continued to faithfully follow the path until she finally spotted the entrance to a building which it appeared the dirt trail led directly towards. Quite unusually, Leah silently observed, the structure that the dirt path led up to wasn't an actual house or a home and the building didn't seem to even remotely resemble an office block or a shopping mall and it looked to Leah like some kind of palace or castle although it certainly wasn't grey or made out of stone and was in fact, formed from neat rows of glossy golden bricks.

An electric current of excitement seemed to suddenly rush through Leah's form as she drew closer to the building and as she neared the structure, she noticed that the glossy golden bricks shone in the sunlight as each one happily and silently greeted the Sun. The walls of the structure which had been formed entirely from the golden elegant looking bricks that sat in neat lines as each column towered towards the sky, looked very impressive and so as Leah walked towards the building she smiled in joyful satisfaction because it all appeared to be absolutely splendid and totally spectacular.

Despite the fact that Leah had personally designed every single one of the eight emotional journeys inside Spectrum because the system literally had thousands of possible unique combinations made up from a diverse range of scenarios, challenges, activities and layouts that could be generated and combined in numerous different ways that meant, not even Leah herself could accurately predict what would happen inside Spectrum on any given visit. How each of those various elements would be combined during a consumer's journey within Spectrum was determined by a totally random process that Spectrum controlled which again had been another aspect that Leah had intentionally programmed that way, in order to make Spectrum more exciting for consumers and their experiences more spontaneous and so her visit that day, was and would be totally unpredictable in every single way that it possibly could be.

Another additional functionality that had been built into the Spectrum system actually allowed each user to save any incomplete emotional journey that they had visited which meant that although Leah would not complete her whole journey of joy that day, she could visit it again at some point in the future to complete it, if she wished to do so. The emotional journey of joy that Spectrum had generated for Leah that day already looked as if might be very pleasant and since she would have to cut her first visit short, Leah at least felt joyfully reassured that she had built a functionality into Spectrum that would allow her to enjoy the final two hours of that experience at a later date.

Quite interestingly but rather strangely, Leah noticed as she began to walk towards the glossy golden structure, around the perimeter of the castle like building there appeared to be a very wide moat but there wasn't actually much water inside it and so that meant, the watery border looked more like a shallow paddling pool than a deep body of liquid. Despite the lack of water however, for some inexplicable reason, the moat had a very wide, large bridge that lay across it which led directly into the entrance of the shiny, golden castle like structure that hardly seemed worth all the effort in Leah's mind because the rather skimpy dribble of water certainly didn't look as if it needed a structure that size just to cross it.

"Such a huge bridge, a few planks of wood would have probably done the job just as well and more than sufficed." Leah whispered to herself as she grinned. "Perhaps I just came along at the wrong time, maybe the tide is out or perhaps the moat is having a bad day, or maybe the moat is under the weather today and so it didn't manage to fill itself up."

At the very least however, the extremely grand looking, huge moat bridge did mean one thing for absolute certain, Leah quietly concluded as she began to walk across it and that one thing was definitely positive because it meant that she could cross the moat without getting her feet wet and that she could greet her adventure head on without any possible slippages. Once Leah arrived at the other side of the bridge, just a minute or two later, she found herself directly underneath a large, glossy golden arch which led into a cobbled courtyard that seemed to be formed from the same glossy golden bricks as the castle's walls though each brick that contributed to the floor of the courtyard was of course, much smaller in size.

Everything about the glossy golden castle like structure looked absolutely spectacular and as Leah quietly absorbed her surroundings in total wonder, she really was in absolute awe because the building looked so very grand and what one might even consider regal which correlated well with her dress and the pretty gemstones scattered across it. Some gentle, cautious steps were taken as Leah stepped inside the courtyard and when she arrived at the very center of its large interior, she suddenly came to a complete standstill as she silently began to inspect her surroundings and look for any indications that might provide a clue as to what she should do next.

A current of excitement silently kept Leah company and ran through her form as she thoughtfully, visually inspected and absorbed her wonderful surroundings which were truly fairy tale like and situated a million miles away from her usual haunt, the dowdy basement that she usually spent most of her days inside. The fictious, immersive, fantasy environment that Leah was now just about to experience, she could not wait to dive into as she prepared to dip her toes, mind and simulated form into the potential adventures that Spectrum contained with joyful and eager anticipation because from what Leah had seen so far, Spectrum had absolutely delivered.

Much to Leah's surprise however, before even a minute had passed by, a rather strange looking fellow suddenly popped out of a stable door situated in one of the interior walls of the courtyard itself and then he briskly strode confidently towards her and it almost seemed as if her arrival had actually been expected. Rather strangely, Leah observed, the man's body was clothed in a very unusual, bright yellow and bold red costume that looked extremely baggy and as it literally hung down from his body, it almost seemed to swamp his entire frame. All in all, the outfit was rather odd looking and it looked as if it had come from centuries ago because it was totally unfashionable which immediately prompted Leah to smile as she began to visually inspect it, purely for her own amusement.

Perhaps, Leah thoughtfully concluded as she silently began to absorb and digest his rather comical appearance, the weird eccentric look was preferred inside castles and perhaps, just perhaps, his outfit was all the rage amongst the castle's occupants. Despite the fact that the man's outfit was absolutely huge, Leah noticed as he walked towards her that his actual frame looked to be a bit on the skinny side which meant, his clothing was definitely way too big for him and so purely to entertain herself, Leah silently began to try and estimate how many sizes too big his outfit might actually be. From what Leah could see, from her quite rough, quick visual inspection, the outfit looked to be at least twenty sizes to big for him but that hugeness didn't seem to bother him in the slightest or restrict his movements in any way and as he rapidly drew much closer to Leah, her estimate remained politely unspoken and her conclusion locked firmly behind her lips as she plastered a courteous smile across her face and prepared to greet him.

“Princess Leah, your presence is now required inside the Castle of Joy because you are to host the Joyful Dance this evening.” The strangely dressed man announced as he neared. “So first of all, you'll have to prepare yourself for the Royal Hunt and then later today, you'll be able to attend the Joyful Dance and the Feast of Plenty, all of which you will be required to host as part of your royal duties.” He boomed before he paused for a moment and then glanced at her face just before he began to leap energetically around the courtyard.

"Right now?" Leah asked as she grinned.

Irrespective of the man's strange choice in clothing that oozed eccentricity and his energetic leaps which seemed totally random, very chaotic and extremely haphazard, Leah noticed that the clownish male who looked to be in his mid-thirties and approximately five years older than Leah herself, definitely seemed friendly and harmless enough. A jovial smile seemed to spread out across his face in direct response to Leah's question and Leah felt a sudden urge to laugh bubble up inside of her as she continued to watch him in fascinated amusement due to his comical behavior and some jangly noises that appeared to accompany his chaotic leaps which it seemed emanated from some bobbles attached to a floppy hat upon his head.

In many ways, the quirky man's appearance reminded Leah a bit of a clown, due to his behavior which seemed slightly strange and quite erratic but he didn't have a shiny red nose or tons of bright makeup plastered across his face and so she rapidly concluded that it was highly unlikely that he was an actual clown. A hand was swiftly placed over Leah's mouth however, as she attempted to mask her amusement, since to laugh at someone you had just met could perhaps be interpreted as slightly rude and it really wasn't the done thing as Leah was fully aware.

"Yes, we have to go right now Princess Leah." He suddenly urged as he paused for a moment and then turned to face her.

"We do?" Leah asked.

"Yes, we really do." He insisted as he gently took her arm and then began to lead her towards a pair of huge golden doors situated at the top of the courtyard.

“Where are we actually going?” Leah enquired as she politely humored his request and obediently started to follow him as she walked just a step or two behind his form. "And who exactly are you?" She ventured to ask as a soft giggle managed to escape from her lips.

Suddenly, the slight, slim, quirky looking man froze in his tracks almost as if he had been struck by lightning and due to his very abrupt halt and sudden variation in pace, Leah almost stumbled over his feet as she came to an immediate stop right behind him. Upon the man's face, Leah noticed that there was now a slightly apologetic expression as he immediately turned to face her and then began to introduce himself.

"How astoundingly rude of me Princess Leah, I've not introduced myself, I'm Sebastian." He explained as he flashed her a grin. "I'm the court jester of the Joyful Kingdom and today, I'll be your guide."

An amused smile instantly spread out across Leah's face in direct response to his words as she immediately accepted Sebastian's explanation because now, his outfit and appearance suddenly made total sense to her since she had created such a guide inside Spectrum. However, despite that sudden enlightenment that still didn't answer the question of where Sebastian actually wanted to take Leah which continued to linger in the air, unanswered and unaddressed because as yet he hadn't furnished her with an actual answer. The explanation that Sebastian had provided to Leah had however, definitely correlated with the fact that she had created guides within Spectrum to guide users through each emotional journey and so that meant, he was therefore there to guide her through that particular emotional plane, or part of it and so now at least, she felt partially satisfied by his divulgence of that information.

Guides inside Spectrum as Leah already knew, could be allocated to specific tasks which varied in accordance to which emotional plane they featured and appeared in and their main role was to direct users towards the various activities that they were supposed to engage in throughout their visit in order to optimize their experiences. Since Leah had created thousands of guides that could function across all the emotional planes inside Spectrum that could lead users in a variety of ways however, that meant that their appearances could be very unpredictable, absolutely random and totally unique inside any given journey that a user embarked upon and so Sebastian's appearance and presence in that particular emotional journey was in most respects, an unexpected surprise and an unpredictable variable. Some guides appeared in human form, since Leah had created them that way but others did not and Sebastian it had now transpired, was Leah's very first encounter with an actual guide inside Spectrum with a human looking form, albeit a rather eccentric, extremely quirky one.

"Does that outfit come with the job Sebastian?" Leah teased playfully as she began to inspect his garments once again with an amused expression upon her face. "It's very unusual and are you sure it's the right size for you?"

The very baggy yellow and red corduroy suit was extremely large and so Sebastian's slender frame, Leah thoughtfully observed, hardly seemed able to cope with the mass of material that hung from it which almost appeared to completely drown him. Some strange bobbles hung down from some woolly threads that had been stitched into the top of a floppy, triangular shaped hat that Sebastian wore which sat rather clumsily on top of his head and each one swung back and forth and bounced mischievously around every time he moved his head which amused Leah somewhat. Inside each bobble there appeared to be a bell and every time one hit Sebastian's face, the bobbles jingled and the noises prompted Leah to giggle as she watched him move his head around as she waited for him to answer her question.

"This is a court jester's uniform Princess Leah." Sebastian explained. "It has to be very big so that I can fit all kinds of things inside it because I have to keep the good people of the court in the Joyful Kingdom fully entertained."

"Right, I guess that makes some kind of sense Sebastian. I

think I'll just stick to pretty dresses and leave the entertainment to you because if I wore an outfit like that one, I'd probably trip over it so often that I would spend most of my day on my butt on the ground." Leah replied as she smiled. "So where are we actually going Sebastian?" She asked again.

"First of all Princess Leah, you'll embark upon and participate in the Royal Hunt which takes place in the Savage Woods nearby and then you'll return to the palace to host and to attend the Joyful Dance which will be followed by the Feast of Plenty." Sebastian announced triumphantly. "It's going to be absolutely splendid but first, you'll need to visit your chamber to prepare for the Royal Hunt."

"What happens at the Royal Hunt?" Leah enquired.

"Well, the Royal Hunt is a very special event that is only held once a year and you'll get to ride a very rare, black unicorn which you will use to chase wild game through the Savage Woods which at some point, you'll then have to catch and kill." Sebastian explained. "Once the hunt party has collected enough game for the feast, you'll then return to the Castle of Joy so that the spoils of the Royal Hunt can be prepped, cooked and served to the guests that will attend the Feast of Plenty this evening."

"That sounds absolutely amazing Sebastian." Leah replied as she nodded her head enthusiastically and smiled. "I probably can't go out on a hunt in this dress though that probably wouldn't work."

"You certainly can't Princess Leah." Sebastian agreed. "That's why you have to visit your chamber inside the Castle of Joy first to prepare."

"What happens at the Joyful Dance?" Leah asked.

"The Joyful Dance happens just before the Feast of Plenty and it is a very special occasion because all the nobles from across the realm attend to present themselves, so quite a few princes and princesses will be in attendance." Sebastian explained. "Some will make betrothals whilst others will simply present themselves to all the other royal families that are present for the very first time and then everyone will have a chance to participate in the traditional dances of the Joyful Kingdom, it's usually lots of fun." He continued. "Once the Joyful Dance is over, a huge feast is then held and there's lots of wine, food and entertainment and I'll actually be entertaining you this evening, so it's going to be absolutely wonderful because I'm always great fun."

Despite Sebastian's odd mannerisms and his quirky strangeness, he seemed harmless, sincere and funny enough and so as Leah nodded her head, she quickly accepted his explanations at face value. Regardless of what did or did not happen next as Leah fully appreciated, she had no actual choice but to accept Sebastian's guidance because at that point in time, he was the only guide that she actually had and so essentially that meant, for the time being he had to be trusted and allowed to guide her through that particular emotional plane.

Since Leah was currently situated in a totally foreign environment and Sebastian was an allocated guide in that environment assigned to her emotional journey on that particular occasion, there really was no valid reason to dispute anything that he related to her any further and so she prepared to fully cooperate with his suggestions. Although Sebastian was really quite strange, strangely enough he was at the very least, quite comical with that strangeness and even what one might describe as fairly pleasant and so it wasn't difficult for Leah to feel totally at ease with his presence as she began to appreciate his quirky but friendly, warm approach.

"Right Sebastian, now I totally understand." Leah swiftly confirmed as she smiled. "I have to get changed now so that I can participate in the Royal Hunt, please lead the way."

"Yes, you do, so please come with me Princess Leah." Sebastian immediately agreed as he gently held onto her arm and then began to guide her across the remainder of the enclosed courtyard.

A pair of very large, shiny golden doors seemed to guard the entrance to the interior of the Castle of Joy and so as the two resumed their walk towards the doors, Leah began to silently wonder what the interior of the building might actually look like because so far, the exterior had been absolutely spectacular. When the two arrived directly in front of the two huge doors, Sebastian immediately began to push one of the doors open and as Leah watched him, she waited in total silence so that she would not distract him from his task because the doors actually looked rather heavy. Some very loud creaks emanated from the large golden door as it moved as it gave way to the request from another presence to open and fully cooperated and to Leah in some strange way, the creaks almost sounded as if the door itself had actually spoken to them both and as if it had politely invited them to step inside the interior of the magnificent, regal golden structure.

Just on the other side of the two large, heavy golden doors, Leah rapidly discovered that there was a very long hallway with glossy white walls and she immediately began to silently marvel at how immaculate and spotless the interior of the building actually looked as she stepped into the hallway and then began to follow Sebastian along it. The two walls that now surrounded Leah were a brilliant, glossy white and as she walked, each wall seemed to shimmer and shine as particles of light bounced silently of each one from a row of windows that lined one side of the hallway. Unlike the walls however, Leah immediately noticed that the floor appeared to be formed from the darkest, black marble stone that she had ever seen and that each surface appeared to compliment the other absolutely immaculately and so from what Leah had seen so far, the interior of the building seemed to be very elegant, absolutely splendid and totally spectacular.

In terms of Leah's current surroundings, everything inside the building appeared to be very majestic and what one might consider rather regal but the overall tone was much more modern and far more fashionable than any castle that Leah had ever seen before in photographs and so it was perhaps an artificial simulation of what a castle might look like, if built in current times. Since Leah had never ventured into or stepped foot inside a real castle before, not even once in her entire life, she couldn't be totally sure that it was truly reflective of what the interior of a castle would really look like but since she had created the Castle of Joy herself, she happily began to accept her surroundings because they were truly amazing, seemed very realistic and looked utterly fabulous, just as she had planned and then created them to be. Despite the fact that it wasn't actually a real experience and the reality that the Castle of Joy did not really exist, the interior of the structure certainly looked realistic enough to Leah and it was a huge improvement upon the basement that she usually spent most of her days inside, tied to various pieces of equipment and so she prepared to just relax, appreciate the moment for what it was and to enjoy her surroundings, since after all, she had actually created them.

Once the two had walked along the long, glossy, white hallway, they arrived at the other end of it where the long narrow space suddenly opened out into a large square lobby which had five large, golden doors situated in one of the walls and then much to Leah's surprise, Sebastian came to a very abrupt stop. For a moment Sebastian stood completely still as he stared at the five doors and as Leah glanced at his face, she noticed that he actually seemed to look quite confused as she watched him suddenly start to scratch his head as if he was in very deep thought as he inspected the doors directly in front of them both. Much to Leah's surprise and amusement, it actually felt as if Sebastian wanted to wait for one of the doors to speak to him and tell him which one he should actually open. The five doors however, Leah observed with a smile, despite Sebastian's confusion remained totally silent and it was highly unlikely as she already knew that any of the doors would attempt to speak to either Sebastian or Leah herself in order to provide either of the two with any kind of direction, no matter how long Sebastian or even she stared at each door and that was a highly predictable fact.

An extremely amused expression remained upon Leah's face as she continued to wait for Sebastian to either speak or walk towards one of the doors as she internally considered how strange his position and actions seemed to be because he was supposed to be her actual guide during that particular emotional journey that day. Since Sebastian was supposed to be Leah's actual guide and he didn't actually seem to know where to go next and which door to open, she began to wonder how she would find anything herself within her current environment because he certainly seemed to know much more about the Castle of Joy than she did and even he seemed to be a bit lost.

"It's definitely this one Princess Leah." Sebastian finally confirmed with a playful grin as he suddenly broke the silence that had gathered between the two inside the lobby and then nodded his head. He held onto Leah's arm and then gently began to lead her towards a door situated on the very right-hand side of the large square space. "It's definitely this door."

"Are you absolutely sure Sebastian?" Leah asked as she grinned.

"I'm very sure Princess Leah." Sebastian replied as he immediately gave her a certain nod in response. "It has to be this one."

Much to Leah's amusement, a few jingles suddenly emanated from the bobbles attached to Sebastian's floppy hat as he assertively nodded his head and as each bobble playfully bounced of his face, Leah smiled as she began to follow him towards the mysterious door. The bells inside Sebastian's bobbles continued to jingle away as the two approached the door as Sebastian wiggled his head around as he walked towards it which instantly provoked Leah to laughter and so much so that she even released some amused giggles because the jangly noise from the bobbles really was rather funny and very unusual.

"You certainly wouldn't get lost in a snow storm Sebastian." Leah teased playfully. "Not in that outfit and especially not in that hat."

"I know." Sebastian agreed. "But this hat can be very helpful at times Princess Leah, it lets you know when I'm around, even when you can't see me."

"Yes, you'd be hard to miss with that hat on your head." Leah joked as she started to appreciate the court jester's playful nature. She suddenly began to suspect that he had really known which door he was supposed to open all along because she had designed and created him to amuse and he definitely seemed, well equipped to deliver and so she continued to tease him as she began to participate with and encourage his quite quirky, eccentric sense of humor. "But don't worry Sebastian being unmissable can be a great quality at times, especially when people are lost."

"How very true Princess Leah, how very true." Sebastian agreed as he pushed the door open. "You can prepare yourself for the Royal Hunt inside your chamber and you should be able to find everything that you require in there but if you can't, I'll be back shortly." He reassured her as he politely held the door open. "I have to go back to the courtyard now because I have to prepare your mount but I'll come back and get you, when it's time for the Royal Hunt to begin."

Leah nodded and smiled appreciatively as she prepared to step through the now open door directly in front of her. "Thanks very much Sebastian." She replied.

"It's no trouble at all Princess Leah." Sebastian said. "I'm just glad to be of service because that is what I'm here for."

When Leah stepped through the actual door of what had been referred to as her chamber, she was immediately stunned and almost totally blown away by what she discovered inside the very large space because it appeared to be far more than just a changing room. A very large lounge area instantly greeted Leah's eyes which had an adjoined bedroom section at one end of it and a couple of other smaller rooms led off from the huge main room, one of which appeared to be an en-suite bathroom and so as she stepped further into the vast space, her surroundings immediately thrilled her because every inch looked absolutely luxurious and extremely grand.

The main area which appeared to be a cross between a lounge and a bedroom had a very high ceiling that was dome shaped and the lounge area almost looked as if several normal sized lounges could fit inside it and so Leah rapidly concluded that all in all, the space that she had been given to prepare herself and change in, was absolutely enormous. Situated at one side of the room there were two large French window doors that led out onto a small patio and everything about the huge space that Leah had been provided with seemed absolutely spectacular as she began to quietly absorb every intricate detail appreciatively.

For the next few minutes Leah did nothing else but admire the contents of the main room as she started to walk around it because even the white glossy walls looked very grand due to some shiny, silver flecks that ran through each one that made the four walls shimmer, sparkle and shine as particles of light bounced off each surface. Absolutely everything about the large, main room, Leah noticed as she silently inspected it, seemed to be spectacularly stunning and immaculately color coordinated because even the sparkly silver and white furniture matched the walls with total precision. Nothing inside the room from what Leah could see, felt or looked out of place and everything inside it seemed to compliment everything else and so she began to smile a very satisfied smile as she visually inspected every inch of the lavish, extravagant luxury that surrounded her which almost took her breath away.

Suddenly, the huge door that led into the chamber banged shut and the noise distracted Leah for a moment as she quickly turned around to face it because the noise immediately reminded her of Sebastian's presence or rather now, of his absence since he had completely and utterly vanished. No further discussions Leah noticed had taken place and Sebastian had simply departed and left her totally alone and so now, she had to find something appropriate to wear to participate in the Royal Hunt all on her own, although what exactly one wore to a Royal Hunt was still a total mystery.

"Such a strange chap." Leah whispered to herself as she gently shook her head and then glanced around the room as she began to visually search for a wardrobe that might contain some kind of suitable attire. "Funny but definitely very strange."

Essentially, because Sebastian hadn't actually said goodbye to Leah as he had parted and there had been no further discussions between the two, Leah suddenly began to realize that all his interactions appeared to be quite functional in nature and perhaps even what one might consider, slightly mechanical. Fortunately however, the humorous, quirky, upbeat edge to Sebastian's character and his eccentric, energetic, unpredictable approach really seemed to suit the environment that Leah was currently situated in and so his persona added pleasurably to her overall experience because he seemed to make everything around her feel slightly more enjoyable and much more natural and so his sudden departure didn't worry her too much, in the greater scheme of things.

"I do enjoy being called Princess Leah though, so I'd definitely invite Sebastian round for dinner and introduce him to Zidane." Leah admitted to herself. "Then I'd be like, you see Zidane I'm a Princess and you didn't even know, you're not very observant, are you?"

Despite Sebastian's rather abrupt departure and his total desertion, Leah was still mindful that she did now actually have to prepare herself for the actual Royal Hunt and so she began to make her way towards the huge bedroom area as she tiptoed across the dark, black marble floor. Every inch of Leah's surroundings was silently inspected as she went and although she felt slightly intimidated by her current environment because everything around her really was so very grand, it was pleasantly grand and definitely something that she could get used to.

"I could live here forever." Leah acknowledged as she arrived next to the huge, king-size, white and silver four poster bed, sat down on top of it and then bounced playfully up and down. "If only I could sleep in a bed like this in real life, even for just a night, how marvelous would that be?"

Some contemplations filled with absolute intrigue and delightful curiosity, suddenly began to tease and dance through Leah's thoughts and mind as she quietly admired the sheer extravagance and very luxurious nature of her chamber which pleasantly distracted her for a moment. In every single way imaginable, the bedroom was far more glamorous and much more luxurious than any other that Leah had ever seen before and it certainly wasn't like the rather humble bedroom or any part of the quite simple home that she shared with Zidane every day and night. A vast array of plump cushions that were various shapes and sizes lay strewn across the top of the luxurious sleeping facilities which instantly comforted Leah as she lay back down upon the bed and as her shoulders nestled gently against each comfortable, small dollop of luxury, she smiled mischievously.

“I wonder what it would be like to make love to Zidane on this bed?” Leah asked herself thoughtfully as her mind was suddenly drawn back to her very real life and the love of her real life once again. "Now that would probably be a lot of fun."

Much to Leah's surprise, an extremely loud horn suddenly and very unexpectedly sounded out and as it blasted through the air all around her and the noise flooded into the large room, it caused not only vibrations in her ears but she also almost jumped out of her skin because it rather rudely interrupted her mind, her thoughts and quickly put an end to her playful mental saunter, very abruptly. Due to the unexpected noise which definitely seemed to relate to the Royal Hunt, Leah's attention was immediately drawn back towards the activities that lay directly ahead of her, just upon the horizon of her day which required not only her attendance but also her full cooperation and participation and so as the noise came to an abrupt, very sudden end less than a minute later, she quickly sat up and then jumped of the bed.

"I guess that rather loud noise was something to do with the Royal Hunt, I better get ready." Leah advised herself. "So that means now, I actually have to find something appropriate to wear."

In terms of the actual noise itself, Leah noticed that the sound of the horn had not held any musical appeal and that it had certainly not been very pleasant as it had rumbled loudly through her ears but it had definitely been extremely loud and unapologetically bold and it seemed to have been an intentional attempt to alert the castle's occupants to the activities that were due to occur shortly. The Royal Hunt was due to commence very soon and so Leah was expected to be ready when it actually did so and she definitely wasn't because she had not even made a start yet.

"Such a beautiful bed, so comfortable and so absolutely splendid." Leah admitted to herself as she gave the lavish bed one final appreciative glance and one last look of total adoration. "I'd love to take you home with me bed, are you committed to this bedroom, or are you open to other opportunities and willing to travel? I don't really like to cheat on my own bed but for you, I would definitely be unfaithful and I'd even initiate actual divorce proceedings."

Nothing but total silence greeted Leah in response however and so she smiled as she began to walk towards two wide mirrored doors that she instantly assumed concealed the interior of the wardrobe behind them which seemed to be built into one of the walls inside the large bedroom area. The pretty dress that currently adorned Leah's form certainly wasn't suitable attire for the activities that were just about to occur and she definitely knew it, even though she had never been on an actual hunt before and so something suitable had to found inside the wardrobe's interior and found very quickly.

"I really need to get ready now." Leah whispered to herself. "And I haven't even started yet, though I have absolutely no clue what someone wears to a Royal Hunt, or any other kind of hunt for that matter."

One of the large mirrored doors was quickly slid open as Leah began to internally deliberate over what exactly she should wear but she still had no idea as she peered into the interior of the wardrobe and then started to assess her available options. The interior of the wardrobe, Leah rapidly discovered, was absolutely huge and it contained rows upon rows of clothing that hung from long rails which sat in neat lines inside of it and every inch was literally filled to the brim with outfits that looked as if they could suit every possible occasion imaginable.

"Well, I do know one thing for sure, I know I can't wear this dress and that I do know for absolute certain." Leah gently reminded herself. "So many choices and so little knowledge but I still have to find something appropriate to wear and find it in a timely fashion. What exactly is appropriate attire for a Royal Hunt though?" She asked herself as she continued to thoughtfully inspect the contents of the wardrobe. "Perhaps I should take this entire wardrobe home with me too, or maybe just the outfits inside it. The outfits in this wardrobe would definitely be sufficient and they would fill my wardrobe a thousand times over but all these outfits still don't give me a single clue about what I should actually wear right now."

No answer to Leah's question however, seemed to be

forthcoming as she continued to visually scan the interior of the wardrobe and none of the outfits it appeared, wanted to contribute to her discussion because no item of clothing eagerly leapt out at her, volunteered to be worn or even wished to advise her as each one just hung down limp and still with an attitude of total indifference from the hangers that they silently clung to. Rather frustratingly for Leah, procrastination and indecision suddenly seemed to grip her form for a moment and she completely froze as uncertainty rapidly began to set in and as she stood rooted to the same spot and just stared at the interior of the wardrobe with a frustrated expression upon her face, she waited hopefully and impatiently for a lightning bolt of ingenuity to strike.

The question of what one wore to an actual hunt continued to linger in the passageways of Leah's mind, unanswered and unsatisfied for a few more minutes as her eyes continued to scan the interior of the wardrobe and she frantically searched her thoughts for any possible answers but unfortunately, she still came up totally blank. A vast array of clothing was currently on offer to Leah but it was absolutely impossible to tell exactly which outfit she should wear for such an occasion and there really were no guarantees that when she did finally choose an outfit that it would be appropriate for the purposes for which it was required.

"You're not much help." Leah suddenly announced to the packed clothing rails as she shook her head and then frowned at the mass of outfits directly in front of her. "I guess I could always attend the Royal Hunt naked." She joked as she started to giggle. "Then I wouldn't need to choose any outfit at all and that would solve that problem."

Suddenly however, fortunately for Leah, she noticed a painting which hung from one of the walls that was situated quite close to one end of the mirrored wardrobe door that she had slid open and as it attracted her attention, she immediately began to walk towards it because it was a painted image of an actual hunt gathering. Since Leah had never ever attended a real hunt before, she fully appreciated that right now she needed all the guidance and help she could get and although she had researched such activities when she'd initially created Spectrum, she had literally researched thousands of different activities and so it was hard for her to remember exactly what kind of attire one should wear for such an occasion. A hopeful wish now existed in Leah's mind however that she would find some actual answers upon the brightly colored canvas that didn't seem to exist anywhere else as she enthusiastically and eagerly approached it.

Much to Leah's total relief, the painting immediately offered her an instant ray of hope because it silently furnished her with a very comprehensive answer as to what exactly she should wear for the Royal Hunt as she quietly began to inspect it. Every inch of the canvas was decorated with beautiful, vivid illustrations that looked as if they had been meticulously hand painted and Leah almost gasped in delight as she stared at the imagery contained in the oil painting directly in front of her because it was not just a visual treat but it also answered Leah's question, very precisely.

Each one of the human bodies featured in the painting and dotted around the courtyard, appeared to be just about to embark upon an actual hunt and as Leah quietly inspected it, she could clearly see some leather, strappy outfits were present which adorned and decorated each hunter's frame, albeit rather sparsely. Inside each person's hands they clasped an assortment of weapons which included bows, arrows and spears and those items further clarified and confirmed that the group were indeed, definitely just about to venture out on an actual hunt which was just about to commence and that they had dressed for the occasion. The group of people in the painting certainly seemed to be adequately equipped for a hunt and so the painting silently confirmed exactly what Leah was supposed to wear in a helpful but nonverbal manner as it rapidly chased her doubts away.

Only one task now really remained for Leah to actually perform in that she had to find a similar strappy looking, leather garment inside the interior of the huge wardrobe so that she could wear it and then essentially, her immediate problem would be solved because then she would be appropriately dressed for the Royal Hunt that was due to occur shortly. A satisfied smile crossed Leah's face as she walked back towards the mirrored doors of the large, elegant wardrobe as she prepared to resume her search once more because now at least, she had an actual answer to her question and now at least, she knew exactly what she had to find inside its very large, densely populated interior.

Delightfully for Leah the interior of the walk-in wardrobe looked so large that it almost gave her the impression that if she stepped inside it, she might get lost within it and then be unable to find her way back out of it again and so just for a moment, she began to wish that her own wardrobe at home had the same capacity and contents. The clothing rails seemed to go on and on forever and the garments hung down in neat rows as far as Leah's eyes could see and so she began to wonder for a moment as she perused its interior, if perhaps a whole family could live inside the actual wardrobe itself because it certainly looked large enough. Elegant dresses, royal robes, beautiful skirts, stunning blouses, tailored tunics and smart trousers lined every inch of the wardrobe's interior and the immense number of clothing choices on offer to Leah, teased her eyes, thrilled her thoughts and absolutely stunned her as she began to visually seek out the actual outfit that she required for the afternoon's activities.

Excitement rapidly began to mount inside of Leah as she began to wander around inside the wardrobe and as she searched, her heart seemed to beat more quickly than usual as she tried to find a strappy, leather outfit like one of the hunt outfits that she'd seen featured in the oil painting and the kind of outfit that she now desperately needed to attend the actual Royal Hunt that afternoon. Fortunately for Leah, her search didn't actually take very long and within just a few minutes she had managed to find a black, strappy, leather outfit very much like one of the outfits that she'd just seen and so she quickly slipped it off the hanger and then stepped back out into the bedroom with a triumphant smile upon her face as she prepared to put it on.

Once Leah had stripped down to her underwear and when she was almost naked, she then started to attach the all in one strappy, sparse leather skirt and bodice to her body as she attempted to comply with the dress code of the actual hunt that she was supposed to embark upon shortly. When Leah felt satisfied that she had dressed herself in the rather skimpy, scanty outfit correctly, she then faced one of the mirrored wardrobe doors and began to inspect her reflection, just to ensure that everything was indeed, in the correct position and the right place.

"Zidane would absolutely love this outfit." Leah advised herself decisively as she started to twist and turn in front of the mirrored wardrobe door and enthusiastically began to admire her appearance. "If you can actually call it an outfit, there's not much to it really but what it lacks in material, it certainly makes up for with sensuous appeal because it does possess a lot of sexual allure."

The black, leather, strappy attire, Leah definitely felt, looked absolutely stunning as she continued to admire her reflection in the mirrored wardrobe doors for a few more minutes because it courteously accentuated and politely complimented her frame in a way that somehow, gave her tons of instant sexual allure, a sensuous factor that had been very sorely missed in Leah's real life in recent times. When it came to the actual issue of the outfit itself, Leah had already noticed that there really wasn't much of it to go around but she didn't let that rather minor detail worry her too much as she smiled with total satisfaction and then nodded her head in absolute certainty.

Regardless of what was and wasn't there, the outfit was definitely suitable for the activities that lay ahead in Leah's now, more informed opinion and so she rapidly accepted that the outfit was indeed, highly appropriate and a perfect fit for the occasion. The strappy nature of the leather skirt would provide Leah with maximum flexibility which would enable her to mount or dismount any animal that she rode very quickly, if that was actually required on the hunt itself which she felt, it probably would be and so Leah began to relax in the knowledge that at the very least, she had managed to locate the correct outfit inside the huge wardrobe as she gave her reflection another quick visual scan because that really had been a task in itself.

For some inexplicable but very pleasant reason, Leah noticed that the outfit itself actually made her body look much stronger and far more powerful than usual and as she quietly inspected and absorbed her reflection once again, a surprised gasp suddenly escaped from her lips. Somehow and in just a matter of minutes, Leah felt as if she had been completely transformed into an Amazonian princess and the results of that transformation as far as she was concerned, were totally and utterly breath-taking.

Each leather strap that the hunt outfit composed of looked sexy and rugged and the flaps of dark black leather that formed a skirt, albeit a very scanty one, clearly showed off Leah's thighs which poked out from in-between each flap and the whole outfit was not only delightful for Leah to wear but also to look at. In so many ways, the outfit was an absolute treat for Leah to adorn her form with because it reminded her of some of the sexy, seductive outfits that she had worn in the past for Zidane which instantly rekindled and evoked several very fond memories inside her mind that involved past moments of sensuous pleasure and historical moments of excited passion that the couple had shared.

Recently, life and Leah had become very dull and so too had the couple's daily routine and the outfit clearly illustrated and silently highlighted to Leah just how dull her own real life had now become back inside the very real world. Once upon a romantic time Leah had made so much effort for Zidane on so many occasions to keep the sparks of love, romance and passion ignited, alive and rekindled between them both but in recent times, due to Leah's additional hours inside the basement as she had worked upon Spectrum, it almost felt as if those romantic sparks inside of her had dimmed, or as if those passionate sparks had just taken a vacation from their relationship and as yet, had not returned.

"I think I might need to buy an outfit like this when I get home." Leah advised herself as she smiled. "It seems to really suit me."

Not more than a few steps away from the end of one of the mirrored wardrobe doors a silver dressing table stood in its allocated spot that brimmed with accessories as it awaited Leah's attention and as she glanced at it thoughtfully, she smiled and then began to make her way swiftly towards it. A huge mirror was situated on top of the dressing table and as Leah looked into it, she hurriedly sat down in front of it as she began to quietly consider some of the cosmetic changes that might perhaps compliment her hunt outfit. Some final touches, Leah definitely felt, were required to enhance and complete her exotic hunt look which was not only extremely sensual but also very attractive and so she prepared to make those additional final touches as she stared into the mirror's reflective surface and at her own reflection.

The large mirror itself looked absolutely spectacular due to some flowery patterns that had been very skillfully etched into the edges of its mirrored surface and so as Leah absorbed every intricate detail, she began to silently admire the workmanship on display. Every lavish, luxurious and elegant inch of Leah's current surroundings had amazed, delighted and surprised her and as she gasped at the sheer sophistication that she was currently immersed in and hungrily digested every minute, glorious, fabulous detail, she thoughtfully appreciated the beautiful mirror which was it seemed, another gorgeous refinement that had not escaped her attention.

For that day inside Spectrum, Leah was definitely, fully immersed in another world that sat not only a world away but quite possibly, even a galaxy away from her own world and the rather bland, subterranean laboratory that she spent most of her life inside and the majority of her days in. The quite moderate bedroom that Leah shared each night with Zidane, suddenly seemed pale in comparison to her current surroundings and it was as if a tadpole in an ocean had just swum alongside a huge whale as she thoughtfully compared both venues for a moment. This world was another lifestyle entirely and because Leah really wasn't used to the extravagance that currently surrounded her, it almost made her feel like a pauper because it was all so magnificent and all so very splendid.

Suddenly, a polite but gentle knock at the door interrupted Leah's thoughts and her final preparations and her mind was rapidly drawn back to the issue of the Royal Hunt that she was now actually, just about to participate in and so Leah quickly tied back her hair, slipped on some earrings and then rose to her feet as she prepared to answer it. The actual knock at the door could only really be one person and that one person was of course Sebastian because he was her allocated guide at the present time and the only person who knew what she was supposed to do next which meant, he had definitely returned just as he had promised he would.

Every inch of Leah's appearance now looked extremely presentable and so as she crossed the room and walked towards the door, she definitely felt appropriately dressed to take part in the first set of activities that had been planned for her participation that day, namely the Royal Hunt. Once Leah was situated directly in front of the large, golden door, she took a deep breath and then began to pull it open as she prepared to greet Sebastian once more in person and to attend the actual Royal Hunt with a smile upon her face and an ounce of nervousness inside her form because it really would be such a vastly different experience for her.

"Great Princess Leah, I see that you've managed to find something suitable to wear." Sebastian immediately teased as he greeted her with a cheerful grin. "That's wonderful because your mount is now ready for the Royal Hunt."

"Well, I did struggle for a minute or two Sebastian because there were just so many outfits to choose from." Leah replied as she smiled. "In fact for a moment, I almost thought I'd have to borrow one of your very bright, extremely colorful outfits because it really was so difficult to actually decide."

"That wouldn't have been a problem Princess Leah but the bobbles on some of my hats might not be very conducive to the actual hunt itself. They would probably get in your way and then you might even end up pricking yourself with a spear." Sebastian replied with a cheeky grin.

Leah chuckled. "Yes, the bobbles on your hat do seem to bounce around rather a lot Sebastian." She agreed.

"We should go now Princess Leah because the hunt party have already gathered inside the courtyard and they're waiting for you." Sebastian urged.

"Right." Leah replied as she stepped out into the lobby and then closed the door of her chamber behind her. "To be perfectly honest though Sebastian, I could have stayed in there all day because it really is absolutely perfect."

Sebastian grinned.

On their way back towards the courtyard, the two engaged in some light conversation as they walked as Leah quietly considered the very unusual activities that she was just about to engage in because the Royal Hunt really would be such a vastly different experience for her and not something that she had ever considered before. Despite the fact that Leah had created so many adventurous experiences inside Spectrum, she had never so much as even ridden a real horse before, never mind gone an actual hunt and so she began to wonder for a moment, just how hard it might actually be. Irrespective of Leah's lack of experience however, she was now just about to not only ride an animal but also participate in an actual hunt and as the two neared the main entrance of the castle once more, it suddenly dawned upon Leah that she might actually have to kill an actual animal that same afternoon and the implications of that potential activity, in some ways actually quite scared her.

When the two arrived back inside the exterior courtyard, much to Leah's surprise, she now found that the enclosed area was no longer empty and that it bustled with activity which immediately intrigued her because it was literally jam packed with riders, stable-hands and horses that had appeared as if from nowhere. Several stable-hands nodded politely at the two to greet them as they passed by each one but from what Leah could clearly see, most of the men and women dotted around the courtyard that were dressed for the hunt had already mounted their respective mounts as they clung onto the silver reins which hung down from the bridles that adorned each of the horse's heads. A few of the creatures inside the courtyard, Leah thoughtfully observed, appeared to be quite restless and those horses paced up and down and it was almost as if some of the animals themselves were anxious for the Royal Hunt to begin and as if they were in an eager rush to actually participate.

Just a few animals, Leah noticed as she walked, still remained unmounted and rider-less and those horses predominantly, stood patiently next to their riders as they waited to be mounted whilst their riders made some last minute preparations and fully equipped themselves with arrows, bows and spears. A few more curious glances were observantly cast towards some of the riders as Sebastian continued to lead Leah through the courtyard towards a magnificent black unicorn and she almost gasped with surprise as she began to digest the majestic looking creature that it was intended would be her actual mount that afternoon and for the duration of the Royal Hunt itself. The Royal Hunt was now definitely, just about to actually commence and so Leah would definitely be in attendance at the actual event in person and participate aboard a very noble looking unicorn and as much as that prospect excited and delighted her, it also slightly unsettled her nerves.

"This is Lancelot and this is your mount Princess Leah." Sebastian explained as he suddenly came to an abrupt stop next to the black unicorn and then turned to face her with an excited smile. "Since you are the Royal Hunt's host, you'll be aboard our most prized unicorn. He's extremely fast but also very obedient, so you should enjoy the ride." He encouraged.

From what Leah could see as she quickly glanced around the courtyard, the Royal Hunt was just about to start because everyone else now appeared to be mounted and ready to embark upon the actual hunt itself and so she enthusiastically approached her mount as she prepared to fully cooperate. The jet black, shiny, silent, majestic looking creature stood completely still directly in front of Leah as she drew very close to the unicorn's back and as Lancelot seemed to wait patiently for her to mount, she immediately appreciated the creature's stillness and very calm nature which she actually felt, would at least be helpful since she definitely lacked experience.

Quite fortunately for Leah, unlike some of the other creatures dotted around the interior of the courtyard that were far more restless, Lancelot seemed to be extremely calm, relatively peaceful and very compliant as the animal stood perfectly still in one spot which immediately put her at ease. Rather unusually however, Leah suddenly noticed that there appeared to be no actual saddle attached to the unicorn's back which worried her slightly and so she immediately began to wonder how on earth she would actually be able to ride the unicorn without falling off, or even mount the noble looking creature in the first place.

Very much like Leah had predicted and anticipated, the first few attempts that she made to mount Lancelot were totally ridiculous and an absolute disaster as she approached the unicorn's back, attempted to mount the creature and then rapidly slipped back down to the ground several times. After a few more failed attempts and a few more crash landings, Leah finally surrendered in total defeat as she turned to face Sebastian, gave him a frustrated glance and then shrugged her shoulders because to mount the unicorn successfully, seemed to be an absolutely impossible task for her to realize and to actually achieve.

"I can't even mount him Sebastian never mind ride him." Leah rapidly confessed as she began to shake her head

"Here Princess Leah, you can put your foot inside my hands and then use them like a kind of step." Sebastian politely offered as he quickly drew much closer to the unicorn's back and then cupped his hands together to make a kind of human stirrup.

"Thank you Sebastian." Leah replied gratefully as she immediately accepted his suggestion. "That's very helpful and it's so kind of you to offer."

Once Leah's foot was firmly in position inside Sebastian's cupped hands, he then quickly pushed her form upwards and somehow, just a few seconds later, she actually managed to pull herself up onto the Lancelot's back as their combined efforts seemed to pay off. Two silver reins flowed down across the unicorn's neck which were attached to a silver bridle that was fastened to Lancelot's head and so Leah quickly picked them up and then tried to make herself as comfortable as she possibly could upon the creature's back as she prepared for her very first ever unicorn ride. Each silver rein was gripped onto very tightly as Leah clung to each one through fear that the animal might actually start to move before she was in a totally stable position because there was no other possible means of control that she could see but fortunately for Leah, Lancelot didn't move an inch and seemed to just patiently wait for her instructions.

"When you want Lancelot to move or go faster Princess Leah, you simply tap his sides with your feet." Sebastian explained. "And when you want him to stop, you have to gently pull back on the reins. You can steer him with both the reins and your feet, so when you want to change direction, you simply tap his side with your foot and lead his head with the reins towards either the left or right-hand side, dependent of course upon which direction you'd like to go in."

Leah nodded.

Sebastian stepped backwards and then paused thoughtfully for a moment as he began to scratch his head. "I've definitely forgotten something Princess Leah, there's definitely something else that you'll really need for the Royal Hunt that you don't have yet." He explained as he conducted a quick visual inspection of the two.

"A saddle perhaps?" Leah suggested.

"Princess Leah, during the Royal Hunt it is actually customary for riders to ride bareback because that makes the experience a lot more natural and much more fun." Sebastian explained. He paused for a moment before he continued with a playful grin. "Ah yes, some weapons, how could I possibly forget about those? Sometimes I think I'd forget my whole body if it wasn't attached to my head."

"Sebastian, I'm not sure that me falling of the back of a unicorn will be much fun and especially not for me." Leah replied. "And yes, everyone else does seem to have some weapons, so I think I'll probably need some too."

"Yes, you can't really do much on a Royal Hunt without those." Sebastian concluded decisively. "You'd be like a sitting pudding."

Unlike the other riders that currently surrounded Leah, she had absolutely no weapons at all and so as Sebastian quickly scurried off and then disappeared into a nearby doorway in one of the courtyard walls which led into the stables, Leah sat very still upon Lancelot's back as she patiently waited for him to return. When Sebastian reappeared, just a minute or so later, he held an elegant silver spear and a black, leather, strappy weapons harness in one hand and inside his other hand there was a silver bow and a quiver filled with silver arrows and as he walked back over towards Leah, she noticed that he now had a very triumphant smile upon his face.

"Here you are Princess Leah." Sebastian announced proudly as he carefully handed her the strappy weapons carrier and then the weapons to populate the leather harness. "You are now officially ready for the Royal Hunt."

Suddenly, a flurry of chaotic activity seemed to fill the courtyard as the sound of a loud horn filled the air to indicate that the hunt was just about to commence and so some of the stable-hands immediately began to rush to and fro as they made some final, last minute preparations and frantically equipped the hunt riders with everything that was required for the actual hunt. The interior of the courtyard was now almost filled to the brim with mounted riders and as the horn sounded out a second time, some of the stable-hands rapidly began to disperse as they completed their final tasks and then began to make their way towards the stable doors which were dotted around the courtyard's inner walls.

Once the sudden flurry of activity had died down, Leah noticed that there had to be at least fifty other riders present inside the courtyard besides herself but that unlike her, they all looked extremely confident and very comfortable about the activities that they were just about to participate in. The other riders and members of the hunt party that Leah had seen mount their respective rides, she had noticed had all mounted their rides with total ease and in a much more dignified and smoother manner than her own rather awkward attempts and so she silently admired their ease of ascent and confidence as she glanced at some of their faces. In some ways, Leah felt slightly soothed by the fact that at the very least, she would embark upon the Royal Hunt alongside a group of far more experienced riders than herself and that factor silently encouraged her as she internally prepared for what was due to occur next.

One of the male riders, from what Leah could now see had been responsible for the loud noises because he held the horn that had been blown inside one of his hands and once all the stable-hands had dispersed, he raised it to his lips again and then blew it once more to indicate that the Royal Hunt was just about to commence and all the mounted riders inside the courtyard immediately turned to face him. A very nervous expression crossed Leah's face as she suddenly glanced down at Sebastian as she internally prepped herself to participate in the actual Royal Hunt itself which it now seemed, was just minutes away.

"Are you ready Princess Leah?" Sebastian asked as he smiled.

"Yes and thanks for all your assistance Sebastian. If you hadn't helped me up, I probably wouldn't have even been able to mount Lancelot in the first place. My approach was very clumsy and I definitely needed your help." Leah replied as she grinned. "What happens now?"

"You're just about to find out." Sebastian quickly reassured her. "And don't worry Princess Leah, you'll have the ride of your life because Lancelot is not only very swift but also extremely cooperative."

Just under the surface of Leah's form a current of nerves seemed to silently bubble away as she glanced at some of the other riders that surrounded her and waited eagerly for the actual Royal Hunt to begin. Each one of the rider's legs, Leah thoughtfully observed, hung limply down beside the horses' bellies as they waited to proceed and absolutely none of the creatures from what Leah could see appeared to have any saddles upon their backs which added slightly more danger to the activities that were just about to take place. Curiosity playfully danced across Leah's thoughts as she continued to wait in total silence as she internally prepared to embark upon her first ever hunt and excitement seemed to fill her entire form, overflow and then seep out of her simulated pores which caused her skin to tingle with an eager but nervous sense of anticipation as she sat completely still and hardly dared to even breath.

All in all, the Royal Hunt really was such a huge step for Leah because she had never so much as ridden a real horse before, never mind ridden an actual unicorn in order to hunt down and then actually kill another animal and so nerves chaotically swirled around inside her form as she waited. Eager anticipation seemed to fill the air all around Leah and surge through every inch of her core as she held her breath and just waited for the hunt to begin because the

Royal Hunt was definitely just about to happen and so that meant, she would definitely be an actual part of it.

"Won't you be coming along with us Sebastian?" Leah suddenly asked the court jester as she glanced down at his face.

Sebastian immediately shook his head. "Certainly not Princess Leah, chasing wild pigs and boars around in the woods on horseback and then trying to kill them is just way too wild for me, I like to keep my feet firmly on the ground at all times." He replied as he grinned. "Besides, I'm utterly hopeless on a horse, I'd fall off all the time and then the wild pigs would get away and everyone would starve. The Royal Hunt for me would just be an impossible feat to aspire to, never mind actually participate in. I can't fire an arrow to save my life and if I did fire one, it would probably end up in someone's backside, or I'd end up with a spear in my backside instead of the pigs because I'm totally useless when it comes to weapons." Sebastian continued. He placed his hand upon the silver bridle attached to Lancelot's head as he spoke. "I'd be more of a danger to the hunt party than an actual help and probably, an absolute hindrance." He acknowledged.

"I'm not sure that I'll do any better Sebastian." Leah joked with a playful grin. "I'll probably end up lost somewhere in the woods on my backside surrounded by wild animals that want to eat me and then you might even have to come and rescue me."

"You'll be fine Princess Leah." Sebastian immediately reassured her.

Another loud burst from the hunt leader's horn suddenly sounded out into the air and then the male rider responsible for the noise began to move forward on his mount as he started to lead the hunt party out of the courtyard, through the arch and then out onto the wide moat bridge.

"This is it Princess Leah." Sebastian encouraged as he gave her a smile of reassurance and a certain nod of encouragement. "It's time to go, just follow the hunt leader across the Meadows of Serenity until you reach the Savage Woods and you'll be absolutely fine." He instructed as he pointed towards the male rider with the horn.

The Royal Hunt it now appeared had actually begun and so Leah gently tapped Lancelot's sides just as Sebastian had instructed her to as she prepared to follow the male lead rider out of the courtyard and began to head towards the moat bridge. Much to Leah's total delight, Lancelot immediately began to move forward and as the unicorn did so, her mount actually headed in the direction that she wanted which pleased her no end because the creature at least seemed to be receptive to her silent, non-verbal commands. A small part of Leah had definitely feared that she would be unable to control Lancelot because the reins had initially, actually looked quite flimsy and so she had almost felt that the silver straps were more of a decorative feature than a fully functional control mechanism but fortunately for Leah that didn't seem to be the case.

Despite the fact that Leah was a total beginner when it came to the actual issue of riding a horse or a unicorn, somehow she managed to exit the courtyard although her departure was slightly more rugged and a lot less smooth than the other riders from the hunt party that now surrounded her. Regardless of Leah's personal challenges and her lack of experience however, she somehow managed to persevere and her potential struggle was greatly reduced by the fact that at the very least, Lancelot seemed to be highly receptive and headed in the right direction which in Leah's mind, was definitely a positive start.

One final glance was cast back towards Sebastian as Lancelot stepped out onto the moat bridge as Leah scanned the interior of the courtyard with her eyes and visually searched for his friendly face before it vanished from sight completely. Very comfortingly for Leah, despite the fact that she had already moved, albeit on the back of Lancelot, Sebastian it transpired hadn't actually budged an inch and he still stood firmly rooted to the very same spot that she'd left him in. A cheery grin and a final wave of encouragement were immediately offered in response as Sebastian appeared to notice Leah's slight hesitation and encouraged her to proceed from a distance which immediately put Leah at ease as she nodded at him appreciatively in return.

Once Leah had accepted Sebastian's final gestures of

reassurance, she then turned to face the moat bridge once again and tapped Lancelot's sides as she began to steer him across it and as she did so, nerves continued to jingle around inside her form. Although Leah had never experienced an actual hunt before, she definitely felt extremely ready to ride out into the unknown, to taste a new experience and to savor the excitement that was due to follow and so the cocktail of nervous excitement that mingled with eager anticipation inside her form, was fully accepted and embraced as Leah rode out across the remainder of the moat bridge.

Jolly Jigs Through the Joyful Dance

Just a minute or so later as Lancelot stepped off the other end of the moat bridge, the hunt leader began to lead the riders out across the Meadows of Serenity that lay towards Leah's right-hand side which clearly indicated to Leah that the hunt party was now ready to proceed, regardless of her doubts, despite her nerves and irrespective of her levels of competence. Somewhere on the other side of the meadows, Leah silently began to speculate as she followed the rest of the hunt riders, there would be some woods because Sebastian had already mentioned that the Savage woods would be the hunt group's actual hunting grounds that day and that the woody location would also host the animals that she would expected to hunt down that afternoon but so far, the woods were not even visible to her.

Unlike the gentle saunter across the moat bridge, the pace of the hunt party suddenly began to increase as the lead rider's mount broke out into a trot and then rapidly progressed into a speedier canter and so Leah quickly turned her attention towards Lancelot's speed as she attempted to pick up the pace and follow suit. The direction that the unicorn was headed in suddenly became extremely important to Leah because the bridge was no longer present to restrict Lancelot's movements and so she quickly tried to focus her mind upon the task at hand and steer her mount in the same direction as the rest of the hunt party but as Leah did so, she also tried to actively survey the meadow with her eyes as she silently searched for further clarity regarding the exact location of the mysterious Savage woods.

Due to the swift increase in speed, Leah repeatedly tapped Lancelot's sides with her feet in order to encourage the unicorn to keep up with the rest of the hunt party's pace and to ensure that she would not get left behind because to fall behind on this particular occasion as far as Leah was concerned, would not be very helpful at all. First and foremost, Leah had absolutely no clue where she was actually supposed to be headed to because the meadows still stretched out as far as her eyes could see and there were no signs of any woods anywhere nearby and secondly, since she had never participated in actual hunt before to be left totally alone somewhere in the middle of the Meadows of Serenity without the rest of the hunt group would in Leah's opinion be absolutely pointless.

Fortunately, however, as Lancelot broke out into a steady canter the two rapidly managed to catch up with the rest of the group and then even managed to keep up with the rear of the hunt party which comforted Leah slightly because it meant, there was now less of a chance that she would get lost. Just a few seconds later Leah somehow, even managed to end up alongside the lead male rider himself as Lancelot pushed forward and picked up the pace even more which comforted her even more because she had feared that another rider's mount might lash out at Lancelot with a kick and being at the front of the group reduced the risk of that possible eventuality. From the little that Leah did know about horses and as she was already aware, at times horses could really be quite hostile towards each other and if they were in close proximity to others of their kind, or any other creature that they didn't like, sometimes they could actually be rather vicious and lash out.

Quite unexpectedly, the pace of the hunt party suddenly seemed to increase again as the hunt leader accelerated beyond a gentle canter and his mount broke out into a much swifter, wilder gallop and so Leah once again immediately followed suit as she attempted to keep up. Approximately ten minutes later the hunt party finally neared some woods which seemed to quite suddenly appear directly in front of Leah and as the hunt leader guided the hunt party towards the mass gathering of trees and began to slow down, Leah continued to follow his lead and started to slow down too as she realigned herself with the speed of the party of riders behind her.

Some gaps rapidly appeared in-between the trees as the riders approached the lush green foliage and dense brown wooded gathering and as Leah prepared to enter inside the mysterious looking Savage Woods, she slowed Lancelot down to a walk as she took a deep, excited, eager breath. A search for edible prey was as Leah already knew, just about to commence and therefore a much slower pace was not only required but also extremely necessary because some of the branches of the trees that lay directly in front of her, jutted out of the trees rather unpredictably and the unpredictable path of those branches and sticks would definitely make the woods tricky to navigate and to venture through.

From what Leah could now clearly see, the Savage woods would not be as friendly as the Meadows of Serenity had been due to the brown wooden claws that protruded from each tree which appeared to be quite tightly intertwined. So much so that in some places each branch gripped onto one another as if they were very close friends and so from what Leah could quite easily predict, the unpredictable nature of those brown tree arms and wooden stick fingers would at times, obstruct the hunt rider's and Leah's own passage. In fact, the highly unpredictable nature of those brown wooden claws also meant that perhaps some of the riders might even suffer a few injuries as they made their way through the woods which had obviously been called the Savage Woods for more reason than one and so, Leah silently began to acknowledge that reality as she cautiously entered into the mass gathering of trees because she was by far the least experienced rider in the group and therefore the most likely to actually suffer an actual injury.

Just a few seconds later the woods seemed to gather the riders quickly into its midst and its mass of existence and as the hunt party rode further into the trees, they were rapidly surrounded in every direction that they could possibly face by the brown tree barks that clothed each tree like a uniform which was topped off with green, leafy, frilly shirts. For approximately the next fifteen minutes or so as the riders rode deeper into the Savage woods, trees, branches and leaves seemed to be all that surrounded them until finally, the hunt party stumbled upon a clearing and fortunately for the hunt riders that clearing was full of swine life.

The clearing deep in the heart of the Savage woods, much to the hunt group's satisfaction, was fully occupied and very densely populated by a group of boars and wild pigs that seemed to be totally oblivious to and quite happily ignorant when it came to the actual issue of the riders' actual approach, since each creature had been pleasantly distracted by their own desire to graze and other boorish activities. Despite the ignorance of the swine however, the pigs' presence meant one thing for absolute certain for the hunt party and that was the fact that the actual hunt activities and the pursuit of live prey could now finally commence, irrespective of whether the creatures themselves were actually ready or willing to participate.

Countless chunks and lumps of grubby, muddy pig flesh littered the entire interior of the clearing as the swine continued to graze, either completely unaware of the riders' presence or totally disinterested in it as the riders hid quietly amongst the trees that surrounded the perimeter. Every one of the swine's bodies that decorated the large, green space seemed to completely ignore the intruders that lay in wait who sat behind some of the trees nearby and as the creatures grunted quite amicably amongst themselves, the hunt party waited with baited breath for the signal to proceed as they prepared to pounce upon the group of ignorant creatures.

Suddenly, a horn was blown by the hunt leader and as the group of riders rapidly began to flood into the clearing like a tidal wave of invaders upon their mounts, Leah quickly prepared to follow them as she attempted to join in and participate with the hunt party's activities. Rather unfortunately however, the sound of the horn being blown and the disturbance caused by the riders' entrance immediately startled the group of wild creatures, most of whom quickly glanced up, grunted and then rapidly began to scatter and as a large number of the hunted animals started to dart towards the nearby trees in a frantic attempt to escape, an immediate whirlwind of chaos was created all around Leah and so much so that she almost slipped off Lancelot's back due to the commotion.

Frantic alarm suddenly seemed to fill every inch of the clearing as the wild pigs and boars grunted and squealed as the riders and their mounts continued to flood in from every direction possible but it really was too late for a few of the creatures to escape because some were immediately pounced on, attacked and hunted down. In just a matter of seconds the clearing was rapidly deserted by the majority of the hunted prey that somehow, in the midst of all the chaos, managed to find an actual exit point but some of the riders immediately rushed out of the clearing after them as they began to pursue the wild pigs and boars with their spears and loaded bows at the ready. Most of the riders in the hunt party, Leah now noticed, had very determined expressions upon their faces as they pursued their targets with tenacity and vigor and prepared themselves to maim and kill the prey that they wished to consume for dinner that very same day.

Despite the frantic flurry, Leah swiftly observed that a handful of wild pigs and boars had actually remained inside the clearing and that the smaller bunch seemed to consist of predominantly slower creatures that had not yet managed to move, or move very far in a timely fashion. The handful of prey that were now sprinkled across the clearing however, did not remain still for very long as they suddenly began to frantically seek out ways to escape between the horses' legs as the chaotic commotion continued and as Leah watched some of their escape attempts, she started to consider her actual participation in the Royal Hunt and wonder if one of those slower creatures might be a slightly more realistic target for her.

Danger however, was now actually upon the swine's doorsteps and the group of more docile, slower creatures suddenly seemed to realize that fact and that to remain stationery in one spot was no longer a sensible thing to do, if they wanted to survive and as Leah continued to watch the mayhem unfold, she noticed that even those swine had finally been provoked to move. Each hunted animal that remained, rapidly began to scurry off in different directions and any direction that they possibly could that seemed to offer a space large enough to squeeze through as the clearing transcended into even more chaos in just a matter of seconds and as it did so, Leah tried to maintain her balance as she sat upon Lancelot's back. From what Leah could see as yet there didn't appear to be a suitable target that seemed to be slow enough for her to actually pursue and so she continued to just spectate until she spotted one and to wait patiently for an opportunity to present itself to her.

Due to the riders' relentless pursuit, Leah rapidly realized that an actual escape for some of the slower creatures was not actually guaranteed because even those that had managed to dart through the chaos and that had found a way to penetrate the trees successfully, were eagerly hunted down and pursued by some of the riders who followed them with hunger in their eyes. Each rider eagerly unpacked arrows from their quivers as they rode and aimed their spears towards the slower swine as they prepared to attack and as Leah observed the scene around her in nervous silence, she noticed that some of the creatures were hunted down with utter determination and sheer tenacity in front of her very eyes. Every second that went by seemed to attract more and more riders into the clearing and as Leah watched them surge through the green space upon their mounts, the hunt party pursued the swine with a hungry zeal as each rider wove in and out of the trees and attempted to secure their potential evening meal with relentless amounts of energy, sheer determination and an unbreakable persistence that appeared to Leah almost as if it had been formed from steel.

Despite Leah's lack of experience and all her doubts however, as soon as a rather plump, slower boar suddenly rushed towards her, she immediately seized the opportunity and rapidly began to respond as she swiftly urged Lancelot to follow the creature and eagerly started to tap the unicorn's sides with her feet. The animal which didn't seem to be that fast due to its very large size and plumpness was then enthusiastically pursued as it rushed into the depths of the Savage woods and as Lancelot started to pick up speed, fortunately for Leah, somehow the unicorn managed to avoid all the tricky, awkward branches that poked out from the trees at virtually every turn. In terms of excitement, the ride for Leah absolutely thrilled her and her blood seemed to pump more quickly through her veins, if that was indeed actually possible in her current form and in just a matter of minutes, much to Leah's satisfaction, Lancelot had almost caught up with the plump boar which meant, it was now time for Leah to prepare to launch an attack.

Rather frustratingly for Leah, she rapidly discovered as she plucked the silver spear from the black, leather weapons carrier that had been strapped to her body that hung across her back, this boar was much faster on its feet than she had initially anticipated because somehow, the creature mockingly remained just in front of Lancelot as it ran. Much to Leah's absolute annoyance and total irritation, despite all her preparations and her current readiness, the boar continued to run just ahead of Lancelot's legs and head and so Leah swiftly attempted to speed up again as she tapped the unicorn's sides with her feet and urged her mount to move slightly faster in an attempt to match the boar's sudden, unexpected, quite rapid burst of speed so that she could orchestrate her first attack.

Once Leah felt that the boar was within range of her spear and quite manageable reach, she then prepared to lunge down towards it with the weapon inside one of her hands as she tried to target its flesh but her first attempt, rather unfortunately, fell well short of requirements, totally missed her target and was extremely clumsy. The animal which seemed to sense the danger then rapidly sped up as it ran ahead of Lancelot's head once again and slipped out of Leah's grasp once more and so since she had completely missed her target and almost dropped the spear and fallen off Lancelot in the process, Leah thoughtfully started to consider an alternative weapon for her next attack. Somehow, the wild creature had managed to avoid the deep cut and potential wound that the very sharp, silver spear could so easily have inflicted upon it and although Leah had tried to aim with absolute precision, she had totally missed the boar's flesh by a very large margin and so the spear combined with her rather amateur efforts, she quickly concluded, probably wouldn't yield the best results or the swiftest and so the prospect of another weapon now suddenly appealed to her far more.

Much to Leah's absolute frustration however, the boar somehow still managed to maintain a slight distance between itself and Lancelot for the next two hundred meters or so and so Leah shook her head in absolute disgust as she continued to pursue it but the disgust that she now felt, was actually related to how miserably she had failed at her first attempt. Irrespective of Leah's current close proximity to the boar, rather frustratingly it seemed, this swine definitely did not want to be killed, injured or eaten and so Leah's next attack would have to be slightly more competent than her first attempt, if she actually wanted to injure the creature and if she wanted to return from the Royal Hunt with an edible contribution for the Feast of Plenty that day. A wild pig and boar hunt it had rapidly transpired, certainly wasn't easy and so now Leah fully accepted that Sebastian had probably made a very valid point because the creatures seemed to be rather tricky to hunt down and you really had to know not only how to ride properly but also how to utilize weapons effectively.

Another attempt and a second attack however, definitely had to be orchestrated and so Leah quickly straightened herself up as she prepared to equip her hands with another weapon but this time she opted to implement her attack with the bow and arrow instead of the spear and so the spear was swiftly returned to the strappy, weapons carrier. Technically, although Leah had never fired an actual arrow from a real bow in her entire life before, Sebastian had provided Leah with both a bow and some arrows and so it was indeed, another weapon at her disposal and right now, she truly recognized that she needed all the weapons that she could possibly lay her hands on to tackle the evasive boar effectively. One rather huge thing did worry Leah about the utilization of the bow and arrow however, and that quite obvious drawback was the fact that she would have to let go of both of the reins which formed the main control mechanism over Lancelot's movements which provided her with a degree of command that felt quite secure and so Leah feared what might actually happen, if she actually relinquished that control.

"Lancelot probably steers himself better than I do, so I shouldn't even worry about it." Leah rapidly reassured herself decisively as she prepared to relinquish control of the reins and focus solely upon her attack. "This could get really ugly and become very messy but let's hope it actually doesn't."

Prior to that precise moment in time Lancelot had pursued the boar obediently, consistently and in a very stable manner and so far, the unicorn had managed to avoid all the awkward branches and sticks that had protruded from the trees within the wooded area and not even one had scratched or touched Leah's face or form and so she silently considered that very real, artificial reality. A degree of trust was definitely required however, on Leah's part because if Lancelot suddenly headed off in another direction unexpectedly, Leah knew that she would in all likelihood fall of her mount's back and end up somewhere on the ground on her backside and that was an inescapable and very predictable truth because as Leah had already fully accepted, she really wasn't the most experienced of riders. Since Leah's departure from the clearing however, Lancelot had remained pretty consistent and stable and that stability, now at least provided Leah with the required drop of confidence that she needed to convince herself that Lancelot would not veer of course as she arrived at an actual, final decision and then prepared to act upon it.

In a matter of just seconds Leah's decision was quickly spurred into action as Lancelot suddenly drew much closer to the boar and she leapt upon the opportunity as soon as it presented itself to her and grabbed it firmly with both her hands. An arrow was rapidly, deftly plucked from the quiver and the bow was swiftly retrieved from the strappy, leather weapons carrier that had been strapped to Leah's back and then just a few seconds were spent in very deep concentration as Leah attempted to line the bow and arrow up with the path of boar. Any negative thoughts and doubts were pushed firmly towards the back of Leah's mind as she decisively focused solely upon her aim because the time to take a risk had just landed upon her doorstep and it was a risk that she now, really had to take because she felt extremely unsure that another opportunity to be in such close proximity to the evasive boar would actually arise again.

Some doubts suddenly began to fill Leah's thoughts and to tug away inside her mind as she leant towards the boar and the creature started to swerve from side to side just in front of Lancelot's front legs because there were absolutely no guarantees that she would actually be able to hit the creature, or that she would not fall of Lancelot's back when she tried to do so. Despite all Leah's reservations and self-doubts however, she managed to persevere in the pursuit of her quest as she gripped onto the bow and arrow firmly with both hands and then carefully took aim again as she prepared to fire the weapon at the boar, even though it continued to dart from side to side rather annoyingly.

The first arrow that Leah fired, much to her absolute disgust, zipped rapidly through the air and missed the creature completely and as it landed upon the ground, it fell into the soft soil directly below Lancelot's hooves where it was rapidly snapped in two by the unicorn and as Leah watched, she shook her head in total dismay and then swiftly lined up another arrow. A second attempt was quickly made to aim for the boar's hide once again with the bow and arrow as Leah persisted in her quest with sheer and utter determination because to surrender to defeat now as she already knew, would only render her efforts so far utterly void, absolutely pointless and totally meaningless. On this particular occasion for Leah, failure was not an acceptable outcome as she fully succumbed to the hunt's core purpose and main goal because this was an actual hunt and so that meant, the prey had to be hunted down by everyone in the hunt party successfully, inclusive of Leah herself.

Fortunately for Leah, the second arrow that she fired somehow managed to penetrate the boar's actual flesh and as the arrow ripped into the creature's side, it seemed to cause significant damage to the boar as the animal suddenly squealed out in pain. Despite the damage that had been done to the creature's hide and form however, the boar continued to move rapidly forward and it almost seemed to Leah as if the creature had simply ignored the wound that had been inflicted upon it as it still frantically and desperately tried to escape.

Rather frustratingly for Leah, the pursuit of the creature suddenly became even more complicated as the animal began to move swiftly from side to side in a more erratic manner than before and it somehow, even managed to sped up slightly and so Leah quickly lined up a third arrow which she then attempted to aim towards the boar's flesh. Much like the second arrow, the third arrow actually hit the creature's side and tore into boar's flesh but the animal still continued to run as it very stubbornly ignored the pain and wounds that had been inflicted upon it for a second time.

"Seriously, how many more injuries and arrows is this going to take?" Leah asked herself as she gently shook her head in total frustration. "Perhaps I should try the spear again, maybe this boar has three lives."

Very strangely, despite the fact that the boar had now already been hit twice in the side by Leah and its hide had been pierced quite deeply in two different places, she noticed that the animal had not yet slowed down and that if anything, its wounds seemed to have spurred it on instead because the boar's pace had actually increased which began to irritate her slightly. The pursuit through the Savage woods however, continued as Leah silently, internally deliberated as to whether or not she should try to utilize the spear again as she rode because as she already knew, the spear could create a much deeper wound. A severe wound was definitely required that the boar would not recover from as easily but as Leah already knew, it was just as risky as the bow and arrows, if not even more so because it meant that she would actually have to lean down towards the boar in order to wound it successfully.

Suddenly however, a golden opportunity presented itself to Leah which immediately grabbed the decision straight from her hands and mind and rapidly dispelled her doubts as the boar finally started to slow down and Lancelot swiftly caught up with the creature. Finally, Leah observed, it seemed as if the damage that she had inflicted upon the wild boar had started to have an actual impact upon the animal's movements and so she quickly reached for the spear. The boar it appeared had now begun to struggle due to its wounds and so Leah even managed to actually ride alongside it successfully for a few minutes as she prepared to grab her chance and swiftly equipped herself in readiness with the desired weapon. Victory, Leah silently began to speculate, now sat just at the edge of her fingertips and lay well within her grasp and so she smiled as a wave of gratitude flooded through her mind and washed over her form because she could already taste the sweetness of that well-deserved victory upon her lips.

When the boar was in what looked like quite easy reach, Leah quickly took aim and then she rapidly lunged the silver spear down towards it, hard and fast as she attempted to spike the creature's flesh. In a matter of just seconds, much to Leah's total relief, the spear penetrated and then successfully sank into the boar's side and as the creature fully surrendered to the impact of the blow that pierced and dug into its hide, it rapidly crashed towards the ground as it immediately caved into the severity of an injury that it could not possibly even hope to recover from. A triumphant, satisfied smile instantly crossed Leah's face as she quickly stopped Lancelot and then turned him around to face the boar which still had the spear embedded into its flesh and as she glanced at the limp, lifeless lump that now lay upon the ground directly in front of her, she began to savor her victory as she rode back towards the boar's remains and then came to a complete standstill next to the creature.

For the next few minutes, Leah was unsure exactly what she was actually supposed to do next because although she had known for absolute certain that she had to chase the boar down and then kill it with the weapons that she'd been given, what exactly was meant to happen after that victory had been achieved, still remained for now, very unclear. In fact, the truth was that Leah hadn't really expected, or believed for even a single second that she would actually be able to kill the creature and so to achieve that feat successfully, had been a surprise in itself but as she glanced down at the boar's carcass which now lay strewn across the ground, totally still and utterly lifeless, she found no actual answers. Despite all Leah's uncertainty however, Lancelot it appeared seemed to be far more certain about his role as her mount stood completely still and silently on guard next to the boar's carcass and so Leah sat and waited in an uncertain silence for something else to happen.

Quite surprisingly, just a minute or so later, Leah's unspoken question was swiftly answered as two men emerged from in-between the trees and then rode towards her and when they arrived next to the dead boar, they both came to a complete standstill upon their mounts right beside it. The two men were instantly recognizable to Leah because one was the actual hunt leader that had led the hunt party throughout the hunt up until that point in time and the other was another member of the hunt party who had hidden amongst the trees alongside her at the edge of the clearing in the heart of the woods, just before the hunt party had invaded the swine's grazing spot. Each one of the two men gave Leah a polite nod before they began to visually inspect the creature's remains for a few seconds in total silence and then the second man and the one who was the least familiar to Leah quickly dismounted his horse and plucked a brown sack from a large leather bag that was strewn across his chest after which point, he turned to face the hunt leader and then just waited for him to speak.

"You've done very well Princess Leah." The hunt leader acknowledged as he nodded his ahead in approval. "That is a very plump boar." He turned to face the other rider from the hunt party that had accompanied him before he continued. "Strap it up and take it back to the Castle of Joy." He instructed.

Upon Leah's face there was now a very proud smile as she watched the second male rider approach the boar's carcass and then start to prepare his sack as the lifeless boar lay completely still upon the earthy ground and blood continued to seep abundantly from its open wounds. Although it was a very strange achievement, especially in comparison to some of Leah's more usual achievements, despite that strangeness Leah still felt that it was an actual achievement because that afternoon, she had definitely stepped up to a very unusual challenge and she'd even successfully managed to fulfil the main objective of the Royal Hunt herself.

The remains of the swine that lay upon the ground proved that Leah could grab the boar by the tail and be an actual hunter although the tail of the creature was actually quite hard to clearly see now and barely even visible to anyone anymore since the animal's actual hide was almost totally saturated and soaked in crimson red blood. Dark red fluid now decorated every inch of the creature's outer hide and so from the red stains that were spattered all across the boar's exterior and its stillness, Leah could clearly see that the creature no longer breathed even a single breath of life.

Since Leah had not yet dismounted or gone anywhere near the boar's carcass to retrieve her spear, the silver spear that she had plunged into the animal's flesh still protruded from it and was embedded in the boar's remains and so just before the second male rider began his assigned task, Leah noticed that he quickly plucked the spear from the dead animal's flesh and then politely handed it back to her. An appreciative nod was immediately given in response as Leah swiftly accepted the return of the spear appreciatively, since she had harbored absolutely no desires at all inside her form that had provoked or urged her to try and retrieve the actual spear herself prior to the two men's arrival. Once the spear had been returned to Leah, she then watched in total silence as the second male rider began to prepare the boar's remains for transportation to the Castle of Joy.

When the empty sack had been swiftly and competently pulled over the boar's carcass, a leather rein and strap was then attached to the top of the sack that contained the animal's remains and once the sack had been secured properly, the second male rider then attached the leather strap to another leather rein which ran along his horse's back. The rather elaborate, long leather rein that ran along the entire length of his mount's back went all the way down to the horse's rump and it had been secured under the horse's tail and so once the man had strapped the second rein to it, he then walked his horse forward a few steps so that the full sack would be lifted up off the ground completely. Once the sack had been lifted up high enough and once it was a reasonable distance from the ground, the second male rider then tightened the strap as he attached the sack more securely to the horse's back so that the horse would carry the sack and its contents back to the castle as opposed to the sack being dragged across the ground.

Rather interestingly for Leah, she noticed that once the second male rider had completed his task and secured the sack to the back of his mount, he did not then actually attempt to remount his horse and that he simply faced the hunt leader and then nodded his head which provided a clear but silent indication that he was ready to proceed which also implied that he had a very long walk ahead of him.

"The Royal Hunt is almost over." The hunt leader clarified as he began to turn his horse around. "Which means, we have to go back to the clearing now so that the riders from the hunt can be gathered. All the riders from the hunt must be gathered inside the clearing before we can return to the Castle of Joy." He explained as he continued. "Because the Joyful Dance and the Feast of Plenty cannot start until the hunt party has returned."

Unlike Leah's initial outward journey from the clearing, Leah observed as she began to follow the hunt leader upon Lancelot's back that the pace of the return journey back towards it was far slower because the second male rider followed the two mounted riders on foot but the slower pace allowed the three to remain together and so therefore only a walk was really, actually possible. For Leah however, that much calmer speed and far slower pace definitely, currently suited her mood due to the absolutely chaotic, rather hectic and very wild pace of her ride during her pursuit of the boar and so, a far gentler pace at that point was extremely welcome and so she did not complain or object to the much slower return walk but instead, silently accepted it appreciatively and gratefully.

Despite the hunt leader's brief verbal communications and interactions so far, rather strangely Leah noticed, he did not make any attempts to introduce himself or enter into any conversation with her as the three made their way back towards the clearing which to Leah seemed mildly impolite. Unlike Sebastian and his friendly, personal mannerisms, for some inexplicable reason, the hunt leader remained totally silent and not a single verbal exchange occurred between the two as Leah rode quietly alongside him and he seemed to avoid any kind of discourse with her which puzzled Leah slightly because his quite cold attitude seemed a tad unfriendly. A slight tweak would perhaps have to be performed to Spectrum upon Leah's return to reality, she began to thoughtfully conclude as she rode because that coldness could perhaps be adjusted and the hunt leader's attitude warmed up a tad since his frosty cold attitude made the surrounding Savage Woods feel slightly unnatural.

Approximately fifteen minutes later, when the three arrived back inside the clearing as they entered into the grassy space, the hunt leader immediately separated from the other two and then he began to make his way towards the very center of the clearing where he came to a complete standstill and then paused as he quickly retrieved his horn from his person. The very loud horn, once retrieved, was then swiftly raised to the hunt leader's lips and blown very loudly to summon the rest of the hunt party back to the clearing and as the sound from the horn vibrated through the air and bounced off the nearby tree trunks and branches, a very clear indication was provided to the riders that still remained scattered throughout the woods that the Royal Hunt had now officially, come to an actual end.

A deep sense of pride rapidly began to fill Leah's form as several riders drifted back into the clearing as she accepted that the strange activity that she had almost been too scared to participate in had now indeed, actually finished because it really had been such a huge achievement for her. Not only had Leah managed to survive the actual hunt itself but somehow, she would even also manage to return with the carcass of a boar that she had hunted down herself and that was hugely significant for her because nowadays, she hardly even ventured very far outside the realms of comfort, or the basement of the couple's home.

In terms of Leah's usual achievements, this particular achievement definitely differed vastly and was situated at least a hundred miles outside her comfort zone but as she watched the other riders as they wove their way back into the clearing through the trees, she couldn't help but feel proud of herself because it was so very unusual and she had somehow, managed to take that strangeness in her stride. Although Leah was not a master hunter and probably never would be, she would now definitely return to the Castle of Joy from the Royal Hunt with an edible contribution to the Feast of Plenty and so some seeds of triumphant satisfaction silently began to gather and collate inside Leah's form as she waited for the hunt leader's next instructions.

At least fifty sacks filled with dead animals had been strapped to the leather reins attached to some of the horses' backs and so some of the riders lead their mounts back into the clearing on foot by the silver reins that flowed down from the silver bridles attached to their heads. Each filled sack looked heavy and damp because the carcasses of the swine now fully occupied every one and as blood continued to seep from each sack's interior, the exterior of every sack rapidly became totally saturated. In fact, the brown sacks were no longer actually, really brown because every visible, filled sack was now stained a deep, crimson red from the blood of the dead animals that each one contained and as the horses that carried the full sacks moved around, blood from the swine's carcasses continued to seep out from the interior of each sack and decorate the exterior as the animals even upon their death, silently decorated their graves with the liquid remnants of their slaughter.

Once all the hunt riders had fully congregated inside the clearing once more, the hunt leader then blew his horn again just before he began to lead the group back out into the wooded area and so Leah eagerly started to follow his lead as she silently celebrated her successful participation in the Royal Hunt's activities that afternoon. The pace of the return journey to the Castle of Joy, Leah rapidly noticed as she rode, was far slower because some of the riders and horses in the group had been slowed down by the heavy sacks that had been attached to some of the horses' backs which definitely had an impact upon their speed. No one in the hunt party seemed to be bothered by the reduction in pace however, as Leah watched some of the riders walk comfortably and peacefully alongside their mounts and after the hectic pace of the hunt itself as far as Leah was concerned, the relaxed saunter was an enjoyable conclusion to the Royal Hunt and her very adventurous afternoon.

When the hunt party finally arrived back inside the castle courtyard, the now weary hunters came to an actual stop and then those riders that were still aboard their mounts, quickly began to dismount as stable-hands rushed out of the nearby stable doors towards them, armed with water buckets and cooling rugs. Every thirsty horse inside the courtyard was immediately attended to as water buckets were swiftly placed upon the ground beside their heads and cooling rugs were rapidly thrown over their backs as the creatures lined the interior of the courtyard and the stable-hands attempted to cool each one down as quickly as they could.

Unlike the blankets that usually covered the bodies of human beings to warm their bodies up, Leah immediately noticed that the brightly colored blankets differed in the sense that none had been formed from solid pieces of material and that each one looked more like a large string vest shaped into a blanket due to the multitude of large circular holes in the pieces of material. The blankets, or what there was off them, were rapidly thrown across the backs of the horses that littered the courtyard and as Leah watched in silence, she began to wonder where Sebastian might be because as yet, she had not seen his friendly face and he had not made an appearance inside the actual courtyard itself and so she felt that she should really try to find him because Lancelot was probably in need of some refreshment. Due to the horses' thirst, Leah noticed that the animals responded very swiftly and eagerly to the buckets full of water as their heads were rapidly dipped inside each one and then the refreshing, cool water that formed the contents of each bucket were thirstily slurped up, practically straight away.

Upon Leah's face there was a very satisfied smile, due to her victorious participation in the Royal Hunt as she quickly dismounted Lancelot and then began to visually scan the interior of the courtyard as she searched for Sebastian's friendly face amongst the sea of faces. Quite amusingly, after Leah had dismounted, it suddenly struck her that it had been far easier to dismount the unicorn than it had initially been to mount the noble looking creature before the Royal Hunt had begun because her initial mount of Lancelot had required not only several attempts but also even some assistance.

Since Lancelot probably needed something to actually drink and maybe even a net blanket because all the horses seemed to have one which meant, the material rugs appeared to be some kind of necessity, Leah was quite mindful as she continued to visually search the sea of faces inside the courtyard that Sebastian had to be found and located as quickly as possible. The unicorn in Leah's opinion, she definitely felt had worked just as hard as the horses throughout the Royal Hunt and so, she felt that he really deserved one just as much as the horses did.

Quite fortunately for Leah, she didn't have to search for

Sebastian's face for very long as she suddenly spotted him and as he strode briskly across the courtyard towards her, she noticed that he was not only fully equipped with a water bucket and blanket but also armed with his usual cheeky grin and so Leah immediately smiled at him to acknowledge his presence and his approach. Much to Leah's total relief, she could instantly see that there was a bucket of water which dangled from one of Sebastian's hands and strewn across one of his shoulders there was also a bright red net rug and the sight of both immediately appeased and comforted her mind.

"You must be a mind reader Sebastian." Leah joked as he drew closer.

"Well Princess Leah, I did come prepared because Lancelot will definitely need these. The cooling rug will cool him down to ensure that he doesn't get a chill and of course the bucket of water will quench his thirst." Sebastian explained as he placed the bucket of water down on the ground close to unicorn's head and then threw the cooling rug over Lancelot's back. "How was the Royal Hunt?" He enquired as he smiled at Leah. "Did you manage to bring anything nice back for the Feast of Plenty?"

"It was amazing Sebastian, I even hunted down a boar myself." Leah gushed enthusiastically as she began to nod her head. "I hit it with some arrows and pierced it my spear and then they put it inside a sack and brought it back with us for the Feast of Plenty."

"You see Princess Leah, it was perfectly straight forward and absolutely nothing to worry about. The kitchen will cook that boar up for the Feast this evening and it will taste absolutely delicious." Sebastian reassured her.

A noisy slurp suddenly emanated from the nearby bucket of water which now contained Lancelot's head as the unicorn began to consume the liquid contents that sat inside it and Leah immediately started to laugh as she turned to face the Lancelot.

"Someone's thirsty." Sebastian joked as he grinned. He began to gently stroke unicorn's sweaty neck as he continued. "Don't worry Lancelot, you can rest now because the Royal Hunt is over and so that means, your work is done, for today anyway."

"Yes and thankfully, no one was injured in process, though at one point I did feel as if I was going to fall off Lancelot's back." Leah mentioned as she smiled.

Between the two there was a few minutes of silence as Leah just stood completely still and watched Lancelot as the unicorn consumed the cool water inside the bucket as she once again began to admire the majestic creature's form because it truly was an absolutely magnificent sight to behold. The unicorn's chestnut brown eyes were soft and gentle and since Leah had never been in such close proximity to such a noble looking creature before, she started to appreciate the experience because in some ways, it almost felt as if she was situated next to actual royalty, albeit a royal member of the animal kingdom.

An amused smile suddenly crossed Leah's face as she silently reminded herself that unicorns were not actually real and that in the real world, a unicorn would definitely not be considered animal royalty because they didn't really exist and that in fact, many of the creatures that Leah had created inside Spectrum did not exist in the real world in any capacity at all. So many of the creatures inside Spectrum that Leah had created and given an existence to, albeit in an artificial capacity, did not inhabit the real world in any way, shape or form and that was another delightful aspect in Leah's opinion within Spectrum's environments.

In fact, some of Leah's animalistic creations inside Spectrum had purely been created just for the enjoyment of Spectrum's potential consumers but somehow, Leah now felt as if she had almost created magic because she had breathed life into those creatures and given them some kind of existence that in reality, they could never possibly ever have. For Leah in some ways, her experiences with Spectrum now felt, extremely powerful because although Lancelot had been the first such magical creature that she had given an existence to that she had encountered with her own mind and even been in some kind of close proximity to, she definitely knew that Lancelot would not be the last and that in some highly unusual way, magic had been brought to life through science and technology, the two disciplines that usually stood in direct opposition to it.

"Right Princess Leah, now it's time for you to return to your chamber so that you can prepare for the Joyful Dance and the Feast of Plenty." Sebastian advised. "You only have an hour to prepare yourself and no doubt, you'd like to freshen up first."

"Yes that would be lovely Sebastian, the Royal Hunt has left me looking a little bit grimy." Leah replied before she paused for a moment and then quickly glanced around the courtyard as she watched some of the riders from the hunt party disperse. She turned back to face him and then smiled as she continued. "So right now, I don't really feel or look very much like a Princess."

"I think you'll find everything that you need to resolve that particular problem inside your chamber Princess Leah but if you have any questions about suitable attire, please feel free to ask." Sebastian offered. "After all, I am here to assist."

"Suitable attire for a dance and a feast, I think I can handle this one Sebastian." Leah immediately reassured him as she smiled. "But thanks, it's very kind of you to offer."

The two began to saunter across the courtyard as they headed back towards the entrance of the castle as Leah thoughtfully pondered over which outfit from the vast range on offer she should select for the evening ahead because there were just so many choices available to her inside that huge walk-in wardrobe. Unlike the Royal Hunt, the Joyful Dance and the Feast of Plenty would both be activities that were far more up Leah's personal street of enjoyment and a house of familiarity to Leah that she definitely felt far more comfortable with, not only to visit and step inside but also to spend her entire evening totally immersed in but another tricky decision loomed upon the horizon of her day and so indecision as she already knew, could perhaps become an obstacle to the commencement of her potentially joyous evening.

Inside the Castle of Joy everything was extremely quiet, Leah noticed as the two stepped back inside the structure and then began to walk along the long hallway that led towards the chamber that had been allocated to her earlier that day and none of the hunt riders or stable-hands appeared to be anywhere nearby. Another gentle tweak would perhaps have to be made to Spectrum, Leah considered thoughtfully as she walked because the quietness around her seemed just a tad too quiet and even verged upon being slightly unnatural, after all the hustle and bustle of the busy courtyard and so a few changes to some codes would perhaps correct that slight oversight on her part so that areas that were expected to be populated to some extent actually were.

Although Leah had been given a whole hour with which to prepare herself for the Joyful Dance, she felt slightly unsure as she walked along the hallway and began to make some light conversation with Sebastian that it would actually be possible to achieve that goal in that actual timeframe because she had been provided with such a tremendous, immense range of clothing choices. A lot of preparation would have to be fitted into that hour, Leah considered thoughtfully and those activities would definitely take time because she would be presented that day as not only a host but also a princess which meant, she really had to look like one in every single way, all in the short space of just an hour. True to Sebastian's usual playful, jestful nature, Leah noticed that he continued to make jokes as they walked, some of which were not particularly funny at all and some of which were really quite awful but Leah smiled at each joke he told as if she was amused, just to be polite.

When the two arrived back outside Leah's chamber once again, she noticed that the afternoon had already started to depart and that the evening had now begun to step in to replace it which meant, the day was no longer young as Sebastian politely pushed the door open and then held it open for her. Despite Sebastian's obvious shortcomings when it came to the actual issue of humor which was supposed to be his specialty, he definitely more than made up for that personality shortfall with thoughtfulness and good manners, Leah quietly concluded as she smiled appreciatively at him and then stepped inside the large, main room. Perhaps a tweak to Sebastian wasn't really a necessary tweak to make after all, Leah considered quietly as she glanced back at the door and Sebastian's face because his warm friendly attitude, considerate approach and polite manners really were more than sufficient and extremely pleasant.

Just a few seconds later, the open door that led directly into Leah's quarters was quickly closed as Sebastian rapidly departed once again and Leah smiled an amused smile as he left because Sebastian certainly didn't seem to be one for long drawn out emotional goodbyes. Once Leah was settled inside the large, spacious area that she had been allocated to, she then began to prepare herself for a long soak in a bubble bath which she definitely needed to take because she actually felt rather grubby after the quite wild and rather mucky hunt activities that she had just engaged in and so she eagerly started to make her way towards the en-suite bathroom.

In the very center of the large, spacious en-suite bathroom, much to Leah's absolute delight, she found a huge sunken bath which almost looked like a small swimming pool because it was certainly large enough for one person to comfortably swim around in and her skin immediately started to tingle with excitement as she eagerly approached it. Unlike Leah's bathroom in the real world inside the home that she and Zidane shared, this bathroom was absolutely huge and at least ten times the size and so it almost made the couple's bathroom look like a cleaning cupboard in comparison.

A huge selection of bath salts, bubble baths, wash gels and liquid creams in shiny colored bottles were situated upon a shelf like rim that ran all the way around the bath and so once Leah had started to run some water, she quickly plucked some bottles from it and then began to open each bottle up and inspect the contents as she smelt the beautiful array of aromas that some of the bottles contained. When some bath salts and a bubble bath had finally been selected, Leah rapidly began to pour some of the crystals and a generous portion of the chosen fluid into the base of the sunken bath and then a wash gel was carefully and enthusiastically picked out and set aside with which to wash her skin as she joyfully savored the sheer luxury that surrounded her and fully indulged in its offerings.

Despite the fact that water still continued to flow into the sunken bath as soon as the water was roughly waist high, Leah quickly stripped off and then gently dipped her toe inside it as she prepared to step into the delicious looking warmth that awaited her because she really couldn't wait for the bath to be completely filled up. Directly in front of Leah, a pool of tranquil relaxation and gentle calmness silently awaited her which silently urged her to not only dip her toe inside it but to more fully sample its promises of peaceful refreshment, guarantees of pleasant relaxation and offerings of much needed rejuvenation and due to the size of the bath, the current depth of the water could already offer and fully provide her with sufficient warmth and so she eagerly prepared to sample those serene delicacies and to make the most of every single one.

Several small steps led down into the depths of the sunken bath and as Leah began to make her descent, her body immediately started to embrace and appreciate the water which felt not only extremely fresh but also deliciously warm as each delightful ripple lapped gently against her pores and playfully greeted her skin. Every single drop of water inside the sunken bath seemed to sparkle, shine and glisten and as the drops of water collectively, instantly caressed and revitalized Leah's skin, her body almost became fully immersed inside it as the water level continued to rise.

The delightfully delicious drops playfully began to embrace Leah's shoulders as the water level rose and so she welcomed the refreshment with open arms and a sponge laden with generous dollops of the wash gel that she had selected as she started to clean off the grimy remnants from the woods that she'd collected from and during the Royal Hunt which still seemed to line and linger on the surface of her skin. In real life and back in the real world, a hunt was definitely not something that Leah would have ever dreamed of actual participation in but just for that day, she had dabbled in the unfamiliar pool of new adventures and derived some pleasure from her participation in a very unusual activity that had both thrilled and excited her and it had opened her eyes to a whole new experience.

Approximately twenty minutes later, once Leah had fully indulged in a long, luxurious soak in the bath which hadn't been quite long enough in her opinion, due to the constraints on her time she stepped out of the bath, wrapped herself in a large bath towel and then began to make her way back towards the bedroom area of her allocated quarters. An outfit that was extremely elegant, splendidly sophisticated and deliciously beautiful had to be found inside the wardrobe to wear for the evening ahead because it was a huge evening and so as far as Leah was concerned, she had to be dressed absolutely immaculately.

Fortunately for Leah, inside the huge mirrored walk-in wardrobe which literally contained hundreds of glamourous dresses and tons of regal looking robes, she managed to find a beautiful black and white dress with elegant gemstones sprinkled across it that looked absolutely stunning within no time at all and she smiled as she eagerly slipped it off the hanger. The bottom of the dress Leah noticed, flared out as it flowed down towards the ground in a fishtail style and as she prepared to slip it on, she could clearly see that the dress was not only very elegant and extremely sophisticated but also absolutely divine. Upon Leah's face there was now a very satisfied smile as the beautiful, gorgeous dress was carefully slipped on and then inspected in the mirrored doors of the wardrobe because from what Leah could see at first glance, it fitted her absolutely perfectly and as it clung to her body, she happily noticed that it courteously accentuated every single curve that formed part of her makeup.

"Zidane would absolutely love this dress." Leah whispered to herself as she smoothed the material down against her skin.

Some small jewel like diamonds were sprinkled across the surface of the material and several tailored cut out holes provided a few limited glimpses and displayed some small patches of Leah's naked skin and as she inspected every inch of the dress quietly for a few minutes, she started to admire each intricately designed detail that contributed to the overall sophisticated beauty of the dress. Not only was the dress extremely elegant but it also flattered Leah's physique immensely because it hugged and clung to her every curve and every inch of the material seemed to silently celebrate her femininity in all its fullness but as Leah released a satisfied, content, happy sigh, she quickly began to consider the time once more because her hour of preparation could not possibly be extended and it had by now, almost expired and come a lot closer to its actual departure.

Only twenty minutes, according to the large, silver elegant clock with dark black hands on one of the walls, now remained for Leah to complete her preparations for the activities and evening ahead and although it was still early evening because the evening had only just stepped into the day as she was fully aware, the dress that she had now chosen would be worn for the remainder of her experience in Spectrum that day. Just one hour had been provided to Leah with which to prepare herself and so she definitely knew, she had to be ready by the time Sebastian returned because if she wasn't, she would lose some precious minutes of her experience in that particular emotional journey that day and perhaps also miss out on some of the planned activities that evening all of which sounded truly fabulous and lots of fun. A few crucial preparations still remained to be performed however, as Leah was fully aware because she still had to beautify her hair, adorn her body with some pretty jewelry and apply some makeup to her face and as she already knew, those final preparations would require every single spare minute of the hour that now remained because Sebastian was due to return shortly.

Once Leah had admired the dress in the mirrored wardrobe doors for a few more minutes, she then began to make her way towards the dressing table as she prepared to give her appearance the final few required touches that would fully equip her for the evening ahead. Unlike the uncertainties that Leah had faced earlier that day, when she'd had to find a suitable outfit to wear for the Royal Hunt, this outfit had definitely been far easier to find and it also correlated perfectly with the planned festivities that evening and of that fact, Leah felt absolutely certain as she sat down in front of the dressing table and then smiled. Several other preparations had to be made before Leah's look would actually be complete and those final touches she hoped, would enhance the beautiful dress that she had chosen and give her that additional portion of gorgeousness that she desired and aspired to realize.

Every possible accessory and item of jewelry that Leah could possibly require, think off, or imagine having access to seemed to be on top of that dressing table neatly displayed in glass, transparent jewelry boxes and as she began to visually explore and silently inspect each one, she couldn't help but admire the vast range of gorgeous accessories at her disposal. Each item of jewelry sparkled inside the glass boxes that accommodated every gorgeous piece and as Leah began to rummage through some of the jewelry boxes in total delight as she eagerly sought out the perfect combination to match her dress, every trinket seemed to wait patiently inside their glass homes for Leah's attention to be focused upon them.

Much to Leah's absolute delight and total surprise, inside one of the jewelry boxes she even managed to find some small, pretty, gemstone decorative hair accessories and so once she had placed the strands of her hair in an elaborate, elegant up-style, she then delicately sprinkled some of the gemstones that sparkled and shone across the top of hair. Several makeup sets lay strewn across the top of the dressing table next to the jewelry boxes and as Leah glanced thoughtfully at each one, she began to inspect them as she attempted to pick out not only some pieces of jewelry but also some makeup that would work well with the jeweled accessories and that would also match her outfit.

A diamond necklace, a bracelet that matched it and some long, dangly diamond earrings that sparkled and shone were quickly selected and then swiftly worn before Leah turned her attention more fully towards the application of her makeup which was another aspect of her appearance that required attention and that had to be matched up with everything else already on her person. Despite the fact that the Royal Hunt hadn't quite been Leah's cup of tea with her usual two spoonfuls of sugar, the activities planned that evening were definitely right up her recreational street and much to Leah's total delight, she had found her chamber very well equipped for the evening ahead because the huge selection of attire that had been on offer, extensive range of jeweled accessories and vast makeup selection had more than sweetened up her preparations and made every aspect of those preparations easily digestible. Some fine dining in an elegant dress with beautiful accessories as far as Leah was concerned, would be a very welcome treat after the grimy, messy afternoon that she had just spent in the heart of the mucky woods and so now, she felt extremely excited about the evening ahead.

Fortunately for Leah, just as the last few minutes of the hour ran out, she finally managed to complete the application of her makeup and as she did so, a knock sounded at the door and so she quickly rose to her feet as she prepared to answer it. True to Sebastian's word, he had returned very promptly indeed, just as he'd promised and despite Sebastian's obvious shortcomings when it came to the issue of his sense of humor which definitely lacked hilarity in places, he was certainly very punctual and his time keeping was absolutely immaculate and not something that Leah could possibly fault him on.

One final glance was rapidly cast into the mirror on top of the dressing table as Leah began to absorb her reflection and gave her attire, makeup and jewelry combination one last look of enthusiastic admiration as she prepared to depart with hopeful enthusiasm and joyful expectations inside every inch of her mind and heart. The makeup and jewelry that Leah had selected had definitely enhanced her overall appearance and that satisfied her tremendously as she smiled a very satisfied smile and then crossed the room as she prepared to answer Sebastian's knock. A solitary wish suddenly began to occupy Leah's mind as she approached the door as she thoughtfully considered Zidane for a moment and started to wish that he could be there beside her because in recent times, she fully appreciated the fact that she had not made much of an effort for him because unfortunately as her life had become more fully occupied by Spectrum, Zidane had been left out in the cold and quite unintentionally, pushed to one side.

The beautiful dress that Leah had chosen to wear that evening and the sight of it had filled her with heaps of confidence and that confidence rapidly began to exude from her every simulated pore as a triumphant smile spread out across her face as she pulled the door open and prepared to face Sebastian. For the first time in a really long time, Leah now felt like an actual princess as she faced Sebastian and smiled because the dress that she had worn that evening in her opinion, would be the elegant, sophisticated element that crowned her physical presence and glory and so for the first time that day, she now actually felt that the title Princess Leah really suited her.

Sebastian grinned as he glanced at her outfit. "Are you ready for the Joyful Dance and the Feast of Plenty Princess Leah?" He asked. "You certainly look ready."

"I'm ready Sebastian." Leah replied as she smiled, nodded and then stepped confidently out into the hallway. "Lead the way."

Another route was quickly taken by Sebastian as this time he led Leah towards another one of the five doors and then pulled it open and Leah immediately observed as she stepped through it that it led directly into another long hallway. The two began to walk along the rather long hallway which Leah noticed had several other hallways that led into it in silence and as Sebastian led the way, Leah started to internally reflect upon and appreciate her experiences inside Spectrum so far that day as she walked as she silently marveled at how real, natural and authentic everything around her actually felt. Despite the fact that the Castle of Joy didn't really exist, everything that currently surrounded Leah seemed so very natural and deeply realistic and that had not only satisfied but also thrilled her mind because her objectives with regards to Spectrum had definitely been achieved and if anything, actually exceeded.

When it came to the actual issue of Sebastian, although he wasn't really, actually human and despite the fact that he didn't actually exist, somehow to Leah simultaneously, he still felt real and human enough because his very human like, imperfect mannerisms had helped her to acclimatize herself and when he had held onto Leah's arm and led her through the courtyard earlier that day, his arm had actually felt like a real solid object. In fact, every sensation that Leah had felt that day had surprised her because her neural senses had it seemed, been replicated with total precision and mimicked with absolute accuracy and although there still remained many uncharted, unexplored areas of scientific territory for human minds to venture through and much technological terrain for the human world to conquer, she fully appreciated that Spectrum would now at least, be placed upon the actual map of human discoveries.

At the other end of the very long hallway, the hallway opened out into a luxurious looking lobby where there was a pair of huge, grand doors and as Sebastian led Leah towards them, she took a deep breath as she prepared for her grand entrance to the evening's festivities. In just a matter of seconds Sebastian had not only approached the doors but also opened them both up and as he held them open for Leah, she noticed that this time there had been absolutely no hesitation at all on his part as he nodded his head politely towards her and so Leah immediately began to step through the pair of very large, now open doors.

Suddenly, despite all Leah's confidence due to her elegant appearance, nerves seemed to somersault chaotically through her stomach and the pores of her skin began to tingle with excitement as she stepped through the doors because this was ultimately, the moment that she had waited for all afternoon and even endured a mucky, wild pig chase for. Despite all Leah's sudden nerves however, she remained absolutely determined to fully explore and felt eager to enjoy every single second of the evening ahead in its entirety because it had been such a long time since she had made so much effort for anyone, including herself.

Just beyond the huge set of doors, much to Leah's absolute delight, she found a very large, long rectangular shaped room that instantly reminded her of a banqueting hall and as she stepped inside the huge space, some pleasant musical notes wafted gently through the air and rapidly began to fill up her ears. Each delightful musical note seemed to welcome Leah's form in a way that soothed and comforted her because the music greeted her ears in a calm, peaceful, tranquil manner as every chord and note invited her to step further inside the large banqueting hall, despite her now, slightly more nervous state.

Pretty much like the rest of the castle's interior, Leah immediately noticed that a large part of the banqueting hall had a very dark black, shiny marble floor and she could see a few throne like chairs at the other end of the huge room situated directly behind one of a three long banqueting tables which actually lined three of the walls. In the very center of the room there was a large black and white chequered square portion of the floor which differed slightly from the solid black marble floor that surrounded it and so Leah immediately assumed that the square space must be the actual dance floor and where the Joyful Dance would actually take place.

Not a word was spoken by either Sebastian or Leah as he gently placed his hand upon Leah's arm and then began to lead her through her majestic surroundings towards the three golden throne like chairs at the top of the room, one of which it rapidly became apparent, Leah would be seated upon for the remainder of that evening. Some unknown variables in the form of human faces, Leah rapidly observed, were scattered around the edges of the dancefloor which became more densely populated towards the center of the banqueting hall but as Leah visually searched amongst the sea of strange faces and the waves of random beings as she walked, none of them were instantly recognizable to her from the Royal Hunt earlier that afternoon. Despite being surrounded by strangers however, Leah immediately adorned her face with a warm, friendly smile and she offered polite nods in response to anyone that greeted her as she walked as she silently absorbed all that surrounded her.

Once the two arrived directly in front of the three throne like chairs, Leah took her place upon the chair in the middle of the three as Sebastian encouraged her to sit down upon it and she immediately complied. Just a few seconds later Sebastian hurriedly left Leah's side so that he could attend to his duties and role as Master of Ceremonies for the evening and as he began to flutter to and fro, in and out of the pair of grand doors at the other end of the large banqueting hall as he politely escorted some more guests into it, Leah sat and watched him quietly as she patiently waited for the scheduled activities to begin.

When the banqueting hall was almost filled to the brim with people, the guests inside the large room were then formally introduced to Leah by Sebastian in small groups and as he read each of their names out loudly and boldly from some silver cards inside his hands, she immediately acknowledged each group of guests with a courteous nod and a polite, friendly smile. Once each small group of guests had been officially presented, Sebastian would then give Leah a comical, humorous bow which seemed to differ slightly for each set of guests just before he ushered them towards some chairs positioned next to the long tables that lined the three of the walls.

Some glasses of champagne and wine were swiftly offered to each group of guests as soon as they had been seated by several servers that began to rush in and out of the banqueting hall and as Leah watched the servers flutter to and fro, she simultaneously attempted to greet the remainder of the guests that were presented to her. A rumble of chitter chatter and an eruption of joyful laughter rapidly began to fill the interior of the banqueting hall as some of the guests, once seated, engaged in polite, humorous conversations with those around them and as Leah remained seated in silence, she waited patiently for the presentations to end and for the Joyful Dance to commence. Once most of the guests had been officially introduced and seated, about fifteen minutes later, Leah noticed that some more servers suddenly appeared as they entered into the large banqueting hall and that their arms were laden with trays which had been filled to the brim with an assortment of canapés and appetizers that were then served to each guest and even to Leah herself and so as she continued to wait in silence, her mouth began to water, purely due to the delightful aromas from the delicious selection of appetizers on offer.

Approximately thirty minutes after Leah had initially entered inside the large banqueting hall, almost all the chairs next to the long tables had been fully occupied by both people and laughter and as she quietly began to inspect, appreciate and admire the elegant tailored apparel and beautiful decorative jewelry on display that each guest wore, she started to nibble on some of the edible delicacies on offer. When no actual vacant seats remained, Leah watched in fascinated silence as Sebastian approached the center of the huge room and then clapped his hands together very loudly as he prepared to address all the occupants of the banqueting hall, most of whom were still deeply engrossed and engaged in their own conversations.

Much to Leah's fascination, she noticed that all the guests inside the large, spacious room immediately fell silent as they stopped their discussions in mid-flow, turned to face the center of the banqueting hall and Sebastian and then just waited for him to speak. A blanket of silence suddenly seemed to fall across the room and fill the huge banqueting hall for a few seconds as the soft music that had filled the large room up until that moment in time, rapidly ceased and not a sound could be heard amongst the huge gathering of people until just a few seconds later, Sebastian cleared his throat and then he began to verbally take command of the evening's activities.

"Ladies and Gentlemen, Princes and Princesses, Earls and Countesses, we are gathered here tonight to participate in the Joyful Dance and the Feast of Plenty." Sebastian announced triumphantly as his voice began to boom out across the room. "This year's Joyful Dance is being hosted by none other than Princess Leah herself which is a huge honor for us all." He continued as he suddenly turned to face her, smiled and then nodded his head. Sebastian paused for a few seconds as he started to rummage around inside one of the pockets of his brightly colored, baggy suit and then he triumphantly plucked a second pile of silver cards from it as he grinned. "First of all, I will announce the betrothals which relate to those of you that have been brave enough to wish to spend a lifetime with another soul and then I'll make some formal presentations and after that the Joyful dance will begin."

Several servers still fluttered to and fro, Leah noticed as Sebastian spoke and as they approached some of the long tables with trays filled with a vast array of bite size delicacies which were then laid down upon the tables directly in front of some of the guests, Sebastian continued to deliver his address undeterred. Every single tasty morsel of food which decorated the huge silver tray directly in front of Leah looked absolutely delicious and totally irresistible and so as she continued to listen to Sebastian speak, she continued to sample some of the culinary delights that were currently on offer to her palate.

The large silver tray situated on the table next to Leah which seemed to be solely for her consumption, was still laden with generous portions of barbeque chicken wings, a large sample of marinated lamb and beef in small bitesize chunks and an assortment of vegetarian canapes all of which featured alongside a lavish spread of seafood appetizers. Some chunks of lobster, rings of battered calamari and even some skewered prawns lined the edges of the silver tray, some of which had been decorated with a sweet, spicy, peanut satay sauce that had been drizzled over the seafood delicacies and everything that the tray contained, from what Leah could see and had tasted so far, in her opinion represented absolute culinary perfection.

A small harp suddenly began to play, Leah noticed as the betrothal announcements began and as each newly engaged couple was officially presented to the audience that surrounded Sebastian, he announced the couple's commitment to each other and their romantic relationship in a rather comedic style and quite hilarious fashion. Despite the very serious nature of the actual announcements, Leah observed that Sebastian leapt around each couple in a very light hearted, jovial manner as he introduced each one and that all the other guests inside the banqueting hall watched him with total delight as they listened and laughed.

Once each couple's betrothal had been officially announced, the couple in question would then bow down and curtsy in front of Leah and the rest of the guests seated inside the banqueting hall would clap, smile and nod their heads enthusiastically as they celebrated each romantic partnership and every romantic commitment. After each couple of engaged lovers had been formally introduced, the couples would then return to their seats and whisper amongst themselves as Sebastian beckoned to the next couple who would then approach the center of the floor and prepare to be presented. When all the betrothals had been announced, the solitary harp immediately stopped and another soft tune began to play after which point, Sebastian then began to present some individuals to the guests for the first time and once those announcements had been made and everyone was seated once more, Sebastian then started to cross the room as he approached Leah's throne like chair with a cheerful grin upon his face.

"You did an absolutely splendid job Sebastian." Leah encouraged as she immediately congratulated him and complimented his delivery which as far as she was concerned had been absolutely immaculate. "If I'm ever getting married to a Prince and I need a Master of Ceremonies, I know exactly where to come."

"Thank you Princess Leah and yes, we might have to find you a handsome prince one day too because every pretty princess deserves a handsome prince." Sebastian teased playfully as a mischievous grin spread out across his face. "After all that is in all the good fairy tales."

"What happens now?" Leah asked.

"Now Princess Leah, the Joyful Dance will begin." Sebastian explained.

"Right now?" Leah asked.

"Yes Princess Leah, right now." Sebastian replied. "So you'd better get ready because you'll be expected to join in." He playfully reminded her with a cheerful grin before he turned to face the middle of the room once again as he prepared to proceed with the remainder of the evening's scheduled activities.

Just a few seconds later the middle of the floor was once more graced with Sebastian's presence as he quickly returned to his duties for the evening and as he came to a total standstill in the very center of the huge banqueting hall, some excited chitter chatter began to erupt from the tables that lined each wall and gushed into Leah's ears from every direction possible. Since the Joyful Dance was just about to commence as Leah already knew, she immediately assumed and rapidly concluded that most of the guests present seemed to be quite excited about it which immediately encouraged her because as she also knew, she would be expected to participate in the actual dances themselves.

“Ladies and Gentlemen, the first traditional dance of the Joyful Kingdom will now begin, so please feel free to make your way towards the dance floor for the Pitter Patter.” Sebastian boomed as he flashed a cheerful grin at his audience.

In just a matter of seconds Leah noticed that the dance floor was literally jam packed with people as the attendees inside the banqueting hall, willingly flocked to the center of the large space as the guests began to instantly respond favorably to Sebastian's invitation and enthusiastically abandoned their chairs. The eager participants, Leah observed, whispered amongst themselves in excitement as they exchanged snippets of conversations, polite nods and cheerful grins as they waited for the first dance to begin. Despite the fact that Sebastian's invitation had been very warm and extremely open, Leah herself however, still remained seated purely due to nerves and as she quietly watched the guests in the center of the room, a song suddenly began to play that related to the actual dance itself as the Pitter Patter began to grace the interior of the banqueting hall.

When the first dance came to an end, the next dance was then swiftly announced and as Sebastian spoke, he glanced at Leah and nodded his head as he encouraged her to actually participate and join in. Unlike the first dance, Leah observed that the second dance which was called the Joyful Jaunt, seemed far more upbeat and that it had a slightly faster tempo and as the musicians in one corner of the room churned out the livelier melody, the guests on the dancefloor enthusiastically began to dance to the rhythm. Quite comically, Leah noticed that the music actually sped up as the dance progressed which prompted her to giggle and so a couple of minutes into the dance, she stood up decisively and then made her way towards the dance floor to join in because the dance itself looked really quite simple and very straightforward, despite its speed and lots of fun.

Lines of people cheerfully wove in and out of each other as the men and women inside the banqueting hall crisscrossed the dancefloor in patterns as the music played faster and faster and a smile of delight crossed Leah's face as she enthusiastically began to participate. On several occasions throughout the dance, Leah noticed that the men and women on the dancefloor actually locked arms with each other and then twirled each other around and as she joyfully joined in, peals of laughter filled the air around her and her ears. Every part of Leah's interior seemed to tingle with excitement as she danced and she actually began to feel quite warm because the dance kept her actively engaged as each step quenched her thirst for a lively, joyful experience.

Approximately five minutes later, the music from the second dance finally slowed down and as it subsided, a third dance was then announced by Sebastian and Leah enthusiastically remained on the dance floor as she waited to join in. Quite a number of dances continued to be announced and engaged in as the evening progressed and as the next couple of hours slipped joyfully away, Leah merrily participated in each one as music, laughter and joyful participation continued to flow through the banqueting hall in abundance until the late evening was finally ushered in.

Rather interestingly for Leah, despite the fact that she was completely surrounded by lots of fictitious strangers, she actually felt quite relaxed as she simply enjoyed their companionship and fully accepted the evening in totality for the fun that it was. Essentially, although Leah's primary objective that day had been to test the first Spectrum environment, due to the enjoyable recreational entanglements that had been offered to her, the immersive nature of the activities that she had engaged in and her enjoyment of each event, her goal she suddenly realized had become a secondary and even slightly arbitrary focal point. In fact, Leah considered thoughtfully as the Joyful Dance finally came to an end and she returned to her throne like chair, she had become so engrossed in the joy that had filled her evening that her main objective had now slipped silently down her ladder of priorities completely and instead the enjoyment of the Joyful Dance itself had now taken absolute precedence.

Once Leah was seated, the next part of her evening pleasantly began as she watched Sebastian make his way towards the center of the room once again and then announce the start of the Feast of Plenty and the dance floor rapidly emptied as the guests that still remained upon it, quickly returned to their seats. An air of excitement seemed to fill the room, Leah noticed and that excitement seemed to float around inside the large banqueting hall as a sea of expectant faces waited in eager anticipation for the

Feast of Plenty to begin and the edible proceeds from the Royal Hunt to be served. For Leah, the Joyful Dance had certainly been a very pleasant experience and she had definitely really enjoyed herself and so her appetite for enjoyment now felt quite satisfied, even though the Feast of Plenty had not yet actually begun.

Some servers suddenly flocked towards the tables inside the banqueting hall with trays in their arms, laden with piping hot, seasoned wild pig and boar meat as the main course from the Feast of Plenty was served to all of the guests in attendance and Leah watched in eager anticipation as she waited to sample some of the culinary delights on offer that she herself had hunted down earlier that day. An apple had been stuffed inside every one of the mouths of the wild pigs and boars upon each tray and the slabs of meat had been cut prior to cooking and a variety of marinades, seasonings and spices had been rubbed into each groove and so Leah's mouth immediately began to water. According to Sebastian, the meat had been grilled on an open fire and so as the aromas that emanated from the server's trays flooded through the room and wafted into Leah's nostrils, she noticed that every meat filled tray smelt, totally divine.

Eager anticipation seemed to simmer just below the surface of each guest's face as Leah watched the Feast of Plenty begin as the first trays were laid down upon some of the tables and some of the guests dove straight into the feast of plentiful provisions directly in front of them. Suddenly, the divine aroma grew even stronger as a server placed a tray of meat down upon the table directly in front of Leah and as the smell gently caressed her senses, she smiled in absolute delight. Despite the fact that Leah had slaughtered an actual boar herself that day as she glanced curiously at the wild pigs and boar faces that filled each of the trays as she prepared to tuck in, she didn't recognize a single one of them and nor could she tell which one she had actually hunted down herself.

None of the pig's faces from what Leah could see was even remotely recognizable to her and so she quickly shook her head and smiled as she accepted that it was a far more efficient use of her time to actually consume the delicious looking meat that had already been placed in front of her that now awaited her consumption. An inspection to clarify the possible identity of a dead animal that had been served to someone for dinner, served no actual purpose to Leah or to anyone else, she quickly concluded and since the trays filled with meat were already being rapidly consumed such a task would be even less likely to render any actual results. Actual consumption of the feast before Leah's eyes would be a much wiser utilization of her time, she quickly decided because time was no longer on her side that day since both her emotional journey and her enjoyment were due to end fairly soon and that reality was a highly predictable fact.

Directly in front of Leah there was now a huge tray filled to the brim with dark pink, barbecued boar meat and so she smiled as she prepared to consume the prey that she had hunted down so persistently inside the woods earlier that day. Since the feast in front of Leah was not actually real, it seemed slightly strange to her for a moment that her appetite appeared to be so deeply tantalized by the sweet, spicy smells that emanated from the chunks of meat directly in front of her that now waited patiently and silently to be consumed but nonetheless, everything still smelt absolutely delicious and so the wonderful aromas continued to tempt and urge her to join the actual feast itself.

Several chunks of meat were enthusiastically ripped from the huge slab of meat upon the tray and as Leah slipped each morsel of food into her mouth, the meat seemed to melt on her tongue as she began to savor the mouthfuls of food that the delicious feast had to offer. An eager stomach seemed to welcome each mouthful as Leah ate as her body immediately embraced the morsels of food and then rapidly began to digest each one.

Just as Leah began to enjoy her meal however, suddenly and without any warning at all the banqueting hall rapidly disappeared right before her very eyes and as she woke up, she found herself back inside the transparent Spectrum capsule that she had entered into earlier that afternoon. All the splendidly dressed people were gone, the huge, lavish banqueting hall was gone and so too was the cheerful Sebastian and quite sadly, all that now surrounded Leah as she issued a voice command and the transparent lid of the capsule started to ascend, was a very dark, quite dismal looking basement.

An amused smile crossed Leah's face as she glanced down at her body and found herself once more dressed in her plain white lab coat and simple black trousers which were unfortunately, still present. The real clothes that Leah had worn that morning were definitely still there but the lavish, fictitious, elegant, sophisticated, gorgeous dress that she had worn throughout that evening had now sadly, completely disappeared.

Reality for Leah, unfortunately, certainly wasn't as majestic as the Castle of Joy, or as fun as the Joyful Dance but it was now definitely time for Leah to spend some real time in the real arms of the man she really, really adored since her visit to Spectrum had now come to an end, for that day at least. Now, a very real return to reality was overdue for Leah because Zidane, the very real man in her very real life had waited patiently to hold her in his arms all evening and Leah's reality was definitely worth more to her and far more precious in her sight than any artificial royal title that Spectrum could ever possibly give to her. In terms of Leah's first exploration of Spectrum however, and as far as she was concerned, her adventure and day had been a tremendous success and although it was now technically over for that day at least, she had really enjoyed her participation.

For some unknown and inexplicable reason, Leah considered thoughtfully as she began to dismount the Spectrum capsule, although her joyful dabble, deep dive and fun delve inside the world of the Joyful Kingdom had been amazingly interesting, deliciously enjoyable, intensely engaging, highly fascinating and extremely pleasant, the day's activities had completely, mentally worn her out because her visit had quite unexpectedly, expended a significant amount of mental energy. Despite Leah's weary state, she could at least take comfort in the fact that at least her first visit to Spectrum had been a tremendous success and although she was mentally worn out, she now had a list of small tweaks to perfect over the next few days in order to make the consumer's experiences of Spectrum absolutely perfect although her visit to the Joyful Kingdom as far as she was concerned had been as close to perfection as it could possibly be. A hopeful wish however, now lay inside Leah's heart and mind as she walked towards the steps that led back up towards the ground floor of the couple's home that reality and Zidane's real smile would refresh her mind and restore her weary thoughts because his smile truly, always brightened up her day.

In real life, Leah silently considered as she walked, although she certainly wasn't a real Royal Princess in Zidane's and her kingdom of love and life, she definitely was as far as she was concerned and he was her very real prince and that delicious thought comforted her immensely because a real life, simple fairy-tale was definitely worth far more to Leah than a luxurious fictitious one. The couple certainly didn't have a huge banqueting hall and their home in terms of luxury was situated a million miles away from the elaborate, lavish Castle of Joy that Leah had just spent some of her day in but the home that they lived in and shared was certainly pleasant enough for Leah because their companionship and love adorned it with more jewels than any crown could ever possibly hold.

A Saunter into the Heart of the Fearful Forest

According to the calendar of life, the next weekend arrived for Leah as expected and in what seemed like no time at all and as it landed in Leah's city and upon her doorstep, the Saturday morning offered her another chance to indulge in Spectrum once again because all the minor tweaks from her first visit had by that point, been successfully performed and achieved. The Saturday was bright and sunny as Leah arose and then enthusiastically greeted the day with a cheerful, hopeful smile and although Zidane was absent, due to a work trip, Leah prepared to spend her weekend with her creation Spectrum as she took a quick shower and then dressed.

Quite unusually for the couple, Zidane was and would be away from the couple's home for the entire duration of that particular weekend and so he would not return until the Sunday evening due to an emergency situation at work which had meant that he had been asked to visit another office and city, situated a three hour flight away. Occasionally, when technical issues arose that only Zidane could resolve, he would have to travel to various corporate sites to resolve those technical issues and sometimes that meant, the couple would spend their weekends elsewhere. In this particular instance, a daily return to the couple's home and the city of Rankford each evening would be totally impractical for Zidane and quite unusually, Leah had opted to spend her weekend at home alone because she had wished to complete her tests on Spectrum as quickly as she possibly could.

When such rare incidences usually occurred, Leah would normally accompany Zidane and they would then both spend their weekend nights together in a hotel in another city, close to his overtime location but because Leah had wanted to perform the walk-through tests on Spectrum more quickly, she had opted to stay at home that weekend. Usually, whenever such work emergencies had arisen in the past and Zidane had been asked to travel somewhere else for work which hadn't been very often, since he rarely had to visit other sites, he had returned to the couple's hotel room quite late at night, completely worn out and very tired which had meant that during the weekend days Leah had normally had to find ways to amuse and entertain herself throughout the day in his absence. On this particular occasion however, Leah had decided to allocate her entire weekend to the performance of some of the final walk-through tests on the Spectrum environments instead of her usual accompaniment of Zidane because that plan had seemed to align more efficiently with the couple's overall long-term goals and so it had therefore been deemed to be the optimal utilization of her weekend by Leah herself.

In terms of Zidane's current employment, although as Leah knew, many wouldn't consider it glamorous in that he was a helpdesk consultant and systems administrator for a large technology company with offices situated all over the world but it definitely paid the bills and kept a roof over the couple's head and it was at the very least, financially stable. Usually, Zidane worked at head office in the heart of the city of Rankford where the couple lived but due to his specialist knowledge, when problems occasionally arose elsewhere his weekly work routine would differ slightly and diverge from the norm because he would then have to visit other locations to resolve those various technology issues in person and so this weekend was one such occasion.

Due to Zidane's absence that weekend, fortunately for Leah that meant, there would be no routine for her to adhere to because her usual performance of household chores and the preparation of the couple's evening meals were a weekday commitment that she usually undertook at certain times of the day, predominantly for Zidane's benefit. Although the couple's weekends usually differed slightly in the sense that Zidane would sometimes cook and at times, the two would go out together, none of those activities would actually happen that weekend either which meant technically, Leah could eat meals when and if she wanted to and purely as her hunger determined and dictated to her human body. Since that weekend there would be no requests or demands placed upon Leah's time, she did not need to go anywhere or do anything else besides visit Spectrum and so she had ultimately decided that her approach to life and the weekend could therefore be really quite undisciplined because her weekend was completely free and so any considerations towards anyone else and their needs for once, could be totally thrown out of the small window of the basement that she worked inside.

Once Leah had showered and dressed, she cooked a light brunch and then consumed it before she headed eagerly towards the basement with heaps of excitement but also with a slight dash of nerves because the next environment inside Spectrum that Leah was due to visit that day was one that would be filled with fear. Since an adventure filled with fear was a far less glamorous prospect than the last adventure that Leah had dipped her toes inside when she had fully enjoyed the Castle of Joy, a sense of nervousness definitely tinged Leah's senses as she prepared to dive into the fearful unknown and embark upon a more fearful exploration of Spectrum which held the promise of potential scariness firmly by the hand. Despite the guaranteed lack of happiness however, Leah remained hopeful as she walked down the steps that led into the basement that it would be equally as interesting for her because although fear was generally regarded as a negative emotion as Leah already knew, it could also thrill in equal measure.

On this particular occasion, since it would be Leah's second visit to Spectrum, she had already decided to make some slight personality adjustments to her persona inside Spectrum so that she would be slightly more timid, a tad more cautious and even a little bit more sensitive to heighten her experiences on that particular emotional journey. Just a few tweaks to Leah's personality, she had definitely felt, would make the fearful environment much more fearful and since she definitely needed to test the impact of various personality tweaks anyway, the tweaks she had planned to implement that weekend would align with her overall walk-through test objectives in more ways than one.

Since Zidane would be absent for that entire weekend that meant Leah could visit and participate in Spectrum's environments not only undisturbed but also at her leisure which meant that she could fully explore as many environments as she could squeeze in to her weekend, without any pressure to cut her visit short to any given world inside it. Essentially, since this would be Leah's second chance to participate in her next emotional journey inside Spectrum, she felt quite eager to make a start that morning as early as she possibly could and so, she had already cooked up a quick brunch and then headed down to the basement by the time eleven that Saturday morning had arrived.

A whole weekend awaited Leah that was her very own to utilize as she wished to and so she had planned to allow her work upon Spectrum to drench and fully saturate her entire weekend because technically, there would be no other huge demands placed upon her time. Several other delicious environments and emotional journeys as Leah already knew, still awaited her attention and participation and so she was therefore absolutely determined to indulge in at least one, possibly even two emotional journeys in Zidane's absence that weekend because it was rare that Leah ever had such large blocks of time to herself, due to her daily household and romantic commitments.

The basement itself, Leah noticed as she stepped off the final step and then eagerly bounced across the room towards the transparent Spectrum capsule, looked very still and sounded extremely quiet as she prepared to be transported to another fictional place and another mysterious location. A dash of slight nervousness mingled with the enthusiastic excitement that Leah felt swirl chaotically around inside of her as she stepped up the small steps that led towards the Spectrum capsule and then slipped into it and rapidly lay down. In a matter of seconds, Leah issued a voice command to close the capsule lid, tweaked her desired adjustments according to the personality changes that she wished to make that day just before she initiated the actual launch of the next emotional environment through several more voice commands as excitement and nerves continued to flood through every inch of her body and swirl around inside her mind like a whirlpool of uncertain but expectant thoughts.

A deep, excited inhalation was taken by Leah as she lay inside the Spectrum capsule and then closed her eyes as she began to prepare her mind for the next emotional journey that she was just about to embark upon which would essentially be one filled with fear. Every inch of the interior of the capsule was rapidly filled with the sleeping gas that seeped into the transparent case and as it surrounded Leah and infiltrated her senses in a matter of just minutes, her body started to silently succumb to the invisible substance as she began to drift peacefully off to sleep.

Despite the fact that Leah had only just woken up a couple of hours ago, she quickly fell back into a deep state of slumber because the sleeping gas was very effective and it had an almost immediate impact upon her body as she rapidly slipped into a dream like state of consciousness. The real world was quickly left behind as Leah's mind left the basement and silently entered into the emotional plane of the fearful environment that she had chosen to visit that Saturday as Leah began her second visit to Spectrum which in this instance, would last for a whole ten hours and the entire length of an actual emotional journey.

Since Zidane would not be seated inside the lounge, or anywhere else in the couple's home that day, evening or night, Leah could that weekend fully indulge and participate in Spectrum's environments more freely in his absence without any constraints and lavish her attention fully upon Spectrum all weekend and so she had eagerly prepared to do so. No time constraints would govern Leah's Saturday and so she had set the timer inside Spectrum to wake her up in exactly ten hours' time and once her emotional journey would be complete because that was as Leah already knew, the required amount of time it took to enjoy an entire emotional experience in one visit and so a whole emotional journey could be experienced and fully enjoyed that day for the very first time.

Just a minute or so later, Leah awoke and she immediately found herself strewn across the ground in-between some absolutely huge tree roots which protruded from the ground around the base of a very large, circular tree trunk. The enormous tree roots that surrounded Leah amused her for a second or two as she glanced at each one because it almost looked as if every root wanted to be recognized as a plant or tree in their own right as they silently demanded to see the light of day for themselves and refused to remain buried below the ground. Everything else around Leah seemed to be very still and extremely quiet as she quickly stood up and then silently began to inspect her surroundings which were certainly nothing like her basement laboratory because she seemed to have woken up on this occasion, in the heart of an actual forest.

Some grains of dirt and crumpled leaves it seemed had accumulated inside the folds of Leah's clothes and so she quickly dusted herself off as she glanced down at the outfit that her form had now been fully clothed in which she hoped would be as elegant as the pretty golden dress from her first visit. Much to Leah's disappointment however, on this particular occasion there was no pretty dress to be found or elegant attire present that adorned her frame and all she found was a very simple, quite dowdy pair of black combat trousers and a khaki top which crossed over her body as it silently hugged her form and embraced her chest along with the rest of her upper torso.

"I think I prefer the pretty dresses personally." Leah mumbled to herself as she screwed up her nose. "But I guess this is a Fearful Forest, so even my outfit has to be fearful and I'd definitely be scared to wear this out on the street."

Unlike Leah's last visit to Spectrum and her joyful jaunt around the Castle of Joy where she had enjoyed not only the Joyful Dance but also the attire that had accompanied that environment which had predominantly been elegant, stunning, royal and lavish, quite sadly on this particular visit, she had found herself dressed for a very different kind of adventure. Rather unfortunately, Leah glumly predicted, this adventure would probably require some physical intimacy and an up-close personal involvement with dirt and mud but one small consolation did exist however, in that her top was at least, slightly acceptable because it looked far more tailored and even quite stylish in comparison to the baggy combat trousers and so that slight dash of elegance comforted her mind slightly.

Attire and style aside, Leah quickly concluded as she began to thoughtfully, visually inspect her surroundings, the Fearful Forest now awaited her attention and participation and so she had to explore its existence and journey through its heart. Although Leah did have ten hours to explore the Fearful Forest, every second that she spent in internal deliberations over clothes as she fully appreciated, would be a second less with which to complete her actual emotional journey that day and so she eagerly began to prepare herself to embark upon her second adventure.

All around Leah, in every direction that she now faced or looked, there sat a vast number of trees which immediately confirmed to her that yes, she was definitely situated inside an actual forest but she had no clue as to what she was supposed to do next or inside that particular environment. The trees and foliage that surrounded Leah, she quickly considered, probably contained a vast array of forest animals, creatures and beasts and so that was one slight worry that lurked inside her mind as she began to quietly digest her surroundings and search for an actual indicator that could perhaps provide her with some kind of direction with regards to her next course of action.

From Leah's first impressions of the Fearful Forest, she could see nothing particularly fearful about the forest itself yet but as she was also fully aware, she had not yet actually delved deeper into its confines. Once Leah ventured out into the depths of the Fearful Forest, she felt absolutely certain that she would find all kinds of fearful creatures that lurked inside every inch of the foliage around her that she would not only definitely fear but also wish to avoid and so she began to prepare herself for that rather fearful possibility.

A tapestry of fearful events and encounters that would scare Leah, definitely lay hidden deep inside the Fearful Forest itself and that much she already knew because that particular emotional experience had been designed to deliver fear and so fear was virtually promised and to be expected. When exactly the fearful creatures would appear and how each fearful event would unfold however, was extremely unpredictable which meant, Leah could expect them to show up and present themselves randomly to her at any point in time throughout her ten hour emotional journey and that unpredictable factor would definitely keep Leah on her toes. Every step and action that Leah took inside this environment as she already knew, would trigger the fearful, unpredictable events that were due to occur and as each scary element presented itself to her, she would then have to brace herself, face each one head on and find a way to cope with the challenges presented to her and so on this particular Spectrum visit as she was fully aware, she would definitely have to air on the side of caution.

Despite all Leah's uncertainty about the fear that was due to follow shortly however, the actual forest environment itself that surrounded her truly stunned and totally amazed her as she quietly absorbed some of the intricate details of its existence because it almost appeared to be alive due to the rich tones that decorated, celebrated and embraced the landscape in abundance. Every object inside the forest from what Leah could see at first glance, seemed to be adorned in vibrant, lush green, frilly dresses and shirts and some had auburn or dark brown suits and as each tree trunk, branch and blade of grass stood politely to attention in its assigned spot, it was almost as if each one waited patiently for whatever might, or might not actually happen next in order to play their designated role. Emerald green leaves generously coated the trees and as the leafy, frilly shirts and dresses wafted around in the air silently as a slight breeze playfully caught their wafer-thin edges, it was almost as if each one waved at Leah politely as she quietly processed, absorbed and accepted their silent welcome.

Quite intriguingly for Leah, she noticed that all the items inside the forest that surrounded her seemed to breathe life and it was almost as if each item had a human existence as they patiently waited for the events to unfold that each one may or may not participate in. Every event that was due to occur, Leah considered thoughtfully as she began to visually scan and inspect her surroundings once again and performed a more thorough search, would prompt each required object to spring into action so that they could fulfill their intended purpose but some objects as she also already knew from her last visit to Spectrum, may not be required at all and were purely there for decorative purposes.

Although Leah's surroundings appeared to be very cooperative in nature, she still felt quite unsure regarding what exactly she was supposed to actually do next because the forest that surrounded her just seemed to observe her every move and watch her in total silence and it did not contribute in any way to her lack of direction, her decision making or her uncertainty. No indicators or signs seemed to be present or exist that would provide Leah with any kind of direction that she could see and so for a moment as she remained completely silent and totally still, she continued her visual inspection of her current environment as she sought out any directional clues and wondered how exactly this particular adventure was actually supposed to begin. Rather unfortunately on this particular occasion it seemed, unlike the Castle of Joy and the Joyful Dance, there was no likeable, eccentric, quirky character like Sebastian to greet Leah or at least if there was, they hadn't shown up yet which meant, she was supposed to do something else before a guide might actually appear, if an actual guide was due to appear at all but that was another unpredictable element about her current environment over which there was no actual certainty.

Uncertainty governed Leah's mind and form as it seemed to quickly wind itself around her steps as she suddenly forced herself to move forward and venture deeper into the forest so that she could explore some of the mysteries it might contain as Leah made an attempt to kickstart her adventure and accepted the reality that for now, she was indeed, completely and utterly, truly alone and extremely unsure as to what exactly she was supposed to do next in her solitude. However, no sooner had Leah begun to walk through the trees than some noises suddenly started to erupt from a clump of trees situated directly in front of her and as the twigs and branches began to break frantically and snap in abundance, the noises immediately attracted her attention and instantly made her feel slightly nervous. A tidal wave of fear and nervous hesitation rapidly started to flood through Leah's mind which quickly washed over and gripped her form as she quietly began to consider what the possible source of those noises could be and so she held herself completely still for a few minutes as she hesitated, paused and waited in one spot, just to see if the actual source of the noises would actually appear.

Very suddenly, some angry growls and scary snarls began to erupt that seemed to emanate from the depths of the trees themselves that snapped through the air and rapidly surrounded Leah and as some nearby branches simultaneously started to rustle quite vigorously, she immediately started to tremble in direct response. Deep down inside, Leah didn't feel entirely sure that she was ready, or even equipped to face the creatures that might lurk inside the Fearful Forest alone and those scary noises rapidly confirmed to her that the trees did indeed contain some very scary creatures.

After a few minutes of total stillness on Leah's part however, fortunately for Leah, no fearful creatures had appeared and so she resumed her walk-in the same direction but as she did so, she kept her eyes peeled for the possible sources and narrators of those fearful, angry growls. For the next few minutes as Leah continued to walk-in total silence, each scary noise seemed to grow louder and louder with every step that she took and not a single sound subsided or disappeared as she ventured deeper into the lush green foliage and dense population of brown trunks that surrounded her and before very long, the scary sounds had actually escalated into a crescendo and had fully erupted into a fearful volcanic opera of scary growls.

Some strange vibrations suddenly seemed to shake the ground below Leah's feet as she walked and her body continued to tremble with fear with every step that she took because whatever was making those horrible, scary noises and those strange vibrations, didn't sound or feel very friendly to her ears or form at all. In fact, as Leah already knew, it was highly likely that the beasts that inhabited the forest were directly responsible for the wealth of growls and snarls that now emanated from its depths and those beasts sounded not only very scary but also absolutely huge.

"I don't think I really want to meet any of those growlers in person." Leah whispered to herself.

Suddenly, a very loud rustle emanated from a nearby tree and so Leah immediately turned to face the source of the noise and much to her absolute horror and total disgust, she spotted a bright orange snake perched upon a branch that it seemed to have taken a liking to and so much so that it had wound its entire body around the brown, leafy stick and it looked, extremely comfortable. Every inch of Leah's form rapidly began to shudder as she stared at the creature, came to a total standstill and then just watched it for a moment because she really hated snakes and harbored absolutely no desires at all inside her form to be anywhere near one in any capacity and so her close proximity to the creature now, deeply worried her.

Fortunately for Leah however, the snake definitely seemed to prefer the branch of the tree that it was coiled tightly around to her company which was a total relief to her because at the very least, the snake hadn't actually curled up around her body when she had initially arrived in the forest and had been strewn across the ground. Despite the snake's lack of interest in Leah which was certainly preferable to the alternative, Leah's form still remained totally frozen and her feet completely glued to the spot for a few more minutes and she seemed to be totally paralyzed by fear and so, she began to question her own response to the creature's presence which made absolutely no logical sense whatsoever due to the snake's lack of interest in her presence.

Just a minute or so later, fortunately for Leah, she finally managed to somehow shake herself out of her state of paralysis as she silently reassured herself that the snake didn't seem to be that interested in her and that it would probably remain in its present spot for a while. The reptile seemed to be very attached and attracted to the branch of the tree that it had chosen to rest upon, for the time being at least and it didn't look to Leah as if the snake was in an actual hurry to move from its current position which was at least in some ways, a small comfort to her.

Fear in this instance, Leah silently convinced herself, was a highly illogical response because the whole environment that she was currently situated in wasn't actually real and so that meant, the snake couldn't really, actually harm her and since she had created Spectrum herself, it made very little sense now that she should fear anything inside it. A slightly nervous smile began to cross Leah's face as she silently pushed herself to continue with her exploration of the forest and as she began to walk-in the same direction once again, the answer of what she was supposed to actually do next suddenly seemed to land upon her lap as she glanced in the direction that she was headed in and noticed a tree just a few trees away that clearly displayed a very colorful arrow upon its trunk.

Quite fortunately for Leah with regards to that particular tree and the branches that jutted out of its thick, prickly trunk there appeared to be no snakes wrapped around any of its wooden arms or fingers and so she began to rush enthusiastically towards it. Finally and thankfully, Leah had now been provided with an actual sign that clearly indicated just how she should actually proceed and so a wave of immense gratitude seemed to silently wash and flow over Leah's form as she embraced that hopeful symbol and eagerly made her way towards the tree that it was displayed upon. The bright yellow arrow definitely stood out and it was hard to miss because it was very large and so as Leah happily approached it, she smiled as she rapidly concluded that perhaps this particular tree wasn't as attractive to snakes because the bark did look really rather prickly and very uncomfortable.

Since the arrow pointed towards Leah's right-hand side, once she had approached the tree and as she began to walk past it, Leah immediately started to walk-in that direction as she followed the directional indicator that had been provided to her. A bit of guidance had now at least, finally been provided but colorful arrows, Leah definitely felt, were far less interesting for her than the quite quirky, slightly lame jokes and eccentric companionship offered by Sebastian which she suddenly began to appreciate a whole lot more. The Fearful Forest quite sadly it seemed however, didn't provide any such comforts, or stretch to such luxuries and so far Leah had noticed that it just housed some very horrible snakes that slithered, some awful creatures that snarled and some ferocious sounding beasts that growled, none of which looked or sounded very friendly at all.

Once Leah had walked a distance of approximately two hundred meters, she found another bright arrow situated upon a second tree but this time it was orange and much to her surprise, she also found a metal key attached to a piece of string that had been nailed to the bark which sat directly below the arrow. The silver key dangled idly down from the piece of string it was attached to and it rapidly struck Leah that she should actually try to pluck it from the tree that it had been nailed to and so she quickly stretched her hand out towards it, untied it and then gently pulled it off the piece of string. Fortunately for Leah, the key wasn't tied up in lots of very elaborate knots and so it was relatively easy to access and once it had been collected, Leah then quickly headed off in the direction that the orange arrow pointed towards which on this occasion was towards the left hand side of the tree that it had been displayed upon.

The density of the forest rapidly seemed to thicken as Leah walked and as she made her way deeper and deeper into its dense existence, she silently followed the twisted, unmarked path and variances in direction that the arrows led her in. Although the twisted variances in Leah's route through the forest seemed to make absolutely no logical sense whatsoever, her venture through the forest continued and as she discovered more and more arrows marked upon some of the trees, she managed to collect some more keys along the way which it rapidly transpired, were strewn across the forest in a somewhat sporadic manner just like the arrows. Despite the fact that Leah had absolutely no understanding at all with regards to why either the arrows or the keys were present and even less understanding as to why she was supposed to follow the arrows and collect the keys, she diligently collected every single key that she came across meticulously as she made her way through the vast collection of trees that seemed to have no actual end.

Somehow and despite all Leah's nerves, she actually managed to press on firmly ahead, even though the scary noises and angry animalistic expressions that could be heard continuously all around her, truly alarmed her because the noises seemed to emanate from every direction possible and literally surrounded her. Internally however, the battle between fear and determination was somehow won by Leah's sheer tenacity, diligence and persistence as she successfully collected all the keys that had been nailed to the trees across her path and diligently followed all the arrows that she saw which guided her through the forest, despite the scary distractions. An avid eye was kept wide open for any creatures or animals that might suddenly to decide to pounce and jump into Leah's path as she walked but fortunately for Leah, she didn't actually have any close encounters with any terrifying animalistic entities and the narrators of those very scary growls as she made her way through the forest.

All in all, Leah noticed as she suddenly paused for a moment by a tree and then began to inspect the contents of her trouser pockets as she had ventured through the forest she had managed to collect nine keys in total in a relatively peaceful manner which as far as she was concerned, due to the fearful nature of the noises, was quite an achievement in itself. Every one of the nine shiny keys was quickly physically inspected and then swiftly tucked away back inside Leah's trouser pockets before she resumed her walk towards the tree that she could clearly see a tenth key nailed to and as Leah approached the tree, she released a grateful sigh as she began to hope that the tenth key would be the final one that she was supposed to collect.

No wild, scary animals had so far presented themselves to Leah and since the growls and snarls that surrounded her had not yet materialized or presented any kind of direct threat to her form, she began to feel slightly less intimidated by the loud, angry, animalistic noises. Much to Leah's total relief, no grizzly bears had jumped out of the trees and pounced upon her and the only real creature that she had seen so far had been the snake which was now no longer even visible to her and that slithery, slippery reptile had it seemed, been totally disinterested in her presence. Absolutely no vicious tigers had leapt out of the trees and threatened to tear Leah's limbs apart and so regardless of all the loud growls and angry snarls that surrounded her, she could at least find comfort in the fact that her walk through the forest so far, despite her nerves and fears had actually been, really quite calm.

The lack of any scary confrontations with any kind of vicious beast up until that point, was a tremendous comfort to Leah as she sighed a sigh of relief as she walked towards the tenth key and the tree that it was nailed to with a hopeful spring in her step. Since Leah felt very unsure as to whether she could handle any aggressive meetings that might potentially occur with any of those growlers because she had no actual weapons with which to defend herself and no other means of defense at all, the fact that they hadn't turned up to act upon their growly threats and hadn't crossed her path in any capacity, relieved her immensely.

One slight fear did however, still manage to lurk at the back of Leah's mind as she approached the tree in that as she already knew, a confrontation with one of those scary creatures could happen at any given moment because their lack of appearance up until that point did not detract from the reality that they did still currently surround her. A growly, snarly, animalistic manifestation could therefore occur at any given moment and some kind of creature could leap out of the trees and pounce upon Leah at any given second and so she kept her eyes peeled and remained vigilant as she walked. Although the animalistic noises intimidated Leah slightly less now because to some extent, she had grown accustomed to them as she fully appreciated that didn't mean that the actual source of those noises had actually disappeared and so Leah actively, visually scanned her surroundings as she drew near to the tenth key and the tree that it clung to.

Rather strangely however, as Leah drew much closer to the tree, the bright red arrow marked upon it and the tenth key, suddenly the key actually disappeared which confused her and so she paused for a moment directly in front of the tree as she internally began to wrestle with her total confusion. The tenth key, for no apparent reason it seemed, had just completely vanished but as Leah started to step back from the tree, much to her absolute and total horror, the ground below her feet suddenly started to very unexpectedly give way at which point, she was then rapidly plunged into the depths of the earth. An alarmed gasp managed to escape from Leah's lips as she started to fall downwards extremely quickly and as Leah frantically attempted to stabilize herself, she tried to cling on to anything that she possibly could to stop her downward descent but her desperate efforts were to absolutely no avail.

Instead of Leah's arrival at the tree and the collection of the tenth key nailed to it as she had planned, the ground had suddenly swallowed her whole with absolutely no warning at all and now it seemed, she was just about to be chewed up by the muddy, circular, narrow tunnel that she'd fallen into as the muddy hole started to digest her via its spiral, slippery slope which it appeared, intended to hurtle Leah very swiftly towards the heart of the earth. A frustrated, alarmed shriek somehow managed to escape from Leah's lips as she tumbled further down into the muddy confines of the ground because her fall had caught her totally off guard and so Leah's unexpected departure from the surface of the forest had actually taken her completely by surprise. No matter how much Leah shrieked however, it rapidly transpired that her downward descent could not actually be prevented, stopped or avoided and as she suddenly, totally lost sight of the trees and forest above her head, she began to completely surrender in totality to her actual fall.

One silver lining did however, accompany the very large, grey cloud of alarm that now hung over Leah's head and that was the fact that quite fortunately, her downward descent only lasted for a few minutes and as she suddenly landed on the ground on her backside, she appeared to have fallen into what seemed to be an underground cave. Despite the fact that Leah had fallen down an actual hole which had plunged her into the depths of the ground as she began to inspect herself, Leah quickly realized and appreciated, the fact that she didn't seem to have suffered any actual injuries, much to her total relief and so that was at least one small comfort and minor consolation to the rather rough, very unexpected fall.

Once Leah had reacclimatized herself, just a minute or two later, she began to conduct a quick visual scan of the underground cave and fortunately, from what she could see at first glance, there didn't appear to be any immediate threats from any kind of scary creatures anywhere nearby. The fact that there seemed to be no immediate danger present, instantly provided Leah with an ounce of comfort as she quickly rose to her feet and then began to visually inspect and mentally dissect her new surroundings as she searched for a possible way to actually proceed.

However, much to Leah's absolute horror, once she had stood up and just as she tried to take an actual step forward, once more the ground below her feet seemed to give way again as the mud suddenly started to suck her form downwards. The pool of mud that Leah had actually landed upon it rapidly transpired, was definitely not friendly or even stable enough to walk on and the muddy pond it appeared, did not intend to allow Leah to walk across it without a fuss as it rather stubbornly silently opposed, slowed down and even began to obstruct her actual movements. Situated not too far away from Leah's current position however, she rapidly noticed that there was a muddy bank which looked slightly firmer than the mud directly below her feet and so she began to try and reach it in order to stop her downward descent.

Every step that Leah tried to take through that pond of mud, she swiftly noticed as she started to try and wade through the thick liquid mud that surrounded her, seemed to be a total struggle and it was by the midway point, almost waist deep. Each breath that Leah took seemed to grapple with the thick muddy liquid that now clung very tightly to some of her limbs and quite strangely, the liquid dirt seemed to be very attached to her form although Leah herself, certainly did not share the same fascination or sentiments. Despite all Leah's efforts however, the grimy brown substance it rapidly transpired would not depart as it stubbornly clung on to every inch of her body that it could possibly reach and clothed her frame all the way up to her waist but despite that rapid progression, it showed absolutely no signs of surrender as the mud continued to pull her limbs further down and deeper into its murky, muddy, dirty brown, earthy depths.

An undercurrent of panic and alarm, suddenly started to engulf Leah's mind and form as she let out a rasp of fear but the mud only seemed to cling on to her skin even more decisively and tightly in response, despite all her internal and external objections. Somehow, it almost seemed as if the mud was alive and fully aware of Leah's presence and absolutely determined to achieve its goal as it clenched very tightly onto every single one of her limbs that it could reach and continued to try and pull her body downwards and due to the mud's stubborn attitude and tenacity, Leah's panic stricken fear rapidly became even more frantic as her steps became stronger and stronger but less and less effective. No matter what Leah had hoped and wanted to achieve, it now seemed as if the mud that surrounded her which clearly had her form in its grasp was in direct opposition to her own objectives and an obstruction to her actual goals which meant, she would definitely have to intensify her efforts and make them a lot more effective, if she actually wished to reach the much firmer muddy bank.

Thankfully however, just a few minutes later, much to Leah's total and utter relief, her somewhat hectic struggle with the muddy pool of liquid dirt finally ended as she managed to wade towards the bank at the other side of the mud bath, arrived beside it and then quickly stretched out her hands towards a root which dangled down from the muddy ceiling just above her head. Rather conveniently, the root was actually reachable for Leah and so as she grabbed onto it and then utilized it as leverage, she somehow managed to pull herself out of the dark brown, muddy pool completely. Unlike the mud, the root very kindly seemed to willingly assist Leah in her quest in silent cooperation, she observed and as it rescued her from the dismal, brown pond of filth that had wanted to drag her down into its depths and claim her as its own, Leah sighed with absolute relief as she finally managed to exit the dark brown pool of liquid dirt.

Once Leah had managed to crawl further up onto the much firmer muddy bank, she then lay quietly upon the ground for a few minutes and just rested because her struggle with the mud that had almost seemed to be alive had actually, completely and utterly worn her out. In fact, due to the struggle that Leah had just endured, her form now felt slightly drained and it was almost as if all the energy had been sucked out of it and siphoned away by the strenuous effort that it had taken to actually reach the bank and then climb out of the muddy pool. A few minutes of rest was definitely required to recover, Leah silently concluded as she just lay absolutely still and attempted to recuperate because the intensity of her battle with the dark brown substance had actually caused her form to ache slightly as she had attempted to escape from its grimy clutches, grubby stubborn attitude and muddy tenacious grip.

When Leah felt that she had gathered sufficient strength with which to resume her adventure once more and that she actually felt strong enough to proceed, she then sat up and began to check the large, square pockets of her black combat trousers. The nine keys that Leah had collected so far and stored inside each one, much to her total delight and despite her struggle with the mud, were all still actually present and that as far as Leah was concerned, was at least one small consolation as she silently and thoughtfully inspected each one and appreciated the fact that none had been lost. Once Leah felt satisfied that the nine keys were not only still present but also intact and she had fumbled around with the metal objects for a few more minutes, she then slipped each one back inside her trouser pockets and stood up as she began to search for what she was actually supposed to do next, or where she was supposed to go from her current position.

At one end of the muddy bank, Leah suddenly noticed that there was a dark dirt tunnel which appeared to burrow into one of the muddy walls of the underground cave that she was now situated inside which appeared to be the only way out and so Leah quickly accepted that it was probably her only real means of exit as she began to walk cautiously towards it. Since it was now virtually impossible for Leah to go back the way that she had arrived, the muddy tunnel appeared to be her only real current option because there seemed to be no other real, viable, alternative to consider and as Leah already knew, to claw her way back up via the muddy, slippery tunnel would be an absolutely impossible mission. In fact as Leah fully appreciated, there was no way that she would be able to reach the surface and return to the forest that now lay silently somewhere above her head via that particular route because it was now ultimately, unreachable and untouchable from her current position and such an attempt would surely be an insurmountable task and not one that Leah really, actually wanted to consider.

The dark tunnel formed from dirt, Leah swiftly accepted as she entered inside its interior, now seemed to be the only accessible way out and so Leah held her breath for a few seconds as she silently began to visually scan the area directly in front of her. An undercurrent of fear definitely lingered in Leah's mind and form that some fearful creatures might lurk in the earthy tunnel walls that might pose and present a direct threat to Leah's actual form and so she diligently searched and visually scanned the area in front of her as she began to walk along the tunnel's interior. Fortunately for Leah however, the tunnel appeared to be clear or at least the distance as far as her eyes could see seemed to be free of any kind of entities other than herself and so as she started to walk along its earthy interior, Leah began to rejoice in the fact that now at least, the ground was actually firm enough for her to walk upon.

After Leah had scurried about two hundred meters or so along the tunnel, she noticed that the tunnel rather abruptly ended and that it led out onto an actual ledge but as she neared the ledge, much to her total horror and absolute disgust, she rapidly discovered that it was in fact, a very high ledge situated above a very large expanse. In fact, the actual base of the huge expanse which was formed from muddy ground, Leah rapidly observed, was now situated at least three hundred meters below her and so it was totally unreachable from her current position but some root like ropes hung down from the muddy ceiling above her head and one was even situated directly in front of her face and so as Leah began to process the presence of the roots, she started to tremble as she stared at the offensive objects. The roots however, seemed totally indifferent to Leah's predicament as each one just dangled silently in mid-air but each one seemed to communicate non-verbally with her as the roots provided a silent indication to Leah that she was supposed to utilize the root ropes to swing her way across the very large expanse.

Extremely uncomfortably for Leah, she now had to suddenly face one of her biggest real life fears and then actually somehow, overcome it and so she winced as she began to silently accept what she was expected to do next as her body continued to tremble. The root ropes in front of Leah's face provided a very clear directional indicator as each one clearly and silently expressed to her that she would have to swing out across the expanse via the roots, if she wished to cross the large expanse at all and that on that particular point it appeared, there would be no actual negotiations.

From what Leah could clearly see in her current position, there were no other choices currently available to her and so she released a frustrated sigh and disheartened groan as she prepared to participate because an attempt to overcome one of her deepest, largest, real life fears had to be made before she could proceed any further. This particular challenge would certainly not be one of Leah's favorite moments, she nervously concluded as she viewed the distance between the ledge and the ground below her because heights were not attractive to her in any way, shape or form and in fact, heights were actually a very personal challenge that really worried and intimidated her in a very personal way.

A haphazard formation of root ropes hung silently down at regular intervals across the huge gap directly in front of Leah and in the middle of the large expanse, she noticed that there was a pillar formed from dirt which had a small, square platform at the top of it, upon which there appeared to be an earthy pedestal. On the other side of the huge expanse, Leah could see that there was a second much larger, far wider platform also formed from dirt which she hoped would somehow lead back up to the surface and provide a way out of the underground tunnels, if she could first cross the huge gap but it had become quite apparent to her by that point that she would probably have to swing her way across the entire expanse, in order to reach both platforms.

For the next couple of minutes Leah did absolutely nothing as she just stood completely still and her heart froze with fear because it was such a huge ordeal for her since heights really were one of Leah's biggest, real life fears. The fact that Leah was now situated inside a simulated, artificial environment didn't seem to comfort her in the slightest, reduce her nervousness, or make that fear feel any less real and as Leah began to internally prepare herself to proceed, a nervous, awkward lump seemed to gather inside her throat. Another few minutes went silently by as Leah quietly considered the possibility of a return to the slippery, muddy tunnel, a choice which now suddenly began to hold far more appeal for her because an actual attempt to claw her way back out of the subterranean tunnels had swiftly become the preferable option to the roots and heights.

Suddenly, the impossible mission held far more appeal and it had even started to seem slightly more possible to Leah because heights really did scare the living daylights out of her and so exposure to them was something that she really felt quite anxious to avoid and usually did avoid very successfully. However, in this instance, the heights and roots seemed to be totally unavoidable and so as Leah silently mulled over the two options, one of which wasn't really a viable option at all, she spent a few more minutes in pointless internal deliberations which didn't really comfort her in any way, since there was no actual real choice or real decision to be made and as Leah already knew, her surrender in totality to the root ropes and heights, would eventually, definitely have to actually happen. Deep down inside, Leah ultimately knew that it would definitely be a complete waste of time to even try to return to the surface via the tunnel that she had initially slidden down but nonetheless she silently entertained the thought for another minute or two before she made any actual attempts to proceed.

This particular confrontation with heights was something that Leah had to finally, as much as she hated it, fully accept because she definitely had to face that particular challenge in order to return to the surface once more and perhaps then she would be able to retrieve the tenth key that she'd seen vanish but she certainly wasn't looking forward to it. Heights as far as Leah was concerned, really were just a disgusting challenge in life and an unnecessary evil that rarely had to be faced, if you were wise enough to keep your feet firmly on the ground which she usually was.

In the very center of the large expanse, upon the small, earthy pillar and platform that protruded from the ground below it, Leah noticed as she began to inspect it slightly more closely that the earthy pedestal upon it had a bright red arrow on one side which clearly indicated the actual direction that she was supposed to proceed in, once she had landed upon it and from that point onwards. A nervous knot suddenly seemed to form inside Leah's stomach however and keep the nervous lump in her throat company, as she glanced at the arrow and then swallowed nervously because it really was such a scary prospect for her and not one that she would enjoy in any capacity at all.

Before Leah moved an inch however, one final, last, reluctant, hesitant visual scan was very thoroughly and pedantically performed as she attempted to ensure that she hadn't missed out on any alternative forms of exit and another possible escape route because an easier option was definitely preferable, if one was available but unfortunately, no other options seemed to exist. Once Leah felt totally satisfied that the root ropes were indeed the only way that she could actually proceed and that no other solutions could be found, she then prepared to swing out across the roots as she took a deep breath and tried to muster up all the courage that she could find from within herself. If Leah wished to resume her adventure inside the Fearful Forest, the root ropes were it seemed, the only real way to proceed and since she would not wake up for at least another seven hours, being sat upon a muddy ledge for the remainder of her emotional journey and all of that time, truly wasn't a feasible solution or an acceptable option.

The tenth lost key seemed to possess some kind of special significance, Leah silently began to conclude, because she had noticed by now that it really was much harder to not only locate but also to retrieve although as yet, she still had no idea where the tenth key actually, currently was. A quick visual scan was rapidly conducted as Leah strained her eyes and tried to visually inspect the two dirt platforms as she visually searched for the tenth key from a distance, just to ensure that the tenth key was actually situated upon one of the two piles of earth and actually present.

Unfortunately for Leah however, due to the distance between the ledge and the two mud platforms, it rapidly transpired that it was actually very hard for her to visually determine whether or not the tenth key was situated upon either muddy platform from her current position and so surrender rapidly appealed to her. Just a couple of minutes later, Leah decisively, quickly abandoned her visual quest in total defeat as she prepared to proceed because the visual search she finally concluded, had really been quite pointless. In order to find and perhaps retrieve the tenth key, if that was indeed actually possible, Leah decided as she readied herself to press ahead, she would have to proceed even with all her uncertainty because she had fallen and the key had fallen but where exactly it had gone, she had absolutely no idea yet and neither muddy platform it seemed, currently wished to provide any answers to that actual question.

Although Leah had now technically, reached a final decision, nerves still seemed to rattle around inside her mind and tease her form which made her skin almost feel as if it crawled with fear as Leah stretched her hand out towards the first root rope which hung limply down from the earthy ceiling above her head, totally still and seemingly indifferent to her dilemma. A nervous gulp was released as Leah rather reluctantly grabbed on to the root rope with both her hands and then firmly gripped it between her fingers and palms just before she started to take a few steps backwards as she prepared to swing out across the large, huge gap directly in front of her. Every part of Leah's form trembled as she prepared to tackle the challenge that now lay directly in front of her head on and as a wave of fear washed over her, she began to silently conclude that the Fearful Forest was indeed a very scary place because she had already met some of her deepest fears within its vicinity, namely snakes and heights and as she already knew, her emotional adventure and journey that day was still far from over.

Just a few seconds later Leah finally forced herself to take action as she silently dismissed the fearful procrastination that resided within her and bravely clung onto the first root rope as she leapt out across the first part of the muddy expanse that lay silently below her. Luckily and very fortunately somehow, Leah actually managed to grab the second root rope mid-flight and then she even managed to swing out towards a third root which she quickly grabbed and then clung on to and as she swung out across the remainder of the first divide via the third root rope, just a few seconds later, much to Leah's total relief, she actually managed to drop down onto the small square platform in the center of the expanse.

A huge sigh of relief escaped from Leah's lips as she landed safely upon the earthy platform and as soon as her feet touched the ground, she quickly attempted to stabilize her form as she rapidly straightened herself back up. Despite Leah's achievement and the fact that she had just managed to overcome one of her deepest fears however, unfortunately there was nothing much to found on the first platform except a brightly colored arrow and the dirt that it had been formed from as she quickly inspected the platform's earthy surface and the tenth key, much to her total dismay, was sadly nowhere to be seen.

Another root rope hung idly down from the earthy ceiling directly in front of Leah's face, she observed as she turned and faced the second platform which rapidly confirmed to Leah that her root rope swings for that day, were far from over and so a rather reluctant sigh and a frustrated groan managed to escape from Leah's lips as she glanced at the root rope in total dismay. Some tiny part of Leah had harbored a small glimmer of hope that once she had finally managed to land upon the first mud platform, something else might be present, another event might be triggered and occur, or another exit might even appear and be provided that would spare her from anymore root rope swings but sadly, as she had now discovered that was not the case. Unfortunately, it had rapidly been confirmed to Leah upon her arrival that several more unstable, dangerous swings high above the ground on flimsy root ropes would have to be performed and endured before she could even hope to leave the underground area and that appeared to be absolutely non-negotiable because there was no other way for her to actually proceed. Technically, Leah was now stuck in the center of the huge expanse until the remainder of the root rope swings had actually occurred and had been fully actioned successfully and so Leah began to prepare herself for some swings across the root ropes once again.

"Just some more flimsy root ropes and even more horrible

heights." Leah muttered under her breath as she shook her head in total frustration.

Before Leah made any actual attempts to proceed any further however, she paused for a minute or two, just to catch her breath and to reorganize her thoughts because once again her courage had to be mustered from deep inside herself before she could swing out across the remainder of the expanse. A quick nervous glance was cast cautiously down towards the muddy ground below the earthy pillared central platform as Leah continued to face the direction that she was headed in and peered over the edge and as she did so, Leah rapidly began to notice that the ground on that particular side of the earthy platform, looked very much like a muddy liquid pool which seemed to be alive as it swished chaotically around in a rather hectic, haphazard fashion.

"I hope it's not sinking mud like the mud inside the cave." Leah whispered to herself. "If I fall down into that mud, there's no way I'll get out of it."

Suddenly and much to Leah's total disgust however, she began to realize the actual reason behind the liquid mud's rapid movement as the pool of dirt continued to swish around hectically below her. Unfortunately for Leah that movement it rapidly transpired, was not due to the actual mud itself and as she screwed up her eyes and just stared at it for a few more minutes, jùst to be totally certain, she managed to visually identify and establish exactly why the mud appeared to be so alive and the reason was far from pleasant. Much to Leah's absolute horror as the real explanation presented itself to her eyes and mind, it became very apparent to her that this particular pool of mud was extremely different in nature to the mud that she had encountered inside the muddy cave and that this liquid mud was horrifyingly, even more dangerous.

Unlike the pool of mud that Leah had initially landed upon and fallen into when she had tumbled down the slippery, muddy tunnel in the ground, the grungy mud below her swirled around rapidly at a very fast pace indeed and it almost looked as if it was alive because it actually contained creatures that were actually alive. Some very large, hungry, blackish brown creatures it appeared, inhabited the actual mud pond itself which were now, more clearly visible to Leah as each one swam around haphazardly inside the liquid dirt and although the mud definitely wasn't alive, the creatures certainly were.

"Nope, this muddy pool is definitely different because this one has creatures in it." Leah advised herself. "Very hungry looking creatures."

For the next few minutes, Leah just stood completely still in total silence as she watched the creatures swim around below her and as she did so, she observed that a few even leapt in and out of the liquid mud pool and then snapped their large, razor sharp, jagged teeth at each other. Fear suddenly seemed to run rampant and somersault through Leah's mind and form as she started to tremble because the creatures looked as if they could tear her apart in seconds but despite their presence as Leah already knew, she still had to cross the remainder of the divide and so she began to thoughtfully analyze and plan her next steps.

"These creatures don't even look like they like themselves and they look as if they would eat each other." Leah whispered to herself.

Unfortunately for Leah, the creatures all looked extremely hungry and she had absolutely no desire at all to fill their empty stomachs and to be their actual lunch and there were no guarantees that she would not fall down into the liquid muddy pond, if and when she tried to swing across it. The slippery, muddy tunnel that Leah had initially fallen down, suddenly seemed to hold even more appeal to her but to leave the subterranean area without the tenth key that it perhaps contained as Leah already knew, would be absolutely pointless because after all, she had ventured quite far along this route already. A fall from the root ropes was not a desirable outcome however, to Leah's next steps as the creatures below her consistently confirmed as they snapped their teeth at one another aggressively because one bite from them would seal Leah's fate and then she would become no more than a mouthful of food and a late lunch snack.

"Dear ugly, horrible creatures, I taste really nasty, I promise."

Leah whispered as she stared at the liquid pool of mud below her and the hungry, savage animals it contained. "And I've not even been seasoned, marinated or cooked properly, so you'd have indigestion for months."

Although Leah's words had actually been whispered out loud, there had been no real intention on her part to verbally express even a single word to the hungry looking audience below her and her comment although directed towards them had merely been expressed to comfort and to reassure herself. In fact, no actual attention was desired, wanted or required by Leah from those very hungry creatures and so each word had been spoken softly, quietly and almost under her breath because the less attention that Leah attracted in that respect, the better it was for her own safety and of that reality, she felt absolutely certain.

Once again however, another root rope dangled down directly in front of Leah's face from the earthy ceiling above her head and as she glanced at it, Leah noticed that the root remained very still and totally uncooperative and that it almost appeared as if it wanted to wait for Leah to make an independent decision as the root rope seemed to politely avoid any contributions or attempts to influence her internal deliberations with a stagnant, unwilling, eerie stillness. Perhaps the root rope was uncertain, Leah began to consider, about whether it would lead its rider to the safety of the second mud platform or to the possible death that lurked inside the muddy pool below it and hence it was reluctant to contribute towards that actual choice in any way and so it did not move a single inch or encourage anyone to take any particular course of action.

Finally, after more than just a few minutes, Leah's uncertain pause which had lasted slightly longer than her usual moments of fearful hesitation due to the additional dimension of fear that was now actually present, came to an end as her internal deliberations were pushed firmly towards the back of her mind and she somehow managed to muster up the courage required to move forward. A deep breath of bravery was taken by Leah as she hoped that the air around her form would fill up her simulated, artificial lungs with any particles of courage that it might contain because whether she liked it or not, the hungry, horrible creatures were not going anywhere which meant, Leah had to venture out across the remainder of the expanse or she would spend the rest of her adventure upon that earthy pillar in a state of paralyzed fear, tied up in knots of hesitation and bound to it in a frustrated state of fearful limbo.

Rather unconvincingly for Leah, the root rope that continued to dangle down in front of her face remained completely motionless and it seemed totally disinterested in both Leah and her plight because it did not sway and commit to lead her to safety but hung silently from the earthy ceiling with an attitude of total indifference. Despite the root rope's lack of interest however, Leah finally plucked up enough courage to lean forward and grab it with both hands as she took a nervous, hesitant, very deep inhalation and clung on to it. One fateful plunge could perhaps land Leah inside the mouth of a hungry creature as she very well knew which added another dimension of fear to the next few swings that she would have to initiate and complete successfully, if she wished to retrieve the tenth key and if she wanted to return to the forest's surface with her form intact but as Leah now fully accepted, despite the additional fearful elements, the root rope swings definitely had to actually occur.

Just a few seconds after Leah had clasped both her hands securely and tightly around the root rope, she then took another deep breath and stepped backwards as she prepared to bravely and energetically swing out towards the next mud platform which was situated just a few swings away. Fortunately enough for Leah, as she swung out with all her might she actually managed to grab onto the second root rope and then she even successfully swung out towards the third and as she grabbed onto it and swung across the remainder of the gap, she was able to reach the much larger, second platform in less than a minute and even more fortunately, arrive in one piece. Despite the fact that Leah's initial landing actually seemed to be quite successful however, as she slipped down towards the ground and landed on her backside on the edge of the second earthy platform and released a sigh of relief, it rapidly became very messy because she totally lost her balance within just a matter of seconds and then almost slipped of the platform completely.

Several root ropes were scattered across the second earthy platform that hung down over its earthy edge and so as Leah started to slip off the platform luckily, she spotted a few root ropes nearby which seemed to offer her a possible form of salvation that appeared to be within easy reach and so she was immediately provoked to stretch her arms out towards any that she felt could reach. Once the root ropes had been grabbed, Leah then clung on to each one for dear life and fortunately for Leah, the root ropes managed to hold her actual weight and so she was able to utilize them as leverage as she quickly pulled herself back up onto the dirt platform and back to safety just a few seconds later.

Since the second platform was much larger, it was quite easy for Leah to fully stabilize herself relatively quickly and once Leah felt that she was in a position of safety once more, in an upright but seated position, she then cast a fearful glance back down towards the hungry creatures below her and just watched them for a few minutes in total silence. One small thought comforted Leah tremendously as she watched the creatures' hungry interactions as they continued to snap at each other and bite each other aggressively and that was the reality that thankfully today, she would not be their actual lunch because that gruesome fate had so far, luckily been totally avoided.

Rather scarily however, Leah rapidly observed that the creatures below her had now gathered at the base of the second platform and it was almost as if they could sense her presence upon it, the possible fall that might have occurred as she had swung out over their hungry bodies, or the fall to the muddy ground that could have possibly happened, if her slippage had been far worse. Each hungry creature that was visible to Leah looked extremely eager to snack on her limbs, she silently concluded and so Leah hurriedly started to crawl as far away from the edge of the earthy platform as she possibly could before she even prepared to stand up again in an attempt to reduce the risk of anymore potential slippages.

On the second platform which like the first platform appeared to have been formed from particles of dirt and from earthy soil, Leah swiftly discovered, much to her sheer relief that there was a bright red arrow marked upon an earthy wall at one end of the platform which actually led directly towards the tenth key. However in this instance, Leah rapidly realized as she began to walk towards the tenth key, this key was not simply nailed to a piece of string and it appeared to be situated inside some kind of bamboo cage that had been embedded into the actual earthy wall.

Despite the potential obstacle that Leah would now have to face however, the tenth key had at least, at long last actually been found but as yet, since it was still not in Leah's actual hands, possession or pockets, she could not yet actually rejoice in her discovery. A gentle sigh of relief escaped from Leah's lips as she walked towards the small bamboo cage that the tenth key was encaged inside because to finally find the metal object after all her struggles with the mud, root ropes and heights, she definitely felt, was quite an achievement in itself.

Upon closer inspection of the actual bamboo cage itself however, it rapidly became apparent to Leah as she stood directly in front of the structure formed from sticks and mud that although the bright red arrow was very visible, easily accessible and hard to miss, the same could not be said about the actual tenth key which looked to be very securely housed behind the bamboo sticks. The bamboo stick cage had been embedded into the actual mud wall which meant, Leah would either have to open the cage and put her hand inside the bamboo structure, if she wanted to retrieve it or smash the cage to pieces in order to access the metal key that it contained.

After just a few minutes of quiet consideration, some much closer scrutiny and some cross visual examination, Leah enthusiastically and without too much hesitation, stretched her hand out towards the bamboo cage as she attempted to open up the stick door and retrieve the actual tenth key. Since none of Leah's biggest fears appeared to be present or involved in this particular challenge, namely heights and reptiles that slithered across the ground, no actual hesitation was present on Leah's part and much to Leah's absolute delight, she rapidly discovered that the door of the bamboo cage opened up easily enough as she quickly slid it upwards.

An eager hand was rapidly slipped inside the bamboo cage as Leah made the most of the easy access that had been provided to its interior but just a second or two later, much to Leah's total surprise and absolute shock, she seemed to be punished for her bravery as the bamboo cage door suddenly, very unexpectedly, snapped back down on top of her arm and her hand actually became trapped inside the cage. Unfortunately, despite all Leah's efforts and her courage, no rewards currently appeared to be on offer to her and rather strangely, the task that she had actually, initially perceived as slightly easier had suddenly become far more complicated in nature and the cage door had actually delivered a sharp, short, painful shock directly to her arm.

"Ouch that hurt." Leah moaned as she winced.

Every part of Leah suddenly started to panic as she began to process the fact that for now, her arm was well and truly stuck inside the bamboo cage and calmness seemed to rapidly desert Leah's form as it totally abandoned her and as fear stepped in to replace it, it almost felt as if that fear wanted to run rampant across the surface of her skin which once again, started to crawl. Some grains of courage were quickly sought from deep within Leah's mind as she attempted to convince herself that there was no real cause for alarm since her arm was not actually in any real danger, or at least not yet and so Leah took a deep breath as she attempted to calm herself back down and prepared to face the two challenges directly in front of her, instead of just the one. Initially, Leah had only faced one challenge which had been to retrieve the tenth key but now, she faced two because she not only had to retrieve the key but she also had to free her trapped arm and hand, if she possibly could.

Although Leah's hand and a large chunk of her arm were now technically trapped inside the bamboo cage, she quickly tried to extend her trapped hand towards the key and reach out for the metal object as she made a rough attempt to grab it. Since the actual tenth key now lay within Leah's actual grasp, she definitely felt motivated and propelled to at least try and collect it and the fact that her arm was trapped hadn't deterred or managed to dissuade Leah from her overall objective which was to retrieve the tenth key. To make no actual attempts to try and collect the key, Leah definitely felt would be absolutely pointless, since it actually looked reachable, seemed more accessible to her and appeared to be potentially attainable and her arm would still remain trapped either way.

"I still have to retrieve the tenth key, whether my arm is stuck or not." Leah gently reminded herself. "And today, defeat is not an option because I've come this far now, so that's the least I can do."

For Leah to leave the actual underground area without the tenth key that afternoon, would simply render all the struggles that she had endured up until that point, completely meaningless, absolutely pointless and totally void hence as far as Leah was concerned that possible eventuality was not a desirable outcome to the problematic issue of the bamboo cage. Some very dangerous swings had already taken place across some very high heights, a sinking mud pool had been wrestled with by Leah and she had even managed to avoid the possibility of being eaten for lunch by some very horrible, extremely hungry creatures and so Leah was absolutely determined not to leave empty handed and unrewarded. All those difficult obstacles had been overcome by Leah and those achievements had not only taken tremendous effort but also a huge amount of determination.

A realization suddenly struck Leah that until she actually retrieved the tenth key, she felt extremely uncertain that she could even leave the subterranean area anyway because as yet, she had seen absolutely no signs of an actual exit anywhere upon the second earthy platform. The tenth key absolutely had to be retrieved because that would probably unlock Leah's method of exit and provide her with a means to return to the forest's surface once again and so in a way, the key would unlock her actual return to the surface of the forest, although no visible, locked door could be seen.

Once Leah had jiggled her hand and arm around for a few minutes inside the bamboo cage, fortunately and much to Leah's satisfaction, her fingertips finally managed to touch the metal edge of the key and so Leah quickly leant forward as she attempted to push her arm inside the bamboo cage as far as she possibly could. Sheer determination propelled Leah to push her arm and hand further into the bamboo cage, even though she still remained unsure that she would be able to retrieve either her arm or her hand from the bamboo structure, once she had the tenth key in her possession and towards the back of the cage where the key was currently situated in order to reach it. Defeat seemed to silently loom like a dark cloud of failure directly above Leah's head as she sought to fulfill her goal which drove Leah to pursue her objective even more persistently as she once again attempted to grab the key from the nail that it hung from as through her tenacious actions, Leah sought to dismiss any possible notions of failure, despite her lack of success up until that point.

"Success really has to show up for me now and actually happen because I absolutely do not have any other choice." Leah whispered to herself. "I'm not going to swing back across those root ropes again because those hungry creatures will eat me alive if I fall and I really don't want to tempt fear or their stomachs."

Some hungry, horrible, savage creatures lurked close by as Leah already knew and as far as she was concerned, a few more risky swings above their savage heads and hungry bodies to go back the way she came, was now totally out of the question. Despite Leah's desire to depart as quickly as possible because she really did not want to stay in the vicinity of the horrible, savage creatures below her for more than a second than she actually had to, the cage door still remained firmly clamped against her elbow and so Leah began to feel quite frustrated by her current predicament. Somehow however, Leah still managed to persevere as she continued to stretch her arm more deeply and further into the cage as she refused to accept defeat but at first Leah's actions seemed to provide absolutely no tangible results because the key remained upon the nail and her arm still remained trapped.

Just a few minutes later, much to Leah's sheer relief, somehow and almost miraculously she finally managed to slightly dislodge the metal key which she was then able to pluck from the small nail that it hung from and as her efforts were more fully rewarded, Leah smiled a very satisfied smile. Once the key was in the palm of Leah's hand and actually in her possession, Leah eagerly once again tried to slip her arm back out of the bamboo cage but rather confusingly and very frustratingly, the door of the bamboo cage would not budge a single inch. Since the cage stick door remained firmly clamped against Leah's arm and in exactly the same position as it stubbornly refused to move even a centimeter, it rapidly became apparent to Leah that her arm would not be as easy to free as the key had been and that it was still indeed, very stuck. Several more attempts were made with Leah's free hand as she tried and tried and tried to slide the cage door upwards again and to free her arm which she definitely felt she needed but her approach seemed to render absolutely no results at all and her arm still remained trapped.

Despite all Leah's efforts, the cage door absolutely refused to budge and as panic, alarm and fear once more started to gather inside Leah's form and crawl across the surface of her simulated skin, Leah began to hurriedly, visually scan her surroundings and search for anything that might assist her in her quest to free her arm. The cage door would definitely require a more forceful approach which Leah felt would be far more difficult to achieve with just one available hand and one hand for now, was all that she actually had access to.

Suddenly and much to Leah's total dismay, the situation rapidly worsened as she glanced at the interior of the cage and noticed that the rear earthy wall inside it started to move and as it slid upwards, a large black, hairy spider with red markings all over its body began to crawl out of the actual gap. Every part of Leah's form immediately began to respond as she started to shake with absolute fear as panic rapidly started to escalate and accumulate inside of her because she definitely feared that the spider might try to crawl onto her hand or across her arm. The crawly saunter that the spider would embark upon inside the bamboo cage was extremely unpredictable and since Leah's arm and hand were still trapped inside it, such an eventuality was indeed, entirely possible.

Spiders didn't generally frighten Leah and especially not the small black ones that people usually encountered that on occasions had chosen to wander around inside their homes but this spider was very different because this spider was much larger. Some bright markings upon the spider's body gave the impression that it could be dangerous and since Leah's hand was still very much trapped inside the cage, she suddenly felt, extremely vulnerable. An urgent response was now required from Leah and the spider's presence and so that meant that her efforts to free her arm and hand from the bamboo sticks that constrained had to be much more effective.

Some more frantic efforts were made as Leah began to attack the bamboo sticks with much more zeal but one eye was still kept on the spider as it crawled around inside the interior of the bamboo cage without a care in the world. Deep down inside Leah, a small glimmer of hope existed that since the cage had been formed from sticks, it might actually be possible to break it in order to retrieve her arm before the spider found it an object of interest and attempted to crawl across it but that freedom of movement was not as Leah knew, totally guaranteed and hence it was still subject to her ability to free her own arm. Several fears now crawled through Leah's thoughts and lurked inside her mind and then started to crowd her thoughts with panic and alarm as she desperately tried to free herself, one of which doubted her ability to achieve her goal in a timely manner as she watched the spider crawl quite close to her actual hand and began to tremble.

Since any kind of contact with the spider was a highly undesirable outcome, Leah's attack against the bamboo sticks rapidly became even more vigorous with every second that went by and as she began to hack away at the cage more aggressively, Leah tried to tear the sticks that the cage door was formed from to pieces but time as she already knew, was definitely in short supply. The potential course of action that Leah had embarked upon might not even be possible or may not be achievable in a timely fashion which meant, her hand was now very much at risk from the spider's approach.

Fortunately for Leah however, just a minute or so later, suddenly her frantic efforts seemed to pay off as a couple of the bamboo sticks started to snap and break which encouraged her to attack the remainder of the cage door even more aggressively and with renewed enthusiastic vigor. Once a few of the bamboo sticks had been broken, much to Leah's sheer delight and total relief, her arm and hand were both finally, totally freed and so she quickly slipped her arm out of the bamboo cage.

"Now that was very close." Leah whispered to herself as she quickly stepped back from the earthy wall.

A bit of distance between Leah and the spider, she definitely felt, was required as quickly as possible and since her arm was now technically free and she had managed to retrieve not only her arm but also the tenth key that distance could therefore happen immediately. Much to Leah's utter relief, she had finally managed to free herself before the spider had taken a wander across her arm or hand and so actual contact with the ugly, crawly creature had on this occasion been successfully avoided but her adventure that day as she already knew, was not yet over. However, one small fearful factor still restricted Leah's movements slightly as she began to move further away from the broken bamboo cage and earthy wall and that was the reality that the distance between herself and the spider couldn't be too large since there were still some very savage creatures below the earthy platform that still appeared to be extremely hungry.

Quite unexpectedly however, and before Leah could even totally catch her breath or resume her search for a possible escape route, much to her complete surprise and very suddenly, the earthy platform that she was situated upon started to move upwards. A large hole instantly appeared in the earthy ceiling directly above Leah's head and so a smile of sheer delight and absolute relief immediately spread out across her face as she was rapidly elevated towards it because she felt extremely grateful to finally be provided with an actual exit from the underground dirt dungeon of horrors. The Fearful Forest as Leah had already discovered, was a very fearful place to explore and extremely tricky to venture through and she had not only realized but also experienced those fearful facts and so now, she deeply feared what might actually come next because the horrible heights, savage, hungry creatures and the creepy, crawly spider had all scared her mind to the very core along with her simulated bones and artificial flesh which had trembled with fear and shuddered in absolute horror numerous times already.

Inside the Tree of Discontent

Once Leah arrived back on the surface and inside the dense forest once again, she found herself not too far away from the spot that she had initially fallen from and quite close to the same offensive tree that had resulted in her slippery, unexpected departure. The tree that Leah had tried to approach, just before she had sunken into the depths of the earth, was now positioned on her left hand side and although Leah could still clearly see it, she had absolutely no desire at all to return to it and so as she hastily glanced at the tree, she shook her head in total disgust as she prepared to head off in another direction entirely.

Directly in front of Leah and just a few meters away from her current position, she noticed that there was now a much larger tree which seemed to tower miles above her head and in the center and at the base of that giant tree trunk, Leah noticed that there was a large hole that gaped which was filled with nothing but a very black, still darkness. Curiosity rapidly began to take Leah firmly by the hand and so she immediately began to walk towards the large, dark hole which looked a bit like a doorway and as she walked, she noticed that the tree itself differed vastly from the other trees that surrounded it, purely because of its size and that largeness instantly provoked and aroused her curiosity.

Due to the size of the giant tree, Leah thoughtfully began to speculate as she walked towards it that a small house could probably be built inside its interior but since she had absolutely no desire whatsoever to spend the remainder of her life inside the Fearful Forest that particular quality which the tree definitely seemed to possess, didn't seem to be very useful as far as she was concerned. Whether or not the tree was habitable and if it housed actual entities that had chosen to reside in its confines was another issue entirely and not one that Leah could answer with any certainty until she had stepped into its interior but she braced herself for those potential discoveries as she approached the entrance to the actual tree.

"If our house ever gets repossessed, I know exactly where to come, though to be perfectly honest, I'd probably prefer my chamber inside the Castle of Joy as an alternative living space." Leah joked playfully as she paused for a moment just in front of the large hole in the tree trunk. "Apparently, in some parts of the world, treehouses are all the rage and I could definitely live inside this tree, if I really wanted to because it's certainly large enough."

No other instructions or directional indicators appeared to be present and so Leah instinctively, immediately assumed that she had to enter inside the tree's interior in order to proceed with her emotional journey because it felt and seemed as if it was the logical thing to do. The dark archway that led directly into the tree, now stood silently just a step away from Leah as she thoughtfully observed that the tree did not invite her to step into its confines but as Leah already knew, nothing that she had encountered so far that day inside the Fearful Forest had been particularly friendly or warm and due to the nature of that particular emotional journey, no warmth or comfort could really be expected.

Invisible needles of discomfort seemed to prick Leah's form as she began enter into the silent darkness as she quietly considered what might possibly lie on the other side of that darkness and on the other side of that moment, once she had actually managed to walk all the way through that very still, eerie darkness and had emerged from it because it held only one promise for Leah, the promise of more fear and so she did not doubt, not even for a second that fear would definitely be fully delivered. No answers however, appeared to be present or were provided as to exactly what form that fear would take and so the only real way for Leah to find any actual answers to her questions as she already knew, would be to emerge from the other side of that darkness, if she could actually find an accessible way out of the dark, black stillness.

"I hope there are no spiders, snakes or muddy pools filled with carnivorous creatures inside here." Leah whispered to herself as she cautiously and carefully tiptoed through the darkness. "But the very high heights thing is starting to look highly probable."

A definite fear now lurked inside Leah's mind that perhaps some of creatures that haunted and occupied the dense forest that surrounded her would be on the other side of the darkness and that perhaps some might even appear as they lay in wait for their next meal to arrive and she had absolutely no desire to be their next meal. Another fear also lined Leah's mind as she tiptoed through the blackness which related to the ground below her feet and so each step was taken very cautiously and extremely carefully because she had absolutely no wish to disturb the ground too much, just in case it opened up again and swallowed her whole.

Despite all Leah's fears that were now quite firmly lodged inside her heart and mind however, fortunately as soon as she stepped out of the other side of the darkness and entered more fully into the interior of the tree, each fear remained unrealized and totally without merit and so she began to relax slightly as she started to inspect the tree's interior. A wooden, circular internal wall now surrounded Leah which was decorated in places with knots, grooves and growth rings which implied that the tree was far more ancient than any other tree she had ever seen before in her entire life and for a moment the tree's artificial age fascinated her.

"You're probably older than any human being alive on the face of the planet." Leah whispered as she ran her finger across some of the growth rings and smiled. "At some point, you might want to think about retirement, though I'm not sure that you'd get much of a pension for your lifetime of leaf contributions." She advised the tree.

Inside the tree's interior, Leah rapidly observed that there was a large, earthy, stick staircase which silently clung to the tubular, wooden internal wall of the tree that appeared to consist of not only mud and dirt but that had also been formed from broken branches and sticks, all of which had been neatly woven together in order to create each step. The staircase which wound its way silently upwards in a spiral as it willingly and politely decorated the interior of the tree seemed to lead directly towards the top of the tree, Leah immediately assumed, although from her current position she could not actually see either the top of the tree or the end of the spiral staircase and so she could not be absolutely certain. Due to Leah's fear of heights however, the top of the tree was certainly not a destination that she wished to visit and especially not that day because she had already had to confront that particular fear several times already, so in this instance she was perfectly happy just to accept and live with her assumption because she had absolutely no desire to find out if it was true and if it was indeed, actually a correct assumption to make.

"Sometimes an assumption can be a comfort, irrespective of its lack of merits." Leah advised herself. "But heights on the other hand, are just a disgusting obstacle that can be completely avoided, if you're smart enough to keep your feet firmly on the ground which I usually am."

Unfortunately for Leah, the personality modifications that she had made earlier that day to her personality and hence to her form inside Spectrum for the purposes of her interactions and for the duration of that particular emotional journey had really worked against her and had made her time in the forest so far, much more of a fearful challenge. The various tweaks had not only made Leah's natural fear of heights far worse but also the Fearful Forest itself, a lot more scary and although those personality adjustments had magnified Leah's emotions and her emotional experiences, in this instance since her emotional journey involved fear, the results had been really rather scary and totally fearful. Despite that setback however, so far that day Leah had somehow, still managed to not only face some of her fears but also to some extent, actually overcome one of them several times as she had striven to face each challenge head on but as Leah was fully aware, her emotional journey that day was not yet over and so quite possibly, some of her fears would have to be conquered again.

Suddenly, some strange but stifled noises attracted Leah's attention to the rear of the spiral staircase which she could not see through since it comprised of blocks of mud and wood and each component had been tightly knitted together to make very solid blocks which were not transparent or see through in any way. In order to satisfy the sudden prickles of curiosity that started to needle away inside Leah's thoughts, she immediately began to walk towards the rear of the staircase as she attempted to establish the source of the noises and much to Leah's total surprise, she found a larger than life, reddish brown squirrel strewn across the ground at the rear of the staircase that at first glance, appeared to be wounded and not just wounded but wounded very badly.

Due to the angle that the squirrel lay in and its current position, the creature had initially been hidden from view by the spiral staircase when Leah had entered into the tree's interior but she could now, see the animal very clearly and as it lay in a heap upon the ground and groaned in pain, the severity of its wounds rapidly became more visible to Leah as she began to visually scan its damaged, fragile, delicate form. Numerous very deep, open gashes unpleasantly decorated the squirrel's frame which Leah's attention was immediately drawn to as she drew much closer to the creature and then began to inspect its present condition and its body seemed to shake in pain as it released every weary, stressful groan which Leah could clearly hear as each pain filled complaint emanated directly from the squirrel's mouth.

The sharp cries of anguish that correlated very precisely with the deep wounds that accompanied each one which still dripped with blood gave Leah the immediate impression that the actual injuries had actually been inflicted upon the squirrel very recently because each cut looked extremely fresh and so Leah winced as she silently continued to inspect each one. Every cut into the animal's fur and flesh looked not only very current but also extremely painful and so a minute or so later, Leah began to visually scan the large ground floor and base of the tree as she searched for something that might possibly alleviate, dim or even slightly reduce the severe pain that the animal so obviously felt but sadly, there was nothing to be found and no remedy from what she could see.

Quite a few things really worried Leah as she faced the squirrel once again and continued to digest the scene directly in front of her, one of which was the fact that the wounds that had been inflicted upon the squirrel's form were actually all over its body and not even an inch of flesh seemed to have been spared. The second thing that worried Leah about the squirrel's condition was the possibility that the perpetrator responsible for those wounds might still be somewhere close by and she had absolutely no desire whatsoever to meet or face the party responsible for that particular attack because it looked to have been extremely vicious. Another final worry that lurked inside Leah's mind was the possibility that perhaps the animal responsible might even return to finish off what they had started and she really did not want to be there if and when they decided to return but she didn't want the leave the squirrel all alone at the base of the tree unprotected either.

Since the squirrel looked rather on the heavy side, Leah doubted that she would be able to move the animal to a position of safety on her own and since it looked as if the creature could not move an inch on its own due to the severity of its wounds, she didn't feel that she would be able to offer any kind of assistance yet in any capacity. An offer of a shoulder of strength or an arm of support would be absolutely pointless in the squirrel's current condition, Leah thoughtfully concluded because it would not fix those deep gashes and wounds and she doubted that she would even be able to provide sufficient strength to enable the squirrel to move from its current position. Upon the squirrel's face there was a very painful expression of total anguish and as it glanced up at Leah's face, its severely damaged body rapidly confirmed to Leah that to try and move the squirrel would probably inflict even more pain and damage upon it and cause the creature even more discomfort than it was already in.

Whatever battle this squirrel had just engaged in, Leah silently concluded as she glanced nervously around the ground floor of the tree's interior, it sure hadn't been pretty and in fact, it appeared to have been extremely ugly and very vicious and there was a pretty good chance that the savage offender responsible for the attack was still in close proximity to not only the squirrel but now, also to Leah herself. A very vicious attack had been orchestrated upon and against the squirrel's form and so the creature responsible was definitely something to fear and as Leah began to process that fearful reality, fear began to run rampant and silently somersault through the passageways of her mind as she began to freeze and her feet quite suddenly became firmly rooted to the spot.

"This is absolutely ridiculous and my response is absolutely ridiculous." Leah gently reminded herself as a minute or so later, she verbally attempted to shake herself out of her paralysis and prepared to be brave. "I created this environment and everything inside it, why should I be scared of it now?" She asked herself as she knelt down beside the squirrel and then started to gently stroke its head.

Inside one of the squirrel's paws, Leah suddenly noticed that there was a solitary nut as the creature glanced up into her eyes with a sad, regretful expression which it held onto almost as if it was a prized jewel that had to be protected with its very life. Despite the seemingly timid creature's obvious pain however, there was not a lot that Leah could actually do to assist because she was a technological scientist not a veterinarian and so she gently shook her head in frustration as she stroked the creature's fur softly in an attempt to try and soothe the animal's pain. Just a couple of minutes later Leah rather reluctantly rose to her feet as she accepted that whilst her efforts might temporarily soothe the squirrel, she could not actually change anything because her hands were limited and were only able to offer minimal comfort to the wounded animal.

"I'll go and see if I can find some help." Leah promised as she glanced down at the creature's face and then shook her head. "I'll be back soon."

No form of assistance appeared to be available on the ground floor and at the base of the tree and that Leah could already, very clearly see and so she had decided to venture further up the tree to see if she could find some help from someone or something else. One very negative aspect of Leah's potential search for assistance meant however, that she would now actually have to climb the earthy, twig spiral staircase and venture higher up the tree and so she began to worry that she'd perhaps have to face her own fear of heights once again but as she gave the squirrel a final glance, Leah sighed as she prepared to surrender, cooperate and participate fully with that possible fearful eventuality.

Unlike the root ropes, the spiral staircase which wove neatly upwards around the inner circumference of the tree seemed to be easy enough to climb, Leah rapidly discovered as she stepped onto it and tackled the first few quite large steps but no sooner had she started to get used to the steps when a sudden crash from the foot of the tree, immediately stopped Leah in her tracks. The very loud noise instantly attracted Leah's attention and as she turned to face the source of the noise, quite alarmingly Leah rapidly noticed that now, an actual iron gate covered the entrance and more importantly, the only exit from the tree's interior which was now suddenly, well and truly, totally blocked. A departure from the tree was now no longer actually possible, Leah quietly concluded, which did worry her immensely but since there was not much that she could really do about it, Leah rapidly began to accept that rather tricky reality as she turned around and then resumed her ascent as she headed towards the first landing which she could now actually see at the top of the first flight of steps.

When Leah arrived at the top of the first flight of steps and upon the first landing, she immediately noticed that it was actually, really quite large and that at one side of the landing, a small pile of nuts had been stacked which Leah immediately assumed must belong to the injured squirrel that she had just encountered at the base of the tree. Every nut in the pile, from what Leah could see, had been stacked neatly up against the internal wooden wall of the tree and just a meter or so away from the pile of nuts, there were some small tree stumps dotted around a large slab of wood which sat upon some wooden stump legs that had been neatly positioned upon the landing which almost looked like an actual table and chairs.

Even more surprisingly for Leah, seated upon one of the wooden, tree stump chairs she found a mature woman clothed in black, velvet robes that looked to be at least one hundred years old and as Leah came to a total standstill and just stared at her face, she noticed that the woman immediately smiled at her and that her smile at least, seemed friendly enough not to be feared. Directly in front of the woman, on top of the large wooden slab, Leah noticed that there appeared to be some kind of large crystal object that was almost shaped like a diamond but that the illuminous object possessed much rougher, far more rugged edges and as Leah thoughtfully, began to visually inspect the mature woman, the crystal and the makeshift table and chairs, she started to absorb her current surroundings. A doubt suddenly started to silently form and then began to more fully occupy Leah's mind as she swiftly concluded that the woman would not actually be able to assist her because neither the wooden slab or the rugged crystal looked like the kind of objects that could help the injured squirrel that Leah had promised that she would return to assist but nonetheless, she immediately offered the woman a warm, friendly smile in response.

"Please, sit down my dear." The woman offered politely as she motioned towards a vacant tree stump chair. "And I'll tell you, your future and what lies on the horizon of your life."

Irrespective of whether or not the woman could actually assist Leah, she definitely seemed friendly and polite enough and her offer did amuse Leah slightly as she began to silently consider and internally speculate as to what secrets her future might really, actually hold. Since Spectrum was an artificial environment as Leah already knew, it was therefore highly likely that any future predicted for her inside its confines would be artificial too and that any such revelations would merely relate to her immediate future inside Spectrum and within that particular emotional plane but despite that artificial fact, Leah obediently sat down upon a wooden stump directly opposite the woman and then flashed her a polite external smile as she prepared to participate. A polite nod was given by Leah as she prepared to accept, embrace and entertain the woman's polite invitation but as she did so, Leah hoped that her future would not be as fearful as the rest of the Fearful Forest.

Some efforts were made by Leah to discreetly mask her internal amusement as she began to try and make herself as comfortable as she possibly could upon the wooden stump which was a task in itself because it was a very hard lump of wood. The fact that Leah was just about to be told her fictitious future by a fictitious stranger had definitely amused her because she was very much a staunch believer that absolutely nothing in life could be predicted with any degree of accuracy, unless it related to facts, figures and hard codes but Leah hoped that her polite smile would mask her internal amusement which could quite possibly be interpreted as rude.

Once Leah had wriggled around a bit and made herself reasonably comfortable upon the wooden tree stump, she watched and waited in total silence as the mature woman began to stare into the rugged, illuminous crystal situated upon the makeshift wooden table directly in front of her. A vast array of images rapidly flickered through the crystal's core as Leah continued to watch and as she waited, the questions inside her mind seemed to grow and grow, until they almost felt as if they would burst from her lips. Rather frustratingly for Leah, there were definitely more than just a few questions that she now wanted to ask which seemed to dance around inside her mind eagerly and impatiently but since the whole future telling process looked really quite intense and deeply involved, Leah held her tongue since she had absolutely no desire to interrupt the woman's concentration which it seemed was solely focused, very intensely, upon her task.

Lots of deep lines and grooves appeared to be etched into the mature woman's weather beaten face, Leah observed as she stared at the woman and then silently began to inspect each one and the lines immediately reminded her of a road map because it almost seemed as if each groove had been engraved into her flesh with a very specific purpose. If the woman was a real person in the very real world, Leah quietly considered, each line engraved into her face would perhaps represent the routes that she had taken throughout her experiences in life and those would be the lines which marked each journey that she'd embarked upon and the grooves would then represent the lessons that she had learnt, the trophies of bravery that she'd earnt and the victories that she had achieved from the various challenges that she'd managed to overcome along the way. In terms of the woman's age, she had to be at least one hundred years old, Leah silently concluded as she continued to inspect the woman's face and in her eyes there seemed to be pools of wisdom which contained all the secrets of the universe and held all the answers to the mysteries of life itself and so, Leah definitely hoped that the woman would be able to provide her with some useful guidance and some drops of wisdom that would help in her quest that day.

“What's actually inside this tree?” Leah suddenly asked, after just a minute or so as her curiosity finally managed to get the better of her and urged her to speak. She smiled as she continued to verbally break the silence that had gathered between the two as another question managed to pop out of her mouth. "It's a very large tree, why is it so huge?"

“This tree my dear is the Tree of Discontent.” The woman explained. “And all who venture inside this tree are eventually filled with unquenchable desires that they will go to any length to fulfil because a curse lies inside this tree that is known as the curse of discontent."

“What happened to the squirrel?” Leah enquired.

For a few seconds there was nothing but total silence as the woman paused for a moment, stared at the crystal directly in front of her and some silver strands of hair that hung down from her scalp fell down across her face in a limp, lifeless manner before she looked up again and then just stared at Leah's face. A few more silent seconds went by before the quietness was suddenly broken as the woman retrieved the loose bits of hair and then swept each one behind her ears as she prepared to respond.

“Ah yes, the squirrel. Well, he wanted more nuts because due to the curse and his current state of discontent, the huge pile that he had already collected didn't seem to be enough for him and so he actually tried to steal some from the Chief Squirrel's store which was not a very wise thing to do." She explained. “Squirrels can be rather vicious sometimes, especially when it comes to the issue of their nuts and especially towards others of their kind."

"Really but squirrels seem so cute and so gentle." Leah replied. "It hadn't even crossed my mind for a single second that he might have been attacked by one of his own kind. I didn't know squirrels could be so aggressive."

"Yes my dear, they can be very aggressive and unfortunately, the Tree of Discontent has that effect upon most creatures, regardless of their usual nature." She advised.

"What am I actually supposed to do inside here?" Leah asked as she urged the woman to provide her with more answers. "And what's your name?"

"My name is Gretchen and I'm the Guardian of all the trees inside the Fearful Forest." Gretchen explained as she introduced herself. "And though I don't have all the answers to your questions because each person has a different journey inside the Tree of Discontent, my crystal may be able to provide you with some of the answers that you seek. You just have to give me a couple of minutes because it usually takes the Crystal of Wisdom a few minutes to warm up."

"Right. Well, it's lovely to meet you Gretchen and I'm Leah." Leah replied as a grateful smile spread out across her face. "You're the first person that I've met since I arrived in the forest and to be perfectly honest, I'm glad that you're around really because I thought I might have to stumble around in here on my own for hours."

Some answers would it appeared, soon be provided and so Leah felt slightly reassured by that fact and even started to relax a little because clarity was generally a positive thing although she wasn't entirely sure that clarity on this particular occasion would necessarily be enjoyable since after all, it was the Fearful Forest. Once Leah had more information about some of the mysteries that lurked inside the Tree of Discontent however, she had no doubts at all inside her mind that she would then be able to accomplish whatever it was that she was actually supposed to achieve inside the tree's wooden interior and so she prepared to wait patiently for Gretchen to attend to her crystal once more. Since Leah had absolutely no desire whatsoever to stumble around upon the spiral staircase aimlessly for hours, she definitely felt that some additional portions of patience were required, totally necessary and should be silently given because Gretchen would hopefully provide some answers shortly and some of those answers might save Leah a lot of time and heaps of misguided effort.

"Let's see exactly what your future holds Leah." Gretchen said as she peered into the crystal.

All of a sudden, Leah observed, the two black eyes in Gretchen's face seemed to shine more brightly and glisten with excitement as she spoke and as Leah watched her lean forward and then start to interact with her crystal once again, she noticed that there was now a joyful expression of total delight upon her face which provoked Leah to smile too but for very different reasons. For the very first time in Leah's entire life, she was actually just about to have her future predicted by an actual fortune teller and that notion really fascinated Leah since she was generally, very much a realist and outside of Spectrum she rarely encountered anything mystical or magical in any capacity at all. In just two visits to Spectrum however, Leah had now participated in at least two activities that she would never have ever dared to participate in back inside the real world and Leah's own participation in these highly unusual activities intrigued and amused her because each one really was situated so far away from her real life and her usual activities.

Since the couple's real lives were both so deeply rooted in science and technology, an actual visit to a fortune teller was just something situated so far away from that and so Leah couldn't imagine either herself or Zidane ever wanting to pay one a visit, never mind actually listening to a single word that they said. No doubt, Leah thoughtfully considered as she waited patiently for Gretchen's verbal impartations, instructions and guidance, if Zidane could see her right now he would probably find the whole scene absolutely hilarious because it was highly unlikely that he would ever entertain such activities himself and he would in all likelihood, classify the whole interaction as superstitious nonsense.

Suddenly, a quite solid image of a branch began to form and appear in the center of the crystal directly in front of the two women and so as the image grew larger and larger, Leah quickly turned her attention towards it as she waited for a verbal explanation to tumble from Gretchen's tongue, lips and mouth. A large, golden, shiny apple, Leah noticed, was attached to and silently hung down from the branch and as she stared at the crystal and the golden piece of fruit, the vision inside the crystal rapidly became clearer and clearer until it was almost as vivid as the interior of the tree itself.

“That is a golden apple of contentment.” Gretchen started to explain as she gave a certain nod. “Anyone inside the Tree of Discontent that is infected by the curse can overcome it, if they eat a golden apple." She continued. "Everyone who enters inside the Tree of Discontent is immediately affected by the curse of discontent and so if they don't eat an apple of contentment, they can become consumed with discontent and then they either become lost inside the tree forever, or just until the discontent inside of them drives them to their own doom."

"Where can I find a golden apple?" Leah asked.

Gretchen glanced nervously around the landing for a few seconds before she continued. “You have to climb out onto the branches of the tree and then you'll be able to pick some apples and if you pick a few, you can even bring some of the apples back with you and then give them to the creatures that dwell inside the tree or to those that have simply become stuck here due to the curse." She explained. "The golden apples can break the curse that has gripped and consumed any of the creatures trapped inside the tree and then they'll be able to leave the tree and they'll finally be able to escape.”

"Like the squirrel?" Leah asked.

"Exactly." Gretchen replied. "Some creatures at times seek refuge inside the tree from the savage beasts in the forest because they do not know that this particular tree is cursed."

“What about you Gretchen?" Leah enquired. "Should I bring a golden apple back for you too?”

"There's no need for that my dear." Gretchen immediately confirmed as she started to smile. "I'm the Guardian of all the trees that exist and reside within the forest, so my spirit is stronger than the curse of the tree which means, it doesn't affect me at all but at this point I should advise you that the further you venture up the tree, the stronger the power of the curse becomes. In fact, the higher up you go, the more powerful the discontent inside of you will be and so you must be careful."

"Really?" Leah asked.

“I'm afraid so and you can easily fall victim to the snare of discontent because you are human and so quite possibly, the curse of discontent has already started to poison your interior which means, you have to find a golden apple and then eat it as soon as you can before discontent fully floods through your veins, seeps into your pores and then drowns your soul." Gretchen advised.

"How do I reach the branches of the tree? Do I have to leave the tree and then climb up onto the branches?" Leah asked.

"No, further up the stairs you'll find some exits and those exits will take you to various places and although some of those exits lead to the tree dweller's homes that have been built upon the tree's branches and some exits will take you to other places entirely, some of those exits will actually take you out onto the branches of the tree, where you can then pick some apples of contentment." Gretchen explained.

"But if I venture further up the tree and go higher up the stairs, won't I be more at risk from the curse of discontent?" Leah asked in a confused tone because the instructions and advice that she had been provided with seemed slightly contradictory in nature.

A deep sense of reluctance definitely existed inside Leah's form which now fully occupied her thoughts because although Leah had accepted Gretchen's words as truth that truth wasn't really and truly something that she now wished to actually face. Inside Leah's mind there was a real aversion to being any higher up from the ground and the base of the tree than she actually had to be, since heights truly were a disgusting obstacle for her to have to face. Another potential fearful activity however, loomed upon the horizon of Leah's day that she had absolutely no wish to participate in because now, it had transpired that she would actually have to climb out onto the branches of the tree itself which meant, she could actually fall from the tree branches and that fearful possibility she felt extremely anxious to avoid, if she possibly could. Upon Leah's face there was a very nervous expression as she waited for Gretchen to speak and to clarify that no matter what, she would have to venture further up the tree and even climb out onto the branches high above the ground.

"You do make a very good point my dear but the curse of discontent has already infiltrated your form and that unfortunately, has already happened and so now, it's a race against time and a race between you and the seeds of discontent that have already been sown deep inside your heart." Gretchen wisely pointed out. "I'm afraid you have no other choice Leah, you have to venture further up the tree to win that race or you'll end up like the squirrel."

"Did you collect all of the ten keys of courage from the Bravery Trail that were scattered around inside the forest and nailed to trees?" Gretchen asked.

"I did." Leah immediately replied as she nodded.

"If you give them to me, I can give you this bottle of courage which will help you to face your fears and it should even help you to overcome them." Gretchen offered as she slipped her hand inside her black robes and then pulled out a small silver bottle.

"What is made from?" Leah asked.

The silver bottle which was shaped like a small lantern was no larger than Gretchen's hand, Leah rapidly observed and it seemed to glow because the liquid that the small bottle contained shone out from its interior almost as if it wanted to escape from the glass case that had captured its very essence. Upon Leah's face there was a glum expression as she started to silently, visually inspect the bottle and began to fully surrender to the notion that she would now, definitely have to climb out onto the branches of the tree but Leah managed to find a slight glimmer of comfort in the fact that at least now, she could retain the hopeful wish that it would not be too awful for her because she'd have some kind of assistance that might help her to overcome her greatest fears. Each explanation that Gretchen had provided to Leah and the small bottle of brightly colored fluid seemed to be all there was which meant, her only real means of escape from the tree and its curse was to cooperate because to leave the tree now, due to the iron gate that blocked the exit, would be an absolute impossibility as Leah already knew.

"This bottle of courage my dear is made from the essence of bravery and it can temporarily disable all your fears." Gretchen clarified as she held the small silver bottle up in the air. "If you drink this liquid which comes from the forest dew and the forest raindrops, you won't be scared of heights anymore, well not for a while anyway.

I must warn you though, it doesn't last forever and it wears off after some time but it will definitely last long enough for you to climb out onto the branches of the tree so that you can pick some apples."

"I'll definitely need it then." Leah immediately acknowledged as she quickly plucked the ten keys from her trouser pockets and then placed each one down upon the wooden slab directly in front of her.

Gretchen eagerly picked up every single one of the ten keys and then slipped each one inside her black robe. "Here you go, drink this and then you'll have the courage of a lion." She instructed as she placed the small silver bottle down on top of the makeshift wooden table directly in front of Leah and then smiled. "You have to drink it all for maximum affect."

"Right." Leah agreed as she quickly picked up the small silver bottle, unscrewed the silver cap and then started to drink the silvery blue liquid that the bottle contained. "It tastes very sweet Gretchen, almost like syrup." She mentioned as she paused for a second or two.

"Yes, courage is generally one of life's sweeteners. When bravery fills the heart and then holds on to one's hand, life really can be much sweeter and far more enjoyable." Gretchen replied.

A smile crossed Leah's face as the final remnants of the delicious, syrupy substance drizzled down the back of her throat because the liquid seemed to make her form tingle all over as it was consumed and digested. Whether or not the liquid would actually make Leah braver when it came to the actual issue of heights, was another issue entirely but at the very least, the contents of the small, silver bottle did taste pleasant enough which made it easy to drink and easy to enjoy.

"I can also give you this to help you on your way." Gretchen offered as she leant swiftly down towards the ground and then lifted up the lid of a small straw basket that was situated beside her feet and underneath the wooden table. "Since you have given me all of the ten keys."

For a few curious seconds, Leah observed, both Gretchen's hands completely disappeared as her hands were dipped inside the straw basket and then just a few seconds later, when her hands re-emerged, something seemed to be clasped inside her hands, although Leah couldn't actually see exactly what her hands contained, since they remained tightly closed. The object that had been retrieved from the straw basket remained concealed for a few more seconds and as Leah watched Gretchen in total silence, Gretchen straightened herself back up and then placed her clasped hands on top of the table. Although not a word was spoken by Leah, her curiosity had definitely been aroused, provoked and stirred up and so she watched Gretchen in fascinated silence as she waited for the mysterious object to be revealed.

Just a few seconds later Gretchen finally satisfied Leah's curiosity as she slowly opened up her fingers and revealed a tiny, silvery, bluish dragon like creature which now occupied and sat upon the actual palm of one of her hands. Much to Leah's complete surprise, the tiny creature seemed very tame as it sat very comfortably upon Gretchen's hand and as it started to groom itself, Leah silently observed its movements in total delight. Although the arrival of the small creature had been very unexpected, Leah was absolutely delighted by its appearance and as she focused upon the small, feathery, dragon like animal, she stared at it in total fascination as Gretchen began to stroke the creature's head and it immediately gave a contented coo as it eagerly lapped up the attentiveness displayed towards it.

"This is Roto and he'll be your guide. He can't carry any apples yet but he can fly short distances which might be helpful." Gretchen explained. "He's still a baby really."

"How old is he?" Leah asked as she stretched her hand out towards the creature and it immediately leapt onto the palm of her hand. "And what exactly is he?"

"He's just one hundred years old which is actually very young for a dragbird." Gretchen replied. "Roto is half eagle and half dragon which means, he's a dragbird but don't worry, he's very friendly and he doesn't bite at all."

"Can he actually breathe fire like a dragon?" Leah enquired as she watched the small creature jump and hop playfully around inside the palm of her hand and then weave in and out of her fingers.

"Well, yes and no." Gretchen started to explain. "He's quite young and he is only half dragon, so little puffs of smoke and small sparks yes but huge balls of fire, quite frankly that would be a bit too much of an ask. Take good care of him though because dragbirds are extremely hard to come by and once you lose them, they may never return."

Leah smiled as she watched Roto for a few more seconds as she silently admired the tiny creature because the dragbird really seemed to be very gentle, extremely friendly and rather playful. "I'd better get a move on now Gretchen, since I have already drunk the bottle of courage and like you said, it doesn't last forever." She suddenly mentioned as she swiftly rose to her feet. "Thanks for all your help."

"Yes, you really should before that bottle of courage wears off." Gretchen agreed as she smiled.

On the other side of the landing the mud and stick stairs continued to spiral upwards in the opposite direction from the steps that led back down towards the base of the tree and so as Leah turned and faced the next set of stairs, she began to prepare for the task that lay ahead which she definitely felt, was going to be far from pleasant. Fortunately for Leah however, Gretchen's mysterious concoction felt as if it had already started to assist her because even the stairs now intimidated her slightly less and so that was at the very least, a small comfort to her mind. Although Gretchen herself had looked slightly untidy and what one might even consider a little rough around the edges, she had actually been extremely helpful to Leah and so she really couldn't fault Gretchen on that because she had provided Leah with some encouragement, useful instructions, a helpful bottle of courage and even an actual guide. A quick final appreciative glance was rapidly cast back towards Gretchen before Leah departed and as she gave Gretchen one final, grateful smile, Leah leant across the wooden table and then hugged her affectionately.

Much to Leah's surprise however, just a few seconds later when she straightened herself back up, Leah noticed that Gretchen's hair and clothes, for some inexplicable reason had suddenly changed and that she now seemed to look much tidier and that everything about her appearance looked a lot less drab. The lines on Gretchen's face had completely vanished and from what Leah could see, she now looked at least forty or even fifty years younger and as Leah glanced at her face and observed the immediate transformation, it was almost unbelievable because Gretchen hadn't moved an inch or left Leah's side for even a single second.

"A drop of appreciation is like a ray of sunshine my dear." Gretchen explained as she smiled. "Cleans out, washes away and sweeps up all the cobwebs of negativity."

Despite Leah's curiosity and her desire to quench it because she now had even more questions for Gretchen that related to her sudden change in appearance, she avoided the temptation to delve into any deeper discussions as she hurried herself along and began to make her way towards the second flight of stairs. Time had definitely slipped rapidly out of Leah's grasp and so she now felt quite eager to fulfil the next part of her mission and to retrieve the golden apples that seemed to be required because the squirrel could not be assisted until that part of her mission had been fulfilled and achieved and as Leah also knew, the courage concoction that Gretchen had provided could wear off at any given moment.

Every step that Leah took up the second flight of steps now seemed much easier and lighter than the first flight of stairs had been to climb as Leah bounced enthusiastically up each step which she quickly attributed to the bottle of courage that she had just consumed. In the palm of one of Leah's hands Roto sat quietly and attentively and the dragbird didn't seem to move an inch as she followed the stairs upwards that spiraled around the inner circumference of the tree. A solution and antidote to the curse of discontent that Leah herself had now been infected by had to be found as quickly as possible as she already knew, and so a climb up the tree was therefore absolutely unavoidable and totally necessary but due to the bottle of courage, quite intriguingly for Leah that task no longer seemed to intimidate her anymore.

Approximately fifty steps later Leah found a second landing but the second landing was slightly different in comparison to the first one in that this landing had an opening at one side of it carved out of the tree bark and pulp which it seemed, led out towards the exterior of the tree. A huge hole gaped directly in front of Leah that was covered by a strange light green mist and so as she bravely approached it and attempted to overcome her fears, she leant fully upon the bottle of courage that Gretchen had provided to her that now seemed to lighten her steps.

"I guess this is where the golden apples are Roto." Leah mentioned as she paused for a moment directly in front of the large arch shaped hole.

"Yes, this is definitely the correct way to go." Roto suddenly replied as he gave her a certain nod.

Very surprisingly and totally unexpectedly, Roto had provided Leah with a sudden verbal response and she almost jumped out of her skin as she glanced at the dragbird's face and then just attempted to absorb the vocal expression which she certainly hadn't anticipated or expected. The mature, sophisticated, deep, refined male voice that had emanated from the dragbird's small form seemed slightly unusual for a creature that size but as Leah began to thoughtfully process what Gretchen had told her, somehow at the same time, it also made perfect sense.

"Roto, you can actually speak?" Leah asked as she marveled at the dragbird's vocal capabilities in total fascination. "I didn't know you could speak."

"I usually only speak to those that I'm entrusted to during the allocated time period that I'm supposed to be their guide." Roto explained. "Because if I speak to people at other times, it seems to confuse them. I tend not to talk to strangers much at all because one minute people seem to understand you and then the next minute they don't." He mentioned as he scratched his head with one of his small, scaly, feathery claws. "Communication with human beings seems to be very complicated, it's definitely too much for my tiny, young brain to understand."

Leah laughed. "I know exactly what you mean Roto. Human beings can be like that all the time, one minute you understand them and they understand you and then the next minute, they do something very strange and you realize that you don't understand each other at all. I mean, I'm human and even I don't always understand the other human beings around me, even when we both speak the same language." She concurred. "I'm really glad you can speak though that might come in handy."

"Yes, communication can be a real necessity and extremely helpful at times." Roto agreed.

"Right Roto, we better do this." Leah insisted as she glanced at the hole directly in front of her.

"Ready when you are." Roto replied with an eager nod.

The strange green mist that covered the hole that gaped directly in front of Leah made it impossible for her to see through the hole to the other side but even though the mist obstructed Leah's view, she began to walk bravely towards the silent hole that awaited her in the hope that some golden apples might soon be found. Despite the fact that the mist hampered Leah's visibility and blinded her, Leah still felt reasonably confident as she walked towards the large hole and prepared to step through it because the bottle of courage that she had consumed, somehow seemed to silently encourage her and invisibly spur her on.

Fortunately for Leah and much to her total relief, on the other side of the hole she found a large, stable, flat branch which she immediately stepped out onto and luckily, the large branch seemed more than able to hold her weight as Leah placed her feet upon it which provided her with the instant reassurance that at the very least, her first few steps would be reasonably safe. The branch did not seem to sway or waver in any direction at all, Leah noticed as she began to walk further along it and it actually appeared to be very firm and reasonably strong which was definitely a comfort to her, since she was now indeed, actually situated quite high above the ground.

Once Leah arrived at the mid-point of the large branch, she paused for a moment and then began to survey her surroundings and she quickly noticed that branches now hung down around her in almost every direction that she could possibly face. Unfortunately for Leah however, none of the nearby branches appeared to carry any actual fruit and so she quickly began to visually scan the area that surrounded her as she searched for other branches situated slightly further away from her current position that might actually possess the required and desired golden apples. After just a few seconds, luckily for Leah, her visual search was finally successful and some golden fruit was actually spotted that hung from a branch situated not too far away and so Leah began to plan her route towards the golden fruit as she started to discuss the matter with Roto.

"I'll have to climb up there Roto." Leah swiftly pointed out as she pointed towards the golden apples with her free hand. "But that could be slightly tricky."

"Don't worry, the apples are not that far away." Roto immediately reassured her as he glanced up at the branch. "They should be easy enough to climb up to and if you get really stuck, I could always blow a little bit of fire in that direction and burn the actual branch so that it falls down and then you'll be able to reach the golden apples much more easily."

"Great suggestion Roto." Leah replied appreciatively. "Can you actually breathe enough fire to do that?" She asked.

"I can breathe flames in little spurts and spouts." Roto explained. "But it's not like an eruption of lava from a volcano or anything. I'm not old enough to unleash a lake of fire yet."

Leah grinned. "Never mind Roto, save those fiery sparks for now and I'll let you know if I need them." She swiftly reassured him as she began to turn her attention back towards her quest and the golden apples.

From Leah's current position, she could clearly see five golden apples that looked as though they would be quite straight forward and easy enough to reach, once she climbed up onto a couple of higher branches and so as Leah internally prepared to embark upon her estimated route, she hoped that it would allow her to collect each one without too much fuss. Once a feasible route had been fully formulated and totally decided upon inside Leah's mind, she then began to climb out onto some nearby branches as she started to head upwards and further up the tree but as Leah went, she carefully avoided any downward glances. The five golden apples that Leah could clearly see, she had already decided should all be picked because Gretchen had advised her to pick a few apples and so it made total sense to Leah to collect all those that were visible and within easy reach, since she had to climb further up the tree and step out onto more branches anyway.

Fortunately for Leah, she rapidly discovered that the tree itself wasn't particularly difficult to climb and so she arrived at the branches that the apples hung down from in what seemed like no time at all and each golden apple was carefully plucked from the branch that it clung to and then placed inside Leah's trouser pockets. Once Leah had finished her task, she then eagerly began to make her downward descent and the bottle of courage that Gretchen had given to Leah, somehow seemed to silently strengthen her and make her task actually possible but deep down inside herself, Leah fully appreciated that she would never have been able to achieve her mission without it. In fact, as Leah was well aware, without that liquid provision of bravery she would have probably lost her balance within seconds and then rapidly tumbled from the tree's branches and plunged towards the ground below her.

"That wasn't actually as hard as I thought it would be Roto." Leah announced triumphantly just a few minutes later as she arrived back upon the sturdy branch that led back into the tree's interior and paused for a few seconds to catch her breath.

"Now you have to actually eat a golden apple." Roto immediately reminded her as he smiled. "And break that ugly curse."

"Right." Leah replied as she nodded in agreement. "What about you Roto, would you like one?" She asked as she dipped her hand inside one of her trouser pockets and plucked a golden apple from its interior.

"Yes please that would be helpful." Roto immediately confirmed.

A second golden apple was quickly plucked and rapidly retrieved from Leah's trouser pockets and as she placed the first apple on the palm of her hand next to Roto, a smile spread out across Leah's face because Roto's frankness definitely amused her. When it came to Roto's verbal expressions, Leah had already noticed that he didn't beat around the bush or seem to feel afraid to express himself very directly to her and that not only amused her but also truly delighted her because human verbal exchanges were so often masked, coated, marinated and laced with slithers of pretention. However, a question did start to form and linger in Leah's mind as the golden apple sat completely motionless in the center of her palm just next to Roto as to how Roto was actually going to eat the apple, since it was nearly as big as his rather small dragonish, bird like form.

For the next few seconds Leah remained completely still and totally silent as she glanced at Roto's face with a puzzled expression and just waited for the dragbird to respond to the apple's close proximity to his form and just a few seconds later, Leah's unspoken question was very swiftly answered. Suddenly and much to Leah's total surprise, a huge, dark hole rapidly appeared as Roto opened and stretched out his mouth and an amused giggle managed to escape from Leah's lips as she watched Roto wolf down the entire apple and swallow it whole in one actual mouthful. One of the dragbird's capabilities had suddenly become extremely visible and very apparent to Leah and she felt absolutely stunned by Roto's feeding capacity because it had been absolutely huge and had far exceeded Leah's own human capacity. The deft, bold approach by Roto and his rapid consumption immediately encouraged Leah to take a bite of her own golden apple as she raised it to her mouth and prepared to join in and as she bit into the golden flesh, she noticed that the apple tasted exceptionally sweet and extremely delicious as the fruit juices started to run down the sides of her mouth.

"Boy Roto, you sure were hungry." Leah teased playfully in-between mouthfuls as she grinned at him.

"I was." Roto agreed. "And I haven't had a golden apple for quite some time. I really like apples, especially the golden ones, they're my favorite and they taste so much nicer than rats or spiders."

"I'd definitely agree with that though I can't say I've ever eaten a rat or a spider before." Leah replied as she grinned. "Right, now that we're both immune to the curse of discontent, what do we do next?"

"Now we can go back inside the tree." Roto immediately pointed out.

"Yes and I have to give the injured squirrel a golden apple." Leah swiftly reminded herself. "I did promise the squirrel that I would return."

"Yes, we should go. A promise is a very serious commitment, especially when it's made to someone that is injured." Roto advised.

Quite intriguingly and rather surprisingly for Leah, approximately ten minutes later, once she had entered back inside the tree and then walked back down the steps that led towards the first landing where she'd initially met Gretchen as she arrived back upon the landing, she found that the tree stump chair that Gretchen had previously occupied had since her departure actually been vacated. In Leah's absence it seemed, Gretchen had completely vanished and Gretchen's absence actually surprised Leah immensely because she had expected to find Gretchen still seated upon the tree stump chair when she returned.

"I guess it's just you and me now Roto." Leah mentioned.

Roto nodded. "Don't worry about Gretchen." He explained. "She's a bit of a wanderer, she comes as she wishes and goes as she pleases."

Leah nodded.

Since there seemed to be absolutely nothing else for Leah to do upon the first landing, just a few seconds later she decisively began to head back down towards the base of the tree and as Leah made her descent, she kept her eyes avidly peeled on the ground floor of the tree. A definite worry lurked inside Leah's mind as she made her way back towards the injured squirrel that the Chief Squirrel might decide to turn up again in order to finish off what he had already started and Leah had absolutely no wish to experience a possible attack herself, if she got in the creature's way. Fortunately for Leah however, the leader of the squirrel's tribe was nowhere to be seen and so as Leah arrived back on the ground floor she quickly approached the injured, damaged creature and it rapidly became apparent to her that the squirrel had not moved even an inch since her departure because the creature still lay in the exact same spot and exactly the same position that Leah had initially found and then subsequently left the wounded animal in.

One of the three golden apples that still remained inside Leah's trouser pockets was quickly plucked and retrieved from her trouser pocket as Leah knelt down by the squirrel's side and then swiftly offered it to the creature as Leah rapidly fulfilled her promise to assist. The gift of the golden apple now occupied and sat in the center of Leah's free hand and the hand that was not currently occupied by Roto and as she prepared to administer the required remedy to the squirrel, she noticed that the creature glanced up into her eyes, somewhat weakly.

After just a few silent seconds of slight hesitation on the squirrel's part, the creature seemed to accept Leah's gift as it suddenly stretched out its tiny paws towards her hand and then plucked the golden apple from the palm of her hand. Despite the squirrel's very weak state, in a matter of just seconds, much to Leah's total surprise, the apple that she had provided had rapidly been demolished and very quickly consumed and Leah noticed that not even a stalk or seed remained after just a few, hungry mouthfuls as the apple, stalk, core and all, totally disappeared.

Rather mysteriously and absolutely astoundingly, Leah immediately noticed that once the apple had been consumed the wounds in the squirrel's form that had mangled its fur and distorted its flesh, rapidly started to heal and in just a matter of seconds, each one had actually, totally vanished right before Leah's eyes. Once all the creature's wounds had completely disappeared, the squirrel then immediately sat up on its hindlegs as if it had never actually been injured at all and as Leah witnessed that seemingly miraculous event in almost total disbelief, the iron gate that had fallen over the entrance of the tree prior to Leah's trip up the stairs, suddenly started to rise.

For the next few minutes Leah did nothing but sit and watch as the squirrel rubbed its fur and then began to silently inspect its body because she felt, totally captivated and utterly mesmerized by the creature's speedy recovery which had been almost instantaneous and not even the now open tree entrance could distract her from what she had just seen. Just a few seconds later however, the creature surprised Leah even more as the squirrel glanced at Leah's face with what looked like a smile upon its face and then to Leah's total surprise, the squirrel actually started to converse with her.

"Thank you very much." The squirrel suddenly said in a slightly rough, low pitched masculine tone. "I've been lost inside this tree for so long now, I'd almost forgotten who I actually am."

"You can actually speak too?" Leah asked. She glanced down at Roto with a slightly confused expression upon her face before she continued. "Can all the animals in the forest speak, or is it just you two?"

"I don't think so. I think we can only speak to humans and be understood by them, when we're both situated inside the Tree of Discontent." The squirrel replied. "But I was so wounded just now, I could hardly even breathe never mind speak."

"Speak for yourself." Roto interjected. "I can speak in a human tongue all the time and anytime I want to and in fact sometimes, I never stop, especially when I have a lot to say but that doesn't mean however, that people always understand me which is another issue entirely. Gretchen gave me a special ring that I wear on my claw which allows me to speak in a human tongue and understand human speech any time I want to and I definitely make the most of it and if the people around me don't understand what I say, then I speak to myself." He continued as he raised his claw with the ring attached to it up in the air, puffed up his chest and then blew a small circle of smoke out into the air in front of his face. "I talk and talk and talk and then when I'm finished, I talk some more. I'm probably the only one though because it was a very special gift and Gretchen doesn't give her special gifts to just any creature in the forest foliage."

"Yeah, the snake I saw in the forest definitely didn't speak, well not to me anyway but then I didn't really try to strike up a conversation." Leah reflected thoughtfully. "I was in too much of hurry to get as far away from it as I could as quickly as I possibly could, though what a snake might actually have to say to anyone is another question entirely. Can I eat you, perhaps?"

Roto laughed. "Yeah, or can I coil up around you and squeeze the life out of you? Don't worry about the snake, when I get older and bigger, I'll eat snakes for breakfast, lunch and dinner." He insisted. "And I'll hunt down all the snakes inside the forest and pursue their species until they're extinct."

"Would any of you like one of my nuts? I've collected this batch of nuts for quite a while now, so there's definitely enough to go around." The squirrel offered politely. "Consider it a token of my appreciation, just to say thank you, after all you did both save my life with a golden apple."

Leah immediately shook her head in response. "Thanks but I'm okay." She replied.

"Nah I'm good, keep your nuts." Roto piped in. "I know how precious your nuts are to you, so there's really no need." He glanced at Leah's face before he continued. "Squirrels love their nuts."

Leah giggled.

"I'd like to go and see my family now because I want to take them some nuts." The squirrel explained. "That's why I collected so many, the nuts are for my family."

Leah nodded.

Upon Leah's face there was an amused expression as she watched the squirrel scamper towards the other side of the spiral staircase and then bounce up each step as the furry animal made his way towards the pile of nuts on the first landing.

"Should I offer to help Roto?" Leah suddenly asked as she glanced at the dragbird that was still situated in the palm of her hand.

Roto immediately shook his head. "Nope, there really is no point, you would only get in his way, he's much faster than you are. He can make three trips whilst you, you'd still be making your first." He rapidly pointed out.

Leah smiled. "True." She replied.

Much to Leah's total fascination, for about the next ten minutes the squirrel scampered up and down the stairs repeatedly between the ground floor and the first landing as the creature retrieved some of the nuts and meticulously piled each one up next to the entrance of the tree. Once the squirrel had retrieved all of the nuts and stacked them up in a neat pile next to the entrance of the tree, Leah then watched in silence as the squirrel turned to face her and Roto and as the creature prepared to leave the tree, she began to admire the furry animal's seemingly tireless dedication. Upon the squirrel's face, Leah now noticed that there was a very proud smile as the creature stood boldly next to the pile of accumulated nuts and she immediately smiled in response because that happiness really was such a different emotional state from the condition that she had found the animal in when she'd initially arrived and stepped inside the tree's interior.

"How on earth will you manage to carry all those nuts through the forest on your own?" Leah asked.

"I won't, I'll call my family and they'll come and help me." The squirrel replied.

Leah smiled and nodded as she watched the squirrel pick up the first nut and then dart towards the entrance of the tree. "Are you sure we shouldn't offer to help Roto?" She asked once again.

"No, we really shouldn't." Roto insisted as he shook his head. "Squirrels are very proud creatures and they're very particular when it comes to the issue of their nuts. They are generally extremely protective of their nuts and so it's better not to get involved really, unless they specifically ask you to do so." He advised. "No one likes to come between a squirrel and their nuts because things can become ugly, very quickly indeed."

Approximately five minutes later, once the squirrel had very deftly and extremely competently, completely removed its precious cargo from the base of the tree, a task which Leah noticed had been performed with the utmost care and almost as if the creature's actual life had actually depended upon it, the squirrel returned once more and then faced Leah with a proud smile and upright tail. Despite Leah's lack of interest in nuts, she definitely appreciated and admired the nimbleness of the squirrel because all the nuts had been moved very quickly indeed and the creature seemed to be very light footed because unlike a human frame that was much more heavy and far more cumbersome, the squirrel it appeared, had been built to move extremely fast.

"My family have arrived now and they're just outside." The squirrel swiftly confirmed. "So sadly, it's time for me to bide you both farewell."

"Right." Leah replied as she smiled. "Well, you take care now and mind how you go because there are snakes in the forest and snakes can be dangerous."

"Yes and mind your nuts." Roto piped in.

"I will and thank you again for the golden apple." The squirrel mentioned appreciatively. "If I hadn't eaten that apple you gave me, I might have been stuck inside this tree forever."

"Yes, so don't come back to this tree ever again, it's a very bad tree. The curse of discontent is a very powerful curse." Roto warned.

The squirrel nodded in agreement. "I won't." He replied.

A polite salute was swiftly given as the squirrel flicked up his tail, held it up against his head with a paw just before it turned and then quickly scampered back towards the entrance of the tree and as Leah watched the furry creature depart, she began to consider whether or not she should leave the interior of the tree herself and return to the forest. Two golden apples still remained on Leah's person but it appeared, there was no one else around to actually give them to and so for now, she decided to retain them inside her trouser pockets as she prepared to leave the Tree of Discontent, since that seemed to be the logical thing to do next.

No indications or signs seemed to present themselves that opposed Leah's plan of action and since Leah had absolutely no desire to stay inside the tree for any longer than she really had to because the protective provisions from the golden apple and her current immunity to the curse as she already knew, might wear off at any given moment, she now felt anxious to depart before the curse infected her form again. Quite strangely and very surprisingly for

Leah however, as she began to walk towards the entrance of the tree Roto suddenly jumped down onto the ground as the dragbird rapidly vacated her hand rather abruptly.

"I can't leave the tree just yet." Roto explained. "I have to wait until my father comes to collect me, he's going to take me snake hunting today."

"Will he come soon Roto?" Leah asked. "Does he already know where you are and that you're here?"

Roto nodded. "Yes, Gretchen sent him a message earlier and so, he should be on his way now." He rapidly confirmed.

"Well, it was lovely to meet you Roto." Leah said as she began to accept the dragbird's unexpected departure.

"Yes, you too and I really enjoyed our adventure." Roto replied. "If we ever meet again, I'll take you snake hunting with my father."

Leah giggled and nodded. "Sure." She agreed.

In a matter of just seconds and without any further ado, Roto had hopped speedily across the ground back towards the foot of the spiral staircase and as Leah watched Roto in a thoughtful silence, the first flight of mud and twig stairs were swiftly tackled as the dragbird departed. Despite the fact that Leah understood and accepted Roto's departure, deep down inside herself, she still felt quite sad to see the dragbird leave her hand and side because the hybrid creation really had been such a pleasant companion. Essentially, Leah had hoped, assumed and even expected Roto to be her guide for the remainder of her emotional journey inside the Fearful Forest that day and so, his sudden desire to depart, reluctance to accompany her any further and then his actual departure had really taken her by surprise.

Once Roto had vanished completely and disappeared from Leah's sight, she then began to prepare herself to face the Fearful Forest once again as she faced the entrance to the Tree of Discontent and then began to walk very slowly and slightly reluctantly towards it. All the beings and creatures that Leah had met inside the Tree of Discontent had now, abandoned her completely it seemed and so she definitely felt that it was time to depart and time to seek out her next adventure in that particular emotional plane.

For the most part, Leah considered thoughtfully as she walked, her experiences inside the Tree of Discontent really hadn't been as fearful as the earlier part of her day which had been spent inside the underground dirt chamber of horrors and some parts of it had even been what one might consider slightly pleasant. However, as Leah already knew, her journey through the Fearful Forest wasn't quite over yet and what remained to occur was extremely unpredictable and was likely to be very fearful since that was after all the nature of the emotional journey that she had embarked upon earlier that day. A slight sense of reluctance did still linger and occupy Leah's mind and form as she walked as she internally prepared to venture back out into the Fearful Forest once again because she had enjoyed Roto's companionship immensely but once she stepped back out into the forest as she was fully aware, she would once more have to face the Fearful Forest again, totally alone.

"It would have been so nice if Roto had been able to come along with me." Leah whispered to herself as she paused for a moment and glanced at the mud and twig steps thoughtfully. "He's definitely a cute companion and the Fearful Forest is rather creepy. At least I don't have to climb any further up the tree though because that courage concoction that Gretchen gave me, probably wouldn't have lasted for very much longer and it's probably on its last few drops by now."

Unfortunately for Leah, it had suddenly transpired that Roto had other matters to attend to that day but as her guide inside the Tree of Discontent for a short period of time, he had definitely performed his role absolutely meticulously and so his presence in the palm of her hand would certainly be missed. In terms of Roto's character and personality, Leah definitely felt that the dragbird was an extremely likable companion and that he had been an absolutely exemplary guide and he'd been as pleasant to spend time with as Sebastian and so, she felt saddened as she gave the steps one final glance, shook her head and then resumed her gentle saunter towards the entrance of the tree.

Very suddenly and rather shockingly however, without any

warning at all Leah's gentle saunter was abruptly and rudely interrupted when just a few steps away from the actual entrance of the tree, much to Leah's absolute horror, the ground below her feet gave way again and opened up. Once again Leah was quickly gobbled up by a muddy, slippery hole and swallowed whole by another earthy tunnel but this time her descent to the underworld was even more rapid and was over in less than a minute.

After approximately forty seconds Leah landed quite gently upon a huge but soft pile of hay which was situated it appeared in the center of a dark, dreary underground cave. The soft pile of hay however, fortunately for Leah, broke her fall in a reasonably pleasant manner and as she quickly slid off it, she began to dust off her clothes which she noticed had collected some stray strands of hay en-route. Due to Leah's rather abrupt, very unexpected departure from the Tree of Discontent, Leah still felt quite shocked as she began to visually inspect and absorb her surroundings because she really hadn't expected to be plunged once more into the depths of the ground and so her fall had caught her completely by surprise.

"The Fearful Forest isn't exactly elegant." Leah whispered to herself as she shook her head. "And all this underground mudslide action is really starting to mess with my hair." She mentioned as she gently smoothed some loose strands of hair down against her head.

Suddenly, some very loud female screams shattered the silence that surrounded Leah and the screams which definitely possessed enough shrillness and sharpness to make one's blood curdle because each one was so very loud, almost caused Leah to jump out of her skin as the noises began to penetrate and infiltrate her ears. Some vibrations from the screams rapidly shook through Leah's mind and form and as the noises filled her ears up right up to the brim, she almost thought that her eardrums might actually burst because the screams seemed to pierce every part of her being. Each noise seemed to grate against Leah's bones as it infiltrated her body because the screams not only frightened her but also completely and utterly horrified her since each one sounded so panic stricken and so absolutely desperate.

For the next minute or so Leah stood completely still and did not move an inch and it was almost as if she had been frozen to the spot until the screams came to an end and then she swiftly began to shake herself out of her paralysis as she began to creep quietly out of the earthy cave. Deep down inside as Leah crept out of the cave, she felt a definite urge to provide assistance, if she possibly could but since the party in need was not visible to her that meant that Leah first of all had to follow the screams.

A small exit at one side of the subterranean cave led Leah directly into another cave and on the other side of the second underground room, Leah could see a dark, earthy tunnel which she quickly made her way towards. The braveness of Leah's steps however, was slightly overshadowed by a fear that began to form and lurk inside Leah's form as she headed in the direction of the screams that questioned whether she should walk towards the screams or stay away from the loud, panic stricken noises completely. Although the screams had sounded like a female in trouble, a doubt now silently lurked inside Leah's mind that the source of those screams might not even actually be human at all and that fearful prospect and notion crept around inside her thoughts almost like a silent robber that aimed to steal any comfort that might exist inside Leah's mind because such a notion worried her profusely.

Unfortunately with each step that Leah took, her doubts seemed to grow and grow and even developed into a full scale cowardly temptation which seemed to lurk and linger inside her thoughts which could not merely be shaken off and so when she arrived at a sudden fork in the tunnel, Leah paused for a moment as she began to face her own internal dilemma. Partially, Leah now felt tempted to travel further along the tunnel in the direction that led away from the screams instead of towards them and that created an inner conflict that she silently began to wrestle with as she thoughtfully considered her next steps.

Some pangs of guilt definitely existed inside Leah's mind and as each one wrestled with the cowardly temptation that lurked in her thoughts, Leah continued to internally deliberate as to her next course of action because although the easier option would be to avoid the screams completely, as she already knew that would be an act of total cowardice on her part and so she bravely prepared to swallow her fears. The guilty pangs that hounded Leah's thoughts silently pushed her to be braver and so as Leah started to succumb and surrender to her wish to assist, she turned to face the tunnel on the right-hand side which led directly towards the screams as she prepared to face not only the screams but also the source of those noises.

Guilt suddenly seemed to be Leah's only companion and her own guilt it seemed, would not walk away or allow Leah to either as some of her own sentiments which appeared to be absolutely determined, compelled her legs to not only step into the tunnel on the right-hand side but then also to walk further along it. The frantic screams had very clearly indicated that someone might be in danger and that possibility disturbed Leah's heart and mind as she walked and from what she already knew that person was definitely female because the screams had sounded very feminine. Every part of Leah's being as she made her way along the tunnel fully understood that those screams meant that someone needed urgent assistance and that female someone had now invoked a deep sense of compassion inside her and that compassion, she could not just walk away from and so she fully caved into it and then began to actually embrace it.

One slight worry did keep Leah company as she continued to walk however, despite her sudden burst of bravery and that was the fact that nothing since Leah had initially arrived inside the Fearful Forest that she had encountered had been what it had seemed or appeared to be and so, she still felt a slight reluctance to follow the noises and to actually find the source. An undercurrent of fear continued to run rampant through Leah's thoughts as she walked that predominantly revolved around the possibility that the screams might actually belong to some kind of creature or another kind of entity that might even attack Leah herself and so her steps towards the source of the screams remained quite cautious and even slightly hesitant.

Despite all Leah's doubts however, she silently persevered as she continued to make her way along the twisted tunnel towards the source of the screams and as Leah followed her chosen path, she began to accept that irrespective of who or what was responsible for the actual noises, she was now on a direct collision course with the entity responsible. Once Leah arrived at the end of the tunnel, she discovered that it led into another underground cave which she quickly entered into and as Leah stepped cautiously into the dark, dismal space, she tried to muster up some final grains of courage from deep within herself because she was absolutely certain that the screams had to have come from somewhere very close by.

At first glance the interior of the cave appeared to be totally empty but it was rather difficult for Leah to see anything situated more than a few inches in front of her because the cave's interior was covered by a blanket of darkness however, Leah's eyes soon began to adjust as she became more accustomed to that darkness as the blackness began to silently dissolve. No actual screams emanated from inside the cave itself and so as Leah began to inspect its interior, she began to silently wonder if the screams had actually originated from that cave in the first place or perhaps from somewhere else because as yet, she still could not see the source of the noises. Just as Leah was about to seek an exit in order to explore the underground area further and perhaps venture along another underground tunnel however, as Leah's eyes became even more accustomed to the darkness that surrounded her, she suddenly noticed a movement in one corner of the cave where there appeared to be a woman curled up on the floor, next to the earthly cave wall.

In some ways, although the woman did look quite human to Leah at first glance, in many other ways she was almost unrecognizable as one because the dirty, matted hair that decorated her head was caked in dried up mud and her face looked dark, muddy and grubby. Every one of the woman's limbs that were visible to Leah looked very grimy and her neck and hands were totally saturated in filth and dirt, Leah noticed as she quietly began to visually inspect the woman and so for a moment, Leah didn't even dare to utter a single word to her because Leah's own tongue and mind silently feared that the woman might turn into some kind of monster at any given moment.

Once Leah had mustered up enough courage from deep within herself to finally approach and speak to the woman however, she began to walk very slowly towards her as she prepared to communicate with the source of the shrill screams and perhaps even comfort the seemingly human source of those noises. Although Leah had summoned up all the bravery she could find inside herself, a remnant of fear still remained as she walked which it appeared her bravery could not dispel which doubted that she would be greeted with warmth and it was far more likely as Leah already knew that she would be greeted with hostility or fear.

Each step that Leah took towards the woman was slow and cautious and provoked questions deep inside her mind as to why the woman was actually there in the first place and what could possibly be going on in those underground caves that would make her scream in the way that she had but there appeared to be no obvious or instant answers. Inside the actual cave itself there seemed to be no immediate threat to the woman's life but her screams had sounded blood curdling and as if there actually was but from what Leah could see as she drew closer, only two female human entities were actually present inside the cave and one of those entities was herself.

When Leah was in close enough proximity to the woman, she carefully and cautiously stretched out one of her hands towards the woman and then gently placed her hand upon the woman's shoulder in a manner that was intended to calm, soothe and reassure. A deep, tense, fearful breath was taken as Leah slowly knelt down beside the woman as she began to prepare to hold an actual conversation with the source of the very alarmed, frightened screams. Despite all Leah's warm efforts however, nothing but fear seemed to greet her as the woman huddled up against the cave wall even more and flinched at Leah's touch and so it rapidly became quite apparent to Leah that the woman would require more than just the reassurances that she had attempted to provide in order to be convinced and persuaded that Leah's intentions were not harmful or meant to cause any discomfort.

"What's wrong?" Leah asked softly. "Why did you scream? Are you afraid of something or someone? Why are you down here alone?"

"I'm afraid of them." She replied as she began to sob.

Every part of the woman's form seemed to be saturated and drenched in absolute fear because Leah immediately noticed that her voice wavered as she spoke and that her eyes looked haunted and glassy as her body started to tremble. The expression upon the woman's face looked extremely scared and it was almost as if even just a discussion about what she feared, made her even more fearful and so as Leah glanced into her eyes, she immediately sympathized with the woman's tearful, fearful state.

"Who or what are they?" Leah asked as she urged the woman to provide her with more details.

"Millipiders. If they hear you, they come to find you and then if they find you, they eat you alive. You can't sleep, you can never sleep." She whispered.

"But if you scream doesn't that actually let them know where you are?" Leah asked as she began to ponder over the contradictory nature of the woman's response and how illogical it sounded. "Doesn't that make things worse?"

"No, the screams are the only thing that keep them at bay. If they hear you and then they start to look for you, you have to scream to keep them away." The woman explained as she immediately shook her head. "The high pitch noises scramble their brains and confuses their ears which drives them away." She insisted.

"What exactly are they?" Leah probed.

"They are like giant millipedes but they can also spin webs like spiders so people call them millipiders. They have a hundred legs and so if they chase you, you'll never escape." The woman explained. She lowered the tone of her voice again almost to a whisper as she continued to speak. "If they catch you, they wind your body up in their web and then they eat you whilst you're still alive."

"Is there a way out of these caves at all?" Leah asked. "Have you ever tried to leave?"

"There's only one way to leave the millipider's tunnels." The woman acknowledged as a glum expression crossed her face and her eyes clouded over with frustration and hopelessness. "You have to cross the Lake of Fire and the only way to cross it safely is via a rope bridge that is very heavily guarded by goblin guards and it's not very stable."

Leah stood up and then nodded her head in understanding. "Right, let's go to the Lake of Fire and see if we can find a way to cross that bridge." She suggested as she extended a hand towards the woman crouched on the ground and politely offered to pull her to her feet. "Since I'm here anyway, we should at least try and see if we can find a way to escape together after all, there's no point us both sitting around inside this dark cave all day is there?"

A slightly suspicious expression crossed the woman's face as she glanced up at Leah and it almost seemed as if she felt uncertain as to whether Leah was actually a friend or foe and that Leah could already sense, due to not only her facial expression but also due to her hesitation. Inside Leah's mind, a few questions definitely lingered as she once again visually inspected and silently absorbed the woman's physical appearance and began to wonder how long she had been stuck inside the caves below the ground and how long she'd had to fend off carnivorous monsters alone as she had defended herself purely with screams because the woman certainly looked as if she had been there for a while.

"I'm Leah by the way." Leah said as she suddenly remembered to introduce herself and made a discreet attempt to convince the woman that she meant her no harm.

"Hi Leah, I'm Jade." The woman replied.

"How do you actually survive down here Jade? What do you eat?" Leah asked but almost as soon as she had verbally presented her questions, she regretted doing so because the answers she imagined, would probably be completely foul, absolutely putrid and certainly not something that she would actually, really want to know. "Perhaps I don't really need to know the answers to those questions

Jade because if the answers are disgustingly awful, sometimes ignorance can be the better option."

"Sometimes I eat mice." Jade replied. "And when I can't find any mice, at times I eat insects or even rats but rats are much harder to catch. It all depends on what I find inside the traps that I leave around the caves. When I catch something, I make a small fire and then I cook whatever I've found." She explained. "There's nothing else to eat down here, absolutely nothing."

"Well, your dietary intake is certainly not an a la carte menu by any stretch of the imagination. How long have you been down here?" Leah enquired as she winced and shivered in disgust. "How long has it been since you saw another human being, or ate a proper meal?"

"A very, very long time, I'm not even sure how long it's been anymore. I lost count of the days and weeks a while ago." Jade explained solemnly. "And now, I've almost forgotten what it actually looks like up there." She paused for a few seconds before she continued. "I waited and waited and I hoped and hoped but none of the forest dwellers ever came to find me, so I haven't seen anyone for a while and in fact, you're the first person I've seen since I've been down here."

"Let's go and find the bridge Jade." Leah urged as she stretched out a hand towards her once again and offered to pull her up to her feet.

Jade nodded appreciatively as she finally accepted Leah's offer of assistance and rose to her feet. "Thanks for coming to find me Leah." She replied. "I know you really didn't have to."

"No problem Jade. Let's try and get out of here, you can't be down here on your own forever." Leah insisted. "Which tunnel leads to the Lake of Fire?"

Jade pointed towards a tunnel entrance nearby. "We have to go that way." She explained.

Leah nodded.

Unfortunately, the dark, dismal tunnel entrance was filled with the same dreary darkness as the cave itself and so Leah quietly began to speculate as to whether it might actually house a millipider inside it as the two women started to walk towards it. Since the tunnel was so dark and probably even darker than the actual underground cave, it was almost impossible to see much further along it than a few steps ahead but nonetheless the two women approached it and then hopefully, stepped inside it as they began to make their way towards the Lake of Fire. Despite the darkness, the two women immediately began to walk along the tunnel quite quickly but also slightly cautiously and as they did so, Leah began to consider the possibility that perhaps a millipider might suddenly appear because that was an actual real possibility.

"Just get ready to scream again if you have to Jade." Leah whispered as she walked. "We might need a vocal shield."

"Right and I've had a lot of practice, so I'm really quite good at it now." Jade replied in a whisper. "I've practically become an expert in screaming since I've been stuck down here."

Leah smiled.

When the two women had gone just a short distance, they suddenly heard some noises that startled them and so they both immediately froze as they glanced at each other's faces with horrified expressions. The threat from an actual millipider was now perhaps just about to present itself to them both because the noises that they had heard, confirmed that something was definitely nearby and as both women already knew, that something would not be friendly.

Jade began to nod. "They're coming Leah." She warned. "So now, we have to run."

Fear rapidly began to flood through every inch of Leah's form as Jade swiftly grabbed her arm and then pulled her further along the tunnel more quickly and the two women ran through the remainder of the tunnel until they finally reached the other end of it. The cave that the two entered into at the other end of the tunnel had at least ten exits, Leah immediately noticed, which led off in various directions and Jade seemed to hesitate as she glanced at each one for a few seconds and it almost appeared to Leah as if she felt slightly unsure about the precise route and correct exit to take.

"We have to hurry Jade." Leah urged as she glanced back at

the tunnel behind her that the two had just left. "They're coming remember."

"I think it's this one Leah." Jade replied as she began to walk towards the tunnel entrance on the very right-hand side of the cave.

"You mean you're not sure?" Leah asked as confusion rapidly began to grip her form. "I really need you to be sure right now Jade because your uncertainty will make us their evening meal."

"All the tunnels look the same sometimes, so it can be hard to remember." Jade explained as she attempted to justify her slight hesitation.

"Now is not a good time to pick the wrong tunnel." Leah rapidly pointed out.

"I think it's this one." Jade rapidly reassured her as she stepped into the tunnel entrance. "In fact, I'm very sure it's this one."

"Right, we better run." Leah replied.

Despite all the doubts that now lurked inside Leah's mind as to whether or not that particular tunnel was indeed the correct one, she grabbed onto Jade's arm and then swiftly began to run along it as she urged Jade to rush and although Leah had no actual idea where she was going, she attempted to lead the way because she felt unsure that the women's speed up until that point would be fast enough to outrun the current threat. The millipiders as Leah fully appreciated, would definitely not care about the two women's uncertainty or about their saunter along the tunnels in search of an exit and so that meant, they absolutely had to find the way out and the Lake of Fire extremely quickly, before the millipiders caught up with and actually found them.

Once the two women arrived at the other end of the tunnel, they entered into another cave which had three more tunnel exits and Jade quickly led Leah towards the one situated on their left hand side as they continued to rush through the underground maze. The second tunnel that Jade led Leah along, led directly into a very large, long rectangular cave which had huge stone pillars inside it that ran in rows across it and there was a wide, open exit at the other end of the large space and as the two women entered into the rectangular, pillared area, Jade held onto Leah's arm and then led her towards the first pillar which she silently urged her to stand behind.

"They're here now." Jade whispered.

"How do you know?" Leah asked her in a hushed tone.

"I can smell them, they have a very distinct smell." Jade replied. "We have to get to the other side of this cave because that's where the Lake of Fire is."

Leah nodded.

"We can hide behind these pillars as we make our way towards the exit." Jade advised. "That'll be safer."

"Okay, let's go." Leah urged as she nodded in agreement.

Fortunately for the two women, the stone pillars provided a degree of cover and so as the two women started to cross the large expanse, for the most part they actually remained hidden from sight as they darted and dashed from pillar to pillar and hid behind each one. Once they arrived at the final stone pillar which was the pillar closest to the exit, they paused for a few seconds as they peeped out from behind it and attempted to evaluate their potential escape route, just to ensure that it was indeed, all clear.

Much to Leah's absolute horror however, she rapidly discovered that right next to the entrance of the bridge that she had hoped would lead the two women to safety and allow them to cross the Lake of Fire, there was a huge, giant goblin like creature which seemed to sit on guard and he looked like he wasn't going anywhere. The potential obstruction that the goblin presented was indeed significant enough to completely sabotage the women's entire escape plan because he silently blocked their route to both safety and the bridge and so as Leah began to process and absorb the goblin's presence, she began to shake her head in frustration as she noticed that he had an extremely large club by his side to match his extremely ugly persona and presence.

Suddenly the goblin, who Leah observed for now seemed to be totally oblivious to the two women's presence, stood up and then to make matters even worse, he actually began to pace up and down in front of the entrance to the bridge as the two women watched him in total silence. Due to the huge ugly warts that decorated the goblin's appearance, Leah almost winced as she watched him as he began to scratch one of them, swigged on a tankard which seemed to contain some kind of beer and then belched extremely loudly.

"He's a goblin guard." Jade explained in a whisper.

"Do goblins eat people Jade?" Leah enquired in a worried whisper as she began to consider and explore what the actual implications of being captured by a goblin guard might actually be.

"I'm not sure but he can definitely kill us both with his bare hands." Jade whispered. "And he definitely won't let us cross the bridge."

"What if we lead the millipider to the goblin that might get rid of the hungry millipider and the ugly goblin at the same time." Leah suggested. "Because then they can eat and kill each other."

"How will we do that?" Jade whispered back.

"One of us will have to act as bait." Leah replied quietly. "If one of us runs around close to the entrance of the bridge and near the goblin, both the millipider and the goblin will be enticed."

"Okay, you be the bait and I'll stand behind this pillar, just in case I have to scream." Jade suggested. "Millipiders are totally blind, so they rely purely upon their senses of smell and hearing to actually hunt their prey down which in this instance could actually work in our favor because we are the prey."

Leah nodded. "The millipider will probably rush out from behind one of the pillars as soon as I make a move." She concluded. "But I'll give it a try."

Since Gretchen's concoction of courage had not yet totally worn off, Leah still felt slightly braver than usual and as she stepped out from behind the pillar and then rushed towards the entrance of the bridge and the goblin guard, she fully leant upon that bravery. The goblin guard continued to pace up and down just in front of the bridge as Leah rushed over the rocky ground towards him and suddenly, much as Leah had fearfully predicted, a millipider darted out from behind a nearby pillar and then rapidly began to scurry towards her.

"A scream might be good right now Jade." Leah called out as the millipider neared her form.

Two spiky horns protruded from the huge, ugly millipider's head and it appeared to have a hundred legs as Jade had mentioned and as it rushed towards Leah very quickly, she started to panic and then totally froze. The dark black skin that covered the creature's form had bumps all over it and so in some ways, it reminded Leah slightly of a spider and as she glanced at the fictitious creature that she herself had created, nothing but a current of chaotic alarm surged through her mind. Somehow, paralysis had suddenly set in but Leah quickly attempted to shake herself out of her stillness and then began to rush towards the giant goblin and the bridge once again as the millipider continued to follow her movements and pursued her with relentless determination.

The giant goblin, who it appeared had now become aware of the sudden commotion, suddenly turned to face both Leah and the millipider as they both raced towards the entrance of the bridge and ultimately, the goblin's current position and as Leah neared the goblin, she quickly crouched down and then rolled across the ground which took her straight through the goblin's huge, hairy legs. Quite fortunately for Leah and somehow miraculously, she actually managed to land upon the start of the actual bridge which was an absolute miracle in itself and although her body aim had really not been that precise, she had managed to completely avoid the goblin guard and the huge club that the he held inside one of his huge, giant hands.

Somehow, the ugly, aggressive looking goblin hadn't really noticed Leah it seemed and had paid more attention to the millipider, probably due to its much larger size which meant that the creature posed more of a threat to the goblin itself and as she took a few steps then paused, she visually searched for any sign of Jade's face. A huge sigh of relief escaped from Leah's lips as she watched the millipider rush towards the goblin's form as both the goblin and the millipider prepared for battle and as the goblin prepared to slay the millipider, the goblin's heavy club was quickly raised. Just as those events took place and Leah's plan started to manifest and occur, Leah also noticed that Jade quickly reacted to the distraction as she slipped out from behind the pillar and then rushed towards the bridge and towards Leah herself.

An aggressive battle rapidly commenced between the goblin and the millipider quite close to the entrance of the bridge and as Leah began to watch the two engage in battle, she remained still as she waited for Jade. In a matter of just a few more seconds Jade had managed to catch up with Leah and so, Leah quickly took hold of Jade's arm and then began to lead her across the bridge. Due to the threat from the goblin and the millipider, Leah felt quite anxious to put as much distance between the two women and their ugly enemies as soon as she possibly could and so she rushed Jade along the bridge in total silence. An opportunity had been given for the two women to escape from their two enemies who continued to do battle in a very ugly clash and so Leah felt absolutely determined to make the most of the opportunity to escape from the goblin's club and the millipiders deadly web as the two women left duo of death well behind them and crossed the remainder of the bridge.

Once both women were safely at the other end of the bridge and had fully crossed it, they smiled at each other as they stepped onto a firm earthy bank and then paused for a moment as they glanced back at the two enemies that had now been left firmly behind them, locked in a battle of death with each other. Just for a moment, Leah thoughtfully reflected upon the millipiders that she had ultimately created because although she'd formed a hybrid creature which was a cross between a centipede and a spider inside Spectrum, the creature that she had just encountered had seemed absolutely huge, especially when it had risen up on its hind legs because it had towered high above her human head which made their presence seem, extremely scary and totally fearful. The unexpected increase in the creature's size, Leah immediately attributed to the fearful environment and it rapidly became quite apparent to her that the Spectrum system itself had adapted the creature's size to make the hybrid more fearful in nature which was another programmable functionality that she had actually built into the system herself.

"What happens Jade, if you fall into the Lake of Fire?" Leah suddenly asked as she turned to face her and pointed towards the lake.

"You burn to a crisp within seconds." Jade replied.

"It would have been absolutely impossible then to cross that lake without the bridge." Leah acknowledged.

"We should go now Leah." Jade urged as she held onto her arm. "Before they realize that we've escaped."

Leah nodded.

At one end of the firm earthy bank there was an earthy platform and as Leah was led towards it by Jade and then the two women stepped onto it, the platform immediately started to rise and as it elevated them both, it moved rapidly upwards towards the surface of the forest. The Fearful Forest it quickly transpired, still lay directly above the two women's heads and as they broke through a thin, muddy skin that covered the earthy ceiling and then the platform tipped them gently off it, they were pushed gently back into the heart of the forest and back onto artificial solid ground once more.

"Thank you so much Leah, you helped me to get out of there." Jade said appreciatively as she turned to face her and then smiled. "I think I might still be suffering from the curse of discontent though because I did live amongst the roots of the tree for so very long."

Leah smiled. "Thank you too Jade, without you I don't think I'd have managed to find a way out of there myself. I still have two golden apples left and if you eat one that will break the curse of the tree." She replied as she immediately plucked the two golden apples from her trouser pockets and then handed one to Jade.

"Thanks." Jade said appreciatively as she immediately accepted the apple with a grateful smile and then started to eat it. "You should eat that last apple yourself Leah, it might give you some extra strength and get rid of any final remnants from the curse of discontent that might still reside within you." She advised in-between mouthfuls of fruit.

"Yes, I think that's a good idea." Leah agreed as she nodded her head and then raised the final golden apple to her lips.

Just as Leah bit into the juicy flesh of the final golden apple however, the Fearful Forest suddenly started to evaporate and disappear and as her surroundings rapidly began to change, a few seconds later she woke up and found herself back inside the Spectrum capsule and back inside her basement laboratory. The entire Fearful Forest had completely disappeared, Jade had totally vanished and so too had the golden apple which had been held firmly inside Leah's hand.

Upon Leah's face there was a relieved smile as she issued a voice command and the lid of the Spectrum capsule started to open and then she began to enthusiastically clamber out of it as she rejoiced in the fact that at the very least, her basement laboratory still looked exactly the same as when she had initially entered inside the capsule earlier that day.

Once Leah had collected her cellphone from the top of the shiny worktop where it had been placed earlier that day, she then began to walk towards the steps that led back up towards the ground floor of the couple's home and as she walked, she glanced down at the screen. Much to Leah's absolute delight, she rapidly discovered that she had received a text message from Zidane that had been sent to her over an hour ago and so Leah smiled as she enthusiastically opened it and then began to read its contents because as usual his words were full of loving sentiments, devoted affection and contained the warmth of his love.

'Just finished working on Spectrum and getting ready for bed now, miss you lots. Lots of hugs, kisses and all that good stuff. xx' Leah quickly replied as she attempted to reassure Zidane that he had not been ignored or forgotten, merely due to his physical absence.

For that night as Leah already knew, the bedroom that the couple usually shared, unusually would only be occupied by her own physical body and that saddened her slightly as she suddenly began to deeply miss Zidane's physical presence. Perhaps, Leah considered quietly as she began to mount the basement steps, she could actually call Zidane once she was upstairs and see if he was still awake and that would perhaps slightly reduce the physical distance between them both and appease their solitude.

"Fink, it's time to shut down." Leah commanded as she prepared to totally abandon the basement and Spectrum for the day.

"Shutting down now." A male, metallic voice suddenly replied as all the lights inside the laboratory and the large, wafer screen attached to one of the walls switched off and rapidly went dark.

Leah smiled in response. "Zidane's not here but at least Fink is and I guess that male presence will have to do for now, although he's not a great conversationalist and he is definitely not sweet like Zidane usually is." She reminded herself playfully. "Fink is just a small glimmer and tiny flicker of artificial masculine companionship and comfort really."

Despite the fact that Leah had not done anything physical all day, for some strange reason she now felt quite mentally drained as she walked up the remainder of the steps that led back up towards the ground floor of the couple's home and more importantly, the bedroom which she now definitely, wearily required. Tonight, Leah would sleep totally alone but at least, she would still have Fink and Fink's voice which would be in easy verbal reach and that would provide a blanket of comfort to her because Fink's voice was in many ways, an audio reminder of Zidane since the whole voice control system that had been created by Leah herself when the couple had initially moved into the home that they shared, had actually been formed from Zidane's actual voice.

When Leah had created the voice controls that she had applied to the various appliances around the couple's home, not just the basement, the actual voice of Fink had been created with Zidane's audio input and so in some ways, Fink's voice actually sounded quite like Zidane's real voice, albeit a slightly clunkier, more metallic version. The voice control system that Leah had designed allowed the couple to control the alarm system, lights and various appliances around their home but Leah rarely utilized it outside of the basement, unless she was feeling exceptionally lazy, or the couple were out somewhere and then she would remote access Fink through her cellphone. Regardless of Fink's convenient applications and comforting tone however, Leah now fully appreciated that Fink could never be an actual substitute for Zidane's presence because Fink did not have two warm loving arms to cuddle into and nestle against and so as she stepped into the couple's empty bedroom and released a weary sigh, she began to fully accept that choices really were so much easier to make than to live with because now, she had to spend her whole night in a cold, empty bed, totally alone and Fink would now be her only actual companion.

Adventures within the Ark of Anticipation

When the Sunday morning arrived, Leah embraced the world with a hopeful smile upon her face as she woke up and then enthusiastically arose because the day was bright, peaceful and pleasant. Since as Leah already knew, Zidane would return to the couple's home later that day in the late evening that joyful thought, sprinkled a pleasant dew of hopeful anticipation across her mind, heart and morning as she began to prepare for the day ahead. Due to Zidane's absence Leah had already decided to make the most of her weekend and to actually explore two Spectrum environments in those two days and so another trip to a Spectrum environment had been planned to occur that Sunday because once Zidane returned, it wouldn't be as easy for Leah to spend a whole day inside Spectrum and to experience a full emotional journey in one recreational sitting.

In terms of the couple's relationship, Zidane wasn't a particularly demanding lover but, on the weekends and evenings when the couple were supposed to spend time together, he definitely seemed to appreciate the chance to spend some quality time with Leah undisturbed and he certainly appeared to enjoy her companionship and so she appreciated their mutual interest in each other. Since Leah's additional work on Spectrum in recent times had far exceeded her usual hours by a very large margin, she now fully accepted that her additional time spent inside the basement had definitely put a strain upon the couple's relationship and that she had to some extent, starved Zidane of the attention that he usually really treasured but Leah hoped that Spectrum would soon be complete and that then Zidane's days of hunger would be officially over.

Fortunately for Leah, the Spectrum environment that she was due to visit that day involved an emotional journey which would revolve around and that would be focused purely upon anticipation and so as she showered, dressed and then stepped inside the kitchen, she felt tremendously excited about her potential adventure. Unlike the Fearful Forest as Leah already knew, this particular emotional journey would be full of nice surprises, pleasant experiences and lots of eager excitement which meant, she would be fully immersed in joyful positivity for the remainder of her day. The fact that Zidane was not actually due to return to the couple's home until ten that Sunday night also meant that Leah could enjoy her visit to Spectrum that day at her leisure and also that she could even complete her whole emotional journey before he was due to return.

A lavish brunch was planned that morning however, and so the required food items were quickly and enthusiastically sought out so that Leah would have a full meal to consume that morning which she had planned would satisfy her dietary intake for both breakfast and lunch that day. When it came to dinner that evening, Leah had already planned to prepare the couple's evening meal once she had finished inside Spectrum because she wished to consume it with Zidane later that night and so that morning, all Leah really had to do was actually feed her own body.

Each item of food that Leah had selected for her brunch was quickly tipped into the frying pan and placed upon the grill as Leah began to thoughtfully consider Zidane's potential return later that day and his steadfast support which had not wavered or swayed, even as the years had slipped by. Not only had Zidane given Leah and their relationship his total dedication over the years but he had also fully committed himself to the couple's romantic future in a way that was second to none and so she hoped that Spectrum would in the end, provide the couple with the additional financial resources that they required to live the life that the two had planned to enjoy together.

Despite the slightly inconvenient and very unusual nature of Leah's professional ambitions, she definitely fully appreciated that Zidane had always stood by her, supported and encouraged her in an truly selfless manner and so how much time they spent together or apart, hadn't yet really become a huge issue for either of them.

The many late nights that Leah had spent inside the basement as she had fine-tuned, adapted, modified, refined and tested Spectrum hadn't yet actually taken their toll upon the couple's relationship and for that reality Leah felt extremely grateful because Zidane as she was fully aware, had the patience of a saint and his financial and emotional support really were not only incomparable but also absolutely irreplaceable.

Deep down inside Leah truly hoped as she plonked her brunch down onto a plate that all the sacrifices that the couple had made would soon be worth it and that her long hours inside the basement would be justified by the eventual payoff and financial compensation that Spectrum would provide to them both. Although the capital sum and financial payoff that the Spectrum prototype would finally provide was for now, extremely uncertain and very unpredictable, Leah hoped that it would be quite large and large enough to lubricate the wheels of couple's future which would allow them to jump over the current financial hurdles they faced and that it would give them the future that they wished to enjoy and had planned to spend together. Fortunately however, in the meantime, despite all Leah's additional long hours and the lack of attention shown to Zidane, Spectrum had not yet pulled the couple's relationship apart at the seams due to Zidane's patience, his love for Leah and his tireless devotion to her and so Leah fervently hoped that all the couple's efforts would soon be rewarded but before that could happen as she already knew, the Spectrum prototype had to be actually finished.

The actual design and creation milestones for Spectrum had now all been met, achieved and realized but Leah still had to actually perform the walk-through tests within each environment that she had created in person and then tweak and fine tune every single one, according to any additional required refinements. Unfortunately for Leah however, the final stage of her work on Spectrum it had now transpired, seemed to be just as time consuming as the initial time spent upon Spectrum's creation, design and development and at times that really frustrated Leah as she strove for total and utter perfection.

Every environment in Spectrum had to be very thoroughly tested so that Leah could identify any problems or imperfections and then resolve those issues after which point, she would then have to test each area again just to ensure that any corrections and changes that had been made, actually produced the desired results. The thorough nature and criteria of the tests therefore meant that the duration of the testing period was highly unpredictable and that if any complications arose, it was entirely possible that it could go on for weeks or perhaps even months and so Leah felt very uncertain as to when it would actually end and when the Spectrum prototype would actually be fit for the purposes intended.

Once Leah had hungrily consumed and totally devoured her brunch which had consisted of a few rashers of bacon, a couple of eggs, some slices of French toast and a couple of sausages, she eagerly began to prepare to visit the basement as she quickly washed up her now empty plate. A definite air of excitement now surrounded Leah because she had planned the rest of her Sunday absolutely meticulously so that she could make the most of every single second, minute and hour and so now, she felt quite eager to actually make a start.

"That brunch was absolutely delicious but totally fattening." Leah admitted to herself as she placed the now washed up plate into a slot in the dish drainer to dry off and then glanced up at the black clock that clung to one of the kitchen walls.

Since the Sunday morning had not yet totally expired and it wasn't quite eleven, Leah felt comfortably certain that she would definitely be able to complete her Spectrum journey by nine that evening which meant that she would still have a spare hour to utilize which would allow her to prepare the couple's evening meal before Zidane returned to the couple's home. The fried bits of food that Leah had prepared that morning which had formed part of her brunch as she already knew, weren't particularly healthy but that meal had definitely filled up the empty gap inside her stomach and it had tasted absolutely heavenly and it also meant that she was now sufficiently fueled up for the day ahead and officially ready for her third visit to Spectrum.

Just a few minutes later Leah began to eagerly make her way towards the basement because she had aimed to be inside Spectrum and to have embarked upon her third emotional journey by eleven that morning and as she walked, she thoughtfully considered all the support that Zidane had provided to her over the years. Fortunately for Leah, she had been given a decent sized bursary with which to fund some of her work upon Spectrum but since that had fallen well short of her actual living requirements, Zidane had financially stepped in and supported her as he had plugged any financial gaps and shortfalls with some much needed financial resources and so Leah had not had to attend an external location each day in order to perform a regular nine to five corporate laboratory job.

Although the bursary that Leah had been given for the past few years hadn't been particularly huge, it had definitely been large enough to satisfy most of the expenses that had related to Spectrum and it had also been accompanied by Zidane's contributions which had always been and were far more generous. Since both amounts combined had managed to cover all aspects of Leah's financial upkeep and her monetary requirements, those two sums of money had therefore enabled Leah to keep her head well and truly above water and had even kept her professional aspirations alive.

Somehow with Zidane's support, Leah had managed to completely avoid having to work inside someone else's research laboratory in order to pay the bills and she had actually managed to buy everything that she'd required which had enabled her to realize her own research goals which had almost been an achievement in itself. The financial provisions from Zidane had allowed Leah to achieve something that she now fully appreciated, she would never have achieved alone and so she felt extremely grateful for his loyalty, his support and his financial commitment to their future. Hopefully soon however, Leah hoped as she stepped of the final step into the basement where her invention lived, those financial sacrifices would be returned to the couple when Spectrum had been sold and then everything that the couple had worked so hard for would finally make total sense to them both.

Much as expected as Leah began to visually scan the basement and glanced around its interior, the subterranean space still looked exactly how she had left it the night before and it remained undisturbed by another living soul and untouched by another pair of human hands. In fact, much to Leah's satisfaction, everything inside it seemed to silently wait for its sole occupant and resident owner to return with an air of very still but loyal expectancy.

A satisfied smile crossed Leah's face as she began to walk towards the center of her laboratory and the Spectrum capsule as she started to internally prepare for her third Spectrum experience and her emotional journey that day which she hoped would be truly delightful. The still silence that surrounded Leah comforted her as she walked towards the transparent capsule situated in the center of the room because it reminded Leah that her workspace had always been totally her own which also meant that no one ever disturbed or tampered with any of her scientific creations.

Visits to Leah's basement laboratory by foreigners were in fact, extremely rare and Leah was the only real citizen that regularly occupied and resided in its confines and although Zidane would pay the occasional visit and pop down now and again on the weekends, he rarely entered into that area during the week without prior notice. Essentially, Zidane seemed to understand the very solitary reality that when Leah was inside the basement, she really had to focus solely upon her professional tasks and that she had to really concentrate. Any disruptions to Leah's concentration as she performed the intricate scientific tasks required as she worked towards Spectrum's completion, would simply disturb Leah and prolong the work that she had to conduct and that fact, quite possibly, Zidane already, fully understood. The more frequently Zidane interrupted Leah and distracted her from her tasks, the longer it would actually take her to complete the Spectrum prototype and hence he seemed to avoid doing so very often and his patience, tolerance and devotion, Leah definitely felt, somehow silently helped to sustain their relationship and enabled Leah to dedicate herself more fully to not only her work but also to the couple's future.

Once Leah arrived beside the empty, transparent capsule that seemed to wait silently and patiently for her to occupy it, she quickly began to prepare herself and Spectrum for the emotional journey that lay ahead just upon the horizon of her Sunday as she instructed the Spectrum system to switch on and initiate. Just a few seconds later Leah mounted the small steps which led up from the basement floor towards the capsule and then she slipped inside it and quickly lay down as she prepared to be transported to another world, albeit an artificial, imaginary location.

Due to Leah's walk-through tests which meant that she had to test each emotional journey, some of the Spectrum environments and the overall system as thoroughly as possible, once the initiation sequence for that particular emotional journey had been activated, she rapidly began to modify and tweak her personality slightly. On this particular occasion and during this visit to Spectrum, Leah wanted to be slightly more confident and more optimistic than usual which she hoped would drive her excitement to higher peaks and allow her to experience greater heights of enjoyment. Personality modifications to a user's persona were easy enough to make inside Spectrum and could be configured almost instantly because Leah had developed that functionality specifically for the Spectrum system and so the required changes were not very difficult for Leah to make that morning. However, as Leah made the required adjustments for her third visit, she began to thoughtfully consider what life might actually be like and how much more simple it would be, if such adjustments could be made to actual human beings' personalities in real life as a playful smile crossed her face.

Less than a minute later a verbal command was issued by Leah and the capsule lid automatically descended and closed down over her body after which point, Leah closed her eyes as she prepared to be transported to another world and another adventure. The sleeping gas instantly began to seep out into the capsule and rapidly started to infiltrate Leah's very real human biological structure and so as Leah waited for sleep to fully embrace her, she began to silently consider her potential adventure that day enthusiastically which she hoped would be extremely positive. Since anticipation was generally and predominantly considered to be a positive emotion, there were absolutely no reservations at all on Leah's part or inside her mind as she fully cooperated with Spectrum and swiftly slipped into a peaceful, gentle slumber as she prepared to awaken in the midst of a pleasant unknown.

When Leah woke up, just a minute or so later, quite intriguingly and rather curiously, she found herself strewn across the grass at the edge of a huge field and although the field itself wasn't much to look at as she sat up and then began to visually scan the rest of her surroundings, she noticed that a huge, glossy, black and white structure situated in the very center of that field of grass, definitely was. A magnificent looking ark stood very boldly and quite magnificently in the middle of that grassy field and the structure literally shone as rays from the Sun above Leah's head bounced playfully but silently off the structure's surfaces. Unlike some of the images that Leah had seen in the past of traditional arks however, this ark was not plain or brown or even wooden and it had been formed from glossy, white and black materials that gave the ark's exterior a fashionable, chequered modern look that even verged upon being slightly stylish.

"The Ark of Anticipation." Leah whispered to herself as she smiled and then started to pick herself up of the ground. "I think I'm going to really enjoy this emotional adventure." She predicted cheerfully as she stood up.

At the very front of the ark, Leah observed that there was a large, wide, glossy black boarding ramp which it appeared led directly into the structure's entrance from the field and so as soon as Leah spotted it, she began to walk eagerly and briskly towards it. Excitement seemed to bubble away and swirl around just below the surface of Leah's form like a whirlpool of emotional warmth as her senses were playfully teased with each enthusiastic step that she took towards the magnificent looking, very grand structure directly in front of her which held the promise of a day filled with pleasant, delightful, joyful experiences firmly by the hand.

According to Spectrum's design and the parameters that Leah had created within the system, every structure that appeared within any Spectrum environment could be utilized in a flexible manner which allowed every single venue and location to function in a variety of ways. The flexibility that Leah had built into the system therefore meant that any structure or location that she had created could appear in any emotional journey that a consumer wished to embark upon and a great deal of effort had gone into the design and creation of those structures and locations to ensure that they not only looked authentic but also that each structure that should, looked utterly splendid and so as Leah visually scanned the ark's exterior she felt immensely satisfied. From what Leah could see at first glance, the Ark of Anticipation's exterior was definitely no exception to the standards of perfection that she had tried so hard to reach and it not only looked extremely spectacular but also very modern and so as she stepped onto the boarding plank and prepared to board the stationery vessel, a ripple of excitement began to silently flow through her form and core.

The potential exploration of the structure itself, fascinated Leah for several different reasons and one was simply because she had never even once set foot inside an actual ark before and that prospect held intrigue firmly by the hand as she began to walk up the boarding ramp. Since Leah had built so many possibilities into Spectrum, she expected her adventure that day to be not only full of excitement and thrills but also to be extremely unpredictable and even more so than her prior visits to Spectrum which had involved her visits to the Castle of Joy and the Fearful Forest due to the nature of that particular emotional journey which centered purely upon anticipation.

Once Leah had walked up the plank and once she was directly in front of the entrance to the Ark of Anticipation, she then enthusiastically stepped through what would basically be considered to be the ark's front door without any reservations at all as she embraced her current environment without any doubts, any uncertainty, or any fear. This emotional journey as Leah already knew, would definitely be very different in nature from the Fearful Forest due to the fact that anticipation was generally considered to be quite positive in nature and so, Leah felt almost certain that it would be very enjoyable and pleasant which meant, no hesitation was present on her part because she knew in advance that no horrible, scary, fearful surprises awaited her.

Much to Leah's complete surprise however, no sooner had she stepped through the entrance of the ark than the boarding ramp, suddenly retracted and the door of the ark actually closed behind her which rapidly confirmed to Leah that she would not be able to exit the ark until her emotional journey had been travelled through in its entirety. The timer on Spectrum had already been set for the full ten hours which meant, Leah would experience that whole recreational journey that very same day and since Zidane would not arrive home until ten that night, she felt fairly relaxed about her potential day ahead because there would be no distractions or any requests from anyone else to attend to.

Directly in front of Leah there appeared to be a maze of pathways as she began to inspect the interior of the ark, all of which seemed to lead in various directions towards a variety of doors and the doors came in all shapes, sizes and colors but there appeared to be no directional clues or indicators to suggest which path she should follow first. The internal architecture of the ark itself however, literally amazed and astonished Leah as she began to admire every inch of the ark's interior because when she had initially created the various structures inside Spectrum, she'd had no idea that they would look so realistic, natural and authentic and so she was now in total awe of the artificial reality that she had not only managed to create but had then actually managed to deliver. Although Spectrum was still technically a few tweaks away from perfection, the manifestation of Leah's years of tireless efforts, professional devotion and patient dedication had definitely artificially lived up to Leah's real expectations and if anything, had even exceeded them and that silent trophy of achievement, now totally thrilled her.

Some of the pathways in front of Leah, she thoughtfully observed, playfully crossed over each other and wove in and out of other paths and whilst some spiraled up towards the ceiling, others dove down towards the deep base of the ark itself which made the interior of the structure look extremely complex, intricately designed and very elaborate. In fact from Leah's current position and the wide, large ledge that she had stepped onto from the boarding ramp, Leah could clearly see that some of the paths twisted and turned down towards the ground right down to the very base of the ark which was now situated quite far below her feet. However, the start of each path, Leah noticed, was situated not more than a few steps away from her current position which meant that each one was extremely accessible to her and that every path was indeed, a viable option that could be pursued. Much like the exterior of the ark, each path had been formed from the same black and white glossy materials and as Leah glanced at some of the paths and then began to inspect a few slightly more closely, she began to thoughtfully consider which path she should actually follow first because the choices currently on offer to her were infringingly numerous.

"There has to be at least fifty paths here, if not more." Leah whispered to herself. "So many choices and so many possibilities, it's absolutely glorious and totally delightful."

Due to Spectrum's very intricate, sophisticated design as Leah already knew, there were literally thousands of possible occurrences, eventualities and combinations because it was a highly complex, recreational system that Leah had planned extensively before she had actually created it. The complexity of Spectrum's design however, meant that it was virtually impossible for Leah to predict which path would actually lead her to any particular adventure without an override of the administrative functions prior to her visit and so that day, she was none the wiser as to which path would yield the most enjoyable experience. In fact, the complex infrastructure of Spectrum, namely the random generation of adventures and the unique combination of various variables, were a couple of the major reasons that it had taken Leah three years to actually build the system into a workable and fully functional, artificial, recreational environment because she had wanted to create a system that would generate adventures that no one could predict with even a speck of accuracy.

One of the main objectives of Spectrum was to totally immerse each user inside any particular world that they entered into in an unpredictable manner which Leah hoped would provide consumers with the ability to participate in each emotional journey not only in random environments but also in different capacities as many times as they wished to. Every activity inside any emotional environment therefore had to be randomly generated in order to meet Leah's overall objective effectively in order to give consumers an element of spontaneity and to keep them on the edge of their seats. Each artificial structure could also function inside any environment and so as Leah already knew, the journey of fear that she taken the day before could so easily have taken place in another location in that she could have visited the Castle of Fear and the forest could have easily been the location for the Joyful Forest Dance because the settings for each emotional journey could vary to such a large degree.

A deep blended sense of excitement, intrigue and mystery delightfully existed inside Leah's mind and form as she continued to visually inspect the current paths on offer to her because she could not predict what might lie ahead on the other side of any of those pathways and the actual potential implications of any particular choice that she might make. Due to the vast nature of Spectrum's programming and the random complexities involved, what might happen if Leah followed a particular path was highly unpredictable and the subsequent results were absolutely impossible to foresee with any degree of accuracy but on this particular occasion, Leah relished and savored that element of uncertainty, since any outcome was virtually guaranteed to at least be enjoyable and pleasant.

One particular path however, seemed to attract Leah's attention slightly more than others and so as she finally attempted to commit to one path, she repeatedly glanced at it because it twisted and turned in a manner that intrigued and fascinated her. The path itself twisted and turned downwards in an almost circular spiral towards the base of the ark and although it was slightly longer than several of the other alternative paths that Leah could have chosen that surrounded it, she decisively committed to her choice and then assertively stepped onto it as its appeal silently tugged away at her thoughts and urged her to follow it. Once Leah had committed to her instinctive choice, she then followed the twisted, spiral path diligently until she arrived at the other end of it where she found a black, glossy door.

At first glance Leah could see that the door appeared to be embedded into the wall of the ark and as she paused for a moment directly in front of it, she rapidly observed that there seemed to be some kind of puzzle on the actual door itself which appeared to function as a lock. Since puzzle locks on doors had been a feature that Leah had built into the inner workings of Spectrum herself to make some doors inside Spectrum slightly trickier to open, she instinctively knew that the door would not budge a single inch until that particular puzzle had actually been solved and so Leah began to prepare herself to tackle the challenge that she now faced. The additional feature of puzzle locks had been designed and added by Leah herself and it was a challenge that had been created very intentionally, in order to add more mystery and intrigue to important doors inside Spectrum because it forced users to engage in their choices before they actually embarked upon their chosen adventure.

Just a couple of minutes were spent in silent inspection as Leah began to visually assess the nature of the puzzle and what she actually had to do to open the door because her actual first adventure that day could not begin until that puzzle had been solved correctly. An amused smile crossed Leah's face as she stretched out her hand towards the puzzle lock which now sat mockingly directly in front of her as she prepared to attempt to solve the puzzle which it appeared involved some decorative patterned pieces.

Some small black and white squares sat in a small square block and there appeared to be a couple of small square gaps at the very top of the block, one of which had a hole in it and it seemed to Leah as if each small patterned, square piece had to be moved around the block and eliminated in a particular order to actually open the door. However, as Leah began to move some of the small squares around, she rapidly discovered that if a small square fell through the hole in the incorrect order, it would then reappear back inside the square block just a few seconds later.

Once Leah had tinkered around with the puzzle for a few minutes, much to her absolute delight and total satisfaction, all of the puzzle pieces finally fell through the gap in the correct order and didn't reappear and so, the door in front of her suddenly unlocked and then automatically swung open. A satisfied smile crossed Leah's face as she was finally granted access to whatever lay beyond the black, glossy rectangular obstruction as she prepared to walk through the gap that now sat directly in front of her.

Rather intriguingly, just beyond the door, Leah could see some rays of brownish light and as she stepped through it those amber rays started to flood over her form until the rays of light had almost swallowed her whole. In fact, as Leah paused for a moment inside the rectangular gap and then glanced down at parts of herself, she could now see that every inch of her skin glowed with a brownish tint and it was as if every inch of her form was completely saturated and totally drenched in the rays of light that emanated from just beyond the open door. The rays of light however, quickly started to fade away just a few seconds later and as the brownish rays evaporated, an earthy looking tunnel was suddenly revealed and left behind in their place which Leah then eagerly began to walk along.

Much like the path that Leah had followed to arrive at the actual door itself, the earthy tunnel continued the downward trend and it even tapered and became much smaller and far narrower as Leah ventured deeper inside it and travelled further along it which forced her to crouch as she walked. Just a hundred meters or so along the tunnel, Leah found that she actually had to crouch so much that she even began to crawl on her hands and knees because it became virtually impossible to proceed any further without doing so but she participated obediently and cooperated fully with the tunnel's decrease in size as she attempted to reach the other end of it so that she could embark upon her first adventure.

When Leah arrived at the other end of the tunnel she found herself in a maze-like room with a very low ceiling which had several more tunnel entrances inside it that led off in various directions but absolutely no directional indicators seemed to be present. A few minutes were spent in silent thoughtful deliberations as Leah visually inspected and quietly considered each tunnel entrance and which one she should follow, although there didn't appear to be much of a difference between any of them that she could see. Since no obvious answers immediately leapt out of the silence that surrounded Leah, she rapidly began to conclude that there was nothing else to do except pick a random tunnel and then just follow it because there were no signs to guide her and absolutely no maps it appeared which could be followed to arrive at a particular destination.

"I can't actually predict what lies at the other end of any of these tunnels." Leah whispered to herself as she gave each tunnel entrance a final glance. "So, I should just pick any one and hopefully, I won't have to crawl along dirt tunnels for too much longer."

Unfortunately, however, as Leah rapidly discovered, her crawl along the dirt tunnels was far from over as she stepped inside the tunnel that she had chosen and it quickly decreased in size, much like the first tunnel had done which therefore meant, her crawl along the ground would continue for a while longer. Despite that minor, rather irritable setback however, Leah managed to persevere as she carried on with her exploration of the underground maze which as yet didn't really amount to much because there was nothing much to see but an earthy tunnel in every direction that she faced. Fortunately for Leah however, on this occasion and unlike the Fearful Forest, no wetness or liquid mud seemed to be present despite the very earthy nature of the tunnel's interior and for that one small mercy, Leah felt extremely grateful because she definitely felt that she had spent enough time in the mud the previous day whilst inside the forest.

Much to Leah's surprise however, as she crawled along the second tunnel, suddenly some very strange, unusual, muffled rustles emanated from somewhere in front of her and so, she immediately paused for a moment and then just listened to the noises that she could hear. A few seconds were spent in thoughtful deliberations and speculative considerations as Leah strained her eyes and searched for the source of the noises as each sound wafted and floated into her ears but the source of the sounds still remained unseen and was not it appeared, even remotely visible to her.

Due to Leah's current lack of visibility, she cautiously began to wonder whether or not the noises were a cause for concern but as she listened attentively to each noise, Leah rapidly began to conclude that the noises sounded innocent enough not to cause any alarm, fear or discomfort. Quite reassuringly, the rustles didn't appear to be hectic or aggressive but rather a soft, gentle welcome and in some ways, the noises even reminded Leah a little of the kind of noises that someone would make when they read a paper newspaper and flicked through the pages and so that soothed Leah's mind to some extent as she prepared to resume her crawl and to proceed.

Just a few seconds later and before Leah had actually begun to move forward again however, the noises seemed to evolve from a mild rustle to a muffled scurry but even as the sounds changed and grew slightly louder, it still remained unclear who or what exactly was responsible for those sounds. No matter how hard Leah peered along the earthy tunnel, she could still see absolutely no one and nothing and so she quickly resigned herself to the reality that she would have to seek answers and further clarity, further along the tunnel itself. Someone or something was definitely nearby and Leah had absolutely no idea who or what that someone or something actually was, no matter how hard she looked but the noises didn't seem to be vicious or savage in nature and so, Leah hoped that the source of those noises would at least be warm and friendly, despite her current ignorance.

Another minute or so was spent by Leah on her hands and knees as she continued to crawl through the earthy, tubular space as it twisted and turned in various directions until the tunnel suddenly, rather abruptly ended as Leah arrived at the edge of a wood clearing. Once Leah had crawled out of the tunnel, she immediately stood up and then released a grateful sigh of appreciation, simply due to the fact that her crawl along the narrow space had now finally ended just before she began to quietly visually scan, mentally process and thoughtfully absorb her new current surroundings. Every inch of the clearing which appeared to be situated in the heart of some woods, looked absolutely immaculate from what Leah could see at first glance as she visually inspected the area that now surrounded her that appeared to be peacefully pleasant which made a nice change from the Fearful Forest that Leah had encountered the previous day.

Around the perimeter of the clearing sat a collection of trees which silently adorned its edges that Leah rapidly observed had been dressed in smart mahogany, reddish, brown trunk suits which had been topped off with frilly, leafy, emerald green leaves that made everything around her look very natural, rich in color and pleasantly vibrant. Each mahogany tree trunk present inside the clearing seemed to contrast perfectly with the vibrant, green leaves that seemed to clothe every tree like a tailor-made garment that had been made specifically to fit each one and as Leah silently admired the seemingly, very natural beauty that wasn't really, actually natural at all, she smiled a very satisfied smile. Rather interestingly, Leah contemplated as she continued to absorb the scene, each tree stood around the edge of the clearing as if they been stationed there like soldiers on guard and it almost felt if something or someone very precious had to be protected as each one stood silently to attention in regimented positions and guarded their post.

In the very center of the clearing, Leah suddenly noticed that there was a deep golden pond which shimmered and shone as golden water gently nestled against the emerald blades of grass that adorned and decorated the circular shaped banks that sat silently around it. Due to the highly unusual color of the water inside the pond, the beautiful collation of water immediately fascinated and intrigued Leah and so, she rapidly began to make her way enthusiastically towards it and towards a small mahogany tree stump that was also visible from Leah's current position which was situated right next to the golden pond.

Once Leah arrived next to the tree stump, she felt a definite urge to sit down upon it as she started to fully embrace and admire the beautiful clearing that surrounded her which seemed to be totally serene, joyfully peaceful and very pleasant. After the longish crawl that Leah had just endured inside the two tunnels, the urge that she now felt to park her rear on top of the tree stump seemed to be only natural and the logical thing to do and so as Leah sat down and started to make herself comfortable, she began to relax for a few minutes as she simply appreciated and started to digest the peaceful beauty that currently surrounded her.

Some curious deliberations and internal speculations swiftly began to form, silently gather and then fully occupied Leah's mind as she glanced into the depths of the pond with deep admiration as she began to wonder what could have possibly made the water such an unusual color. No explanations however, seemed to exist as to why the water looked so golden and although Leah stared at the pond for a few minutes as she considered the matter further as she watched the golden water ripple due to the movement of some fish that occupied its golden collation of drops as each ripple softly lapped gently against the grassy edges that formed its perimeter, no actual answers it appeared could be found in its depths. A number of brightly colored fish seemed to occupy the pond's interior, Leah observed and as she watched some of the small aquatic creatures, swim chaotically around inside the pond, she noticed that each one looked extremely busy and rather intriguingly, actually glowed as they moved around and their brightness instantly fascinated Leah because they looked not only amazingly bright but also highly unusual.

For the next few minutes Leah just sat and relaxed her mind as she simply appreciated the calmness and collective beauty that the clearing composed of and as Leah's mind began to wander, she started to wish that her own back garden at home could contain such a beautiful pond. Sadly however, all Leah's back garden currently contained was a bunch of weeds because the couple rarely had any time to maintain it and so it had overgrown due to the lack of care and attention that it had been shown.

Quite unexpectedly and much to Leah's surprise however, suddenly her thoughtful meander was interrupted by a small dark beige, sandy colored, furry creature which appeared as if from nowhere and the animal's sudden arrival caught Leah completely off guard because it really was so unexpected. The rustles and scurries that Leah had heard whilst inside the second earthy tunnel had to have come from someone or something and so she immediately assumed and attributed the noises to the small hybrid creature that had suddenly made an appearance as she began to stare at its form with an amused expression upon her face.

Fortunately for Leah, this particular hybrid creature looked a lot more cuddly and way cuter than the millipider that she had encountered inside the Fearful Forest and so there was a smile upon her face as the creature walked boldly towards her and drew much closer. Not an inch of fear seemed to exist on the creature's part as Leah watched the hybrid approach her and the animal didn't seem to be intimidated by her presence at all, despite its quite small physique. Although Leah was currently in a seated position, she quickly began to estimate that if she stood up the creature's height would only reach up to just above her knees, if that and so due to the animal's quite short stature, Leah remained seated upon the tree stump, simply because she did not want to alarm, intimidate or scare the creature away.

"Where on earth did you come from?" Leah asked the animal politely even though she didn't actually expect a response.

"Actually, I'm always here." The creature replied in mature male voice. "You however, are not so, perhaps I should be the one asking you that question instead."

The very astute, intelligent response by the small furry animal immediately caught Leah by surprise and so much so that she almost fell of the tree stump that she was seated upon as she discreetly tried to mask the giggles that bubbled away inside her form which threatened to erupt from her being and spill out of her mouth. For the next minute or so, a closer inspection of the hybrid animal in front of Leah was silently, curiously and rapidly conducted as she began to examine and inspect every intricate detail of the creature's makeup and external appearance and then started to scan her mind for answers with regards to what he could possibly be but her mind came up totally blank.

Some strands of dark golden, sandy brown hair, Leah observed, hung down from the top of the creature's head which glistened as rays of sunshine seeped into the clearing from the sky above the trees and he had small, bald, hand like paws which rested on top of his large stomach. Despite the creature's quite short stature, Leah noticed that his stomach and feet protruded out in front of him rather prominently and a dark paddle like tail that was really quite long which brought a smile to her face as she began to appreciate his presence because he looked slightly comical albeit in a quite serious, unintentional kind of way.

Due to the creature's unique appearance, Leah already knew that he definitely belonged to one of the Random Hybrid Animal Groups that she had created inside Spectrum where she'd mixed various species of animals in a completely random manner and blended some of their characteristics. Some of the creatures in one of those hybrid groups had specifically been given the ability to speak in a human tongue but what kind of animal exactly he was, Leah still felt slightly unsure because she had literally created thousands of hybrid creatures and this creature's form wasn't one that was immediately recognizable to her.

Suddenly Leah's visual inspection was interrupted however, as the creature gently cleared his throat and then opened up some kind of parchment which had been tucked under his that appeared to contain a large, pair of glasses with a solid, black, thick frame that he plucked from it and then perched on top of his long, sandy brown nose. Once the visual aid was securely in place, Leah watched in total silence as he swiftly spread the parchment across the ground directly in front of him which appeared to be a small map. For some inexplicable reason, the creature's actions amused Leah immensely as she observed each movement in thoughtful silence but she immediately attempted to mask her laughter and any giggles that threatened to erupt from her being with a hand that she rapidly placed over her mouth.

In every way imaginable as Leah already knew, laughter was definitely an incorrect response in her current position and so, she quickly suppressed each giggle that threatened to escape from her lips which would definitely shatter the peaceful quietness that currently surrounded her. The small, furry creature looked extremely serious and as Leah fully appreciated, to offend someone so serious through a sudden expression of amusement and outburst of hilarity might perhaps be interpreted as rather rude and since she was totally reliant upon that hybrid animalistic entity for guidance and since that entity knew more about her current position than she did, it really wasn't the wisest thing to express. Quite often, as Leah fully appreciated, laughter could be interpreted by others as an insult, especially when someone was extremely serious about everything around them and about themselves and if she insulted the seemingly helpful creature, he might then refuse to actually assist her and so, Leah attempted to control her facial expressions and interact with him in a very serious manner as she sat totally upright upon the tree stump and straightened up her face.

"Who are you, if I may be so bold?" Leah asked as she watched him.

No answer to Leah's question was immediately given however, as the creature remained completely silent for a few more seconds and continued to study the map that he had just retrieved from his person which by now he'd placed upon the ground directly in front of him and quite close to the tip of Leah's feet. Approximately thirty seconds later, the creature suddenly, finally looked up at Leah's face as if he had just remembered that she was actually there and that she had asked him a question and upon his face, Leah noticed that there was now an apologetic expression as he turned his attention back towards her and quickly abandoned his inspection of the map that lay on the ground directly in front of him.

"A thousand apologies." He replied. "I don't get many visitors down here, so sometimes I forget the basic rules of social etiquette and my manners slip. I'm a mudmarsh and my name is Mindstone." Mindstone clarified. "I'm the keeper of the map and you were actually quite fortunate to find me because I'm the most useful mudmarsh to find in the Marshland Underground Tunnels and who might you be?"

"I'm Leah. I wandered down a tunnel from the Ark of Anticipation which I had to crawl through and somehow, I ended up here." Leah explained as she smiled.

"Ah, now I understand." Mindstone replied.

Everything about the mudmarsh's diplomatic explanation and his very polite introduction instantly impressed Leah as she rapidly began to conclude that he was definitely well mannered despite his initial slight hesitation. According to the hybrid creature groups that Leah had originally created and formulated within Spectrum coupled with Mindstone's appearance, he appeared to be a cross between a beaver and a kangaroo which suddenly made total sense to Leah because she had crossed those two species to create a hybrid species that she'd then called mudmarshes. The fur on Mindstone's body was predominantly a sandy, beige brown and some golden patches decorated the creature's frame in a few places, inclusive of his stomach pouch and the hair upon his head. Two long, dark brown feet protruded from below the creature's frame, Leah observed, which were slightly longer than one would usually expect to belong to an animal of his size and so they almost looked like paddles and a third tale like paddle which was slightly smaller in size protruded from Mindstone's rear.

Despite the creature's rather odd appearance however, Leah quickly decided that mudmarshes seemed to be very logical, highly organized creatures and that if Mindstone was an accurate reflection of the rest of his species, they were generally very amicable and didn't seem to be wild or untamed in any capacity at all. Since Mindstone appeared to be quite knowledgeable, it seemed only natural for Leah to present him with some more questions and the next logical question that lingered inside her mind and to expect a logical, intelligent answer to her questions because he seemed to be intellectually capable and appeared to be able to handle her verbal enquiries. Right now, as Leah fully appreciated, Mindstone definitely knew a lot more about her visit to his domain than she did and hence he was actually better placed to advise Leah about what she was actually supposed to do next and so she enthusiastically prepared herself to communicate with him more freely.

“What exactly am I supposed to do down here Mindstone?” Leah asked as she smiled.

“Well Leah, you are now situated inside the Marshland Underground Tunnels and each tunnel leads to another clearing and within those clearings, you'll find another mudmarsh and each mudmarsh that you find will require your assistance." Mindstone began to explain as he drew slightly closer to the pond and the tree stump upon which she was seated. "If you choose to assist a mudmarsh and perform the task that they require successfully, each mudmarsh will then point you in the direction of a tunnel that will lead you closer to the exit. However, if you fail a task, they might send you further away from the exit and if you choose not to assist them at all then you'll have to find your own way out and that can be pretty tricky." He advised.

The explanation that Mindstone had provided made it immediately apparent to Leah that if she failed to perform the tasks required or didn't bother to help any of the mudmarshes that she met along her way, she could actually be stuck in the Marshland Underground Tunnels for eternity, or at least until she woke up and left Spectrum later that day. On the brighter side of that quite dismal notion however, Mindstone's remarks also implied that if Leah assisted the mudmarshes successfully, she would then be able to leave the underground tunnels more quickly which definitely appealed to Leah because an entire day spent on her hands and knees as she crawled through the earthy tunnels wasn't exactly her idea of a great adventure.

"Right, so which tunnel should I go through first Mindstone?" Leah asked as she silently processed the explanations and instructions that had just been provided to her which it seemed, really were non-negotiable.

Suddenly however and much to Leah's surprise, Mindstone leant over the golden pond and then quickly dipped one of his hand like paws inside the water as he seemed to become distracted from their conversation for a moment and just a few seconds later, when it re-emerged and reappeared, Leah noticed that there was now a golden fish clasped inside it. Upon Mindstone's face there was a very satisfied smile as he began to hungrily lick his lips and glanced at the object of desire that was now in his actual possession which immediately prompted Leah to smile as she watched him in amused silence.

Irrespective of Mindstone's manners, diplomacy, intelligent dialogue and social etiquette, Leah thoughtfully observed, it had now transpired that he also possessed a rather short attention span which had been shortened and reduced even further by his animalistic, primal instincts which had definitely just kicked in along with his hunger. Just for a moment, Leah silently reflected, Mindstone's concentration had totally lapsed and his focus had rather amusingly, completely slipped and it had been solely focused upon the pond, the fish and his hungry stomach as he had temporarily abandoned not just the map but also their conversation.

A few seconds later Leah watched in amused silence as Mindstone popped the fish straight into his mouth and as she did so, Leah managed to suppress the giggles that threatened to escape from her lips because he had eaten the whole fish in one very wide mouthful which had absolutely stunned her. Suddenly, a rather loud gulp was heard as Mindstone actually swallowed the raw fish whole and Leah almost fell of the tree stump with laughter as she watched him smack his lips together in joyful satisfaction.

"Apologies Leah, I haven't eaten breakfast or lunch yet." Mindstone explained in a quiet tone as he sheepishly glanced back up at her face once more as a wave of embarrassment washed over him. "How rude of me, would you like a fish?" He asked.

Upon Leah's face there was a very amused smile as she glanced at Mindstone's face because he really seemed to be quite ashamed of the fact that he had forgotten his manners and that he had actually consumed a whole fish without even so much as an offer being made in Leah's direction. The lack of attention to Leah's form as she already knew, could perhaps be interpreted and regarded in some circles as slightly rude but as Mindstone had already mentioned to her, he rarely received any visitors which made total sense since Spectrum wasn't actually, fully operational yet which meant that day, Leah was his first real human visitor. Technically that day, Leah was Mindstone's actual guest and not only had she swooped into his domain unannounced and very unexpectedly but she had also required his actual guidance and so she could fully understand his obvious embarrassment along with his subsequent apology which like his manners, appeared to be a little rough around the edges but definitely seemed to be sincere enough to accept.

“No thanks Mindstone. I'm good, honestly.” Leah replied cheerfully as she politely flashed him a pleasant smile in an attempt to reassure him that everything was perfectly fine. "Thanks for the offer though, I really appreciate it and it's very kind of you."

Everything about Mindstone's offer almost made Leah wince because a raw fish that hadn't been cleaned, scaled or attended to in anyway and her stomach, certainly weren't a match made in heaven and it sounded to Leah like something that would actually turn her stomach over not fill it up. Quite strangely, Leah suddenly noticed that the water inside the pond and the fish that Mindstone had scooped out of it were actually the same color which instantly intrigued her as she began to consider for a moment how Mindstone had managed to spot the golden fish in the first place because she hadn't even noticed any golden colored fish inside the pond. The fact that Mindstone had noticed the golden fish however, silently confirmed to Leah that Mindstone's eyesight with his visual aid in place was now razor sharp but due to his visual aid, she couldn't really be certain that this characteristic was something actually common to his species in general.

"Which tunnel should I go through now Mindstone?" Leah asked again as she attempted to steer their conversation away from the consumption of raw fish and focus it once more upon her actual adventure.

"Yes, let me direct you so that you can proceed." Mindstone replied.

"Well, it's been lovely to meet you Mindstone and although I've never actually met a mudmarsh before, it's been an absolute pleasure." Leah mentioned as she quickly rose to her feet.

"I've never met a human being before, so it's been a first for us both and I must say Leah, it's been a very pleasant experience for me too." Mindstone acknowledged. "Right, in order to proceed, you have to go this way." He instructed as he began to walk towards a tree situated at the edge of the clearing.

Once Mindstone arrived next to the tree, Leah watched as he leant upon the actual tree trunk and then the whole tree started to slide backwards and to one side and as he did so, a kind of passageway appeared in the gap that it left behind as Leah's means of exit was swiftly revealed. For a few seconds before Leah even attempted to depart, she quietly reflected upon how polite Mindstone seemed to be and she wondered for a moment how Zidane would feel, if one day she returned from Spectrum with a mudmarsh in tow that could speak in a human tongue and then suggested that the creature should live inside their back garden.

The couple didn't actually have any animals at home and had never even once discussed the accommodation of a pet before but if Leah ever wanted to share her living space with any kind of animal, a mudmarsh in her opinion, would definitely be the kind of animalistic companion that she would welcome, enjoy and appreciate because Mindstone seemed, absolutely delightful. However, as far as Leah was now concerned, Mindstone so closely resembled an actual human being in terms of his nature that he could hardly be regarded as a pet and so, if Leah brought Mindstone home one day, she definitely felt that the couple would probably have to build him a small guest house of some sort in the back garden to reside in and have to consider him an actual guest.

Suddenly, it was as if a blanket of sadness had fallen across Leah's form as she glanced at her exit point once again that she could now clearly see and then began to walk towards it. Once Leah arrived beside Mindstone and next to the entrance to what looked like a narrow dirt path that led into an underground tunnel, she paused for a moment and as Leah turned to face him, she prepared to bid Mindstone a sad and solitary farewell. The next part of Leah's adventure inside the Marshland Underground Tunnels definitely awaited her but Leah felt slightly saddened by the fact that Mindstone would not be any part of that adventure and that she now had to leave him behind because he really was such a polite and pleasant chap and so, she had definitely started to become accustomed to his presence.

"Well Mindstone, until we meet again." Leah said as she smiled and then stretched her hand out towards him.

"Yes, oh and I almost forgot to mention Leah, if you assist my mudmarsh friends and you fulfill their requests successfully, some of them will actually give you gifts." Mindstone replied as he smiled and then gently shook her hand.

"Right, gifts are good. I'll try my best to be as helpful as I can." Leah immediately reassured him before she turned to face the quite narrow passageway and then prepared to exit.

Two tightly knitted rows of trees lined the narrow dirt path which restricted any possible deviation from the path itself, Leah observed as she left Mindstone's side and then began to walk along it and so there wasn't much of a chance that she could get lost en-route to the next Mudmarsh. Approximately thirty meters along the dirt path, it dipped below the ground where it continued in the form of a earthy tunnel and then about fifty meters or so along that earthy tunnel, Leah discovered that the nature of the tunnel changed as it tapered and dove much further down into the depths of the ground. Apparently, it had rapidly transpired and as Leah had quite swiftly discovered, her crawl through small underground tunnels and earthy subterranean spaces that day was far from over and had probably really, only just begun as Leah immediately surrendered to the reduction in size and ended up on her hands and knees once again.

Hopefully, Leah wished as she began to crawl along the earthy tunnel, the rest of Mindstone's species and especially those that she was due to meet that day would be as polite and respectful as Mindstone himself had been because she had truly felt extremely comfortable in his presence, despite his slightly animalistic tendencies. A hopeful wish now resided in Leah's heart and mind as she crawled towards and sought out the first mudmarsh that she was supposed to assist that the tasks that she would be asked to perform that day would not involve anymore underground tunnels because the lengthy crawls through the dirt just to arrive at their current locations, would certainly be more than enough crawls for one day as far as Leah was concerned.

Sadly by now, Leah observed as she suddenly paused for a moment, turned and then inspected the earthy tunnel behind her,

Mindstone the polite mudmarsh, the peaceful clearing that he resided in and the beautiful golden pond had all completely vanished from Leah's sight and nothing but earthy tunnel walls were all that could be seen. Unfortunately, all that now surrounded Leah in every direction that she faced and could possibly look at was an earthy tunnel wall and so in order to amuse herself as Leah resumed her crawl, she began to consider for a moment what it might actually be like if mudmarshes existed in the real world and not just inside Spectrum because Mindstone had totally fascinated her.

Irrespective of Leah's fascination however, as she started to consider that actual possibility she fully appreciated the very human reality and that if an animalistic species that possessed real intelligence like the mudmarshes existed upon the face of the human planet, they would probably be completely wiped out in no time at all. Since mudmarshes could communicate, reason and verbally express themselves in a human tongue, they would probably pose a tremendous threat to humanity's dominance of the planet and so for such creatures to exist on the surface of the Earth, would probably not be in that species long term interests as Leah was already, fully aware. Such creatures would defy the current laws of both science and nature and any logical characteristics that they displayed, would surely be perceived as a threat to humanity and so, human beings would only slaughter them and ruin their existence and Leah totally understood that very sad, human reality.

The creatures that Leah had created inside Spectrum purely for human amusement as she already knew, could never possibly exist or live inside the real human world because they would not survive. Each species would be hunted down and then sold for profit until they were either endangered, extinct or all caged up and some would perhaps be utilized as a form of entertainment whilst others would perhaps, be hunted down, roasted and then eaten for dinner. Human beings as Leah was already aware, weren't always kind to other species and especially not towards those that they deemed less capable or less human than they were and so mudmarshes on the face of the human planet would all in likelihood, be extinct within a decade.

Inside Spectrum Leah had created well over a thousand animal species and although some of those species were very much like the animals in the real world in that they did not have the ability to communicate in a human tongue and even reflected some aspects of their physical forms in various ways, at least one third were hybrids and about a third of those hybrids, like the mudmarshes, were what Leah referred to as hybrid differentiations. Hybrid differentiations were instances where two species had not only been mixed together but each hybrid differentiation also possessed some characteristics of another species beside the two and although most had been given animalistic characteristics, some species within that group had actually been given a few human characteristics and so some of the hybrid differentiations were really quite special and some even what one might consider, slightly peculiar.

Since as Leah already knew, human reality could really be quite dull at times in that only human beings could communicate with each other which limited the human existence to some extent, Leah had decided to give some creatures inside Spectrum enhanced capabilities that would allow them to communicate with human life forms. In some ways, through Leah's creation of Spectrum and the creatures inside it, Leah felt as if she would perhaps challenge the human world with her hybrid creations to consider what life might actually be like, if such creatures really existed upon the face of the very human Earth because that possibility had always intrigued her.

"Perhaps it is safer this way and perhaps my hybrid creations that can speak in a human tongue are safer inside Spectrum." Leah finally concluded and verbally acknowledged as she continued her crawl along the tunnel. "They just wouldn't be safe in the real human world."

If another species could communicate with others of their kind and understand human beings, Leah thoughtfully considered as she suddenly spotted a dot of light directly in front of her and then began to crawl more quickly towards it, they would probably plot to overthrow mankind, have an actual revolution and then end humanity's reign over the planet as soon as they possibly could. Humanity as Leah already knew, weren't always gracious or even very tolerant towards the planet's other occupants because the Earth was very much seen by human eyes as a human domain and as humanity's own to do with as they wished to and that was it seemed, absolutely non-negotiable. The human assumption of Earth's human ownership meant that other species were generally perceived as and deemed to be secondary to human agendas, human objectives and human lifestyles and as far as Leah was concerned that was by now, a very well established, unspoken term of humanity's earthly existence and humanity's planetary occupation but at times, she often wondered what the world might be like if that human assumption had been successfully challenged.

Approximately three hundred meters after Leah's crawl had begun, despite all her internal deliberations regarding her hybrid creations, the earthy tunnel finally came to an end and as Leah crawled out into the second clearing, much to her absolute delight, she found another mudmarsh situated inside it just as Mindstone had mentioned. In the second instance and inside the second clearing however, the mudmarsh in question that greeted Leah with a warm smile and friendly manner appeared to be a female member of the mudmarsh species that had a furry pouch on her stomach who quickly introduced herself as Divine and so Leah politely introduced herself too as she prepared to cooperate with Divine's request.

After just a couple of minutes and once a few more pleasantries had been exchanged, a polite request for assistance was made by Divine that revolved around the construction of a stick and log lodge home that she wished to build next to a second golden pond situated in the center of the clearing because according to Divine that is where she wished to reside. Once Leah had agreed to assist and the two had agreed upon what exactly the task ahead entailed, they then both set to work and somehow, much to Leah's surprise, the two actually managed to build the lodge home within thirty minutes which absolutely astonished Leah because initially, she had felt and estimated that it would have taken their artificial forms slightly longer.

Rather satisfyingly for Leah, the end results of their combined efforts seemed to please Divine immensely as she watched Divine pop in and out of her newly constructed lodge several times with a huge smile upon her face as Divine inspected its interior and its exterior in utter delight. A curiosity suddenly began to form, wander across Leah's mind and then linger however, as she waited for Divine's inspection to end as she silently speculated as to whether or not she would be given a gift for her assistance like Mindstone had mentioned and what kind of form that gift might take because Leah could currently see nothing inside the clearing that she felt might satisfy that criteria.

Suddenly, just a few minutes after Divine's inspection had started, Leah noticed that it rather abruptly ended as Divine turned to face a small stone furnace that was situated just a couple of meters away from the newly built lodge and then began to walk towards it. For the next couple of minutes Leah continued to just watch and wait in silence as Divine arrived next to the stone structure and then picked up a clay bowl which sat on top of it.

Once the small clay bowl was situated securely in one of Divine's hand like paws, Leah noticed that Divine then began to walk towards the golden pond and that when she arrived beside it, the clay bowl was quickly dipped into the golden water and filled just before she returned to the furnace. When Divine arrived next to the furnace once more, this time Divine actually opened the stone structure up and as Leah kept her eyes firmly fixed upon Divine, she noticed that Divine then collected a small, clay tray from interior of the stone structure which appeared to be some kind of mould. The golden liquid inside the clay bowl sparkled, glistened and shone, Leah observed as it was swiftly poured from the bowl into the mould tray by Divine after which point, the filled clay tray was then rapidly placed inside the stone furnace and from what Leah could see, it appeared as if Divine wanted to make something with the clay mould, the golden water and the stone furnace.

For the next few minutes, once Divine had returned to Leah's side, Leah listened politely and attentively as Divine chattered cheerfully away as she discussed the various small rooms inside her newly built home and what items of furniture she would like to seek out, create and make from the nearby trees and then place inside it. A few cheerful nods were given at regular intervals as Leah listened to Divine's excited chitter chatter until just a few minutes later, a very loud crackle suddenly interrupted Divine mid-flow and as Leah continued to listen and watch, Divine immediately fell silent and then turned to face the furnace after which point, she politely excused herself.

Upon Leah's face there was a curious but amused smile as she watched Divine return to the small stone structure, open the furnace up and then retrieve the clay mould from its interior. Once the clay mould had been removed from the furnace, Leah noticed that Divine then quickly placed it on the top of the stone structure and just a few seconds later, much to Leah's surprise and delight, a pretty, golden, jeweled bracelet that sparkled and shone was plucked from the clay mould. A huge smile crossed Divine's face as Leah waited for her return and Leah noticed that Divine still clasped the with the beautiful bracelet inside her hand like paw as she walked back towards Leah which silently answered her unspoken question because it implied that the bracelet would perhaps be one of the gifts that Mindstone had referred to.

"This is a token of my appreciation and my gratitude Leah." Divine explained with a grateful smile as she handed her the bracelet. "You can keep this inside your treasure chest and whenever you want to, you can wear it upon your wrist."

"Thank you Divine, it's very pretty." Leah replied as she immediately attached the small piece of decorative jewelry to one of her wrists in order to illustrate her appreciation. "It's absolutely stunning and very unusual."

Although the bracelet certainly wasn't like some of the luxurious, diamond embedded affairs that one usually found on display inside the jewelry shops in the heart of Leah's city, she definitely felt that it was very unique and it was certainly, delightfully pleasant to look at. Some rays of sunlight seeped into the clearing from the sky directly above Leah's head and as each ray bounced playfully of the bracelet's jeweled surfaces, Leah held her wrist up and then began to visually admire and inspect the pretty bracelet slightly more closely as she noticed that every ray seemed to make it sparkle and shine even more brightly.

Just a few minutes later and once the two had exchanged a few more pleasantries, Divine then politely escorted Leah towards a nearby tree which it rapidly transpired, currently concealed Leah's exit point from that particular clearing behind its mahogany trunk. Much like Mindstone had done in the first clearing and instance, the second tree was then swiftly moved aside by Divine in a similar manner as Leah watched and waited for her exit point to be revealed. The entrance to a second tree lined dirt path swiftly appeared and quickly opened up just a few seconds later which Leah could see led directly into another underground tunnel and so once Leah's exit had been fully exposed, she immediately prepared to leave the second clearing behind as she bade farewell to Divine and then stepped onto the narrow dirt path.

Quite sadly, Leah left the second bright clearing behind that housed the very amicable and exceedingly pleasant Divine behind as she began to walk along the second narrow dirt path which led directly into another underground tunnel. Once inside the underground tunnel, Divine and the second clearing quickly disappeared from Leah's sight and could no longer even be seen with a backward glance but as Leah resumed and continued her journey through the Marshlands Underground Tunnels once again, she made her way optimistically towards the third mudmarsh as she admired the bracelet upon her wrist and speculated as to what her next challenge might actually be. Upon Leah's face there was a satisfied smile as she went as Leah delighted and rejoiced in her day so far which had been extremely pleasant and deliciously peaceful, except for the earthy tunnel crawls of course but somehow, despite their uncomfortable nature, even those hadn't yet managed to detract from Leah's overall enjoyment.

For the remainder of Leah's afternoon that day, she continued to eagerly assist the exceedingly polite mudmarshes, all of whom seemed to be very appreciative of her efforts and so much so that Leah even managed to collect several more gifts as she ventured through the Marshland Underground Tunnels and went along her way. Once a few very pleasant hours had slipped by since Leah's initial entrance into the Mudmarshes' Tunnels and once Leah had assisted at least another five mudmarshes, she finally found herself at the exit to the Marshland Underground and as she prepared to leave the mudmarshes and their cute, pleasant, peaceful underground world behind, she smiled a sad but very satisfied smile.

Everything about the mudmarshes had totally delighted Leah from their witty, intelligent conversations to their deft reactions and they seemed to possess an excellent blend of animalistic instincts and slightly human characteristics. In fact, as far as Leah was concerned that delightful combination had truly intrigued her because it had been impulsive but fun, sophisticated but relatable and overall, extremely comfortable for her to spend a large part of her afternoon with. Rather intriguingly, although Leah had noticed that the mudmarshes could be deft and swift like predatory animals and that they were at times, driven by natural animalistic impulses somehow simultaneously, they were also intelligent, mature and even what one might consider dignified like decent human beings and so she had found that their unique mixture of characteristics had provided her with an afternoon of very pleasant companionship. Quite surprisingly, Leah had also discovered that all the mudmarshes she had met seemed to possess excellent manners and the complexity of their makeup that she had now experienced in person had not only surprised her but also captivated and truly thrilled her because it really was so very unique.

Much to Leah's total delight, her afternoon had gone by very peacefully and extremely pleasantly indeed and so she actually felt quite sad when she stepped through a door at the end of the final tunnel that led her back out onto the ledge inside the ark. However, since Leah's emotional journey was not due to end just yet because she had not yet spent more than four hours inside Spectrum that day, Leah began to silently prepare to select another path and another door as she bid a final silent farewell to the mudmarshes and their tranquil underground world.

A Surprise Flight on the Wings of Intrigue

A quick glance was cast towards some of the other paths as Leah began to thoughtfully consider her next choice because although technically, she could actually return to the Marshland Underground Tunnels if she wished to, Leah really wanted to experience another adventure that day and so she wanted to follow another path. Due to the crawls through the mud tunnels that Leah now felt anxious to avoid, she kept her mind solely focused upon the tunnels that led in an upward direction as her silent deliberations continued in the hope that one of those paths might render a slightly more favorable outcome and less time spent on her hands and knees.

After just a few minutes of further consideration, Leah finally picked out a path from the multitude of options and then enthusiastically stepped onto it but unlike Leah's first choice, the second path actually led upwards and towards the very top of the ark's internal structure. For the next few minutes Leah rushed cheerfully along the second path as she headed towards a shiny, white door that she could clearly see situated at the other end of it and when she arrived in front of the door, Leah rapidly discovered that much like the first door that she had approached, another puzzle lock had to be solved before it would actually open.

Just a few minutes were spent in thoughtful silence in front of the second locked door as Leah attempted to figure out the puzzle lock and then enthusiastically began to tackle it so that she could embark upon her second adventure. Much to Leah's total delight, just a few minutes later and once the puzzle lock had been solved the second door automatically swung open and some rays of sky blue light instantly flooded through the open door and as Leah eagerly stepped through it, she noticed that she was rapidly, totally engulfed and drenched by the rays of light which quickly saturated her entire frame.

Once the rays of blue light evaporated, just a few seconds later as Leah emerged from the doorway, she suddenly found herself in the middle of a large, green, grassy enclosure of some kind that had some small tree trunk poles scattered sporadically across it which initially appeared to be randomly dispersed. A bed of plush green grass decorated the interior of the enclosure which Leah instantly noticed cushioned her feet as she began to walk across it and as Leah started to survey the rest of her surroundings, she also noticed that some small gate like structures littered the green enclosure in a similar manner to the tree trunk poles.

Upon further inspection Leah began to conclude that the small gate structures and tree trunk poles appeared to be in some kind of formation since each one appeared at quite regular intervals around the enclosure though what exactly the structures would be utilized for, Leah still remained unsure. In some ways, the gate like structures and tree like poles seemed to form some kind of pattern and overall, their appearance reminded Leah a bit of a show jumping course that had been designed for horses but as she glanced around the expanse and visually scanned her surroundings, she couldn't see any horses situated anywhere nearby.

At one end of the enclosure there appeared to be a large, fixed structure that looked to Leah like some kind of barn and as she stared at it and then began to visually inspect it, she silently considered whether or not she should approach it to see what it contained and if it contained anything at all. The structure itself was black and white and it had a glossy, modern finish to it, much like some of the other structures that Leah had already seen inside Spectrum and much like the exterior of the ark and although it wasn't a palace or a human home of any kind it still had an elegant and sophisticated feel to it.

"Now that's the best looking barn I've ever seen." Leah whispered as she smiled.

Suddenly however, before Leah could even start to make her way towards the structure, a tall, handsome, dark haired man appeared from the rear of the barn like building and then began to walk briskly towards her. A hand was politely extended towards Leah as the extremely attractive man drew much closer to her form and she could clearly see that his face carried a huge smile upon it which seemed friendly, warm and even what one might consider, slightly seductive.

“Hi I'm Toran and I'll be your guide today.” He explained. "This is the Mountaflump Stables where I train and look after mountaflumps and I also raise some dragbirds, so I'm a tour guide for the Dragbird Sky Tours."

Upon Leah's face there was a joyful smile as she listened to Toran speak and a wave of instant appreciation seemed to flow across her form as she admired his deep husky voice and as he released each word, every single one seemed to float gently through the air and then softly caress her ears. A very attractive male guide had suddenly presented himself to Leah and so as she began to accept his presence, she quickly embarked upon an expression of mutual reciprocation and responded to his warm, friendly gesture as she stretched out her hand towards him and then shook his hand.

Inside Leah's form and thoughts there now lived a very hopeful wish that her final experience that day would be with Toran and that their companionship, albeit an artificial simulation of companionship, would last for the remainder of her emotional journey because his masculine presence seemed to absolutely ooze with charm and looked totally delicious. Although Leah had listened to Toran speak and now partially understood why he was there, in some ways that purpose didn't seem to matter much in the larger scheme of things and in Leah's sight because he was just simply there and simply, extremely fine.

For the very first time inside Spectrum, it suddenly dawned upon Leah that she would now experience part of her emotional journey alongside a masculine human form that represented exceptional eye candy and that element of sensual anticipation hugely excited her. The remainder of Leah's time spent inside that particular plane that day, now held the actual possibility of what could and might be explored between the two and that potential passionate, sensual excitement had stirred Leah more than anything else that she had encountered inside Spectrum so far. A delicious, seductive possibility now lay at the tip of Leah's fingertips and so, she felt utterly determined to appreciate, savor, enjoy and explore that possibility that seemed to naturally accompany her current environment and naturally stir up sensual ripples of excitement inside her being.

Not even a word had been uttered yet in response by Leah but deep down inside, she almost felt as if an opera of romance had begun to play as a warm, sensual sensation that tingled, lingered just below the surface of her skin which immediately confirmed to Leah that she was definitely, deeply attracted to the handsome male guide that now stood directly in front of her. A powerful pulse of passion had suddenly gripped Leah's being that seemed to cause her heart to race and her form to tingle all over with sensual excitement as a surge of electric romantic attraction rushed through every ounce of her existence as she glanced at Toran's face and then smiled.

"Hi Toran, it's nice to meet you, I'm Leah." Leah finally replied in an almost breathless, hushed tone as she began to break the few seconds of seductive silence that had gathered between the two. "What are mountaflumps?" She asked. "And what do you do exactly with dragbirds?"

Every part of Leah's being now felt extremely curious about Toran's presence and since she was possibly just about to spend the remainder of her time inside Spectrum that day with him, she wanted to know everything about him that she possibly could. Rather strangely for Leah however, the attraction that she currently felt, suddenly began to raise a few questions inside her mind despite the fact that it was extremely pleasurable because it prompted her to question whether or not her natural reaction was somehow a betrayal of her feelings for Zidane. For the first time ever, since Leah had entered into an environment inside Spectrum, she actually felt attracted to and aroused by one of her own fictitious creations and by another male presence and that hadn't actually happened to her since she had been in a relationship with Zidane and so, she had just stepped into very unfamiliar, sensual territory and though it excited her, it also felt simultaneously, quite strange.

Some internal whispers of uncertainty suddenly began to tease Leah's mind and run rampant through her thoughts as she silently deliberated for a few more seconds about how such sensual urges could even be remotely possible inside Spectrum but there seemed to be no logical explanation as to why Leah currently felt the way she did. In many ways, Leah had actually lived quite sheltered life for the past three years since she had spent most of her time inside her basement laboratory but she began to wonder for a moment, if perhaps that lack of exposure to the outside world and the men that resided within it had somehow made her more vulnerable to such passionate desires and such sensual urges.

For the past three years the reality was that Leah had hardly even spent a moment with another man besides Zidane, due to the fact that she spent most of her life inside the couple's home and so, Leah began to conclude that somehow that solitude had now begun to take its toll. On the occasions that Leah had ventured outside the couple's home for occasional shopping trips, she would at times interact with store owners and cashiers but most of those people were either female, over sixty years old or below twenty five and so they fell well outside Leah's romantic age bracket and so she thoughtfully considered if perhaps that lack of exposure to other men had made her more sensitive and susceptible, especially when it came to the issue of attractive men. The presence of an attractive male stranger had now it appeared, somehow aroused Leah and that male stranger wasn't even real but was merely a fictitious male creation that she herself had created and that attraction slightly confused her for a moment as she glanced at Toran's face.

"Well Leah, I train and raise both mountaflumps and dragbirds and then once they're ready and fully trained, I take them to the market and sell them." Toran explained.

"What on earth are mountaflumps?" Leah asked again. "I've never seen one before."

"Come with me and I'll show you." Toran invited as he pointed towards the stables at the other end of the green enclosure. "There are some mountaflumps in the stalls inside the stables."

"Okay, sure." Leah replied with a nod.

Some ripples of sensual excitement seemed to flow through Leah's form as she began to follow Toran very willingly and allowed him to lead her towards the stables and as the two neared the entrance of the building, Leah smiled a satisfied smile as she accepted that whilst Toran wasn't a real life, physical Zidane, he was certainly a very handsome, fictitious male companion. Once the two entered into the stables which it rapidly transpired housed three animals that were tied up individually in one of five stalls that lined one side of the structure, Leah watched in silence as Toran quickly approached one of the occupied stalls and the three creatures inside each stall immediately looked up as if they had noticed the sudden entrance and presence of the two human forms.

The three majestic creatures that the stables housed from what Leah could see at first glance, were definitely not horses and could perhaps belong to the Hybrid Differentiation Group, the Mythological Creatures Group or the Hybrid Mythological Creatures Group that she had created inside Spectrum. Although the three animals had a similar appearance, their appearance was also very unique in comparison to other animals and so Leah felt slightly confused as she stared at them because she didn't remember their initial creation at all. Some very dark hair adorned each of the creatures slim frames and the skin of the mountaflumps, Leah immediately noticed, was slightly shiny and a deep charcoal black and whilst they looked quite light in terms of their weight in comparison to other creatures of their height, they actually had five legs instead of four which rapidly clarified that they were not horses or even close relatives of horses because their appearance differed so vastly.

Unlike the hooves of horses, mountaflumps it appeared had soft feet that seemed to possess the capability to grip onto surfaces and objects and their toes almost looked like claws, Leah observed as she silently admired their forms and began to inspect their physical structure slightly more closely. Situated at the end of each of the mountaflumps long, giraffe like necks were large, round, silver, moon like faces and their mouths were thin, long and narrow and as each one stuck out in front of their faces, they reminded Leah somewhat of an aardvark. Rather intriguingly, Leah noticed that the lips and mouths of the mountaflumps looked a bit like a narrow funnel and seemed to form some kind siphon as she watched one of them suck up some water through its mouth like it was a straw from a water bucket on the ground directly in front of its soft feet.

Although three of the stalls were currently occupied by mountaflumps, the other two stalls that lined one side of the stables, Leah thoughtfully observed, were completely empty and vacant which indicated that perhaps Toran had recently trained and sold a couple of mountaflumps and that he had not yet replaced the absent creatures. Not a word was spoken by Leah however, despite her many questions as she watched Toran enter into a stall and then come to a standstill beside one of the mountaflumps heads after which point, he turned to face Leah and then politely began to introduce the animals that he was responsible for.

"These Leah are mountaflumps." Toran explained as he stood next to the creature's head and then started to gently stroked its neck. "I only have three at the moment because I sold two just yesterday. Do you fancy a ride?" He asked playfully as he grinned. "You can ride one if you like and fortunately for us both, they aren't out in the paddock today, so I won't need to catch them first which can be another task in itself."

Leah nodded her head enthusiastically. "Sure Toran, I'll give it a try." She replied.

Attached to the rear wall of the occupied stall that Toran currently stood in, Leah noticed that there was a shelf upon which there appeared to be a silver saddle and a silver bridle hung from a large hook directly underneath it and as Leah watched Toran, he began to make his way towards both items. When Toran arrived next to the shelf and the hook, he then quickly picked up the saddle and put it over one of his arms before he plucked the bridle from the hook which he then rapidly hung upon his shoulder after which point, he returned to the mountaflump's side.

Just a few seconds later Toran began to stroke the creature's neck in a gentle manner before he proceeded to tack the mountaflump up so that it could be mounted and ridden and as Leah waited quietly, she began to wonder what it would actually be like to ride one of the creatures because they seemed to be a bit on the tallish side. Since the creatures were much taller than any of the horses that Leah had ever seen in real life, she definitely appreciated the fact that in this instance, there would at least be an actual saddle to sit in because she couldn't even begin to imagine how such large creatures could be successfully mounted or ridden comfortably without one.

"Mountaflumps can be a real handful at times and sometimes, they are even quite stubborn and uncooperative, so you have to approach them carefully." Toran advised as he gently placed the saddle down upon the creature's back. "They have a very playful streak inherent in their nature that can be very unpredictable, so you have to handle them with care."

"Why do they have five legs?" Leah asked.

"Well, mountaflumps usually carry riders over very rocky terrain and so their additional leg allows them to alternate their active four legs so that they can rest one at any time during a journey which can be really quite useful at times because it means that they tire less easily on long journeys." Toran explained. "But that fifth leg is also why they can be a nightmare to catch because they rarely get tired when they are not being ridden and when they run around freely, they can be extremely fast."

"Why are their feet like claws?" Leah enquired.

"Their soft feet allow them to grip onto the rocks and enable them to tackle rocky mountain surfaces more easily which they are actually well accustomed to because the mountains are their natural habitat and so the mountain areas are where you can usually find them, when they live out in the wild." Toran replied as he began to attach the silver bridle to the mountaflump's head. "They're called mountaflumps because people usually ride them when they wish to venture over mountainous terrain since they are very resilient and extremely flexible."

"Are they very hard to control?" Leah asked.

"Sometimes." Toran replied as he smiled. "But once you actually catch them and then mount them, they tend to settle down and of course, I'll be around to assist you, so it should be much easier for you."

Despite all Toran's explanations and the presence of the three mountaflumps inside the stalls, Leah still couldn't remember the actual creation of mountaflumps during her original creation of all the species groups inside Spectrum and that puzzled her slightly. However, as Leah prepared to embark upon her very first ever mountaflump ride, she silently pushed her curious questions and puzzled thoughts to one side as she prepared to just live in the moment and to enjoy it because as she already knew, her time that day inside Spectrum was limited and so, she wanted to make the most of her time with Toran and the sensual sensations that he seemed to arouse within her.

In what seemed like no time at all Toran had actually tacked the creature up and as Leah watched, he suddenly began to untie the rope that bound the mountaflump to the wall of the stall and then began to lead the creature out of its home. Inside Leah's form as she began to follow Toran out of the stables, a chaotic stream of nerves suddenly seemed to leap and somersault around in the depths of her stomach because Leah felt very unsure that she would actually be able to handle the very tall creature that she was now just about to mount and ride.

Quite unexpectedly, when the two arrived at the top of the grassy green enclosure once more which Leah had automatically assumed would be the location of her lesson, Toran suddenly began to lead the mountaflump towards the rear of the stables and so Leah immediately followed him obediently as she accompanied him in fascinated silence. Directly behind the stables there was a small fenced off paddock and as Toran steered the mountaflump towards it, Leah quickly followed them both and as they neared the entrance to the paddock, she noticed that the second enclosure differed vastly from the grassy green enclosure due to its wood chippings floor. A wooden pole fence which appeared to be made from small tree trunks surrounded the paddock, Leah observed, which was shoulder high and there was a small gate situated at one end of the fence that Toran walked towards and as Leah continued to follow him, Toran lead both Leah and the mountaflump directly towards the gate and then opened it up.

Once inside the paddock, Toran rapidly came to a total standstill and as he turned to face Leah and then smiled, she prepared to embark upon her first mountaflump ride as nerves continued to rattle around inside her stomach. Much to Leah's total relief however, at least in this instance there was an actual saddle present and that provision provided her with a small glimmer of comfort as she glanced at it and then began to prepare herself to mount the mountaflump's back.

"Do you think you'll be able to mount the mountaflump on your own Leah?" Toran asked. "Or do you need a hand?"

"I'm not sure but I'll give it a try." Leah replied optimistically.

Toran nodded. "Okay, give it a try and if you have any problems then I'll assist you." He offered.

Leah nodded.

From the saddle that had been attached to the mountaflump's back, Leah rapidly observed that two metal, shiny stirrups hung down on either side of the creature's frame which were definitely reachable and accessible to her hands and feet and so she began to approach the saddle quite enthusiastically and very hopefully as she embarked on her first attempt to mount the mountaflump. When Leah felt that she was as close to mountaflumps back as she could possibly be, she then held on to one of the stirrups and tried to slip her foot inside the metal foothold but unfortunately, her efforts were not well rewarded and were in fact, a total disaster. The second that Leah actually tried to utilize the stirrup as leverage in order to mount the mountaflump's back, much to Leah's frustration, her foot rapidly slipped straight back out of the metal foothold and she immediately fell backwards and then landed upon the wood chippings on her rear with a gentle bump.

"Perhaps I will need a hand Toran." Leah swiftly acknowledged as she glanced up at his face and then gently shook her head. "It's slightly trickier than I thought it would be."

Toran smiled. "Don't worry about it Leah that happens all the time, mountaflumps are actually quite awkward creatures to mount due to their height and build." He immediately reassured her.

A steady hand was rapidly placed upon the reins of the bridle as Leah watched Toran stabilize the creature and hold the animal in a stationary position just before he began to walk along the mountaflump's side towards Leah's current position. Once Toran was in very close proximity to Leah, he then politely offered her a hand which she gratefully, immediately accepted and as he began to pull her to her feet, she smiled due to his masculine presence and the almost electric surge of attraction that she instantly felt run through her form.

Suddenly and quite delightfully for Leah, just as she stood back up, Toran's form and her own form became much closer and as their faces almost touched, Leah inhaled and then released an excited gasp as her body began to immediately respond to their close physical proximity and tingled even more with passionate excitement. Although Leah couldn't really, fully understand why her form seemed to respond in such an electrifying manner whenever Toran was actually in close proximity to her, the sensation itself seemed to be an immensely pleasant one and not a sensation that Leah wanted to reject, or that she wanted to end but it did provoke some deeper questions inside her mind with regards to why she actually felt that way.

All around the two there was nothing but a seductive silence for a brief moment as everything around Leah suddenly seemed to freeze and the internal passion that she felt, somehow seemed to transport her to another place and that delicious, fictitious place within another fictitious place, was somehow situated inside Toran's masculine arms. Just a few seconds later however, Leah rapidly began to shake herself out of her paralysis as she silently reminded herself that she was actually supposed to mount the mountaflump directly in front of them both and that she was actually due to have an actual riding lesson.

The creature, despite all Leah's delays and her hesitation, continued to wait silently directly in front of Leah but as she drew closer to the mountaflump's back in order to try and mount the creature again, Toran's form pressed gently against her own which instantly made Leah's heart start to race and flutter with excitement and so, she paused and hesitated once again. A vacant saddle now sat directly in front of Leah's face that waited to be occupied but for a few seconds, she seemed to lose her breath as a sensual, passionate surge which overpowered her senses flowed chaotically through her form as Toran's warm breath, caressed her cheek gently from behind. Some more random even more hectic surges of passion suddenly seemed to swirl around inside Leah almost like a storm as the chaos of attraction and a whirlwind of desire fully gripped every part of her form as she silently accepted that a frantic undercurrent of passion had now, very unexpectedly, totally and utterly conquered her being and that this particular storm of passion had almost rendered her completely breathless.

Despite that fact that Leah had become very caught up in the moment between the two however, an unexpected grunt from the mountaflump directly in front of her, suddenly politely interrupted that passionate flow and so Leah began to smile as she thoughtfully accepted that the creature had now, quite possibly, become bored of being ignored. For a few more brief seconds however, Leah continued to stall as she began to quietly consider whether or not she should actually attempt to mount the creature at all, or whether she should just succumb to her sensual desires and her attraction to Toran and attempt to quench those passionate urges instead because a very strong undercurrent of desire continued to silently tantalize Leah's thoughts. Just a second or two later however, Leah's thoughts were suddenly interrupted as Toran began to speak to her in a soft, deep, husky voice and as Leah listened to him speak, her form continued to tingle with excitement as his voice added even more passion to the romantic, sensual flames of desire that leapt around inside of her.

“Once you've had a mountaflump riding lesson Leah, if you'd like to, we can then go for a ride on a dragbird and I can show you around the Hilltops of Hope?" Toran offered. "And we could even go for a walk down by the River of Expectations.”

"Sure that would be absolutely lovely Toran." Leah gushed as she eagerly, immediately accepted his suggestions which sounded as if each one possessed heaps of romantic potential which fully aligned with her own thoughts that were certainly hopeful that some sensual expectations would perhaps be fulfilled between the two at some point later that day.

Something had definitely stirred deep down inside Leah and so now, she felt extremely tempted to explore that sensual sensation much further with Toran and that exploration definitely wouldn't be about the terrain, the scenery, the hilltops or even the river. Irrespective of what potential enjoyment the rest of Leah's day might hold in its seconds, minutes and hours however, she quickly attempted to focus her mind once more upon the task at hand and make a second attempt to actually, finally mount the mountaflump directly in front of her who had by now waited patiently for more than just a few minutes. Rather intriguingly and very distractingly for Leah, a handsome stranger had now crossed her path quite suddenly, albeit a fictitious male stranger and as a result, Leah's concentration had definitely lapsed as he had stepped into her life, albeit in a fantasy, artificial capacity and as a result, she had now become distracted from her main objectives and her form had somehow, become totally engulfed and consumed by the intense physical attraction that she currently felt towards him.

Usually, in real life and in the real world, Leah managed to ignore and control any passionate desires and sensual attractions to other males very easily whenever they arose which was extremely rare, due to her minimal contact with the outside world and the very high levels of romantic satisfaction that Leah usually felt, experienced and fully enjoyed from her current romantic partnership but that day was definitely different. Something it seemed had shifted and changed inside Leah herself and that something definitely felt, very different and as she began to analyze that difference, Leah quietly began to consider for a moment that it could perhaps be related and attributed to the personality adjustments that she had made to her own personality earlier that day via the Spectrum system.

Perhaps, Leah considered thoughtfully, the personality adjustments that she herself had made that morning had placed her in a unique position where natural impulses and sexual passions had been more easily stirred within her and those passionate desires now seemed to be almost impossible to contain and quite difficult to control. Some sensual desires had definitely been invoked inside Leah's form, purely due to Toran's presence and those desires it seemed now required some kind of actual satisfaction because she felt a very deep hunger within and the flames of passion that now seemed to burn frantically deep inside her form, seemed to yearn to actually be extinguished.

Just a few seconds later Toran gently clasped onto one of Leah's thighs with one hand and then provided some additional support to her other leg with his other hand as he began to push Leah's form up onto the mountaflump's back and into the saddle. Once Leah was on top of the mountaflump's back, she quickly began to wriggle around as she attempted to maneuver herself into the correct position and a comfortable spot as she more fully occupied the saddle just before she started to straighten herself up. Upon Leah's face there was now a very appreciative smile as a few seconds later, she glanced down at Toran's face and then started to thank him appreciatively because at the very least, she was now in the correct position, although it hadn't been purely due to her own efforts which so far had rendered nothing productive for her and had just delivered a bump on the ground directly to her derriere.

"Thank you Toran." Leah said as she smiled. "I don't know what I would have done without your help."

In the real world and throughout the usual course of Leah's every day real life, she had very little contact with animals and so generally speaking, a ride upon an animal of any kind wasn't something that Leah usually participated in because the city of Rankford that the couple lived in wasn't abundantly populated with animals. Due to Leah's lack of experience it had certainly made her task slightly more complex that day but at the very least, Leah definitely felt appreciative of the fact that at least a guide had been provided to assist her in this instance and that had made the challenge a lot more fun and way more enjoyable for her to face, tackle and then eventually, actually overcome.

"You're very welcome Leah, just give me a nod when you're ready to proceed and then we'll begin." Toran replied.

Once Leah felt fully comfortable with her position and had given Toran a certain nod, he then began to lead the mountaflump forward towards the outer edge of the paddock's interior and as the mountaflump started to walk around the paddock, Toran remained close to the creature's head. The mountaflump riding lesson which lasted about an hour or so, was extremely thorough as Toran covered all the basics and taught Leah how to start and stop, how to walk, trot, canter and even how to jump over some little tree pole fences that were dotted around inside the paddock and Leah really enjoyed it because it was far more relaxed and much more controlled than the hectic hunt trip which had spun her through the woods at a very fast pace indeed.

Although the mountaflump was much larger than a horse in terms of height and far taller than the unicorn that Leah had ridden on her first visit to Spectrum, the creature's frame was much more slender than either which meant it could move slightly faster and so Leah noticed that it swiftly tackled the small pole fences with total ease. When Leah's riding lesson finally ended Toran politely offered to help Leah dismount, an offer which she immediately, gratefully accepted due to the size of the creature and once Leah was safely back on artificial, simulated firm ground once more, he began to lead the mountaflump back towards the stables.

After the mountaflump had been tied back up inside its stall and once the creature had been untacked and given a fresh bucket of water by Toran, he then immediately abandoned the stables completely as he started to lead Leah back outside. Some more activities had definitely been planned for Leah's participation that day by Toran and so as he walked, Leah listened to him as he began to verbally present to her the next activity that he had planned as he asked her to participate.

"Would you like to ride a dragbird now Leah?" Toran asked.

Leah nodded. "Sure Toran but are they actually big enough to ride?" She asked as she suddenly remembered how tiny Roto had been.

"Yes, they definitely are but only when they're fully grown adults." Toran explained. "I keep some adult dragbirds in the barn at the bottom of the paddock, so we can go there now if you like?"

"Sure, lead the way." Leah replied.

The two began to walk towards the rear of the stables once again as Toran led the way, only this time he walked around the exterior of the paddock and then towards the bottom of it as he guided Leah towards a barn like structure which apparently, contained some adult dragbirds. Once the two arrived in front of the huge barn, Toran quickly slid open the metal door and then the two stepped inside the structure and as they did so, they made some light conversation amongst themselves as the two discussed what exactly Toran's training of dragbirds actually entailed.

Inside the interior of the barn which Leah immediately noticed was extremely quiet, there appeared to be several stalls that looked quite similar to the ones inside the mountaflump stables but unlike the stalls in the stables, these stalls had no walls at either side and simply some small gutters that divided each one. The dragbirds that occupied each stall immediately intrigued Leah because she instantly noticed that they were much larger in size than Roto as she began to reflect upon how tiny Roto had been because essentially, Roto hadn't even been large enough for an actual human being to mount, never mind ride anywhere and Leah had even carried him around in the palm of her hand. However, the three adult dragbirds that Toran was responsible for that occupied and lived inside the barn, were far larger than any actual human being that Leah had ever seen and appeared to be almost the height of a small bungalow.

One of the three dragbirds, Leah rapidly observed, was a dark, orangish red and the creature suddenly stepped forward as it drew much closer to the edge of its stall and then cooed softly and as she watched, Toran quickly walked towards the dragbird, entered the stall and then began to gently stroke the creature's head. Once a few initial pleasantries had been exchanged between the two and Toran had greeted the dragbird affectionately and sufficiently, Leah continued to watch as he then left the stall and made his way towards the other side of the barn where Toran plucked a black harness down from a shelf attached to the wall as he prepared to tack the dragbird up.

Some small chunks of fish were quickly plucked from the interior of a nearby bucket just before Toran stepped back into the stall and he then began to feed the creature a few small morsels of food as the dragbird cooed in absolute delight. The black harness which looked to Leah like it was made from leather, was then slipped over the dragbird's head and attached to various parts of its body and as Toran attended to his task, he continued to feed the dragbird some more small chunks of fish. Once the harness was fully in place and had been attached correctly to the dragbird's frame, Leah watched in fascinated silence as Toran suddenly turned to face her and then nodded his head just before he began to lead the dragbird out of the stall as he prepared to exit the barn.

"Let's go outside now Leah." Toran suggested as he walked. "Clément is ready to be ridden now."

"How come these dragbirds are so large Toran?" Leah asked as she started to walk alongside him. "The dragbird I saw in the forest was absolutely tiny."

"Well Leah, dragbirds are usually tiny until they reach about five hundred years old which is when they become fully grown adults and then they suddenly, shoot up to their full height and that's when you can ride them." Toran explained as he exited the barn. "Not many dragbirds actually manage to reach five hundred years old though because usually, they're eaten by snakes."

"Yuck." Leah replied as she winced. "I hate snakes."

"Yes, snakes can really be a problem for dragbirds when they're small but when they are fully grown then dragbirds become a problem for snakes too. Snakes and dragbirds are a match made in hungry hatred." Toran joked as he smiled. "When dragbirds are young, snakes hunt them down and eat them but then when dragbirds become fully grown adults, they hunt snakes down and eat them, so that hungry hatred is mutually reciprocated, albeit in a delayed form on the part of the dragbirds.

Once the two had walked just a few meters away from the

entrance of the barn, Toran suddenly came to a complete standstill and then turned to face the dragbird which Leah immediately noticed now stood totally still right next to him as the creature waited obediently to be mounted. Unlike some of the other animals that Leah had seen inside Spectrum so far, the dragbird didn't pace around or appear to be restless in any way, she observed as it just waited in one spot and remained completely motionless and it almost felt to her as if it had been glued to the spot of ground that it stood upon.

In some respects, Leah actually felt a lot more worried about this potential ride than she had about the mountaflump ride that she had just experienced because this ride would actually involve a dragon like bird that would carry her high up in the air and across the actual sky. Some very serious implications accompanied those high heights and as Leah already knew, the potential ramifications of her sky ride could be far more severe than just a gentle bump on the ground which meant, there was a lot more to fear. Quite possibly, Leah could actually fall off the dragbird's back and if that happened whilst the Clément was high up in the sky that fall would certainly not be as gentle as her bump to the ground inside the paddock and that potential eventuality worried Leah as she glanced at the dragbird's face. The face of the dragbird however, from what Leah had seen so far, at least looked quite kind and amicable and the creature's patient demeanor, stillness and calm nature indicated that it would perhaps be a pleasant journey though there were no guarantees that she would not fall off the Clément's back mid-flight.

"I'm a little bit worried Toran that I might fall off mid-flight." Leah mentioned nervously.

"Don't worry Leah, since it's your first time, we'll ride Clément together." Toran reassured her.

Fortunately for Leah, the dragbird was rather large which meant, Clément could potentially carry both Toran and Leah's weight quite easily and so at the very least that was not a concern that Leah felt she had to worry about as she glanced at Clément, quickly assessed the dragbird's capabilities and then nodded her head in agreement. In terms of Clément's height, Leah had already noticed that the dragbird towered high above both their heads and that Clément seemed to be almost the height of a small bungalow and hence she felt the dragbird was definitely powerful enough to fly through the air with both of them seated upon its back. From either side of the creature's large frame which composed of a large oval shaped body, two muscular arm type legs and two longer chunky hindlegs protruded along with two large wings and the two wings looked extremely strong, physically powerful and very sturdy, Leah noticed as she visually inspected each one.

Rather interestingly, Leah observed as Toran enthusiastically approached the dragbird and then mounted Clément, the dragbird politely lowered its form almost to the ground as it obediently enabled him to easily climb onto its back which clearly indicated its full cooperation and absolute willingness to be mounted and then ridden. Once Toran was in position and firmly seated upon the dragbird's back, quite close to the base of the creature's neck, Toran then turned to face Leah and stretched out a hand towards her as he offered to assist her and invited her to join him.

"Will Clément be able to carry us both?" Leah asked as she sought out final clarification about the dragbird's capacity.

Toran smiled and nodded. "Don't worry Leah, Clément is stronger than an ox or even five oxen, she can definitely carry us both." He replied.

A strong, firm hand was rapidly accepted by Leah as she drew much closer to the dragbird and then Toran began to pull Leah gently up onto Clément's back after which point, she wriggled around for a few seconds until she had found a comfortable position to sit in directly front of him. Due to the ride that was just about to take place which as Leah already knew, would be sky high and situated many miles above the ground, she held onto the black harness that adorned the dragbird's frame tightly and clung onto the leather straps with both hands as she prepared to be lifted up off the ground.

"Are you ready for the ride of your life Leah?" Toran asked.

Leah nodded. "Definitely Toran." She replied.

Just a few seconds later Leah watched and listened in total awe as Toran gently nudged the dragbird's form with his feet and then called out some verbal commands and Clément, immediately responded as she puffed up her chest and then spread out her huge wings as the dragbird prepared to take off. Unlike the wings of a bird, Leah immediately noticed that Clément's wings were absolutely huge in comparison and although they did look quite similar to a bird's wings in shape, they looked far more powerful, much more muscular and even appeared to be webbed.

Once again, Leah considered thoughtfully as the dragbird began to waft her powerful wings and then took off, she would have to face her pet hate of heights but at least, she would have a handsome male companion by her side as she did so and that was at the very least, a small comfort to her. Everything on the ground rapidly began to shrink as Clément soared up into the sky and as Leah began to marvel at the sheer exhilaration and power of the ride, she clung onto the harness around Clément's frame extremely tightly. Despite the leather harness and Toran's presence directly behind Leah, she tried her best however not to look down at the ground below her too often as Clément ascended into the skies due to her fear of heights but the fact that one of Toran's arms was now secured firmly around Leah's waist provided her with a tremendous amount of comfort as their distance from the ground rapidly increased.

For some strange reason, Leah considered quietly as Clément rose higher and higher up into the sky, Spectrum had definitely brought out the braver side of her character because there was absolutely no way that she would have ever mounted such a creature in real life, never mind actually allowed such an animal to elevate her even an inch above the ground. A quick glance was suddenly cast back down towards the ground as Clément circled above the stables, barn, paddock and enclosure as Leah finally succumbed to the temptation to look at the ground below her from a very high height and she rapidly observed that the buildings now looked almost like matchboxes.

Several more verbal commands were called out by Toran as he directed Clément and the dragbird instantly began respond as the two were swiftly flown away from the area upon the dragbird's wings and as Leah continued to listen to Toran and watched Clément respond, she noticed that some hilltops suddenly began to appear. The stables, paddock and barn had by that point Leah observed, completely vanished from sight as Toran proceeded with his planned flight via Clément's wings and as a river, some structures, some more hilltops and even some woods rapidly appeared and then swiftly disappeared below the three, Leah began to visually explore and marvel at the various complex landscapes inside Spectrum from the skies above. Somehow just Toran's presence and his arm around Leah's waist seemed to reduce her fear of heights and so highly unusually, she actually felt quite comfortable, even though she was situated many miles above solid ground, albeit a fictitious form of solid ground.

Approximately fifteen minutes later Clément flew towards some very large hilltops which Toran steered the dragbird towards and a valley that Leah rapidly noticed, sat neatly in-between two of the hilltop peaks. Several more verbal commands and instructions were issued by Toran and as Leah watched and listened in silence, she noticed that Clément immediately, obediently responded to each one as the dragbird began to head towards the valley and prepared to land. Just a minute or so later Clément swiftly swooped down towards a suitable landing spot and as the dragbird began to make her descent, Leah clung onto the harness with all her might and as the dragbird actually landed with a gentle bump, an excited gasp escaped from Leah's lips.

"Let's stop off here for a while Leah and take a walk down by the River of Expectations." Toran suggested as the dragbird came to a total standstill and he prepared to dismount. "Then when you're ready to return, we'll fly back."

"Yes that'll be nice." Leah immediately agreed.

Although the flight had truly thrilled Leah, it had also for some inexplicable reason worn her out and the landing bump had also slightly surprised her, even though it had been quite gentle but it had almost nudged her off the dragbird's back and so a little time to recuperate and relax was definitely deemed to be required before a return journey could be embarked upon. The dragbird's back was lowered towards the ground once again and Toran rapidly dismounted and then politely offered Leah a hand which she graciously accepted as she prepared to dismount.

"Can dragbirds speak Toran?" Leah asked as she dismounted. "I met one inside the forest that could speak."

"They usually can't but they can be trained to understand and to cooperate with basic human verbal commands." Toran replied. "Perhaps you met a very special dragbird."

After the two had vacated the dragbird's back, much to Leah's amusement, Clément immediately began to wander off and approached the nearby river which was full of golden water. An assumption had clearly been made by Clément, Leah swiftly concluded as she watched the dragbird with an amused smile that the river would contain some fresh fish and since fish it seemed, were a major part of a dragbird's diet, Clément's immediate interest in the river was therefore totally understandable.

The river itself in this instance, Leah immediately observed as she watched Clément make a beeline for it, seemed to be formed from the same golden water that she had seen inside Mindstone's pond and the water glistened and shone as rays from the sun gently bounced of the surface as it gurgled and bubbled gently along the riverbed. Less than fifty meters away from Leah's current position, she could see that there was a rocky cliff face which was adorned with a large waterfall and as the golden water cascaded down from the top of the waterfall, it fell into a deep golden pool just below it which seemed to form the river's source.

"Clément's on the hunt for some fish." Toran quickly pointed out as he grinned. "Well, she'll probably find a lot of fish in that river, golden rivers and ponds are always full of very fresh fish."

"Are dragbirds always hungry Toran?" Leah asked as she watched the dragbird step into the river and then start to splash around enthusiastically.

Toran nodded. "Absolutely always. Adult dragbirds have a huge appetite and they can eat more than any other creature I've ever seen." He rapidly clarified. "Are you hungry Leah, if you are I can make you something to eat?"

"Yes, something to eat would be nice, thanks Toran." Leah replied as she nodded.

Some fish leapt in and out of the golden water from the river nearby, Leah noticed as she glanced at Clément and then watched the dragbird splash around for a couple of minutes as the dragbird bounced clumsily around in an attempt to catch each and every single fish. Unlike mudmarshes, dragbirds it appeared were extremely powerful and very strong but they didn't seem to possess the same deftness and sharpness of movement that mudmarshes did and as Leah watched Clément's struggle and rough attempts to capture some fish that major difference in the two hybrid species become increasingly apparent to her.

Around the perimeter on the near side of the deep golden pool of water there was a grassy bank and as Toran began to lead Leah towards it, they discussed the beauty of their surroundings and made light conversation and as Leah walked, she silently rejoiced in her current environment which appeared to be peaceful, pleasant, tranquil and serene. The deep depths of the golden pool shimmered and shone as Leah sat down upon the grassy bank and then glanced at it and as she did so, she noticed that Toran approached a nearby tree and then broke off some of the smaller wooden branches which she immediately assumed he required to make a fishing rod to catch some fresh fish. Once a seemingly sufficient number of small branches had been gathered, a roll of wiry thread was then plucked from one of Toran's trouser pockets and as Leah watched him, he started to make several fishing rods from the broken branches and the wiry thread which he cut to size with two sharp edged rocks and once he had finished, a small glass container was quickly slipped out of his other trouser pocket that appeared to be filled with bait.

"I keep this bait handy because the dragbirds eat a lot of fish." Toran explained as he attached some bait to the end of each rod.

"They sure do." Leah agreed. "They could eat enough fish in a day to feed an entire neighborhood."

Just a few minutes later and once the three fishing lines had been cast into the golden pool, the branch ends were quickly propped up on the bank against some small rocks and Leah started to relax as Toran sat down next to her and the two began to converse. Upon Leah's face there was a smile as the two spoke as she silently considered how simple Toran's life seemed to be in comparison to her own work filled, stressful days but as Leah already knew, lifestyles like her own were common place in any human city. The real human world had definitely become very complex and so too had modern life and so Spectrum in some ways, now served as a reminder to Leah of how simple life could actually be and how simple life at one time had actually been for humanity.

In fact that was possibly one of the most attractive qualities about Leah's emotional journey that day because it had illustrated to her how Spectrum could provide a kind of escapism to consumers since it had allowed her to delve into an environment where the complex realities of the real human world that usually demanded so much from people and even from Leah herself, just seemed to melt away and the horizon of life no longer seemed to be so cluttered with complexities. Sadly, as Leah now fully realized and began to appreciate, the human world had evolved over centuries built upon the mass accumulation of human knowledge but for one reason or another, it seemed far more stressful now than it had ever been and that was a rather solitary grim truth that sat silently upon the shelf of human discontent and modern discomfort. The evolution of humanity and the realization of all mankind's achievements to date had not made the human existence any easier for human beings to live with and if anything, had actually made human life far more complex, much harder and mentally tougher to endure and so as Leah now accepted, a strange human paradox had been created that humanity itself could not even begin to try and resolve and although civility had improved, the stresses of human life due to modern complexities had also increased alongside those improvements, very significantly.

Before very long the fishing lines that Toran had set, suddenly began to tug as eager, hungry fish attacked each one and tried to consume the small grubs of attached bait and as Leah watched,

Toran quickly rose to his feet and then walked towards the three fishing lines. Once Toran arrived next to the fishing lines, the three lines were then quickly reeled in within a matter of minutes and as Toran started to silently inspect the three fish that had been caught, Leah continued to watch him in a thoughtful silence as she noticed that the fish were extremely bright and very colorful. One of the fish appeared to be a glittery gold color whilst another sparkled and was bright red and the final one from the three, was a deep, shiny brown color and as the three fish were removed from the fishing lines, Leah noticed that the glow which had initially surrounded their form, rapidly began to fade.

When the three fish had been removed from the fishing lines, Leah noticed that Toran placed the fish on top of a small rock and then he attached some more bait to each line and cast the lines back out into the golden water once again. The sight of the three raw fish immediately reminded Leah of Mindstone as she began to consider for a moment how they would actually eat the fish that Toran had caught because technically, right now the fish were still in a raw state and as far as Leah was concerned, completely inedible.

"It's not actually that hard to find something good to eat around here when you're hungry Leah. You can find these fish in any river or pond." Toran explained as he started to search the nearby foliage.

Leah nodded.

Despite Leah's initial reservations with regards to the current state of the fish however, her mind was quickly put at ease just a few minutes later because not only had Toran gathered some herb and spice leaves, pods, stems and twigs from the nearby trees but he then proceeded to descale each fish and clean out their interiors. The herb and spice leaves, pods, stems and twigs, Leah noticed, were then placed upon a large rock and crushed into a pulp with a smaller rock and as Toran ground the ingredients into a comprehensive marinade, Leah smiled as she thoughtfully admired his culinary skills. Once the marinade mixture had been fully prepared, the three fish were then spilt open with a small, army pocket knife that Leah saw Toran pluck from one of his trouser pockets just before the mixture was rubbed into the grooves and all over the exterior of each fish so that all the flavors would be fully captured and Leah's mouth rapidly began to water as she watched Toran work because it seemed as if he could really, actually cook.

Much to Leah's total satisfaction, once the fish had been fully prepped Toran then collected some branches and sticks from the ground underneath some nearby trees which he placed in a pile and then put a small grill on top of that he had cut and wound together from some yellow twigs. The grill itself, quite strangely Leah observed had been formed from sticks that had been collected from a tree with a strange, yellow trunk and as Leah had watched Toran gather the required items, she had noticed that he had woven the yellow sticks together with the same thread that he had used to make the fishing lines but as she watched him position the firewood which had been placed under the grill, she began to thoughtfully consider and question his actions.

"Won't the grill burn Toran?" Leah enquired as her curiosity urged her to seek further clarity and prodded her thoughts.

"No because these sticks are sticks from the Evershot tree and they are the only sticks that you can actually make a grill from." Toran explained as he pointed towards a yellowish tree trunk nearby. "Sticks and branches from the Evershot tree never burn."

Once the three marinated fish had been placed on top of the grill and the fire had been lit, Leah watched as Toran started to cook the fish and turned each one over to ensure that every one was cooked thoroughly and as the daylight began to fade, the duskiness of the evening silently danced into the valley to replace it. At the same time, Leah observed that Toran still also kept a close eye upon the three active fishing lines and once the first three fish had been cooked to absolute perfection, one was politely handed to Leah which she hungrily and immediately started to eat as she watched Toran pluck another three fish from the fishing line and then start to prepare the second batch of fish for consumption.

Rather amusingly, Leah observed as she ate, Clément continued to potter around in the nearby river as the dragbird attempted to catch some more fish and although Leah knew that a few raw fish had already been caught and eaten by Clément, it appeared as if the dragbird never seemed to tire or fill up and as if Clément had an appetite that was almost as deep as the valley itself. The satisfaction of hunger appeared to be Clément's only mission since the three had initially arrived in the valley earlier that day and ever since the second that the dragbird had spotted the nearby river and so the shallow edges of that river had been searched continuously as Clément had hunted for as many fishes as it had been possible to find, catch and then consume. Due to Clément's seemingly tireless energy and the dragbird's very persistent pursuit which hadn't seemed to yield many results so far, Leah was absolutely fascinated by Clément's chosen activity which it appeared had fully occupied and captured the dragbird's time, attention and total focus and so she watched Clément for a few minutes as she ate.

Occasionally, since the three had arrived in the valley, Leah had heard a bit of a commotion emanate from the river as Clément had flapped around and fought with some of the larger fish that the dragbird had managed to grab a hold off that it had appeared, had not been willing to be caught and had no desire to be eaten but for the most part, the dragbird's pursuit of food had been really quite peaceful. Some of the larger splashes however, had definitely amused Leah as she had watched Clément fight to keep each fish, no matter how large they had been and a hilarious battle would then be fought, until each fish either surrendered and had been consumed or until the fishes had managed to slip out of the dragbird's grasp which a few of fish actually had.

"Dragbirds can be quite funny, can't they Toran?" Leah mentioned as she watched some of Clément's antics and then started to giggle.

"They can be but they're extremely hard to keep because when they are fully grown, they have an absolutely huge appetite." Toran explained. "They can eat a small mountain of fish in a week."

"Yeah, I could definitely see that happening." Leah replied.

Later that evening, once the two had eaten their fill and Leah could eat no more, Toran invited her to take a dip inside the golden pool and she immediately agreed, even though she had no actual swimsuit to wear. Despite the lack of suitable attire however, Toran quickly stripped down to his underwear and then Leah began to follow suit as she completely abandoned her reservations which predominantly revolved around her lack of swimwear and eagerly joined in.

Fortunately for Leah as she slipped off the grassy bank into the golden pool, she noticed that the water felt very warm and absolutely delicious as each drop seemed to welcome her into its midst and each golden ripple appeared to invite her to come and join its gathering as the soft waves lapped gently against her skin and silently caressed her form. For at least the next hour, the two enthusiastically splashed around playfully, almost like schoolchildren as they swam around the pool of water and made the most of the evening and the remainder of Leah's time that day inside Spectrum.

After the two had enjoyed the water and their swim as much as they possibly could, they then returned to the grassy bank as the evening silently turned into night and as they lay upon the grassy bank beside each other, they watched as the night wandered across the sky and darkness started to enter into the day. Directly above their heads, the sky began to darken and as Leah stared at it thoughtfully, she once again appreciated the serene simplicity and tranquil pleasantness of the environment that she was currently situated within as she basked in Toran's companionship.

Everything inside the positive Spectrum environments that Leah had visited so far had felt so perfect, so beautiful and so picturesque and inside those worlds, Leah felt as if she would never need or want a single thing ever again and as if she could exist inside Spectrum forever and never have to worry about anything ever again. Finances, deadlines, work, biological clocks, potential inventions or even capital sales to secure a decent future just didn't factor into Spectrum in any way at all and the pleasant environments that Leah herself had created had given her a peaceful place to exist where nothing was expected form her and where she could just exist.

"If only my life and the real world was this simple." Leah

whispered to herself under her breath as she lay upon the grassy bank and stared up at the sky above her head.

Essentially, Leah knew that her considerations with regards to humanity and the complex modern world were absolutely true because if life was far simpler, many more people would live much longer and enjoy life a whole lot more and there would not only be longer human lives but also far less heart attacks, less stress, less depression and definitely a lot more happiness. Modern complexities and the agenda of progress certainly didn't always amount to and correlate well with a peaceful, enjoyable human existence, or lie very comfortably in a bed beside each other and progressive agendas had definitely contributed to more human deaths than increased the longevity of human lives and so at times, Leah wondered what progress humanity had really, truly made over the centuries and how much joy humanity had ultimately sacrificed in the name of supposed advancement.

Suddenly, Toran stretched out a hand towards Leah as he gently interrupted her thoughts and as he began to stroke her arm, her form immediately began to react as every inch of her flesh started to tingle with sensual excitement because this tender interaction had been desired with eager anticipation since the very first second that she had first set eyes upon him earlier that day. Just a few seconds later Toran gently turned Leah's face towards him and as she turned to face him, their faces brushed and as they did so, he began to softly kiss her lips and Leah's form immediately surrendered to him as waves of pleasure instantly washed over her. In a matter of just seconds, the two were locked in a sensual, passionate embrace and as Toran's hands began to search every inch of Leah's form, she encouraged him to fill her feminine form with his masculine presence.

The truly awful reality was that Leah had actually wanted Toran ever since she had first laid eyes upon him and now it seemed, there was absolutely no escape from those passionate desires but she suddenly began to feel very guilty about her internal passion which appeared to be unstoppable and uncontrollable. Every part of Leah's being had longed for Toran to provide satisfaction to her internal desires and those desires she had silently held inside her core since the two had met, albeit artificially and fictitiously. A desire to be intimately and sensually adored by Toran and to make love passionately and frantically to him had definitely grown inside Leah's mind and now, she wanted him to thrust his masculine presence inside of her and for their sexual exploration to commence.

Rather suddenly and abruptly however, the sensual moment between the two was silently interrupted as Toran and the grassy bank rapidly, completely disappeared and Leah woke back up inside the Spectrum capsule and back inside her basement laboratory. Since Leah had programmed the Spectrum capsule very precisely, the sudden departure had taken her by surprise but as she also fully appreciated, her meander into some extracurricular activities with Toran that day had strayed quite far from the path of her actual emotional journey and had fallen well outside the scope of the usual experiences that Spectrum provided which had consumed some additional amounts of time. Just as Leah had taken a deep dive into the pool of sensual lust that had welled up inside of her that day however, she had been woken up and returned to her own very real life at the most inconvenient moment and as she commanded the capsule lid to open and then sat up, she began to gently shake her head.

"Now that was a very inconvenient reawakening." Leah admitted to herself as she climbed out of the capsule and then began to make her way towards the foot of the basement stairs. "I should have spent less time swimming around."

Once Leah's feet were firmly back on real ground and her mind back inside her real life, she verbally commanded Fink to shut down and to switch everything off inside the basement and the large, wafer thin screen that clung to one of the walls swiftly darkened. The lights inside the basement rapidly began to dim all around Leah as she started to mount the steps that lead back up towards the ground floor of the couple's home but as she prepared to vacate the basement for the remainder of that day, a mischievous temptation suddenly tugged away inside Leah's thoughts which teased her mind as just for a moment, she considered whether or not she should perhaps extend her emotional journey and indulge in another thirty minutes with Toran.

Since Leah did have full administrative powers over the entire Spectrum system that possibility was indeed, technically possible but it would definitely reduce the time that she would have left with which to prepare the couple's evening meal and Zidane was due to return from his work trip quite soon. In fact as Leah was fully aware, quite shortly not only would Zidane actually arrive at the couple's home but then the two would eat their evening meal together, discuss their respective weekends and laugh together and later that night, they would even sleep inside the bed that the couple usually shared and so those factors definitely had to be considered. If Leah didn't leave the basement on time and cook the couple's evening meal and then spend the rest of her evening with Zidane, he would probably feel very insulted because they hadn't even spent a minute together all weekend.

One final glance was swiftly cast around the basement's darkened interior as Leah prepared to step back into the ground floor of the couple's home as she thoughtfully considered how throughout that entire weekend, Zidane's presence had really been so very absent. Unlike the weekday evenings when Zidane usually steered well clear of the basement, at times on the weekends he would wander down and pay Leah an unexpected visit as she worked because he seemed to be slightly less willing to abide by his own general rule on the weekends. Sometimes, Zidane would suddenly appear without any warning whatsoever and pop down with a spot of lunch and although Leah had enjoyed the weekend that she had just spent inside Spectrum as she thoughtfully reminisced on how pleasant it had been, a part of her had definitely missed Zidane's occasional weekend interruptions and his masculine arms each night.

Another dabble in the emotional journey that Leah had just enjoyed as she already knew, would definitely have to wait for another day because Zidane would be very upset, if she choose to extend it that night and missed his return and so that was not an acceptable choice for Leah to make to either member of their romantic partnership. Deep down inside, Leah really loved the fact that she was so loved and truly wanted by Zidane and so any time spent with him and any time spent inside his arms was extremely important to her too because Zidane had never once rejected her in any capacity at all and that consistent acceptance warmed every inch of Leah's heart as she stepped off the final basement step and then began to prepare herself for the night ahead. Although the weekend had almost drawn to a close, Leah's night as she already knew, had only really, just begun because the couple had a whole weekend to make up for which meant, a passionate, sensual night definitely lay ahead for the couple with as much adoration, companionship, sensuality, passion and desire as they could possibly fit into one night.

Rides of Heartbreak Upon the Waves of the Sea of Sorrow

Approximately one hour later, when Zidane arrived home, Leah greeted him with open arms, an affectionate smile upon her face and a hearty home cooked meal and as the couple sat down inside the lounge and then started to consume it, Zidane verbally leapt into a discussion about his truly awful, hectic weekend. Apparently, it rapidly transpired as Leah listened to Zidane speak and empathized with his frustrations, he had spent his entire weekend up to his neck in problems because the support team in the city that he had visited hadn't implemented the company's procedures correctly or the software that they had been provided with properly and they had remained uncooperative despite the fact that their lack of adherence to company guidelines had been the root cause of the chaos to begin with.

Since Leah had enjoyed her weekend for the most part, she predominantly kept silent throughout most of their meal as she simply listened to Zidane verbalize and voice his frustrations because to discuss her enjoyment in his absence felt totally insensitive. Some words of sympathy as the couple ate dinner together however, were considerately and swiftly offered as Leah attempted to put Zidane at ease and tried to help him relax because his stressful weekend it seemed, had created some tension in his being.

When dinner had been consumed and once the dishes had been washed, the couple then strolled casually towards their bedroom hand in hand as Leah prepared to passionately celebrate the night with the very real love of her very real life and as she walked, she hoped that some tender sensual affection would help Zidane to wind down and de-stress himself. The couple didn't have very far to walk because their bedroom was situated less than thirty meters away from the lounge and the kitchen because their home was really quite compact but for Leah that smallish size often suited her just fine because it meant that there was less to keep clean and tidy, so that also meant that more time could be spent upon her creations, her professional aspirations and Spectrum.

In terms of the couple's quite moderate home, it had been chosen very precisely to suit their current needs and so it only had two bedrooms inside it, one of which was the couple's own bedroom and the other bedroom that had been allocated by the couple to be a guest bedroom. Although the spare guest bedroom had been furnished as an actual bedroom, just in case the couple ever had any guests, it usually remained unoccupied for the most part but at times, the couple would tease each other about it and make jokes about its interior. A playful agreement existed between the couple that if they ever disagreed, or if someone had failed to live up to the other party's romantic expectations and it was deemed that they deserved to be punished, they would be sent to the guest bedroom where they would have to sleep and remain until forgiveness had been granted to them by the offended party. The agreement about the guest bedroom was purely a joke however, and since the couple rarely disagreed that eventuality had so far, never actually occurred and so the guest bedroom had remained unutilized by the actual couple themselves.

"It feels so nice to be home Leah." Zidane whispered in her ear as he led her into their bedroom. "And since I haven't seen you all weekend, next weekend we definitely have to make up for it."

"I know Zidane, my work on Spectrum has kept me down in the basement so much lately but don't worry next weekend, I'll take a whole weekend off and we'll do something really nice together." Leah immediately reassured him.

"Now that will be nice." Zidane replied as he turned to face her.

Inwardly, Leah vowed as she paused for a moment and then turned to face Zidane that once her work on Spectrum was complete, the couple would spend a lot more time together because it really had consumed so much of her time and by then she also hoped that their financial resources would have increased so that there would be no more working weekends for either of them. The promise that Leah had just made to Zidane as she already knew, she really could not afford to break because in recent times, his tolerance levels had really been pushed to absolute breaking point. In terms of their relationship, if Leah attempted to stretch Zidane's tolerance much further, she feared that their relationship would end up shipwrecked upon the rocks of romantic destruction and torn apart the jagged edges of total heartache which would negate all of the sacrifices that they had both made for each other up until that point in time and render her time in the basement absolutely worthless.

Unfortunately for Leah, the walk through tests that she had started to perform upon Spectrum so far had proven to be just as time consuming, if not more involved than the actual creation and development stages and that had now become a point of frustration for both members of their romantic partnership to some degree, albeit for slightly different reasons. Regardless of Leah's commitment to Spectrum however, there was definitely one thing that she was absolutely certain about, she had to honor her promise to spend a full weekend with Zidane the next weekend because if she didn't, she knew it would impact negatively upon their relationship and a failure on her part to focus upon him and allocate sufficient time to his needs, would be totally unjustifiable. In every romantic way, Zidane didn't really ask for much from Leah and she silently reminded herself of that reality as she nestled peacefully inside his arms and so, she really had to be mindful of his dedication and faithfulness and she really had to appreciate both because men like Zidane really were worth their weight in gold.

For the next few days Leah managed to resist the urge to enter back inside the Spectrum capsule as she attempted to wrap up her work inside the basement before eight each evening as she focused purely upon tweaks from her findings and then spent most of her evenings with Zidane. Time as Leah knew, was the one luxury that they could both share and enjoy together that didn't cost either of them anything and so, it was an easy sacrifice to make as she sought to please some of Zidane's needs and wants and placed Spectrum slightly further down her priority ladder for a few days. A few pleasant evenings were spent in Zidane's faithful arms as Leah emerged from the basement each evening at a decent hour and then spent the remainder of her night with Zidane who as Leah already knew, was in desperate need of some affection, attention and some tender loving care, due to his very long working weekend the previous weekend.

However, by the time the Thursday morning arrived and due to Leah's promise to spend the coming weekend purely with Zidane, she could resist the urge to indulge in a Spectrum environment no more as she prepared for the day and night ahead on the Thursday morning and her potential trip to Spectrum that day. A simple evening meal was quickly prepared before lunch was made and by the time twelve noon arrived, Leah began to make her way towards the basement as she prepared to take a deep dive into the next Spectrum environment which would be centered upon an emotional journey of sorrow.

Once inside the basement, Leah programmed the Spectrum system with her preferences and adapted her personality to be slightly more empathetic, a bit more confident and she even enhanced her levels of bravery because she was just about to embark upon a sorrow filled journey and so those personality tweaks she felt, would enhance her experiences. Since this fourth visit to Spectrum was expected to be a much sadder experience than Leah's last emotional journey which had been full of excitement, intrigue and pleasant anticipation, Leah had opted to increase her levels of bravery, just in case any challenges that involved heights showed up again because she had remembered her experiences in the Fearful Forest.

Although Leah couldn't predict with any accuracy where she would end up that day, unless she accessed the administrative back end of Spectrum which she had no wish to do as she mounted the Spectrum capsule and then lay down inside it, she began to prepare herself for what might lie ahead. The emotional journey that Leah was just about to venture into and embark upon that day held the promise of a day filled with sadness which was definitely a much heavier emotion and so Leah could at least predict that this emotional journey wasn't going to be filled with joy or laughter.

Just a second or two later Leah issued a verbal command to Spectrum and the transparent capsule lid began to descend and close down over her body and as usual, once the capsule lid had closed, the sleeping gas immediately started to flood through the interior of the capsule and seep into Leah's biological system. A peaceful slumber was quickly entered into as Leah embraced the state of sleep that wrapped its arms all around her as she entered into a deeper state of consciousness and began to enter into her next adventure.

Approximately a minute or so later, when Leah woke back up, she found herself strewn across a smooth, golden, sandy beach and just about thirty meters away from her current position and the spot where she lay, waves that were an aqua, turquoise blue lapped gently against the honey colored sands and it was almost as if the waves and the sands were involved in an actual conversation with each other and in the midst of deep discussion. Each wave seemed to gently wash further up the sands with each visit and then the waves would quietly subside as the sea and the beach happily conversed back and forth in an almost in a rhythmic fashion and as Leah watched for a few minutes in total fascination, it almost appeared as if the tide conducted the waves of the sea like an orchestra and as if it was determined to play each note on the scale to total perfection and in complete harmonious unison.

Suddenly however, a movement further along the beach rapidly attracted Leah's attention and she noticed that a short, elderly man with grey hair stood on the edge of the shore, just a few steps into the water, right next to an actual boat and so she stared at him and the boat for a few surprised seconds before she finally began to stand up as she prepared to approach him. One of the man's hands, Leah observed, tightly clasped onto a large pole which was currently in an upright position that had been dipped into the shallow water around him and the grip he had upon the long pole seemed so very tight that it was almost as if his life actually depended upon his retention of the pole and so Leah began to thoughtfully consider whether or not she should actually walk towards him before she took an actual step in his direction.

Unlike Leah's uncertainty however, the man himself didn't seem to harbor the same reservations or any fears as he suddenly turned to face Leah and then beckoned to her to draw closer as he actually invited her to approach him. Due to the man's friendly gestures which seemed at least to be harmless, Leah enthusiastically began to walk towards him as she started to cooperate with his invitation and hoped for the best and as soon as she was close enough to the boat, he then invited her to actually step into the boat itself.

"When you're ready, you can get into the boat and take a seat." The man offered politely. "I'm your guide and I'm here to take you on your journey."

Since the man's invitation seemed genuine enough and he had verbally expressed that he was an actual guide, Leah began to nod as she slipped off her shoes, paddled a few steps towards the boat and then started to climb into the vessel. No other signs anywhere nearby implied that there was an actual choice or that Leah was supposed to do anything else and take an alternative course of action and despite the man's strange appearance, he seemed harmless enough.

In terms of the man's appearance, from first impressions and what Leah could see at first glance, he certainly wasn't cute like Roto or as electrifyingly handsome as Toran and he definitely lacked the comical appeal of Sebastian but as Leah was fully aware, every guide in Spectrum had been given a unique appearance and a unique set of personal attributes because she had intentionally created each guide to be different. According to Spectrum's internal architecture and processes, any guide could appear in any emotional journey and turn up anywhere which meant, each one could participate in those emotional journeys in a variety of ways, so it was almost impossible for Leah to predict where or when a particular guide would show up and what they would actually do when they appeared because this was another aspect that was subject to the random generation process of the Spectrum system.

“Are you ready to start your trip?” The man asked.

Upon Leah's face there was an amused smile as she nodded

her head and then just stared at his attire which composed of a long black overcoat, a black woolen jumper and some thick dark black trousers which struck Leah as slightly strange because he was situated upon a sunny beach and the weather certainly wasn't gloomy. Due to the man's second question which implied that he was very certain about his function, Leah suddenly felt quite obligated to verbally respond because it seemed a bit rude to ignore him for a second time and she definitely felt that a verbal response would be far more polite.

"Who are you and where are we going?" Leah asked as she sat down, slipped her flat, black shoes back on and then straightened herself back up.

Although Spectrum was an artificial, simulated environment, Leah had absolutely no desire to find out if her shoes would be soggy, if she had actually kept them on and then stepped into the water and so she had slipped them off and then back on again, according to her desire to keep them dry because ten hours spent in soggy shoes, wouldn't be a great part of any adventure. Despite Leah's successful efforts to keep her shoes dry however, as she glanced up at the man's face something very unusual swiftly began to puzzle her because upon closer inspection, he definitely didn't appear to look totally human.

Some aspects of the man's physique seemed to possess some quite strange characteristics which definitely didn't fit in with the usual expectations of a human form and his ears looked slightly pointed which reminded Leah somewhat of an elf. A thought rapidly sauntered across Leah's mind that perhaps he was an elf or a dwarf, or perhaps even some kind of hybrid because she had created some hybrid guides but as Leah also knew, he could also be just a very odd looking human being because she had also created some odd looking human guides but there was no actual way to clarify that issue, unless she asked him directly. The pepper grey, black and white dusty hair that sparsely covered the mature man's head suggested that he was very mature in years but his beige colored skin actually looked clear and youthful and it glowed slightly and from what Leah could see, no wrinkles or lines appeared on his face and so, she began to wonder if perhaps the water around her possessed some kind of skin rejuvenation qualities which perhaps had contributed to his youthful appearance.

"I'm Delta and I'm here to guide you through the waves of the Sea of Sorrow." The odd looking man explained.

A sigh of relief was released from Leah's mouth as she began to appreciate that at least on this occasion, her guide had turned up before she had because the forest which sat in the not too distant distance, looked quite dense and a wander around a dense forest that might be riddled with strange creatures probably would not have been very pleasant. Fortunately however, Delta appeared to know how to man the boat effectively and looked equipped to do so which was another positive aspect of his presence because Leah had no idea how to row or steer a boat on her own through a mass of water and so his early appearance removed those two highly unattractive possibilities from Leah's potential emotional journey and adventures that day.

"Why is this sea called the Sea of Sorrow?" Leah asked as she wriggled around and tried to make herself as comfortable as she possibly could upon the boat's hard wooden bench.

"Well, it's said that the lost souls of all the people who die at sea are drawn here because their bodies cannot be retrieved from the ocean and so no proper burials take place." Delta explained. "They come here to rest for eternity because they are filled with sorrow because they never had a chance to say goodbye to those they love and their loved ones never had a chance to say goodbye to their physical remains and due to that lack of peace, their sorrow fills the sea, rides through the waves and gushes through every tide."

Suddenly, Delta pushed the pole against the sandy ground and the boat which had been wedged against it began to move and as it was silently released, the vessel began to move slowly further out into the sea and as Leah left the comfort of the shoreline, she held her breath in uncertain excitement as her journey across the Sea of Sorrow began. Rather curiously, Delta the guide that Leah had been allocated by Spectrum on this particular occasion didn't seem to speak very much as the boat drifted further and further away from the shore and even started to pick up speed and it appeared that he didn't seem to offer any information unless it was directly requested from him which worried Leah slightly because that meant that he would perhaps not actually tell her anything that she did not specifically ask him.

From Delta's sparse explanations so far however, Leah clearly understood that the fun, joy and pleasantness experienced during her two past visits to the Joyful Kingdom and the Ark of Anticipation, would not be present or form any part of this particular emotional journey and that no such positive emotions would be evoked in any capacity because this was definitely going to be a different kind of journey altogether. Despite the potential lack of joy and the definite sadness that was due to follow, as Leah already knew, the Spectrum environment of sadness definitely had to be tested nonetheless and to do that effectively, it had to not only be visited but also travelled through and each challenge participated with in its fullness.

The water seemed to gradually change color, Leah noticed as Delta maneuvered the boat as it drifted and as he steered the vessel out towards deeper waters with his long pole, Leah watched in silence as the two ventured further from the shore and the sandy beach was rapidly left behind. Quite interestingly, Leah thoughtfully observed as the boat glided across the water, although the water got slightly deeper it didn't actually seem to get much deeper and as the vessel continued to move further out to sea, she also noticed that Delta no longer utilized his pole as frequently to steer the vessel and that finally he stopped altogether.

Despite the lack of physical input from Delta when it came to the direction of the boat as he sat down on a second wooden bench, directly opposite Leah and then placed the long, wooden pole across his lap, she realized that the tide seemed to carry the boat further out to sea even more rapidly which struck her as slightly strange as the vessel seemed to pick up speed. Although no actual other changes had occurred inside the boat, Leah noticed that the waves around the vessel were now a much richer, royal blue as she began to inspect the water around her and that the aquamarine green waves that had lapped gently against the sandy shore had completely disappeared. Each wave seemed to silently, playfully caress the sides of the vessel and although the change in the water's color had surprised Leah, it didn't seem to be a cause for concern as the boat continued to move further across the sea.

All of a sudden however, as the boat continued to move towards its destination and cut silently through the waves, the air around Leah began to change as it rapidly became chilly and breezy and directly above her head, the sky suddenly, swiftly started to darken as the initial warmth that Leah had enjoyed, was chased silently out of the air by an invisible foe. A light mist suddenly seemed to gather around the boat very unexpectedly as the sunshine rapidly disappeared and as it hovered and clung to the vessel's occupants, Leah glanced up at Delta's face with a slightly confused expression as she silently questioned the quite abrupt change in atmosphere. Due to the sudden changes an actual explanation was expected from Delta as Leah stared at his face and waited expectantly but no answers it appeared, would be offered to her as he remained totally silent, stagnantly fixed and just stared directly ahead of him almost like a statue.

Rather curiously, the strange mysterious mist seemed to thicken as the boat moved which alarmed Leah slightly, especially when she glanced backwards and quickly realized that she could no longer see anything beyond the vessel. Despite the mist and all Leah's alarm however, the boat continued to silently cut through the waves and as it moved, she peered over one side of the vessel and then started to inspect the water that surrounded her which it seemed had changed color once again and it was now a far deeper, much darker blue.

Much to Leah's total shock however, just a few seconds later as she continued to stare at the water, she almost jumped out of her skin as a face inside the waves suddenly, actually appeared to stare right back up at her. Just below the surface of the water there appeared to be a pale skinned female face that didn't flinch or even move an inch and a pair of dark black eyes that didn't blink and that sight caught Leah completely off guard as the eerie looking face startled her. A pair of soggy, dark, sunken eyes stared up at Leah from just below the surface of the water that definitely belonged to the face of a woman but from what Leah could see, her face was not attached to any body or any kind of female form.

Suddenly however, the soggy, sunken eyes that belonged to the mature looking, weather beaten face blinked and Leah shrieked in absolute horror as she immediately jumped of wooden bench that she was seated upon and then scrambled towards the other side of the vessel. The steps that Leah took as she tried to distance herself from the side of the boat that had offended her as quickly as she possibly could however, were counterproductive as her foot and ankle got caught and became tangled up on the edge of the small wooden bench. Unfortunately and to make matters even worse, Leah almost stumbled at that point and then nearly fell over the side of the boat as she lost her balance completely and as that occurred, she nearly joined the face and landed in the sea itself next to the source of all her alarm and distress.

"Who is she?" Leah demanded as she turned to face Delta with a horrified expression upon her face. "Who does that face belong to?"

"I wouldn't look into the water." Delta advised her as he solemnly began to shake his head. "You might not like what you find there. The Sea of Sorrow is only a peaceful resting place for the dead, it's not a comfort to the living."

Due to Leah's sudden scare, a possible return to the shore suddenly became an option that deeply appealed to her inner core as she began to consider for a moment whether or not she could actually try to return to the sandy beach that she had initially arrived and landed upon. Any notions that Leah had of a possible wade or swim back to shore and a departure from the actual boat however, were quickly chased out of her mind as she silently reminded herself of the female face that she had just seen inside the water and then shuddered with fear because a long wade through water filled with the faces of the lost at sea, really would be a very traumatic wade.

Just for a moment Leah began to silently wonder and entertain the possibility that perhaps, she could ask Delta to turn the boat around and that he might then direct the boat back towards the shore with his pole because that was a viable option which would not involve a scary clamber through a body of water that from what Leah now knew, was obviously full of dead, haunted faces. The face that Leah had already seen, was definitely enough of a reason alone to put her off a departure from the actual boat, never mind the actual distance that she might perhaps now be from the actual shore she had first arrived on. Inside Leah's form, a pool of fear suddenly seemed to rapidly grow and squeeze every positive thought from the depths of her being as she glanced at Delta's face and then prepared to actually raise the possibility with him.

"Delta, would it be possible to return to the shore?" Leah enquired slightly nervously as she swallowed her fear and attempted to utilize her vocal chords effectively but each word seemed to grate against her throat as she spoke as a sudden dryness gripped her.

“I'm afraid that won't be possible, this is a one way trip.” Delta replied as he began to shake his head. “The Sea of Sorrow can only carry vessels in one direction and so once you've begun the journey through the sea, you have to complete it.”

"What an uncomfortable fact." Leah whispered as she sat back down upon the wooden bench, lifted her feet up from the ground and then hugged her knees.

From the depths of Leah's form a sudden wave of discomfort seemed to wash over her as she began to yearn for the companionship of Roto, Toran or Sebastian once more because they at least had an attitude of cooperation which Delta it had rapidly transpired, clearly didn't. Even Sebastian's quite pale attempts at humor, Leah silently concluded, would be very welcome in comparison to Delta's rigid, determined, stubborn mindset which frustratingly for Leah, did not seem to waver and was not fluid in any way, unlike the waves that currently surrounded them both and that lapped gently against the sides of the boat.

Approximately ten minutes later and after a period of total discomfort for Leah which she had noticed that Delta appeared to be absolutely indifferent to, she noticed that a large cliff face suddenly appeared which seemed to have a huge, dark, black hole in its face. Rather mysteriously, although Delta did not move an inch as Leah watched both him and the boat in silence, the boat swiftly began to change direction and the vessel appeared to accelerate as it headed towards the large black tunnel entrance which rapidly became much more visible. Due to the sudden change in direction and acceleration in pace which had definitely startled Leah, she instantly clung onto the wooden bench below her form with two sweaty, nervous palms as the boat drew closer to the black tunnel that burrowed into the cliff face and a stream of worries began to flood through her thoughts like a train at top speed.

Once more, Leah observed as she cast an eye over one side of the boat and glanced down at the water that now surrounded the vessel, the color of the water had changed and it now appeared to be a very murky, dark gray color that almost looked black. Since the water contained a host of horrors that Leah had absolutely no desire to be in close proximity to, she silently accepted as the boat approached the tunnel entrance that no matter what happened next, she would have to participate because a return to the golden sandy beach was highly unlikely at that point and a wade through the murky gray waters was totally out of the question.

Although Delta sat inside the boat alongside Leah, the only real companion and presence that she could really feel, was the fear that seemed to run rampant through her mind that gripped onto her thoughts as the boat began to enter into the dark, dingy tunnel and that fear seemed to hold her hostage as her form trembled and attempted to shake of the drops of fearful uncertainty. Due to the unusual nature of Leah's emotional journey that day, she couldn't be totally sure what might happen next or what she was just about to face but whatever was due to occur, she felt absolutely certain that it certainly wouldn't be pretty as the boat slipped inside the still, dark blackness.

Fortunately, due to the initial adjustments that Leah had made to her personality that day, she had somehow managed to remain inside the boat up until that point but everything that surrounded her was very eerie and so she could definitely feel her usual calmness slip from her grasp. Although there had been some additional bravery instilled into Leah's personality upon her entrance to

Spectrum that day, she really couldn't feel that bravery and it certainly didn't feel as if was inside her form or anywhere inside the boat.

A solitary thought wandered across Leah's mind as the tunnel's blackness gathered the boat and its occupants into its midst as Leah began to speculate that perhaps if she hadn't actually made any personality adjustments at all that day, by now she would have screamed hysterically and would have already jumped off the boat. Inside Leah's form, she finally managed to find a grain of calmness as the last glimmer of light disappeared and the blackness completely engulfed her and as the darkness appeared to swallow the boat literally whole, she gently reminded herself that this was not supposed to be a fearful environment but a sad one which comforted her slightly.

Nothing but darkness seemed to surround Leah as the boat began to travel further along the tunnel that was burrowed into the cliff face and she rapidly noticed that everything in front, behind and all around her was dark, dismal and dreary and it was almost as if the tunnel wore an actual uniform of blackness that mourned. Not a single word was uttered by Delta, Leah observed as he sat quietly at the other end of the boat, stagnant and still, much like the black water that surrounded the vessel because the water inside the tunnel from what Leah could see, did not even lap or appear to move as the boat cut silently through it and it merely appeared to part in silent obedience. Some jagged rocks littered the dark, black waters but Leah noticed that the boat seemed to steer itself around each one with a silent certainty as the vessel rode along the current and entered deeper inside the stagnant, dreary, black darkness and it was almost as if the boat could see the jagged edges which it wished to avoid.

Suddenly, a forlorn song seemed to emanate from the depths of the actual waters and as each note echoed around Leah, the melody washed over her ears almost like a wave as the sorrow filled tune drifted into her mind. On either side of the boat there were some rocky walls but Leah could barely see each one because it really was so dark and as the dark confines of the tunnel hungrily consumed the vessel and the boat ventured further along it, no one inside the boat uttered a single word as the strange melody grew louder and louder.

Every note of the sorrow filled lament seemed to lap in and out of Leah's ears much like the sea had lapped against the sandy beach that she had initially arrived upon and as Leah listened to it in total silence, she began to empathize with the sadness it contained. Nothing but teardrops of sorrow seemed to drench every single note of the lament that sounded not only beautiful but also soaked in despair, saturated with tragedy and laden with heartbroken remorse and so Leah's heart swiftly began to weep as the sorrowful melody wept with pain, exuded tragedy and mourned with loss.

A sorrowful silence seemed to linger between the two occupants of the boat as the vessel continued its journey because neither party inside the boat uttered a single word to each other and as Leah just sat and listened to the mournful tones that ascended and descended in sad unison, she noticed that each voice sounded out in perfect harmony. No actual words however, could be heard as the song continued and as Leah searched the melody for some kind of message, she began to silently absorb the sadness that the tune contained that seemed to cling to her heart but no message could be found.

Not even a single word could be distinguished and no actual language seemed to be present as the loudest female voice that Leah could hear continued to lead the choir of heartbroken despair. The female voice that led the group of voices almost sounded to Leah like a woman who grieved that had lost her family through some kind of tragedy and Leah could almost feel the profound heaviness of her grief as it bore down upon her shoulders like a heavy weight of sadness.

"What song are they singing Delta?" Leah finally asked as she surrendered to her curiosity, stared at him and broke the silence that had gathered between them both.

"That melody is the Song of Sorrow." Delta explained.

"It's very beautiful but it sounds so sad. What language are they singing in?" Leah asked. "I don't understand it at all."

“There are no actual words and so it's not sung in any language." Delta replied.

"What is the song about?" Leah enquired.

"The Song of Sorrow is the song sung by lost souls that have been lost at sea." Delta explained. "It's a song sung by those who mourn and grieve beyond their mortal life. A song sung by those who wish that their departure had been different and that they'd had a chance to say goodbye."

Much to Leah's surprise, just a few seconds later, a rock platform suddenly appeared directly in front of the boat and as it protruded from the water, it seemed to block the way completely as the boat came to an immediate and abrupt standstill right next to it. Rather intriguingly for Leah, the boat seemed to react to the rules of the Sea of Sorrow that surrounded it and as soon as the vessel had been commanded to stop, it had obediently come to a sudden halt. Several questions scampered through the passageway of Leah's mind as she glanced at Delta's face but as he turned to face her, she silently reminded herself that she was now inside Spectrum and that the laws of science and nature on the face of the real world, no longer actually applied.

“This is your stop.” Delta rapidly pointed out as he motioned towards a nearby rock path that led up towards the top of the rock platform.

"What's up there?” Leah asked as her curiosity provoked her to probe him for more information and further clarity as to where the actual rock path led before she even attempted to step foot outside the boat.

“This tunnel is the Tunnel of Despair and inside this tunnel there are many, many different caves and each cave is a potential stop for any boat that travels down the tunnel with a passenger." Delta explained. "The boat can stop anywhere along this tunnel beside any cave at any point in time and where it will stop is totally unpredictable and because there are so many caves I can't possibly tell you what lies inside each one. Every journey is different and so I cannot tell you where the Sea of Sorrow will stop a boat because that is not a decision that I can make or something that I can control."

Leah nodded.

An eerie silence suddenly seemed to engulf the boat as the sorrowful lament came to an abrupt end and as the even sadder silence seemed to wrap its arms around Leah, she froze for a moment. Despite Leah's hesitation, the vessel it appeared however, was not prepared to move any further along the Tunnel of Despair until she had complied with Delta's instructions and the rock platform remained stubbornly in place as it blocked the way ahead and silently forced her to participate, irrespective of her slightly fearful reservations.

After a few minutes of inaction and total silence, Leah finally accepted that the boat was really not going to move any further forward until she had actually stepped out of its confines and then participated in whatever was due to occur next. An interaction of some kind lay at the top of that rock platform and as much as Leah felt reluctant to leave the safety of the boat as she already knew deep down inside, nothing else would happen until she did so.

Much to Leah's astonishment, despite all her hesitation, she noticed that Delta remained totally silent and very still and as she glanced at his face with a quizzical, bemused expression and just watched him for a few seconds and he actually reminded Leah of a statue that refused to budge even an inch which worried her slightly. Since Leah had automatically just assumed that Delta would leave the boat alongside her, his lack of interest in a departure from the vessel slightly confused her as his form remained completely still, absolutely stationery and totally stagnant, much like the still black water that surrounded the boat or the water that one might find inside a very dirty pond that hadn't been cleaned out for years. No matter how hard Leah stared at Delta however, no attempts to stand up or leave the boat were made on Delta's part and so his lack of participation in what was due to occur next became quite visibly apparent to Leah as she continued to wait patiently and watch him in silence.

"When do we leave Delta?" Leah suddenly asked.

“This part of your journey, you must face alone. I don’t leave the boat and I don't come along with you." Delta rapidly confirmed. "Don't worry though, when you return, I'll be waiting for you here."

Some part of Leah definitely felt slightly frustrated by Delta's lack of support and the fact that he would not accompany her into the heart of the rocky mountain which meant, she had to now face a very sorrowful, eerie unknown, totally alone. In many ways, Leah had already noticed that Delta was definitely a tad on the cold side and his frosty attitude was another small tweak that Leah felt that she might perhaps need to correct on her return to the real world because it was just a touch to cold and it did absolutely nothing to calm her nerves. When it came to the issue of Delta, Leah had already begun to conclude that although he was a guide, he was really quite a reluctant ally but she rapidly considered that perhaps a reluctant ally was better than no ally or guide at all because things would have been far worse, if she'd had to row the actual boat across the Sea of Sorrow alone and by herself first.

A fearful shiver began to run down Leah's spine and nerves seemed to rattle around inside her form as Leah gave Delta's face one final glance and then prepared to leave the boat. The fearful possibilities of what might actually lie ahead had no predictable elements at all and so as Leah bravely rose to her feet and prepared herself to face the unknown and whatever interactions might lie at the top of the rock platform, minus the reluctant ally that had actually brought her there, she remained totally silent as a bunch of fearful worries held her tongue completely captive.

Several worries swirled around inside Leah's mind and nibbled away at her form as she nervously stepped out of the boat and placed her two feet upon the start of the rock path directly in front of her but shivers and trembles continued to keep Leah company as pensive apprehension seemed to totally grip her core. Although Leah's steps appeared to be quite confident and even what might consider brave, she definitely felt far from either as she paused for a second and then quickly glanced back at Delta, just to see if perhaps he had changed his mind but unfortunately for Leah, he just remained seated in the same position and merely nodded his head at her as he encouraged her to proceed.

"He's definitely honest, just not particularly helpful at times." Leah whispered under her breath as she began to walk up the rocky path towards the rock platform.

Despite Leah's nervous state and Delta's noncompliance with her wishes, she tried to mask her fear and emotional discomfort as she walked as she plastered a look of bravery across her face because as Leah already knew, his lack of support would not change and he would simply sit completely still inside that boat until she had visited the cave. The small, thin rocky path that had been carved out of some large jagged rocks led directly towards a smooth rock platform and at the end of that platform and from what Leah could see from her current position, there appeared to be another thin, narrow path which led directly towards a dark tunnel entrance.

Since just a few more steps now lay between Leah and the smooth rock platform, she began to feel slightly intimidated by the dark tunneled entrance that sat carved, chiseled and burrowed into the rocks on her left hand side because she had no real desire to step into that dark, dismal, dreary looking space. Further along the Tunnel of Despair, as Leah stepped up onto the smooth rock platform she could now actually see that there were a lot more caves as Delta had already mentioned, although whether or not the boat would stop at any one in particular as it travelled further along the tunnel, was not something that Leah could predict with any accuracy.

One final glance was cast back towards Delta and the boat as Leah began to walk across the smooth platform as she began to prepare herself to enter into the cave but she rapidly noticed that he had not budged even an inch and still sat in the same position that she had left him and so a smile crossed her face. Despite Leah's departure and her absence, Leah observed that Delta continued to remain seated in exactly same spot as he clung onto his long, wooden pole which was gripped firmly inside his hands. Just like Delta's attachment to the boat, his attachment to the pole seemed extremely important to him and it was almost as if the pole was the most important thing in the world and as Leah thoughtfully stared at him, just for a minute his consistency amused her. At the very least,

Leah thoughtfully concluded as she paused for a moment, Delta definitely seemed to be very consistent, even if that was consistently stubborn and consistently uncooperative.

In some ways, Leah quietly concluded, Delta had at least provided her with some kind of companionship, albeit in a very loose sense of the word, despite his strange mannerisms, his very stubborn streak and his deep personal attachment to the boat which seemed to be an unbreakable bond that not even she had been able to convince him to break or breach. Some small glimmers of warmth however, had been provided to Leah by Delta in that he had managed the boat and had even answered some of her questions but as Leah glanced at the dark cave entrance, she wished that those inklings of warmth had been far more substantial and that he had accompanied her because now that she had to step out into the unknown alone, uncertainty and doubts began to run rampant and flood through her thoughts and form.

The chilliness of solitude gently tugged away at Leah's thoughts as she prepared to leave the familiarity of both the boat and Delta firmly behind her because this challenge would definitely as Leah already knew, have to be faced totally alone and as the icicles of fearful uncertainty began to collate inside her form, a cold fearful shiver ran silently down her spine. Some wisps of cold air suddenly began to whisk rapidly around Leah's form which added to the internal coldness that she felt and it was almost as if each wisp wanted to lash Leah's flesh and tear into her skin as some kind of punishment for her hesitation.

From Leah's lips, a gentle sigh managed to escape and as it was released, she finally surrendered and then turned to face the tunnel as she prepared to enter inside it because no matter how long she remained rooted to the same spot in paralyzed hesitation that would not change the challenges that she was ultimately due to face totally alone that now lay directly in front of her. A few drops of bravery still remained inside Leah's form, she discovered as she took a deep breath, dug deep inside herself and then desperately clung onto each one and although it almost felt as if bravery had completely abandoned her, disgusted either by her quest or by her nervous hesitation, Leah tried to muster up any remnants that had decided to stick around and that appeared to remain.

Rather unfortunately for Leah, the only way forward for her now lay inside the dark, dreary, dismal cave entrance directly in front of her and there would be no going back to the pretty sandy beach, at least not for the next few hours and that was a highly predictable fact. Due to the stubborn stony obstruction that had suddenly appeared, to return to the boat now as Leah already knew, would be absolutely pointless because it would not move anywhere until she had faced the challenges that lay inside the dark, rocky cave. Unlike Delta who seemed to be paralyzed with stubbornness, Leah's paralysis was more due to her own fear but as she inhaled deeply, she prepared to force herself to move forward and to actually enter inside the tunnel.

“Everything will be absolutely fine.” Delta suddenly called out. “I'll be waiting right here.”

"Right." Leah shouted back as she glanced at him and then turned back to face the cave.

Once more Delta had thrown some more verbal promises Leah's way and his encouragement compelled her to step into the dreary, dismal darkness that seemed to wait to devour her form as Leah's legs were suddenly propelled to move and carry her body forward and into the interior of the cave. In a matter of just seconds, the black interior of the cave seemed to swallow Leah's entire form whole, all of which swiftly became dark just like the cave. The dark, still, stagnant darkness it rapidly transpired however, led into not only a cave but that cave appeared to have a tunnel burrowed into one of the walls and so as Leah's eyes swiftly began to adjust to the cave's interior, she enthusiastically started to walk towards it.

"This is not the Fearful Forest." Leah convinced herself in a whisper as she walked. "It's the Sea of Sorrow which means, I should not be scared."

For the next fifty meters or so, as Leah entered into the tunnel and then began to tiptoe along it, the still darkness silently surrounded her but suddenly, she spotted an actual pinprick of light which immediately lifted her spirits and so, she began to rush eagerly towards it. The hopeful sign that the pinprick of light provided, immediately comforted Leah because it was a symbol of hope that the darkness that had been present all around her, would not continue or last for very much longer and that her surroundings would soon be much brighter.

Fortunately, much as Leah had hoped, the speck of light grew larger and larger as Leah walked briskly towards it and before very long, she found herself situated inside a wood clearing as the tunnel suddenly ended and bright sunlight seemed to flood all over her simulated form as rays of light silently began to replace the darkness. Some enthusiastic rays of sunshine which consisted of deliciously warm beams, suddenly drenched, saturated and soaked Leah's simulated skin as each one poured in from the sky and the opening above her head and to Leah's complete surprise as she stepped further into the wood clearing, she actually found a woman seated next to a golden fountain that sparkled and shone as golden drops of water cascaded down over every inch of the golden structure.

Unlike the golden fountain next to the woman and the golden ledge around its base that she was seated upon, Leah rapidly observed that a long, emerald green dress gracefully adorned her form which flowed down to the ground and even spilled across some of the grassy blades which her dress almost seemed to match in color. Some rich chestnut, brown ringlets crowned the woman's face which cascaded gently down onto her shoulders and as each strand of hair embraced her face and neck eagerly, every spiral seemed to silently celebrate her femininity. In one of the woman's hands there appeared to be a dark, reddish brown clay urn which it seemed, she wished to fill from the fountain but as Leah began to walk towards the woman, she immediately paused for a moment and then politely turned to face Leah. Just a second or two later the woman swiftly rose to her feet as she rapidly abandoned the fountain and then started to walk away from not only the golden water but also her task and so Leah politely prepared to greet her and to interact with her with a warm friendly smile.

“Oh you're here now.” The woman remarked. "I've been

expecting you but I wasn't sure when you would actually arrive."

"Yes, I'm here." Leah replied. "But what am I supposed to do here?"

A hopeful wish lay inside Leah's mind that the woman would provide her with more satisfactory answers to her questions than Delta had, who had been quite obscure, very ambiguous and even slightly evasive when Leah had attempted to establish the kind of activities that this particular emotional journey would actually entail.

"Well, you're here to visit some of the lost souls from the Sea of Sorrow, so that you can help some of them to find some peace. I'm Medina, the guardian of the woods." The woman explained as she drew close to Leah and then came to a standstill. "We have to go this way." She continued as she pointed towards a tunnel entrance at the other side of the wood clearing.

At the other side of the wood clearing and the opposite side from which Leah had entered, another tunnel entrance was situated and as Medina gently placed her arm upon Leah's arm and then led her towards it, Leah began to cooperate and follow her lead. Unlike the first dark, dreary tunnel however, this tunnel which actually led further away from the boat and Delta, was grey and shiny and as the two women stepped inside the circular space, Leah noticed that their reflections bounced off the surfaces that surrounded them. The two women continued to walk further along the tunnel and as their reflections followed them, almost like shadows, they made their way towards the other end of it as Leah began to quietly wonder where it might lead to.

Just a couple of minutes later the two women arrived at the other end of the tunnel where much to Leah's curiosity. she found there was a large expanse, the floor of which was covered in very shallow water that appeared to be only a few inches deep. The huge space which was white and very shiny, seemed to be completely bare except for one very thin, tall tree which stood firmly planted and rooted to a spot in the center of the space and as Leah absorbed her surroundings in silence, she began to wonder what might actually happen next.

Rather strangely the tree itself, Leah observed, looked almost as if it was dead because it had a dark, greyish, black trunk that contrasted very sharply against the white surfaces it was surrounded by which made it immediately stand out. Much to Leah's utter surprise however, when she turned round to face Medina so that she could ask her question about the tree, the mysterious, fairy like woman, Leah suddenly discovered had totally vanished without even a farewell or a sound and she had left Leah completely alone.

"I guess it's just me now." Leah whispered as she shrugged and then began to walk towards the tree. "I don't think it was personal, she probably just remembered that she has to fill the jug with water."

Once Leah arrived next to the tree and once she was close enough to touch it, she began to stretch her hand out towards it but just as she did so, a rather haughty female laugh suddenly interrupted the silence that surrounded her, filled up the expanse and echoed out all around her. Since the loud laughter had caught Leah completely by surprise, she almost jumped out of her skin as she began to visually scan the area as each sound continued to vibrate through the air and rattled around her ears but the person responsible, rather strangely, was nowhere to be seen, despite the bold noises that seemed to mock Leah somehow. Due to the size and thickness of the tree as Leah already knew, no one could possibly hide behind it as she quickly inspected it from a variety of angles but as she attempted to establish the source of the laughter, she could find nothing to account for the loud cackles of laughter and the tree was so thin that it would be virtually impossible for a person to hide inside its trunk.

Much to Leah's surprise however, just a few seconds later, a woman suddenly stepped out from behind the tree as if she had always been there and then she walked towards Leah in a very strange manner that almost looked and felt like an actual threat. Even more strangely, the woman actually looked exactly like Leah in that her face, body and clothes were the same and she almost seemed to be like a reflection but as Leah glanced at her and began to inspect her, she appeared to be slightly older manifestation of Leah herself. Due to the creepy nature of the woman's facial expression and approach, Leah automatically took a step backwards as the woman came to a sudden standstill directly in front of her.

Another few nervous steps were taken backwards as Leah attempted to put a bit of distance between the two because the woman's presence made her feel very uneasy but as Leah stepped back even further, the woman began to follow her and then even started to circle around her. Suddenly and without any warning at all, the situation rapidly changed and much to Leah's total shock, not for the better as the female reflection actually pounced towards Leah, leapt upon her and before Leah could even recover from the shock, the woman then started to actually wrestle Leah to the ground.

Nothing but total confusion engulfed Leah's form as she began to try and recover from the shock and deal with the agile female form that had gripped onto her neck but Leah's form buckled in seconds as she crashed to the ground and was easily overpowered, due to the sheer speed and agility of her female foe. The attack upon Leah's physical person was unprovoked and so it absolutely horrified her because it seemed to have no purpose as Leah struggled and attempted to cope with the consequences of being victimized in that fashion. In just a matter of seconds Leah's muscles seemed to tighten as spasms gripped her body as she tried and tried to wriggle around on the ground and free herself from the woman's grip however, the woman's weight which appeared to be far heavier than Leah's own actually pinned her down and so her efforts were fruitless.

"Why are you doing this?" Leah finally managed to blurt out as some words found her lips and stumbled out of her mouth. She searched the woman's eyes for a grain of compassion as she continued. "I don't understand what this is about."

“You can’t understand someone else’s sorrow until you have first felt your own.” The female reflection scorned as she leant over Leah's face and sneered at her mockingly. "And sometimes, your biggest sorrow in life will be when you have to face your own actions and your own self."

Some vibrations seemed to grate and bump all the way through

Leah's form as all her deliberations and speculations were rapidly cast aside because why the woman had attacked her no longer seemed to matter as much as Leah focused solely upon her struggle. However, Leah still felt absolutely horrified because this woman's grip was far tighter than the liquid mud that she had encountered in the Fearful Forest had been and the woman did not appear to wish to release Leah from her steadfast hold. Not a single ounce of compassion appeared to be present inside the woman's form as Leah remained trapped upon the ground and so Leah began to realize that the woman would not free her until she had managed to overpower her and had found a way to free herself.

Due to the woman's tight, cruel grip, Leah decisively started to try to fight her way out of that lock and hold as she began to wriggle and squirm around more frantically and after a few minutes, finally Leah managed to free one of her arms, one of her legs and then her upper torso from her captor's hold. Once Leah had mustered up her strength, she then tackled the woman with a hard push and the woman, surprised by Leah's sudden retaliation, rapidly fell backwards and onto the ground herself.

Just to ensure that the female reflective form would not pounce again, Leah quickly leapt to her feet and then pounced on the woman and as Leah began to grapple with her, Leah pinned down in much the same manner that Leah herself had been pinned down just a few minutes beforehand. A few pieces of material were quickly ripped from Leah's simple black top and then utilized like bits of rope as Leah attempted to bind the hands of the aggressive reflection in an attempt to restrict her from the orchestration of any further attacks. Once the woman's hands had been bound, Leah then quickly turned her attention towards the woman's feet and legs and bound those together too as she secured her own safety and left no possible room for any margin of error on her part.

Quite strangely, Leah realized as she began pull the woman onto her feet and then began to lead her back towards the rear of the tree, although the woman's grip had constrained Leah's movements, she hadn't actually caused Leah any real pain or done any actual damage to her actual form. The strange, aggressive woman had just caused Leah some severe discomfort and had restricted her but hadn't actually injured her person in any way but as Leah pushed the woman back towards the place where she had first appeared, her reflection suddenly seemed to accept defeat as the woman froze and then just a few seconds later, totally evaporated.

Once the woman had fully vanished, Leah walked a few feet away from the tree and then dropped down onto the ground as she attempted to gather her thoughts and tried to recuperate because she now felt completely worn out by the unexpected wrestle that had caught her totally by surprise. However, as Leah rested, she kept an avid eye upon the tree, just to ensure that no more aggressive reflections suddenly appeared, jumped out from behind it and popped out of it because she really didn't want to be caught off guard again.

Only a few minutes had passed by however, before a young man suddenly appeared from behind the tree much like the reflection of Leah had done and as he stepped out from behind it, Leah rapidly began to stand up. Quite strangely, it almost looked and appeared as if he had been a part of the tree itself or hidden inside it and as he began to walk towards her he smiled politely at her. Unlike Leah's reflection however, this male form seemed a lot more friendly and far less harmful as he extended a hand towards her and wore a warm smile upon his face which seemed like a friendly gesture. Due to the male form's peaceful gesture, Leah immediately reciprocated his sentiments and extended a hand towards him but it was slightly more cautious than usual because Leah definitely feared that his attitude might change at any given moment and so, she continued to keep her guard up a little.

"I really need your help." The man explained.

"Who are you?" Leah asked as her curiosity began to overpower her fears and provoked her to be slightly bolder.

“I'm Forlorn.” He replied. “You have to come with me please but we have to go quickly because we don't have much time.”

Suddenly a flat, square raft made from wooden planks floated into the area upon a wave of crystal-clear water and as it came to a complete stop next to the two, Leah watched in silence as Forlorn immediately stepped onto it and then turned to face her and urged her to do the same. The raft, Leah observed, appeared to be very simple and it looked as if it had been formed from the same dark, greyish black wood as the dead looking tree that Forlorn had stepped out from because the wooden planks were identical in color.

A long pole lay on top of the raft and Leah noticed that Forlorn quickly picked it up as he prepared to depart and the raft which was flat, square and not very thick, seemed to float gently on top of the shallow waters as it rested upon each drop. Since Leah had been invited to step onto the raft, she began to cooperate with Forlorn's request as she prepared to be taken wherever she was supposed to go next because it made very little sense to Leah to remain there on her own and besides that she had absolutely no desire to hang around and wait for another aggressive reflection that might decide to suddenly materialize and appear from behind the tree which may then subsequently try to attack her again.

When Leah had stepped onto the very basic vessel, Forlorn swiftly began to maneuver the raft as Leah quietly contemplated whether or not the shallow waters the vessel was situated upon could actually accommodate the weight of both their bodies because the depth of the actual water below it was extremely shallow. Suddenly however, Leah's question was answered as the raft started to move, despite her doubts, regardless of her questions and without any further ado and as Forlorn began to guide the vessel's direction with the long pole, it quickly became apparent to Leah that the physical dimensions of the raft and their combined weight didn't appear to be an issue at all.

In real life, Leah knew that she would never usually be so compliant and that she would never have usually participated in a stranger's request so willingly, if indeed a stranger had suddenly appeared and then invited her to board a strange looking raft because in real life Leah's response would definitely have been very different and trust would not have been given so easily. Inside Spectrum however, Leah's responses differed greatly and were not defined by the normal rules that she usually clung to in real life which governed her interactions with other human beings in the very real world because inside Spectrum, everything was totally different and so the rules of social interactions were as far as Leah was concerned, totally unwritten, varied according to the situation and were pretty much to be made at her own discretion as each situation arose.

A foggy mist suddenly seemed to blanket and envelope the raft as the two ventured out deeper into the white expanse that lay beyond the tree and even though Forlorn was situated only a few steps away, on the other side of the raft, the mist that settled all around his body made it difficult for Leah to see him properly for at least a few minutes. The mist however, Leah observed, didn't remain for very long and it rapidly suddenly seemed to clear just a few minutes later, much like a companion that wished to depart from their company but as it departed, the raft suddenly grounded against what appeared to be a bank and as it did so, Forlorn quickly stepped off the raft.

"We're almost there now." Forlorn explained as he gave her a quick nod and then rapidly secured the raft against the grassy bank with the long pole. "We have to go quickly, time is in short supply."

After Forlorn had secured the vessel, he beckoned towards Leah as he encouraged her to leave the raft and to follow him and so Leah immediately complied with his request as she stepped off the raft. Once Leah had stepped onto what pretty much looked like normal land once again, she followed Forlorn quietly as he led her across the grassy bank which seemed to greet her feet politely with lush, soft, green grass that cushioned each step that she took.

For about one hundred meters the two continued to walk-in silence and Leah noticed that there was a small hill directly in front of them that Forlorn seemed to be headed towards. A few minutes later the two arrived at the top of the small hill and on the other side of that hill, Leah rapidly noticed that there appeared to be an actual muddy swamp. The two continued to walk together in silence as Forlorn led Leah down the other side of the hill and towards the swamp and as they drew closer to it, Leah could see that there appeared to be a woman stuck on a small mound of solid grass in the center of the swamp.

"Help me please Forlorn." The woman suddenly called out.

Rather curiously, Leah observed, the woman appeared to have been stuck in the center of the swamp for some time because her facial expression looked strained and tense and she had not only noticed Forlorn's arrival but the two seemed to know each other because she had called out his name as she had welcomed his presence. A look of sheer relief seemed to cross the woman's face as she glanced at Forlorn and so Leah immediately assumed that she had probably been waiting for some signs of a possible rescue for quite some time.

In direct response to the woman's pleas, Leah noticed that Forlorn suddenly started to rush around the edges of the swamp as he began to collect and gather some pieces of wood from underneath the trees that surrounded it and so Leah quickly followed suit and joined in. Once what appeared to be enough wood had been collected, Forlorn then tied the pieces of wood together with a vine like rope that he had stripped from a nearby tree as Leah watched him prepare to try and rescue the woman with a makeshift bridge of sorts. Each piece of wood, Leah observed, was joined together and when it looked as though the wooden bridge might be long enough to reach the woman, Forlorn rapidly slid it towards the swamp and towards her current position.

The wooden contraption was pushed out towards the mound of solid grass as far as it would go as Leah watched Forlorn in silence and then he sat down upon one end of makeshift bridge to stabilize its position. Once the wooden bridge was in place, the woman immediately clambered onto the bridge and then took a few steps as she began to walk across it as she attempted to assist Forlorn in his rescue attempt and make her way to safety.

"Yes, just try to walk across the bridge Christine. If you can walk across the bridge, you'll be okay, I promise." Forlorn called out enthusiastically.

Although Leah wanted to assist Forlorn in his rescue attempt, she suddenly froze as she just watched the two in total silence because she felt unsure that her input would actually help and that it may even make things worse. A few more cautious but successful steps were taken across the bridge as Leah watched Christine attempt to reach safety and as Christine's confidence started to grow, Leah noticed that her steps became much bolder in that each one was slightly larger and even slightly faster.

Suddenly however, something seemed to go wrong and from what Leah could see, Christine's steps seemed to go off track as she lost her balance and her progression across the makeshift bridge was hampered. For the next couple of minutes Christine stood in one place as she tried to restore her balance and struggled to straighten herself up and just as Leah thought Christine was about to regain her composure, much to Leah's absolute horror, Christine suddenly appeared to slip. Some pieces of wood, Leah rapidly noticed, suddenly appeared to melt into the swamp which each one had rested delicately against just seconds before and the vine rope started to snap as the flimsy, makeshift, wooden bridge started to fall to pieces and ultimately, began to sink.

Every part of Leah's body started to tremble as she watched Forlorn quickly lay down upon the ground and then try to stretch his arm out towards Christine who by this point had travelled too far along the flimsy bridge to return to the solid mound of grass. From Christine's mouth, a very loud shriek suddenly pierced the air and then shot straight into Leah's ears as she watched Christine began to slip down into the muddy swamp that surrounded her but no matter how hard Forlorn tried to reach Christine's hands or arms, his quest appeared to be absolutely impossible because the distance between the two was just too great to bridge with his arm. The sight before Leah's eyes continued to frustrate her but she felt absolutely powerless to assist as she continued to watch Christine sink and her desperate attempts to grab onto Forlorn's hand but as Leah could already see, the situation was totally impossible because Christine was unable to reach or grip onto the hand that Forlorn had offered to her.

A terrifying moment gripped onto Leah's thoughts as she watched Christine disappear below the surface of the muddy swamp but just a few seconds later, Christine suddenly seemed to claw her way back up to the surface as she spluttered and coughed. Some frantic attempts were made by Christine as she resurfaced to grab onto some nearby pieces of partially submerged wood as Leah saw her attempt to raise herself back up out of the mud that had almost consumed her but the muddy swamp just continued to ruthlessly pull her downwards and so within minutes, she disappeared from Leah's sight again. Horrifyingly for Leah as she watched, the pieces of wood vanished alongside Christine and Forlorn's efforts, she rapidly realized, were now almost totally pointless because Christine could not even possibly hope to reach his hand from below the mud but as Leah watched Forlorn respond, she noticed that he made another attempt to try and save Christine as he crawled out across the bank and closer to the swamp itself.

The frantic crawl of Forlorn almost broke Leah's heart which began to weep as she watched him try to stretch his entire body out towards Christine and as Christine continued to wrestle and fight the muddy swamp, Forlorn frantically fought the liquid mud too which it appeared, wanted to consume her and drag her body down into the depths of its grungy, muddy death bed but his efforts were futile. Just a few seconds later, sadly and unfortunately, Forlorn's own body began to sink into the depths of the muddy swamp and as Leah stood on the bank, she shook her head as she was suddenly kicked into action and then started to rush towards him. Much like the liquid mud that Leah had encountered in the Fearful Forest this muddy swamp it appeared, wanted to claim any human bodies that it could lay its muddy claws upon as its own and it was a ruthless predator that seemed intent on capturing any innocent captives that it had managed to intertwine in its muddy, deadly embrace.

Some tears began to trickle and then stream down Leah's cheeks as she tried to kneel on the lower part of Forlorn's legs in order to keep them on the bank and a large dark brown branch which was on the ground close to Leah was then quickly grabbed and placed in one of Forlorn's hands. Just a few minutes later however, Forlorn's legs began to slip from Leah's grip and as Forlorn slipped down into the mud completely, Leah knew that there would be no actual rescue for either of them because she would never be able to pull them both out of that muddy swamp and certainly not in time to save them.

Nothing but total defeat seemed to gather, fill, occupy and line Leah's heart and thoughts as she collapsed onto the grassy bank in a conquered heap and mourned as she began to accept that the battle with the muddy swamp had now been lost and that instead of one life, it had managed to claim two victims in one foul swoop with its heartless muddy tentacles of death. The whole situation had absolutely traumatized Leah and as tears continued to stream down her cheeks and her body continued to shake with sorrow, she could not find any comfort at all upon that grassy bank because no matter how she mourned, neither of the two returned.

Deep in the Rocky Caves of Reconciliation

Just as Leah was about to be consumed in the depths of sorrowful grief however, Medina suddenly reappeared and then began to walk towards Leah and as she did so, Medina stretched out her hand as she smiled. A confused expression crossed Leah's face as she glanced at Medina and then shook her head as a few sobs were released from her lips. Once Medina was close enough, she held onto Leah's arm and then gently pulled Leah to her feet and although Leah didn't particularly want to stand up, she reluctantly began to cooperate as she rose to her feet and then turned to face Medina.

"Why Medina?" Leah asked. "Why did they have to die?"

"You can't save everyone Leah. No one can. No matter how much you try or how much you want to." Medina explained. "But it's time for you to go now, there's nothing more you can do here and there's something else you have to do."

Despite all of Leah's sadness, she began to follow Medina's lead as Medina guided her away from the bank of the swamp towards a cave like hole that was burrowed into the hill that Leah and Forlorn had walked down to arrive at the swamp. Some part of Leah inwardly continued to mourn as she walked over her inability to intervene because she had not been able to save the couple who had fought so desperately and frantically with the muddy swamp grave for the right to their own lives. The swamp had finally consumed both people and Leah had been completely unable to assist or help them in any capacity at all and she still felt unable to accept that harsh, grim reality.

When the two women stepped into the dark, black cave, Leah noticed that it was very silent and as Medina led her towards the right-hand side of the cave, Leah could see that there was a tunnel burrowed into the hillside and the wall of the cave. Once the two women had entered into the tunnel's interior they followed it until the very end as Medina remained by Leah's side but just a step ahead of her and held onto her arm. At the other end of the tunnel there was a large opening which led into another subterranean, rocky cave where Leah could see a woman in her early forties all dressed in black, seated upon a rocky pedestal with a very sad, downcast expression upon her face. Just a second or so later, Leah watched in silence as Medina began to walk towards the woman as Medina left Leah's side and when she arrived beside the woman, Medina touched her shoulder gently and the woman immediately glanced up.

"I've brought someone to help you Celia." Medina explained.

Celia nodded. "Thank you, Medina." She replied as she wiped a tear from her eye and released a sob.

A quick glance was cast towards Medina's face as Leah tried to search for answers as to what exactly she would help with or instructions of how she might possibly help the woman but no clarity could be found in Medina's face and she not a single word came from her lips.

"How can I help?" Leah asked. "I couldn't help the people in the swamp."

"Don't worry, this will be different because you are going to help Celia put her soul to rest." Medina explained as she turned to face Leah. "She'd like to sleep peacefully now and you can help her do that."

Suddenly, the rocky cave that the three women were situated inside transformed all around Leah and as Medina smiled at Celia reassuringly and then nodded, the other two women began to fade away as Leah was left alone not inside the cave but inside what looked like the lounge of a house. Once the cave's interior had fully evaporated and the lounge had fully formed all around Leah, it appeared that she had just arrived inside a house where there was a funeral gathering which confused her slightly because at least twenty people dressed in black were dotted around the interior of the room. A few seconds were spent in introspective consideration as Leah glanced at the sea of strange faces around her and searched for an indication of what she was actually supposed to do next. No answers however, seemed to jump out and into Leah's hands or thoughts and since no one seemed to welcome Leah or even acknowledge her presence, she waited awkwardly and silently at one side of the room as she continued to watch the guests.

Not more than a minute or so later, a young boy stepped into the lounge that looked to be around ten years old and Leah noticed that he walked towards a man situated on the other side of the room that was surrounded by three other adults and the group of adults which consisted of two other men and a woman continued their discussion despite his approach. For the next couple of minutes, Leah noticed that the boy seemed to just stand politely at the edge of the group as he waited to be addressed and that he appeared to be reluctant to interrupt the group in mid-conversation as he remained completely silent as he waited and so Leah smiled as she thoughtfully appreciated his exceptionally good manners.

After a few minutes had gone by, the mature man in his late forties that the boy was closest to, suddenly glanced at him and then excused himself from the group of people that surrounded him and as he turned to face the boy and then drew much closer to him, the adult male began to address him directly. The man, who Leah immediately assumed was his father, due to his attitude, tone and conduct, then led the boy across the room and when they were quite close to Leah's position, the adult male came to a total standstill, faced him and then began to speak to him.

"You should go to your room now Wesley." He instructed. "This gathering is really for adults."

"I just wanted to say goodbye to my mum." Wesley replied.

"Yes well, you've done that now, so you can go to your room." The older man reiterated in a slightly sterner tone as he attempted to dismiss the boy from the lounge and the funeral gathering.

"Yes father." Wesley replied obediently as he nodded his head and then prepared to vacate the lounge.

Due to the close proximity of Wesley and his father, Leah had managed to overhear every word of their brief discussion and as she continued to watch them both, she noticed that Wesley began to walk slowly towards the lounge door as his father turned, then walked back across the room as he re-joined the same group of guests. Some pricks of curiosity suddenly began to needle Leah's mind as she watched Wesley accept his dismissal and leave the room with his head hung low and she noticed that he did not utter a single word to anyone else inside the lounge as he vacated the room.

Since Wesley's father had by that point returned to his conversation and had fully turned his attention back towards his guests, Leah began to follow Wesley out of the lounge because deep down inside, she felt a sudden desire to comfort him. Strangely, Leah noticed that Wesley hadn't spoken to anyone else inside the lounge besides his father and so, Leah wondered as she walked, if perhaps his grief had silenced him but then no one else had spoken to him either and it almost felt as if he was somehow, invisible to everyone around him.

Quite curiously, Leah observed as she followed Wesley out into the hallway of the house, he didn't approach the start of the staircase as she would have expected him to because that was where the bedrooms in the house, she immediately assumed, would actually be situated. Instead of Wesley going up the stairs, much to Leah's surprise, he paused for a moment and then just glanced at the foot of the stairs before he turned and then walked in the opposite direction as he did an about turn and headed towards the kitchen which it rapidly transpired, was situated at the rear of the building on the ground floor. Since Wesley had gone against his father's wishes, Leah noticed that he made his way into and through the kitchen on tiptoes as he headed towards the back door and as she watched him, she continued to follow him quietly.

Once Wesley arrived at the back door, he quickly opened it up and then slipped out into the back garden as Leah continued to follow him and vacated the interior of the house as she walked just a few steps behind him. The back garden seemed to be reasonably well kept and decently manicured and there appeared to be a row of apple trees along one side of it and some neat rose beds which adorned a few large rock gardens that Leah immediately noticed, appeared to cover most of the gardens quite large enclosed space and a few neatly trimmed hedges lined a garden path and also the outer edge.

At the very bottom of the garden however, Leah observed that despite the well-maintained areas, there appeared to be an extremely shabby looking shed which seemed to be very run down and in desperate need of repair and as Leah watched Wesley head towards the shed and then enter inside its confines, she continued to follow him quietly. Despite all the people inside the family's home, Wesley had remained pretty much alone since Leah had arrived inside the lounge but she noticed that his solitude seemed to be quite comfortable for him because the funeral gathering appeared to be for one of his relatives. Grief as Leah already knew, was such a strange phenomenon and it struck different people in so many different ways and often people would surround themselves with silence and solitude in order to cope with life and an unexpected departure from it as their minds were thrown into the deep depths of heart-breaking loss and they tottered around on the torn edges of traumatic despair and that solitude, it was often extremely difficult to actually retrieve their hearts from.

When Leah stepped into the shed, suddenly Wesley glanced up at her face, seemed to notice her arrival and then politely stood up but up until that point, Leah had thought u that no one could see her because absolutely no one so far had acknowledged her presence in any capacity at all. However, Wesley it transpired, could actually see and hear her and had actually responded to her presence, unlike the people in the lounge who had totally ignored Leah as she had walked through the room.

"Are you one of my mother's friends?" Wesley asked politely.

"I guess in some way I am." Leah replied as she nodded and smiled.

"You weren't at the funeral service." Wesley mentioned.

"No, I wasn't. I think I'm actually here to see you." Leah suggested.

"Why?" Wesley asked.

"I'm not sure yet." Leah replied honestly.

"Is my mum okay?" Wesley enquired.

"Yes, your mum is fine." Leah immediately reassured him. "She misses you a lot."

"Would you like to sit down?" Wesley asked as he pulled a small, empty crate across the ground towards her. He quickly pulled a cloth from a nearby shelf and then dusted of the top of the crate before he continued. "You can sit down if you like, no one comes in here except me."

"Sure." Leah replied as she nodded and then politely sat down on the top of the empty crate. "Do you know why I might be here Wesley?"

For a few seconds a blanket of uncertain silence seemed to fall across the interior of the shed as Leah watched Wesley shake his head and then just stare across the shed at the shed door in a thoughtful silence. Just a few seconds later however, Leah watched as a spark of recognition suddenly seemed to appear in and light up Wesley's eyes and face as he appeared to recall something that could perhaps shed some light on the matter. A hand was eagerly slipped inside one of Wesley's pocket, Leah observed and then a crumpled slip of paper was swiftly retrieved which looked like some kind of booking receipt.

"Perhaps you're here because of this." Wesley suggested as he handed the crumpled piece of paper to her. "I found this on the floor outside my father and mother's bedroom yesterday. I was going in there to look for a bracelet that my mother loved, I wanted to keep it just because she loved it so much, she wore it almost every day." He explained. "I gave the bracelet to my mother for her birthday last year."

"What is it?" Leah asked.

"It's a booking receipt for a boat that was hired for a boat trip that my mother and father went on the day that she died but my mother absolutely hates boats." Wesley replied. "I wasn't supposed to go anywhere near my father and mother's bedroom, my father told me not to since she passed away but I really wanted to keep the bracelet, I didn't want anyone else to have it."

"What happened on the boat trip?" Leah asked.

"I don't know but she never returned from it." Wesley explained solemnly as he shook his head sadly. "My father just said there was some kind of accident."

Due to Wesley's explanation which sounded slightly suspicious, Leah immediately began to uncrumple the small booking slip and then started to inspect, examine and read the quite sparse details upon it but there wasn't much to really explore since it had been written quite vaguely. A few details were to be found like a time, a date and the name of a boat and so it didn't take Leah very long to complete her inspection. Once Leah felt satisfied that no further answers lay inside the shed, or inside her hands, she quickly stood up and then began to pace the interior of the shed as she quietly considered what it might all mean but no obvious answers leapt out at her.

"Is the boat hire office nearby Wesley?" Leah asked.

Wesley nodded his head. "Yes, it's in walking distance." He replied.

"Can we go there now?" Leah enquired.

"Yes, it's just about a ten-minute walk from here." Wesley explained as he nodded again. "I can take you there right now." He continued as he stood up and then walked towards the shed door.

"Should you tell anyone where you're going?" Leah ventured to ask.

Wesley immediately shook his head. "My father will be busy for hours, he won't even know or realize that I'm not at home." He mentioned.

"I think you could be right about that." Leah agreed. "He did seem to be rather tied up with visitors."

Just a few seconds later the two stepped out of the shed and then Wesley began to lead Leah discreetly away from the house and further down the garden towards a small, metal gate which Leah noticed was situated at the very bottom of it. Once the two stepped out of the garden through the gate, Leah continued to follow Wesley as he led her along a small, dirt lane which ran along the end of the garden and as the two walked, Leah noticed that they both remained silent and it almost felt as if fear had silenced them both due to their close proximity to Wesley's home.

At the other end of the dirt lane was a main street and as the two stepped out onto it, Leah began to ask Wesley some questions about his mother as they walked, all of which he politely answered and the answers rapidly confirmed to Leah that Celia was definitely, actually Wesley's mother. Before very long and once the two had crossed a few more streets, they arrived outside the boat hire venue and so Leah enthusiastically prepared to enter inside the small retail venue with a glass front that looked really quite small and more like an office with a counter than anything else. A large framed, auburn haired, busty woman in her mid-fifties, sat behind the counter itself and as Leah stepped into the venue, she noticed that Wesley quickly followed her inside and that the woman stood up as she prepared to greet them both with a huge jolly smile upon her face as they walked towards her.

"What can I do for you both today?" The woman asked politely as she lifted up the counter hatch and stepped through it. "Would you like to hire a boat?"

"I'm not sure." Leah replied honestly because she actually wasn't very sure why the two were there yet. She smiled as she handed the woman the crumpled booking slip as she continued. "I came to ask you about a recent booking."

"Ah yes." The woman acknowledged as her face suddenly changed and a frown rapidly spread out across the lines of her skin. "That day, there was a terrible tragedy, it was the first accident that we've ever had. It's absolutely never happened before on one of our boats. Never ever."

"Can you show us the boat please that was hired that day?" Leah asked.

"I definitely can, it's moored by the pier today." She explained as she began to walk back towards the counter.

"Right." Leah agreed as she began to follow her.

"I'm Melanie by the way and I already know you of course Wesley." Melanie said as nodded her head at him. "Aren't you growing into such a polite and responsible young man, your mother would be so proud. I'm so sorry about what happened Wesley and anytime you need anything at all, you know where I am."

"Yes, thank you Mrs. Peterson." Wesley replied graciously.

"I'm Leah." Leah said as she quickly introduced herself. "I'm a friend of Celia's."

"Ah okay, nice to meet you. I'll just get my keys so that I can lock up the shop front for a few minutes." Melanie said as she walked towards a cabinet, opened it up and then plucked a set of keys from it.

A few silent seconds went by as Melanie attended to a few more things behind the counter as Leah watched and waited for her beside the door alongside Wesley in silence. Once Melanie had switched the phone to answering machine and put the computer on standby, she then began to walk towards the door, Leah and Wesley with a cheerful smile and as Leah watched, she observed that Wesley pulled the door open for them all.

"Thanks." Leah said appreciatively as she stepped through the door.

"Yes, thank you so much young man." Melanie agreed as she followed Leah.

Quite interestingly for Leah, by this point it had struck her that Melanie could actually see her and so for a moment, as the three left the booking office behind and then began to walk along a concrete path, she wondered if perhaps visibility of her form in this particular world was attributable to some kind of spirit-based sight. In some strange way, it felt as though only the people that were connected to Celia favorably or the people that were supposed to assist Leah in her quest, were perhaps the only people that could see Leah's actual form it appeared because the people in the lounge at Wesley's home hadn't even given her a second glance.

Some discussion was held as the three continued to walk along the concrete path towards a few wooden piers where the boats were moored as Melanie chatted away with Wesley as they walked and Leah listened to the two converse. Most of the conversation seemed to revolve around Wesley's mother and father, Leah noticed as she listened to the two communicate and discuss various things, none of which she knew anything about and as the three stepped onto the relevant pier and then started to walk along it, Leah glanced at each boat they passed with as she began to inspect her surroundings and the vessels moored to the wooden structure.

Once they had arrived beside the relevant boat, Melanie immediately invited them both to take a look around inside it and so Wesley and Leah climbed up onto the boat and then walked across the top deck of the boat as they prepared to inspect it quietly. The boat itself was quite small in comparison to some of the other larger vessels that were moored alongside it, Leah observed and it seemed to only have a capacity to carry about ten passengers although it did have a lower deck which possibly meant, it could actually house and squeeze in a few more on a journey, if required.

"I can't possibly stay with you but please feel free to look around as much as you want to, this boat is not booked out to any clients today." Melanie offered politely as she unlocked the lower cabin. "I have to get back to the booking office just in case there are any customers." She explained. "When you're finished, just let me know and I'll come back and lock up."

Leah nodded. "Thanks Melanie." She replied.

"The journey the boat took that day is actually charted in the voyage records which you can find here." Melanie mentioned as she walked towards a screen inside a small enclosed space on the top deck. "Just in case that might help, I'll switch it on for you just in case you need to check anything." She explained as she touched a panel on a raised part of the deck and it immediately lit up. "If you need anything else, I'll just be inside the booking office."

"Thanks, we'll let you know if we need anything else." Leah replied with an appreciative smile.

Just a few seconds later and once Melanie appeared to feel satisfied that she had done all that she could to assist the two, Leah watched her depart as she left the two alone to conduct their inspection of the interior of the boat. The charted records of Wesley's mother and father's voyage were quietly inspected as Wesley and Leah huddled together inside the enclosed area which had a thick transparent case. A pen and paper lay on a shelf just below the screen itself and as Leah continued to study the screen, she noticed that Wesley quickly picked it up and then began to map out the path that the boat had taken and the voyage that his mother had never returned from. The contents of the screen were swiftly and roughly sketched out on the piece of paper and even though Leah could see that it was quite a rough sketch, it was still definitely understandable and easy enough to follow because Wesley had the charted various landmark that the boat had sailed past that awful, tragic day clearly upon it.

"We should follow the path of the boat and visit all the places that they passed by that day. I've charted them all on my map, just like the voyage records." Wesley explained as he finished his map sketch, held the piece of paper up in the air and then placed the pen back upon on the shelf.

"Yes, we should." Leah agreed as she nodded her head. "Let's check the rest of the boat first." She suggested. "Melanie left the lower deck unlocked, so we can have a look."

Wesley nodded.

For approximately the next ten minutes the two searched the interior and top deck of the boat but there appeared to be nothing particularly helpful or useful and so the two left the boat and then returned to the boat hire office to thank Melanie for her assistance and to bid her farewell. Once the two had left the boat office, they then began to wander along the shoreline in accordance to the charted journey on the map that Wesley had sketched as they attempted to re-enact and travel along the boat's steps that day, albeit on solid land. The first two landmarks and plot points were pointed out to Leah by Wesley as the two walked as he attempted to trace the route that the boat had taken until they reached the third and final plot point which was actually a small cottage.

Unlike the first two landmarks which had simply been unoccupied buildings and structures, the last third plot point on Wesley's sketched map, Leah rapidly discovered, was actually a person's residence that sat upon the top of a low cliff that jutted out over the sea which sat underneath it and just below the cliff face where there appeared to be a picturesque sandy bay. Since Wesley had already begun to walk towards the door of the cottage, Leah swiftly followed him as she prepared to face a total stranger with a bunch of questions which they may or may not answer and once Wesley had knocked upon the front door, the two waited for a few seconds in silence as they waited for the occupant to respond.

Approximately sixty seconds later a man in his late fifties opened up the cottage front door and then he looked at the two stood on his doorstep quietly for a few seconds and Leah observed that his visual scan appeared to be laced with some light traces of cautious suspicion. In terms of the man's appearance, his clothes looked ruffled and very quaint, Leah noticed and there even seemed to be some cobwebs in the folds of his long, black overcoat which hung from his frame and almost swamped him. Although Leah wanted to be polite since the two were in pursuit of information from this stranger that might help them, she couldn't help but screw up her nose in response as she tried not to inhale for a moment, just in case any undesirable aromas that might emanate from his person wafted through the air uninvited which could then perhaps penetrate her nostrils.

"What do you want?" The man suddenly asked in a gruff voice.

"We're just here to ask you something, if you don't mind." Leah started to explain as she attempted to justify why the two were actually there and then paused for a moment as she searched her mind for something that might sound reasonably acceptable but not divulge too much information.

Although the man didn't appear to be very friendly and didn't sound very helpful, he was the first person that could possibly shed some light on Celia's disappearance and so Leah began to swallow her reservations and her disgust as she gave him a strained smile and prepared to ask him a few more questions. However, much to Leah's utter relief, before she could utter another word, Wesley actually, bravely stepped forward and then began to embark upon a conversation with the man.

"We were wondering if you could help us please. A woman disappeared about a week ago on a boat and the boat passed by this cove that day." Wesley explained as he slipped a photo of his mother from his pocket and then showed it to the man.

A few seconds of uncomfortable, awkward silence passed by as the suspicious, unfriendly man glanced at the photo and the two stood directly in front of him and then his face, Leah observed, suddenly seemed to change as a glimmer of recognition flickered across it.

"You'd better come in." The man suddenly said as he took a step back from the front door of his cottage. "The doorstep really isn't the right place to discuss such sensitive matters."

Since the man appeared to be the first person that could assist the two in a in some capacity which therefore meant that they had little choice, Leah prepared to accept his invitation and to cooperate, despite its lack of appeal but she held her breath discreetly as she bravely stepped towards the front door of the cottage. The rough, unkempt man led the two inside his home as they stepped through the front door which led straight into a large lounge with a kitchen area at one end of it and the interior of the cottage, Leah swiftly noticed, appeared to be just as rough, dusty and disheveled as his physical appearance.

At one side of the room there was a large, dusty window which had a telescope and a set of binoculars attached to a stand next to it which pointed out of the window and towards the sea and as Leah glanced at it, she wondered how much one could possibly see out of the dirty grime that surrounded it. Despite all Leah's reservations however, she held her tongue as she prepared to participate nonetheless because to verbalize and to release such doubts from her lips as she already knew, would definitely not help Wesley, Celia or herself. Since the two that were present were in pursuit of information and the facts that revolved around the events of that day which this person quite possibly held some crucial details to and quite possibly even the key to Celia's tragic accident, Leah knew that to anger or offend him would be counterproductive to their actual visit and at least so far, he had been polite enough to open the door and then invite them both into his personal residence which definitely deserved an ounce appreciation.

"I do watch the seas sometimes, just in case ships and boats come by because there are some jagged rocks on the other side of the bay that can be very treacherous, especially if there's a storm." The man started to explain. "My family have lived here for over a century and I guess it's just a kind of responsibility that we've taken on board. We're a bit like lighthouse keepers I guess you might say, just we don't get paid for it. I'm Vernon and we like to call ourselves Sea Guards." Vernon continued as he smiled.

"Did you see the boat that day?" Wesley urged as his eyes suddenly filled with fresh hope.

"I did." Vernon replied. "And I noticed that there was a couple on the boat and that the man pushed the woman in the photo into the water but it all seemed quite playful and so I just assumed that they were lovers and involved in some kind of romantic game. I didn't see her reappear or swim but then I didn't watch them for long."

Wesley nodded his head and then thanked him appreciatively. "Thank you so much Vernon that's very helpful, it really wasn't a romantic game, my mother couldn't swim." He mentioned as he began to slip the photo of his mother back inside his pocket.

After a few more minutes and once a few more words had been exchanged, the two felt satisfied that there were no more answers to be found inside Vernon's cottage and so, Leah and Wesley thanked Vernon and then left as they began to make their way back towards Wesley's home. Some of the things that Vernon had said continued to churn around inside Leah's thoughts as she walked and as she discussed them with Wesley, they tried to piece together what might have happened on that tragic day but there still seemed to be some missing details and crucial plot points that didn't relate to any landmarks at all and so, Celia's accident just didn't seem to make any kind of sense to either of the two.

Once the two arrived back at Wesley's home, Wesley led Leah back inside the building and this time instead of the stairs being ignored, he actually began to walk up them as he headed towards the upper floor of his home and the bedrooms. When the two reached the upper landing, Wesley began to walk on tiptoes towards a bedroom door but once he had taken just a few steps, he suddenly paused for a moment, turned to face Leah and then urged her to follow him.

"There's still one last place to look." Wesley whispered. "My father's bedroom."

"What if you get caught?" Leah whispered back.

"I don't care. This is my duty, this is for my mother." Wesley replied in a whisper as he gave an adamant shake of his head. "I'll just say I wanted to look for something that belonged to my mother." He reassured her and then he began to walk towards the door once again on tiptoes.

"Okay." Leah whispered as she nodded her head and then started to follow him on tiptoes.

A dim, dull, dark room greeted Leah's eyes as Wesley pushed his father's bedroom door open but Leah rapidly noticed that the bedroom itself was quite large in size and although it had a huge pair of windows at one side of the room, neither window appeared to let much light in due to a pair of very long, dark red curtains that hung down generously over each one. In terms of the bedroom itself, there appeared to be nothing particularly fancy or special about it and it looked quite plain and rather moderate in comparison to some of the bedrooms that Leah had seen in other people's homes but as Leah watched Wesley, she noticed that he made his way towards one of the bedside cabinets and then began to search inside it.

"What exactly are we looking for Wesley?" Leah asked in a whisper as she crossed the room and joined him.

"I don't know yet but we'll know when we find it." Wesley replied with a determined nod. "Have a look around and if you see anything unusual just let me know."

"Right." Leah agreed.

Every part of Leah's form trembled with nerves as she tiptoed towards a nearby chest of drawers, opened up the top drawer and then began to rummage around inside it although she still felt quite unsure as to what exactly she wanted to find. A hopeful wish however, lay inside Leah's heart and mind that she would recognize that something unusual when she actually came across it because Wesley seemed to feel absolutely certain that not only did something have to be found but also that the something unusual that had to be found, was situated somewhere inside his father's bedroom.

Besides some male attire, for a few minutes Leah found nothing particularly helpful or that unusual inside the drawers but finally, her rummage seemed to strike gold as she found a small bottle that seemed to contain some kind of liquid inside it that had a warning label on its exterior. Since the warning label was small and barely even visible and no other label appeared to be on the bottle itself, it immediately aroused Leah's suspicions as she glanced across the room at Wesley and then held it up as she showed it to him.

"Do you think this could be anything to do with what happened?" Leah whispered.

Wesley nodded as he paused. "Probably, we should try to find out." He crossed the room and then plucked the bottle gently out of her hands as he began to inspect it

Suddenly however, the two were interrupted in the middle of their search as some giggles wafted through the bedroom door that emanated from the hallway just outside the room and so Wesley quickly grabbed onto Leah's arm and rapidly shut the open drawer. A finger was swiftly placed over Wesley's lips as he warned Leah to be totally silent and then rushed her towards the pair of large windows and curtains at one side of the room. One of the curtains was swiftly utilized to mask Leah's body from view as Wesley hid her from sight just before he hid behind the second curtain and concealed himself.

For a few seconds an awkward, uncertain silence filled the interior of the bedroom, Leah observed as the two just waited expectantly for the source of the giggles to enter inside the room and as Leah waited, she hoped that the giggler's entrance would not lead to their actual discovery. Just a few seconds later two people stepped inside the room and from the laughs, snippets of conversation and giggles that emanated from both parties involved, Leah could immediately tell that one of those parties was indeed, Wesley's father. Since Leah could peek around one edge of the curtain without being noticed, she had a quick glance and as she did so, she caught a glimpse of Wesley's father with his arms wrapped around a younger woman that was all dressed in black. The couple it appeared were clearly engaged and involved in an extremely flirtatious exchange from what Leah could clearly see and as she watched them touch each other affectionately for a few seconds, she hardly dared to even take a breath through fear of discovery.

"How long do you think we should wait Stuart?" The woman suddenly asked in a very serious tone as she smiled at Wesley's father.

"We have to wait a while Patricia. Celia's only just gone." Wesley's father replied. "Wesley took it very badly and so will the rest of her family, if you move in straight away and we get engaged next week. A few months perhaps."

"I can't wait that long Stuart." Patricia demanded as a frown suddenly crossed her face. "I've waited ages already."

"Let's just see how things go." Wesley's father replied. "It'll take Wesley a while to adjust to his mother's death."

"Can't you just ship him off somewhere?" Patricia asked. "You could always send him to a boarding school, or you could just get rid of him like you got rid of his mother."

"He's my son Patricia, he's my own flesh and blood." Wesley's father quickly pointed out as he shook his head.

"And she was your wife." Patricia mentioned as she shrugged. "What's the difference?"

"Look I'll sort out Wesley, you just worry about yourself." Wesley's father advised her. "Perhaps boarding school in a month or so is a good idea though that wouldn't look suspicious and it would just seem natural. The actions of a husband consumed with grief and unable to cope after the loss of his beloved wife." He added as he kissed her passionately on the lips and then stroked her hair. "Yes, that would make some kind of sense, you're definitely more than just a beautiful face Patricia."

"We better go back downstairs now Stuart; your guests are waiting and you still have to play the part of a grieving husband." Patricia quickly reminded him as she began to lead him back towards the bedroom door.

"Yes, you're absolutely right." Stuart agreed as he began to follow her towards the door.

The bedroom suddenly emptied, amidst another bunch of sniggers and giggles from the two lovers but Wesley and Leah remained hidden for a minute or so longer as they waited patiently to ensure that the lovers did not actually intend to return. When Wesley felt satisfied that it was highly unlikely the two would actually return, he then stepped out from behind the curtain and motioned towards Leah to do the same.

"Your father actually killed your mother Wesley." Leah said in a horrified tone as she walked towards him and verbally regurgitated some of the overheard snippets of conversation. "It's absolutely horrific. You can't possibly stay here, with him, you might be next." She insisted as she absorbed the ugly, horrific, painful truth.

"I can go and stay with my Auntie perhaps." Wesley mentioned. "She's my mother's sister."

"Yes, you have to go somewhere else because you can't stay here." Leah agreed.

"Aunt Marie will look after me." Wesley reassured. "I'll be safe there."

"Will she be willing though?" Leah asked

"Definitely, she never really liked my dad anyway." Wesley explained as he nodded. "The whole family on my mother's side, didn't really like him much, they married very much against her parent's wishes."

Leah nodded.

"I'll go and ask her now and I can probably leave today." Wesley explained. "She's downstairs."

"Is there anything you want me to tell your mother?" Leah asked.

"Yes, you can tell her that I love her and that she was the best mother that a boy could ever possibly have." Wesley replied as he faced her and smiled. "Tell her that I miss her and that I'll try my best to be a good man, like she taught me and like she wanted me to be."

Leah smiled and nodded. "I'll tell her all those things Wesley and if she was here right now, I know she would be so proud of you."

She reassured him. "You're a very good son and any mother would be proud of you and please don't worry about your mother, she's in a place of rest now."

"Thanks." Wesley replied. "We should get out of here and I should go downstairs and speak to my Auntie Marie."

"Yes, of course." Leah agreed.

Once the two felt satisfied that it was actually safe to do so, they walked towards the bedroom door as they prepared to leave Stuart's bedroom and as Wesley opened the bedroom door, he peeked out into the hallway just to ensure it was actually clear before the two attempted to vacate the room. Since the upper landing appeared to be clear, Wesley quickly led Leah out of the room and towards the stairs but quite strangely as Leah began to follow him and stepped through the door instead of her arrival on the landing, suddenly she found herself back inside the subterranean cave once more next to Celia who was still seated upon the rocky pedestal.

"Thank you so much." Celia said as she suddenly stood up and then walked towards Leah. "I couldn't return to the world of the living to help my son because my soul has already joined the souls of dead."

Upon a part of the cave wall, Leah could see an image of Wesley's home which displayed Wesley's form within it and as she watched him step inside the lounge, she observed that he approached a woman that was seated in one corner of the room on her own. The woman looked slightly older than Celia but very much like her in many ways and there was definitely an obvious physical resemblance between the two women and as Leah watched and listened to Wesley as they started to converse, he quickly entered into a discreet but deep discussion with her. Since most of the conversation between the two was conducted in whispers, no one else in the room paid much attention to it, Leah noticed as the two spoke but Celia rapidly reassured Leah as she too listened to the them both speak.

"She's my sister Marie." Celia explained as she nodded. "Wesley will be well taken care off now, so thanks for all your help."

"That's okay, really." Leah replied graciously.

Suddenly, Medina entered the cave and as she walked over towards the two women, she smiled as Leah prepared to greet her. A polite nod was given to Celia and then Medina gently took Leah's arm and began to lead her towards a nearby tunnel burrowed into one side of the cave wall.

"You can go now Leah. Your work here is done." Medina reassured her.

Leah smiled. "Okay." She agreed.

Quite strangely, once the women had stepped into the tunnel, much to Leah's surprise, instead of a dark circular space she found herself once more back inside the wood clearing where the golden fountain was situated. The golden water cascaded down as Leah stood in silence rooted to the spot and just watched it for a few seconds with a bemused expression upon her face before she turned to face Medina.

"It's time for you to go back to the boat now Leah." Medina explained. "I don't come with you. You leave me here."

"Okay." Leah replied as she nodded and prepared to depart.

A smile crossed Medina's face just before she turned and then walked towards the golden water fountain once again as Leah prepared to depart and to return to the boat and as she began to walk towards tunnel that would provide her with a means of exit, she suddenly began to appreciate the real life that she and Zidane shared. The couple had a life that was peaceful, harmonious and enjoyable and their shared life definitely lacked the misery and heartache that so many others seemed to not only face but also suffer from.

However, that day Leah's eyes had truly, definitely been opened to the various ways in which some members of humanity suffered and the Sea of Sorrow had challenged and changed her perceptions of the world and the people that lived in it. How some people coped with life, how they faced and attempted to overcome the various obstacles that had been placed in their path and how love could touch other people's hearts and make them risk their lives for those they loved had now been fully demonstrated to her by Spectrum that day and so, she would now return to her real life with slightly more compassion and understanding than she had left it.

Just a few minutes later Leah arrived at the other end of the tunnel and as she stepped out of it and then began to walk back along the rocky path that led towards the boat and Delta, she smiled as she glanced at his face. Rather amusingly, Leah noticed as she drew closer to the boat that Delta was still in exactly in the same spot as he had been when she had left him hours and hours ago and it appeared that he'd not even moved an inch, since she'd actually left the boat.

“Ah, you've returned?” Delta announced triumphantly as he glanced up at her face and gave her a certain nod.

"I definitely have." Leah replied politely as she stepped back inside the boat and then sat down upon the small, wooden bench once more.

Once Leah was safely seated inside the boat, the rocky platform in front of the vessel that had blocked the boat's path suddenly started to sink and the boat began to gently shake as it prepared to move off once again. Since the end of Leah's journey that day was near as the boat started to move through the waters and continued to make its way further along the Tunnel of Despair, Leah didn't expect the boat to stop off anywhere else although she could clearly see lots of cave like holes in the tunnel's walls as the boat moved.

"Will we be stopping anywhere else Delta?" Leah finally ventured to ask as she sought final clarity from him with regards to her assumption.

"No, I don't think so. People usually only visit one stop off point on any given journey." Delta explained. "How did you find your stop off?" He asked.

Leah sadly shook her head. “It was truly awful Delta.” She replied softly. “I watched two people die and there was absolutely nothing that I could do to save them.”

"I'm sorry, such sorrow does weigh very heavily upon the heart." Delta replied.

“Why couldn't I save them Delta?” Leah asked.

“You are not the giver of life and nor can you decide when life is taken away.” Delta explained in a solemn tone. “I really don't know what you see when you leave the boat because I have no control over the Sea of Sorrow, much like you do not have any control over life and death. Everyone's journey is different and so I can only say that today perhaps, you saw and experienced what you needed to in order to help you understand life a little better."

Despite Delta's logical, diplomatic explanation, Leah's mind continued to wrestle with the events of the day inwardly as the boat floated further along the tunnel and towards the other end of it. The wooden bench that Leah was seated upon provided absolutely no comfort as she tried to silently console herself and hugged her knees and simply felt hard, wooden and totally indifferent to what she had just experienced. One small comfort soothed Leah's heart however, as the boat neared the end of the rocky tunnel and some rays of light could clearly be seen ahead and that was the warmth that Zidane would provide when she returned to his loving arms and his tender touch and he would hopefully, ease some of the frustration and hurt that she felt deep down inside.

Approximately fifteen minutes after the boat had resumed its journey along the Tunnel of Despair, the vessel finally arrived at the other end of the tunnel and as it started to float back out into the bright sunshine once again, Leah tried to console herself with the knowledge that at least she had provided someone with some comfort that day. Although Leah's journey through the Sea of Sorrow and the Tunnel of Despair had been saturated in sadness, she could at least find some grains in comfort amongst the ashes of pain because that day, she had helped Wesley's mother find some kind of peace.

The golden, sandy beach that Leah had initially arrived upon however, was not seen by her eyes again as when the boat had fully exited the dark, dismal tunnel, Leah suddenly woke up back again inside the basement and found herself once more inside the transparent Spectrum capsule. Everything that had just surrounded Leah, the boat, Delta, the Sea of Sorrow and even the exit to the Tunnel of Despair had totally vanished and as Leah began to reacclimatize herself with her usual, real surroundings, she began to process and accept that her adventure for that day at least, was completely over. Although Leah's emotional journey that day had differed vastly from some of her more pleasant experiences inside Spectrum, she definitely still felt appreciative of the fact as she prepared to leave the basement that every minute and experience that it had contained, had translated into a valuable life experience that had deepened her understanding of life.

Much to Leah expected, a few minutes later when she arrived inside the lounge, she found Zidane strewn across the sofa where he had dozed off, tired and worn out from his working day and so she began to consider for a moment if she should simply curl up on the sofa beside him or wake him up. The temptation to sleep on the sofa however, was a far less attractive idea than sleeping inside the couple's bed which was far more spacious and a lot more comfortable and so Leah quickly shook her head and swiftly dismissed the idea which as she already knew, really wasn't wise.

Unlike the Spectrum capsule which was perfectly formed to house a single human form and the couple's own bed, the sofa definitely wasn't as well shaped as either facility which meant, if two people actually slept upon it for an entire night, they would usually wake up with stiff necks and various aches and pains from the awkward sleeping positions that their body had endured. Such unnecessary experiences would add nothing to the couple's day the next morning when they actually woke up as Leah already knew and so as she stretched out her hand towards Zidane's arm and prepared to wake him up, Leah dismissed those lazy thoughts from her mind and refused to surrender to them.

In less than a minute, Zidane began to stir as Leah gently touched his arm and tried to awaken him with playful, tender, sensual strokes and as Zidane began to open his eyes, Leah noticed that a smile immediately crossed his face. Upon Leah's face there was an affectionate smile as she sensually kissed his lips and as Zidane began to sit up, he rubbed his eyes as he glanced down at the shiny, black and gold wristwatch that decorated his wrist.

"Is that the time Leah?" Zidane asked. "We should eat and then go straight to bed."

Leah nodded. “Yes, we will Zidane don't worry.” She insisted.

A warm, affectionate smile adorned Leah's face as she rose to her feet and then began to make her way towards the kitchen as she internally celebrated the couple's romantic partnership and shared life which as always, was full of love, oozed with mutual adoration and contained heaps of affection. Unlike the Sea of Sorrow that Leah had just spent her day inside as she now more deeply appreciated, the couple's life was full of joy, peace and tranquility and that was something that no amount of money could ever buy and something that Leah now really, actually had to start to truly treasure.

Lost in the Maze of Trust

When the next Monday morning sauntered gently into Leah's life, she prepared for her next adventure as she attended to her daily hygiene routine, the household chores, the couple's evening meal and then stepped into the basement. In accordance with Leah's promise to Zidane the previous week, she hadn't visited the basement at all during the prior weekend and on the Friday that had preceded that weekend, she had actually just spent the large part of her day on some modifications and tweaks to Spectrum in order to avoid being totally worn out and so, Leah felt really quite anxious that morning to get on with her planned walk-through test schedule and to return to it.

The artificial simulated emotional plane that Leah was supposed to visit that Monday would revolve around an emotional journey of trust and so Leah felt really quite excited about the potential adventures within that simulated plane as she began to walk towards the Spectrum capsule because it was highly likely that her visit would be both enjoyable and pleasant. Since a few days had passed by since Leah's last visit to an emotional plane inside Spectrum, she felt really quite refreshed that morning because her mind and body had definitely had enough time to fully recuperate from her last intensive ten-hour experience. Unlike Leah's very intensive experiences inside Spectrum however, as she was fully aware, most consumers would only usually visit the emotional planes of Spectrum for a few hours at a time on any given visit and would not be focused upon every minute detail and so, their experiences would not be drain them as much as her recent, very complex, far longer visits had.

An excited smile crossed Leah's face as she began to walk up the small steps that led towards the Spectrum capsule as she started to prepare herself for another adventure, the prospect of which she silently began to savor even though it had not yet actually begun. Since Leah felt that this emotional journey would be very different in nature from her last visit and that those differences would intrigue her in numerous ways, she felt really quite optimistic about the day ahead because it would differ so vastly from her last visit to Spectrum. Unlike Leah's last visit which had been drenched in total sadness as she already knew that day's adventure held the promise of some pleasantness firmly by the hand but as Leah paused for a moment on the steps, she thoughtfully reflected upon and began to appreciate the Sea of Sorrow that she had experienced because it had actually illustrated to her some of the types of sadness that some people faced, experienced and had to cope with as they journeyed through life.

On the Thursday night, when Leah had finally emerged from the basement, she had actually discussed her visit to the Sea of Sorrow with Zidane and she'd even divulged some of the details to him and he had seemed quite surprised by the levels of intensity that Spectrum provided as well as been very sympathetic towards Leah due to her sad experiences. Some tearful drops of sorrow had fallen from Leah's eyes as she had related her experiences that day to Zidane and he had faithfully held her close to him and then had wiped away her tears and as each sorrowful tear and sad reflective thought had been gently washed away by the ripples of tenderness from Zidane's touch, he had somehow provided an immediate form of relief to the sorrows that Leah had felt. Somehow, Zidane's touch and his words of comfort had instantly soothed Leah's sadness, had swiftly strengthened her mind, had rapidly cleansed her thoughts and had even discreetly nursed her broken heart and so that morning, she felt fully recharged and absolutely ready for her next adventure.

Quite interestingly however, Leah considered thoughtfully, on that actual Thursday night Zidane had also made some very wise, extremely insightful observations and useful comments as he had held her in his arms and had comforted her downcast spirit and so, Leah began to quietly reflect upon each one as she prepared to enter into the Spectrum capsule. Since Spectrum was now in the final stages of actual completion and it was expected that the prototype would be sold once the walk-through tests had been performed successfully and any required corrections, tweaks and modifications had been made, Leah knew that Zidane's observations and the issues that he had raised, now sat upon the near horizon of her life and so, he had brought such considerations to the forefront of her mind.

"Spectrum is a very powerful invention Leah and so, you'll really have to make sure that it's utilized wisely." Zidane had warned her.

Every single part of Leah knew that Zidane had been absolutely right as she glanced into the interior of the Spectrum capsule and then slipped inside it because it was a very powerful recreational tool that could definitely be utilized either constructively or negatively as any potential buyer saw fit and it certainly possessed the ability to be utilized in both capacities. The extremely vivid, very believable and almost realistic experiences that Leah had enjoyed so far inside Spectrum had really opened her eyes to just how easily her invention could be manipulated, exploited and used in a detrimental manner, if someone did indeed wish to utilize it in that particular manner.

Although Spectrum was a tool that could easily export a user into a magical world, it also possessed the potential ability to temporarily dissolve the quite often stagnant realities of the real world and it could perhaps even replace real life with a lucid existence that thrilled where anything could happen and Leah had seen that herself with her own two eyes because she had hungered to experience more. A time would definitely come as Leah already knew, when she would have to find an actual buyer for Spectrum and so as she now fully appreciated, a lot of care would have to be exercised in the arrival at that decision and the final buyer that she sold the Spectrum prototype to would have to be vetted prior to the actual sale in various ways. In fact, on that particular point Leah definitely not only fully agreed with but also wholeheartedly appreciated Zidane's thoughtful, wise and insightful observations because the reality was, the damage that Spectrum could cause if placed in the wrong hands and placed in the wrong powerful hands, was extremely unpredictable and so that meant, the subsequent fallout from an unwise decision on Leah's part might be absolutely horrendous.

Once Leah had lain down inside the Spectrum capsule as she began to press ahead with her walk-through tests, she issued some verbal commands and just a few seconds later the transparent capsule lid began to descend and close over her body just before some particles of sleeping gas rapidly began to infiltrate the interior of the capsule itself. In order to heighten Leah's experiences on her fifth visit to Spectrum, she had made some small tweaks to her personality which meant that she would be far more reflective and much more introspective and also slightly more indecisive than usual because she had felt that those changes would make her experiences in that particular emotional journey a lot more interesting. Each hurdle and every obstacle that Leah would face throughout her journey of trust that day she wanted to really challenge her inner being and to provoke her to dig deep within herself in order to actually overcome each one and so, Leah definitely felt that the selected tweaks to her personality would make her visit to Spectrum not only much more of a challenge but would also help her to achieve multiple objectives with regards to the performance of her walk-through tests.

In a matter of just minutes the sleeping gas had successfully begun to infiltrate Leah's human biological structure and as the particles of gas hit her senses like a warm blanket of comfort, she rapidly slipped into a dreamlike state of consciousness. Just a minute or so later, when Leah reawakened, she found herself in what looked like the grounds of an old abandoned estate house which appeared to be full of greenish, brown hedges that seemed to be organized into overgrown rows. At the top of the grounds, in an elevated and prominent position, sat a very large estate house which nestled gently against a small hill that appeared to sit directly behind it and as Leah glanced at the building and began to visually inspect it, she noticed that the house was absolutely huge and that it almost looked like a top hat as it silently adorned and topped off the hedge walls that ran across the grounds below it.

Nearby, Leah observed and quite close to her current position, there appeared to be a hedge lined grassy path and so she quickly and enthusiastically stood up and then began to make her way towards it and as she walked, Leah remained hopeful that it would lead towards the huge estate house which as far as she was concerned, was her intended destination. Suddenly however, much to Leah's complete surprise, a small furry creature darted out from under one of the hedge walls nearby and then crossed her path and even more surprisingly, just a few seconds later, the animal came to a complete standstill a short distance away from her. Much to Leah's amusement, the creature actually perched up on its hindlegs and then turned to face her and once it had done so, it didn't move an inch for a couple of minutes as the animal seemed to wait for something else to happen and so, Leah began to silently, visually inspect the dark coat of dark reddish almost black fur that adorned the animal's body and that clung to its features and frame.

In some ways, Leah definitely felt that the creature looked a bit like a squirrel but that it also seemed to bear a quite strong resemblance to a raccoon due to the mask like dark black patches of fur around its eyes with white outlines, a pointed nose that protruded from its face with two thicker white stripes on either side and a bushy tail formed from some reddish black and white furry rings. Due to the creature's appearance, Leah rapidly concluded that the animal was probably a racrel as she continued to visually inspect it and just watched it with total intrigue, utter fascination and in absolute delight because it really did look extremely cute and unlike some of the scarier hybrids that Leah had already encountered on her previous visits to Spectrum, she gratefully accepted that at least this one was definitely not one to be feared.

One of the hybrid species that Leah had created inside Spectrum was a cross between a squirrel and a raccoon and so, she had named that species racrels and the creature in front of her, Leah definitely felt, certainly seemed to match that species group in terms of its overall appearance and its visible features. When it came to the actual issue of the creature's appearance, Leah swiftly noticed that not only was it exceptionally cute but also that it looked slightly larger than a squirrel in terms of its size and that its face seemed to look very intelligent which puzzled her slightly as she glanced at the creature and continued to visually inspect every single visible minute detail. For some inexplicable reason that Leah couldn't quite put her finger on or explain, the racrel's face looked very wise but since there had been no actual communication between the furry animal and Leah, there was no real way to verify that her assumption was indeed, actually true.

After another few minutes of silent stillness and mutual visual inspection by both Leah and the racrel had gone by, Leah watched in fascinated silence as the creature suddenly began to move off again as the pathway directly in front of the racrel was once more decorated by its movements. Quite amusingly however, Leah swiftly observed, although the creature seemed to leap and bounce playfully across the path very energetically, the racrel actually seemed to remain in pretty much the same spot and hardly seemed to move forwards or backwards at all.

For a few more minutes Leah just stood and watched the creature's frivolous antics with an amused expression upon her face, since she wasn't particularly in a rush until just a minute or so later, the creature suddenly turned to face Leah and then did an about turn. Much to Leah's surprise, the racrel not only scampered eagerly back towards her but then the creature also passed by her legs as it began to head off in the opposite direction from the actual estate house which struck Leah as slightly strange because she had just assumed that the estate house was to be her first stop off point. Once the creature had gone a distance of about ten or twenty meters, the racrel paused again and then it turned back to face Leah once more as the creature perched up on its hindlegs and as she watched the racrel in total fascination, it almost looked to Leah as if the racrel had decided to wait until she had started to follow its movements.

"Well, why not?" Leah asked herself as she smiled, shrugged and then began to walk towards the creature's current position. "I'm definitely intrigued, though I'm not quite sure where you actually want to take me."

The next fifteen minutes passed by peacefully and pleasantly enough as Leah followed the racrel along the hedge lined path as it moved off again and as she was led through various twists and turns, the racrel scampered playfully along the path just a meter or so ahead of her. Finally, the two arrived at the edge of a very deep, large chasm which surprised Leah slightly because the deep groove had appeared so suddenly and very unexpectedly but that surprise on Leah's part wasn't actually coupled with optimism and rather, was completely filled with dread. Unfortunately, and much to Leah's total dismay, it rapidly transpired that the wide chasm only appeared to be crossable via a very flimsy looking, shaky, weak wooden bridge which joined both sides together, albeit somewhat reluctantly as it sagged down below the nearest edge just a few steps away from her current position and wafted around in a breezy wind that seemed to run through the depths of the deep divide.

Rather strangely, Leah swiftly noticed, just like the path that the racrel had taken the bridge actually seemed to lead further away from the large estate house that Leah had initially assumed that she was supposed to visit not towards it and in another direction entirely which puzzled her slightly for a moment as she just stood and stared at the bridge and the deep divide. Since Leah had actually already mentally prepared herself to make her way towards the estate house, the continued deviation from the direction of the large residential building was really quite unexpected and so, she began to adjust and realign her expectations in accordance with the racrel's movements which at that time, appeared to totally go against the grain of her own logical instincts.

Much to Leah's absolute disgust, the flimsy bridge that joined the two pieces of land together looked as if it had literally been thrown together in a matter of minutes and so, it definitely lacked any kind of appeal in her sight. In fact, everything about the bridge's existence added to Leah's internal desires to follow her own greatly preferred natural instincts since the scrappy structure, wobbly contraption and shaky excuse for a bridge really didn't look like very much fun and more of an awful experience than anything else which convinced her to avoid it completely, if she possibly could.

A few more silent seconds went by as Leah continued to visually inspect the flimsy wooden contraption a bit more closely and as she did so, she started to wince and shudder with absolute fear. However, as Leah silently examined, inspected and analyzed the flimsy wooden structure which it appeared was held together with just a few pieces of rope, she suddenly noticed that the racrel didn't seem to share her sentiments or her fears in any capacity at all and that the creature started to bounce across the shaky contraption with total ease and it appeared, without a single care in the world.

Just a minute or so later, since the racrel had already bounced across at least a third of the bridge by that point and Leah had noticed that the creature hadn't suffered any actual injuries or fallen off the wooden contraption, she suddenly began to feel slightly more convinced and much more motivated to make an actual attempt to cross the flimsy bridge herself and so, she began to take her first step onto its woody frame. However, as Leah cautiously stepped out onto the first plank of the bridge and then cast a swift, nervous downwards glance towards the base of the deep chasm, she rapidly noticed that it was actually situated miles below the flimsy, shaky bridge and that the ground was formed from a multitude of jagged rocks that jutted proudly out across its depths as each lump of stone seemed to silently celebrate their rocky formation and stony existence.

Suddenly, Leah's fear of heights was now once more directly in front of her face, or more precisely directly under her feet and the unsteady structure that she was supposed to utilize to cross that deep divide formed from just some basic wooden planks held together by a few rope rails, didn't look very secure or even very safe and so, she definitely lacked confidence. A nervous lump rapidly began to gather inside Leah's throat as she quietly processed and silently absorbed the simulated reality that she would have to walk across the entire bridge and actually conquer her fears once again. Sadly, on this particular occasion however, and much to Leah's disappointment, there appeared to be no potion of courage that could be consumed and there would be no friendly guide by her side which definitely worried her profusely.

Since the weak, fragile, flimsy bridge that adorned the chasm almost looked as if it had been forced to decorate the large gap that it bridged, Leah started to tremble with fear as she bravely stepped out onto the second plank of wood because as Leah was already aware, she would definitely have to face this particular challenge not only head on but also on her own. Whether Leah liked it or not as she already knew, the flimsy bridge certainly wouldn't change and neither would the deep chasm that now lay directly below her despite all her doubts, regardless of her nerves and irrespective of her lack of confidence and since she definitely had to cross the whole bridge at some point, nervous hesitation served absolutely no useful purpose to her and so it made very little sense. A frustrated sigh was released from Leah's lips as she swiftly attempted to silently pull herself together as she prepared to force herself to walk across the remainder of the bridge but reluctance seemed to be the only companion that had remained by Leah's side because by that point, the racrel had bounced eagerly ahead and had almost reached the other side of the bridge.

"Perhaps racrel, I shouldn't have followed you anywhere in the first place and perhaps, just perhaps, you have actually led me in the wrong direction." Leah whispered as she glanced at the creature and then shook her head. "In fact, maybe I should just turn around right now and return to the path." She considered thoughtfully for a moment. "I could even make my way back towards the estate house."

For the next minute or so, Leah totally froze as she wallowed in her hesitation and her indecision both of which it seemed had absolutely paralyzed her because a retreat from the shaky, flimsy bridge and the high heights definitely held a lot of appeal for her. Inside Leah's form a definite tug of war had begun between bravery and her more cowardly, natural instincts which leant well away from the very high heights and flimsy shaky bridge and so, she felt really quite tempted to follow those much more cowardly instincts, purely for the sake of comfort.

Perhaps, Leah silently considered, she really had misread the signs when she had followed the racrel along the path that it had taken and since there had been no real logical reason to do so, Leah continued to wonder if perhaps, she hadn't actually been meant to follow the creature anywhere at all. No signs or any other clear directional indicators had existed and had actually been present that had provided Leah with any kind of clarity upon her initial arrival in the grounds of the estate house that had affirmed to her that the racrel was indeed, actually a guide inside that particular environment and so for a minute or two, Leah began to wonder if perhaps, she had been mistaken. In some ways, the racrel's presence and the creature's behavior had seemed like the only real direction that had been provided but Leah suddenly questioned whether she had misinterpreted the racrel's behavior and if she had then subsequently been led in another direction entirely than the one she should have taken due to her own incorrect assumptions.

Despite all Leah's internal deliberations however, as she glanced up at the racrel again she noticed that by that point the creature had actually, almost crossed the entire bridge on its own and that the racrel seemed to scamper across each plank with total ease. Once the racrel arrived at the other side of the bridge, Leah watched in total silence, intrigued fascination and in absolute awe as the creature sat down perched upon its hindlegs and then faced her and as it looked back across the flimsy contraption, the creature just seemed to stare at her face expectantly. For the second time the racrel actually seemed to wait for Leah to follow its movements, she observed as she continued to thoughtfully analyse the creature's bold actions, brave scampers and expectant stillness in total fascination but the bridge really was such a scary ordeal for her to have to face and so, she definitely feared the thought of making an attempt to cross the remainder of it.

Due to the racrel's now stationary position and the creature's total standstill, it rapidly became blatantly obvious and very apparent to Leah that the animal would not move any further forward until she actually did and until she had crossed the entire bridge which meant, she definitely had to cross the remainder of the flimsy, awful, shaky bridge. A deep breath was swiftly taken as Leah started to step out onto the third plank as she tried to convince herself that she had already stepped out onto two planks so far and that she had not yet actually fallen off the bridge and that somehow, almost miraculously, the bridge had even actually managed to hold her weight which reassured her to some extent, albeit very slightly.

Another deep inhalation occurred as Leah decisively braved the fourth plank of the shaky contraption and as she stepped out onto the rectangular shaped piece of wood, she noticed that the flimsy, wooden structure wavered slightly which instantly unnerved and scared her. Rather unconvincingly, in-between each wooden plank there was a length of rope which held the planks together, albeit in a slightly casual manner and across the top of the bridge ran two skimpy rope handrails all of which Leah felt, definitely lacked a proper sense of commitment to the bridge that each piece had been attached to but nonetheless, she immediately clutched onto the two handrails more tightly in the hope that the rope rails would perhaps steady her slightly or perhaps even stabilize the actual bridge itself.

Irrespective of the lack of certainty in Leah's mind that the bridge could and would, actually hold her weight until she arrived at the other side off it, Leah tiptoed onto the next plank cautiously and carefully as she hoped for the best and feared for the worst and just tried to make the best of the awful, tricky hurdle that now stood in her path. The whole wooden contraption not only looked very delicate but also sounded extremely unstable because the wooden planks had creaked under the strain of Leah's weight every single time she had stepped onto one and that worry gushed through her mind like a sharp undercurrent of fear as she continued to make her way across the planks of wooden uncertainty.

Once Leah arrived at the sixth wooden plank however, much to her complete and utter horror, the situation suddenly took a turn for the worse as some of the planks of wood behind her actually started to fall down and parts of the bridge seemed to totally collapse. A shocked gasp managed to escape from Leah's lips and mouth as she quickly turned to face the gaps in the bridge and surveyed the full extent of the damage and as Leah stared at the now broken bridge directly behind her which clearly indicated to her that the wooden contraption definitely had a mind of its own that seemed to care very little about Leah's fear of heights, she shook her head in total disgust and absolute disbelief.

An actual return to the side of the bridge that Leah had just come from was now no longer an actual or realistic option and so she began to process that fact or rather that simulated reality as she watched the planks of wood hurtle towards some of the jagged rocks that formed the base of the deep chasm directly beneath her. Due to the jagged, sharp rocks as each plank made a very rapid, extremely swift descent, Leah began to tremble with absolute fear because the wooden planks as she already knew, were well on their way to total destruction and she really didn't want to experience a similar departure from the bridge herself in any capacity at all.

Rather predictably, less than a minute later as Leah continued to watch, the wooden planks actually hit the jagged rocks and as each one shattered into over a hundred pieces of splintered wood, Leah began to shake her head in shocked dismay. Very uncomfortably, as Leah watched the fallen planks from the bridge shatter into tiny pieces of splintered wooden bits, she began to tremble with absolute fear because not only had several of the planks from the bridge fallen but with each one's departure and destruction, the planks of her own bravery had departed too and had then been destroyed as each plank had hurtled towards the ground and so now, all that really remained, were some shattered pieces of broken bravery torn apart by the jagged rocks of horrified shock. Although Leah's form had been absolutely abandoned and totally deserted by each plank of bravery that had held her mind and form together when she had begun to cross the bridge that had been required to fully conquer her some of her deepest fears, as she already knew, the divide would still have to be crossed whether the rest of the bridge behind her collapsed or not and so she bravely prepared to continue.

A quick glance was cast back towards the portion of the bridge that Leah had already crossed and much as she expected, that visual inspection rapidly confirmed that now some awful, large gaps had formed as a result of the planks sudden departure which had rendered the bridge in that direction, totally uncrossable. Since the gaps silently confirmed to Leah that now there would definitely be absolutely no turning back, the only real but simulated choice that she really had was to carry on across the remainder of the bridge because no other choice existed and so, Leah bravely faced in the direction that she was headed as she prepared to continue.

A few fearful, feverish shivers suddenly ran silently down Leah's spine and as fear rapidly gripped every part of her form, a wave of total alarm quickly swept over her and as it did so, Leah's hands swiftly became as cold as ice as the feverish sweat rippled across the surface of her skin and a nervous lump seemed to gather, expand and then cling onto the walls of her throat. Some doubtful fears definitely still lurked and lingered inside Leah's mind which haunted her thoughts and so, she tried to push those fearful doubts firmly from her mind and to one side as she prepared to move forward once again and took her first step across the remainder of the shaky, wooden contraption.

Despite all of Leah's internal fears, she tried to force herself to be brave and to press ahead as she pushed herself to reach the other side of the bridge as quickly as she possibly could but due to the shaky nature of the bridge itself, the rest of her journey across it was more of a fearful wander and hesitant saunter than a bold, confident, fast paced stride. Just a few minutes later however, and much to Leah's sheer relief, somehow she actually managed to arrive safely on the other side of the bridge and as she did so, Leah released a grateful sigh because she had crossed the remainder of the planks almost on tiptoes and had feared that she would slip of the bridge with every single step and so, it had been a huge achievement from her point of view, just to reach the other side of that deep chasm successfully.

Quite strangely however, as Leah began to visually scan the grassy, woody area that she had now reached as she started to search for the racrel, it appeared that the creature had by that point, completely vanished because the racrel was nowhere to be seen and suddenly seemed to be actually absent. A frustrated sigh was released from Leah's lips as she began to process and accept the racrel's absence but it did seem slightly strange to Leah that the very creature that had provoked her to cross the flimsy, horrible bridge and that had encouraged her to brave those awful high heights in the first place had now, rather suddenly, actually, totally disappeared. Rather frustratingly for Leah, it also seemed as if the racrel had led her absolutely nowhere because all that she could see and all that she appeared to be surrounded by was a grassy bed that carpeted the ground which led directly up to some clumps of trees that seemed to form the edge of a densely wooded area.

Just a few seconds later however, Leah suddenly spotted a narrow dirt path on her right-hand side that seemed to be naturally woven into some of the trees that could perhaps lead to somewhere and since that path started about twenty or thirty meters away from her current position, she eagerly began to make her way towards it. Since a return to the estate house via the broken bridge was now totally out of the question because several more planks had hurtled towards the ground as Leah had crossed the remainder of it, the bridge was now totally uncrossable and so that uncrossable bridge was a definite obstacle to that potential course of action which meant, Leah's alternative plan was no longer actually viable and so, she quickly succumbed to her only real option, the narrow dirt path. Deep down inside Leah began to silently accept as she walked towards the path that not only was the bridge totally uncrossable but also that the racrel had completely abandoned her and that the creature was highly unlikely to return which implied that Leah's solitary status would remain that way for the unforeseeable future which also meant, she would have to face the next part of her emotional journey, completely and totally alone.

For approximately the next fifteen minutes Leah diligently followed the dirt path as it wove its way through the grass and trees because that course of action seemed to be the most natural and only logical thing to do until it finally led into a large open clearing situated in the heart of the wooded area. All around the perimeter of the clearing, Leah noticed that not only were there trees but also that there were some large hedge walls which looked quite similar to the hedges that she had seen in the grounds of the estate house but that these hedges had been properly trimmed and well maintained and that some hedge like chunks decorated and littered the interior of the clearing which seemed to be shaped like very large chairs. In the very center of the large clearing there appeared to be a long mahogany slab of wood which rested upon some big, chunky wooden tree stump legs and the whole wooden arrangement and hedge accompaniments looked a bit like a dinner table because the hedge chairs seemed to be plonked around the large slab of wood at varied but quite regular intervals however, from what Leah could see at first glance, almost all of the hedge chairs appeared to be vacant and unoccupied.

Not more than a few seconds later and much to Leah's surprise however, she suddenly spotted an attractive male in his late thirties seated upon a throne like hedge chair at the head of the wooden makeshift table that appeared to be in the midst of the consumption of a meal and his presence almost startled her because it was so very unexpected. For the next couple of minutes Leah remained totally silent and completely still as she froze and just watched the male form since he had not yet it appeared, noticed her arrival and as she stood on the perimeter of the wood clearing, Leah just waited patiently for him to spot her as he continued to consume his meal. Quite amusingly, Leah observed as she waited, the man even started to hum a song as he raised a shiny glass filled with wine to his lips and although she definitely felt curious about his presence, since the man hadn't yet actually noticed her and seemed to be in the throngs of a delicious, hearty meal that looked to be very enjoyable, Leah held back for a minute or two longer as she waited for him to either notice her or take a break from his meal.

Suddenly however, the attractive male form glanced up, looked at Leah and then just stared at her face as he came to an immediate and very abrupt stop and as Leah continued to observe his movements, she kept completely still and totally silent for a few more seconds. After a few more seconds of absolute silence and total stagnant stillness on both parts had gone by, much to Leah's delight, the man suddenly began to nod his head, swiftly rose to his feet and then began to stride briskly towards her and so, Leah quickly offered him a warm, friendly receptive smile as she prepared to greet him.

“How frightfully rude of me, please won't you join me?" He invited as he motioned towards an unoccupied hedge chair next to the table. "I'm Ravid and you are?"

"Thanks that's very kind of you Ravid. I'm Leah." Leah replied as she eagerly introduced herself and then began to make her way towards the vacant hedge chair that she had just been invited to occupy.

The kindness of Ravid's invitation prompted Leah to smile as she sat down and once Ravid had returned to his own hedge chair, Leah noticed that he immediately picked up one of several bowls full of food that had been strewn across the table directly in front of him. Just a few seconds later the full bowl was politely placed much closer to Leah's position and then Ravid nodded his head as he encouraged Leah to join him in his feast.

"Please help yourself Leah." Ravid invited.

A large wooden jug was quickly lifted up and as Leah watched Ravid, she noticed that he rapidly began to fill a shiny glass with the liquid it contained which looked as if it had been formed from some kind of precious crystal or perhaps even diamond materials. Once the shiny glass had been filled, it was then gently placed back down on the table directly in front of Leah and so, she nodded her head appreciatively as she began to acknowledge Ravid's very kind and extremely polite gestures.

"Thanks, Ravid." Leah replied as she accepted and welcomed the glass of wine on offer and enthusiastically picked it up. "It's very kind of you to share your meal and your wine with me."

"Well Leah, I don't get visitors very often so the pleasure is all mine." Ravid admitted. "Just a few creatures come by now and again but more often than not, the conversation really lacks and it's usually a bit of one-sided discussion."

Leah giggled. "I can imagine it would be." She teased.

Some rays of sunlight shone directly down from the sky above Leah's head and she noticed that each ray bounced silently off her glass and made both the glass and the liquid it contained glisten and shine even more as she began to drink some of the dark crimson red wine that Ravid had just poured inside it. An empty, mahogany wooden plate which sat upon the makeshift table, Leah observed, was quickly picked up by Ravid and then filled with an assortment of barbecued meat, some chunks of fresh bread and some slices of fruit from some of the bowls of food that adorned the wooden slab and once full, the plate was then politely handed to Leah as Ravid encouraged her to tuck in and participate in the meal on offer.

Due to the truly delightful aromas that emanated from the now full wooden plate, Leah heartily and enthusiastically, immediately started to tuck into her meal and as she hungrily began to devour the contents of the plate, some of the juices from the spicy meats which tasted absolutely divine ran down the sides of her mouth and somehow, totally against her wishes, even managed to escape from her lips. Although Leah tried her very best to capture every single morsel of food and to savor every single one of the glorious flavours on offer to her palate as the meaty juices coated her fingers and as the chunks of meat melted on her tongue, she silently began to accept that some tasty dribbles would probably escape from her eager lips which also meant that some wastage was totally unavoidable because the meaty chunks really were so very juicy.

Rather intriguingly, Leah noticed as her plate rapidly emptied and then she eagerly refilled it, Ravid's invitation had seemed very natural and so, it had seemed even more natural for Leah just to accept it, although technically, she had actually only just met him a few minutes ago. Hunger, curiosity and an undercurrent of passionate attraction had definitely completely overridden logic and reason in this instance, Leah thoughtfully concluded and those impulses had propelled her to join Ravid without even a second thought as to who he might actually be or why she should accept his invitation.

Luckily and fortunately for Leah, the heavenly chunks of meat, fluffy breads and delicious fruits that she assumed had been prepared by Ravid himself, seemed to be perfectly safe to consume and so, she eagerly continued to tear off chunks of meat and bread and to pick up slices of fruit which she then eagerly slipped into her mouth. The rich spicy sauces that coated the meaty chunks, the fluffy fresh dough of the bread and the sweet fleshy pulps from the fruits tantalized Leah's senses as she hungrily tucked into her second plate without any kind of restraint because as Leah fully realized and joyfully appreciated, simulated food couldn't really, actually add any weight to her body mass or be considered as over indulgence and so that meant, she could dabble and consume to her heart's content.

For some inexplicable reason, Leah began to silently conclude, the food that she had actually consumed so far inside Spectrum had predominantly tasted far superior to most of the meals that she had eaten in real life which definitely intrigued her. Over the years Leah had visited some very upmarket, fine dining culinary establishments not only in the city which the couple lived but also in other cities when she had accompanied Zidane to other places on his working weekends but the refined, vast array of tastes on offer in Spectrum had not only delighted her palate but had also absolutely thrilled her.

Inside Spectrum however, as Leah fully appreciated, those tastes would be based on freshly picked or recently caught raw ingredients which had been cooked with minimal chemical inputs and so, in some ways that superiority in flavors made total sense to both her mind and her taste buds. The truly wonderful aromas and scrumptious flavors that Leah had experienced so far inside Spectrum had definitely enticed not only her mind and eyes but also her tongue and stomach because each one had teased her senses and enthralled her taste buds and fortunately, the actual consumption of those foods had proven to be even more delicious than originally anticipated.

Once Leah had eaten her fill and she couldn't possibly squeeze or pack in anymore, she swiftly washed her meal down with what remained of the sweet, fruity, full bodied glass of wine that Ravid had poured for her and as each drop drizzled and trickled down the back of her throat, the simulated liquid seemed to quench her thirst immaculately. For the next few minutes, since Leah had been both fed and watered to her total satisfaction, albeit artificially, she just sat and watched Ravid who it appeared hadn't quite finished his meal yet and as Leah glanced at his face, she began to visually inspect and quietly examine the attractive male form that was currently seated less than two meters away from her.

Much like Leah's visit to the Ark of Anticipation where she had of course met Toran the handsome male guide, although Ravid differed vastly in terms of his appearance, Leah definitely felt that he was just as attractive in her sight and so, she felt really quite fascinated and slightly intrigued by him as she just sat and waited patiently. Essentially, being that it was now the second time inside Spectrum that Leah had actually encountered an extremely attractive man, who it appeared might be her guide for the remainder of that emotional journey, the prospect of what might occur between the two definitely intrigued her because Ravid was just as, if not even more attractive than the first handsome male guide Toran and so passion seemed to linger silently in the air all around Leah's form and dance across the surface of her lips as she continued to wait.

Just a few minutes later Ravid finished his meal and then he quickly stood up and as he walked towards Leah's hedge like chair, he politely stretched out a hand towards her as he offered to pull Leah onto her feet. An undercurrent of excitement suddenly seemed to rush through Leah's form like a pulse of passion as she began to participate with Ravid's silent invitation and welcomed his masculine offer of assistance as she swiftly accepted his affectionate gesture, arm of friendship and warm hand of kindness and allowed him to pull her gently to her feet with absolutely no objections at all. Drops of excited passion seemed to gather on Leah's forehead as she waited for Ravid to direct their steps and guide her into the adventures that would take place within that emotional plane as she wished and hoped that the activities involved would include some close physical proximity, albeit in a simulated capacity and that some intense interactions between the two would be required.

"We have to go this way Leah, now that we've eaten I'd really like to show you something." Ravid explained as he walked towards one of the large hedge walls and then pushed part of it backwards.

Beyond the hedge lay a narrow dirt path that was lined with trees and so as Leah glanced along it, she attempted to see where it led to but due to a twist and turn in the path, it was virtually impossible to see very far along it. Once again therefore, Leah swiftly realized, she would have to put her trust and faith in another entity with no proper explanations just as she had done when she had first arrived in Spectrum that day and had followed the racrel along the path but as she glanced at Ravid's face, Leah felt slightly more certain that at least Ravid would not suddenly disappear and abandon her like the racrel had done. Since the two had just shared a meal together and since they had both actually engaged in an actual conversation, Leah definitely felt that it was much more likely that Ravid would hang around and so, she immediately readied herself to cooperate and participate with Ravid's directional input.

"Sure Ravid." Leah replied as she nodded her head and then prepared to follow him. "Please, lead the way."

Every part of Leah felt tremendously excited as she started to follow Ravid out of the clearing and stepped onto the narrow dirt path as she willingly participated with his request and began to internally speculate as to what he might possibly want to show her. Since the path was lined with trees on both sides and it was really quite narrow, the two walked along it quite slowly but Leah definitely felt that their relaxed pace was probably, partially due to the large amounts of food that they had both just consumed because her stomach still felt absolutely packed to the brim and so the slower pace was definitely welcome and quite comfortable for her.

Some light conversation was engaged in as the two walked which Leah fully participated in as the two playfully teased each other about the large meal that they had just enjoyed and how much they had both eaten. Due to the large glass of wine that Leah had just consumed which had definitely infiltrated her senses by that point, her mood had become much lighter and far more relaxed which was a very welcome change from her earlier state of mind which had of course involved fear and alarm due to the shaky bridge that she'd actually had to cross, the sight of which had absolutely terrified her.

Interestingly for Leah, she rapidly discovered that the second dirt path also seemed to lead further away from the large, mysterious estate house not closer to it, which definitely struck her as slightly strange but as she walked, Leah began to accept that perhaps she was not actually supposed to explore the inside the large estate house just yet. Some tree branches were woven very tightly together directly above their heads, Leah observed as she ventured further along the dirt path by Ravid's side which made everything around them both look slightly darker and a bit gloomier than it normally would and should have because those branches let in very little light in from the sky above them. Despite the quite dismal semi-darkness however, Leah continued to make light, cheerful conversation with Ravid as she walked as she hoped and wished that whatever was due to happen next would at least be pleasant and enjoyable.

Once the two had walked for about two hundred meters, Leah noticed that the dirt path carved into the two lines of trees suddenly ended, rather abruptly and as the trees and branches that had surrounded them so far ceased to form two organized but twisted lines, a grassy mountain top immediately stepped into the dirt path's place. Much to Leah's total discomfort and absolute disgust however, the sudden change in landscape wasn't exactly beneficial to her form because as she rapidly discovered, although the dirt path had completely disappeared and a plush, cushiony, soft green grassy bed had stepped into replace it which usually would have been regarded as quite a pleasant sight, this particular grassy bed was less than fifty meters long and it actually led to somewhere far worse, an actual clifftop.

Although Leah definitely harbored some fears inside her form due to the sudden appearance of the cliff edge, she rapidly noticed that Ravid didn't seem to be bothered by the presence of the cliff at all or the potentially huge heights that might have to be faced which lay just over the edge of that clifftop, if the cliff face was to be tackled in any capacity. Unlike Leah who hung back in reluctant silence, she noticed as she watched Ravid that he quickly strode right towards the edge of clifftop and then actually, enthusiastically leant over it as he began to survey the actual cliff face itself and due to his relaxed approach, it almost looked to Leah as if he had just opened a small window inside someone's home and then leant out of it.

Due to Leah's internal fears, although she still continued to follow Ravid's movements, this time it was at a far slower, much more reluctant pace because another meeting with very high heights that day held nothing but absolute worries for her. Quite suddenly and very unexpectedly, Leah had found herself slap bang at the edge of an actual cliff face and that cliff it rapidly transpired as Leah arrived at the edge and peeked out over it, was in fact a very steep, extremely rocky and rather high cliff that towered way above the valley below it.

"Leah, it looks like we'll have to rescue some dodovarks first from those ledges because they seem to be stuck inside those nests." Ravid suddenly mentioned as he surveyed some of the ledges that ran across the cliffs' rocky surface, turned to face her and then pointed towards the occupied ledges. "Then afterwards, I'll show you what I wanted to show you."

"What are dodovarks please Ravid, I can't quite remember?" Leah asked as she turned to face him. "And why would they climb so high up a cliff that they would become stuck?"

"Well, since dodovarks are a cross between dodos and aardvarks, they like very high and very low places because they feel that those places will protect them from predators and so sometimes, they try to build nests in high places but more often than not, they usually dig and make burrows in the ground." Ravid explained. "Although they can't fly, I think they really do wish that they could and so, they tend spend some of their time in high places and on muddy ledges that they can climb onto which is not actually very wise because they can be plucked from those high places very easily by predators. This time though, I think they were probably plucked from the ground and the bottom of the valley itself because they usually like to find ledges on muddy hills to nest on not rocky cliff faces."

"They do look a bit like birds actually but their wings are much shorter and they also have two short, stumpy forelegs with claws at the end of each one, how very unusual." Leah replied as she visually inspected the creatures that sat inside some of the nests on the cliff ledges below her. "Yes, dodovarks that makes total sense now."

"Unfortunately, those four spadey like hoofey webbed feet are no good to them right now because they usually use them to burrow into mud or dirt, or to climb up soft surfaces and since their feet are quite hard, their claws can't really grip onto rocky surfaces very well." Ravid pointed out. "When it comes to their noses and mouths which are hard and long, those siphon snout beaks can be very useful at times, when they want to suck food out of dirt mounds or suck things up from shallow waters but right now sadly, such natural utensils aren't really much use to them. Their two stumpy, furry, feathery wings are more of a decorative feature than anything else because they really can't utilize them to fly anywhere because dodovarks cannot fly even an inch which means for now, they are well and truly stuck."

A smile crossed Leah's face as she stared at the dodovarks as she began to accept that inside Spectrum, some miracles could actually be achieved that could never possibly exist in the real world because technically, she had brought dodo birds back from extinction, albeit in an artificial capacity. Absolutely everything about the dodovarks seemed almost magical and totally delightful to Leah as she continued to visually inspect the creatures, from their unusual bluish, sandy, grey coloring to their spiky feathery, furry tails that sat attached to the rear of their frame and their large pointed ears which reminded Leah a bit of a rabbit or a donkey's ears flapped and wriggled around enthusiastically as they waddled around.

Some very high pitched, alarmed squawks suddenly darted through the air as Leah continued to watch and listen to the creatures in total fascination as the dodovarks jumped up and down, waddled around from side to side and even flapped their short stumpy wings in a hectic fashion. The dodovarks urgent tone seemed to indicate that they were in a distressed state and their large pointed ears seemed to flap around chaotically as they called out to each other and it was almost as if their ears wanted to challenge their wings and enable flight but no matter how hectically their ears flapped around, the dodovarks unfortunately, remained firmly upon the ledges, stuck inside the nests and totally flightless.

"Are dodovarks always that loud and frantic Ravid?" Leah suddenly asked as she turned to face him. "They seem to be very upset about something."

"No, usually they're quite peaceful, pleasant and cheerful but if you notice the nests that they are situated inside are very large which means, those nests definitely do not belong to the dodovarks and since the nests are so huge, the nests obviously belong to a far larger creature." Ravid swiftly clarified. "In fact, I would say that those nests actually belong to dinobirds because these cliffs are a well-known habitat for dinobirds which means right now, they are in a lot of danger and so, they can probably sense that danger and desperately want to escape from it. Since dodovarks are very social creatures, whenever they're in close proximity to one another they like to communicate frequently and even more so when there's cause for alarm and so that call is a distress call."

"What are dinobirds Ravid, are they a cross between a bird and a dingo or something else?" Leah asked as she smiled. "I've created so many hybrids, so sometimes I forget a few and could the owners of those huge nests come back at any given moment and are we even safe here ourselves?"

"Yes and no I'd say. Dinobirds are cross between dinosaurs and birds and they can be extremely powerful, very vicious and absolutely ruthless." Ravid replied. "And yes, the vicious dinobirds could return at any second."

"Where do you think they are right now?" Leah asked as she nervously glanced across the skyline.

"I guess right now, the dinobirds are still out on their daily hunt. Usually, dinobirds hunt all day during the daylight hours and sometimes, even at night because they have absolutely huge appetites and so, they only really take a break when they want to eat something that they've caught." Ravid mentioned. "The dodovarks probably waddled into the valley earlier today and then ventured near the base of the cliff face at which point, the dinobirds must have spotted them just as they were about to embark upon their hunt and so, the dinobirds would have plucked them from the ground and then plonked them inside their nests for a late lunch appetizer, a mid-afternoon snack or perhaps even for a dinner desert. So, the dinobirds that caught these dodovarks are probably out on a hunt right now which means, they could be anywhere and return at any time."

"How are the dodovarks going to get off those ledges, if they can't climb or fly?" Leah asked.

"Well Leah, we'll have to climb down and rescue them and we should really try to do that as quickly as we possibly can because if the dinobirds return, they'll probably be very hungry and if they are, they will swallow each one of those dodovarks whole in a single mouthful." Ravid rapidly confirmed. "When it comes to the actual issue of our own safety, once we step of the clifftop to start our rescue mission and climb down towards the ledges, we will be in as much danger as the dodovarks."

"Can't we just lower a rope or something else down to them Ravid?" Leah asked as she glumly peeked out over the edge of the clifftop once again and then reluctantly surveyed the rocky ledges and the very high heights which unfortunately, had not changed or moved a single inch, despite all her hopeful, internal, silent wishes. "It's just I'm not really good with heights and those ledges are very high up."

"There's no way the dodovarks can escape Leah, even if a rope or vine was lowered down to them it would be very tricky for them to grip and latch onto anything of that nature because they really don't possess the capabilities to hold onto vines and ropes in that manner." Ravid explained as he shook his head. "And if we attached a basket to one end of the rope and then sent it down, it's highly unlikely that the dodovarks would understand that plan well enough to participate with it and so, we would still have to climb down to the ledges anyway to actually put them inside the basket ourselves before we could pull them up. Another worry is that the dinobirds might not be that far away which means, they could return whilst a dodovark was inside the basket and then the dinobirds would probably either just pluck the dodovark from the basket and dump them in another nest and that other nest might be even trickier to reach, or they could even just eat them on the spot and swallow both the basket and the dodovark inside it whole."

"How on earth will we rescue them though Ravid?" Leah asked.

"We don't have any equipment and to be perfectly honest, I'm not sure that I'd fare very well, if there was an actual attack from a dinobird."

"Look Leah, I'll go and look for some wooden stumps and I already have some rope and a bunch of wooden pegs so with all those useful things I can make a rope ladder that should be long enough to reach those ledges." Ravid suggested enthusiastically. "Then we can utilize that rope ladder to climb down onto each ledge, rescue the dodovarks from the dinobirds' nests and carry them back up to the top of the cliff on our backs.

"What happens if they don't stay on our backs?" Leah asked hesitantly. "What if they jump off, or even fall off when we try to carry them?"

"Now that's a very good question. We'll have to tie them to our backs with some rope so that way, they don't fall off and that way, we'll be able to climb back up the ladder much more easily." Ravid swiftly concluded.

"Okay, I'll give it a try Ravid but I'm not totally sure that I'll actually be much help." Leah agreed. "I do have to warn you though, I'm not very good with heights as in heights are one of my biggest, deepest fears."

"Well, things should be okay Leah as long as the dinobirds don't actually return whilst we're still on one of the ledges." Ravid immediately reassured her.

"What happens if they do return?" Leah asked.

"Then I'll have to fight them off and you will have to climb back up the rope ladder very quickly because they can be extremely vicious, especially if they think that we're trying to steal their food." Ravid explained. "We have to rescue all five of them, so this is not going to be very straightforward or a lightning fast rescue mission because I don't think that I'll be able to carry two dodovarks up the rope ladder at the same time because Dodovarks are actually quite heavy and way heavier than they look. So that means between us both, we'll have to make five trips down the ladder in total."

"Okay, well I probably won't be able to manage more than one dodovark at a time either." Leah mentioned. "Especially not with the high heights, a rope ladder and a possible attack from savage creatures. In fact, to be perfectly honest Ravid, it'll be a huge achievement for me if I can even manage to rescue one."

"Trust me Leah you can do it and I'll be right beside you, so there's nothing to fear." Ravid rapidly reassured her.

"Except those huge, vicious, savage dinobirds." Leah joked.

"Yes, except for those huge, savage dinobirds." Ravid agreed as he smiled. "Right, I better go and look for those stumps of wood." He said decisively.

"Okay, I'll wait here and keep an eye on the dodovarks." Leah replied.

"Yes, that's a good idea." Ravid agreed. "One of us should keep an eye on them really."

For the next few minutes Leah was left totally alone beside the cliff edge as Ravid rushed off and started his search and as she listened to the five dodovarks' distress calls from the ledges below her, Leah visually checked their positions every few seconds, just to ensure that they were all indeed actually still present and okay. The air around Leah seemed to rapidly became quite clammy, rather muggy and very taut with tension as she empathized with the dodovark's fear and their obvious distress which was by that point, very evident and increasingly obvious with every second that went by and as she waited for Ravid to return a definite fear lingered and lurked inside her form that one of the dinobirds might return before Ravid did. Since Leah had absolutely no weapons at all with which to tackle an unknown savage foe alone and none of the dodovarks were within arm's reach, the dinobirds as she already knew, would just devour all the dodovarks in one go and she would not be able to stand in their way or stop them.

Much to Leah's sheer relief however, despite all her nerves, fears and worries, when Ravid finally returned about five minutes later all the dodovarks still remained present upon the ledges, intact and uneaten. Although Ravid had a bundle of wooden stumps tied together with some rope that dangled from one of his hands, Leah swiftly noticed as he strode towards her that he also had some weapons in the form of two spears which he had wedged under one of his arms, the sight of which immediately, slightly comforted her.

An actual potential dinobird attack now lay upon the horizon of Leah's day and since she was currently not only unarmed but also totally defenseless, Leah felt that the provision of the spear at least provided her with some reassurances that she could defend herself, if she really had to although the actual practical utilization of that spear was another issue entirely. When it came to the actual issue of physical confrontations and direct attacks upon Leah's person, self-defense, physical battles and violent conflicts were definitely not something that she had experienced in the real world and so being that it was very unfamiliar territory to her, the possibility of an actual battle made her feel slightly lost. In fact, never once in Leah's entire life had she ever had to fend of an attack from a vicious creature and certainly not a huge, prehistoric bird like creature such as a dinobird and so the sight of the two spears was a very welcome sight and instantly put Leah slightly more at ease as she began to clasp on to the hope that perhaps the weapons would offer an effective means of defense.

In just a matter of minutes, much to Leah's absolute astonishment and total awe, Ravid had not only roped the rope ladder together but then he had also handed Leah a spear and offered to demonstrate to her exactly how it functioned and how she should utilize it. Once a quick demonstration had been given, Leah waited patiently and cooperated fully as Ravid then secured the two spears to their backs with some rope so that the spears would not obstruct their movements but would still remain reachable and easily accessible.

"I collected these two spears from one of my weapon stashes in the woods Leah." Ravid explained as he tied the final knot in a piece of rope to secure the spear to her back and then turned to face her. "I always keep some weapons hidden in a few of the hollow tree trunks around this clifftop just in case because the cliff face is a well-known nesting spot for dinobirds. The spears might come in handy, if a dinobird attacks."

Leah nodded in agreement. "Yes, because my hands certainly won't be any use without some kind of weapon." She admitted.

"I'll just knock some pegs and stumps into the ground to secure the rope ladder and then we can start our rescue mission." Ravid said as he plucked a small wooden mallet from one of his trouser pockets.

A couple of minutes went by as Leah just stood close to the edge of the cliff in total silence as she watched Ravid tap the wooden pegs and stumps into the ground with the wooden mallet and as she waited patiently for him to complete his task, a few watchful glances were cast down towards the dodovarks upon the ledges just to ensure that they were indeed, all still actually present. Once the wooden pegs and stumps had been secured and appeared to be firmly enough in position to hold the rope ladder in place, Leah watched as Ravid cast one end of the rope ladder over the side of the cliff and then turned to face her with a grin.

"Right, now that the rope ladder is in place Leah, we better get a move on before those dinobirds actually come back." Ravid urged as he leant down towards the top of the rope ladder. "Once I reach the first ledge, you can start to make your way down the rope ladder that way there won't be too much weight on the ropes at any one time. The good thing is that at least some of the dodovarks are on the same ledges, so that makes our task slightly easier."

"True and that means less trips up and down the rope ladder." Leah agreed as she nodded and smiled.

When Ravid had climbed down the rope ladder and once he had arrived parallel to the first ledge, Leah took a deep nervous breath as she watched him step off the ladder onto the ledge as she prepared to follow him and to climb down the actual rope ladder herself. On that particular ledge as Leah already knew, there were two dodovarks present and so she automatically assumed as she began to climb quite nervously down the ladder that Ravid would rescue one of the creatures and that she would be responsible for the rescue of the second dodovark.

Approximately five minutes later, once Leah had made her quite nervous descent and once she had arrived successfully parallel to the first ledge, she carefully stepped off the rope ladder onto the rocky surface and then stood and watched in fascinated silence as

Ravid picked up the first dodovark and then tied the creature securely to his back. Some soft, gentle coos floated into Leah's ears as the two dodovarks situated upon the ledge that they had come to rescue seemed to realize that a rescue operation was currently underway and immediately welcomed the two human forms and fortunately, much to Leah's total relief, she noticed that the first creature cooperated with Ravid's presence without any fuss and so, Leah eagerly began to approach the second dodovark. The second creature, in direct response to Leah's approach, rapidly started to waddle enthusiastically and eagerly towards her and towards the side of the nest that it was actually stuck inside and so Leah smiled as she drew closer to the dodovark and prepared to make her first actual rescue attempt.

Unfortunately, however, Leah swiftly noticed, since the dinobird's nest had rather high sides which reached almost all the way up to her waist although the dodovark had managed to waddle to the side of that nest and as close to Leah as it possibly could, it seemed to struggle to actually climb out of the nest. Once a few eager but very unsuccessful attempts to escape had been made, Leah swiftly concluded that a definite effort was required on her part to make the rescue operation slightly easier, far smoother and much faster because although the dodovark might eventually be able to finally clamber out of the nest unassisted as Leah already knew, time was definitely in short supply.

Just a few seconds later Leah politely leant over one side of the nest and then stretched her arms towards the dodovark's position as she prepared to lift the creature up and out of the dinobird's nest. Fortunately, it rapidly transpired, no entity present upon the rocky ledge wanted to be eaten and snacked upon by the dinobirds inclusive of the dodovarks themselves as the creature quickly participated and willingly allowed Leah to lift it from the interior of the predator's nest and as Leah placed the dodovark on the rocky ledge beside her, Ravid rapidly began to walk towards her in order to assist her.

"Once I get to the top of the rope ladder Leah, start to make your way up the ladder as quickly as you can." Ravid advised as he picked up the second dodovark and then strapped the creature to her back with some rope. "In fact, I think you should probably go first that might be safer."

"Right Ravid, I'll do that." Leah agreed as she nodded and then immediately started to action his suggestion. "The dodovarks don't seem to mind being strapped to our backs." She mentioned as she suddenly noticed how cooperative the creature had been and how the dodovark had instantly accepted the constraints with minimal fuss.

"They're probably just grateful to finally get off these ledges." Ravid replied as he smiled. "Dinobirds can be very savage and so, they've probably managed to work out that they are on the afternoon snack menu.

"Dodovarks are actually quite heavy, aren't they? I've just discovered how heavy they are and it seems as if, the more you carry them around, the more they seem to weigh." Leah joked as she smiled.

Much to Leah's total surprise, she had rapidly discovered that the dodovark was rather heavy and even heavier than she had initially expected the creature to be but as Leah reflected upon some of Ravid's earlier comments, she remembered that he had actually mentioned that fact to her. The actual dodovarks themselves, Leah noticed, seemed to reach almost waist high in terms of their height and they were very round and plump which meant, the creatures waddled as they walked which normally would have amused her but, in this instance, laughter and smiles remained far from Leah's lips since the rescue mission was so very urgent. Unfortunately, the rescue mission that Leah had volunteered to participate in that day, not only involved several ledges at horribly high heights, some very heavy cargo but also some savage, vicious foes that might return at any given second and that scary possible eventuality, definitely worried Leah profusely.

"Yes, they really are quite heavy and that's another reason why we have to move swiftly because we can't really carry them around on our backs for very long." Ravid agreed as he walked towards the rope ladder and then held it steady.

"I can see why a dinobird would want to eat you." Leah mentioned to the dodovark as she placed a foot onto a rung of the rope ladder. "You are very plump and so, they probably thought that you'd make a great snack because there's definitely enough of you to fill a gap in a hungry creature's stomach."

Approximately five minutes later, Leah arrived back at the top of the rope ladder with her heavy cargo in tow and as she stepped off the final rung and then clambered on to the safety of the clifftop, she peered back down the cliff face and then gave Ravid a certain nod, just to let him know that the ladder was now unoccupied so that he could proceed. Once Ravid had arrived at the top of the rope ladder, just a few minutes later and he too had clambered back onto the clifftop, Leah smiled as he swiftly offered to unstrap the rather heavy dodovark from her back which was definitely a very welcome offer that was instantly accepted because the longer Leah carried the creature around, the heavier the dodovark actually seemed to become.

After Ravid's polite gesture had been actioned and the dodovark had been placed on the ground next to Leah's feet, a huge sigh of very welcome, extremely grateful, immensely appreciative relief escaped from Leah's lips as she began to silently rejoice in the fact that now at least, the heavy creature's weight had been removed from her simulated limbs and frame. For the next couple of minutes and once Leah had helped Ravid to unstrap the second dodovark that had been attached to his own human frame, Leah just stood and watched as the two creatures were reunited because it truly was a very pleasant sight to see as the dodovarks began to welcome each other with affectionate familiarity and flapped around each other in excitement. The two dodovarks not only eagerly cooed around each other's furry, feathered forms as they greeted each other but as Leah watched the creatures interact, she swiftly noticed that they even began to groom one another affectionately which amused her no end and even prompted her to smile.

"I can rescue the third dodovark one on my own Leah, since it's on a ledge on its own and then after that we can rescue the final two from the third ledge together." Ravid suggested as he began to stride enthusiastically back towards the edge of the clifftop. "That way, you'll have a chance to recuperate and a chance to recover.

"Sure, I won't argue with that action plan Ravid." Leah swiftly agreed.

Although Leah wanted to actively participate in the rescue of all the dodovarks, the suggestion of a slight break before her second and final trip down the rope ladder was definitely greatly preferred and so, she gladly succumbed immediately and instantly accepted Ravid's plan of action with absolutely no objections whatsoever. For approximately the next ten minutes or so, once Ravid had vacated the clifftop, Leah just sat and relaxed on a spot of grass near the two rescued dodovarks as she watched them playfully interact which brought a smile to her face and amused her no end because their mannerisms really were quite humorous. Not only did the dodovarks appear to be quirky and funny, Leah observed but they also seemed to be very social creatures as they groomed each other politely, flapped around each other in little circles and exchanged coo after coo and so Ravid's absence was barely even noticed as each minute slipped by very quickly.

When Ravid actually returned with the third dodovark, once he had released the creature and it had joined its two comrades, Leah began to discuss the third ledge with him and the final trip that they would both make down the rope ladder to rescue the two dodovarks that still remained stranded upon the third and final ledge. Although Leah still felt very nervous about the high heights and the rope ladder climbs, she wanted to complete her third trip down the rope ladder as soon as she possibly could because that would be the last and final rescue attempt which meant, her trips down the rope ladder would finally come to an end. Since Ravid had promised to show Leah something else, Leah really hoped and wished in her heart of hearts that the something else he had referred to would be far more pleasant than their rescue mission and she also hoped that it would not involve anymore rope ladders, cliff faces or the threat of any savage creatures.

"I just hope the dinobirds don't return whilst we're on the final ledge Ravid." Leah said as she gave the dodovarks one final glance and smile, then rose to her feet and began to walk towards him.

"Well, we only have two more dodovarks to rescue now Leah." Ravid swiftly pointed out. "So, it shouldn't take too long and hopefully, the dinobirds will stay away from their nests a bit longer, or at least just long enough for us to rescue those final two."

Leah nodded. "Yes, I definitely agree with that because the climbs up and down the rope ladder, the high ledges and the heavy dodovarks all in one go, really are enough of a challenge for me." She admitted.

Since a firm action plan had been agreed that would hopefully usher in an end to the awful heights and rocky ledges, Leah felt slightly reassured as she began to follow Ravid towards the edge of the cliff once again that quite soon, their dodovark rescue mission would not only be successful but also actually complete. Just one final ledge had to be tackled and reached to complete the dodovark rescue mission and then the two dodovarks trapped upon it had to be rescued and so, Leah's fear of heights would definitely have to be conquered once again but at the very least, she could find comfort in the fact that Ravid was around and that his two masculine arms seemed more than ready to assist, if the need arose.

For the next few minutes Leah remained both totally silent and completely still as she waited at the top of the rope ladder and watched Ravid as he headed down towards the final ledge and as she did so, Leah noticed that his descent occurred at a far quicker pace than her own initial trip down the rope ladder had which amused her slightly. A lack of confidence definitely existed on Leah's part when it came to high heights because she had never actually climbed down any rope ladders or cliff faces in real life and so, she really wasn't used to either activity which meant, she had felt very challenged which had been the main reason why she had made her first descent much more cautiously, carefully and more slowly than Ravid's far bolder downward swings.

Once Ravid had stepped of the rope ladder onto the ledge, Leah began her own descent for a second time which was definitely hampered by both nerves and fear which seemed to rattle around inside her simulated form as she went and even made her arms and hands tremble and shake. Approximately five minutes later, when Leah arrived parallel to the ledge, she nervously stepped of the rope ladder and onto the ledge as she prepared to collect and rescue the fifth and final dodovark that she was responsible for and as she did so, Leah noticed that Ravid had already strapped the fourth creature to his back and form.

"You can carry that dodovark over there Leah." Ravid said as he pointed towards the fifth dodovark. "I've got some more rope with me, so I can strap it to your back now."

Leah nodded.

Due to the threat of a possible dinobird attack which as Leah already knew, could happen at any given moment she quickly began to walk towards the nest and then leant over the side of it and swiftly lifted the dodovark from the nest's interior. Since as Leah was already aware, the dodovark would struggle to leave the nest by itself, some assistance was definitely required and so was eagerly offered and provided to the creature without any hesitation in order to save time, minimize fuss and to achieve the rescue mission as efficiently as possible. However, just as Leah started to walk back towards Ravid so that he could strap the fifth dodovark securely to her back, things suddenly took a turn for the worse as the owner of the actual nest actually returned.

Suddenly it seemed, the huge monstrous dinobird had decided to put in a live, very personal appearance and as the huge dinobird swooped down towards the ledge and its nest, Ravid hurriedly started to strap the fifth dodovark to Leah's back. A few nervous shivers ran down Leah's spine and she began to tremble with absolute fear as she waited for Ravid to make the final adjustments to the rope knots because the dinobird looked absolutely huge and extremely powerful and so her fear was certainly justified. Some nervous gulps seemed to gather and stick inside Leah's throat as she waited for Ravid to secure the dodovark to her back and tie the final pieces of rope around its form that would hold the creature securely in place as the dinobird headed rapidly and directly towards not only the ledge but also towards the human forms and dodovarks situated upon it.

Nothing but fear seemed to run rampant upon the rocky ledge as Ravid finally finished his task a few seconds later, then he gently held onto Leah's arm, nodded his head and began to lead her quickly towards the rope ladder as the dinobird drew much closer to the ledge and then swooped in. Much to Leah's absolute horror however, the rope ladder which was situated just a few steps away from her current position, suddenly became unreachable as the dinobird not only swooped in towards the ledge but also blocked Leah and Ravid's path as it hovered next to the rocky ledge and the rope ladder as the creature obstructed their actual escape route.

"Look Leah, I'll try to distract the dinobird and then you can climb back up the rope ladder." Ravid suddenly called out as he began to walk speedily towards the other end of the rocky ledge.

"What about you Ravid?" Leah asked. "Will you be alright?

"I can handle a spear quite well so hopefully, I should survive." Ravid quickly reassured her as he flashed her a grin. "At least if you go, one of us will be safe and so will another dodovark."

Although Leah really didn't want to leave Ravid alone on the rocky shelf with just a vicious, savage creature for company, she knew that it made very little sense to stay since she couldn't really utilize a spear very well which meant, she probably wouldn't be able to help him very much. Currently as Leah could clearly see, it was virtually impossible to clasp onto the rope ladder never mind actually place her feet upon the wooden rungs and climb up due to the dinobird's position because the creature still remained situated between Leah and the actual rope ladder so that meant, an actual escape was also absolutely impossible.

Just a few seconds later however, and much to Leah's sheer relief, the dinobird suddenly seemed to notice Ravid's movements and as it responded to his actions and began to circle around the ledge, the savage beast started to move towards the other end of the rocky surface. A nod of encouragement was given by Ravid as Leah glanced at his face as he silently reassured her and encouraged her to make an escape but Leah hesitated for a few seconds as she looked at the dinobird once again and then watched in total fear and absolute horror as the creature swooped in towards the other end of the rocky ledge and towards Ravid.

Despite the fear that ran rampant inside Leah's form however, she noticed that Ravid bravely brandished his spear as he prepared for the dinobird's attack as the savage creature drew closer. A silvery, mysterious glow seemed to emanate from the spear inside Ravid's hand, Leah observed as she watched him prepare to defend himself with it and as the spear suddenly extended into a much more sophisticated, intricate looking weapon, Leah cast a fearful glance back towards the huge blackish, grey, savage dinobird which from what she could see, definitely looked more than ready to pounce on Ravid's form and to launch an actual attack.

Technically, Leah's route to the rope ladder was now actually clear and so as she began to shake herself out of her shock and her frozen state, she started to rush speedily towards it as she prepared to abandon the rocky ledge completely and to carry the dodovark to a place of safety. Fortunately for both Leah and the dodovark tied to her back, Ravid's distraction seemed to have worked which meant, the dinobird was now focused solely upon Ravid and the other end of the rocky ledge but as Leah rushed towards the rope ladder nothing but absolute fear seemed to occupy, reside and surge through her form.

The second that Leah arrived in front of the rope ladder, she quickly clung onto it and then a nervous foot was rapidly placed upon the nearest wooden rung as Leah prepared to flee but just before she committed to her escape in totality, she cast one final glance back towards Ravid and the other end of the rocky ledge. Since the dinobird had by that point already swooped down onto the ledge, the savage creature now appeared to be engaged in what looked to be a very aggressive attack against Ravid's form and although Leah couldn't actually assist him because she wasn't particularly good with weapons of any kind, she tried to find some comfort in the fact that unlike her, at least Ravid knew how to utilize a spear effectively.

After just a few wooden rungs had been climbed, Leah paused for a moment as she glanced back down at Ravid once more and the ledge and as she did so, Leah noticed that his efforts to fight the dinobird had been like a mere drop in the ocean and had not gone very well at all because even as she watched, he was knocked completely of his feet. Despite all Ravid's efforts and his prior experience, the spear that he held and that he had swiped at the dinobird had not yet managed to touch, pierce or penetrate the dinobird's hide and from what Leah could see as she continued to watch the two engage in battle that failure to damage the vicious creature had meant that the dinobird had continued to attack him with relentless vigour and determined tenacity. Due to the continuation of the vicious attacks by the dinobird, Leah felt absolutely horrified as she watched Ravid be savagely tossed against the rear wall of the cliff ledge like a ragdoll but courage was definitely in short supply because Leah felt unsure that she could handle the spear effectively enough to actually be of any assistance to him.

Almost mockingly, the dinobird repeatedly swooped in and out of the rocky ledge and cliff face several times and as Leah stared at the creature in total horror she noticed that each time it did so, the dinobird swept one of its huge scaly, webbed, feathery wings towards Ravid on every visit. Every single swipe seemed to knock Ravid against the rear rocky surface of the cliff ledge and so, Leah began to doubt that he would actually be able to escape because the dinobird seemed to have him pinned to that end of the rocky ledge and had almost completely demobilized him.

Deep down inside Leah's simulated form however, a small but noticeable surge of courage suddenly seemed to pulse through her mind which urged her to respond to Ravid's predicament and that spurt of motivation urged Leah to not just jump back down off the rope ladder onto the ledge itself but also to launch an actual attack upon the dinobird. Although heroic acts and very high heights were definitely not a great duo or coupling that appealed to any of Leah's personal internal instincts, in order to help Ravid overcome the creature's relentless pursuit she felt compelled to respond to his plight and to act upon that small glimmer of bravery that had finally managed to visit her and had somehow, slipped into her mind.

An actual spear was currently in Leah's possession because

Ravid had very politely provided her with a weapon and so, she now felt compelled to put it to good use because as Leah already knew, two spears would definitely be less likely to miss than one spear and could cause a lot more damage to the horrible dinobird. In every way imaginable it had started to look to Leah as if the dinobird and its repetitive attacks had overpowered Ravid and it now seemed as if he would not be able to leave the rocky ledge at all because the dinobird had trapped him at the other end of the ledge and there was no other escape route as Leah already knew which meant, she was now Ravid's only hope.

Despite all Leah's nerves which seemed to rattle away chaotically inside of her, she suddenly assertively and bravely climbed back down the few wooden rungs and then jumped back down onto the rocky ledge. Since the dinobird actually looked as if it could easily swallow Leah whole in one mouthful, some courage had to be swiftly mustered from deep within as she reached for the spear and then began to walk towards the other end of the rocky ledge. Once Leah had retrieved the spear as she held it boldly inside her hand and continued to walk towards the other end of the ledge, she noticed that it began to glow quite mysteriously as it extended in much the same manner that Ravid's spear had done just before the dinobird's attacks had begun.

A few more slashes, Leah observed as she walked towards Ravid, were aimed at the dinobird's dark blackish grey hide as she watched him continue to try and defend himself as the creature swooped down towards the ledge again and again but his efforts seemed to make absolutely no difference at all. Not even a single stoppage occurred, Leah observed as she watched the savage beast attack Ravid relentlessly and aggressively and since Ravid now looked totally defeated, Leah doubted that the dinobird would actually leave him alone long enough to allow Ravid to regain his strength and so it was highly unlikely that he would be able to injure the creature in any way.

Unfortunately, as Leah neared the dinobird and Ravid, the creature's attacks seemed to worsen and become even more aggressive in nature as the dinobird swiped its huge wings in

Ravid's direction and he rapidly lost his balance completely as he was swept towards the edge of the ledge. Since the rocky ledge was pretty much just a large, stony shelf on the cliff face, there was it appeared absolutely nowhere for Ravid to run to and there was nowhere that he could possibly hide and so as Leah could clearly see, there were no shields that Ravid could utilize to try and protect himself which meant, her attack had to happen very soon.

Another huge swipe was taken as the dinobird swooped in towards the rocky shelf and this time as Leah watched in total horror, Ravid was swept off the rocky ledge completely by one of the creature's huge wings. On this occasion however, Leah actually lost sight of Ravid completely and so, she held her breath as she froze in a state of absolute shock and total fear as she continued to watch the scene unfold not more than a few steps away from her current position.

Just a few seconds later and much to Leah's total relief however, she noticed that Ravid had somehow managed to grab onto the rocky ledge with one of his hands as he suddenly began to reappear and then he even made a brave attempt to grab onto the rocky surface with his other hand so that he could pull himself back up onto the ledge. Since Ravid had almost fallen off the rocky ledge completely, a distraction Leah felt, was definitely required from his now, very vulnerable state and as she already knew, the only other distraction on that rocky ledge was Leah herself and so, she bravely, boldly brandished the spear as she prepared to step forward and to attack the dinobird.

Due to the whirlpool of fear that Leah felt chaotically spin around inside her form and Ravid's current position, she hesitated for a few seconds before she proceeded to tackle the dinobird and then started to tremble because the small particles of bravery that had been mustered up and that existed inside of her had definitely been rapidly diluted by the gushes of absolute fear that seemed to run rampant through her veins. For a moment, Leah began to question whether she should make an attempt to rescue Ravid first and then face the dinobird or whether she should launch her attack first because Ravid now faced two dangers, the dinobird and a potential fall from the rocky cliff and both those dangers as Leah already knew, could be equally as dangerous.

"What should I do Ravid?" Leah called out as she bravely held the now fully extended spear up in a bold attack position. "Attack the dinobird, or help you back up?"

"Just keep the dinobird busy for a couple of minutes please Leah, if you can." Ravid replied. "I'll be fine."

Leah nodded.

In accordance with Ravid's guidance and instructions, Leah immediately readied her spear to launch an attack upon the dinobird and as she drew closer and neared the dinobird's position, she prepared to also defend herself because the dinobird seemed very angry that the two human forms had not only interrupted its late lunch but had also stolen its potential meal. Rather frighteningly, Leah swiftly noticed that the dinobird looked even larger close up than it had done just a few minutes beforehand when she had been at the other end of the ledge and a few rungs up the rope ladder but she didn't really have much time to consider that largeness because the dinobird swiftly continued its attacks but this time the attacks were actually directed towards Leah herself. Another swoop towards the ledge and the human forms upon it, swiftly occurred as the creature suddenly seemed to notice Leah's presence and pay much more attention to it and so, Leah trembled as she bravely stuck the spear out rapidly in front of her as the dinobird swooped in towards her.

Fortunately for Leah and much to her total amazement, her first efforts actually seemed to pay off as the spear dove straight into the creature's hide, pierced its flesh and a deep gash suddenly appeared across the dinobird's chest. Very satisfyingly for Leah, not more than a few seconds later, she heard a very loud shriek and then the dinobird actually started to fall from the sky as it swiftly weakened and as Leah watched the creature's involuntary retreat due to its wound, she could hardly believe that her aim had managed to render so much damage to such a savage, scary, vicious foe so quickly.

A few seconds later Ravid eagerly rushed towards Leah and

then he gently held onto her arm, since by that point he had actually managed to not only stabilize himself but had also managed to clamber back up onto the ledge.

"We need to get off this ledge right now Leah." Ravid urged as he began to lead her towards the rope ladder. "There might be more dinobirds nearby."

"Right." Leah immediately agreed as she followed him towards the rope ladder.

"You know Leah, you have a pretty good aim." Ravid teased as he paused in front of the rope ladder and then held it steady as he turned to face her. "Are you sure you haven't done this before?" He jokingly asked.

"Nope, definitely not that lucky strike was just beginner's luck I guess." Leah replied as she smiled.

Approximately five minutes later, when Leah arrived back on the clifftop, she noticed that the dodovark tied to her back seemed to be extremely excited by the sight of the other dodovarks and so, she quickly unstrapped the creature from her form and then politely placed the dodovark upon the ground. Due to Leah's scuffle with the dinobird which had definitely shocked her, Leah still felt slightly uneasy as she watched the fourth dodovark enthusiastically join its other three comrades but a smile managed to wander across her face as coos of delight were swiftly expressed amongst the four as the creatures began to scurry, waddle and flap around each other and then started to groom the fourth dodovark affectionately.

Once Leah felt satisfied that the fourth dodovark had been safely reunited with its three feathery, furry companions, both amicably and peacefully, she then quickly turned her attention back to Ravid as she returned to the cliff edge and peeked out over it. Since by that point Ravid had almost reached the top of the rope ladder, Leah felt a great sense of relief as she watched him climb up the final few wooden rungs before he clambered back over the edge of the cliff and back onto the safety of the clifftop.

"Now that last rescue was slightly trickier than I expected it to be." Ravid admitted as he released the fifth and final dodovark and placed the creature upon the ground.

"Indeed, it was." Leah agreed as she nodded.

"We should sit down for a few minutes and rest Leah." Ravid suggested as he began to walk towards a small grassy knoll nearby and then sat down upon it.

"Sure." Leah immediately agreed as she began to follow him and then sat down on the grass beside him. "Will we be safe up here Ravid?"

"Yes, we should be. The dinobirds rarely come up here because the Woods of Curiosity which you and I walked through are very difficult to fly through and so any prey that they might try to pursue up here, just seeks refuge in the trees which really frustrates them." Ravid explained. "So, we should be pretty safe here."

A few more pleasant minutes slipped peacefully by as Leah just enjoyed the serenity that surrounded her as the two sat upon the grassy knoll on the clifftop and took a moment to catch their breath as they watched the five dodovarks playfully interact with each other. Since there were no longer any potential threats from the savage dinobirds, Leah noticed that the dodovarks no longer seemed to be filled with alarm and that they did not exhibit any signs of distress anymore and that in fact, the fluffy, feathery creatures appeared to look totally at ease as they frolicked and cooed amicably and playfully amongst themselves and fussed over their comrades. The animalistic pleasantries exchanged and the affectionate rituals performed between the dodovarks continued to amuse and fascinate Leah for another few minutes as she just sat in silence and continued to watch them as she attempted to recuperate and began to wonder what the next part of her adventure that day might entail because Ravid had said that he wanted to show her something and so she felt intrigued and increasingly curious about what that something might actually be.

Leaps of Courage Across the Clifftops of Trust

Quite unexpectedly however, Leah noticed that a mature man who looked to be in his early sixties suddenly appeared from the same path that Leah and Ravid had walked along to arrive at the clifftop prior to their actual rescue mission and as she fell silent and then began to watch him approach the grassy knoll, Leah noticed that he wheeled a large cart in front of him as he walked. The large cart looked almost empty, Leah observed as the man drew closer but as she started to visually inspect its interior, she could see a handful of small objects that appeared to litter the base which looked, from a short distance away, almost like soft toys. Once the cart had been swiftly parked and then left in a stationery position just a meter or so away from where Leah and Ravid sat, Leah watched in silence as the man strode enthusiastically towards them and the grassy knoll that they were both seated upon.

Interestingly for Leah, she noticed as the man walked towards their seated human forms with a warm, friendly smile upon his face that the dodovarks suddenly seemed to notice the man's presence and as they did so, the creatures instantly responded to his sudden entrance both extremely favorably and in a very amicable manner. Much to Leah's amusement, a gush of soft gentle coos were enthusiastically, suddenly released and a flurry of excited flaps as the dodovarks welcomed and greeted the man like an old friend as he came to a total standstill next to Ravid's form. Due to the positive signs from both parties, Leah immediately began to conclude that the dodovarks definitely, already knew the man and that he was deemed to be a friend not a foe because his appearance had not caused any alarm, any distress or any discomfort in their midst and so she began to relax as she waited for him to speak.

Unlike the predatory, vicious, savage dinobirds which Leah had observed had filled the dodovarks with total alarm, absolute distress and bundles of fear, this man's presence seemed to soothe, excite and interest them in a very positive and affectionate way as the dodovarks eagerly started to waddle towards him. Upon the man's face Leah could clearly see that there was an affectionate smile as he glanced at the dodovarks and then released an amused chuckle which further reinforced the fact that not only was he very familiar to them and vice versa but also that there seemed to be some deep sentimental and emotional bonds that ran silently between the man and the five dodovarks.

Just a few seconds later however, the man suddenly turned to face Leah and Ravid once more and as Leah watched him, she noticed that he nodded his head to acknowledge their human presence just before he greeted Ravid politely which also indicated to her that the two men already knew each other and that they were acquaintances of some kind. Quite amusingly, as Leah continued to watch the man, she noticed that one of the dodovarks boldly approached him before the creature came to an actual standstill beside one of his legs which much to Leah's surprise, the dodovark then rubbed their plump body affectionately against.

Due to the friendly and humorous actions of the dodovark, Leah immediately giggled as she absorbed the scene in front of her in total delight because those friendly interactions clearly indicated to her that the man did indeed have a very close relationship with the dodovarks that was not only pleasant and warm but also what one might even consider deeply affectionate. An amused smile remained upon Leah's face as she watched the other four dodovarks gather around the man's form just before he started to greet the creatures both affectionately and playfully as he began ruffle their furry feathers and started to discuss the group's departure from his care earlier that day.

"What have you been up to today my feathered, furry friends?" The man asked as he laughed. "You've been missing all day you have."

"Well Ham, I can tell you that they must have waddled into the Valley of Perils and then approached the Cliffs of Bravery which as you and I both know, is renowned dinobird territory and not a very wise thing to do." Ravid explained as he suddenly stood up. "Then the dinobirds must have spotted them and plucked them from the foot of the cliffs and dumped them inside their nests for dinner. So, we had to rescue them before the dinobirds returned from their afternoon hunt, otherwise they would have been gobbled up and eaten."

"Well, well, well that was quite an adventure." Ham replied as he began to gently shake his head. "I don't know how Ravid but they managed to find a way out of the enclosure this morning and I had absolutely no idea where they'd gone."

For a few seconds Leah watched in intrigued silence as Ham started to inspect the dodovarks with a slightly suspicious expression upon his face as he continued to shake his head in disapproval. One of the dodovarks that was slightly larger than the other four suddenly seemed to attract Ham's attention far more than the others, Leah noticed and as Ham's focus remained fixed upon that particular dodovark for a bit longer, she listened to him in silence as he suddenly began to scold the dodovark in a rather stern and very firm voice.

"Sinbad, you are a very naughty dodovark." Ham scolded. "You not only took your friends out today without permission but you also led them towards that rocky cliff, didn't you?" He demanded crossly. "You know the Valley of Perils is a very dangerous place for dodovarks don't you?"

Much to Leah's total amusement, the dodovark that Ham had addressed in a cross voice, suddenly seemed to try and hide its head under a furry, feathery, stumpy wing and as Leah watched the creature's reaction, she began to smile because it appeared to be so sincere and quite strangely, actually verged upon being slightly apologetic.

"Yes, I think they were on a wander around the valley and that they waddled right up to the cliff face and that the dinobirds found them there and then just snapped them up." Ravid agreed. "The dinobirds probably thought that it was their lucky day, since some food had just appeared voluntarily, landed quite close to their nests and virtually waddled right onto their rocky nest front steps."

"Sinbad, those cliffs are a very dangerous place for everyone not just dodovarks because the rocky cliffs are where the dinobirds live and everyone knows that." Ham insisted as he continued to scold the dodovark in a cross voice. "And I have told you that many times now." He turned to face Ravid before he continued. "I don't know what to do sometimes Ravid, you can feed them, train them, groom them and try to keep them safe but they really have got a mind of their own. I try my best but sometimes, they behave like very mischievous, naughty children."

Leah smiled.

"Yes Ham, I can imagine, they do seem to be very lively and they do look like they can be a handful sometimes." Ravid concluded. "Just a little bit too adventurous perhaps."

"Adventurous or reckless, it's a fine line and today, Sinbad definitely crossed it." Ham replied as he shook his head. "He's the leader of the group and so, the rest of the dodovarks usually just follow his lead and today that almost got them eaten." He turned to face the dodovark once more before he continued. "If you don't behave Sinbad, I'll find another dodovark to lead your group and then you won't be the leader anymore." Ham paused for a moment and then turned to face the rest of the dodovarks as he clapped his hands together. "Right ladies and gentlemen, it's time for us to leave and Sinbad, there'll be no treats for you today."

Leah smiled.

"Right Ham, I'll walk you to your cart." Ravid said politely as he rose to his feet. "Are you coming Leah?" He asked as he turned to face her. "So, we can say goodbye to our feathery, furry friends properly."

Leah nodded and rose to her feet. "Sure." She replied.

"Thanks very much Ravid for all your assistance, if you hadn't retrieved them from those dinobird's nests and rescued them today, goodness only knows what would have happened to them." Ham mentioned appreciatively as he began to walk back towards his cart. "In fact, I have absolutely no doubts at all that instead of eating their dinner, they would have been eaten for dinner by the dinobirds."

Rather amusingly, Leah noticed as she walked that the dodovarks immediately started to follow Ham enthusiastically and eagerly as he made his way back towards the cart and that as soon as he reached it, they waited patiently beside the cart and beside him until he picked each one up and then placed them inside it. Unlike the dodovarks earlier distress whilst stuck on the cliff ledges however, Leah observed that no distress or upset now seemed to be present as Ham handled the creatures with total ease and they cooed softly and cheerfully as he picked each one up. Once all the dodovarks were safely positioned inside the cart, Leah continued to watch in satisfied silence as Ham prepared to depart but just before he vacated the area, he paused for a moment and then turned to face both Ravid and Leah as he began to address them once again.

"Thank you both so much for all your help today, I probably wouldn't have ever seen my dodovarks again, if you hadn't saved them. Unfortunately, I don't have much with me right now that I can offer to you, or give you but I can give you this." Ham said appreciatively as he opened up his long, dark coat and then plucked out a golden chain from an inside pocket. He handed the necklace to Leah and then encouraged her to wear it. "This necklace will give you much more physical strength and lots more courage whenever you wear it around your neck, it's called a Chain of Strength." Ham explained. "These necklaces are very, very rare and exceptionally hard to find because they are forged from not only gold but also encased in and molded with resin from the tree of bravery. I actually forged this one myself just last week."

"Thank you very much Ham, it's lovely." Leah replied as she graciously accepted the necklace and then quickly slipped it around her neck and fastened the clip so that the piece of jewelry hung in the correct position.

"Is there nothing for me Ham?" Ravid teased. "Don't I get a gift?"

"Now why would I give you a Chain of Strength Ravid?" Ham joked as he laughed. "You're stronger than ten bulls and more courageous than a lion so, you'd probably never even wear it but I'll tell you what I will do, I'll drop by a bottle of cherry wine tomorrow morning." He promised as he winked at Ravid and then smiled. "Since I know that is your favorite and I just made a fresh batch."

Ravid laughed. "I'll hold you to that promise Ham, I do love a glass of cherry wine and you do grow the best cherries in your orchard."

"Right lads and girls, let's go home." Ham teased as he glanced at his cart and the five dodovarks inside it. "It is way past your bedtime now."

Some merry coos and eager flaps immediately emanated from the cart and the dodovarks inside it as Ham lifted up the cart handles and then prepared to depart and as he started to push the cart back towards the path, Leah noticed that Ham spoke to the dodovarks almost like human beings as he walked.

"The dodovarks seem to get along very well with Ham don't they Ravid?" Leah concluded as she turned to face him.

"Yes, they do but the dodovarks must be really quite tired by now because they usually sleep in the early afternoon each day and then wake up in the middle of the night and after that they stay up until the next afternoon. So, they're probably ready to drop off right now and must be quite glad that Ham, who is their keeper, came by when he did to take them home." Ravid explained as he smiled.

"Yeah, they probably didn't expect to be captured by dinobirds." Leah replied conclusively.

"True but they did wander around the Valley of Perils and waddle right up to the foot of the Cliffs of Bravery and those cliff faces are well known dinobird nest zones." Ravid acknowledged as he began to shake his head. "It was almost predictable that they would be snapped up by dinobirds."

"Never mind, they probably won't do that again in a hurry." Leah mentioned as she smiled.

"They might not Leah but today you've certainly earned that Chain of Strength because you not only managed to cross the Valley of Perils via the flimsy, shaky Bridge of Uncertainty to reach the Woods of Curiosity which not many people manage to do but then you also faced the Cliffs of Bravery and a dinobird with nothing but a mere rope ladder and a spear." Ravid said as he congratulated her.

"You should be very proud of yourself."

"They call that bridge the Bridge of Uncertainty?" Leah asked. "How unusual."

"Yes because no one is ever really very sure that they'll actually make it all the way across that bridge to the other side and sometimes, quite strangely, it actually moves around and it can lead to different places entirely." Ravid explained as he smiled and shook his head. "At times it even falls apart too and so, I usually have to find it and rebuild it about once a month."

"I absolutely hated the bridge but the dodovarks were lovely." Leah admitted as she watched the cart full of dodovarks disappear from sight. "How come Ham seems to be able to cart them all around so easily, they are very heavy?"

"He's probably wearing a Chain of Strength himself." Ravid replied as he laughed. "Right, now that the dodovarks are safe and on their way home Leah, I better show you what I was supposed to show you before we embarked upon our rescue mission."

Since Ham was no longer visible and the dodovarks had been returned to their keeper, Leah felt a great sense of peace as Ravid gently held onto her arm and then began to lead her towards a second dirt pathway which burrowed its way into the woods as it neatly and silently divided the trees on either side of its earthy substance. Although Ravid had not divulged to Leah where he wanted to take her or even exactly what he wanted to show her just yet, she walked quietly alongside him as she followed him along the path and as she accompanied him along it, she started to silently wonder, where it might actually lead to.

Not more than ten minutes later however, Leah's question and curiosity were answered in part as the two walked out onto a grassy clifftop and which surprised Leah somewhat because she hadn't expected to see another clifftop that day. However, the second clifftop differed vastly from the first in one sense in that there were many other small clifftops situated all around it and although the other clifftops remained separate, they were situated not too far away from each other and just a little distance apart. The close proximity of the clifftops instantly struck Leah as quite unusual because they looked almost reachable from her current position, albeit with a long leap but since heights and Leah were definitely not friends, she harbored absolutely no desires inside of her to find out if they were indeed, actually reachable.

"These are the Clifftops of Trust Leah." Ravid mentioned. "We have to jump across them to reach the Hilltop of Serenity."

"Jump across the actual clifftops?" Leah asked as she glanced at him and then began to gently shake her head. "Are you sure we can make it Ravid?"

"Yes, I'm very sure." Ravid immediately reassured her. "Every leap of courage Leah, is a leap of trust plus you do have the Chain of Strength on now, so that means you can definitely do it."

"I'm not really much of an athlete Ravid." Leah admitted as she glanced at his face. "I probably wouldn't be able to jump that far."

"Nonsense Leah, you can do anything that you set your mind too." Ravid insisted. "Trust me, you can do this."

Much to Leah's complete and utter surprise, just a few seconds later as she watched Ravid in total silence and complete awe, she saw him approach the edge of the clifftop and without any hesitation at all, he suddenly leapt out over the large gap between the first clifftop and a second clifftop quite close to it and then he even managed to land successfully in one piece.

"Please join me Leah." Ravid called out as he looked back at her and encouraged her to participate with a smile. "It's really quite fun and very easy once you get the hang of it."

Although Leah's reluctance to move was detailed all across her face, she noticed that Ravid didn't seem to be dissuaded by her fear which had now, effectively frozen her and gripped every part of her form. Unfortunately for Leah, the wine that she had drunk earlier that afternoon whilst it had made her slightly more relaxed hadn't quite been enough to render her totally reckless and so her internal inhibitions were quite hard to shake off in just a few seconds which meant, her mind would not allow her to just leap out in a totally foolhardy way. An actual attempt to defy the laws of nature and gravity sat just a tad beyond what Leah felt comfortable with and totally confident about and so, she really doubted that she could actually make such a large leap, even though Ravid had achieved a similar leap with total ease.

Due to Leah's hesitation which Ravid suddenly appeared to notice and sense as she continued to watch him, he quickly leapt out across a second gap and onto another clifftop nearby and then he paused as he turned back to face her and just waited for Leah to participate. A nervous lump seemed to collate, gather and stick in Leah's throat as she prepared to cooperate with Ravid's request and to follow him because cliffs and heights were definitely not Leah's friend but as she bravely prepared to participate, Leah began to take a few steps backwards, so that she could run up to and then jump across the gap.

Since Spectrum was subject to different rules than the real world and an artificial, fantasy environment, Leah silently reminded herself of that fact as she prepared to fully abandon her fears and inhibitions because fantasy permitted things that reality did not allow which meant, the leap could actually be quite possible for her to make successfully. The courage and confidence that Ravid had just displayed however, had totally astonished and completely surprised Leah as she marveled at the agility and boldness which had seeped from his interior and then leapt via his exterior across those gaps and across those very high heights. Neither courage nor confidence were particularly good friends to Leah when it came to high heights but Ravid it appeared, unlike herself she swiftly realized, obviously had an abundance of both and possessed no fear of heights it seemed or off anything else and he appeared to utilize both his courage and his confidence in a totally fearless manner that Leah felt, was very impressive.

“You'll definitely make it Leah.” Ravid suddenly called out to as he continued to try and encourage her and provide her with some verbal reassurances despite the distance that currently stood between them both. “You just have to trust me.”

A few more seconds were spent in nervous hesitation as Leah attempted to convince herself to make the run up and leap and although the first gap really wasn't actually that large, its largeness seemed far larger to Leah's eyes mainly due to the undercurrent of fear and gushes of doubt that ran through her form. Despite all Leah's nerves however, she finally began the run up to the edge of the cliff and then bravely leapt out across it and as she did so, she caught a rapid flash of the ground below her which just looked like a deep dark divide with a muddy base at its foot.

Fortunately for Leah, somehow, a few seconds later she actually managed to land upon the second rocky clifftop and as she did so, she quickly attempted to stabilize herself and tried to regain her balance. From Leah's lips a sigh of relief was gratefully released as she glanced back at the gap that she had just leapt over and it suddenly struck her that her own fear had definitely worried her and rocked her nerves more in the end than the actual leap itself had done. Once Leah was firmly positioned on top of the second small clifftop and she felt reasonably secure, she glanced up at Ravid and then smiled as she began to nod her head.

"You see Leah, it's easy and once you get the hang of it, you'll see that it really can be quite a lot of fun." Ravid swiftly reassured her as he smiled. He turned to face the next clifftop enthusiastically as he prepared to plough ahead and make another leap as he continued. "The leaps of courage test not only your agility but also your self-belief, you can really do a lot more than you think you can Leah and today you're going to see that."

For as far as Leah's eyes could see there were rocky platforms scattered sporadically across her line of vision and as she glanced at them as she caught her breath, she began to wonder how many clifftops she would have to jump across before the two finally arrived at the Hilltop of Serenity. Some of the rocky platforms, Leah swiftly noticed, appeared to be larger or smaller in size and some narrower or wider than others and the gaps that sat in-between each one also seemed to vary and so a slight undercurrent of nervousness remained inside her form as she prepared to proceed.

Once Leah had bravely jumped across a few more gaps, she finally caught up with Ravid and landed on the clifftop that he was situated upon and as she did so, she noticed that he politely leant out to catch her as soon as her feet touched the ground. Just for a moment Leah almost lost her breath as any physical space or lack of proximity that had existed between the two prior to that moment in time was quickly eradicated and as Leah's body began to surge with excitement, the two locked positions and as they did so, she entered into Ravid's masculine arms very willingly. A quiet stillness suddenly seemed to surround Leah as intense waves of passion washed and rippled over her form that not only gripped her interior but also her exterior and an intense electrical current of physical attraction seemed to run rampant through Leah's mind that not only penetrated but also infiltrated every ounce of her being.

"You see Leah, I was right." Ravid whispered.

From deep within Leah could almost feel her heart pound away more rapidly inside her ribcage as she began to cherish, savor, delight, relish and revel in every second spent in Ravid's arms. Suddenly, it struck Leah that she was now uncontrollably, totally and undeniably attracted to this unusual attractive man that she had only just met a few hours beforehand and although it intrigued her, it also made her feel slightly curious because these sensual attractions to and intimate interactions with male guides weren't actually something that Leah had factored into or built into Spectrum's actual creation. How exactly Ravid fitted into Leah's emotional journey of trust, she wasn't entirely sure just yet and what he was actually there to do in his role as her guide was another matter entirely but she definitely felt very attracted to him and so she didn't need a guide or any kind of assistance to work that much out.

"Don't worry Leah, we'll be out of the Maze of Trust soon and when we reach the Hilltop of Serenity then we can relax a bit." Ravid reassured her.

"This is a maze Ravid?" Leah asked as she sought to clarify that she was indeed inside some kind of maze that related to the emotional journey of trust and that she had actually experienced what she was supposed to experience whilst inside that particular emotional plane. "It doesn't really look like one."

"Yes well, it's a strange kind of maze really because it's built from and based upon your fears, anxieties and insecurities and not only does it challenge you to face and tackle each one but it also helps you to try to overcome and conquer them." Ravid explained.

"The Maze of Trust and the challenges it presents differ for each person and so, it can very unpredictable and vary greatly each time it is entered into and explored, just like these gaps that we have to leap over in order to reach the Hilltop of Serenity."

"I didn't realize." Leah replied as she gently shook her head.

"It definitely is a Maze of Trust." Ravid confirmed. "Think about it Leah, you trusted me when you jumped out across the clifftops and participated in the leaps of courage, you trusted the rope ladder that I had made when you climbed down the cliff face to rescue the dodovarks and you trusted yourself when you fought the dinobird."

"And the spear, I definitely trusted the spear, probably even more than I trusted myself." Leah teased.

Suddenly Ravid's explanations made total sense to Leah as the realization suddenly struck her that since the very first moment of her emotional journey that day, she had actually been tasked with placing trust in the various things that she had discovered inside that emotional plane. When Leah had followed the Racrel over the flimsy, wooden Bridge of Uncertainty, she had trusted the creature and had stepped out onto a contraption which had looked less than fit for purpose and in the Woods of Curiosity, when Leah had been wined and dined in the clearing by Ravid, she had trusted him and then embarked upon a rescue mission with him which had involved cliff faces, rope ladders and very high heights. In fact, all of those activities that Leah had participated in so far inside the emotional plane of trust had stood in direct opposition to her own internal fears and so each one had definitely challenged her. Everything that Leah had experienced and encountered since she had initially, actually arrived in Spectrum that day had required trust and Leah had not only had to place her trust in others but also in herself and now she could actually, clearly see that simulated reality and the challenges of trust that Spectrum had discreetly and subtly thrown in her path.

Quite strangely, Leah now fully realized that so far that day inside the emotional plane of trust she had actually faced her biggest fear several times in various different forms and that the emotional journey that she had embarked upon earlier that day, had actually been extremely complex in nature. Despite the strange, complex path that the emotional journey of trust had involved and had taken Leah on however, she could at least find some comfort in the knowledge as she started to follow Ravid's lead that there had been a courageous, deliciously handsome male guide by her side and that had definitely been one of the highlights of her experiences in Spectrum that day.

The leaps of courage across the clifftops continued for a while longer as the two carried on until they arrived at a plush, green hill top and as the two landed upon it, Ravid triumphantly announced and confirmed to Leah that it was indeed the Hilltop of Serenity. Due to the huge leaps of courage that Leah had just made, she immediately collapsed on a heap upon the grass and was rapidly joined by Ravid as she began to internally celebrate her achievement and started to silently rejoice in the pleasant day that she had just spent in the Maze of Trust which had been full of challenges but actually, really quite pleasant.

In some ways, Leah considered thoughtfully as she lay by Ravid's side, it felt really quite strange to her that she had just spent a large part of her day facing one of her biggest fears several times but that she had actually had fun whilst doing so because usually such fears triggered nothing but total distress and absolute alarm in her being. Somehow however, Ravid's presence that day or perhaps the Chain of Strength that Leah had been given and worn had given her the courage to not only face her fears head on but also to finally conquer them and even enjoy doing so. Rather intriguingly for Leah, the pleasant combination of those two very positive factors had worked together side by side and hand in hand, Leah swiftly concluded as she lay on the hilltop and attempted to catch her breath, and both had somehow managed to erase and remove all of the fearful tendencies that usually restricted Leah in her own very real life.

A part of Leah deep down inside however, somehow wished that she could take even just a dash of that strength and courage back into the real world and inject it into her own very real life when she returned to it because in some ways, she actually felt quite liberated, if only for a moment in time and albeit a fictitious moment.

Unfortunately, as Leah already knew, Spectrum was an artificial environment but if she could find a way to transport and transfer some of that courage and strength into her real personality back in the real world, Leah definitely felt that she would because such an addition to her real life would be a very positive outcome to her day and a pleasant souvenir to bring back from her fictitious journey.

For the next few minutes as the two lay on the grassy hilltop together not a word was spoken until Leah finally turned to face Ravid and then smiled at him and as she did so, a lock of hair fell across her face which he gently moved and then courteously placed behind her ear. Just a few seconds later, somehow the two touched again and Leah almost gasped in excitement as Ravid suddenly pulled her closer to him and then began to gently caress her body with his hands. Since Ravid's touch was very pleasant, extremely seductive and amazingly sensual, Leah felt absolutely no desire at all to stop him and deep down inside, she definitely, actually longed for him to continue.

Unfortunately, excitement had been on a vacation from Leah's life for a very long time due to her long hours in the basement that had swamped her in hard work and the daily household chore routine which had bogged her down with conventionality both of which had diminished her zest for life and so, the sensual excitement currently on offer to her, invoked some very deep passionate undercurrents of desire that Leah now truly longed, to fully satisfy. Every part of Ravid's masculine form seemed to exude masculine charm and it appeared to ooze from his every simulated limb and although as Leah already knew, she hadn't technically, actually built a functionality into Spectrum that enabled sexual interactions with guides or anyone else, she decided not to question it because it all just felt so natural and so naturally passionate, absolutely delicious and thoroughly enjoyable.

Nothing but total silence surrounded the two, Leah observed, since neither uttered a single word and as she just basked in the delicious moment and Ravid's companionship, a sensual prospect seemed to teasingly and silently linger all around her that held the promise off a romantic interaction that remained as yet unexplored, unrealized and unfulfilled. Quite suddenly, their two faces somehow touched as Ravid moved his head and Leah lifted hers and then as she swiftly became caught up in a moment of intense sensual passion, Leah suddenly found herself locked in a passionate kiss with Ravid's lips which made her body surge with excitement as a wave of lustful desires swept rapidly over her form and she felt filled with an intense sexual hunger that she now, eagerly and hungrily longed to actually fulfil.

The issue of Leah's very real life and her real romantic commitment to Zidane didn't seem to hinder her in any way or even prick her conscience in the slightest, Leah noticed as she fully succumbed to the flames of desire inside of her that now longed to be extinguished and sensual passion seemed to rule her form in a way that excited her immensely. An artificial affair, Leah had in the end decided, could be considered a purely artificial indulgence and so she had dismissed any guilt in advance so that it would not hinder her in any way which also meant, Zidane was barely even given a second thought as Leah began to sensually succumb to her own passionate desires and fully participate with every single one. Since technically, the male forms inside Spectrum didn't really actually exist in the real world, Leah had already concluded prior to her Spectrum visit that day that she would participate in any sensual activities that might occur purely to see how realistic they felt because she really didn't consider any potential, fictitious sensual splurges that occurred inside Spectrum to be an actual act of betrayal of Zidane on her part.

For Leah, the rationalization of her conduct had already been justified inside her mind as an exploration off the various sexual liaisons that a user could participate within whilst inside Spectrum and that attitude would allow her to paddle through the shallow, murky waters of infidelity without any undesirable invocations and subsequent pangs of guilt. Since guilt as Leah already knew, would only weigh her down and tie her actions up with the rope binds of fidelity that would probably restrict her in some ways, Leah had already dismissed her usual faithful notions as being inapplicable during her walk through tests of Spectrum, due to the fictitious nature of the environment that she was currently situated inside and her main justification for that dismissal being that she had to fully test every single element of Spectrum prior to any potential sale. Quite intentionally, Leah had somehow, completely avoided the issue inside her mind of how she would feel if Zidane did the same thing to her and she had not even given it any consideration at all as she'd kept the Pandora's box of moral deliberations firmly shut, simply ignored any deeper implications, fully entertained her own sensual meanderings and then had just ploughed full steam ahead with some deep dives into her own sensual desires and her own passionate curiosities.

Somehow inside Spectrum, Leah's conscience and guilt, she now fully realized and totally accepted as she entered into and entertained a brief moment of reflection had been allowed to take an actual vacation from her form but Leah felt that it was somehow, absolutely acceptable inside Spectrum, although normally, she definitely wouldn't. The real-life romantic commitment that Leah had made to Zidane had been pushed to one side and totally ignored as so far, she had allowed herself to live freely and fully explore whatever sexual meanderings occurred and it was almost as if her commitment to Zidane inside Spectrum had become completely irrelevant but Leah felt absolutely powerless to stop her departure from it. For some inexplicable reason and for the very first time since the couple had initially met, Leah felt that she really couldn't tear herself away from her own passionate desires inside Spectrum and even though Leah herself had created the fictitious males in question, that very real fact didn't seem to matter in the slightest, or appear to detract from the attraction that Leah now felt.

In the space of just minutes and very rapidly indeed, the two bodies on the hilltop became passionately intertwined and as Ravid searched every inch of Leah's skin with his lips, tongue and hands, his lips suddenly, sensually tickled her naval which sent a surge of sensual passion through Leah's form and any thoughts of Zidane rapidly fled from Leah's mind. Some electric surges of passion and lust seemed to chaotically flow through every ounce of Leah's form as the desire inside of her swiftly heightened and their two forms continued to merge as the two began to make love passionately and frantically and without any reservations at all. The night started to embrace the hilltop and as the last drops of daylight scampered off quietly into the distance as the day silently departed, Leah barely even noticed its departure as passionate, sensual desires took absolute precedence over her mind and form.

A deep current of passionate lust seemed to have not only been stirred but now, completely reigned over and ruled Leah's form as the last drops of daylight abandoned the two completely as Ravid continued to penetrate her and she groaned with pleasure. Excitingly, Leah observed, their two human forms seemed to completely merge in sensual unison until she could no longer actually tell where Ravid's form ended and her own actually began as passion seemed to blend their simulated limbs into a union of sensual desire that rocked every ounce of her being in passionate harmony. The actual fulfilment of animalistic, sexual desires was not really something that Leah had ever fully explored in her entire life up until that point and since she was currently situated inside a fictitious environment, Leah felt that Spectrum was the perfect environment in which to experiment in that manner and so, she had allowed Ravid to take her on a sexual adventure which had very little to do with actual trust and far more to do with lust.

Although such overt sexual behavior was completely alien and totally foreign to Leah, she just couldn't resist her actual participation as a couple of hours flew swiftly by on the wings of passion fueled by her hungry, thirsty, sensual desires. In real life as Leah was fully aware, she would never have sexually explored another man or even any other man except Zidane as freely as she done inside Spectrum and so her behavior in that respect, definitely fell well outside the usual scope and remit of her usual participation in reality and real life. Self-control and a cautious attitude around strangers were definitely an approach to life that Leah felt extremely comfortable with but that day, Spectrum had unexpectedly flown her totally out of her usual comfort zone and intriguingly for Leah, it had been an extremely enjoyable experience.

Once Leah felt completely worn out, totally exhausted and the last drop of her unconsumed passion had been satisfied, she rested her head upon Ravid's chest as the two lay on top of the hill together in satisfied silence and although it felt slightly wrong to Leah, strangely and curiously, simultaneously it also felt totally right. For a few minutes neither spoke as Leah lay in Ravid's arms and began to quietly contemplate and consider whether Spectrum had actually liberated her from her own fears and insecurities that day in more ways than one.

Somehow that day, Leah wondered if perhaps Spectrum had liberated her from her own strict guidelines and characteristics that usually governed and controlled every aspect of her everyday life in a very rigid format and so, just for a moment, she began to wonder if the Leah inside Spectrum was in fact, the real Leah and who she actually was. A bondage of conformity had perhaps tied Leah's conduct to her usual lifestyle and so perhaps, Leah silently considered, Spectrum had simply allowed her to explore and to enjoy the desires that she usually kept hidden away from the world and maybe Spectrum had in fact, enabled passionate urges that she usually harbored inside of her that she normally avoided and perhaps at times, she even subconsciously suppressed those desires in reality.

Due to the many questions that seemed to flood through Leah's mind, the issue of Zidane and her very real life suddenly zoomed once more to the forefront of her thoughts as she silently reminded herself of the main purpose of her visit to Spectrum that day which had absolutely nothing to do with moments of passion with a fictitious stranger. Reality continued to nag away at Leah's mind as it urged and prompted her to act as she began to accept that whilst her passionate moments with Ravid had definitely quenched a few flames of passion, reality now required her return, her full participation and her reawakened mental presence because her real relationship with Zidane, now required her actual return to their real life, their real daily routine and their very real shared home.

"I think I have to go now Ravid." Leah suddenly whispered as she reluctantly broke the silence between the two. She glanced up at his face with a slightly apologetic expression and then began to fix her ruffled, disorganized attire. "I think my journey of trust is almost over now, for today at least."

"Don't worry Leah, I understand. I'll show you the exit." Ravid agreed as he smiled, nodded his head and then began to arrange his own clothing.

For the next couple of minutes barely a word was spoken by either of the two as they organized their respective items of clothing but as Leah dressed herself back up, in some ways she almost wished that she didn't actually have to leave. The two began to make their way down the hillside just a minute or so later and as Ravid led Leah towards the base, she began to reflect internally upon his remarks about the maze of challenges that had challenged one of her deepest, darkest, inner fears but in such a highly unusual, very positive and even quite enjoyable manner. Although the Maze of Trust had been a lot for Leah to absorb in one day and in one ten-hour visit, Spectrum that day had definitely added an additional layer of intrigue to her life, albeit in an artificial capacity, with scenarios that had been deeply relevant to Leah personally and that whole notion, absolutely fascinated her.

Approximately fifteen minutes later the two arrived at the bottom of the hill and as Leah watched Ravid in silence, he walked towards a nearby hedge wall that surrounded a wooded area which he swiftly pushed aside to reveal the clearing in the heart of the Woods of Curiosity once again. The wooden slab makeshift table still remained intact along with the hedge chairs and that amused Leah slightly as she walked through the gap in the hedge and the entire interior of the clearing rapidly became more visible to her.

"Would you like another glass of wine Leah before you leave?" Ravid offered politely as he began to make his way towards the wooden slab table.

Leah immediately shook her head in response as she smiled. "As much as I'd love to Ravid, I'd better not." She replied.

"Okay Leah as you wish, I'll show you the exit now then." Ravid rapidly confirmed as he suddenly turned to face one of the hedge walls around the perimeter of the clearing and then began to walk towards a portion of the hedge. “If you follow this path, you'll be able to find your way out of the Maze of Trust in no time at all." He explained as he swiftly pushed a portion of the hedge backwards and then pointed towards a dirt path which was exposed that started directly behind it.

A grateful smile crossed Leah's face as she glanced at the path as she began to prepare herself to leave Ravid, their moments of shared sensual passion, the Woods of Curiosity and the highly unusual Maze of Trust behind.

"Thanks for everything Ravid." Leah said appreciatively as she walked towards him and then hugged him. She released him a few seconds later and then smiled at the handsome stranger in front of her, who despite the moments of passionate intimacy that they had shared that day, was still very much a stranger in terms of her own reality and her very own real life. "You really helped me get over my fear of heights."

"Anytime my lady." Ravid answered as he smiled. "I'm always here since the Woods of Curiosity are my home and there's usually enough food and wine for more than one so, you are always welcome."

Leah nodded. "Thanks, I'll keep that in mind." She replied softly. "It's always nice to feel welcome somewhere in this world."

Some drops of sadness seemed to silently gather and collate on Leah's forehead in the form of sweat as she prepared to depart as she silently accepted that there really were no more meaningful words to exchange with Ravid that day and then turned and began to walk along the dirt path that she had been directed towards. Once again as Leah was fully aware as she walked along the quite narrow tree lined path, it was time to return to and to face the real world once more which meant, her adventures in Spectrum for that day, were now almost over. Initially that day Leah had set the timer for a ten hour visit to Spectrum and although she felt slightly unsure as she walked as to how much of that ten hours still actually remained, she did feel absolutely certain about one thing and that was the fact that the drops of those ten hours had by that point, almost been fully consumed.

Rather intriguingly for Leah, the promise that Ravid had made to her that he would always be there and that she would always be welcome at his table in the Woods of Curiosity, comforted her slightly as she walked even though his presence inside Spectrum was as she already knew, purely fictitious. The eternal reassurances offered by Ravid however, seemed to provide Leah with some kind of warmth as she silently began to accept that since the two had now parted ways, she might never actually see the fictitious Ravid ever again.

Not more than ten minutes later, when Leah arrived at the end of the two lines of trees, she discovered that the dirt path led directly into a hedged passageway that disappeared rapidly underground and as she continued to follow the path, she stepped into a hedge lined underground tunnel. Nothing but hedges and earthy soil seemed to surround Leah for the next few minutes as she continued to diligently walk along the path until she suddenly found herself in a large underground cave which appeared to house a large golden pool of transparent water in the very center of the enclosed subterranean space. The golden water looked absolutely delicious as it seemed to silently invite Leah to step inside it and as she drew closer to it and then stared into its depths, Leah began to search for some kind of sign to guide her steps because she felt slightly unsure as to whether she was supposed to enter inside the golden watery substance which seemed to have a sparkly presence and a beautiful brightness that shone out from somewhere deep below its surface.

Suddenly, much to Leah's absolute surprise, there was a slight rustle from directly behind her and as Leah swiftly turned around to face the entrance to the hedge lined tunnel, she noticed that the hedges that lined either side of the earthy tunnel had started to move and that the twigs of the hedges had actually begun to quickly wrap themselves around each other. Each stick and every twig seemed to eagerly embrace each other as the pieces of wood swiftly tied each other up in knots and crept across the actual entrance until they had swallowed up every inch of light from outside and it almost looked as if the actual hedges were actually alive as Leah just stood and watched the wooden twiggy movements for a few seconds in a very nervous, still, fearful silence.

Just for a moment, Leah started to panic as she felt a sudden surge of alarm begin to swirl around inside her interior but despite her inner turmoil, Leah still tried her best to remain calm as she attempted to grip onto, limit and contain her chaotic state of total panic and tried to control the fear that had suddenly struck her mind which it seemed had swiftly, gripped and latched onto almost every single part of her simulated form. Since Leah still felt quite unsure that she was actually supposed to enter into the golden pool of water, she immediately headed back towards the hedged entrance that was now completely covered in wooden brown twigs, sharp edged sticks and greenish brown leaves. A nervous hand was stretched cautiously out towards the hedge itself as Leah began to try to snap and claw her way out of the underground cave but even as she tried to do so, the hedges simply continued to weave themselves over the entrance of the cave even more tightly and much to Leah's total frustration, some twigs even started to curl quite firmly around her hand.

In less than a minute the gap that had been the actual entrance to the underground cave had been completely swallowed up and filled with hedge twigs, sticks and leaves and so, Leah began to silently accept that it was no longer an accessible form of exit and as she began to absorb and process that reality, she rapidly pulled her hand away from the hedge's twiggy grip. A quick visual scan of the interior of the underground cave which had darkened slightly but fortunately for Leah, was still quite visible due to the golden light that emanated from the golden pool itself, rapidly confirmed to her that the now covered entrance, had indeed been the only actual entrance or exit to the subterranean area in the actual earthy cave walls as her eyes were swiftly met with and found no alternative gaps.

Due to the lack of exits as Leah was fully aware, only one option now really remained as a viable possibility and so, she swiftly accepted that reality as she started to walk slowly back towards the golden pool of water and prepared to search for an exit amongst the collation of golden drops. Once Leah arrived quite close to the water's edge, she sat down on the earthy ground near the golden pool and then started to maneuver herself towards it as she bravely prepared to dip her hands inside it. From what Leah could see at first glance and feel from the safety of the quite firm, dirt bank as she dipped her hands cautiously inside the watery collation of golden drops, the water was not only delightfully warm but there also appeared to be a much brighter source of light that emanated from somewhere below the surface of the water itself.

Much to Leah's sheer relief and absolute delight, a delicious freshness seemed to embrace every one of her fingers and as each one began to pleasantly tingle, the water seemed to welcome her hand in a non-intrusive manner, unlike the hedgy twigs that had actually tried to hold her hand and fingers captive. In addition to the pleasant sensations that the water evoked and to add even further to Leah's surprise as she continued to conduct her visual inspection of the golden pool and stared into the water's depths, she rapidly noticed that close to the bottom of the golden mass of water, there appeared to be a much brighter source of golden light that emanated from a circular hole in one of the golden brown earthy walls which actually looked large enough to swim through.

No other possible form of exit seemed to exist inside the cave from what Leah had seen and she swiftly confirmed that fact once again as Leah gave the earthy walls and ceiling another quick visual scan which meant, she would definitely have to fully enter into the golden pool and then swim down to that hole, if she actually wanted to leave the cave. Since the circular hole held the potential promise of a tunnel that might lead to an actual exit, Leah felt that an underwater swim would definitely have to occur, if she wanted to leave the underground cave which worried her slightly because as far as Leah was concerned that hole was laced and adorned with countless drops of uncertainty which occupied the fringes of her thoughts and none of those uncertain drops of worry and nervous speculation in Leah's mind, were either beautifully bright or golden.

Despite all Leah's worries and doubts however, she quickly removed her shoes and then she cautiously dipped the tips and toes of her bare feet into the golden water, an action which was followed just a few seconds later by the rest of her two feet as she rapidly surrendered to the only choice on offer. Since the water felt deliciously warm and didn't seem to present any kind of threat to Leah, she then eagerly prepared to plunge her form more fully into the golden pool and to swim down towards the hole which she had already assumed, would lead into some kind of underwater tunnel and hopefully, to an actual exit.

Although as yet Leah hadn't actually removed any of her clothes, namely the top and trousers that she had woken up in, she didn't feel that it was necessary to undress, especially since she had no actual idea where the tunnel might lead to or where she would actually resurface. A risky factor which worried Leah slightly as she prepared to fully immerse her form in the golden drops and to lower herself into the water, was the actual possibility that the other end of the underwater tunnel might be situated quite a distance away because as Leah already knew, human abilities to hold their breath whilst underwater were really, actually rather limited.

After a few more seconds of thoughtful consideration however, Leah finally took the plunge as she lowered the rest of her body into the golden water, held her breath and then began to swim down towards the circular hole. The deep dive that Leah had now embarked upon as she already knew, was the only possible way out and so, she fully accepted that reality since it made very little sense to delay that departure any further, purely due to speculation and deliberations which served absolutely no useful purpose at all.

Fortunately for Leah as she swam down to the lower depths of the pool, the golden water remained deliciously warm and as she held her breath, she made her way as quickly as she could towards the actual hole itself with some strokes of eagerness and some powerful kicks of determination. Much as Leah had suspected and expected as she approached the circular hole and actually swam closer to it, she found a tunnel entrance that definitely led to somewhere and since she had absolutely no desire to stay in the cave until the Spectrum timer ran out and woke her back up, she quickly swam into the underwater tunnel's golden interior. The underwater tunnel, quite strangely Leah noticed as she began to swim along it, twisted and turned in various directions which meant, she could see no actual exit yet but she increased her hopeful swim strokes and optimistic kicks as she attempted to reach the other end of the tunnel as quickly as she possibly could.

In some ways, an actual gamble had been taken on Leah's part and she definitely knew it as she continued to diligently travel further along the tunnel because she had entered into the tunnel in the hope that it would end before her breath ran out. Due to that very risky factor, Leah's body felt taut with tension as she continued to swim along the tunnel's interior as worries started to run rampant through her mind and core, some of which even seemed to cling onto her simulated limbs which appeared to have an impact upon her progress, speed and movements and seemed to slow her down. The other end of the tunnel however, was still not yet in sight even after Leah had swum along a few twists and turns and so, she started to feel more and more alarmed as she swam because a definite fear now existed that the tunnel might actually become her watery grave.

Much to Leah's sheer relief however, just a few seconds later she suddenly spotted a pinprick of brighter light and so, she enthusiastically began to swim more quickly towards it, spurred on by the fresh hope that an exit was now indeed quite near and within actual reach. The need to breathe by that point almost felt like a heavy weight, Leah noticed as she swam more frantically towards the dot of light which gradually grew larger and larger in size and as the light grew larger and larger, the pressure to breathe also seemed to increase with every stroke and kick as Leah's mind grappled with her simulated bodily functions.

Quite unfortunately, just as Leah was about to exit the tunnel her body suddenly, actually caved in and so, Leah was forced to take a deep breath as her lungs demanded air and actually forced her mouth to open as her interior finally defeated her mind's reluctance to allow them to be filled. Nothing but absolute horror filled Leah's mind for a few seconds as she gasped, spurted and splurted air but much to her complete surprise and total relief, she quickly discovered that she could actually breathe underwater and that there had been in fact, no actual real need to hold her breath at all. A wave of gratitude seemed to rapidly wash over Leah's body as she silently accepted the freedom and luxury that her newly discovered ability to breath under water offered and afforded to her and as a result, Leah felt her confidence levels instantly increased and so, she swiftly and boldly swam out of the tunnel as she entered into a second large pool of golden water.

From what Leah could see at first glance as she swam into the depths of the second golden pool, it appeared to be very similar to the first and so, she quickly made her way towards the surface so that she could climb out of the watery pool. Once Leah arrived at the surface, she immediately noticed that there was a firm bank nearby which she then rapidly swam towards it and when Leah arrived beside it, she eagerly clambered onto it as she swiftly discovered that the interior of the second cave looked pretty much like the first underground cave. However, luckily for Leah, upon closer visual inspection and much to her total relief, the second cave did seem to differ from the first in one sense in that this cave actually had an accessible exit that appeared to be free from any twigs, branches, leaves and hedges and so, Leah enthusiastically began to quickly make her way towards it.

Quite surprisingly for Leah, she noticed as she walked towards the potential exit that her clothes, hair and skin were not wet at all and that everything related to her person was in fact, bone dry which pleased her no end. The prospect of being dressed in saturated, soggy clothes that would cling to Leah's form for an indefinite period of time as she searched for an exit, really didn't hold any appeal for her and as Leah already knew, wouldn't have been very pleasant and so that was one positive but curiously strange outcome from her swim that comforted her slightly but also slightly confused her as she walked. Whilst the water had felt wet to Leah when she had actually dipped her hands inside it and then had subsequently swum through it, her clothes, skin and hair all seemed to have managed to avoid any kind of saturation but since the effects of that lack of saturation were really quite positive, Leah decided not to question or worry about it too much.

"Now I wish I'd kept my shoes on." Leah whispered to herself as she walked. "Oh well, I guess I'll just have to complete the rest of this journey with nothing but my bare feet."

Although the lack wetness intrigued Leah slightly and she definitely had some internal questions that niggled away at her curiosity, she decisively picked up the pace and then began to rush towards the exit as she eagerly continued to seek out a viable, fully accessible means of departure from the underground caves undeterred. A stop off search for answers due to the lack of saturation as Leah already knew, would definitely take time to satisfy and time on that day on that particular emotional journey was now, in very short supply and another curiosity actually occupied Leah's mind that she felt far more curious about. Since Leah wanted to see exactly how the emotional journey of trust that she had embarked upon that day would end that element of uncertainty compelled her not to make any unplanned stop offs because she felt much more curious about that aspect of her journey than her bone-dry state.

In fact, the reality was that Leah now actually felt quite eager to return home not only to the comfort of Zidane's presence but also to the couple's very comfortable, warm bed both of which she knew, definitely awaited her presence and attendance. Both those two factors of comfort silently spurred Leah on and so, she felt motivated to try and leave the underground caves as soon as she could because she actually felt, really quite mentally drained and totally worn out. Although Leah had enjoyed her now, almost ten-hour visit to Spectrum that day and although she had successfully managed to explore a whole emotional plane filled with adventures in one recreational sitting, a hearty, real meal and some real affection were definitely something that Leah wished to experience and to enjoy that night that Spectrum would never ever be able to provide to her as she was well aware.

Once Leah had exited the cave as she stepped through the exit, she immediately found the start of another hedge lined, underground, earthy tunneled path that sloped upwards which she hoped as she enthusiastically began to walk along it, would not only lead back towards the surface but also back towards the couple's home and Zidane's arms. Just a few minutes later Leah arrived at the end of the path and as she exited it and stepped back out onto the surface, she suddenly found herself back at the bottom of the gardens below the old estate house and where she had initially woken up when she'd first arrived in Spectrum earlier that day however, a few huge things about the landscape had definitely changed and those changes instantly, caught Leah by surprise.

Very intriguingly, Leah swiftly observed and discovered, the estate house itself now looked polished, well maintained, clean and loved and the brownish, unkept hedges that had obstructed Leah's path and that had previously sat below it, had by now totally vanished. Instead of the brownish hedges that had looked as if they had been on their last sticks in their place there now appeared to be some pretty, well maintained flower beds and rock gardens that nestled decoratively against the slope that led towards the building itself which confused Leah slightly for a moment as she began to absorb and process the very large changes. Since Leah's potential path towards the estate house was now actually clear, she immediately began to rush towards the entrance of the large building as she started to weave her way around the pretty flower beds and the small decorative rocks that appeared to be scattered sporadically across the grounds with a smile upon her face because she would now finally perhaps, actually discover what was inside the huge, now very grand and luxurious, mysterious estate house.

A huge pair of large, black, iron doors seemed to adorn and guard the entrance to the grey, stone building and so as soon as Leah reached them, she swiftly attempted to push open one of the iron doors which began to creak quite loudly as it started to move. The actual door it appeared, seemed to be slightly reluctant to participate with Leah's request and as a result, it opened very slowly indeed and it was almost as if the door itself felt weary and tired from all of the years that it had spent standing upright and on guard to the building that stood directly behind it and that it had committed to and as the door creaked and groaned as it moved, it seemed to overtly express that fatigue directly to Leah's ears.

Quite amusingly for Leah, once she had opened the door widely enough to step through it and then had actually stepped through the space that the open door had left behind, she suddenly found herself back inside her laboratory and back inside the basement as she woke back up inside the Spectrum capsule. An amused but satisfied smile crossed Leah's face as she prepared to dismount the Spectrum capsule because although she had really enjoyed her adventures that day inside Spectrum and her visit to the Maze of Trust which had been full of intrigue as far as Leah was concerned, it also felt very nice to return home, not only to her real life but also to return to a very real Zidane.

The familiar surroundings of Leah's basement laboratory silently comforted Leah as she commanded the capsule lid to open up and then began to dismount the Spectrum capsule and although as she already knew, Zidane would have probably dozed off on the sofa already, she silently vowed to make it up to him the next evening and to spend some quality time with him. A few more verbal commands were issued to shut the Spectrum system down and to switch off the lights inside the basement as Leah stepped onto the basement floor and then began to walk towards the steps that led up towards the lounge of the couple's shared home as Leah hoped that Zidane's doze had not yet transcended into a fully-fledged, deep slumber because if it had, she would feel slightly awkward about actually waking him up from it.

Just a few minutes later Leah arrived in the lounge and she found it completely silent and very dark as she instantly observed that even the entertainment center had already been switched off which she immediately attributed to Zidane's tiredness and the long working day that he had endured and returned from. Since Leah had spent more time than usual in Spectrum that day and it had cut into the couple's evening, she knew that Zidane would definitely be upset about it because he really treasured their evenings together and that meant, she would have to offer apologies and attempt to make amends somehow to the love of her life the next day, since his needs for that day had definitely not been met, even though Leah's needs actually, already had.

Although Leah did at times divulge some of the details about her adventures in Spectrum to Zidane and she did sometimes verbally relate her experiences to him on this particular occasion, she decided not to as she paused by the lounge door and then glanced at the sofa for a few seconds in thoughtful silence. For just a moment as Leah stood and considered the couple's potential conversation when Zidane actually awakened, she swiftly concluded that it wouldn't be very wise to discuss her journey of trust because effectively that day, in some ways, she had perhaps broken the trust that Zidane held in his heart and mind for her, albeit in a fictitious capacity which actually was a contradiction to the very nature of trust itself. Since Leah had dabbled that day in fictitious sexual meanderings with a fictitious lover that was a complete foreigner to her body, mind and heart and she had not only totally ignored Zidane's needs completely that evening but had also fully explored her own with a fictitious someone else, a guilty silence definitely hung-over Leah's mind and heart as she prepared to wake Zidane up.

Only three more areas of Spectrum still remained to be tested as Leah already knew and as she began to consider that constraint upon the couple's evenings thoughtfully, she approached the sofa and Zidane who was faithfully plonked upon it as she hoped that the final three areas that remained to be tested would be straightforward and that the Spectrum prototype would be complete soon. A definite tug of war had started inside Leah in recent times because she now felt a tremendous sense of urgency to meet the professional aspiration that was expected to financially lubricate the couple's future which faced not only the pull against her daily household routine but also the required maintenance of her romantic relationship which due to the tugs of time consumption from Leah's work demands had not been its usual self for a very long time. The recent much longer hours that Leah had undertaken as she had occupied the basement and worked diligently on Spectrum had definitely, already taken their toll upon the couple and had even started to place their relationship under pressure and Leah didn't need a walk-through test or a formula to figure out that reality.

Usually, as Leah already knew, such in-depth, intricate, technologically and scientifically complex inventions would require a whole team of scientists and technicians and that team of professionals would then split the long hours and the tasks involved between them which would ultimately, make the workload involved much lighter and more manageable. However, since Leah carried and bore the sole responsibility for Spectrum's delivery and that was a responsibility that lay firmly on her doorstep and directly under her feet that meant, she not only had to complete the project on her own but also that she had to do every single thing herself which at times, wore her out. The large workload however, as Leah fully accepted, was the price that she had to personally pay in order to retain full ownership rights to her work but now as she also realized, Zidane had also borne some of that cost as he had been denied the time and attention that Leah usually gave to him so willingly.

Several years had gone by since Leah had started the Spectrum prototype and although Zidane had always been very supportive and extremely patient, recently due to the much longer hours that she had put into Spectrum, Leah had noticed that his patience had started to wear a little thin and that it had even showed some external signs of actual wear and tear. On several occasions Zidane had actually complained about her absence throughout the evenings that they usually spent together in the past month or two as he had expressed his dissatisfaction verbally and voiced his concerns directly to Leah and he had also requested some undivided attention however, Leah felt absolutely powerless to change anything. Due to Zidane's recent verbal expressions of dissatisfaction, Leah now partially feared that if the Spectrum prototype wasn't finished soon, it would just be a matter of time before Zidane would seek out other leisure activities and other forms of companionship with which to decorate his evenings with that Leah's increased involvement in Spectrum had in recent times, actually denied to him because he had expressed that dissatisfaction several times.

An apologetic smile crossed Leah's face as she prepared to wake Zidane up from his snooze and as she began to ready herself to sort out the couple's evening meal but just for a moment, Leah paused as she emphasized with Zidane's frustrations which she felt were really, very reasonable. Just like herself, Leah swiftly concluded, Zidane was a mere human being and although at times, he was delightfully patient, extremely sincere and very committed, he too had very human feelings, needs and desires and she had perhaps mistakenly begun to ignore those very human factors at play as she had soldiered on, totally dedicated to her task and completely oblivious to the world around her. Unfortunately, that day, Leah silently accepted, she had totally ignored Zidane's very human needs, desires and emotions as she'd eagerly fulfilled her own, albeit in a fictitious capacity and even though his dedication, patience and loyalty had not yet wavered, it was just a matter of time before the sands of his commitment and patience finally ran out and there was absolutely nothing artificial as Leah knew deep down inside, about that highly probable, potential eventuality.

Another worry started to dwell and linger in Leah's mind as she stretched a gentle hand out towards Zidane and then started to wake him up and that was the possibility that someone else might notice Zidane's tireless dedication and his lack of satisfaction before the Spectrum prototype was actually complete. A danger definitely existed as Leah now fully realized that if she didn't take the time to fulfil Zidane's needs and desires that someone else might step in and that they might do what Leah had in recent times, chosen to ignore. The excitement of fictitious environments, artificial sensually loaded scenarios, fantasy love affairs and deliciously handsome simulated lovers as Leah knew, would not prevent or obstruct Zidane's departure, if and when he actually decided to leave and that was one thing she knew for absolute certain and the reality was that if Leah continued to ignore his needs, she ran the risk of losing Zidane forever.

One day Leah hoped, Spectrum would actually be valuable and the income from the sale that the prototype generated would then provide the couple with the future that they both wanted and the future that they had waited years to enjoy but all her hard work would be almost pointless, if Zidane was no longer by her side. The future that Leah hoped that the sale of Spectrum would usher in would be a future for the couple free from financial struggles, a future where they did not have to plan and pinch every penny that they made and spent, a future where their children would have the comfort of a large home, their own bedrooms and even a large garden to actually play in and a future where their romantic partnership would be totally free from the worries of tomorrow. An uncertain tomorrow definitely lay at the foot of the couple's door each morning and Leah wanted to reduce that risk and to contribute positively to the couple's future financial stability but as she also now fully accepted, to lose the person that she loved in the meantime, due to her lack of romantic care, would be counterproductive to her overall goals.

Upon Zidane's face there was a smile, Leah observed as he suddenly stirred and began to wake up and as she prepared to engage him fully in conversation, she began to consider how much Spectrum might actually be worth. In monetary terms there was as Leah already knew, no actual certainty when it came to Spectrum but the couple had been infused with excitement when a few potential corporate buyers had purchased other recreational products that had offered far less than Spectrum for a substantial price and so she truly hoped that the couple's investment, namely the time, effort and sacrifices that they had both made coupled with Leah's individual hard work, would one day be rewarded very generously.

The couple had planned to have at least two children in the future and a huge wedding for all their family members and friends to attend and they had even discussed the future purchase of a large family home, situated just outside the city but as Leah knew, with their current financial means, such discussions were purely just discussions. If the Spectrum prototype sold for the expected sum however, Leah knew that the sale would definitely pull the couple's plans into the income bracket of their combined financial reach but for now, those plans currently stood well outside their current financial comfort zone, since Zidane's salary was quite moderate and Leah's bursary even more moderate which almost made such plans seem absolutely impossible and look totally unrealizable in reality.

"We should go out somewhere nice this weekend Leah."

Zidane suddenly said as he began to awaken more fully. "We're just getting snowed in by life and buried by an avalanche of worries."

"Yes, we really should Zidane." Leah immediately replied as she nodded in agreement. "You're totally right, we really shouldn't be tied down by uncertainty or enslaved by the worries of tomorrow."

"We'll always have us Leah and that will always count for something in our hearts." Zidane reassured her as he rose to his feet. "Let me help you sort out dinner, you look quite tired."

Leah nodded. "Sure, yeah it was a very long day." She acknowledged.

Despite all Zidane's reassurances as the couple made their way towards the kitchen and began to talk, laugh and joke with each other, Leah continued to worry about the future because as she knew, Spectrum was a form of hope for the couple that could help them to realize their goals in a much quicker timeframe. In every way imaginable, as Leah was fully aware, Spectrum was ultimately, the couple's best chance of achieving everything that they had aspired to be and do in life since the very first day that they had met, without enduring a whole decade of hard sacrifices and difficult struggles beforehand. For that reason alone, Leah had felt absolutely determined to complete Spectrum as quickly as she possibly could, so that the couple could finally live the life that they yearned to live, free from the shackles of financial worries or monetary concerns.

One day, Leah considered as the two stepped into the kitchen, she hoped to marry the man who had stood by her so faithfully for years and she really wanted to give birth to his children and then to raise them alongside him because that for Leah would definitely be a life that was as close to heaven on earth as she could possibly get. Since Zidane was as Leah had already seen throughout the years, such a pillar of unshakable strength, a tower of dedicated fidelity and a rock of complete devotion there was no other real man on the face of the planet that Leah felt would give her that peace of mind, such loyal support and his total dedication and so, she definitely wanted to spend the remainder of her entire life with him. Whether Spectrum yielded the expected return or not, Zidane's love was something very certain and Leah's heart definitely knew it but she wished and hoped as the couple began to warm up their evening meal that in the midst of all that uncertainty that the Spectrum sale would in the end, be all that they had wished for, all that the couple had hoped it would be and all that they had sacrificed so much for.

A Deep Dive into the Disgusting Dimension

Despite the tugs of curiosity and intrigue that Leah felt deep down inside herself as the next morning and Thursday stepped into her life, she managed to discipline herself for the first part of the morning and to resist the urges as she stuck to the ground floor of her home and completely avoided her basement laboratory. Although those urges definitely tempted Leah to pop down to the basement in order to explore and venture into the next Spectrum environment, she knew that a break was definitely required for Zidane's sake because she had worked more very late nights than usual in recent times. So, for once that day, Leah had decided to place Spectrum on a back burner of her life for the entire duration of that day and since she had committed to her decision that meant, she would focus solely upon the couple's home, the daily household routine and their evening meal as she attempted to zoom in on Zidane's and even her own human needs in a devoted and dedicated fashion.

Due to the excitement that Leah had experienced on her last visit to Spectrum, a definite seductive current lingered just below the surface of her skin which held some strands of curious intrigue as to what adventures the next environment might actually hold, so a pulse of excitement accompanied her throughout the day as the morning began to silently depart and the afternoon arrived to step into its place. In fact, the pulse of excitement that resided inside of Leah was so strong that every time she passed the entrance to the basement, the excitement that rested gently on the outskirts of her skin and pores seemed to suddenly ignite and rapidly, voluntarily reawaken without any further provocation which created some internal and external tugs of desire. Every tug of temptation that teased Leah's bodily form, she observed, seemed to make her skin tingle as each tug of excitement teased her interior and exterior and every one clearly belonged to her next potential adventure which as Leah already knew, lay firmly at the foot of the basement's steps and dangled silently upon the horizon of tomorrow.

Since Leah's next adventure which she had planned to embark upon the next morning was actually due to be an emotional journey of disgust, Leah was well aware that it would probably not be as pleasant as her last visit to Spectrum but she still hoped that it would be filled with as much intrigue and mystery as her last emotional journey. Despite the lack of pleasantness that might occur the next morning however, a tremendous amount of personal satisfaction had filled Leah's mind as she had gone about her tasks that morning because in every imaginable way, Spectrum had definitely turned out to be all that she had planned it to be. Although as Leah already knew, there were still some minor tweaks that remained to be performed, the system itself was almost as perfect as she had hoped it might be which had satisfied her mind and her professional aspirations immensely.

Everything that Leah had experienced inside Spectrum so far, had seemed extremely natural, amazingly authentic and very realistic and so the system that she had created herself, Leah definitely felt as she started to attend to her list of afternoon tasks, fulfilled its actual purpose. In fact, as far as Leah was now concerned, Spectrum possessed a unique blend of mystery, intrigue and excitement which seemed to co-exist alongside some highly engaged, individually tailored experiences that triggered very deep levels and depths of emotional involvement in any given journey. Every element of interaction inside Spectrum from what Leah had seen first-hand up until that point had seemed very unique and deeply personally and so in some respects, Spectrum had managed to not only meet some of her professional aspirations but had also even exceeded her own hopeful personal expectations.

However, since Leah knew that one step inside the basement would definitely tempt her to indulge in another Spectrum environment, she intentionally kept as far away from the basement as she possibly could as she dug into her afternoon tasks and kept herself busy. A much more elaborate weekday evening meal was diligently prepared as Leah kept her mind focused upon Zidane and their evening together which on this occasion would involve the consumption of one of Zidane's favorite dishes lamb tagine and since she had actually marinated the meaty chunks that morning, by the time the afternoon had arrived the lamb was fully prepped and ready to be slow cooked inside the oven.

Quite strangely, Leah realized as she slipped the dish of lamb tagine into the oven, set the timer and then began to prepare to make an apple crumble for desert, the excitement that Spectrum offered to her, now seemed quite hard to resist and those tugs of excited interest that lay inside her own mind, definitely intrigued her. In fact, in some ways, it almost felt as if Leah had developed a taste and appetite for her own fantasy environment that had actually grown in unison and alongside her artificial experiences inside Spectrum and that growth in her hunger and appetite for Spectrum puzzled Leah for a moment as she began to core, peel and slice the apples.

Later that afternoon Leah finally ventured outside as she embarked upon a trip to a local store to purchase some double cream for the apple crumble which was one of Zidane's favorite deserts but as Leah attended diligently and affectionately to Zidane's needs in his absence, it suddenly struck her that her external outing in some ways, really felt quite strange. Since it had actually been a while since Leah had stepped foot outside the house alone and the lamb tagine which was not just a firm favorite of Zidane's but also Leah's own palate hadn't been eaten inside their home for at least a year, the day was highly unusual in the sense that Leah had gone that extra mile in terms of effort. However, as Leah fully appreciated that additional effort on her part, was totally justifiable and so it definitely had to be made because Zidane's heart desperately required and needed some kind of comfort.

Recently, as Leah already knew, Zidane had definitely been left alone during the weekday evenings on one too many occasions and he had been so patient and so faithful not just to her heart but also to the couple's potential future. Every weekday inside the basement, in recent times, Leah had waded through task after task, shoulder deep in her quest to reach the shores of completion and Zidane had not fallen short one single time but for once that day, Leah would try to make some amends and she would make an actual attempt to render some form of restitution to Zidane's heart. For once that week, Leah wanted to give Zidane something to actually smile about as soon as he arrived home from work that weekday evening and so she had pushed the boat of effort out slightly further than usual and quite far away from the usual shores of comfortable convenience and so as she waited for Zidane to arrive home from work that evening, Leah hoped that her efforts that day would be enough to encourage and to restore his heart.

When Zidane arrived at home and as soon as he stepped into the couple's home, Leah immediately greeted him and welcomed him with open, affectionate arms before she proudly, triumphantly and attentively served him the lamb tagine that she had labored over earlier that day. The couple spent a few peaceful hours together that evening as they relaxed, ate dinner together and enthusiastically discussed his day along with a few other topics of interest as the evening hours gently slipped away. For the most part that evening, finally and much to Leah's total relief, she felt some actual peace inside her heart because she had made the effort to pay some well-deserved attention to Zidane's heart which over the years, had stood so faithfully next to her own and as she could see from the appreciative smile on his face throughout that entire evening, it was very gratefully received which definitely set her mind at rest, albeit temporarily.

The couple's dreams for the future were given some verbal attention and mental consideration as the evening progressed and the night arrived as the couple discussed the potential purchase of a large family home situated on the outskirts of the city that Leah hoped one day might be within their financial grasp. Since the couple had actually planned to have two children, Leah hoped that the large family home would be the residence of not just the couple but also the home to their two offspring but as they both already knew, that dream still sat quite far outside their current, combined financial capacity. Although both those hopes for the couple's future held the promise of a pleasant, peaceful, enjoyable life both goals remained quite unreachable at that time due to their current financial constraints but Leah still hoped and felt that both those goals might actually be achievable, if the Spectrum sale managed to realize and meet her actual expectations.

Unfortunately, and quite frustratingly for the couple however, as Leah already knew, their hopes for the future rested firmly upon one thing and that one thing was Spectrum. In fact, the reality was that in order to climb up the financial ladder of prosperity so that the couple would be in a position to make such a large purchase, Leah would not only have to complete the Spectrum prototype but then also sell it to a buyer for a significant sum and so she definitely felt that it had to be as perfect as possible. Perfection on Leah's part would ensure that any potential buyer would want to purchase the Spectrum prototype without any compromises being made on the issue of price and so as far as Leah was concerned that was a crucial component to actual completion.

Sadly, as Leah was already fully aware, the actual completion of the Spectrum prototype, would definitely result in less time being spent between the couple for at least another month because Spectrum's requirements ate greedily into their weekday evenings together. Essentially, Spectrum placed a strain upon the couple's relationship which at times as Leah could now clearly see, was really quite hard for Zidane to actually carry but as she also knew, that strain was for the meantime, totally unavoidable. At times Leah had felt tempted to work at a slightly slower pace and to place less strain upon herself but rather curiously, she had recently discovered that as she had drawn closer to Spectrum's actual completion that she had felt more compelled to speed things up in order to finish Spectrum as soon as she possibly could. The slower pace option had therefore in the end been completely ignored and had not even been given any real further consideration as Leah had striven to meet her goals and had if anything, actually sped things up.

Once the late hours of the night arrived as Leah snuggled in Zidane's arms inside the couple's bedroom, they began to share and enjoy some moments of tenderness together which rapidly progressed into some deep dives into passionate affection as Leah began to enthusiastically shower Zidane with some generous helpings of sensual adoration. A couple of hours later and once Zidane tired, Leah then watched him fall asleep as she prepared to rest herself however, quite frustratingly, Leah found that sleep didn't come to her as easily that night as it seemed to have done for Zidane because her fictitious sins from the previous day seemed to silently haunt her thoughts and gnaw away at her peace.

In some ways, it almost felt to Leah as she lay quietly beside Zidane and began to reflect upon her day as if the additional efforts that she had made that day had almost been like a form penance which she had felt a duty to deliver to Zidane's mind, body and heart. Earlier that day, almost instinctively, Leah now realized that she had perhaps embarked upon that course of action in the hope that it might relieve her mind of the guilty remnants and distasteful residue that the previous day and her simulated actions inside Spectrum had left behind but as yet it appeared, despite all Leah's efforts, her guilt had not yet fled from her being.

Unfortunately for Leah however, it now seemed that those acts of dutiful penance still hadn't fully repaired or provided a sufficient form of actual restitution for the acts of simulated betrayal that she had indulged in because she could not successfully push them out of her mind. Somehow, even though Leah was no longer actually present inside the simulated planes of Spectrum and she had made some form of restitution that day, it now appeared that her sins seemed to have followed her out of that artificial environment and back into the real world because visions of her betrayal continued to flood through her mind and crowded her thoughts with guilt as sleep continued to silently avoid her.

For the next few minutes Leah attempted to divert her thoughts as she silently brushed off the dusty, guilty specks from her mind and then stared at the ceiling as she began to consider once more whether Spectrum's potential value would ever actually, materialize in reality as she waited for sleep to embrace her. The reality was as Leah already knew that the material rewards from Spectrum's sale were extremely hard to predict and since that materiality was absolutely uncertain, at times that material and financial uncertainty definitely worried her. So much of Leah's time and life for the past few years had been invested into Spectrum and so, she definitely hoped that every hour of her effort would be generously rewarded but as she was well aware, there really were no actual guarantees.

Unfortunately for the couple, when it came to the actual issue of Zidane's job, Leah knew that he performed a basic run of the mill, lower level corporate job which certainly wasn't enough to provide them with much luxury and so, it was more like a wooden raft than a glossy, luxurious yacht. However, it was highly unlikely that there would be much change in that financial reality and certainly not in the immediate future because opportunities for progression in that particular corporate entity and Zidane's department, from what Leah had seen so far, didn't come by very often and so Zidane's actual income was likely to remain quite stagnant and was unlikely to increase for a while. Although Zidane's income had kept the couple's boat of life financially afloat over the past few years as Leah was fully aware, his income would definitely be stretched beyond breaking point, if the couple moved to a larger property never mind actually had two children to raise.

No certainty existed however, when it came to the actual issue of Spectrum's sale and so, no matter how hard Leah stared at the ceiling, nothing could remove the financial worries that niggled away at the back of her mind most nights because Zidane's current job certainly couldn't provide her with the certainty to erase any of those worries and concerns. The only possible hope that the couple had as Leah already knew, really was Spectrum's completion and a large sale which would not only erase all her worries permanently but also lubricate their future sufficiently but that sale still seemed a million miles away from her current position.

When it came to the actual matter of Zidane's job, his current corporate commitment as Leah was fully aware, wouldn't probably be considered very upmarket or even remotely impressive by many in that he simply worked for a large company on their technology helpdesk. However, in Leah's sight, Zidane was definitely far more impressive than his current position gave him credit for, especially when it came to his professional efforts, his dedication and his tireless additional support. Despite the rather basic impressions that Zidane's position might conjure up in one's mind, as Leah knew full well deep down inside, he definitely deserved more in life than his current corporate portion because he worked far longer hours than a traditional nine to five job and he always worked overtime and on weekends whenever he was asked to.

Every single time any additional technological, corporate assistance was required, Leah had seen Zidane cooperate and participate very enthusiastically and on occasions, he would even travel to other cities and Leah knew that for a fact because she had accompanied him many times to several different places. On those working weekends Leah had even stayed in hotels with Zidane in those city locations and whilst the various destinations had added a bit more scenery to the couple's life, Leah had noticed that Zidane had never once been given any of the promotional opportunities that he had applied for, even though he had served the company that he worked for Stapletons very faithfully for the past five years.

Somehow and unfortunately for the couple, Leah considered thoughtfully, the corporate ladder at that particular company seemed to have been restricted for Zidane and although there had been no slippery snakes in that he had not regressed professionally, there had been no real rungs of advancement either and so it now almost appeared to Leah as if Zidane was stuck in a very deep professional rut. The monetary compensation from Zidane's job had kept a roof over the couple's head and the bills paid on time but so often, Leah had wished that she could actually add to Zidane's financial provisions positively because they really had to be quite careful financially and so every penny that was spent had to be planned thoroughly in advance.

A quick glance was cast towards Zidane's face as Leah silently considered the next morning when as she was fully aware, she would definitely fully surrender to her desire to resume her work on Spectrum once again which meant, her late weekday nights would definitely return. On the plus side of Leah's quite negative consideration however, it was almost the weekend which meant, a couple of nights that week for Zidane would be more enjoyable and so he would suffer far less interruptions to romance. The late nights in the basement meant only one thing for Zidane as Leah already knew and that was an interruption to the couple's potentially romantic weekday evening together which would leave Zidane plonked on the sofa alone once again.

In every way imaginable as Leah knew, Spectrum had totally drained her attention and her creation had siphoned off almost every single drop of energy that she had and as yet, it still remained a contingent asset which had no actual, certain, measurable value and that wouldn't change overnight or in an instant. However, Leah hoped as she closed her eyes that at the very least, Spectrum would be complete soon and that then at least one issue in the couple's life would be fully resolved. Once Spectrum was complete that completion, Leah felt, would not only give the couple their weekday evenings back but also make Zidane a much happier man and that definitely had to be worth something to both their hearts, even if in the end Spectrum turned out to be worth far less than expected.

Just a few minutes later, fortunately for Leah, she finally started to drift off into the gentle arms of slumber herself as her worries started to depart, chased away by the tiredness of the day and as she fully surrendered to sleep's call, Leah fully accepted that she felt absolutely worn out. The additional hours in the basement in recent times had definitely taken their laborious toll upon Leah's physicality which meant, sleep had now become a far more precious necessity in her sight and so, long gone were the days when sleep could just be taken for granted.

Since worries about the future often occupied Leah's mind which frequently kept sleep at bay and made her feel restless at night, any additional portions of rest that she could enjoy were now regarded as something precious, something valuable and something fervently sought after. Recently, therefore sleep in Leah's sight had not only become something to appreciate, savor and rejoice in but also something to grab with both eyelids and something to fully indulge in because as Leah had begun to realize, to follow one's professional aspirations in life without any established corporate safety net in place was like taking a wade across a deep river of uncertainty.

Unfortunately for Leah, in many ways, she had been totally unprepared for that deep river of uncertainty and since there had been no way to predict the actual depths of that river in some places, it had caused her many restless nights and lots of worries. However, Leah hoped that Spectrum's completion which she felt sure would happen in the next month or two, would finally ease some of that uncertainty and at least provide her with a riverbank of stability that she could finally peacefully rest her head upon worry free.

Much to Leah's absolute relief, the arms of slumber finally seemed to embrace her and started to carry her off into the depths of the night and as it did so, her body finally seemed to succumb to sleep's natural call as her worries about the future along with any guilt-ridden thoughts, seemed to silently vacate her mind. A smile of satisfaction began to cross Leah's face as sleep finally managed somehow, to overcome the unrest that had almost conquered her mind and that had kept her awake for at least another hour since Zidane had drifted off and as she slipped into slumber, Leah welcomed the sleep that had almost avoided her completely as she began to look forward to the next morning and her next visit to Spectrum.

When the next morning arrived and once Leah had woken up, attended to her usual hygiene routine and then made a start on the daily chores, she willingly began to adhere to her schedule as she pushed firmly ahead. A visit to the next emotional plane inside Spectrum was due to be embarked upon just after lunch and so the Friday morning that particular morning, Leah found literally flew by as she attended to the daily household chores as usual but with slightly more enthusiasm than most days, spurred on by her planned potential visit to Spectrum that afternoon.

Once lunch had been rapidly prepared inside the couple's kitchen which on this particular day consisted of a toasted sandwich with some slices of cheese that had been garnished with a few slices of fresh tomato and some chunky, spicy salsa sauce, Leah's quick fix lunch preparations and a cup of tea were eagerly taken out into the back garden. The couple's back garden was quite small but very overgrown and so as Leah sat down in a deck chair near the back door where there was a rectangular weed free space and a couple of deck chairs, she began to consume the melted proceeds of her efforts from the kitchen as she glanced at the weeds around her and then smiled. Since the weather was warm, calm and fairly pleasant being that it was the middle of summer, Leah's short sleeve lab tunic she found was definitely sufficient but as she started to consume her lunch, Leah began to visually inspect the quite messy, untidy garden that surrounded her slightly more closely as she started to consider the state of the actual garden slightly more thoughtfully for a moment.

Very much like the interior of the couple's home, the back garden was really quite compact and it was no bigger than their joint lounge and dining room but rather strangely, Leah observed, it seemed to house rather a lot of weeds in that compact space. Quite close to the set of French windows that led out from the lounge and next to the back door of the couple's kitchen, there was a rectangular, weed free spot that had been cleared by Zidane and so, Leah had put a couple of deck chairs there but as she was fully aware, the whole garden really needed a very thorough clear-out.

An amused smile began to cross Leah's face as a minute or so later, she shrugged her shoulders and then just continued to eat her lunch because as she already knew that day, she certainly wasn't going to spend her afternoon knee deep in weeds inside the garden. Since a new adventure definitely awaited Leah down in the basement, she swiftly began to conclude that the weedy, overgrown, botanic mess could wait, at least until a day on an actual weekend when Zidane would actually be around in the daylight hours to help her tackle that mess and to help pull those weeds up.

Due to the absence of any children in the couple's life, their quite limited social life and their professional commitments, the latter of which frequently spilled over into less social hours than a regular nine to five schedule Leah rapidly concluded that the overgrown weeds really didn't matter that much in the greater scheme of things. In fact, in recent times, Leah had almost come to a place of total acceptance that their messy back garden would probably remain that way for quite a while and for at least the foreseeable future which actually, really didn't bother her that much since she didn't particularly mind the presence of the weeds because the couple hardly spent any time in the back garden most weekends. For the past few years, the couple's main focus had been their life goals and so they had worked tirelessly towards those goals as a couple and as a romantic team, united by love and determined to realize their future together so, Leah didn't really think that the weeds would disappear anytime soon because the couple's weekends were usually spent wrapped up in each other's arms or out in the city engaged in various leisure activities together.

"I think you weeds might just be allowed to live here for a while longer." Leah whispered as she finished her sandwich, glanced at the untidy weeds and then smiled. "Though technically, you are actually squatting, since you weren't officially planted here or invited."

After lunch had been enjoyed and the cup of tea fully drunk, Leah eagerly began to make her way back inside as she headed towards the basement and towards the emotional plane of disgust which promised to be full of disgustingly foul things, quite possibly some grime, dirt and mud and perhaps even some slime. Despite the quite negative connotations that Leah's potential emotional journey that day invoked however, she felt really quite optimistic about her planned visit to Spectrum and her participation in the simulated offerings that she would perhaps experience on that particular emotional journey because every visit to Spectrum so far, no matter how happy or sad had touched Leah's mind and heart in different ways. One element of certainty with regards to Spectrum definitely existed that Leah could fully appreciate and that was the reality that despite all those variances in her visits to Spectrum so far, each visit had definitely had one thing in common in that each one had deeply engaged her thoughts and had provoked her emotions in a manner that had triggered various emotional responses from deep within her inner being.

Once Leah had stepped off the final step that led into the basement, she eagerly began to press ahead as she started to cross the cement floor and headed towards the Spectrum capsule and as she walked, once again, Zidane's needs were swiftly pushed towards the back of her mind. Some intense focus and dedicated attention were definitely required by Leah that day for the performance of her walk-through tests and since the other love in Leah's life aside from Zidane was actually Spectrum, she was more than willing to focus for most of that day, upon her unique, professional creation. In every way possible, Spectrum was Leah's very own in that she had actually birthed herself and then it had been built from her professional aspirations, scientific hopes and technological dreams as her years of hard work had been invested into what she hoped would one day change the couple's life and future but as yet, Spectrum still remained incomplete and an actual sale uncertain.

A fear definitely lurked, lingered and resided in Leah's mind most mornings that drove her to complete her test schedule as soon as she possibly could because she feared that if she didn't complete it soon, Spectrum would never actually reach full, workable completion status or be sold to anyone. In recent times, Leah had not only lived and breathed every aspect of Spectrum's creation without any regrets, shame or even many restraints but she had also frequently dreamt about Spectrum's completion and as that achievement had dangled upon the horizon of a very close tomorrow, it had almost felt like a constant thorn of irritation that had continuously pricked her mind with needle pricks of frustration.

Although Leah had tried so hard to bridge the chasm of incompletion formed from unrealized tasks in order to reach the other side of the divide and actual achievement somehow, much to Leah's irritation, so far achievement had dangled just outside her reach and had lain beyond her professional grasp. The deep divide of incompletion as yet had still not been fully bridged or crossed, even though Leah had firmly put in place so many sturdy, hourly planks of hard work to build that bridge of professional success and even though she had tied so many ropes of effort and dedication to those planks of diligent hard work and so, every waking hour that reality, constantly frustrated Leah's mind.

Throughout Leah's years as a research student, it had been her dream to pursue her own chosen area of research and from that desire, Spectrum had actually been birthed and then as soon as Leah possibly could after her graduation that goal had been fully pursued. Unlike some of the other students that had been in attendance on Leah's program of study prior to her graduation, she hadn't chased after doctoral titles and peace prizes but had instead opted to create something that she could hopefully one day sell that might actually contribute positively to her own future and her own future family's financial stability. Fortunately for Leah, since her graduation, despite the unique nature of her professional aspirations and her meander into very uncertain areas of unexplored technologically scientific terrain, Zidane had not only always stood firmly by her side but he had also supported her and that support had not just been emotional and psychological but also practical and financial.

Every six months Leah would receive a quite moderate research grant that barely even covered the costs of her work and so usually, Zidane would not only cover the bills but he would also contribute financially towards her work as and if the need arose. The financial efforts that Zidane made each month definitely made a huge difference and so, Leah definitely appreciated his input immensely because every single month Zidane would also give Leah an additional allowance which she would then utilize to pay for any personal items that she needed, like clothes, toiletries, accessories and so on and his support seemed as faithfully deep as the ocean.

Due to Zidane's supportive contributions to Leah's life, she definitely felt that his loyalty, support and commitment totally justified the household chores that she did each weekday for them both since the couple did live in their shared home together. Unlike some other women who may not have bothered or that might perhaps have taken a more feminist stance, Leah felt that her contributions to the couple's home and their life were extremely important because that was her contribution to not only the couple's life but also to the upkeep of the home that they both shared. Since the household chores had never been an actual bone of contention between the couple because extreme feminism just wasn't part of Leah's makeup, it had therefore meant that their relationship had virtually run like a smooth engine of romantic peace for the past few years as the couple had operated on a daily basis upon a platform of mutual respect, devoted participation and dedicated cooperation from both parties involved.

Inside Leah's heart however, as she mounted the Spectrum capsule, a deep hope definitely lay that wished that upon Spectrum's completion, Zidane would then be able to seek alternative employment and find a slightly more sociable job that would allow him to return from work at around five or six each weekday and to start no earlier than nine every morning. The life that the couple currently both lived each day as far as Leah was concerned, was a rather hard daily slog and so, she definitely felt that they deserved a slightly easier life than the one they both currently toiled through every week but she remained hopeful as she lay down inside the capsule that a slightly more pleasant life and lifestyle currently sat just a few steps away from the couple's current position in life.

For the exploration of Leah's next adventure, she had already decided to be slightly more bold and a tad more organized because she felt that such tweaks to her personality that day would perhaps provide her with some obstacles that were slightly harder to overcome. Since disgust lay on the opposite end of the spectrum from the attributes that Leah had chosen to modify and increase, she felt that those changes would perhaps heighten her experiences that day which would make that particular emotional plane a bit more off challenge to her which would ultimately, make her walk-through tests much more thorough.

Once Leah had issued a few verbal commands, she then set the Spectrum timer as usual as she prepared for her emotional journey of disgust but on this occasion, Leah shaved off an hour to her visit as she set the timer to wake her up in nine-hours' time.

Although a ten-hour visit was required to experience the whole emotional journey of disgust in one recreational sitting, due to the fact that it was a Friday and since it would be a Friday evening by the time she returned, Leah had already decided to spend just nine-hours in that particular emotional plane that day because she had taken Zidane's heart into consideration and so, she had adjusted her pending visit to Spectrum accordingly. However, Leah definitely feared that if that nine-hour timeframe was reduced any further then she would miss out on the final part of her adventure and some key elements of that particular emotional journey which she had absolutely no desire to do because she wanted her walk-through tests to be performed as seamlessly as possible.

Another factor that Leah began to thoughtfully consider as the Spectrum capsule lowered over her head, was the fact that she could actually return to that emotional journey at a later point in time and so, she rapidly concluded that she would perhaps complete that final tenth hour throughout the next week. Although it wasn't absolutely essential for Leah to pick up the one hour shortfall at all and there was no real pressure to actually do so, usually Leah preferred her visits to Spectrum to be complete for the sake of consistency. Each environment had to be tested not only effectively but also thoroughly so that any required modifications and tweaks could be identified and then made which meant, Leah had to mentally capture every single element of her experiences effectively in order to be accurate which she felt could be tricky, if there was a long time lapse between the entrance into an emotional journey and the completion of that same journey.

Just a minute or so after the sleeping gas had circulated around the capsule's interior, infiltrated Leah's biological system and she had drifted off, Leah reawakened and as she did so, she found herself strewn across the ground in what looked to be a wide, grimy, grubby, earthy underground tunnel. From what Leah could see at first glance there appeared to be a brownish green slimy river that flowed across one side of the tunnel which a foul stench seemed to emanate abundantly from and as Leah began to process the repugnant smell, she immediately screwed up her nose and winced in direct response to the awful aroma that silently wafted into her nostrils.

"Now that smell is definitely disgusting." Leah acknowledged as she glanced down at her clothes and her simulated form for a few seconds before she started to pick herself up off the ground.

Some muddy, earthy particles clung to the folds of Leah's clothes which on this occasion she noticed, appeared to comprise of a black satin jumpsuit and so as Leah stood up, she enthusiastically began to shake the dirt off the all in one item of clothing that she had just woken up in. However and much to Leah's total disgust as she attempted to rid herself of the earthy particles of dirt, she swiftly noticed that some small creatures which looked like a cross between rats and snakes scurried across the muddy tunnel about a meter or so away from her current position.

"And they look like mudrattysnakes. Yucky, yuck, yuck." Leah whispered as she shook her head in total disgust. "How absolutely foul."

Since the mudrattysnakes actually looked quite horrible and really quite scary, for the next few seconds Leah just stood completely still and it was almost as if she was rooted to the spot in fear after which point, since the mudrattysnakes didn't actually draw any closer, Leah began to internally shake herself out of her paralysis. Once Leah had convinced herself that the hybrid creatures were not actually going to come any nearer for the time being and since they didn't seem to be that interested in her simulated presence, she then started to relax a little as she began to inspect the interior of the earthy tunnel.

At the other end of the muddy tunnel and about eighty meters away from Leah's current position, she suddenly spotted an arch shaped doorway with a closed earthy door carved into the muddy earth which appeared to lead to somewhere else. Since Leah definitely harbored a desire to actually be somewhere else and as far away from the mudrattysnakes and the stinky, slimy river as she possibly could be, she enthusiastically began to make her way towards it because it appeared to be the closest exit available to her from the earthy tunnel that was clearly, comfortably populated by mudrattysnakes and the creatures certainly didn't seem to be in a hurry to leave its confines. Due to Leah's desire to distance herself from the awful contents of the earthy tunnel as soon as she possibly could, Leah quickly sped up as she tried to avoid the mudrattysnakes that littered the earthy ground because in all honesty, in her heart of hearts, she really felt quite anxious to leave not only the slimy river firmly behind her but also the filthy, slithery creatures that decorated the interior of the tunnel.

Much to Leah's sheer relief, she rapidly discovered that the earthy door seemed to open easily enough, once she arrived beside it and then began to push it open and so as soon as the door was wide enough ajar, she bravely started to step through it, even though as yet she had no actual idea what was actually on the other side of that door. Just beyond the muddy, earthy door, rather surprisingly, Leah found a large underground room which was actually full of simulated people and though it was almost filled to the brim with unknown human like entities, Leah quickly found an unoccupied spot quite close to the earthy door to stand in.

Rather amusingly, Leah observed as she began to visually scan the subterranean cave, all the people in attendance seemed to be dressed very smartly in that they were either clothed in sharp suits or elegant dresses which prompted her to smile. In fact, the sudden presence of all those sophisticated, clean, sharp items of apparel that clung to the simulated human occupant's forms seemed such a stark contrast from the slimy river, the foul stench and the yucky mudrattysnakes that Leah had just left behind that it almost seemed strange to her that the two spaces could be in such close proximity to each other and yet be so vastly different. At least thirty to forty simulacrums appeared to be present, Leah swiftly estimated, and since the simulated human entities appeared to be in the midst of some kind of meeting, Leah kept and remained completely silent as she continued to visually inspect the interior of the subterranean room which looked very unlike the earthy, muddy tunnel that she had just come from.

The walls and ceiling of the underground area, Leah rapidly noticed, appeared to be lined and adorned with smooth, mahogany planks that literally covered every inch of it and not even a speck of earthy mud was visible or could be seen by her eyes. Apart from the obvious lack of dirt and the absence of any mucky earth as Leah scrutinized her surroundings another positive aspect of the underground cave like room that she found pleasing was the fact that the repugnant, foul smell from the slimy river had completely disappeared by that point. Much to Leah's total relief, she found that she could actually once more breathe freely again and in total comfort without any possible inhalation of any foul fumes from the stinky river of slime which pleased her nostrils no end.

At the opposite end of the cave like space which almost looked like a decorated room inside a home minus the presence of any actual items of furniture, Leah suddenly spotted an attractive looking man that stood in a stationary but prominent position as he addressed everyone around him and so, she started to listen to him as he spoke. Due to Leah's arrival which the attractive man suddenly seemed to notice, he glanced at her face and then paused for a few seconds before he offered Leah a polite smile and nod which she immediately returned and then as she watched in amused fascination, he continued to deliver his verbal address.

Although the actual purpose of the gathering wasn't totally clear to Leah quite yet, she continued to listen to the attractive man speak as she prepared to participate in her surroundings and to cooperate. Each word that was spoken by the attractive male form was attentively listened to as Leah made an attempt to at least try and grasp some kind of understanding via the verbal explanations on offer regarding the main purpose of the gathering and the primary objective of his verbal address. Since no one around Leah appeared to be hostile, she continued to stand quite comfortably at the rear of the wooden, subterranean cave like room as she waited for some more snippets of information from the attractive man who it appeared was some kind of leader and as Leah waited for some verbal drops of enlightenment, she began to admire some of the other attendees' smart apparel.

Suddenly however, the attractive man's address came to an actual end and once it did so, Leah watched in total silence as he quickly strode across the room towards her with one of his hands outstretched and so, Leah quickly faced him as she prepared to greet him. Since the attractive man's address had seemed quite important, Leah had not even dared to interrupt him mid speech but as he began to officially welcome her, she prepared to cooperate with his friendly gestures which at the very least, seemed to be warm and friendly. Apparently, Leah's entrance and presence were not going to slip by unnoticed or unattended to which in some ways made her feel really quite special and so as the male form neared her position and drew closer to the back of the enclosed, underground cave room, she rapidly offered him a hand to shake in response.

"Hello there, I'm so glad you could join us. I'm Jonas." He explained as he began to politely introduce himself and started to shake her hand. "I'm the leader of the rebellion."

"Nice to meet you Jonas. I'm Leah." Leah replied as she smiled, shook his hand and then nodded as if his verbal explanation made perfect sense to her, even though as yet she had no actual idea what the actual rebellion itself was all about.

Rather amusingly, Leah suddenly noticed, everyone inside the wooden plank lined room had turned to face the two which almost made her feel slightly nervous but as she cooperated with Jonas's pleasant welcome, firm handshake and masculine grip, she flashed a polite smile at the sea of strange faces around her. Although the handshake that had been offered by Jonas had instantly put Leah at ease as she glanced around the wooden cave room and inspected the people inside it in a search for answers, their smart apparel did not in any way explain why they were actually there or what the rebellion itself was actually about and so, she waited for Jonas to elaborate further.

"Well Leah, since you arrived in the middle of our meeting I'll explain why we're gathered here today and hopefully that will shed a bit more light upon our actual mission." Jonas started to explain. "We are in a fight against the disgustingness of the Disgusting Dimension and we're trying to bring some joy, refinement, civility and eloquence to an ugly environment but it is an ongoing battle and it's one that we have to fight every single day."

"Okay." Leah replied as she smiled.

The mission of the rebel group it appeared as Leah began to thoughtfully process Jonas's verbal explanation as she watched him turn around and then return to the other end of the room, didn't seem particularly urgent in nature but it was still quite cute nonetheless and so, it definitely amused her. Since Jonas had returned to the front of the gathering and had then even started to address the rebel group once again, Leah silently concluded that their conversation for now at least, definitely seemed to be over but as she watched and listened to him in fascinated silence, Leah noticed that the attendees once again turned to face him which suited her right down to the ground since having a sea of strange eyes upon her had made her feel a tad nervous.

A couple more minutes went by as Jonas continued to speak and as Leah listened to him, she studied his outfit in total fascination which looked very smart but also quite practical since he wore a black waistcoat with some black trousers to match, both of which appeared to have a multitude of pockets and also seemed to be made out of the same velvety cord material. Many of the simulated attendees, Leah observed as she waited patiently to see exactly what would happen next, nodded their head at regular intervals as Jonas spoke and the gathering seemed highly civil and very well organized because the attendees looked extremely cooperative as well as enthusiastically focused.

"Does everyone have a social etiquette handbook, a bag of joy and a transformation kit?" Jonas suddenly enquired as he began to round off his address.

Some eager nods, Leah silently observed, immediately followed in direct response to Jonas's question and some of the attendees even held up some strange looking items inside their hands. For the next couple of minutes Jonas appeared to visually scan the wooden subterranean room which Leah instantly assumed, was just a visual check to ensure that the attendees were sufficiently and adequately equipped for their pending mission. Once Jonas appeared to be satisfied that everything was indeed actually in order, Leah continued to watch him in silence as he began to walk around the subterranean room and as he did so, she noticed that the attendees present were split into much smaller groups of twos and threes before he returned to his former position.

Several more verbal instructions were enthusiastically imparted to the gathering of simulacrums by Jonas as Leah listened to him speak and as she watched the attendees respond, she noticed that there was an air of participation and willingness present inside the wooden cave room as every attendee appeared to immediately accept his instructions with very serious expressions upon each of their faces. Since the rebel group appeared to take their cause and mission very seriously indeed, Leah smiled as she began to accept that just for today, disgust was actually the main enemy and that filth was the major manifestation of that disgusting enemy which therefore meant that the battle ahead, rather amusingly, was to be one filled with hygienic weaponry of various kinds.

"Right Leah, you don't have any equipment, so if you'd like to come with me please I'll get you prepared for the mission ahead." Jonas offered as he suddenly strode back across the room towards her.

Leah immediately smiled and nodded her head in agreement. "Sure Jonas that would be great." She replied.

Much to Leah's fascination as she began to follow Jonas, she noticed that the small groups inside the enclosed cave like area rapidly started to disperse as they left the enclosed subterranean area via some wooden wall panels that they pushed open. For the next minute or so as Leah watched the subterranean cave room empty in thoughtful silence, she began to prepare herself for her actual participation in her very first ever Disgusting Dimension rebel mission as Jonas opened up a wooden wall panel that Leah noticed housed an actual cupboard behind it that appeared to be built into the wall of the room and then began to take something out of it. Since it had now become quite apparent to Leah that Jonas was to be her guide in that emotional plane for the time being which therefore meant that he would direct her towards either some or all of the actual activities that she was supposed to embark upon and engage in during that particular emotional journey, she continued to patiently await his direction because the rebellion was essentially under his command.

"You'll definitely need one of these Leah." Jonas explained as he handed her a small book.

Rather curiously but very splendidly, Leah instantly noticed that the small book had a golden, shiny cover which glistened and shone and that it not only looked amazingly extravagant but also totally luxurious despite its small size. A few seconds were spent in visual admiration before Leah proceeded to open the book up and as she began to flick through the material pages inside the golden cover, she estimated that it had to be around two hundred pages long. Much to Leah's surprise and amusement however, inside the book there were no actual written or printed words to be found and instead each material page contained a smart item of material attire that hung down from a wardrobe like rail that seemed to run through the entire length of the book's interior.

Since the book wasn't like an actual book at all and quite surprisingly, Leah had discovered that it was actually more like a miniature wardrobe filled with very smart miniature clothes, a few giggles managed to escape from Leah's lips as she perused some of the pages. Every page that Leah flicked through seemed to be formed from a different kind of material as opposed to sheets of paper and that notion utterly fascinated Leah because so much care and thought seemed to have gone into the wardrobe book's creation and each page she noticed had a small page number sewn into the bottom of every one. Each small item of clothing that Leah found inside the book's pages looked really quite real and so it almost felt as if each outfit could actually be worn by an actual human being, if only the garments had been large enough to fit an actual human body.

"What is this Jonas, a book or a mini wardrobe?" Leah asked as she paused for a second and then glanced up at his face. She smiled and then resumed her visual inspection. "It's really quite astonishing, very intricate and totally amazing."

"It's a social etiquette handbook Leah and every outfit on each page has its own set of personal codes that can transform the wearer of any outfit chosen which will equip them for any event, any kind of activity, any type of weather or for any occasion imaginable." Jonas explained as he watched her inspect the book's interior and smiled. "You can actually take any outfit from any of the pages and then just enlarge the clothes to the size required, so that you can actually wear any outfit inside the book that you want to." He mentioned. "And each item of clothing instantly transforms the wearer, their personality and their conduct to suit the garment that they have chosen."

Just a few seconds later as Leah watched Jonas stride across the room, she noticed that he headed towards another one of the wooden wall panels on the other side of the room which was then enthusiastically pushed open to reveal the interior of a second cupboard. For the next few seconds Leah remained completely silent as she continued to watch Jonas inspect the cupboard's interior and then pluck a small, black, velvet pouch shaped bag from its confines and a small golden case, both of which looked very similar to some of the items that Leah had seen the gathering attendees hold up inside their hands before they had vacated the room. The small black velvet bag almost seemed to overflow with some kind of golden mass and although Leah felt uncertain as to what the golden mass actually was, she noticed that it sparkled and shone and that it appeared to be formed from thousands of small particles which wriggled around and surged through the interior of the pouch shaped bag that made the golden substance almost look actually alive.

"You'll need this bag too Leah for our mission." Jonas swiftly confirmed as he shut the second cupboard panel door, strode back across the subterranean room towards her and then handed her the small bag.

"What exactly is inside here Jonas?" Leah asked as she accepted the small bag from his hands and then began to peek inside it. "This golden stuff seems to be moving around, is it alive?"

"That is a bag full of joy Leah." Jonas rapidly explained. "We usually give a portion of joy to any of the creatures or any of the people that we meet inside the Disgusting Dimension that we feel, think or can see are in need in order to lift their mood, to lighten their spirits and to provide them with a glimmer of hope. A word of warning however, joy is very hard to make and even harder to find and collect, so try not to spill any please." He advised as he swiftly pulled the drawstrings tightly shut around the top of the small velvet bag.

Before any further conversation could be held and before Leah could ask any more questions, just a second or two later Jonas handed Leah the small golden case which she immediately opened up due to her curiosity. Much to Leah's complete surprise, inside the small golden case, she found a small, shiny golden star shaped object which appeared to be wedged into some protective soft, rubbery foam. No explanations seemed to exist however, inside the small case that accompanied the golden star and so as Leah glanced at the shiny object she began to silently speculate as what it could possibly be and what it might actually be utilized for.

"I give up Jonas, what is the golden star for and what does it do?" Leah asked just a few seconds later as she shrugged. "I just can't seem to work it out at all."

"Now that golden star Leah, believe it or not, is actually a transformation kit." Jonas replied as he grinned. "It can transform anyone or anything that it touches."

"Really, how does it do that?" Leah asked as a puzzled expression spread out across her face.

"Well, if you'd like to come with me, I can demonstrate that to you right now." Jonas offered.

"Sure, I'm intrigued." Leah replied.

"Let's go through this door Leah." Jonas said as he gently held her arm and then began to lead her towards a wooden wall panel nearby. He pushed the wooden door panel open before he continued and as he did so, his voice dropped to almost a whisper. "We'll probably find some humabears down here."

Beyond the wooden plank door and exit there appeared to be another earthy tunnel which Jonas quickly stepped into and then began to lead Leah along and as she started to follow him as he walked, he continued to speak to her in a hushed tone. The second earthy tunnel, Leah observed as she walked along it, had a ceiling that was much higher up than the first and it also appeared to be much wider and unlike the first muddy, grimy tunnel, the second tunnel she rapidly noticed, did not actually have a slimy river inside it but it did have some slimebattymice which flapped around just above their heads as the two walked. Quite curiously however, Leah found that the second tunnel twisted and turned in every direction possible and that it seemed to taper off quite quickly and narrow down quite rapidly as the two walked along it until it became so narrow and small that the two had to actually walk along the remainder of it in single file.

When the tunnel came to an end, approximately two hundred meters or so later, Leah discovered that it actually led out into a large expanse which had some twisted looking clumps of trees scattered across it and a muddy, sticky, grungy base. Some damaged partial tree stumps appeared to be dotted around the interior of the expanse along with some piles of small rocks which appeared at sporadic intervals that seemed to quite happily litter the grungy ground. Since the sudden appearance of the muddy, sticky, grungy ground didn't appeal very much to Leah, or seem to offer anyone a warm welcome, she hung back slightly as she waited for Jonas to provide further direction and a shred of guidance to her.

Unlike Leah however, Jonas didn't seem to harbor any reservations at all as she watched him stride quickly and comfortably towards the center of the expanse and she noticed that he visually scanned the area around him as he walked, although what exactly he was on the lookout for, was at that point in time, extremely unclear. A second or two later however, Leah's silent question was answered as suddenly she spotted a couple of waist high creatures that seemed to have entered into the expanse from another entrance on the other side of it and although the creatures almost looked like small bears, she noticed that they both seemed to have quite human hands, faces and feet. Quite curiously, the creature's faces, Leah observed, seemed to possess very human shaped pointed noses that jutted out from their round, hair lined faces and as soon as Jonas spotted the two hybrid creatures which she immediately assumed were humabears, Leah watched in absolute fascination as he began to quickly stride towards them.

Before the humabears could even try to escape, Leah noticed that Jonas swiftly stretched out one of his arms and then quickly grabbed one of the small hybrid creatures and as he did so, the other humabear glanced at him, let out a shriek and then began to rush out of expanse. By that point in time, Leah noticed that several other similar looking hybrids had started to enter the expanse via a few other entrances but that within a matter of seconds and as soon as the new arrivals had observed the scene or had heard the shriek, they too started to quickly scurry off and from what Leah could see, the hybrid creatures clearly appeared to be rather anxious not to be captured themselves. A smile of amusement crossed Leah's face as she watched the scene unfold in front of her and as the other humabears scattered, she swiftly began to conclude that the humabears weren't particularly loyal to each other since they seemed to quickly abandon each other at the very first signs of trouble.

Once the other humabears had vacated the expanse and Jonas had the captured humabear firmly in his grip, Leah watched in total silence as he began to place a golden transformation star upon the creature's head which he appeared to hold down very firmly as the creature continued to wriggle around. For a split second nothing seemed to actually happen as Leah stood and watched in fascinated silence as the captured humabear continued to wriggle around under the golden star as the hybrid tried to avoid not just the star but also to free itself Jonas's very tight grip. At least another couple of seconds went by before Leah suddenly noticed that a transformation had actually begun and that it now appeared to be underway because the humabear's external appearance had actually started to change and the changes that she could see absolutely intrigued her.

In a matter of just another few seconds, Leah observed in amazed delight that the furry, grubby, mucky hybrid with human features had been completely transformed into a sophisticated, well dressed humabear which actually, totally surprised her. A tailored tweed waistcoat that had trousers to match now adorned and clothed the hybrid's exterior which seemed to fit every inch of the humabear's frame immaculately and Leah almost gasped as she observed the results of the transformation. Every strand of the humabear's former matted brownish black hair, Leah swiftly noticed, was now clean and looked polished as each strand sparkled, shone and glistened and the animalistic grunts that had emanated from the humabear's mouth just moments before, seemed to have ceased completely.

"Jonas my old chap, what brings you down here this fine afternoon?" The humabear politely enquired as he suddenly faced the two human forms and then smiled. "And who is your lady friend? I can't say that we've ever met before, I'm sure I would remember that. Would you both like some tea? I can arrange that for you now if you'd like me to."

Leah giggled.

"Sure, some tea would be lovely Humatine and that's a lovely tweed waistcoat, it really suits you." Jonas replied as he nodded his head.

Much to Leah's amusement, the humabear's voice now sounded very refined and totally human as opposed to the coarse grunts that had initially emanated from the hybrid's mouth and quite strangely, the humabear now seemed to be extremely polite and even what one might consider, well mannered. Just a few seconds later as Leah watched in total delight and sheer amazement, Humatine clapped his hands together and within less than a minute, another humabear suddenly scurried out of a hollow in a large tree trunk nearby and then drew closer to the group. Very much like the initial appearance of the first humabear, the second humabear looked grubby, mucky, muddy and rough and was also about waist high, so Leah rapidly began to assume that the humabears were probably all around that height and that the creatures usually, just seemed to accept and even blended into the disgustingness of the Disgusting Dimension rather naturally which she immediately attributed to their animalistic origins.

"Can you clean Mankin up please Jonas?" Humatine asked.

"Then we can have some tea."

"No problem Humatine, I'll do that for you right now." Jonas immediately agreed as he began to walk towards the second humabear armed with his golden star.

"How come humabears are so small Jonas?" Leah asked as she began to follow him so that she could see the transformation to the second hybrid take place more clearly.

"Well Leah, they're a special kind of bear that usually only grow to around an average human's knee height but because they are half human, they do tend to grow slightly above that usual height but their natural origins do restrict their growth, so they never really grow much beyond waist height." Jonas explained. "Humatine is actually the leader of the humabears, so we were quite lucky to find him here really because the other humabears usually follow his lead and they always obey his commands."

For the next minute or so, Leah watched Jonas in total silence as she stood next to him as he performed the second humabear transformation and as he did so, she noticed that Humatine began to pick up, arrange and organize some small rocks on the ground nearby. Each rock selected by Humatine, much to Leah's amusement and total fascination, was carefully placed in a circular formation and then a much larger flatter rock was placed in the middle of that circular formation and as Humatine went about his task with a very serious expression upon his face, Leah tried not to giggle. Once each rock had been placed in what appeared to be a satisfactory position, according to Humatine's requirements, Leah continued to watch the humabear as the hybrid suddenly turned to face Mankin and then began an extremely polite and very civilized discussion with the second humabear and as some brief verbal discourse was exchanged between the two, Leah listened to the two speak in amused silence.

"Our visitors would like some tea Mankin." Humatine explained.

"Certainly Humatine, I'll organize that straight away." Mankin replied as he gave a compliant nod.

From what Leah could see, it appeared that the second humabear had been adequately briefed and as she watched Mankin in total delight and absolute fascination, the second humabear suddenly rushed back towards the hollow tree trunk that he had originated from and then stepped back inside it. In a matter of seconds Mankin had completely vanished from sight and so, Leah turned to face Humatine and Jonas once more as she began to prepare herself to participate in the humabear's polite offer though what exactly a cup of humabear tea might actually taste like, she was extremely unsure.

"Please take a seat." Humatine swiftly offered as he pointed towards some of the small rocks and directed the two human forms towards the makeshift rocky seats that he had just arranged. "I'm afraid the seating arrangements on this occasion are a bit rough because there aren't any real chairs or a proper table but I've tried my best to make do with that is here, instead of missing out because of what isn't."

Although the invitation from Humatine had been pleasant enough, the rocky chairs did feel slightly uncomfortable, Leah rapidly discovered and so, she wriggled around a little once she sat down on one as she attempted to try and make herself as comfortable as she possibly could. Just a couple of minutes later and once Jonas too had sat down, Leah watched as Mankin suddenly reappeared and she noticed that as the humabear re-emerged from the hollow tree trunk and then began to walk cautiously, carefully and slowly back towards the small rocks that the two simulated human forms had sat down upon, he now carried a large brown tray in his paw like hands.

On the top of the tray there appeared to be four earthy brown, small clay cups that lined one side of it, Leah noticed and in the very center of the tray, there sat an earthy brown, large clay teapot which she immediately assumed contained some kind of tea though what exactly that tea would actually taste like, still remained to be clarified and tasted. Despite all Leah's questions however, she kept completely silent as she watched Mankin place the tray carefully down upon the large, much flatter rock in the center of the circular formation which had a smoother surface and once Mankin had performed his task, Leah continued to watch the humabear in total fascination as he suddenly turned to face her and then flashed her a polite smile.

At that point it appeared, since all the human simulated forms present were actually seated and the pot of tea had now arrived, Leah observed that Humatine also quickly sat down alongside their simulated human forms and that the humabear actually licked his lips as he eagerly prepared for the refreshment that was due to be served. Just a second or two later as Leah watched the two humabears, she noticed that Mankin reached for the dark brown, clay teapot, the contents of which he then proceeded to pour into the four earthy brown, clay cups.

Despite the rough rocky rocks, all in all from what Leah could see, the humabear gathering appeared to be extremely civilized and so, once she had been handed a clay brown cup full of liquid by Mankin, she immediately began to sip on the dark brown liquid it contained as Leah made an effort to fully accept, welcome and appreciate the two humabear's warm gestures. A basic provision of hospitality had been extended towards the two simulated human guests by the humabears and so Leah did not wish to reward that polite kindness with a refusal to participate in their offer of hospitality because she felt that such a refusal on her part, would actually be quite rude.

Unlike the tea that Leah was used to in the real human world, she immediately noticed that this tea had a very sweet, quite spicy almost earthy taste and it definitely tasted as if it contained some ginger as some of the liquid drops drizzled down the back of her throat. Some aspects of the Disgusting Dimension were discussed between Humatine and Jonas as the tea was served and drunk and as Leah listened attentively to the conversation that flowed between them both, she began to wonder if the humabears actually knew that they were a hybrid creation of her own making as she sipped on her cup of tea.

Once a few minutes had gone by Leah observed that Mankin, who was not actually involved in the conversation, suddenly stood up and then rushed off again and as he vanished from sight courtesy of the same hollow tree trunk, she continued to sip on her tea. Since the humabear's promised tea was now actually present and was in the midst of being joyfully consumed, Leah did wonder why Mankin had disappeared again but no obvious answers immediately sprung to mind or presented themselves as she sat and listened to Jonas and Humatine discuss some of the other hybrid creatures that occupied the confines of the mucky, muddy, slimy Disgusting Dimension.

Just a few minutes later however, Leah's unspoken question was silently answered as Mankin suddenly reappeared with another brown tray in his hands but this time the second tray was full of small, brown objects that reminded Leah a bit of chunks of chocolate cake though each one did look far more rugged and more earthier. Much to Leah's absolute amusement, the second tray which she instantly assumed had been stacked with edible items was swiftly presented to her by Mankin and a chunk of earthy looking cake was actually singled out and almost recommended to her as Mankin edged a corner of the tray in Leah's direction and nodded his head. Since the cup of humabear tea had actually tasted quite decent, Leah had absolutely no reservations at all inside her mind as she eagerly stretched out an arm in order to offer a polite response and to accept the humabear's kind offer but just as Leah plucked a chunk of brown rugged cake from the tray, suddenly Jonas turned to face her and then he gently grabbed her arm.

"Thank you so much for your generous hospitality Humatine and Mankin." Jonas said appreciatively as he smiled at the two humabears and then quickly stood up. "Unfortunately Leah, we have to leave now because we have some very important matters to attend to today." He mentioned as he quickly turned to face her and then nodded before he continued to address the two humabears. "So Humatine, I'm afraid we won't be able to stay but thank you very much for the cup of tea. Your hospitality today was absolutely impeccable."

"But you'll miss out on our humabear specialty Jonas." Mankin rapidly pointed out.

"There's nothing I can do about that Mankin I'm afraid, another time perhaps." Jonas replied politely as he offered an apologetic smile. "We really have to go now Leah." He urged as he turned to face her and then swiftly but gently pulled her to her feet. "But before we go Humatine, I'd like to give you this as a token of our appreciation, it might come in handy sometimes and so, I'd really like you to have it." Jonas mentioned as he pulled a golden social etiquette handbook out of one of his pockets and then handed it to the leader of the humabears.

"Thank you Jonas but what is it actually for and what exactly does it do?" Humatine asked with a puzzled expression as he began to inspect both the exterior and the interior of the golden book.

"It's a social etiquette handbook Humatine. So if you have an occasion that you wish to attend, you'll find not only something appropriate to wear inside there but each outfit that you decide to wear will also help you to apply the appropriate social rules to that particular occasion automatically." Jonas explained. "You can enlarge every outfit inside that handbook and then actually wear each garment but try not to lose it because these handbooks are extremely tricky to craft."

"Thank you Jonas, it's very kind of you." Humatine replied as he perused the book's interior. "Yes, I can already see a few nice things in here that I would love to wear, how splendid."

"Well, I don't give many handbooks away Humatine, so you're definitely an exceptional humabear and you've definitely earnt that one due to your good manners and your splendid hospitality." Jonas said as he smiled.

A quick but discreet nod was given to Leah as Jonas suddenly turned to face her again and then urged her to follow him which Leah swiftly did as he began to lead her away from the humabears and away from the rocky makeshift dining formation which had somehow served as an actual table and chairs. Despite Leah's lack of understanding regarding Jonas's sudden rushed departure from the humabears and the expanse, she followed his lead without any hesitation on her part because Jonas's discreet indications had clearly signaled that the two should leave the humabears and their refreshments behind immediately and since he was essentially her guide in that plane and the humabears weren't, it seemed to be the most sensible thing to do.

Since Leah had actually managed to pick up a chunk of the brown, earthy humabear's cake that morsel of food remained inside one of her hands as she continued to follow Jonas out of the expanse and as the two stepped into a muddy, earthy tunnel entrance but as yet, she hadn't actually had a chance to eat it. When the two had walked about twenty meters or so along the tunnel however, Leah noticed that Jonas suddenly stopped and then he gently placed a hand on her arm, just before he turned to face her as he began to shake his head.

"I'm so sorry that I had to interrupt you like that Leah, it's just well, I had to stop you before you actually ate anything." Jonas explained in an apologetic tone. "The food that Mankin offered to you and then gave you, well it just isn't suitable for human consumption."

"Really?" Leah asked as she glumly glanced down at the brown chunk of humabear cake inside her hand. "But the cup of tea tasted rather nice."

"Yes well, the tea was different because that was a special type of tea that humabears usually only give to human guests, although they do sometimes consume that tea themselves but only on very special occasions." Jonas said as he shook his head and smiled. "The chunk of humabear cake on the other hand, now that's something else and although it looks harmless enough, it is actually made from the raw intestines of slimebattymice and so, I don't think that your stomach would be able to digest it or that your internal organs would really enjoy it." He swiftly clarified. "Although I do have to say, it was actually a huge compliment to be offered that cake by a humabear in the first place because it's a very special humabear delicacy that is highly sought after. Unfortunately, however, if we humans try to consume humabear cake, it definitely wouldn't be a complement to our stomachs and it would be more likely to result in injury than any actual enjoyment."

"Thanks for saving my stomach." Leah replied as she started to giggle.

"Yes that particular humabear culinary delicacy is definitely not one that you would even want to try." Jonas teased as he deftly plucked the brown chunk from her hand and then tossed it away.

"Why did they offer it to us?" Leah asked.

"Perhaps they were trying to impress you, after all, they are half human remember and they are both male." Jonas pointed out. "Perhaps they were captivated and swept away by your beauty. They don't receive many female human visitors in this part of the Disgusting Dimension and especially not exceptionally pretty ones like you." He teased with a playful smile.

"Where are we going next Jonas?" Leah asked as she flashed him a flirtatious external smile and inwardly reveled in his complimentary remarks which had definitely flattered her.

"Now we're going to find some more disgusting creatures which we will then transform in order to make them much more socially acceptable and far less disgusting." Jonas replied. "And then Leah, perhaps we can explore the social etiquette between you and I." He suggested playfully as he gently held onto her arm once again and then started to guide her further along the underground tunnel.

Deep within Leah a sudden surge of sensual passion was swiftly aroused which began to flow through her simulated veins, ripple across her simulated skin and sensually somersault through her simulated thoughts as she instantly, silently accepted Jonas's flirtatious offer which promised to be highly seductive and full of passionate excitement. A multitude of deliciously sensual prospects seemed to lighten Leah's steps as she began to walk along the tunnel once again alongside Jonas as she began to imagine what could perhaps lie within his charm filled arms, in his handsome face and what might be stirred inside of her by his sensual touches that definitely held the promise of a wide range of very passionate experiences.

Every single one of Jonas's visible simulated attributes excited and interested Leah in more ways than one because not only was Jonas extremely attractive but he also possessed several other non-cosmetic attributes that had caught her attention which appealed to her in other ways too. The romantic taste buds that formed Leah's palate of male attractions had definitely been sensually tantalized, passionately ignited and accurately matched when it came to the issue of Jonas's simulated persona because every single aspect of his presence seemed to create seductive ripples of sensual excitement within Leah's inner being which felt heightened by his every simulated touch. Some of the finer points of Jonas's simulated masculine existence had definitely come to Leah's attention and so too had his attractive appearance which seemed to become more and more attractive with each second that went by and his seductive remark had it appeared, created a whirlwind of passionate urges that gushed through Leah's mind as she began to sensually speculate as to what might actually transpire later that evening between them both.

Inside Spectrum Jonas would now be Leah's third romantic encounter and so, she internally began to consider that prospect quite thoughtfully as she continued to follow Jonas along the earthy tunnel as the two made some light but playful conversation. Since the first two simulated romantic experiences that Leah had already engaged in with the two other male guides inside Spectrum had been extremely delightful and totally pleasurable, Jonas's suggestion had been met with avid enthusiasm and sensual acceptance because it had aroused Leah's taste buds of desire. In fact, Leah just couldn't wait to sample Jonas's passionate offerings which she felt would definitely light up her emotional journey that day because he had definitely ignited the embers of passion inside of her.

Usually, outside of Spectrum, Leah gave very little or absolutely no thought at all to the men or the sexual experiences that she had enjoyed whilst she had participated inside it and so, she felt that this third experience would be pretty much the same. In some ways, it had almost been as if each sensual experience and passionate occurrence had been totally ignored by Leah in real life as far as had been humanly possible since once Leah had left the confines of that particular Spectrum environment, she had barely even considered the simulated male guides again that she had met inside it.

Inside Leah's mind, the experiences and simulacrum male

guides that she had explored and encountered whilst inside Spectrum had all been fictitious elements and therefore none had been fully regarded as real and so, she had absolutely no qualms when it came to her acceptance of that reality. Irrespective of the lack of any real substance however, Leah had definitely passionately enjoyed her participation in the playful, sexually charged, seductive, fictitious distractions that the two male guides so far, had so generously, sensually provided, albeit just for a brief moment in time and that reality she could certainly not deny, at least not inside the safe confines of her own mind.

Although Leah had taken a couple of artificial passionate meanders inside Spectrum however, her passionate loyalties and real emotions had still somehow remained fully engaged and tied to Zidane's heart in real life bound by strong strings of love and deep bonds of commitment and somehow, Zidane her solid rock of reality had managed to keep Leah focused in real life. At times however, Leah definitely felt as if she existed in a tug of war between a very sensual artificiality and a rather plain, dull reality as she tried to keep her reality and her relationship with Zidane at the forefront of her mind and her thoughts back in the real world. The various interactions that Leah had enjoyed inside Spectrum, as far as she was concerned, had been fully attributed to and deemed totally necessary as part of the essential tests that she had to perform in order to ensure that the capabilities of Spectrum, a system that she had actually created which she was ultimately, fully responsible for, were up to scratch and so her sensual meanders had been totally justified in her sight and fully accepted.

Some of the men that Leah had interacted with inside Spectrum had been devilishly attractive, exceedingly charming and had oozed sexual excitement but deep down inside, she ultimately knew that only Zidane was actually, really real. No matter how delicious those fictitious, simulacrum male entities had appeared to be, what fictitious flames of passion had been ignited inside Leah or what sexual desires had been quenched, not one of those male forms would ever actually possess even an ounce of reality and as she was fully aware, all that they could ever offer her was an artificial romance that had no depths in reality that could never materialize into anything more than an artificial fling.

In some ways, the fictitious nature of the sexual liaisons that Leah had indulged in and experienced inside Spectrum had actually allowed her to relax as she had enjoyed the casual, sexual interactions without any subsequent feelings of guilt to weigh her down. Technically, inside Leah's mind, she had already rationalized and then decided that there were no real emotional attachments since no real sexual interactions had actually taken place which to her mind meant that there had been and was no actual real betrayal on her part and so, she had accepted that rationalization and those justifications in totality. Since Zidane was the man that Leah would have real children with, Zidane was the man that Leah would actually spend the rest of her real life with and Zidane was Leah's real forever, the fictitious males in Spectrum represented very little to her in reality and were considered nothing more than a fictitious exploration of sensuality and a temporary, passionate departure from reality.

Despite the artificial nature of Jonas's existence however, as Leah glanced at him as she continued to walk alongside him, she fully accepted that he was not only masterful and full of charm but also sensually assertive and she definitely felt that he was a successful reflection of her tireless and devoted efforts to create guides for Spectrum that were devilishly attractive, highly engaged and full of sexual allure, albeit in a subtle, fictional kind of manner. Since Spectrum had the capability to allow users to specify which gender of guide they preferred upon each visit or guides could be randomly selected by Spectrum itself, due to Leah's own choices so far those selections had meant that most of her guides had predominantly been male and that the majority of them had been attractive because she had actually, specifically chosen to have male guides several times.

Another feature of the Spectrum system was that it also allowed users to interact without any guides at all and Leah had actually experienced that lack of guidance throughout one of her journeys as she had voyaged through the Fearful Forest. Generally, however, the guide feature had been implemented by Leah to reduce the sense of isolation that a user might experience whilst inside Spectrum itself and due to her own interactions and experiences so far, she definitely felt that the guides added to the whole experience very positively and did not detract from it and so that aspect of Spectrum had really pleased her. Rather satisfyingly for Leah in that respect, Jonas was definitely one of her better fictitious creations, she silently mused and began to conclude as she glanced at his face as they continued to walk along the earthy tunnel alongside each other and not just better but as far as she was concerned, deliciously and mouthwateringly better.

When the two arrived at the end of the tunnel, Leah noticed that it opened out into another expanse but that this one was much larger and far muddier and that in the very center of the expanse, there appeared to be a firm earthy island which seemed to house a very large tree and a clump of swampy bushes. All around the swampy, earthy island there was a quite large brown pool of liquid mud and at the foot of the large tree Leah spotted a dinoleopard which she recognized almost instantly due to its unique, bold bodily markings. The tree and the small island of firm earthy mud that it sat upon appeared to be totally surrounded by the swampy, grimy pool of brown liquid mud that seemed to move around as Leah glanced at it and around the perimeter of the liquid mud that moved, there were some more trees that lined the edge of the expanse which were adorned with some swampy vines that clung onto and decorated some of the branches.

Due to the promise of another adventure that now sat upon the near horizon of Leah's afternoon which was now within visible sight, she quickly started to prepare herself for her next challenge in the Disgusting Dimension and so as Jonas began to walk towards the edge of the muddy pool, she immediately started to follow him. Some cries of alarm and distress, Leah suddenly noticed, appeared to emanate from the large tree and as she scrutinized it further, she managed to spot a nest about halfway up that tree which it appeared contained a baby dirtlizardingo that seemed to actually be stuck inside it. Since the cries sounded full of frustration, full of anguish and full of anxiety, Leah immediately began to shake her head in response as she listened to the cries for help because she had no idea how she could possibly assist the small hybrid creature that was so obviously in a position of weakness because the dinoleopard didn't look as if it wanted to leave the foot of the tree or as if it wanted to go anywhere and certainly not in a hurry.

"Leah, we'll have to stop off here for a while because we have to try and save the baby dirtlizardillo." Jonas mentioned decisively as he suddenly came to an abrupt stop at the edge of the muddy pool.

"Right but how did it actually get all the way up there?" Leah asked.

"It was probably plucked from the ground and then dumped in the nest by a vultger, they can climb trees and fly so I wouldn't be surprised and that nest does look like a vultger's nest." Jonas explained. "The dinoleopard probably just came along and found a ready meal that had been prepared but not yet eaten, so it's probably just waiting for the baby dirtlizardillo to fall out of the nest and to drop to the ground so that it can fill its stomach."

"How will we rescue the baby? I mean that dinoleopard sure looks hungry and if we get in the way then we could become another potential afternoon snack." Leah quickly pointed out.

"Yes, so we'll have to plan our approach quite carefully." Jonas swiftly concluded. "Perhaps I could transform the dinoleopard and then we could safely approach the tree, climb up the branches and then we'll be able to rescue the baby dirtlizardillo."

"How will you transform the dinoleopard Jonas?" Leah asked. "You'd have to hold a transformation star down onto its head and that creature is on a very hungry prowl. I really don't think that the dinoleopard will just stand still or willingly cooperate with that plan."

"Yes that is a slightly tricky issue, perhaps we can offer it some kind of food and then whilst it is eating the bait, we could climb the tree and then I could drop the star down onto its head from one of the tree branches." Jonas swiftly suggested. "If I wait until the dinoleopard has started to eat and then aim the star carefully enough, it probably won't even notice the star until the actual transformation has taken place."

"I hope your aim is good Jonas. One slight issue though, we'll have to pass the dinoleopard to actually get to the foot of the tree." Leah quickly pointed out.

"Don't worry Leah, I have a string dangle tool that I can use and I'll put some sticky tree sap on one side of the transformation star so that the dinoleopard won't be able to shake it off very easily." Jonas reassured her. "When it comes to the actual issue of the tree itself, hopefully the food will distract the dinoleopard and keep it busy for a while which should give us enough time to climb up the tree. If I throw the bait a few steps away from the foot of the tree that should buy us a little more time and who knows, the dinoleopard might even be so hungry that it might not even notice us or bother with us at all." He continued. "Right, now that we've got a workable plan, we need to find some food to tempt the dinoleopard away from the base of the tree."

"You probably won't get the transformation star back." Leah teased.

"Yeah that's okay, I always carry a couple around with me." Jonas replied. "Just in case."

"One other thing Jonas, how will we cross the muddy pool?" Leah ventured to ask.

"Well, the mud shouldn't actually be that deep, I've visited this spot before." Jonas explained as he dipped a foot into the liquid brown substance to prove his point. "Which means, we should be able to wade across it quite easily."

"Okay." Leah replied. "I'll let you lead the way."

"But first, before we attempt to do that I have to sort out the food issue." Jonas mentioned as he grinned. "We can't really bait a dinoleopard with no actual bait."

Leah giggled. "True." She agreed.

For the next minute or so Leah watched Jonas in total silence as he glanced around the expanse before he focused once more upon the large muddy pool which Leah observed, continued to move around as it churned and swirled in a random fashion rather chaotically. Due to the continuous movement of the brown muddy substance, the liquid dirt almost gave Leah the impression that it was actually alive and so she almost feared the prospect of an actual wade across it but as Leah continued to watch Jonas in curious fascination, she noticed that his face suddenly lit up as a look of triumph rapidly began to appear. Something inside that liquid dirt had definitely caught Jonas's attention which had ignited a spark of hope within him and as Leah watched him visually concentrate upon the muddy grunge, she began to wonder what he had actually spotted because all she could see from her position was liquid dirt.

"I know what I can do Leah, I can catch a mudrattysnake and then we can give it to the dinoleopard." Jonas suggested enthusiastically as he turned to face her. "This muddy pool is absolutely full of them."

"Right." Leah immediately agreed as she nodded her head.

A small net was swiftly plucked from one of Jonas's many waistcoat pockets and as Leah began to watch him in total awe, she noticed that he quickly walked towards a nearby tree and then grabbed a branch that was within easy reach that hung down low enough to actually be held onto. Once a long thick stick had been snapped off the first branch, a vine that hung down from a second branch which was also within quite easy reach was then swiftly torn from its position just before Jonas proceeded to wrap the vine around both the net and the long thick stick and as he tied the three objects together, Leah could clearly see his attempts to make an actual fishing net.

"I should be able to catch a mudrattysnake with this net Leah." Jonas swiftly reassured her with a triumphant smile as he gave her a certain nod.

The brown liquid mud, Leah noticed, continued to swirl around as she watched Jonas secure the net to the stick rod more firmly as he tied the vine more tightly around the stick contraption just before he cast it into the large but shallow muddy pool. Since there wasn't very much that Leah could actually do to assist Jonas, she stood completely still in absolute silence as she continued to watch and wait patiently beside the edge of the liquid mud because she had no wish to disturb his focus and no desire at all to interrupt his efforts to catch an actual mudrattysnake which was a key prerequisite and a very essential element of their planned rescue mission.

Approximately five minutes went by as Leah continued to wait and as the two stood by the muddy pool in complete silence, Leah watched in curious fascination as Jonas scraped the makeshift fishing net through the mud which seemed to be his main strategy when it came to capture of the required creature. During that time, since Leah had no actual fishing net herself as Jonas sifted through the mud and filtered the liquid dirt, she remained in the same spot in total silence because as she had already realized and fully accepted, she really couldn't assist Jonas until the mudrattysnake had been successfully captured and so to distract him now, would simply prolong their plan of action and delay it even further.

"Leah, can you grab a small rock for me please?" Jonas suddenly asked as he began to pull the net out of the liquid mud.

"Sure Jonas." Leah rapidly agreed as she eagerly started to visually scan the grungy floor around her in search of a rock.

Fortunately for Leah, in just a matter of seconds, she managed to spot a small rock nearby which she then quickly made her way towards and once she had collected the rock from the ground and as soon as she had it safely in her possession, she rushed back to Jonas's side and then handed the rock to him.

"Thanks." Jonas said appreciatively as he clasped onto the rock and then bent down towards the ground.

Another couple of minutes went by as Leah watched Jonas tip the mudrattysnake out of the net onto the ground beside him and as he did so, she noticed that the creature still wriggled around because it still appeared to be very much alive. Just a few seconds later, much to Leah's surprise, the rock was put to good use as Jonas thumped the mudrattysnake with it a few times until the creature lay still and lifeless upon the grungy ground and then he nodded his head in what appeared to be satisfaction since as Leah already knew, the first part of his plan had been successfully achieved.

"Are you ready Leah?" Jonas asked as he quickly stood back up. "This will be the hardest part because now, we actually have to lure the dinoleopard away from the tree and then climb up the branches of it to rescue the baby dirtlizardillo."

"I think so Jonas." Leah replied as she gave him an eager but slightly uncertain nod.

"Right, let's go for a mud wade." Jonas joked as he prepared to head out across the muddy pool. "It's a bit less elegant than a swim but we should be okay."

Leah laughed. "True but what's a bit of mud for, if it's not for having a good wade in?" She teased playfully. "This is the Disgusting Dimension after all."

"Now that is a very valid point Leah." Jonas agreed as he stepped into the mud and then enthusiastically started to wade through it. "If the Disgusting Dimension wasn't so disgusting, our rebel mission would be absolutely pointless."

Much to Leah's sheer relief, she rapidly discovered that the liquid mud actually only reached up to about the mid-point of her calf and that it didn't seem to get any deeper as she began to follow Jonas's lead and started to make her way towards where the tree was actually situated. Although the mud itself wasn't very deep however, Leah swiftly realized as she waded through the brown substance that it was still actually quite hard work because the liquid mud was slightly more stodgy and far more clingy than she had originally anticipated. However, the stodgy substance was at least, Leah noticed, still quite manageable and so within five minutes, the two had managed to arrive at the center of the expanse and beside the small earthy island.

Since Leah didn't have any actual bait for the dinoleopard, she hung back slightly as she began to watch Jonas approach the foot of the tree and then as he threw the bait towards the other side of the tree, much to her total relief, she saw the dinoleopard rapidly spring into action. Just a few seconds later as Leah watched in nervous silence, the dinoleopard actually pounced on the lifeless carcass of the mudrattysnake and as the creature began to tear into the hybrid creature's remains, Jonas gently held onto Leah's arm and then swiftly guided her towards the foot of the tree.

Once the two arrived directly under the tree as they stood

beside the trunk, Leah began to silently inspect it to see if there was an easy way to climb up the trunk in order to reach the branches but from what she could see at first glance, there didn't appear to be any footholds of any kind. Much to Leah's surprise however, Jonas suddenly pulled some small pieces of rope and some nails from one of his pockets which he then began to attach to the tree to make footholds as he started to climb up the trunk.

"You need to start climbing up the tree now Leah." Jonas urged her as he paused for a moment. "We don't have that much time."

Leah nodded.

Some more nails and ropes were swiftly pushed into the tree trunk as Leah prepared to follow Jonas's lead and as she started to climb up the tree, she noticed that the rope rungs hung down slightly which made them easy to facilitate as footholds. Just a few minutes later, Leah arrived parallel to the vultger's nest and the branch that Jonas was perched upon as she did so, she instantly noticed that the baby dirtlizardillo had by that point, calmed down significantly and that as a result, the hybrid creature's cries of distress had now totally ceased.

Upon Jonas's face Leah could see that there was a warm smile as he immediately welcomed her to the branch and then quickly made a space for her to occupy beside him and as she sat down, Leah released a grateful sigh because at the very least, she had actually managed to arrive at the branch safely. For the next couple of minutes the two just sat next to each other upon the branch in total silence as Leah attempted to catch her breath but as she did so, she began to visually inspect the baby dirtlizardillo's form which was really rather cute in a strange reptilian kind of way which prompted her to offer the creature some gentle human strokes of reassurance. Some touches of warm human comfort were swiftly extended towards the baby dirtlizardillo as Leah placed one of her hands inside the nest and then began to run her fingers softly across the hybrid creature's scaly, armored shell as she attempted to comfort the small hybrid which was obviously terrified of the predatory creature that was less than a stone's throw away from their current position.

Suddenly however, Jonas began to spring into action and as Leah watched him start to embark upon the next part of his plan, she saw him scoop the baby dirtlizardillo out of the nest and then much to Leah's surprise, he actually placed the hybrid creature in her arms. Once the hybrid was safely nestled inside Leah's arms, she continued to watch Jonas as he rapidly plucked a transformation star from one of his many waistcoat pockets and a long piece of string which was fished out of another pocket and as Leah watched him implement the next part of his plan, one side of the golden star was quickly dowsed with tree sap.

For the next few minutes as Leah watched Jonas crawl onto another branch and then all the way along it, she stroked and comforted the baby dirtlizardillo as Jonas made his first actual attempt to transform the dinoleopard. Since the dinoleopard, much to Leah's total relief, still appeared to be quite busy with the food that it had been given from what she could see, Leah felt that the remainder of Jonas's plan would probably occur without any mishaps but that delivery really depended upon Jonas's aim and so, she watched him with baited breath because the prospect of the two human forms being stuck in the tree along with the baby dirtlizardillo did worry her.

When Jonas arrived above the dinoleopard's position, Leah held her breath as she watched him attempt to lower the transformation star down onto the creature's head via the piece of rope that it had been attached to. Fortunately for not just Leah but also for the baby dirtlizardillo, the star actually landed upon the dinoleopard's head and then actually stuck to it on Jonas's first attempt and as Leah watched that occur, she released a sigh of relief as she began to wait for the actual dinoleopard's transformation to start. A couple of seconds of stillness passed by before Leah started to see the dinoleopard's transformation start to occur and as the creature rapidly became much cleaner and far less disgusting, she observed that a dark grey suit now actually clothed the creature's frame.

Although the dinoleopard up until that point had been on all fours, suddenly the creature stood up on its hindlegs and as Leah watched in absolute astonishment, Jonas started to actually climb back down the tree and then even approached the dinoleopard. For a few seconds Leah just sat and listened as the two began to engage in what sounded like an actual civilized conversation before she started to make an attempt to climb back down the tree herself which was slightly trickier then her ascent due to the fact that she now had the actual baby dirtlizardillo in one of her arms.

Just after Leah landed upon the ground which was at least five minutes later, she spotted an adult dirtlizardillo at one side of the expanse and as the hybrid creature began to make its way towards the earthy island and waded through the muddy pool, Leah prepared to return the baby dirtlizardillo to the adult hybrid's parental care. Since Jonas appeared to be on a mission to transform any creatures in the Disgusting Dimension that he could possibly find as soon as the adult dirtlizardillo drew close to the tree, Leah watched in amused fascination as Jonas swiftly approached the hybrid creature and then began to transform the dirtlizardillo via another golden transformation star. Once the actual transformation was well underway, Leah smiled as Jonas strode towards her position with a smile upon his face as she prepared to part ways with the baby dirtlizardillo which by that point, she had actually become rather fond off and quite attached to.

"Right Leah, now that everyone's cleaned up, you better return that baby to its own species." Jonas advised.

"Yes Jonas, I'll do that now." Leah swiftly agreed as she started to walk towards the adult dirtlizardillo. "Are they definitely related?" She asked as she suddenly paused for a second and turned to face him.

"I think so but since that is a male dirtlizardillo, he must be the baby's father." Jonas replied.

A slightly sad expression crossed Leah's face as she arrived in front of the adult dirtlizardillo and then placed the baby down upon the earthy ground but as the two creatures instantly began to greet each other with amicable gestures, Leah began to smile as she watched the baby dirtlizardillo be reunited with its own kind. Much to Leah's amusement as the transformed adult dirtlizardillo attended to its adventurous youngster, a few words of caution were offered as the adult hybrid creature began to warn the baby of the dangers that lurked in the expanse which as Leah already knew, were definitely to be feared because she feared some of the creatures that she'd seen in the Disgusting Dimension herself and she was an adult.

"You really shouldn't wander off like that Dill." The adult dirtlizardillo insisted in a cross voice. "The Swamps of Mischief are full of danger; your mother will be very cross."

After a few minutes had been spent in polite conversation with Jonas, who the adult dirtlizardillo thanked with what seemed to be the utmost sincerity, Leah watched as the hybrid creature lifted Dill onto his back after which point, the two began to leave the expanse. Since the baby dirtlizardillo rescue mission had by that point been fully achieved, Jonas smiled as he gently took Leah's arm and then began to lead her towards an exit and as the two left the expanse and stepped into the entrance of an earthy tunnel, Leah released a huge sigh of relief. The wild dinoleopard had really intimidated Leah and so she had been truly put through her paces in terms of courage, especially when she had been in close proximity to the hybrid prior to its transformation and during her climb up the tree, just for a moment, she had even feared that she might fall out of the tree and land straight in the creature's jaws herself.

The Slimy Rescue from a River of Misery

The exit tunnel that had been chosen by Jonas from several exit points around the expanse had led the two directly into another muddy, earthy tunnel and as Leah walked along its interior beside Jonas, they ventured further along it until they arrived at an intersection which had six more earthy tunnel entrances to choose from. For a few seconds as Leah watched Jonas inspect the earthy entrances, she hung back slightly until he started to walk towards the tunnel entrance on the very right-hand side before she continued to follow him as she allowed him to lead the way, since she had absolutely no idea which tunnel entrance lead to anywhere.

The exit tunnel that had been chosen by Jonas from several exit points around the expanse had led the two directly into another muddy, earthy tunnel and as Leah walked along its interior beside Jonas, they ventured further along it until they arrived at an intersection which had six more earthy tunnel entrances to choose from. For a few seconds as Leah watched Jonas inspect the earthy entrances, she hung back slightly until he started to walk towards the tunnel entrance on the very right-hand side before she continued to follow him as she allowed him to lead the way, since she had absolutely no idea which tunnel entrance lead to anywhere.

Once the second tunnel had been entered into by the two, Leah continued to walk alongside Jonas until they arrived at a huge rocky underground cave which unlike the swampy expanse that they had just left behind, contained absolutely no foliage or any other signs of wildlife inside it. However, the very large, quite circular rocky cave which was almost the size of a small park did contain one thing, Leah rapidly noticed and that was a huge slimy river that ran through the center of it and this particular river of slime, she observed as she glanced at it, certainly didn't look very peaceful. In fact, this slimy river differed vastly from the first slimy river that Leah had come across because it appeared to be very aggressive, extremely chaotic and rather volatile since the dark green, brownish liquid swished, churned and whirled through the interior of the cave in angry, churlish waves.

Although the rocky hard cave wall surfaces should have been a stony grey which was instantly apparent to Leah from some visible patches of rock, she could also clearly see that some of the slimy waves had crashed against some of the large rocks that littered the slime river's path which had made those rocky walls a dark greenish brown in many places. So much so in fact that the muddy, slime splatters were so frequent upon the rocky surfaces that it almost felt to Leah as she visually inspected the rocky cave walls as if the cave had been given some kind of decor by the slimy river via those slimy collisions, albeit a rather filthy, mucky form of decor.

A more thorough visual inspection was swiftly conducted as Leah began to analyze her surroundings as she attempted to work out how the two were supposed to cross the slimy river or get around it because it was highly likely as Leah could see that the exit to the cave lay on the other side of that slimy river. Although no exit point could be seen in the cave walls closest to Leah's current position however, another quick visual inspection was rapidly conducted as she attempted to ensure that she hadn't missed something which might allow both Jonas and herself to avoid the angry slime river's path completely. Unfortunately, however, Leah could see no actual exit from the cave on that side of its large interior as she silently scanned the rocky cave walls closest to her and the slimy river looked totally uncrossable, from what she could see, so there appeared to be no immediate answers to be found from her visual search.

Much to Leah's surprise however, just a second or two later as she turned her focus solely back to the slimy river and began to visually examine the slime that gushed through the cave's interior as she stood just a few steps away from the edge of it, Leah suddenly noticed something else and that something else, unlike the slime, was actually, a simulated presence. Due to a sudden movement and some cries that the simulated entity had made which had managed to catch Leah's attention somehow through all the slime crashes and splatters which were really quite noisy, quite surprisingly, Leah had actually noticed that someone or something was stuck in the midst of all that slime but who or what exactly was stuck, she couldn't actually tell from her current position.

"Is that a person or a hybrid creature Jonas?" Leah asked him in a whisper as she quickly turned to face him and then pointed towards the source of the movement and cries.

"I'm not sure yet." Jonas replied as he leant forward and to one side as he tried to visually establish the identity of the mysterious entity. "It could be either."

For the next couple of minutes Leah moved around slightly as she leant in several different directions to get a better view and after some further intense visual inspection, she finally arrived at the conclusion that in the very center of the angry, slimy river, upon that rocky pedestal, there appeared to be a hybrid form of some kind. Since the angry brownish green slime seemed to decorate every inch of the hybrid's form, it was hard for Leah at first glance to see exactly what kind of hybrid creation was situated upon the rocky pedestal but from what she could ascertain, after some more visual inspection and a few more cries had been heard, the hybrid was definitely female. A couple more minutes slipped by as Leah stood beside Jonas and continued to survey her surroundings but it almost felt to Leah as if the hybrid entity hadn't even noticed the arrival of the two simulated human forms, since they appeared to be very focused upon some kind of injury or upset and quite naturally, the aggressive, chaotic, angry river of muddy slime that surrounded, crashed and flowed all around them.

Some more lamentful cries were heard through the crashes of slime and even some hurtful sobs in-between each slimy wave and rocky collision and so, Leah quickly tried to ascertain if there was any other immediate danger apart from the very obvious and chaotic slimy river as she took a few more steps towards the edge of the slimy river itself. A few of the cries that Leah heard almost sounded like a very sad ballad as she drew closer to the edge of the muddy bank and there seemed to be an almost musical lilt to each expression of pain and hurt but as yet Leah could see no way across the actual muddy slime but as she inspected the river from the very edge of the bank, much to her total relief, Jonas rapidly joined her.

"How do you think she got stuck in the middle of all that slime Jonas?" Leah asked.

"I'm not sure yet but I do know one thing for absolute certain now, she is definitely Rhiannon, the Fairymingo Queen." Jonas swiftly replied. "She does seem to be stuck though, so she'll be glad that we're here."

"How will we reach her to rescue her from all that slime?" Leah asked.

"You'll probably have to find a way to cross the slime via the rocks Leah that's the only way I can see from here. Some of the rocks do jut out above the slime, so it might just be possible." Jonas suggested. "But this river does look like it might be a slimy river of misery, so you'll have to be careful when you try to cross it."

"We're probably going to get drenched in slime ourselves Jonas. I just hope I don't fall into it." Leah mentioned. "And why did you call it a slimy river of misery?" She asked.

"I hope you don't too because slimy rivers of misery can be very hard to escape from because they are made from total misery." Jonas explained as he began to shake his head. "First of all, if you fall into the flow of the slime, you'll be drenched in absolute misery which will then weigh you down so that your limbs become clogged up after which point, you'll hardly be able to move." He continued. "And once you are demobilized by the slime of misery, you might then be swept away by the slime and the misery it contains, so you could end up stuck in any part of the Disgusting Dimension and totally lost. Trust me Leah, a slimy river of misery is no laughing matter and since the misery consumes anyone that the slime touches as you can see from Rhiannon, you wouldn't even be able to help yourself."

A glum expression crossed Leah's face as she began to nod because the slimy river and the waves of slime that crashed against each rock, certainly didn't look very friendly and Jonas had implied that she would have to face that river of slime alone.

"That sounds bad, really bad." Leah replied. "Do I have to

cross the slimy river on my own Jonas?"

"It's definitely bad because you could end up anywhere and it might take me hours just to find you again." Jonas agreed. "And yes, you will have to cross the slimy river of misery alone because I have to stay here to keep this mud bank intact with some bags of joy, or you won't even be able to return to it never mind actually be able to rescue Rhiannon."

"Really?" Leah asked.

"Really because with every minute that goes by, the slimy river of misery rises and that tide of swampy misery will at some point, start to erode the muddy banks that we are now situated upon." Jonas insisted. "Which means, I'll have to stay on this side of the river to sprinkle particles of joy across the edge of the riverbank to keep the slime of misery at bay until you return."

"You mean this slime rises?" Leah asked in an alarmed tone.

"It definitely does." Jonas swiftly confirmed.

Some silent seconds went by as Leah internally waded into and then began to wallow in her own fear as she glanced at the chaotic river of slime directly in front of her because there now appeared to be very little bravery inside her simulated form that she could clutch onto and no planks of courageous confidence or certainty seemed to exist inside her mind either to walk safely across. Just as Leah was about to indulge in an act of total cowardice and back away however, a few more tearful cries were heard which compelled her to at least try and find some planks of bravery inside her own mind to inwardly step onto and to bravely step out with. A few nervous fears were bravely crushed inside Leah's mind as she glanced into the depths of the slime and then began to inspect the rocky stepping stone path ahead of her which as she already knew and could quite easily predict, would be very difficult to cross because the mass of slime that looked almost alive, certainly wouldn't welcome her human simulated presence and if anything, would definitely try to consume her.

"Okay Jonas." Leah replied with a decisive nod. "I'll just try to figure out a safe route across the rocks." She rapidly clarified as she began to visually map out a possible route. "I can see that some of the rocks do have slightly flatter surfaces, so it might just be possible for me to utilize those rocks as actual stepping stones."

"That's the spirit Leah but you'll need to do that quite quickly because the slimy river of misery will continue to rise and it will erode the mud with every minute that goes by which will then make it more difficult for you to return safely, once you've actually rescued Rhiannon." Jonas advised. "This muddy bank won't remain untouched for very much longer because I can only keep the slimy misery at bay for so long."

"Okay. I think, I hope." Leah said as she began to nervously process his response which as she was fully aware, required immediate action on her part.

"Don't worry though Leah, I'll still be here." Jonas swiftly reassured her as he smiled. "So, if you need me urgently, you can just give me a shout."

Just a second or two after Jonas had finished the delivery of his verbal reassurances, Leah noticed that he fished a black velvet, pouch bag of joy from one of his trouser pockets and that he then swiftly started to proceed with his planned task. The implementation of Jonas's actual plan prompted Leah to actually face her journey across the slimy river of misery as it compelled her to act but no part of Leah's simulated form felt confident as she glanced out across the slime and then began to take her first shaky, nervous step forward onto the first rocky stepping stone. Before Leah stepped out onto the second stepping stone however, she nervously gave the stepping stone route that she had mapped out a quick recheck and as Leah tried to calculate the actual distances more accurately between the flatter rocks that littered the slimy river, she hoped that her estimations had been accurate so that she would not end up stranded upon a rock like Rhiannon.

Nothing but total nerves and absolute fear seemed to occupy Leah's thoughts and those negative emotions seemed to be her only true companions as she began to make her way across a few more rocks and some more slime but as she went, her bones seemed to rattle away inside of her form. A viable alternative choice was just not available to Leah at that time because to back out and return to the muddy bank alone, would just make her look like a total coward in Jonas's sight and so that was the last thing that Leah wanted to do and although her heart seemed to beat a hundred times faster than usual, Leah tried to dig deep within herself to find some strands of bravery to grasp and to hold onto as she prepared to continue.

Another quite jagged rock was bravely approached by Leah's foot as she attempted to place her foot in a place of safety and fortunately, her foot was met with some stability, despite the very rocky appearance and extremely jagged nature of that fifth stony step. However, as Leah stepped onto the fifth stepping stone more fully, she began to tremble with fear because the fifth rock really was a lot more jagged than the first four had been and so that fifth stepping stone had definitely pushed her courage to the absolute brink.

After ten more rocky stepping stones had been bravely conquered which fortunately for Leah, weren't any rockier than the fifth rocky stepping stone had been, she released a sigh of total relief because she had finally stepped onto a stepping stone that was slightly larger and one that was also within arm's length of Rhiannon's current position. Quite awkwardly however, as Leah stood upon that fifteenth rocky stepping stone, she noticed that for a few seconds the Fairymingo Queen remained completely silent, even though Leah felt almost certain that Rhiannon had by that point, actually noticed both her presence and her arrival.

"I'm here to help you Rhiannon, if I can." Leah quickly reassured her as she stretched out an arm towards her. "I'm Leah."

"Thank you, Leah, it isn't very often that I need help from anyone but today, I definitely do because quite strangely, I've found myself in a position of great weakness." Rhiannon replied as she began to nod and then stretched out an arm towards her.

Despite the Fairymingo Queen's predicament, Leah noticed that her tone was very gracious, extremely respectful and immensely appreciative and so, Leah quickly gripped onto Rhiannon's arm and then began to gently pull the Fairymingo Queen towards her position as swiftly but as carefully as she could. Fortunately for both parties, Leah found that the slimy substance that surrounded Rhiannon didn't seem to obstruct their passage as she pulled the Fairymingo Queen quite easily across it and once Rhiannon had reached the side of the rocky stepping stone, Leah quickly leant down and then utilized both her arms to pull the Fairymingo Queen up on to the rock.

Every part of Leah's form sighed with relief as just a few seconds later the Fairymingo Queen clambered up onto the rocky stepping stone beside Leah and as Rhiannon joined her, a smile of satisfaction crossed Leah's face because now she had at least, achieved the first part of her rescue mission. Although Leah began to relax a little as she started to prepare herself for the return journey, she also still kept in mind that there was an actual return journey to embark upon which meant that her rescue mission was far from over since that return journey across the slimy river of misery had not yet even begun.

"We have to step across the rocks Rhiannon." Leah explained. "It's the only safe way to cross the slimy river."

"Right." Rhiannon immediately agreed. "I'll follow your lead."

From what Leah could see at first glance as she started to brave the rocky stepping stones once again and Rhiannon began to follow her, the Fairymingo Queen appeared to have two large, silvery, pinkish feathery wings but they were barely even visible due to the muddy slime that caked her entire frame. Unlike the rocky walls which were decorated in spatters of muddy slime, Leah observed that the Fairymingo Queen was completely drenched in the slimy substance and that every part of her form seemed totally saturated which worried Leah slightly because she feared that Rhiannon might slip back into the slimy river, if she didn't offer her a non-slippery, slime free simulated arm of support.

Fortunately for Leah however, as she began to assist Rhiannon politely and courteously for most of the return trip there were no actual slippages but just as the two approached the final rocky step, the Fairymingo Queen almost fell back into the slime as Rhiannon suddenly misplaced her footing. Since Leah was still actually upon the final rocky step when that unfortunate incident occurred, luckily, she was able to grab onto Rhiannon's arm before the Fairymingo

Queen actually slipped off the final rocky step completely and once Leah had a firm grip on Rhiannon's arm, the Fairymingo Queen was swiftly pulled back up to a position of safety and stability quite quickly. However, Leah's response as she was fully aware had been very hectic and extremely disorganized because she really hadn't expected Rhiannon to slip at the very last hurdle and certainly hadn't expected anything to go wrong so close to the muddy bank of safety.

Once the two finally stepped off the final rock and back on to the safety of the muddy bank, Leah released a relieved sigh as she started to visually search for Jonas and not more than a few seconds later, much to Leah's sheer relief, she suddenly spotted him as Jonas speedily began to rush over towards their position. Due to the Fairymingo Queen's weakened, slime caked state, Leah instantly noticed as she turned back to face Rhiannon that the Fairymingo Queen had actually sat down upon the muddy bank but thankfully, Leah swiftly observed, Jonas seemed to have planned for every eventuality as she watched him pull another bag of joy out of another one of his many pockets as he drew closer to them both.

"Fortunately for you Rhiannon, I still have a bag of joy left." Jonas rapidly confirmed as he glanced down at her, smiled and then swiftly opened up the bag of joy. "Whatever are you doing here though? How did you of all people get stuck in a slimy river of misery?"

A smile crossed Leah's face as she began to watch Jonas at work in total fascination and awe because he seemed to instinctively know with absolute certainty which remedy was applicable to each and every situation that they had come across so far. Not even a single discussion had taken place with any of the hybrid creatures that they had encountered prior to the application of his remedies, yet Jonas seemed to know exactly what to do in any given situation and that impressed Leah tremendously because so often in real life, she doubted herself and lacked the confidence that Jonas definitely appeared to possess in abundance.

"I was attacked by a dinobeast Jonas and injured in midair after which point, I fell down into a slimy slide which led straight into this slimy river then I was carried all the way down here and I couldn't even escape because this muddy slime seems to be a liquid source of misery." Rhiannon replied as she released a dismayed sigh. "The misery started to stick to every part of me and it even clogged up my wings then I became so weighed down by that misery that I could hardly even move."

Everything about the Fairymingo Queen looked extremely delicate as Leah glanced at her frame and then began to visually inspect her form more closely and although she looked very slender, Leah suddenly noticed that she also seemed really rather tall. However, due to all the muddy slime that caked and weighed down Rhiannon's frame, Leah noticed that she currently seemed unable to stand for very long which indicated that she was in a very weak state indeed. Some long, silvery, pinkish strands of hair, Leah swiftly observed, appeared to surround and crown her face but because of the muddy clumps and strings of slime that clung onto every strand, those matted clumps were barely even recognizable as actual hair.

"Can you access your fairy powers?" Jonas asked.

"No, I can't Jonas because the muddy slime is all over my wings. My powers emanate from my wings and the muddy slime is very heavy." Rhiannon explained as she shook her head. "Can you help at all Jonas?"

Jonas nodded. "I certainly can." He replied.

"I must have fallen into a slimy river of misery." Rhiannon concluded as she glanced at the slime river with an expression of total disgust. "Usually, slime rivers would be no match for me but this slimy river must be full of absolute misery which is probably why I was totally demobilized."

"Yes, I think so too, this slimy, angry, muddy river does look like a slimy river of misery which is really quite common in the Disgusting Dimension." Jonas agreed as he enthusiastically began to scoop some golden particles from the interior of the black velvet, pouch bag which then started to wriggle around inside his hands. "But don't worry Rhiannon, I've come well prepared and, in this instance, my bag of joy will be a very effective tool because it can eradicate any misery in seconds."

Just a few seconds later as Jonas drew closer to the Fairymingo Queen, Leah noticed that a sigh of relief seemed to be released from Rhiannon's beaky mouth as he eagerly began to sprinkle some particles of joy over the Fairymingo Queen's form. Once a few handfuls of joy had been generously sprinkled over Rhiannon, Leah watched Jonas in total fascination as he quickly plucked a golden transformation star from one of his trouser pockets and then placed it upon the Fairymingo Queen's head.

The actual transformation itself was really quite speedy and Leah noticed that it took less than a minute to actually occur and so, for the first time since their arrival in the rocky cave, Leah finally saw Rhiannon in her natural hybrid state which was truly a wonderful, beautiful sight to behold. Every single inch of the Fairymingo Queen, Leah now observed, seemed to sparkle, glisten and shine with a silvery, pinkish glow and each speck of dirt had completely vanished right before Leah's very own eyes and since all of the slimy misery had totally disappeared, the flamingo fairy hybrid now looked utterly spectacular, absolutely immaculate and flawlessly spotless.

"Thank you, Jonas." Rhiannon announced triumphantly as she began to enthusiastically inspect her form. "Now, I feel like myself again."

"No problem Rhiannon that's what I'm here for to lend a helping hand when and where I can. I barely even recognized you at first with all that slimy misery all over you." Jonas admitted as he smiled. "But now you've been fully restored to your former self and to your former glory."

"Yes, and so now I can return to my people, who will no doubt be wondering where I am." Rhiannon swiftly concluded.

Much to Leah's surprise and delight, just a few seconds later, Rhiannon suddenly spread her large silvery, pinkish wings and then flew up into the air and as the Fairymingo Queen twirled around above the heads of the two human forms and started to dance for joy in mid-flight, Leah watched in absolute delight as Rhiannon began to happily celebrate her restoration. The downcast expressions, Leah observed, had definitely flown away as Rhiannon had not only flown up into the air but also risen to her former glory and each remnant of sadness it appeared had fully abandoned her now beautiful form, chased away and replaced by the sparkles of happiness that now radiated from within her simulacrum being. A joyful smile now adorned Rhiannon's face along with the sparkles of happiness that emanated from her form, both of which Leah noticed, seemed to silently decorate the cave with a lavish warmth as the cave's interior suddenly began to sparkle and shine in harmonious unison.

"You even make that filthy, slimy misery look slightly less disgusting Rhiannon." Jonas teased.

"I'd better return to my people now Jonas but we will forever be in your debt because I doubt that any of the other fairymingoes would have been able to find me in that slimy river of misery." Rhiannon acknowledged as she paused for a moment and glanced down at him. "The muddy slime in those rivers and streams is full of total misery, so it usually blocks all our sensory abilities which means, I might have been stuck inside this cave forever if you two hadn't come along."

"Don't worry about it Rhiannon, it's just a part of our mission to save anyone that we can from the disgustingness of the Disgusting Dimension." Jonas replied.

"Still Jonas, I'd like to give you both a gift, it's a special fairy blessing." Rhiannon insisted. "May your lives be long, productive and peaceful." She announced as she suddenly twirled around and a mass of particles formed from silvery, pink fairy dust fell from her wings which landed directly upon the two human forms below her.

Suddenly a silver, pinkish burst of light and some very bright particles filled the entire interior of the cave and just a few seconds later as the very bright burst of light began to fade, Leah noticed that much to her total astonishment, Rhiannon had completely disappeared. The silvery, pinkish sparkles of dust that remained however, didn't seem to offer any kind of explanation as to Rhiannon's disappearance as they fell silently to the ground but a warm sense of peace did seem to linger inside Leah's simulated form as she began to accept and process the very sudden, rather abrupt departure of the Fairymingo Queen.

"She didn't really say goodbye to us Jonas." Leah mentioned as she grinned at him. "Well, I guess she did say that she had to return to her people now and so, I guess that now, really meant now."

Jonas laughed. "Fairymingoes don't usually indulge in many pleasantries Leah." He explained. "They come, they go, they're not always the most social of creatures plus you have to remember, she is also a queen, so she has her whole hybrid species to lead and to attend to."

"She disappeared very quickly." Leah replied with an amused smile.

"Yes, Rhiannon's magical fairy powers are actually contained within her feathery wings, so once the slimy misery no longer restricted her movements or her powers, she could then leave in an instant." Jonas rapidly clarified. "Fairymingoes are magical beings, so they can do many special things that would be absolutely impossible for anyone else because a fairymingo's wings contain the magic possibility of any impossibility."

"Well, now that we've saved the Fairymingo Queen, where should we go next?" Leah asked.

"Let's go to my house to eat some dinner and on the way, we can perform a tunnel sweep." Jonas suggested. "Then when we arrive at my cottage, perhaps we can explore our social etiquette more thoroughly and if there's enough time, I'll even give you some personal one on one lessons.

Leah laughed. "Now that sounds like a well-tailored plan and an ultra-tidy idea that suits me right down to the ground." She agreed.

"Yes, the hunt for disgusting creatures to free from the disgusting grunge of the Disgusting Dimension can continue tomorrow." Jonas concluded as he dipped his hand into one of his waistcoat pockets and then began to fumble around as he started to search for a device. "Right, now that we've agreed on a plan of action, I'll need my Disgusting Dimension creature detector and hygiene zapper device to clear our path." He confirmed as he swiftly plucked a device from his pocket.

Upon Leah's face there was an amused smile as Jonas placed

his arm gently on her own and then began to lead her towards the rocky cave wall closest to them which he began to scan with the device until it beeped. Once Jonas had seemingly identified the relevant part of the wall, much to Leah's sheer surprise, he then leant upon a part of it and the rocky wall instantly slide backwards.

"Since this device finds hybrid creatures, it's therefore only logical that some should be quite close to any exit point." Jonas explained.

Beyond the large rocky circular hole, Leah noticed that there appeared to be another earthy tunnel and so as she stepped inside it and then continued to follow Jonas's lead further along it, she noticed that he held the creature detector and hygiene zapper device firmly in his hand as he walked. For the next few minutes as Leah walked peacefully alongside Jonas the two discussed the various hybrid creatures that occupied the Disgusting Dimension some of which she had already encountered that day and as they walked and talked, Leah noticed that Jonas kept his eyes firmly on the path ahead of them as he appeared to constantly visually scan their surroundings for any hybrid creatures.

Approximately another five minutes went by with no creature interruptions or hybrid clashes, Leah noticed as the two continued to walk along the earthy tunnel and as they did so, Jonas held Leah's attention firmly by the hand as he verbally related to her some of his past experiences with some of the creatures in the Disgusting Dimension. Some of the hybrid creatures that Jonas mentioned, Leah hadn't actually seen so far that day like swampliongators but as she listened attentively to each descriptive, she winced with disgust because every creature that he described sounded absolutely foul and disgustingly awful which made Leah appreciate the rather cute humabears even more despite their animalistic appetite for the raw intestines of slimebattymice.

The earthy tranquility around the two however, Leah noticed, didn't last for very long as they suddenly arrived at the end of the tunnel which led directly into another large expanse that appeared to contain a slimy, muddy swamp with a rather rickety looking wooden bridge which ran all the way across it. From what Leah could see at first glance, the swampy expanse contained at least fifty hybrid creatures inside it and it literally crawled with disgusting animalistic entities, most of which Leah could recognize but there were some that she had definitely never ever seen before. A few swampliongators, Leah swiftly observed, definitely appeared to be present that were dotted around the swampy area which she could identify from Jonas's verbal earlier descriptive that slide in and out of the swampy liquid that ran under the rickety bridge from some of the firmer muddier mounds that sporadically decorated parts of the slimy swamp in some places, the sight of which sent fearful shivers up Leah's spine.

"Okay Leah, now we have to cross this shaky bridge and as we walk across it we have to zap everything that we can on the way then once we get to the other side, we have to follow another tunnel." Jonas instructed as he gave her a certain nod. "Inside that tunnel we'll then have to perform a tunnel sweep while we venture along it because the creatures from this swamp can get into that tunnel and so they often do venture inside it. So, you'll definitely need a creature detector and hygiene zapper device too." He insisted as he handed her the device in his hand and then began to rummage around inside his waistcoat pocket for another one.

"Does this device do the same thing as a transformation star Jonas?" Leah asked.

"No, not quite." Jonas rapidly clarified as he plucked a second device from his pocket. "This device just scrubs up any target that it hits and it also blocks any animalistic tendencies or attacks that they might present for a while because the Disgusting Dimension tends to bring out the worst in those who occupy it, so the zaps just block that worse for a while. However, this device doesn't actually possess the capacity or capabilities to actually transform any disgusting hybrids into civilized, decently dressed, well-mannered entities."

"How do you actually utilize it Jonas, it looks rather complex?" Leah asked.

"You just aim the device at the target of disgust like this Leah and then you press this button to zap the target." Jonas explained as he held his device up in front of her and gave a quick mock visual demonstration. "Within seconds, any hybrid entity that this device zaps will not only be cleaned up but also a lot more docile."

"Okay but is that bridge actually safe to walk across because it doesn't really look that secure?" Leah asked as she began to visually inspect the shaky, rickety wooden bridge, the start of which now sat just a few steps away from their current position.

"Well, occasionally some wooden planks do fall out of it and as you can see it is tied to some tree branches, so in the past one or two have been known to snap but it's the only bridge around which means, it is the only choice that we have right now, if we want to cross the swamp in reasonably safe way. The only other alternative we have, would be to cross the swamp via the swampy ground and that would be far riskier." Jonas confirmed. "Which also means that for now, the bridge will just have to do. I did plan to renovate the entire bridge at some point but the implementation of such a plan would require effort from more than just myself, so I'll have to plan that renovation with the rest of the rebel group."

"I'm not really very good with heights." Leah nervously confessed.

"Don't worry about it Leah, I'll be right next to you." Jonas cheerfully reassured her. "So, you won't fall of the bridge because if I see you slip or a wooden plank fall, I'll help you straight away."

"That's if you see me slip on time." Leah replied.

"Seriously, I'm a very alert rescuer." Jonas insisted confidently. "Nobody has ever fallen off this bridge before when I've been around, so you're in extremely capable arms and very safe hands. Right, now we'd better make a start, or we'll never get to my cottage."

"Okay." Leah agreed as she nodded her head.

In the back of Leah's throat, she could feel a nervous lump of fear that seemed to have silently gathered and collated but she tried her best to swallow that nervous accumulation of fearful doubts as a few cautious steps forward were taken. Unlike Jonas's confident, brave, large strides as he walked towards the start of the rickety bridge, Leah's steps were much slower, far more nervous and much smaller as she continued to follow his lead and quite reluctantly prepared to cross the actual bridge.

At least a hundred shaky planks of wood had been strapped together, albeit in a rather loose fashion from what Leah could see and so as she began to cross the wooden contraption, she hoped that the ropes of courage that tied her thoughts to her movements would also remain intact and stable as she ventured across it. A few planks of stability, bravery and determination had been positioned very carefully inside Leah's mind in order to prepare for her walk across the bridge but as she already knew, those planks could quite easily fall apart, if the planks of wood began to make a sudden departure from the bridge due to the hungry hybrid creatures below it which definitely evoked and stirred up whirlwinds of fear within her interior.

Unfortunately for Leah, she had by that point noticed that most of the hybrid creatures in the swampy area didn't seem to discriminate when it came to the actual issue of food consumption because they seemed to bite, attack and snack on each other without any prejudice at all as she watched their hungry antics as she walked in absolute fear. Due to the hybrid creature's lack of discrimination when it came to the issue of consumables, a definite worry lurked inside Leah's mind which pricked her thoughts that felt absolutely certain that if she fell off the bridge into that swampy mud then she too would be eagerly snacked upon just as swiftly and just as eagerly as any of the hybrid creatures and that worry slightly undermined her quite brave attempts to tackle the flimsy wooden structure.

"Remember Leah, we have to zap as many hybrid creatures as we can as we cross the bridge, just in case." Jonas advised as he suddenly paused then turned to face her. "The creatures that can fly might swoop down onto our heads and then flap attack us, so they are equally as dangerous because if you try to defend yourself from their attacks, you then run the risk of an actual departure from the bridge, if they manage to destabilize you. So, keep your zapper on full alert at all times."

Leah nodded.

Despite Jonas's comprehensive instructions, confident

reassurances and the zapper device that he had provided, Leah couldn't help but feel nervous as their walk across the bridge began and several hybrid creatures swiftly swooped down towards the two as they walked which certainly didn't do anything to reduce those nerves. However, as Jonas had recommended Leah kept the zapper on full alert as she took a few more brave steps across the shaky wooden contraption and much to Leah's absolute surprise, she actually managed to successfully zap a slimebattymouse as she walked. An immediate small spark of warm comfort seemed to gently ignite inside Leah as she basked in that little victory which instantly provided her with a dash of reassurance that perhaps the walk across the remainder of the bridge might not actually be as fearful as she had first anticipated it might be and that small victory seemed to reduce her nerves, albeit quite slightly.

For approximately the next five minutes Leah continued to follow Jonas's lead as they walked across the first half of the bridge without too many problems but as they walked, she noticed that a few planks of wood shook under her feet which definitely created an undercurrent of fear that flowed all the way through her interior. When the two arrived at the midpoint of the bridge, much to Leah's absolute horror, a plank that she had just stepped onto suddenly began to shake below her feet and then rather horrifyingly, the plank actually slipped out of place after which point, it rapidly began to make a downward descent.

Due to Leah's total shock a sudden, very loud shriek managed to escape from her lips as Leah frantically tried to grab onto anything that she could in an attempt to stabilize herself in order to avoid her own departure from the bridge but her body and hands trembled as she did so in absolute fear. In no way, shape or form did Leah wish to follow that particular plank's downward journey and so she desperately clutched on to some of the ropes that now hung down from the bridge that had been tied around the departed plank prior to its departure as she attempted to avoid not only a dip in the swampy waters that sat below her but also and even more importantly, the jaws of a hungry hybrid creature.

Although the wooden plank had already departed and was now

absolutely irreparable because from what Leah could see, it had fallen straight into the swampy waters below the bridge, she clung onto the tattered ropes that remained as tightly as she could in the hope that assistance was on the way. For a few nervous seconds Leah almost felt as if she was going to fall off the bridge completely as she tried to regain her composure and clung onto the now stringy ropes with all the tenacity and determination that she could muster but her whole body was no longer actually on the bridge anymore which truly alarmed her.

Since Leah's legs and lower torso now actually hung and dangled below the wooden contraption itself, Leah definitely feared that the rest of her form would soon follow suit and that it would just be a matter of minutes before she too would be immersed in the swampy waters below her. The fallen wooden plank as Leah cast a quick, nervous glance downwards was barely even visible anymore and was almost fully immersed in the swampy waters which worried her even more because if she fell, then she would fall straight into those swampy waters herself which would then make the likelihood of being snacked upon by hungry hybrids a highly probable outcome.

Fortunately, however, it rapidly transpired that Jonas had heard Leah's loud shriek, even though he had been at least a few planks in front of her and as she watched him suddenly, rapidly speed towards her, a sigh of total relief escaped from her lips. Once Jonas had lain down upon several of the wooden planks that still remained on one side of the gap, he swiftly offered Leah a helpful, strong, reliable arm and a firm grip as he made an attempt to assist her and so within a matter of minutes, Leah was quickly pulled back to safety and some kind of satisfactory stability. However, as Leah attempted to recover and tried to regain her composure once more upon a plank of the bridge that still remained, she was still fully aware as she stood back up and re-stabilized herself that the rickety bridge couldn't really offer her very much actual stability at all, purely due to its shoddy condition.

A few still seconds slipped by as Leah tried to catch her breath and as she thanked Jonas appreciatively, they both stood on the bridge once more beside each other as they prepared to cross the remainder of the rickety wooden contraption. The close shave that Leah had just experienced however, remained at the forefront of her thoughts as she stuck much closer to Jonas and zapped the hybrid creatures around them both more energetically as the two began to brave the remainder of the bridge.

Unfortunately, once the two arrived at the other side of the bridge and the earthy tunnel which apparently, lead to another junction and the tunnel that would lead them both to Jonas's cottage, Leah rapidly discovered that her hybrid creature battles were far from over. Inside that tunnel, much to Leah's absolute horror, there appeared to be a host of swampy, hybrid creatures because an earthy ramp led directly into the tunnel from the swampy area which provided the hybrid creatures with instant easy access to the tunnel's interior. From what Leah could see the tunnel itself, seemed to be just as populated as the swampy area which also therefore meant that their battle with the swamp's disgusting hybrids had unfortunately, only just begun.

However, as the two started to walk along the tunnel's interior, much to Leah's total relief, she swiftly discovered that Jonas appeared to possess a far more powerful laser ray device which he quickly mobilized and then prepared to operate. Once prepped, Leah watched in complete awe as Jonas aimed the laser ray device at the creatures of disgust which not only zapped them but also swept them quickly away as the hybrids were rapidly knocked further along the tunnel by the rays and then swiftly fled. Since Leah still had her zapper device in one of her hands, she enthusiastically supported Jonas's efforts as the two continued to walk along the populated earthy tunnel as he fired the laser and Leah complimented his efforts with some additional zaps as she walked alongside him.

Approximately the next fifteen minutes or so were spent in battle as Leah and Jonas zapped every hybrid creature that lay in their path and performed a tunnel sweep of cleanliness, so Leah felt really quite relieved when the two finally arrived at the earthy junction that apparently, was quite close to Jonas's cottage. An iron spiky gate guarded one of several tunnels that intersected at the junction and as Leah glanced at it, Jonas swiftly began to walk towards which rapidly confirmed to her that it was the actual tunnel that would lead directly to Jonas's home.

Once the two had stepped into the correct earthy tunnel and as they began to walk towards Jonas's abode which was not actually yet visible, Leah swiftly noticed that the tunnel's interior was much cleaner and far tidier than any of the others that they had walked along, since they had left the first underground cave. In fact, this tunnel's interior, Leah observed as the two travelled further along it, even had some concrete slabs that adorned the base of it and so the difference was immediately noticeable and very apparent. At least another ten minutes went by as Leah and Jonas walked further along the tunnel side by side and since no disgusting creatures littered the interior of the tunnel, Leah began to relax and the two even managed to make some light conversation as they walked.

At the end of the tunnel there was another large clearing but this clearing, Leah swiftly noticed as she stepped into it, definitely differed from the other expanses that she had visited so far inside the Disgusting Dimension because every inch of it looked organized, neat, mud free and slimeless. Not even a drip of slime or speck of mud seemed to be present from Leah could see as she released a sigh of relief and it actually looked quite homely and comfortable.

Some trees decorated the perimeter of the clearing and in the very center of it, Leah observed as she began to inspect her surroundings, there was a neat, compact cottage which nestled gently against the trees that sat around. A small concrete path led up to the door of the cottage which silently carved its way through some well-manicured gardens that sat on either side of it and directly in front of the compact but very tidy, residential structure, the sight of which immediately reassured Leah that there was absolutely nothing disgusting about Jonas's cottage or the clearing that it occupied.

Unlike the earthy, muddy browns, slimy greens and stony greys that Leah had been surrounded by so far in the Disgusting Dimension, this structure was a shiny white, so it glistened and shone as some rays of light from above the trees seeped into the clearing and bounced off its walls. The gardens that decorated either side of the stone path, much to Leah's delight, contained flowers with a multitude of petals that were full of bright vibrant reds, bold loud yellows, courageous fiery oranges, tranquil peaceful blues and there were even some deep dignified purples, all of which provided an instant visual treat to Leah's eyes. Since Leah had initially entered into and arrived inside Spectrum earlier that day, she had almost been fully immersed and totally saturated in grungy, mucky colors courtesy of swampy foliage, earthy tunnels and rocky caves that had been all around her which had contained nothing but grungy browns, slimy greens and dull stony greys and so the contents of the clearing were an absolute refreshment to her visual senses.

"Your cottage is absolutely amazing Jonas; did you build it yourself?" Leah asked as she verbally dug around for more information and further clarity as to the origins of the compact but beautiful structure which had genuinely impressed her. "After all that disgusting filth, it really is a visual treat."

"I did but it took a lot of hard work and a very long time." Jonas explained as he nodded his head. "It was definitely worth it in the end though because it's certainly not disgusting."

"It certainly isn't." Leah agreed wholeheartedly. "Anything but in fact, I'd even call it very impressive in this environment."

"Let's go inside then we can get cleaned up and have something good to eat." Jonas suggested.

Leah nodded.

Some bold steps were enthusiastically taken as Leah allowed Jonas to lead her towards the cottage and towards the front door of his home because unlike the mucky areas that littered the rest of the Disgusting Dimension, the stony path was clean, tidy and so, it looked like it would be a total joy to walk along. Since the path did not contain or host any mucky, hybrid creatures, Leah handed Jonas back the zapper as she began to walk along it because she felt peacefully reassured that she would no longer actually need it.

One small thing did puzzle Leah slightly however, as she

followed Jonas towards the door of the compact structure and that was the fact that she hadn't created any homes for any of the guides that existed inside Spectrum, so the cottage's existence was quite unusual because Jonas had built it himself. A definite question therefore arose in Leah's mind as to why the cottage itself was there in the first place because as far as she was aware, no simulated being actually, really needed a place to live, since they were purely fictitious in both nature and character but Jonas, rather intriguingly, had actually built his own home. However, as Leah walked, she silently began to dismiss her query as over analytical and totally unnecessary because on this occasion that question didn't really, have to be asked or even answered because it was far comfortable, just to enjoy its peaceful, pleasant existence and to welcome the joys that could be explored within the cottage's confines.

According to Leah's programmable commands, Spectrum as she already knew could actually generate some aspects of its own existence randomly from a given set of flexible variables and so, she rapidly assumed that Jonas's home was just one such random manifestation. How those variables had been combined exactly to produce Jonas's home was another issue entirely and not one that Leah could answer with any certainty and so, she dismissed the issue fully as an arbitrary concern as the two neared the front door and just accepted the structure's existence in its entirety as she prepared to cooperate. In fact, Leah was just so glad to see the cottage that she could fully accept its strangeness in totality because she definitely appreciated the change in scenery and the vibrant, beautiful color tones on display and so no further complex examination, analysis and inspection was entered into as Jonas cheerfully opened up the spotless white front door and then politely invited her to step into his home.

Due to Leah's interest in not just the cottage but also Jonas the cottage's main resident, she eagerly stepped inside the structure as she began to consider the possible passionate explorations and sensual voyages that might take place that evening within the cottage's four walls. Everything inside the compact cottage, Leah instantly noticed as she stepped into the large room beyond the front door, looked crisp, clean and tidy which totally refreshed her mind along with her senses because after being immersed in the grungy tunnels, muddy expanses and slimy swamps for so long that freshness was a very welcome sight indeed.

Each item of furniture, Leah silently observed, appeared to be formed from a dark mahogany wood and the walls were a comfortable cream which gave the cottage an elegant but humble feel which instantly put her mind at ease. What the accommodation lacked in terms of luxury, Leah definitely felt, it made up for in terms of cleanliness, warmth and organization and so, the four walls that held the roof of the cottage up over their heads, contained some definite charm that for Leah's eyes and mind, were a total breath of fresh air.

"First of all Leah, we'll clean ourselves up and then we can have some dinner." Jonas suggested as he followed her into the large ground floor room and closed the front door behind him. "We can stay here for a while if you like."

"Sure, that sounds great." Leah swiftly agreed.

"I'll start to make dinner now." Jonas explained as he headed towards the kitchen area of the large ground floor room.

Since Leah had never actually been inside an actual cottage before, for the next few minutes she began to wander around the ground floor as she started to visually inspect the cottage's interior. The main ground floor room appeared to house a large lounge area, a smaller dining area and even a moderately sized kitchen area and although it was quite compact as far as Leah was concerned, it definitely seemed sufficient enough to meet the accommodation needs of one person.

On one side of the large ground floor room, Leah noticed that a door led to a second much smaller room which upon closer inspection, she swiftly discovered, was a bathroom that contained not only a toilet and hand basin but also a large, wide sunken bath. Although the interior of the cottage certainly wasn't huge by any stretch of the imagination, it did feel very homely and so, Leah felt really quite relaxed as she turned her attention back towards the main ground floor room which she continued to silently peruse and inspect for another couple of minutes.

The serene cream walls that adorned the ground floor gave the room a subtle, homely beauty and each one perfectly complimented the deep, dark, burgundy mahogany furniture that had been scattered across its interior. A large mahogany, wooden framed sofa nestled gently against one of the walls of the large ground floor in the lounge area which had some plush, cream cushions scattered across it and so, Leah eagerly sat down upon it as she started to watch Jonas prepare the meal that as she already knew, they would both consume shortly.

Much to Leah's total relief, Jonas was not only brave, kind and assertive but he also seemed to know his way around the kitchen as she watched him marinate some meaty chunks in a mixture of herbs and spices and smiled. A few pleasant aromas began to waft through the air which instantly stirred Leah's appetite and made her mouth water as her form started to eagerly anticipate what each mouthful of food might actually taste like once fully prepped and cooked because the aromas held the promise of tasty perfection.

"Would you like me to run you a bath Leah?" Jonas suddenly asked as he began to walk towards the other side of the room where there was a small fireplace.

"Yes, please Jonas because after all that filthy mud and grimy slime, I could sure do with one." Leah swiftly acknowledged. "My body almost feels weighed down by all the dirt, mud and grim that I've been through today and some of it seems to be glued to my skin."

"Yes, the Disgusting Dimension can truly be a very mucky and absolutely disgusting experience." Jonas agreed as he ignited a spark device which he then utilized to light some paper and some logs in the small fireplace. "Just give me a minute please Leah and I'll sort that bath out for you."

For the next few minutes, once Jonas had prodded the fire a bit until it was ablaze to his satisfaction, Leah was left alone in the main ground floor room of the cottage as Jonas stepped inside the bathroom and then totally vanished from sight. Since Leah had been left to her own devices for a few minutes, she began to quietly consider as she waited for Jonas to return, what she might actually wear once she had cleaned herself up because she had no actual change of clothes.

The black satin jumpsuit that Leah had woken up in was now barely recognizable as one because it was almost brown from all the mud, slime and filth that had been splashed and spattered across it earlier that day and so Leah knew that she definitely couldn't wear it again, once she had bathed. In fact, Leah's outfit now almost felt and looked as disgusting as some of the filthy, slimy mud that she had seen in parts of the Disgusting Dimension that she had visited and so she really felt quite eager to change her clothes because the clean environment that she was now situated inside, made that filth even more noticeable and quite uncomfortable.

Although Leah could no longer see Jonas's face, the flow of the bathwater could actually be heard as she continued to thoughtfully consider possible material alternatives as she waited for Jonas's return. A sudden thought struck Leah's mind that perhaps the golden social etiquette handbook that Jonas had given to her earlier that day might hold a viable solution because it did seem to house a whole wardrobe of possibilities inside it but just as she was about to reach for it in order to explore that possibility, Jonas suddenly reentered the room and her question was swiftly answered.

"Don't worry Leah, I've brought you something clean to wear." Jonas quickly reassured her as he strode enthusiastically across the room towards her with a white, crisp, clean bathrobe tucked under one of his arms which he then handed to her.

"Thank you, Jonas, you must have read my mind." Leah replied as she quickly stood up and then accepted the bathrobe from his hands appreciatively.

"I've run a bath for you now and you should be able to find everything that you need on the bathroom shelves but if not, you can always give me a shout." Jonas clarified.

"Thanks Jonas." Leah said appreciatively.

Just a few seconds later Leah stepped into the bathroom and as she made her way towards the sunken bath, she held the clean bathrobe in her arms as she joyfully began to appreciate just how attentive, thoughtful and helpful Jonas had actually been. A definite desire lay inside Leah's mind that wished to eradicate all the mud and grime that had not only gathered but also accumulated upon her simulated person during her travels through the earthy, slimy tunnel passageways that belonged to the Disgusting Dimension which now seemed to have lined her skin with a muddy brown tinge and a swampy residue.

Inside the bathroom, Leah rapidly discovered that a large, white, crisp, freshly laundered towel now hung from a golden rail that clung to one of the walls just a step or two away from one side of the sunken bath and so, she quickly hung the bathrobe next to it. Since by that point the evening had already started to enter into the day and the air outside the cottage had become far duskier, Leah was very much aware as she walked towards the sunken bath and prepared to delve into the foamy depths that awaited her that time was definitely not on her side. Soon as Leah already knew, her visit to the Disgusting Dimension would be over for that day because every last minute would be fully consumed and so, she really felt quite eager to enjoy every precious minute that remained and not to waste even a single second.

A seductive invitation to participate in an exploration of social etiquette with Jonas had been offered to Leah and so, she wanted to ensure that she saved enough time to explore that invitation more fully. If Leah spent too long inside the bath as she was fully aware as she stepped into the sunken tub, she wouldn't have much time left or a chance to explore or enjoy anything with Jonas at all which meant that this soak could not possibly last as long as the one that she had enjoyed whilst in the Joyful Kingdom.

Quite strangely, although Leah's very real life patiently awaited her return to it from her jaunt inside the fantasy domains of Spectrum that day, she had recently discovered and realized that the more time she spent inside Spectrum, the less desire she seemed to have to rush back to reality. Even more strangely, Leah now found that her strange realization seemed to nestle inside her mind and thoughts quite comfortably as she embraced every part of the simulated world of Spectrum, even though deep down inside herself as she already knew that realization really shouldn't actually be so comfortable amongst her thoughts because reality and especially Zidane, definitely mattered to her heart.

Some delicious bubbles formed a thick layer of foam on the surface of the water and as the warm drops inside the bath instantly began to rejuvenate, invigorate and refresh Leah's skin, the water seemed to seep into every one of her simulated pores and swiftly flush out the mucky remnants of disgust. The grains of muddy grime and dirt that had quite comfortably, up until that point, rested upon the surface of Leah's skin with an uncomfortable familiarity almost like a dusty layer, rapidly started to vanish as she eagerly embraced the water and then began to lay down inside it.

Unlike Leah's previous soak in Spectrum whilst inside the Castle of Joy, this second bath had to be far more functional and a lot less luxurious and so, Leah quickly reached for a soft cloth like sponge which she then proceeded to utilize to cleanse her skin. Since as Leah already knew, time was in short supply and her time in Spectrum that day could not be extended any further because Zidane would definitely be upset, there was now a definite urge to fulfill her hygiene requirements as quickly as she possibly could. Other aspects of Leah's emotional journey awaited her enjoyment and her participation which she hopefully anticipated would not revolve around any elements of actual disgust at all and so, there was now a definite sense of urgency inside her form.

Approximately ten minutes later and once Leah had thoroughly washed her face, her body and her hair as soon as she felt that her skin had been cleansed to her total satisfaction, Leah released the bath water as she unplugged the plug then stepped back out of the bath. Due to Leah's extensive exposure to all the grime, mud, slime and dirt that the Disgusting Dimension had thrown her way that day, quite intriguingly, she had found that every drop of water inside the bath had contained more refreshment than usual and as she glanced down at her now clean skin and then reached for the freshly laundered towel. Much to Leah's delight, the natural hue and glow had once more returned to her form and since no more particles of mucky dirt now clung to her pores, her skin almost felt as if it had now been fully liberated from the disgustingness of the Disgusting Dimension that had stubbornly clung to her body throughout most of that day, much like an unwanted companion.

Once Leah had fully dried her skin as she began to slip on the white bathrobe, rather amusingly, she found that it was absolutely huge and nearly twice the size of her actual body but Leah tried to overcome that slight technicality as she began to wrestle with the mass of material. For the next few minutes Leah remained inside the bathroom as she tried to hang the material in a way that would at least feel comfortable for her, so that she could actually move around in the garment but it was a challenge in itself because it really was so huge. Nonetheless however, Leah attempted to persevere as she attempted to wrap the bathrobe around her body and tie the belt several times as she stood next to the now empty bath.

In fact, since the garment was so huge, Leah actually suspected as she continued to wrestle with the material that it might be worn by Jonas himself since he was not only much taller than Leah but also possessed a frame wider than Leah's own. The material however, Leah swiftly discovered, was not very cooperative and so as it hung down rather awkwardly in a semi acceptable state, Leah began to consider that she would perhaps just have to tie the belt around it and make do with the bathrobe's somewhat saggy fit.

Despite all Leah's efforts, due to the constraints on her time, she finally began to surrender in total defeat as she fully accepted that it would be virtually impossible to find perfection with a garment that was definitely way too big for her and was just a simulated reality. Since Leah had not yet put her shoes back on which were still caked in mud as she left the bathroom, Leah carried them inside her hands as she stepped back into the main large ground floor room of the cottage in her bare feet and then began to walk across the neat polished, mahogany planks that adorned the floor. Each wooden plank, Leah noticed, felt soft, smooth and well sanded as she headed towards a side of the room that seemed to have a clear space on the floor where she then carefully parked the now offensive muddy footwear.

"Did you enjoy your bath Leah?" Jonas asked as he swiftly noticed her return and instantly turned to face her.

"Definitely Jonas, it felt so nice to have a good soak after all that mucky grime and slime." Leah admitted.

"Well, I've prepared some appetizers for you, so you can relax on the sofa and eat those whilst I have a quick scrub up." Jonas suggested thoughtfully as he began to walk towards the sofa with a tray in his hands which was generously loaded with appetizers. He placed the tray down upon a small coffee table next to the sofa and then smiled. "I shouldn't be too long."

"Thanks Jonas." Leah replied as she flashed him an appreciative smile. "Do you go out into the tunnels and swamps of the Disgusting Dimension every day?" She asked as she enthusiastically began to make her way towards the sofa.

"Yes, every single day without fail and each morning, I have to perform a slime river and mud pool search, so my work in the Disgusting Dimension is never done." Jonas explained. "Every night the slimebattymice, mudrattysnakes and swampcattyrats create more slime rivers and mud pools inside the tunnels and expanses of the Disgusting Dimension and so each morning, I have to find them and then clean them up. I usually have to stop the flow of the slime rivers with my slime powervac and I also have to find the mud pools and then plug the holes up with mud stoppers, or slime and mud just ends up everywhere."

"Really, do those creatures do that every single night?" Leah asked as she sat down upon the sofa and then plucked an appetizer from the tray.

"They sure do." Jonas swiftly confirmed. "It can be such a nuisance."

"Now that sounds like a lot of hard work." Leah said as she began to shake her head.

"It can be but it's all just a part of the Disgusting Dimension and the disgustingness that we fight every single day." Jonas pointed out. "I better go and clean up now, I really need to freshen up before we eat dinner together."

A smile crossed Leah's face as she nodded her head and then

started to munch on the appetizer in her hand as she watched Jonas turn around and then walk towards the bathroom. Some thoughts continued to wander across Leah's mind as to how much time exactly she had left in the Disgusting Dimension that day because there was no actual way she could tell and so, she could only really make rough estimations. Another small tweak to Spectrum was definitely required, Leah swiftly concluded that would allow users to see how time they had consumed or how much time remained on any particular visit to it at any point in time because guesswork as Leah already knew, wasn't always accurate or even remotely reliable.

Suddenly, a quite strange realization dawned upon Leah as she plucked a second appetizer from the tray and then glanced around the ground floor of the cottage and that realization was that from what Leah could see, there appeared to be no actual bedroom anywhere on the ground floor of the cottage. Since Jonas had referred to the cottage as his home, it had suddenly crossed Leah's mind that there was nowhere to actually sleep, at least not on the ground floor of the cottage and so, she began to wonder, if there was an actual bedroom because she couldn't see any stairs that might led to an attic area. A definite question had now been raised in Leah's mind as she rapidly consumed the second appetizer and then picked up a third as she began to wonder where exactly Jonas slept every night because although the cottage felt warm and cozy, there appeared to be no actual bedroom adjoined to the main ground floor room and no actual bed that she could see.

"Perhaps Jonas has a home that he doesn't actually sleep in." Leah whispered to herself. "Or perhaps, he doesn't actually sleep, after all he is a simulacrum and perhaps simulated human beings don't require any sleep."

Some black iron lanterns with candles inside each one hung from the four walls of the cottage and Leah suddenly noticed that prior to her return to the large, main ground floor room, each candle had been lit and as she stared at one of the lanterns, she began to watch the flames flicker away. From what Leah could see as the silent rays of light danced across the smooth, cream surfaces that surrounded her, each ray of light appeared to quietly chase the shadows away as she watched in total fascination and it was almost as if each shadow was an unwanted guest that despite being chased away, seemed absolutely determined to return.

The evening had definitely fully entered the day by that point, Leah noticed as she glanced across the room and looked out of the two large, square windows carved into one of the walls of the cottage as she picked up a fourth appetizer and then began to munch upon it. Outside the cottage as Leah could clearly see, the air now looked really quite dark which held the silent promise that the night would soon be sure to follow the evening's path. Since Leah's departure from Spectrum was due to occur at around nine that evening that also meant that her experiences inside the Disgusting Dimension were almost over for that day because at least seven hours had now been fully consumed and thoroughly enjoyed.

Rather intriguingly, Leah considered thoughtfully, although the Disgusting Dimension should have totally repulsed her, she had actually enjoyed her time inside it, mainly due to the presence of Jonas and so, quite unexpectedly, she was not in an actual rush to depart from it. However, as Leah already knew as she finished the fourth appetizer and then selected a fifth, time was definitely in short supply which meant, her curiosity for that day was now definitely on a time limit.

Approximately ten minutes after Jonas had left the main ground floor room and once a few more delicious appetizers had been joyfully consumed by Leah, Jonas finally resurfaced from the bathroom with a smile upon his face and a clean set of clothes which silently clung to his athletic frame. A smile crossed Leah's face as she began to process and appreciate Jonas's appearance because it was almost as if each garment that clothed his frame loved him since each one hung to his body quite tightly which definitely enhanced his masculine appeal and clearly displayed his rugged, fit masculine edges.

Due to Jonas's return and his now extremely attractive appearance, the sensual passion inside of Leah instantly began to stir silently as she leant back against the plump, puffy cream cushions that had been scattered across the sofa and continued to munch on one of the appetizers that Jonas had so kindly provided. Although Jonas was deliciously handsome and also deliciously available to Leah, the two as she already knew, still had dinner to eat which Jonas had actually prepared and so, passion was not yet available or on the actual menu just yet and so those passionate sensual undercurrents that ran all the way through her form, would definitely have to wait, at least until after dinner had been eaten.

"We should eat dinner now Leah." Jonas said as he began to walk towards the kitchen area of the main ground floor room. "All that slime zapping has made me feel really quite hungry."

"Yeah me too and you did put in such a lot of effort." Leah agreed as she quickly rose to her feet and then began to walk towards him. "Can I help at all?"

"No Leah, you should just sit down." Jonas insisted as he pointed towards a vacant chair next to the large mahogany dining table. "Please don't worry about anything because today you are my guest and besides you don't know where anything is."

"Okay, I won't argue with that Jonas." Leah replied as she grinned. "A meal off from the kitchen is always a welcome blessing in my sight."

Another fifteen minutes or so sped by as Leah watched Jonas make the final dinner preparations which included a variety of things that swiftly put to good use the small fire that had been lit earlier that evening which rapidly became an actual culinary tool. The marinated chunks of meat were spiked with some metal skewers as Leah watched Jonas at work, before he placed each one upon a small wire frame that sat just above the flames and as the chunks of skewered meat started to cook, some delicious aromas began to waft through the air towards Leah's nostrils. Since each delicious aroma smelt absolutely divine, Leah's mouth eagerly started to water in direct response to Jonas's culinary efforts in eager anticipation as she continued to wait and silently, admired Jonas tireless efforts in the kitchen which even put her own usual efforts to shame.

Some fruits, vegetables and herbs, Leah observed, were swiftly sliced, chopped and then mixed together in several small wooden bowls before a variety of spices were added to each mixture in order to create some chunky dips. A loaf of fluffy white bread was swiftly sliced and then placed upon a large wooden plate and then the dips and bread were placed carefully down upon the mahogany table directly in front of Leah, the arrival of which made her mouth water even more because now, the delicious aromas were in very close proximity to her actual mouth and palate.

Once a few other edible items had been attended to, inclusive of the delicious chunks of meat and once some more wooden bowls and large wooden plates full of consumables had been placed upon the table, Leah watched in admiration as Jonas smiled at her just before he sat down and joined her. Although the food on offer that Jonas had prepared wasn't as grand as the meal that Leah had been served at the Feast of Plenty or the provisions as abundant, Leah definitely felt that the meal that Jonas had prepared, was still a feast of sorts because it certainly looked and smelt like one.

Rather intriguingly and quite surprisingly for Leah, Jonas had actually managed to prepare a delicious meal in the heart of the Disgusting Dimension which had really impressed her since that emotional plane was actually so filthy, muddy and slimy. The zone that Jonas resided in and that Leah was currently situated, wasn't totally in alignment or very compatible with the notion of a decent meal and so, the preparation of the actual meal itself although it had been a total surprise to her, had been a very welcome surprise because every edible item smelt and looked a million miles away from what one might consider to be objects of disgust.

"Please help yourself Leah." Jonas invited as he picked up the large wooden bowl full of meaty marinated chunks and then began to spoon some chunks of meat onto his plate.

"Thanks, it smells and looks absolutely delicious." Leah replied as she picked up a wooden bowl and then began to serve herself.

For the next few minutes as Leah eagerly filled up her plate, she observed that Jonas actually encouraged her to do so as he handed her several few wooden bowls and wooden plates full of food which smelt and looked hard to resist. A few of the items upon the wooden plates and inside the wooden bowls that lay scattered across the table, Leah didn't actually recognize at all but most of the food on offer was eagerly sampled as she tried to have at least a small portion of everything that was available and offer to her palate and stomach.

"This is a special root vegetable Leah." Jonas suddenly mentioned as he picked up a bowl and then offered the contents to her. "We call them rootyfruity cakes."

"Okay, I'll try some." Leah replied as she plucked a chunk of meat from her plate and prepared to consume it. "What do they taste like?"

"Yes, you should try some, they're very nice." Jonas immediately encouraged her. "Well, rootyfruity cakes are a bit like a sweet potato but a bit fruitier, a bit more spongey and I guess a little bit more pulpy."

"How did you manage to get hold of all this delicious food in the Disgusting Dimension Jonas?" Leah asked as soon as she had devoured the chunk of meat and had then licked the seasonings of her fingers. "I'm very impressed and totally stunned."

"There's actually a trader that visits the Disgusting Dimension about once a week, so most of the vegetables, spices, herbs, fruits and bread I source from the trader but the meat usually comes from the animals that I catch myself." Jonas explained. "We have an agreement, he brings food items from the lands that surround the Disgusting Dimension where such items can actually grow or can be made which I then trade for some of the animals that I catch, so that way, I have all the things that I need to prepare a proper meal."

"What does the trader do with the animals that you catch?" Leah asked.

"Some he trades as pets to people outside the Disgusting Dimension, some he trains to be animal guards before he trades them and then others, he just slaughters and trades the meat." Jonas replied. "He usually tells me what he wants on each visit and then I catch them for him before his next visit."

"Such a simple life Jonas." Leah teased as she smiled. "If only my life and my world were that simple."

"Isn't that just human nature, to want something other than what is actually on one's plate of life?" Jonas asked.

"Now that Jonas is a very philosophical question and not one that I could even attempt to furnish with an actual answer that had any degree of precision, reliability or accuracy." Leah teased. "I think some people are extremely sure about what they want in life and are usually quite satisfied once they have achieved it and some others aren't. Human beings are very individual despite some of our herd like tendencies."

Approximately twenty minutes passed by in absolute pleasantness as Leah hungrily attacked the food on her plate and then even refilled it and as the conversation flowed between the two, Leah wished that her real life could be far more relaxed. Simplicity definitely appeared to have its advantages from what Leah could see and since her life was currently, really quite complex, it was nice for a change just to bask in that simplicity and to fully enjoy it, if only for a moment in time.

After the two had eaten their fill from the main course, Leah watched Jonas as he sliced up some fruits, dowsed each slice and chunk in fruit juices and then added some honey to the mixture to make a fruit salad. The fruits on offer instantly tantalized Leah's appetite as she watched chunks and slices being mixed together because the fruits seemed to represent every single color that one might find in a rainbow and there was no shortage of ingredients from what Leah could see. Once the two had eaten their fill and the delicious fruit salad had been not only served but also fully enjoyed, Leah smiled as she watched Jonas enthusiastically rose to his feet and then walk towards her with his hand outstretched as she internally began to speculate as to what might happen next between them both.

Just a few seconds later and once Leah had risen to her feet, her question was silently answered as Jonas began to lead her towards what looked like a cupboard door in one of the cottage walls which he then pulled open. Much to Leah's surprise and delight, a small, narrow, spiral, mahogany staircase was rapidly revealed behind the cupboard door which seemed to lead up into an attic area. The small spiral staircase seemed to answer not only the question of what might happen next but it also instantly answered Leah's earlier question with regards to if there was an actual bedroom inside the cottage and where Jonas actually slept each night as Leah poked her head through the doorway and then peered further up the stairs as she started to visually inspect the staircase.

"This is another part of my home Leah that you haven't seen yet." Jonas swiftly clarified in a hushed, low tone as he took her hand and then began to lead her up the stairs.

At least thirty steps seemed to form the staircase all of which looked quite easy to climb up and so, Leah eagerly began to follow Jonas's lead as she quietly assumed that those steps would lead to his actual bedroom. Since Leah was about to visit that actual bedroom in person, an undercurrent of sensual tension and excited passion seemed to occupy her form as Leah followed Jonas up the stairs and not a single word was uttered by Leah's lips as she mounted each step. Somehow, it almost felt to Leah as she neared the last few stairs as if the silence and unspoken words that now lay between the two, was a silence of passionate acceptance that they both fully understood because they both knew, exactly what a visit to Jonas's bedroom would entail and what such a visit would actually usher in between them both.

When Leah arrived at the top of the stairs, much to her surprise, she actually found that the staircase led directly into a large attic space which delighted her because she had imagined Jonas's bedroom to be a poky little room that had been squeezed into the rafters. However, the bedroom that greeted Leah's eyes not only looked spacious but also generously sized because it seemed to stretch across the entire width and length of the entire ground floor. The ceiling of the room, Leah noticed was slightly lower than the ceilings of the ground floor rooms but despite that small noticeable decrease, the bedroom was much larger than she had actually expected it to be and it definitely looked as if Jonas had transformed every inch of the whole attic area into a functional space to suit his individual requirements which clearly indicated that the cottage was indeed, very much his home in every sense of the word.

In the very center of the room, Leah noticed as she gave the room a quick visual scan, a huge mahogany bed frame sat that she definitely felt as she glanced at it, seemed adequately equipped for the passions that lay inside of her. A thick, chunky mattress, some soft golden satin sheets, a few beautifully woven plush gold and cream blankets and some plush pillows lay scattered generously across the top of it, all of which held the promise of passionate, sensual comfort to all that might wish to lie upon it.

Since in just a matter of minutes, Leah felt almost certain that she would sample and experience all of the seductive charm that Jonas's bedroom contained in a very up close and personal manner, her heart suddenly seemed to beat away more rapidly inside her simulated ribcage as her visual inspection continued. In fact, just the sheer thought of what might transpire between the two, made every inch of Leah's simulated form rapidly begin to tingle and surge with a current of sensual passion as butterflies of sensual attraction and sexual arousal started to flutter away inside of her which were accompanied by an even faster heartbeat than usual as pulses of passion fully gripped on to every single pore and every part of her simulated presence.

Nothing but sensual, passionate, sexual tension seemed to fill the air as Jonas gently held onto Leah's hand and then started to lead her towards the bed positioned in the center of the room and as he did so, Leah followed his lead extremely willingly. Drops of silent passion seemed to cling onto every particle of air inside the room as Leah fully participated and cooperated with Jonas's suggestive direction and that sensual excitement actually appeared to heighten and grow inside Leah as she moved until it almost felt as if it would spill out of her simulated form and then splurge onto the floor around them both. Fortunately for Leah however, that feeling inside of her remained silently tucked away within her but as Jonas turned to face her and then gently lay her down upon the top of his bed, an excited gasp managed to escape from Leah's lips because she could hardly contain the passion inside of her.

Just a few seconds later Jonas leant down towards Leah's face as he swiftly joined her and lay on the bed beside her after which point, he began to hungrily and passionately caress her lips with his mouth, lips and tongue whilst he ran his hands and fingers across her body. Each sensual touch from Jonas's hands was soft and tender and so, it was easy for Leah to immediately surrender to his passionate advances as she eagerly began to respond with some of the passion inside of her that had gathered since their first meeting earlier that day. A deep sensual hunger had welled up inside Leah's form and that passionate energy now urged her to unleash and release it, due to Jonas's sensual touches and passionate kisses.

Some passionate moans managed to escape from Leah's lips as Jonas swiftly unwrapped the bathrobe that swamped her simulated frame and then began to explore every inch of her naked skin. A definite sensual and sexual hunger lay upon Leah's lips as Jonas massaged and stimulated her with both his hands and his lips and so much so that her back arched with passion as she welcomed his masculine sensual expressions and yearned for him to actually penetrate her. The sexual exploration between the two rapidly became more urgent, rugged and hectic, Leah noticed as Jonas held her in his arms and then suddenly delved into her simulated interior at which point, Leah gasped with surprise and in absolute ecstasy.

At least an hour slipped by as the two made love passionately, frantically and eagerly as Leah instantly succumbed to not only Jonas's desires but also her own as she welcomed his masculine sexual penetration with every part of her simulated form. Every part of Leah rejoiced in and celebrated her femininity through her passionate expressions as sexual climatic crescendo after crescendo was reached, sensually explored and thoroughly, sexually enjoyed. Somehow, the depths of sensual intensity that Leah felt during that entire hour as she allowed Jonas explore every inch of her body and permitted him to make love to her in every single way possible, felt unparallel to anything that Leah had ever experienced before in her entire life in reality and so, the boundaries of her own sexual, sensual, passionate enjoyment had not only been heightened but had also been extended that day.

New depths of passion had definitely been felt by Leah and new heights of sensual pleasure had certainly been reached and so as the two began to relax after their frantic, passionate hour of very sensual indulgence, she thoughtfully began to consider her experiences. Rather intriguingly for Leah somehow, her passionate experiences inside Spectrum that evening had almost made reality look like an inferior, substandard substitute, a notion which totally captivated and even amused her to some extent. However, although Leah had almost lost herself that evening between the passionate sheets of Jonas's mahogany bed and their sexual exploration, quite suddenly thoughts of her real life rushed back to the forefront of Leah's mind which interrupted her focus upon the artificial, fictitious sensual entanglements that she had been absolutely, fictitiously immersed in and passionately, fully wrapped up for a very enjoyable part of that evening.

Every pore of Leah's simulated being had been passionately satisfied, albeit artificially by Jonas that evening but that wild, erotic, sexual excitement and enjoyment as Leah already knew, had been solely her own and Zidane's needs had been completely ignored. Somehow as Leah had lost herself amongst the sheets of Jonas's bed, she had pushed to one side and almost totally forgotten Zidane's heart and needs because although she had fulfilled her own passionate, sexual needs, she definitely hadn't fulfilled any of his.

A deep sense of guilt suddenly began to interrupt and disrupt Leah's mind and her thoughts which up until that point had been comfortably wrapped up in her experiences with Jonas, his golden satin sheets and their moments of passion. Some pangs of guilt suddenly, inwardly urged Leah to not only leave Jonas's side and bedroom but also to return to her own very real life immediately because the day was almost over and Zidane definitely required some comfort, affection and attention. Since Zidane was a real human being that meant as Leah already knew that he had very human needs and whilst she had been getting some of her needs met and sensually fulfilled in an imaginary, fictitious environment by a seductive, fictitious, handsome male lover, Zidane had been totally ignored, abandoned and pushed to one side. Somehow, Leah now fully realized and accepted, Zidane had slipped down her actual priority list when it came to the actual issue of passionate, affectionate and sensual provisions and in terms of his support, loyalty and dedication to her, Leah also knew that the reductions in her provisions to his heart, mind and body, were definitely unacceptable decreases.

Inside Leah's mind a guilt-ridden question now pricked away and needled her thoughts as she began to wonder if Zidane would still be awake when she mentally returned to the real world and the interior of their home. Despite all of Leah's good intentions however, just a few seconds later and before she could even make an attempt to leave Jonas's bedroom, she suddenly felt herself start to drift off to sleep due to fatigue because she felt absolutely worn out. Some internal guilty pricks of discomfort did remain however as Leah lay inside Jonas's arms but as she drifted off, she tried to ignore them as she attempted to enjoy the last few drops of her time inside Spectrum that day.

Just a minute or so later, when Leah reawakened, she found herself back inside her basement laboratory once more and so, she rapidly began to process that sudden change in environment as she started to adjust and mentally prepare her mind for a return to reality. A few verbal commands were swiftly issued to Spectrum as Leah prepared to dismount the Spectrum capsule and as the capsule lid started to lift, she began to sit up and then glanced at the wall clock that clung to one of the basement walls. For once Leah observed, fortunately for Zidane, since it was just past ten she would actually leave the basement that day on the right side of midnight and for that small grain of comfort as Leah already knew, Zidane would definitely be extremely appreciative because he had mentioned several times how much he hated the late nights that she worked and how those late nights never seemed to end.

One final farewell glance was given to the Spectrum capsule as Leah stepped onto the basement floor as she prepared to leave behind not just the basement for the night but also Spectrum and her most recent sensually packed adventures. A temptation at times had definitely occupied Leah's mind as to the possibility of an actual export from Spectrum that involved one of her fictitious creations but as Leah already knew, if she brought a handsome, attractive, fictitious male guide back with her into the real world, Zidane would probably pack his bags and leave her side forever.

Since all the future possibilities that occupied Leah's mind with regards to Spectrum had to be left in the basement for at least the remainder of that night, Leah quickly began to walk towards the basement steps because Zidane would not be impressed by additional indulgences on her part, since Spectrum had already devoured so much of their lives. A gentle but weary sigh was released from Leah's mouth as she began to mount the first step and then issued a verbal command to Fink to shut everything inside the basement down as she started to thoughtfully consider the couple's future and how Spectrum could never be an actual substitute to the children that they could have and raise together. Some years had definitely departed and had left Leah's side since she had met Zidane but the couple hadn't yet managed to realize their desire to have an actual family together and so, those desires remained unfulfilled, unsatisfied and unquenched which definitely created frustration at times because it almost felt as if a financial pause had been placed upon their future.

Once the couple had a couple of children and their future desires had been satisfied to some degree, Leah silently considered, then perhaps she could invent something else but those plans and the creation of their future family, really depended on Spectrum and how much it realized in an actual sale. No amount of money however, as Leah was very much aware, could ever give her back or replace the fertile years that she now lived in and for every year that she spent down in the basement, that fertility reduced to some degree as she walked towards a time in her life when the dream of their own family, would no longer be possible or would be much harder to achieve.

Some additional ribbons of fatigue and ropes of tiredness suddenly seemed to wind themselves around Leah's body as she began to walk up the remainder of the stairs and just for a second, she felt tempted to head back towards the Spectrum capsule and lie down inside it. Since the capsule itself was really quite comfortable because it had soft transparent furnishings that lined the base, it was actually a very nice place to sleep but Leah resisted the urge to return to Spectrum as she pushed herself to walk up the rest of the stairs. Upstairs inside the couple's lounge as Leah was fully aware, Zidane would definitely be waiting for her to emerge from the basement and so, to sleep inside the Spectrum capsule for the entire night would not only really upset him but it would also not be a very nice way to reward his patience.

In terms of the couple's life together, Leah considered as she arrived at the top of the basement steps, the couple certainly weren't royalty, or even very wealthy nor was their life action packed or filled to the brim with excitement but it was definitely all real and all their own. Both their home and lifestyle were comfortable and as Leah knew, deep down inside herself as she began to walk towards the door of the lounge, Zidane had always treated Leah like a real princess and the princess of his heart and so that lack of excitement and action didn't seem to matter in the greater scheme of things. A pleasant, peaceful, tranquil relationship, Leah definitely felt, was a rarity that was actually really hard to find and even harder to keep and so, she could live with the lack of action and excitement although Spectrum had recently highlighted that lack to her in a way that had been hard to deny.

The clock on the wall inside the lounge showed that Leah's plan for the day was still intact as she approached the door of the couple's lounge, glanced at it and hoped that Zidane was still awake. Although the night had already started to grace the city with its presence and time had almost slipped out of Leah's hands that day, fortunately there was still enough time for the couple to eat their usual evening meal together and then she hoped that there would still be a handful of quality time that could be spent in Zidane's loving arms that night before he began to rest. Upon Leah's face there was a warm smile as she began to walk towards the sofa and more importantly, towards Zidane and his real arms because no matter what happened inside Spectrum, he would always be the real love of her life and he had always been there to comfort her, love her and to appreciate her and that reality was not only deliciously real but also all Leah's own to fully enjoy.

For a few seconds Leah paused as she arrived directly in front of Zidane and observed that he had already dozed off as she began to consider their real life together which she definitely felt, was not only happy but also very content and full of love. A humble, beautiful, slightly less action-packed reality as Leah began to suddenly appreciate, was definitely far superior to a luxurious, excitement packed artificial existence that would never render anything to her real life, her real heart or to her real mind in the long term. In as much as Spectrum at times tempted Leah to push the boundaries of her own real life, she now realized as she glanced at Zidane's faithful face that her real life actually contained way more real happiness than she would ever find inside its confines because Spectrum could never make her smile even one single real smile and that was a very real fact.

Quite strangely that day however, Leah's trip to the Disgusting Dimension had highlighted to her just how predictable and dull the couple's life had actually become because it had been full of vibrant activities, despite all the slime and muck so she hoped that once Spectrum was complete things would change for the better. Every part of Leah knew deep down inside that despite the quite boring, mechanical nature of the couple's life that for the time being, boring was really a good thing because every part of the couple's life was stable, consistent and reliable which allowed her to focus and work on Spectrum in peace. Not even once since Leah had embarked upon the creation of Spectrum had she experienced or suffered from the sharp shards of painful hurt or betrayal that so many other people regularly faced and that lack of drama and hurt had allowed the couple to build their future in harmony not only with total peace of mind but also with total peace of heart.

"Don't worry Zidane, soon Spectrum will be finished." Leah whispered as she watched him suddenly stir and reposition himself on the sofa. "And so soon, we'll enjoy the love of our lives every single day, every single evening and every single night and soon, we'll both be much happier."

Zidane suddenly sat up and then opened his eyes. "Are you finished in the basement for today Leah?" He asked as a smile crossed his face.

"Yes, I'm finished now." Leah replied.

"You know Leah, sometimes I really miss you, even though we live in the same house and see each other every single day." Zidane confirmed as he glanced into her eyes.

"I know Zidane but don't worry, it won't be for too much longer." Leah immediately reassured him. "Soon we won't have to cram our minutes of quality time into every night because soon, those minutes will flow in abundance and our love will overflow from our hearts."

"I can't wait for that to happen Leah because I feel like we've lived in a desert for the past few months just searching for an oasis and that we've become totally dried out from the dryness of life." Zidane teased.

"Yeah, sometimes I feel that way too. Let me go and sort out dinner now, I'll be back soon." Leah promised as she smiled and then prepared to make her way towards the kitchen.

Every fiber of Leah's being, every pore of her real skin and every thought inside her mind as she turned to face the lounge door and then began to walk towards it, fully accepted and appreciated that Zidane truly was the kind of partner that her heart, body and mind could never afford to lose. No matter what unexpected things occurred in life, Zidane's heart was not only extremely reliable but his body and mind were also absolutely faithful to Leah in every single way possible and imaginable and so as she fully appreciated, she really could not afford to lose that love for a fictitious reality that might not even render the actual rewards hoped for or expected.

A solemn, silent promise was made by Leah's heart and mind as she stepped inside the kitchen and then began to heat their evening meal up as she vowed to save her next venture into Spectrum until the mid-point of the next week because every time Leah made Spectrum her number one priority, she pushed Zidane's needs and heart further down her ladder of importance. Deep down inside as Leah already knew, Spectrum could never offer her heart the real commitment that Zidane had so consistently provided and so, she could not afford to ignore his heart because unlike Spectrum which could be tweaked, modified, fixed and even rebuilt, Zidane and their relationship, if destroyed, would not be so easy to rebuild or repair and if their love suffered very severe damage, it would perhaps even become absolutely irretrievable and totally inaccessible to her heart.

A Meander Across the Meadows of Surprise

When the next week was ushered in, the mid-point of the week seemed to arrive rather quickly and as Leah prepared for her next adventure on the Wednesday just after she had eaten lunch, she stepped into her basement laboratory at around one with a smile upon her face. For Leah's day ahead inside of Spectrum that day, she hoped that her emotional journey would be one of the more pleasant Spectrum trips because it would involve a visit to the emotional plane of surprise which she expected to yield some unexpected but wonderful events. An appointment with an unknown adventure definitely awaited Leah inside the Spectrum capsule and so, she felt not only eager but also extremely excited as her emotions hopefully aligned in a glorious but silent internal crescendo of harmonious expectations. Every real human inch of Leah's being felt eager to be whisked away to a new fictitious location and so she began to look forward to whatever artificial enjoyment, potential explorations and simulated pleasures that might entail as she approached the Spectrum capsule.

Just a few seconds later Leah started to mount the steps that led to the transparent capsule and as she did so, she issued a few verbal commands to Fink to activate Spectrum so that the capsule and system would be ready to utilize straight away. Once Leah arrived at the top of the steps, she enthusiastically slipped into the capsule and then lay down inside it as she prepared to enjoy the emotional journey that lay ahead which that day promised to be one full of surprises. A few more verbal commands were enthusiastically issued as Leah watched the Spectrum capsule lid close down over her body and once the capsule was closed, the sleeping gas rapidly began to infiltrate its transparent interior.

When Leah awoke, just a minute or so later, she found herself strewn out upon a huge stretch of grass that looked like a meadow which had some sparse trees and bushes scattered around one of the edges in little clumps which she could see from her current position. For the next minute or so as Leah began to visually inspect her surroundings, she searched for any human faces that might be around or any animalistic hybrid entities but there appeared to be none anywhere nearby which instantly confirmed to her that a guide would not immediately be provided on this particular emotional journey. Despite the lack of direction and any form of guidance, Leah quickly stood up as she prepared to head towards the edge of the meadow where she could see that some trees and bushes were situated which held some ripe fruits on their branches and sticks, the appearance of which instantly made her mouth water because they looked extremely delicious.

"The Meadows of Surprise." Leah whispered to herself as she brushed off her clothes.

Quite amusingly, on this particular occasion, Leah had found herself dressed in a bright blue short jumpsuit which definitely amused her because bright blue wasn't a color that she normally wore in her real life but then neither was a short jumpsuit the type of garment that she would usually select or actually purchase. However, despite the strangeness of Leah's attire, she began to thoughtfully consider what course of action she should take and which direction she should actually head in because no obvious signs or clear indicators appeared to be present anywhere nearby.

Apart from the fruit bushes and trees that decorated the edge of the meadow, from what Leah could see there really didn't seem to be much else except grass and beyond the trees there just appeared to be another grassy meadow and so the trees seemed to be a logical place to head to. Since the ripe fruits that hung from the tree branches and that clung to the bushy sticks appeared in a vast array of colors and came in a variety of different shapes and sizes, some of which Leah had never seen before, she felt slightly intrigued by the variety on offer which had aroused and pricked her curiosity. The colors of the fruits on offer seemed vast and ranged from bright ruby reds to deep golden yellows and even included some light greens, dark blues, light turquoises and dark purples and some of the fruits Leah noticed, glistened as rays from the sun above her head bounced off each smooth, prickly or bumpy surface.

Each piece of fruit seemed to dangle down in total readiness as if everyone just waited to be plucked and consumed and so as Leah arrived beside a tree, she eagerly picked a piece of golden fruit from one of its branches and then began to sink her teeth into the peachy shaped fruit. A definite curiosity lay inside Leah's mind as she bit into the fleshy pulp that urged her to establish if the fruit actually tasted as good as it looked and much to Leah's total delight, her taste buds were immediately rewarded as her mouth swiftly filled to the brim with sweet juices and a mouthful of soft, fresh, fruity pulp. The sweet pulp however, didn't remain on Leah's tongue for very long as it melted gently away and as the fruity juices silently drizzled down the back of her throat, each drop embarked upon their journey to Leah's simulated stomach in a very obedient and highly cooperative fashion.

Situated not too far away from Leah's current position there appeared to be a clump of fruit trees that rapidly caught her attention as she ate the golden piece of fruit which contained not only some shiny looking fruits with unusual textures but also comprised of tree branches and tree trunks that actually sparkled and shone. The skins of the fruits that hung down from that particular clump of trees looked extremely different but different in a good way and so, Leah's eyes were instantly tantalized as she enthusiastically began to walk towards the clump of trees which seemed to surround a clearing. Much to Leah's total delight as she walked towards the wooden gathering from what she could see, the small clearing seemed to contain a golden pond set in the very heart of it which looked amazingly serene and extremely peaceful which encouraged her to head towards the golden watery mass.

Once Leah arrived next to the unusual clump of fruit trees and once she had plucked a piece of unusual fruit from one of the tree branches, she then began to make her way into the clearing as she prepared to sit down upon the grassy bank around the golden pond to eat the piece of fruit. The golden water inside the pond rippled and lapped gently against the grassy bank that surrounded it, Leah noticed as she eagerly approached it and then sat down upon the grass and it looked as if the pond was actually occupied by several kinds of aquatic life forms.

For the next few minutes Leah did nothing else but eat the piece of fruit and gaze into the golden water inside the pond as she watched some of the brightly colored fish that occupied its interior swim eagerly around inside the collation of golden drops. In terms of the fish, the aquatic creatures seemed to come in a wide range of colors, shapes and sizes which ranged from glossy shiny silvers to bright fiery oranges and from noble royal blues to bold ruby reds and some of the creature's shapes were highly unusual. Much like the golden water that surrounded the fish, the aquatic life forms sparkled and shone which instantly intrigued Leah because they almost looked as if they could light up a dark night.

At quite regular but sporadic intervals, much to Leah's amusement and delight as she continued to watch the fish, she noticed that quite unexpectedly, some of the brightly colored creatures would suddenly leap out of the water and jump into the air as they performed various forms of water acrobatics. Due to the splashy performances by the fish which definitely amused Leah, she giggled as she watched some of their airy and watery displays as each one that jumped out of the water leapt around and turned in mid-air in a very unpredictable but utterly delightful fashion.

Since the clearing seemed so peaceful and very tranquil, Leah began to relax for a few minutes as she began to savor the serene beauty that surrounded her but after that few minutes had gone by, suddenly something inside the pond caught her attention and then held it firmly by the hand. In terms of the pond itself and its contents that something which had definitely caught Leah's eye and attention seemed rather strange, highly unusual and actually quite out of place and the more she looked at it, the more strange and out of place it appeared to be. Rather curiously, at the very bottom of the pond, there appeared to be what looked like a large golden chunk of precious metal right in the center of it and so, Leah started to speculate for a moment as to why it might be there and what it could actually really be as she thoughtfully considered a closer inspection of the mysterious object in question because it had definitely pricked her curiosity.

A few more minutes slipped by as Leah continued to stare at the golden object in total silence which she felt might actually be some kind of plug for the golden pond before she finally decided that she would try to wade out towards it. The golden water inside the pond didn't actually look that deep, from Leah's current position, so she definitely felt that a paddle to reach it was a viable option and an achievable goal but she considered that decision carefully for a few more seconds as she glanced at the interior of the water and tried to estimate its depth at the deepest points.

When Leah finally arrived at a final decision, once she had weighed up the various risks that a bold paddle might entail, she then began to decisively remove her shoes as she committed to that decision which on this particular occasion simply comprised of a pair of flat plimsolls. Since the rather plain, simple plimsolls were the type of footwear that one might wear to potter around inside the back garden, Leah didn't feel particularly worried if she never saw those plimsolls ever again and so, she eagerly slipped them off and then placed the shoes upon the grassy bank beside her.

Quite delightfully, once Leah stepped into the golden water as she began to take a few watery steps through it, she swiftly discovered that the water not only felt deliciously fresh but also really quite warm which encouraged her to bravely paddle further out into its golden depths since nothing had gone wrong so far. Fortunately for Leah as the golden water lapped gently around and against her ankles and calves, the baggy, loose short jumpsuit that she had woken up in didn't seem to get in the way at all since the material sat just above her knees which meant, it didn't even touch the surface of the water as she paddled through it. Although the water did seem to get slightly deeper when Leah waded towards the center of the pond, she noticed that overall it didn't really rise much above her mid calves and as the soles of her feet squished against the grains of muddy sand, she smiled as the sandy grains seemed to crawl in and out of her toes and gently tickled her senses.

Rather surprisingly and quite intriguingly for Leah, she found that when she reached the center of the actual pond itself and what could perhaps be the golden pond's metal plug, the water around her suddenly changed color. Instead of the golden water that Leah had originally stepped into, the water that now surrounded her had swiftly become a shiny silver which really puzzled her for a moment because there seemed to be no trigger for that change in color except of course Leah's own movements. Although the water still shimmered and shone as Leah stared into its depths, it definitely appeared to have changed color from gold to silver but as she began to accept and process that rather rapid change, another change swiftly started to occur but the second change was even more of a surprise to her and was even more unexpected.

Suddenly, a silvery whirlpool began to form all around Leah which span around in a very fast, chaotic circular motion and so much so that Leah was swiftly knocked off her feet and then sucked down into the whirlpool itself. The surface of the pond swiftly disappeared as Leah was pulled below the surface of the water before she could even try to make a wade or swim for safety and the whole incident caught her totally by surprise as she instantly started to panic. However, as Leah now fully realized, to try and make an actual attempt to clamber back onto the grassy bank in order to escape was no longer a realistic option or goal because she had been fully sucked below the pond's surface by the mysterious whirlpool without even a minute's warning. Due to Leah's sudden change in position, she quickly began to prepare herself to adapt to that very sudden change as she prepared to hold her breathe for as long as she possibly could but even more strangely, before Leah could actually do so, she swiftly discovered that there was no actual real need to which puzzled her immensely and even more so than her actual departure from the clearing.

Very strangely and much to Leah's surprise, no actual water appeared to be present below the surface of the actual pond itself and although Leah had been sucked down into the pond, no water was actually present to restrict her breathing in any way which once again, totally surprised her. Instead of a pond full of water, Leah rapidly observed, underneath the surface there just appeared to be an empty vacuum which quickly sucked her further down into its depths until she landed even more unexpectedly, on an underground path in an underground tunnel that appeared to be made from a combination of dirt and grass. Since Leah landed with a gentle bump on her rear, a surprised but amused smile crossed her face as she quickly began to stand up and then started to brush off her clothes.

"I'm lucky really that no one was around to see that rather clumsy fall, or my less than graceful landing." Leah whispered gratefully to herself as she shook her head and then began to visually inspect the tunnel's interior. "That would have been quite embarrassing."

Some definite fogs of confusion seemed to surround Leah's thoughts for a moment as she silently began to wonder which direction she was supposed to head in next as she visually inspected the dimly lit interior of the grassy, earthy tunnel and sought out some indicators or clear directional signs. Only two possible directions were available to choose from and as Leah already knew, only one was accessible to her at any given time because she simply couldn't be in two places at once and so, she prepared to make a decision in total ignorance because no directions seemed to exist.

Once Leah had made a decision, she then enthusiastically started to take some steps further along the dimly lit tunnel in one possible direction but as she swiftly discovered, just a few minutes later, the first direction that she had chosen only led to a total dead end. The appearance of the rocky dead end rather abruptly clarified to Leah that the other direction was the only real direction that she could actually, really head in, if she wanted to arrive at the next challenge in that particular emotional plane without any further delays and if she wished to proceed and so she quickly began to prepare to return to her starting position. After a few more seconds of quick visual inspection, just to make sure that the dead end was in fact a real dead end, Leah then did an about turn as she began to walk back towards the place where she had initially landed as she retraced her steps and reversed her movements in order to proceed.

For approximately the next ten minutes or so, once Leah had

returned to her initial landing spot, she then proceeded in the only real direction that she could possibly walk-in and although Leah remained totally silent, she was silently hopeful that the earthy passage wouldn't just lead to another golden pond like the one that she had just fallen out off. After a few more minutes' walk further along the wide, earthy tunnel's interior, much to Leah's satisfaction, she found that it led directly into another clearing but that the second clearing, unlike the first one in the meadow which now sat somewhere above her head, was far darker because it was situated underground. However, some dim lights seemed to adorn some of the tree branches around the perimeter of the clearing which made parts of it slightly more visible and as Leah's eyes grew more accustomed to her surroundings, from what she could see there appeared to be a large metallic roundabout in the center of the clearing which spun rapidly round and round in a circular motion.

In the very center of the metallic roundabout contraption, Leah swiftly noticed that there actually appeared to be a woman seated upon the contraption itself who seemed to be in control of the roundabout's movements. However, Leah rapidly observed that the woman didn't seem to notice her arrival because she didn't even glance up at Leah's face and that instead, the woman's focus appeared to be solely upon the roundabout's movements. Since the woman was all dressed in black and she had shiny, jet black hair, Leah felt that she definitely blended into the darkness of the dimly lit clearing rather well but from what Leah could work out, some metal chains appeared to flow directly inwards from the circular edges of the roundabout itself.

Each metal chain rope, Leah swiftly observed, seemed to have been hung on a central pole positioned next to the metallic pedestal that the woman in black was seated upon but the strangest aspect of the metal chain ropes, Leah quickly discovered, was not actually where the chunks of metal had been hung. Much to Leah's total surprise and utter shock as she began to visually follow each of the three chains and then started to inspect the other end of the chain ropes, she could see that there were three male human entities attached to both the chunks of metal and the metallic roundabout contraption which instantly struck Leah as extremely strange.

Every one of the three men attached to the chains and the roundabout, Leah observed as she watched them in silence for a moment, moved around in unison with the contraption and so it definitely appeared as if their movements provided the actual legwork that the roundabout needed to move. An eerie, strange tune appeared to flow out into the clearing from the center of the roundabout which seemed to vary in tempo according to the roundabout's speed as it moved and as each sound floated through the air, Leah's ears began to fill up with the strange noises that only just verged upon a musical melody. In fact, the noises actually sounded far more like a bunch of tins being rattled around accompanied by a sharp object being dragged across some metal surfaces to Leah's ears which almost made her cringe because the noises were actually uncomfortable for her ears to listen to.

The woman, who Leah noticed still seemed to be oblivious to her presence, cackled very loudly as the roundabout continued to go around and round and as the strange tune filled the clearing, Leah watched in silence as the woman cracked a long, black whip across the metal bars of the roundabout as it turned. From what Leah could see, the whip lashes appeared to be definite nonverbal instructions to the three men to increase their speed which Leah also noticed, they immediately, automatically obeyed as she watched them move more quickly around the clearing and the contraption start to spin round faster and faster.

Suddenly however, as Leah watched in total silence, she noticed that the woman paused for a moment as the roundabout owner suddenly glanced in Leah's direction and appeared to notice her arrival which seemed to distract the woman from the roundabout and her tasks. In fact, for the next few seconds, Leah observed, the woman's whip lashes actually ceased as the woman just stared at Leah's face and froze but due to Leah's current uncertainty, she remained totally silent and very still as she stood in a stationery position at the edge of the clearing and just waited for the woman to speak and to address her.

Unfortunately, the reality was that the whip lashes had really intimidated Leah which meant, she wasn't particularly in a rush to break that uncomfortable silence or to approach the metallic contraption that the woman seemed to be engrossed in and enthralled by. For some inexplicable reason, Leah's silence definitely felt slightly safer on this particular occasion than an actual verbal breach of it, especially on her part because the sight of the metal chains attached to the males around the roundabout and every whip lash that she had seen, had looked aggressive and powerful which really worried her.

"Do you see any men that you like?" The woman suddenly asked as she rose to her feet, placed the whip down next to the metal pedestal and then started to walk towards the edge of the roundabout. "You can have one if you want."

Leah smiled politely as she listened to the woman speak. "How much do they cost?" She asked.

For the next few seconds Leah began to silently inspect the woman's black leather dress like robes which seemed to hang from her being like a tent as the woman drew closer to Leah's current position and the edge of the roundabout.

"They don't cost any money my dear, they're pets." The woman in black explained. "I captured them but if you sign a Pet Ownership Agreement then you can choose the one that you want and you can have that man as a pet for the rest of your life, it's really that simple."

"What do they actually do?" Leah enquired as she started to walk around the edge of the roundabout and began to visually inspect the three males attached to it. "I mean what do you actually do with them?" She asked as she noticed that the roundabout suddenly stopped moving.

"Whatever you want to honey." The woman replied as she smiled. She raised her eyebrows suggestively. "They're usually very compliant, especially once I've finished with them, so they'll do whatever you want them to."

"Isn't a bit strange to keep men as pets?" Leah asked.

"No, not at all!" The woman swiftly clarified. "Women have been viewed as sexual objects for so long, so this kind of balances things out a bit between the genders in some small way. In fact, I consider my roundabout of male pets a vital part of the gender balance system, it keeps any male chauvinism on its toes and firmly at bay."

A few seconds of silence sat between the two women as Leah continued to visually explore and inspect the males on offer but no matter how thoughtfully she considered the potential ownership of each man, the offer of a male pet still seemed very strange to her. Although the whole notion had taken Leah totally by surprise however, she prepared to cooperate with the woman's offer as she paused beside one of the men and then began to inspect his face. Quite amusingly, it suddenly struck Leah that if she did make an actual selection and sign the actual pet agreement as the woman had stipulated that she had no clue what she would do with the man in question afterwards because she was currently situated in unfamiliar territory and she had absolutely no idea where anything was or what she was supposed to actually do there herself.

The male that Leah had paused next to, she swiftly noticed, appeared to be in his mid-thirties and as she started to inspect him slightly more closely, his handsome face and athletic frame managed to hold her interest quite firmly by the hand as she remained in close proximity to him. Despite all the natural appeal that the man possessed however, Leah still felt extremely unsure what would happen once she signed the pet ownership agreement and participated in the woman's scheme but as she glanced at the other two men attached the roundabout, she began to make a firm decision about her participation and her potential choice. If Leah had to choose from one of the three men attached to the roundabout then she definitely felt it would have to be the man that she was currently in closest proximity to because he was definitely the most preferable masculine presence amongst the three.

Irrespective of all Leah's doubts with regards to the actual issue of what would happen if she participated in the woman's scheme, she swiftly pushed her uncertain thoughts to one side as she quickly pointed towards the man closest to her, since he appealed to her the most. The woman's verbal interactions and communications hadn't really shed any further light upon any of the questions that Leah had posed and so, she silently decided as she prepared to verbalize and communicate her selection that once the two had left the clearing and Leah had free him that she would then just set him free.

"Okay, I'd like him please?" Leah answered as she began to humor the woman and the very strange choice that she had been presented with.

"Certainly." The woman replied. "And may I just say, he's definitely a great choice, he's one of my better pets." She continued as she stretched out her arm and a long scroll dropped out of her black leather robes. "He's very strong so he never collapses or ever seems to tire."

Not more than a few seconds later Leah heard a soft gentle bump as the bottom of the scroll which appeared to have a small wooden edge, landed on the ground and as Leah watched in total fascination, she noticed that the scroll as well as being extremely long, was actually full of handwritten text. From what Leah could see there had to be at least five hundred lines of written text upon the scroll and the lines of text became gradually smaller towards the end of the scroll by which point, most of the written words were barely even legible at all because each one was so very tiny.

"You'll have to sign here for me please." The woman suddenly insisted as she leant forward. "Then he'll be yours." She swiftly clarified as she scooped some parts of the scroll from the ground that had fallen and landed on top of the wooden edge.

Upon Leah's face there was a look of amused surprise as she looked at the end of the scroll and discovered that a dark bold line appeared to be at the very bottom of it which clearly indicated to her that a signature was definitely required from her. Since as yet, no actual pen had been offered to Leah that lack of provision did confuse her slightly because she had no idea how she would sign the document without one.

A few seconds of uncertain silence went by as Leah attempted to swallow her nerves which seemed to gnaw away inside of her as she prepared to verbally address the woman and present a question to her that related to the provision of an actual pen. Some courage however, was definitely required on Leah's part because the woman looked and behaved in a very dominant, aggressive manner which was really quite fearful and so, Leah began to silently dig deep within herself so that she could present the question to the woman that sat silently behind her lips which once answered, would perhaps allow her to proceed in that particular emotional journey.

"How do I sign the agreement please?" Leah finally asked politely. "Do you have a pen that I can borrow?"

Quite surprisingly, a very loud cackle suddenly filled Leah's ears as the woman started to laugh and as Leah glanced at the woman's face with a slightly confused expression, she started to wonder what had prompted such a loud display of hilarity. The question that Leah had asked, had seemed really quite natural in the circumstances and so, she really didn't understand the woman's sudden expression of amusement. No verbal explanations however, were immediately offered to Leah, and much to her surprise, instead the woman swiftly stretched out a hand towards her, grabbed one of Leah's thumbs with her own hand and then she proceeded to reach inside the folds of her black leather robes with her other free hand.

Just a few seconds later, much to Leah's horror, from the interior of the woman's leather robes, Leah noticed that a large, sharp knife was quickly retrieved which appeared to have been strapped to the woman's leg all along courtesy of a black leather strap which had been concealed by her leather robes. The sight of the sharp blade instantly alarmed Leah because as she had already seen, the woman had lashed the whip very enthusiastically against the roundabout's metallic bars with absolutely no restraint and so, Leah definitely feared what she might do with the sharp-edged weapon.

A nervous lump began to gather inside Leah's throat as the woman's grasp on her thumb remained very tight and as the woman pulled her thumb towards one end of the scroll, Leah tried to quickly step backwards in order to free herself. Much to Leah's total horror however, it was far too late to escape from the woman's very tight grip which felt almost like a metal clamp and as the woman continued to pull her thumb towards the end of the scroll, she then proceeded to quickly prick Leah's simulated skin en-route to the scroll with the end of the sharp, large knife.

"You don't need a pen to sign this agreement my dear, you sign it with your blood." The woman replied mockingly as she started to laugh.

For the next few seconds Leah remained completely silent as a few drops of blood managed to escape from her thumb, just before it was quickly pressed down against the end of the yellowish-brown document. A very sharp pain suddenly shot through Leah's form as her thumb was pressed quite aggressively and very firmly against the scroll which immediately made Leah wince and as she watched some drops of blood seep out of her form, seconds later each one landed upon the document, just above the bold black line.

Once an agreement had seemingly been reached and a few drops of Leah's simulated blood had been shed, much to Leah's surprise, she was then swiftly handed a set of metallic chains. However, very oddly, when Leah began to inspect the other end of those chains, she swiftly discovered that the metal chain rope was actually attached to another male and not the male that she had actually chosen. A confused expression rapidly crossed Leah's face as she began to process the woman's actions which seemed extremely strange because Leah hadn't even wanted a male pet in the first place and now quite strangely it appeared, she'd even had to shed some drops of blood for a male pet that wasn't even the preferred male that she had initially selected.

After a few more seconds of total bewilderment had gone by and a few more baffled considerations had been silently considered, Leah turned back to face the mysterious, strange woman once again as she prepared to question her actions. However, there was definitely a nervous lump inside Leah's throat as she prepared to challenge the woman verbally head on because as Leah could clearly see, the woman still held the sharp knife inside one of her hands.

"Sorry but I think there's been some kind of misunderstanding because he's not the man that I chose." Leah mumbled as she verbally pointed out the woman's obvious mistake as politely as she could.

"You should have read the contract dear." The woman teased as she gave a haughty laugh. "Didn't they teach you that at college? This is the Roundabout of Trickery and so you have to be prepared for tricks not treats."

Quite confusingly as Leah continued to watch the woman, she noticed that the woman suddenly put the knife away and that she then turned to face the center of the roundabout as she began to make a return to her usual routine and her roundabout activities. Just a few seconds later the whip was retrieved from the center of the roundabout once more as Leah watched the woman in total bewilderment after which point Leah observed, it was cracked aggressively against the metallic bars which clearly indicated to the males that still remained attached to the metal contraption that it was time to move forward. The strange verbal exchanges between Leah and the woman, now appeared to be over as far as the woman was concerned and it almost felt to Leah as she stared at the woman in total confusion and watched the roundabout owner tend to her metallic contraption once again as if the roundabout hadn't even been stopped for a second.

Since Leah had rapidly realized by this point that there was not really very much that she could actually do, she quietly concluded that she should try to leave the clearing as she began to accept the second man's presence as non-negotiable. The woman's return to the roundabout had made it absolutely clear to Leah that she no longer wished to discuss the matter with anyone and so Leah began to prepare to depart with the second man in tow, who certainly wasn't the man that she had chosen. Just as Leah started to walk away however, the woman suddenly stopped the roundabout again and walked towards Leah's position as she turned to face her at which point, Leah paused for a moment as she silently began to hope that the woman might have had a sudden change of heart.

"Just a minute, I'll tell you what I'll do." The woman said as she smiled. "Since I'm in such a good mood today and you were extremely polite, I'll let you have the man that you wanted though I must be getting soft in my roundabout turns because it really was your mistake." She continued. "Now, don't say that I'm not a nice pet trader because usually, I have a very strict no exchange or returns policy."

An expression of sheer relief began to cross Leah's face as the chains were deftly plucked from her hands by the woman and then quickly replaced with another chain rope which was attached to the man that she had actually chosen. Unlike Leah's delight however, she noticed that the second man now had a glum expression upon his face as the chains were switched around because ultimately, the woman's actions clearly communicated his return to the Roundabout of Trickery and the woman's pet ownership once again.

Just after the second man had been reattached to the roundabout and Leah had the chosen man securely in her hands, she then prepared to depart quite quickly, in order to ensure that there wouldn't be any spare seconds that might provide the woman with enough time to change her mind again. In every way imaginable, Leah accepted that her bargaining power in this instance was really quite limited because she certainly couldn't risk an attempt to free all the men attached to the roundabout since the woman's whip had truly scared her.

Much to Leah's amusement, the man that she had initially chosen, appeared to waste absolutely no time at all as he enthusiastically began to embrace his freedom and drew much closer to Leah's side. The sudden change in the man's ownership seemed to please him immensely as Leah watched a delighted smile spread out across his face as he welcomed and greeted his release appreciatively and as he drew closer to Leah, he gave her a thankful nod of appreciation as he held gently onto one of her arms.

"We have to get out of here right now." He urged.

"We do." Leah swiftly agreed as she began to walk towards the edge of the clearing where there appeared to be some exit points.

Unlike the first man's release however, Leah noticed as she cast a swift backward glance over her shoulder that the other two men were far less fortunate as the woman swiftly returned to her usual roundabout activities and with a few cracks of her whip set the contraption in motion once again. Since Leah still had the chains inside her hands that the first man was attached to, she continued to hold onto them tightly as she walked because another man swap at this point as far as she was concerned, was totally out of the question. Sheer determination drove Leah eagerly forward as she aimed to reach the edge of the clearing and an exit point before the strange woman could stop the roundabout again and perhaps even demand another exchange. Rather strangely however, Leah noticed as she walked and as she clutched onto the chains that the man was attached to, the chunks of metal actually seemed to coil around her arms and hands, almost like a snake and it almost felt as if the chains themselves were alive somehow.

On the other side of the clearing as Leah and the first man approached it, Leah noticed that there appeared to be at least six exit points and tunnels from what she could see and so as the two walked briskly towards the exits, she began to consider which one might actually result in a successful return to the Meadows of Surprise. Although technically, the first man was now attached to Leah via the chains, quite comfortingly, he walked alongside her as opposed to behind her which reassured Leah in some ways because she had no actual clue where to go from that point and he probably knew a lot more about the underground tunnels than she currently did.

"Enjoy." The woman suddenly called out as she gave another haughty, loud laugh.

Irrespective of the woman's well wishes which seemed in some ways to tease and mock Leah in an almost eerie manner as the woman's laughter echoed out around the clearing, Leah held onto the chains even more tightly as she began to lead the man towards one of the exits. A quick visual inspection was rapidly conducted as Leah walked as she gave the five other possible exits another few seconds of silent consideration but even as she did so, Leah continued to decisively gravitate towards the exit on the very right-hand side because she wished to make a very speedy choice and really rapid exit. However, as Leah started to near the tunnel entrance of the tunnel that she had instinctively chosen, the man that was now in her actual ownership suddenly stepped out in front of her and then stood in the way as he blocked her path which caught Leah totally by surprise.

For a few seconds Leah came to a total standstill as she began to process his interruption because she hadn't even considered for a second that she should consult him, even though he would probably offer her a wiser choice than her own since he knew the underground area better than she did. An apologetic expression crossed Leah's face as she glanced at the man's face and then shook her head as she silently accepted that she really should have consulted him but that she hadn't done so because she had just been in such a rush to leave the clearing.

"Sorry, I should have asked you which way we should go." Leah mentioned apologetically. "I was just in such a rush to get out of here."

"I know and don't worry about it, I totally understand." He gently reassured her as he smiled. "Well, you really don't want to go down that tunnel." He advised as he pointed towards the exit that she had chosen. "We should go another way, this way." He continued as he pointed towards another tunnel close by.

"Are you sure?" Leah asked.

"I'm very sure. I know these tunnels like the back of my hands." He swiftly clarified. "And that tunnel, the one that you've chosen, just leads to the Twisted Paths of Nowhere which is fine if you want to spend hours lost in a maze of complexity made from nothing but dirt and muddy booby traps." He continued. "But this tunnel, on the other hand, this tunnel actually leads back to the Meadows of Surprise. Correct me if I'm wrong but I assume that the meadows are where you wish to go and where I believe you just came from."

"Why should I trust you?" Leah asked as she hesitated for a moment.

"Why would I lie?" The man replied as he shrugged his shoulders. "I have no reason to and it is really up to you but I don't think that you'd want to be stuck inside a maze of tunnels for hours and hours and since I'm going wherever you go, to be perfectly honest, I don't really fancy it very much myself. Since I'd like to return to the Meadows of Surprise myself and you want to go there too, there's no actual reason to lie."

A few silent seconds were spent in thoughtful contemplation as Leah quickly evaluated her position and her reliance upon the words of the man that had actually been given to her in some kind of strange arrangement by the strange pet trader. Since Leah had no actual reason to mistrust him however, she quickly surrendered to his suggestion and then began to head towards the exit that he'd suggested that they should step inside because she had absolutely no desire to embark upon a wander of frustration for hours through earthy tunnels that could lead to absolutely nowhere at all.

Although the recommended tunnel might perhaps lead to another destination and somewhere else that the man wished to go, Leah hoped as they both stepped inside it that at the very least, it would take her back to the meadows because she had found that environment to be really serene and very pleasant. However, this time on Leah's return to the meadows, she silently vowed as she walked, she intended to steer well clear of any golden ponds.

Once the two had stepped into the earthy tunnel and had begun to walk along it, neither of the two uttered a word as Leah silently hoped as she walked that the worst outcome at the end of the tunnel exit would perhaps be that the man might then leave her side which would leave her alone and guideless. Since Leah had arrived in the Meadows of Surprise without a male companion or guide, she swiftly concluded that his presence or his absence wouldn't really have much of an impact upon her but that if he did decide to stick around, she felt that at the very least, his presence might actually be quite helpful because then he might actually show her around.

Approximately fifteen minutes after the two had stepped inside the tunnel, Leah found that the earthy passageway seemed to end rather abruptly as a earthy wall suddenly greeted her eyes which it appeared, blocked the way ahead. Since the earthy wall seemed to block not only Leah's path but also the escape route, she couldn't help but silently wonder for a moment if the man had perhaps tricked and misled her because this particular tunnel it now transpired, only led to a total dead end.

"This is a total dead end." Leah stated as she suddenly turned to face him and then began to shake her head. "I thought you knew your way around these tunnels."

Upon the man's face there was an amused smile as Leah waited for his response which he actually withheld for a few seconds and as he did so, the silence that gathered between them both in the meantime, Leah felt, seemed to fill up the vacant space inside the earthy tunnel completely. Just a few seconds later however, the man actually walked towards Leah before he pushed her gently towards the earthy wall and as she bumped against it, his actions not only really surprised Leah but also almost knocked her off her feet.

"Oh, ye of little faith." He teased.

Very strangely and extremely unexpectedly as soon as Leah's body actually touched the earthy wall which was now situated directly in front of her, the two were quickly catapulted through the air and just a few seconds later, they both landed upon a mound of springy grass. The mound of grass, much to Leah's delight, was actually situated above the ground and quite delightfully, Leah rapidly discovered, the two appeared to have landed with a gentle bump somewhere in the Meadows of Surprise. Due to the sheer exhilaration of the bouncy ride and the gentle bump, a surprised gasp managed to escape from Leah's lips just after she landed because the unexpected catapult journey had truly caught her totally by surprise.

Fortunately for Leah, the mound of grass that the two had landed upon seemed to be very spongey, springy and soft which had at least cushioned her landing and so she had managed to avoid any bruises on her butt, albeit an artificial form of fictitious bruises. The man however, still remained attached to Leah's arms and hands via the metallic chain ropes and so their catapult journey, Leah observed, hadn't changed a thing in that respect but as she prepared to stand up, Leah noticed that he suddenly leapt to his feet before he politely stretched out a hand towards her as he offered to pull her onto her feet. Quite strangely, the fact that the man had been chained to a roundabout and then sold to Leah for a few drops of blood didn't seem to bother him in the slightest or affect him, Leah noticed because his manners and behavior towards her, seemed absolutely impeccable and totally faultless.

"How's your butt?" He joked playfully as he pulled her gently up onto her feet. "After our crash landing."

"Yeah these sudden jolts above and below the ground do seem to happen quite often around here, I guess I'm getting used to that." Leah replied. "Not sure if my butt will survive many more though but you never know, my butt could start to build up a resilience to crash landings."

"Thanks for choosing me by the way." The man said as he smiled. "I almost thought I was going to be stuck on the Roundabout of Trickery forever."

"Yeah, the whole roundabout thing really didn't look like very much fun." Leah teased.

"It really wasn't, it was absolutely horrible." He swiftly agreed. "Now, since I did bring you back to the Meadows of Surprise, if you could just release me from these chains I'd appreciate it immensely."

No obvious reason seemed to exist that Leah felt justified a denial of his request as she rapidly concluded that he seemed harmless enough and even quite polite so therefore, she was definitely willing to release him without any further discussion or any debate. Since Leah certainly wasn't particularly interested in a man being chained to her arm for any length of time as some kind of pet, she eagerly prepared to adhere to his request as she began to try to remove the chains from her arms and hand but the metal chunks seemed to be rather attached to her arm as each chunk of metal stubbornly clung on to her simulated flesh.

"How do I release you?" Leah asked as she struggled to unwrap the metal chain rope once again and then paused for a moment. "How do I undo these chains?"

Suddenly, the man leant towards Leah and as he drew closer to one of her ears, his warm breath caressed one of her cheeks and then much to Leah's amusement, he began to whisper some extremely simple words into her ear.

"You simply let go of the chains." He whispered softly.

Just below the surface of Leah's skin she could suddenly feel some embers of sexual desire burn with passion as the chemistry of attraction seemed to stir and prod the coals of passion inside her form. For a few seconds that sensual passion seemed to silently sizzle and simmer away inside of Leah as her body immediately responded to their close proximity and her own internal desires. However, despite that undercurrent of passionate desires, Leah tried to keep her mind focused upon the task at hand as she began to process the man's logical response and glanced down at the chains that were wrapped around her arm.

"When you try to unwrap the chains, you hold onto them more tightly and so then the chains think that you want to keep them close by and so, they stay wrapped around your arm." He explained. "When I was attached to the roundabout, the chains wouldn't leave because a spell had been placed upon them but up here, things are different, you can just drop them."

"Really?" Leah asked.

"Really." He replied with a certain nod.

A realization suddenly dawned upon Leah that perhaps the man might actually be correct and so she lowered her arms and hands as she attempted to release the chains from her grip and as she did so, much to Leah's surprise, some chunks of metal started to fall voluntarily to the ground. For a few seconds as Leah watched the metal chains begin to depart, she shook her head in almost total disbelief because in the end, it had really been quite simple and very straightforward to actually release the chains and so there had been no real need for her to struggle.

Quite surprisingly in the end, Leah had discovered that the metal, snake like chain rings had relinquished their grasp without any further objections at all and as Leah watched the chunks of metal surrender to her now gentler commands to depart, each metal ring swiftly abandoned the arm which only a moment before they had been so affectionately and tightly entwined around. Once the metal rings had clattered to the ground, Leah noticed that each chunk of metal then sat in a stationery, redundant, discarded, unwanted heap piled up on top of each other and it almost looked as if the metal rings were in an actual sulk because each ring of metal now seemed absolutely lifeless and even looked, slightly duller.

"Well, I didn't expect that." Leah mentioned as she began to grin.

"But this is the Meadows of Surprise." The man teased. "So, you have to expect the unexpected."

"True." Leah agreed. "And it's definitely been full of surprises so far."

For the next few seconds a silence gathered between the two as Leah began to wonder if she should attempt to strike up an actual conversation but just as she was about to do so, the man began to pick up the metal chains from the ground. Once the chains had been gathered, Leah watched in total silence as he tucked the heap of metal chunks under one arm which he was actually free to do now, since he was no longer bound to the arm of a stranger.

Since Leah and the man had managed to escape from the underground tunnels and since the two were now a bit more relaxed, a conversation did seem to be the natural way to proceed, if Leah wished to remain in his company but it suddenly struck her that she didn't actually even know his name yet. In fact, the reality was that Leah had been in such a rush to get out of the underground tunnels that the normal rules of social etiquette and manners that usually governed her social interactions had flown totally out of her mind as instead she had focused solely upon their escape from the Roundabout of Trickery.

Despite Leah's lack of knowledge however, with regards to who the simulated human male entity was and what he was supposed to do in that particular emotional plane or on that emotional journey, she decided to be brave and to try to venture into the realms of a polite conversation with him. Technically, since the man had just been chained to Leah's arm for at least the past thirty minutes, Leah definitely felt that there was a slight familiarity between them both that totally justified a polite, friendly verbal exchange even though he did now look as if he was just about to depart. Since Leah had just freed him from the Roundabout of Trickery however, she hoped that the man would be receptive to her potential discussion and that he would perhaps spare her a minute or two before he actually vanished.

"What's your name please?" Leah asked.

"I'm called Lament." He replied. "And you are?"

"I'm Leah." Leah replied as she flashed him a polite smile. "Lament that's a very unusual name though to be perfectly honest, everything about today has been extremely unusual."

"Yes, it is quite unusual but it's definitely my name, one doesn't make jokes about one's name, it's absolutely unthinkable." Lament replied. "But now my dear lady, I'm afraid, I must leave you and so I will bid you farewell."

"You have to go so soon?" Leah asked.

"Yes unfortunately, I have a lot of matters to attend to." Lament explained. "I didn't expect to be captured and then held for so long. Usually, I'm the hero and the rescuer not the captive." He joked. "So that was a rather strange turn of events and very unfamiliar territory for me but don't worry Leah, I'm sure we'll meet again."

Since the conversation between the two now seemed to be completely over, Leah watched in amused silence as Lament suddenly rushed off as he headed towards a wooded area nearby and then a minute or two later, he vanished from sight completely. A small dent still remained in the grass that Lament's feet had occupied just minutes beforehand and as Leah glanced at it thoughtfully, she began to shake her head as she quietly considered his very rapid, abrupt departure but the vacated space seemed to offer no comfort or explanations to her as each blade simply sprung slowly back up into place.

"Well, that was a very brief conversation." Leah whispered to herself as she began to visually scan the meadows around her.

Whether Leah would actually see or meet Lament again that day was uncertain because he hadn't made any firm commitments or promises to Leah of that kind and so as she began to process her surroundings, she prepared to continue her journey alone. Since no other human or animalistic presence were in sight and Lament was highly unlikely to return, Leah swiftly concluded that there was no real reason to hang around in the same place as she began to ready herself to head off across the meadow. The Meadows of Surprise had already really surprised Leah and so there was one thing that she could at least be certain about as she began to visually scan her surroundings as she prepared to move off and that one certainty was that more surprises definitely lay ahead of her that day although what form and shape those surprises would take was for now, totally unpredictable.

In almost every direction that Leah could face as she stood on top of the small grassy hill that the two had landed upon and tried to find an indication of what she was supposed to do next, she could see a plush carpet bed of green grass which seemed to totally surround her. After just a couple of minutes and a more intense visual scan of the meadows had been performed however, Leah finally spotted a small stream that seemed to run across the meadows that bubbled away enthusiastically and so, she began to make her way towards it, in the hope that it might lead to her next adventure or the next challenge.

Every part of Leah now accepted as she headed towards the foot of the small hill that the two had landed upon that Lament would definitely not return to her side and at least, not for a while, so she started to focus more fully upon the stream and the banks that decorated and lined its watery path. The stream itself seemed to bubble gently along an earthy bed Leah noticed as she walked towards it and when she arrived beside it, she could hear the watery drops gurgle away cheerfully as it went which soothed her mind slightly as she began to walk alongside it and followed it in one direction.

Not more than five minutes' walk along the stream, Leah suddenly spotted a hybrid entity stretched out upon one of the earthy banks and as she drew a little closer, Leah noticed that it was actually, a beavagon which as she already knew, was a cross between a dragon and a beaver. Some golden brownish scales adorned the hybrid creature's frame and from what Leah could see as she neared the simulated entity, the hybrid appeared to be engaged in some food related activities that revolved around the stream which she immediately assumed involved the capture of some fish.

Since the hybrid creature seemed to be very busy and deeply

engrossed in the task at hand, Leah approached the beavagon quietly, since there was a very serious expression upon the hybrid creature's face which clearly indicated that the food related activities were deemed to be quite important. However, as Leah drew much closer, the beavagon suddenly seemed to notice her arrival and then immediately paused as the hybrid creature politely turned to face her.

"Are you hungry?" The male beavagon asked.

Leah grinned and nodded. "Definitely." She rapidly confirmed.

Just a few seconds later the male beavagon dipped his hand into the stream and then plucked a fish deftly from its interior and as Leah watched in total fascination, she marveled at how rapid and swift the beavagon's movements had been. Next to the stream there was a small grill, Leah observed and as she continued to watch the beavagon, the fish along with two others that had been caught prior to Leah's arrival, were quickly cleaned, gutted, descaled, marinated and then placed upon it.

A puff of fire was blown towards the base of the grill to lit some wooden sticks and leaves that sat just underneath it and as Leah watched the fishes upon the grill start to cook, her mouth began to water. Since the beavagon had been so polite, kind and had offered Leah some of the food it had collected, she began to strike up a conversation with the hybrid creature which due to its hybrid origins was about the height of a large adult.

"What's your name?" Leah asked.

"I'm known as Bankon." The beavagon replied. "By those who wish to formally address me."

"Do you always fish here?" Leah enquired. "Does this stream have a lot of fish?"

"Not always but most days I do. I usually spend my afternoons here. I have a family to provide for and the fishing here is generally very good." Bankon explained. "What's your name?" He asked.

"Well Bankon, I'm Leah." Leah answered. "But as you can probably tell, I'm not from around these parts. In fact, today is my first visit." She explained.

"Well, you're more than welcome to join me Leah and you are

more than welcome to eat some of the fish I caught." Bankon swiftly reassured her. "You can sit down if you like."

"Sure, thanks." Leah replied as she sat down upon the grassy bank next to the stream and quite close to the small grill.

Both the politeness of the beavagon and the grilled fishes, which now smelt absolutely delightful since each one appeared to be fully cooked, were hard to refuse as Leah sat on the grassy bank and was swiftly handed one of the cooked fish in a soft leafy kind of napkin. The other two fish Leah observed, were then quickly consumed by the beavagon in two swift gulps as she began to eat her own fish much more slowly.

"Thank you Bankon." Leah said in-between mouthfuls of fish. "This fish tastes absolutely delicious."

"You're welcome. I don't always bother to cook the fish that I catch but since you are human and humans generally prefer to eat fish that way, I made a bit more effort." Bankon admitted.

"Do you often cook fish for people?" Leah asked.

"Not usually. Most of the people that I cross paths with normally just want to trade, so I don't usually prepare any fish for them. When I enter into a trade, I just trade the raw fish with them for the things that I want and then they usually do the preparation bit themselves." Bankon explained.

Leah nodded. "Well, this fish tastes heavenly." She acknowledged. "You did a great job."

The fish tasted absolutely splendid, Leah noticed as she continued to consume it because it had been seasoned with some delightful spices and herbs which instantly woke up and invigorated Leah's taste buds. Each soft flake of fishy flesh seemed to almost melt on Leah's tongue and so, in no time at all she had fully devoured the consumable parts of it.

"Would you like me to help you catch some more fish Bankon?" Leah offered as turned to face him. "I'm not in a rush or anything."

Bankon shook his head. "No don't worry that won't be necessary, I've already caught a lot of fish today." Bankon explained as he suddenly spread out a webby wing and displayed a neat row of fresh fish that lay underneath it which hung down from the top of it.

"Wow that's a lot of fish Bankon." Leah swiftly concluded as she began to laugh. "You've been very busy today."

Suddenly however, before even another minute could go by, the two seated upon the grassy bank were interrupted as a silvery white alaricorn rode up towards them and as the alaricorn's approach attracted Leah's attention, she paused for a moment as she turned to face the mythological hybrid creature. Much to Leah's total surprise and sheer delight as she turned to face the alaricorn and glanced up at the rider that approached, Leah discovered that the rider was actually Lament himself but that now, he looked completely different.

"Sorry to drop in unannounced." Lament teased. "Are you ready to leave Leah?"

"Sure. Where are we going?" Leah asked as she jumped to her feet.

"It's a surprise." Lament replied as he walked his mount towards her.

Rather surprisingly and very unexpectedly, before Leah could even utter another word, Lament quickly leant down, plucked her from the ground and then swept her off her feet as he lifted her up onto the alaricorn's back. Despite all Leah's surprise, as Lament lifted her up, she fully cooperated with his efforts as she not only participated in but also welcomed his arrival and their potential departure which held the promise of some delightful surprises.

"Farewell Bankon." Lament suddenly said as he turned his mount around and then prepared to depart. "We have to head off now." He explained as he offered the beavagon a polite salute.

"No problem." Bankon replied as he smiled and nodded.

Once Lament had bade farewell to the beavagon, Leah held tightly onto the alaricorn's mane as Lament began to move his mount away from the side of the stream. The pace of the ride swiftly quickened, Leah observed as the alaricorn started to trot and then rapidly progressed into a caner as the two headed across the meadows upon the alaricorn's back. Unlike their first meeting earlier that day, when Lament had been dressed in grubby garments and had looked quite rough and rugged, Leah had already noticed that he now looked very smart, extremely cleaned up and even what one might consider slightly regal because some golden velvet robes now adorned his simulated frame. In fact, Lament's transformation was so spectacular that Leah had hardly even recognized him at first, when he had initially ridden up to her at the side of the stream upon his mount but his attire and presentation definitely made him look a lot more handsome and far more refined and so Leah couldn't help but mention it as they rode out across the meadows.

"You've definitely changed Lament." Leah teased. "I barely even recognized you."

Lament laughed. "I wasn't always a pet you know. One day whilst I was out on a hunt, I was captured by Shamania the sorceress and since then I've been stuck down there in her underground world of trickery. She's a male pet trader that captures unsuspecting males which she then keeps trapped and attached to her Roundabout of Trickery until she trades them." He explained.

"Yes, I did notice that." Leah replied. "She did seem quite determined to keep her Roundabout of Trickery fully manned and fully operational."

"Yes, I was just fortunate that you came along when you did." Lament acknowledged. "Or I might have been stuck down there for years."

"Where are we going now?" Leah enquired.

"You'll find out very soon." Lament teased.

"I didn't really say goodbye properly to Bankon and he even gave me a fish to eat." Leah mentioned as she cast a glance backwards towards the stream which by now looked far smaller. "Do you think he'll be offended?"

"Don't worry about Bankon Leah, he'll be fine." Lament immediately reassured her. "He often visits me and I usually buy some of his fish. He's a very nice chap, so I'll give him some extra gold coins next time he comes by, just to say thank you on your behalf." He continued. "Now hold on tight because we are about to speed up."

"Okay." Leah replied as she clutched onto the alaricorn's mane more tightly.

Due to a sudden increase in speed as Lament urged the alaricorn to break out into a gallop, the meadows suddenly started to whiz by Leah's face as the mythological hybrid responded obediently and for the first few seconds, Leah almost felt slightly giddy and dizzy. Although Leah almost lost her balance as Lament's alaricorn galloped faster and faster across the meadows, she was swiftly stabilized again as Lament quickly put an arm around her waist and then pulled her closer to his body which comforted her tremendously. A quick backward glance was cast towards the stream but by that point, Leah rapidly noticed that it was barely even visible to her and so Bankon was now, just a tiny dot on the horizon.

Since Leah had absolutely no idea where the speedy alaricorn ride would end, she began to relax and enjoy the ride which really was quite enjoyable, once she had grown accustomed to the increase in speed as the alaricorn rushed across the meadows. The meadows seemed to flash by Leah's eyes and the scenery around her passed by in almost a blur and as it did so, a gentle breeze whizzed past Leah's cheeks as she gasped with delight and in excitement as she clung onto Lament's arm which remained firmly wrapped around her waist. Despite the awful Roundabout of Trickery and the few drops of simulated blood that Leah had shed, she definitely felt as the two galloped across the meadows that Lament had been worth the rescue, if only for the alaricorn ride afterwards because as yet, Leah still had no clue where the two were actually headed to or what would actually happen next.

Upon the horizon directly in front of the Leah however, just a few minutes later, her question was suddenly provided with an actual answer as a silver palace that was situated on top of a small hill swiftly came into view which from what Leah could see from a distance, looked almost magical. Suddenly, just as that wonderful sight became visible, Leah noticed that the alaricorn began to slow down as Lament's mount returned to a steadier, far gentler canter once more and as the alaricorn headed towards the actual hill and the actual palace, Leah felt absolutely intrigued by the sudden appearance of the magnificent structure. The silvery palace itself,

Leah observed, sat on the very top of the hill but all around it there appeared to be silvery buildings that spiraled downwards around the circumference of the hill which collectively seemed to form a small town but the sight of the town and the palace totally fascinated Leah because it all looked so utterly idyllic.

Since the palace and the buildings that surrounded it all looked quite magnificent, Leah was literally stunned and almost speechless as the two approached a silver perimeter wall upon the alaricorn's back that appeared to enclose the entire town. In fact, Leah swiftly noticed that there only appeared to be one actual breakage in the town's circular base where two silver gates decoratively cut into the perimeter wall but that breakage appeared to be wide enough to accommodate the two large, grand entrance gates that sat in-between the wall's edges. A guard dutifully stood behind the two large silvery gates and as Lament's mount drew closer, Leah watched in silence as the guard suddenly seemed to spot their approach after which point, he quickly nodded his head and then started to open one of the gates up.

Just beyond the silver gates, Leah noticed that there appeared to be a cobbled courtyard formed from silvery bricks and that at the far end of that courtyard, she could see that the cobbled stones appeared to split into four quite narrow, spirally streets. Each of the town's four main streets spiraled upwards in different directions, Leah observed as her eyes visually scanned and then followed each one's path and as the cobbled stones made their way silently and voluntarily towards the entrance of the palace, each one seemed to willingly follow their destined route in total obedience. Everything that now surrounded Leah looked intricately designed, immaculately structured and absolutely amazing and so she was in total awe as the alaricorn stepped through the town's gates and into the cobbled courtyard.

"Is this the town that you live in Lament?" Leah asked. "It looks absolutely splendid."

"It is but right now, due to my prolonged absence, we are actually under siege." Lament explained as he tapped the sides of his mount and then started to guide the alaricorn across the cobbled courtyard. "Some vamptrolls have invaded the town and so that means, we have to be careful how we proceed from here on in because they could attack us at any given moment." He continued as he directed his mount towards one of the four narrow street entrances.

Suddenly, as Lament's mount stepped into the cobbled street, a door flew open on Leah's right-hand side which appeared to guard the entrance to a cottage and as it did so, a man rushed out of it and then headed towards them both. Upon the man's face, Leah could see that there was a look of total alarm which decorated his facial features with a very worried frown but despite that gloomy, fearful expression as he neared the two, he greeted them both with a courteous nod before he swiftly turned his attention and focus towards Lament.

"Prince Lament, there are vamptrolls all over the town and some of them have even taken over some of the townspeople's homes." He explained.

"Prince Lament?" Leah asked as she turned to face him. "Lament, are you actually a prince?"

"Yes, I am Leah, but only on the good days when I'm not chained up to roundabouts by wicked sorceresses." Lament replied as he nodded his head and smiled. "I would take you to my palace but it seems that since I was captured, we have a slight problem because the whole town is now completely saturated in and totally infested by vamptrolls, including my palace. My cousin Samuel, who stepped in during my absence, cannot run a kingdom very well or even defend one because physical combat and defense skills are not things that he has ever bothered with let alone tried to master and so, the whole town was taken over by vamptrolls in my absence as a result." He added as he grinned. "Which means now, I'll have to try and gather some defenders and then we'll have to make an attempt to exterminate the vamptrolls so that I can regain control of my kingdom."

"Does your kingdom have a King or Queen?" Leah asked.

Lament nodded. "Technically yes, my father and mother rule the five kingdoms of the Restorian Dynasty but I've been entrusted with this one which is called Fantoria, along with my cousin Samuel who is supposed to assist me, until my father and mother retire at which point I will then become king of the five kingdoms." He replied.

"That sounds like a huge responsibility." Leah mentioned.

"Well it is but I've been in preparation for that particular responsibility since the day I was born." Lament swiftly clarified. "So, I fully appreciate and totally understand what is expected from me."

"Right." Leah replied as she nodded.

"Okay Foray, I did hear about the vamptroll invasion from my uncle, who I visited en-route to Fantoria and since the vamptrolls still have control of the town, I think that we'll need to assemble some defenders as soon as we possibly can." Prince Lament advised as he turned to face the man that had addressed him. "We'll need at least ten, probably twenty defenders and we'll also have to ask the sorcerer to prepare some vamptroll repellent because that solution can turn those pesky vamptrolls into drops of water which will reduce our reliance upon wooden stakes and weapons forged from silver as our only means of defense." He continued as he verbally responded to the issues that had been raised.

"Okay, I'll do that right now Prince Lament." Foray immediately agreed with a certain nod. "It'll be better if I go alone that way there'll be less chance of anyone being spotted by vamptrolls. I'll keep to the backstreets and stick to the town's underground tunnels which should help me to avoid confrontations with most of them and hopefully, I won't be spotted en-route."

"Right Foray and if you can equip the defenders with some weapons forged from silver like arrows, spears and swords that should be sufficient, if we have the repellent. Before we launch an actual attack however, we will need to douse our weapons in the repellent prior to utilization which should make our attacks more effective and our defenses much stronger." Lament advised. "If we douse our weapons first, we should be able to eradicate some of the vamptrolls quite quickly which should hopefully, drive the rest of them out of town."

"Should I ask Samuel to assist us?" Foray asked as a slightly sheepish expression crossed his face.

Prince Lament immediately shook his head in response. "No, I wouldn't bother Foray, he'll probably just make the situation worse." He rapidly clarified.

Foray nodded.

"Right Leah, we'd better hide out in Foray's cottage for a while, just until the defenders have been fully assembled." Prince Lament advised as he began to dismount and then turned to face her.

"Okay." Leah agreed as she nodded and then started to dismount.

"Yes, you can both wait inside my cottage." Foray swiftly confirmed. "And if you'd like to eat or drink something, just ask my nephew and he'll prepare something for you because you can't do battle with vamptrolls on an empty stomach." He offered as he took the reins of the alaricorn and then gave the two a polite nod. "I'll tie your mount up in the stables at the back of my cottage Prince Lament."

"Thank you Foray." Prince Lament replied. He turned to face Leah before he continued. "Right Leah, we'd better go inside before any vamptrolls show up because the longer we stand out here, the more likely it is that some vamptrolls will appear and since we're not yet armed that means that we'll be an easy target if they do show up."

"I should be back in about thirty minutes." Foray reassured them both just before he started to lead the alaricorn towards a narrow opening at one side of the building.

"Okay." Leah replied.

"Foray, you should be able to get all the silver arrows, spears and swords that we'll need from Igon the blacksmith. He should have enough to equip us all because he's been building up Fantoria's weapon stocks for some time now." Prince Lament mentioned as he gently held onto Leah's arm and then began to lead her towards the open cottage door. "I wouldn't bother with the wooden stakes though because the vamptroll repellent and the weapons forged from silver should be enough."

"Right, I'll pay him a visit Prince Lament." Foray swiftly confirmed as he paused for a moment in front of the narrow entrance. "I'll stop off there on my way back, once I've assembled the twenty defenders."

"Yes that'll be easier for you Foray because you can't carry a load of weapons around on your own." Prince Lament agreed as he paused for a second and turned to face him.

A few seconds later Foray disappeared from sight completely along with Prince Lament's mount and as he vanished from view and headed towards the rear of his home, Leah followed Prince Lament as he stepped through the open door of Foray's cottage. Once the two stepped inside the cottage, Leah watched as a young man that looked as if he was in mid-twenties approached them both and then offered the two a seat inside the lounge area of a large main room which seemed to contain not just a lounge but also a quite compact kitchen and even a dining area. The polite invitation extended to Leah was swiftly accepted as she eagerly sat down upon the sofa after which point, she listened to Prince Lament speak as he began to discuss their presence at Foray's cottage and the vamptroll invasion with Foray's nephew but Leah's silence on this occasion was slightly nervous because as she already knew, she was just about to enter into battle with some of those fearful hybrid entities herself.

"Swinton, your Uncle Foray has gone to gather some defenders and to collect some weapons and so, he asked us to wait here for him until he returns." Prince Lament explained as he sat down.

"Okay Prince Lament, would you like me to organize some food for you both whilst you wait?" Swinton asked. "And would either of you like something to drink?"

"Are you hungry or thirsty Leah?" Prince Lament asked as he turned to face her.

"Yes, a little bit." Leah confirmed as she smiled.

"Yes please Swinton, some food and drink would be greatly appreciated." Prince Lament confirmed with a certain nod.

"Right." Swinton replied as he nodded. He hesitated for a moment before he continued as a worried expression crossed his face. "I just hope that you'll be able to get rid of all of the vamptrolls Prince Lament because right now, they're all over town."

"Don't worry Swinton I'm back now, so things will be different." Prince Lament swiftly reassured him.

In less than ten minutes, much to Leah's surprise and delight, the dining table had been laid with an assortment of foods some of which looked as if they had been prepared prior their arrival after which point, the two were invited by Swinton to sit down beside the table and encouraged to feast on the consumable provisions on offer.

"Please take a seat and help yourselves." Swinton encouraged as he handed the two a silver plate each.

From what Leah could see at first glance the meaty chunks, fishy delicacies, fluffy breads and root vegetables on offer all looked absolutely delicious and there was a huge range of edible supplies and so as soon as she had been handed a silver plate by Swinton, she enthusiastically began to fill the silver plate.

"Won't you be joining us Swinton?" Leah asked as she suddenly paused for a moment.

"No I won't. I've already eaten dinner today." Swinton immediately reassured her. "My uncle and I ate not long before you arrived."

Despite the fact that Leah had already eaten a fish beside the stream with Bankon, the sight of the delicious spread on offer had silently tickled her appetite which now urged her to consume some food, so she heartily began to tuck in as she watched Prince Lament do the same. The evening from what Leah could see as she glanced around the interior of the cottage for a few seconds as she started to fill her simulated stomach had already started to enter into the day because the two front windows in the wall of the main ground floor room clearly displayed the cobbled street outside the building and she noticed that a layer of duskiness had started to fall across the town. Fortunately for Leah however, time still appeared to be very much on her side because the darkness of night had not yet threatened to enter into the world or her current Spectrum visit which meant, for the meantime, there was no actual rush.

Some light conversation was made around the dining table by the two as Leah and Prince Lament eagerly conversed as they continued to eat and after approximately five minutes had gone by, Leah noticed that Swinton finally joined them both as he sat down and gave the two a polite nod. A minute or two later, Leah noticed that Swinton actually joined their conversation and as she listened to him speak to Prince Lament, the discussion between the two men rapidly digressed into the topic of the vamptroll invasion which appeared to weigh heavily upon Swinton's mind. However, since some of the dishes from the vast range on offer had not yet been tasted, experienced, savored or enjoyed, Leah welcomed the two men's vamptroll discussion along with her ignorance when it came to the actual issues of combat and the recent invasion as she focused her attention solely upon her desire to sample as many of the dishes on the table as she possibly could.

Inside Leah there was a definite desire to capitalize upon the edible opportunities that had been offered to her taste buds as she silently appreciated the fact that she had not cooked any of the dishes herself which for some inexplicable reason, seemed to make the food taste even nicer than her usual dietary intake. Since the feast that Swinton had provided consisted off far more food than either Leah or Prince Lament could consume singularly or jointly, she attempted to provide her taste buds with at least a generous mouthful or two from most of the delicious, simulated, edible treats on offer as she heaped some more generous spoonfuls onto her plate as the two men continued to speak. A few of the issues that had arisen in Prince Lament's absence were discussed by the two men as Leah continued to listen as she ate but since most of those issues seemed to revolve around town matters and the lack of leadership from Prince Lament's cousin, it wasn't a conversation that Leah felt that she was in a position to verbally contribute to and so, she remained silent and fully focused upon her meal.

Approximately twenty minutes later and once the two had finished their meal, true to Foray's word Leah watched as he returned with twenty defenders in tow, a vast array of silver weapons and some large circular containers which were rolled into the interior of the cottage. Since the containers appeared to be quite heavy and full of liquid, Leah swiftly assumed as she down for a minute upon the sofa that each one contained the much needed vamptroll repellent that Prince Lament had requested which reassuringly implied that at the very least, the battle ahead might not be as tough or as gruesome as it might have been without it.

The interior of Foray's cottage, Leah noticed, rapidly became quite jam-packed as Foray attempted to squeeze everyone in along with the weapons and the large containers of vamptroll repellent but from what Leah could see, it was definitely a rather crowded fit. Due to Leah's desire to cooperate with the battle plans that lay on the near horizon of her day, she swiftly rose to her feet again just a minute or two later as she made an attempt to at least try and look as if she was relatively calm and reasonably confident. However, deep down inside Leah's simulated form, a whirlpool of silent fear chaotically swirled around every part of her being as she stood in the now crowded room and waited to participate in the battle ahead in nervous silence.

Once all the defenders, weapons and equipment had been packed into the cottage, Leah observed that the large vamptroll repellent containers were then placed in the very center of the main room after which point, some much smaller cannisters were swiftly filled with the brightly colored liquid. The silver weapons that Foray and the defenders had brought into the cottage were speedily doused very generously in the concoction and as Leah continued to watch the scene around her, she noticed that Prince Lament, Foray and Swinton attended to all the defenders present with an attentiveness, eagerness and thoroughness that deeply impressed her. Since Leah had never seen anyone prepare for battle ever before, the three men's actions absolutely fascinated her and so her eyes were literally glued to their movements with sticky fascination which fortunately for Leah, kept her mind focused for some minutes and far enough away from fear to avoid a deep dive into fearful paralysis.

Although the scene inside the large ground floor room of the cottage was quite busy and there was barely even any room to maneuver, much to Leah's surprise as she watched the three men go to and fro, despite that lack of space they seemed to perform their tasks meticulously. Once all of the silver weapons had been fully doused, each one was then handed out to every defender present and as Leah observed the distribution of the doused weapons in total silence, some silver weapons were even handed to Leah herself.

Aside from the weapons that had been given to each defender as Leah watched, at least twenty small cannisters, all of which had been filled with vamptroll repellent, were then swiftly handed out to each of the defenders by either Foray or Swinton or Prince Lament. Every defender in the group from what Leah could see, was not only thoroughly prepared but also fully equipped and totally mobilized in a matter of minutes and as she glanced at some of the defenders in hopeful fascination, she noticed that they slung the leather straps attached to the small cannisters over their shoulders as they enthusiastically prepared to venture out into battle.

A vamptroll battle definitely lay upon the not too distant horizon of Leah's day and from what she had already realized from the powerful weapons on display that battle wasn't going to be a fun filled walk-in the park. However, inside Leah's heart and mind as she nervously continued to spectate, there lay a hopeful wish that the defenders present would offer the vamptrolls a real challenge because as she already knew, her combat skills certainly weren't anything to write home about and were in fact, virtually non-existent.

Chaotic Clashes with Vicious Vamptrolls

From what Leah could gauge, shortly after the cannisters and weapons had been distributed to the defenders, it appeared as if Prince Lament and the rest of the group were ready to depart but just before the battle group ventured outside, Prince Lament began to impart some last-minute instructions to everyone inside the cottage. Some nervous sparks of fear leapt around inside Leah's mind and stomach as she listened to Prince Lament speak and a fearful lump gathered inside her throat as she prepared to not only leave the cottage but also to engage in an actual battle with some actual vamptrolls herself because it would be such a huge challenge for her. Since Swinton, it rapidly transpired, would remain quite close to home because he would be on lookout at the town's gates where he had been instructed to assist the town's guards, if and when required just to ensure that no more vamptrolls entered into the town, Leah swiftly realized as she offered Swinton a polite nod that he would not be in of the vamptroll battle groups which also meant that she would separate from him shortly.

Just a minute or two later, when Prince Lament's brief came to an end, the front door of the cottage was opened up by Foray and as Prince Lament began to lead the group out into the streets, Leah noticed that the defenders started to visually inspect the streets outside the cottage as soon as they stepped out of the building. An active hunt for vamptroll activity was definitely just about to commence and as Leah followed closely behind the main leaders of the group, a strange emotional cocktail of fear and excitement seemed to swirl around inside of her simulated being. A very thorough visual inspection of the town street and cobbled courtyard was rapidly performed as Leah continued to follow the defenders lead and as they began to spread out, she even started to join the visual hunt as she optimistically hoped that their thorough approach would at the very least, keep their numbers intact.

Although the group had left Foray's cottage together, Leah noticed that the defenders quickly congregated into four smaller groups of five as per Prince Lament's instructions, once they had checked and ensured that the area around the cottage and cobbled courtyard were relatively clear. After the defenders had split up into the four smaller groups, Leah then watched as the groups of five began to disperse and as three of those groups started to walk towards three entrances to the main but quite narrow town streets until only one group of five was left behind which was of course, the final fourth group that included Leah herself.

Fortunately for Leah, she had been allocated to the same small group as Prince Lament which meant that they would remain together for a while at least and so that was a huge comfort to Leah's mind as Prince Lament swiftly started to lead the rest of the group further along the fourth town street which was the same street that Foray's cottage lived upon. Although the threat from the vicious vamptrolls was not yet visible as Leah began to follow Prince Lament's lead and started to head towards that as yet uncertain, unseen, unknown, unmeasurable threat, she tried to prepare herself for what might lie ahead but fear was definitely deeply embedded in every part of her being as she walked.

When Leah's group had travelled less than one hundred meters or so along the cobbled street which twisted and turned as it spiraled upwards towards the palace, Leah suddenly spotted their first vamptroll targets which came in the form of three vamptroll entities who it appeared were seated at a table outside an inn. The inn seemed to hold some kind of appeal for the grotesque vamptroll creatures which Leah immediately attributed to the tankards of ale that each hybrid creature held inside their hands and from what Leah could see, the vamptrolls had obviously developed an attachment to the venue which they apparently liked and so much so that three of their number were comfortably seated outside the building. Since the vamptrolls didn't appear to be in a rush to leave the inn, a silent visual inspection was rapidly conducted by Leah as her group drew closer to the structure and as she glanced at their gruesome forms, Leah noticed that the three grisly creatures had slimy, greyish skin, jet black or grey clumpy hair, huge fangs and some very large warts all of which seemed to silently decorate their unsightly exteriors and appeared to celebrate their gruesomeness.

Due to the defender's desire to pounce upon the vamptrolls unexpectedly, the five defenders in Leah's group she swiftly observed, quickly hid from sight as they drew much closer to the inn and as they did so, Leah noticed that Prince Lament gave some nods of approval as he watched the five start to surround the hybrid creatures. On one side of the cobbled street there appeared to be some kind of stand which Leah instantly assumed was a market stall and once the defenders were no longer visible, she began to follow Prince Lament's lead as he gently held onto her arm to guide her steps and silently directed her towards it. Since the market stall stand was in quite close proximity to the inn's entrance but actually had a tarpaulin cover over it, Leah felt that the two would be reasonably safe concealed behind it because it reduced the risk of the two being spotted whilst it simultaneously offered them a bird's eye view of the three gruesome creatures and so she cooperated with Prince Lament's direction very willingly.

Luckily for Leah and for the rest of her group, the three vamptrolls appeared to be totally oblivious to their simulated human approach as they continued to merrily consume tankards of ale as they sat around the table outside the inn which was situated quite close to the entrance of the establishment. Some noisy, drunken, boisterous pranks were played by the three vamptrolls upon each other, Leah observed as she watched them for a few minutes in nervous silence but aside from that everything else around the inn was completely still because from what Leah could see, the defenders had now hidden themselves so well that there were no longer actually any visible signs of any of them.

Suddenly however, Leah noticed that a series of movements occurred that did not originate from any of the three vamptrolls seated outside the inn as a nervous innkeeper appeared at the entrance to the building and then stepped out of the open doorway. Inside the innkeeper's hands, from what Leah could see, there appeared to be a large wooden jug which looked as if it was actually quite heavy because it seemed to require two hands to carry it around and as she watched the innkeeper walk towards the vamptroll's table, she swiftly assumed that the wooden jug was full of more ale.

From the expression upon the innkeeper's face, Leah could instantly tell that he felt absolutely petrified as she watched him attend to the three gruesome guests that had decided to visit his establishment as he began to pour the dark brown liquid from the jug into the three tankards. Despite all the innkeeper's nerves and fear, Leah noticed that he fearfully tolerated the vamptroll's presence as he served the vile creatures more ale and as he did so, she could see that the three vamptrolls mocked him very loudly as they belched in his face and even threw some rude verbal insults at him.

A discreet signal, Leah suddenly noticed, was speedily given to the five hidden defenders by Prince Lament and as Leah's attention turned more fully towards him, she noticed that he seemed eager to seize the moment and to capitalize upon the distraction that the innkeeper had unknowingly, just provided. Not more than a second or two after the discreet signal had been given as Leah watched in total fascination, a rapid reaction started to occur as the five defenders quickly crept into position but as they did so, Leah noticed that they somehow, managed to keep out of the vamptroll's line of vision and so quite fortunately for her group, the defenders managed to slip into their pre-attack positions unnoticed.

The front of the inn as Leah already knew as she continued to watch the five defenders' movements as they prepared for their attack, was far too risky for an actual approach but she noticed that two of the defenders wisely crept towards the rear of the building which was far less visible. Once the two defenders had crept almost to the rear of the inn which silently indicated to Leah that they had a definite attack plan and position in mind, she watched in total fascination as they started to scale one of the structure's exterior walls and headed towards the roof of the building. From what Leah could see so far, she definitely felt that the first two defenders had made good use of the building's exterior but when it came to the other three defenders from Leah's group, she noticed as she turned her attention towards them that they had opted to remain at street level and had hidden behind some temporary structures that littered the cobbled street around the inn in a crouched position.

Much to Leah's nervous amusement, just a minute or so later, she swiftly discovered that the vamptrolls didn't even seem to like their own company very much as a noisy argument suddenly broke out between the three hybrids about an ale related issue. Due to a rapid escalation in the vamptrolls' argument which quickly turned into a series of loud angry shouts accompanied by some aggressive shoves, Leah noticed that Prince Lament speedily gave the five defenders scattered across the cobbled street and perched upon the inn's rooftop a second discreet signal as he immediately responded to the second distraction.

Another helpful distraction had voluntarily, unknowingly been provided to Leah's group and so Prince Lament's second signal which instructed the defenders to fully utilize that distraction to launch an actual attack had been swiftly given. For a few seconds Leah almost froze as she watched the defenders respond as she considered for a moment that in this instance, since the second distraction had actually been provided by the vamptrolls themselves, the savage hybrid creatures were probably their own worst enemy because their aggressive behavior towards each other had blinded them to some extent.

In a matter of just a few more seconds as Leah watched the scene around the inn's entrance unfold, the five defenders launched their attack as the two that were positioned upon the inn's rooftop, suddenly leapt down from their positions whilst the other three charged towards the hybrids from different angles with weapons at the ready. Since the two defenders that had leapt down from the roof landed directly on top of two of the vamptrolls heads, Leah noticed that the hybrid creatures were swiftly knocked off balance as several weapons were not just mobilized but then also aggressively thrust towards the two vamptrolls' exteriors. A doused spear and sword rapidly hit two of the intended targets as Leah continued to watch in nervous silence and as both weapons sank into the fleshy outer skins of the two vamptrolls without even a moment or a split second of hesitation, Leah released a sigh of relief.

A few nervous seconds went by as Leah watched the other three defenders turn their efforts and attention towards the third vamptroll, since the first two vamptrolls had now been successfully tackled and therefore no longer posed as much of a threat. From what Leah could see, the third vamptroll had not yet been wounded but as she watched the attack upon the third hybrid, she noticed that something quite strange but very powerful suddenly started to occur.

Almost miraculously and much to Leah's sheer relief, the two vamptrolls that had been leapt upon from the rooftop and then subsequently injured by the doused spear and sword, suddenly vanished from sight before even a minute had managed to slip by but that strange disappearance happened so quickly that Leah could hardly believe her eyes. In fact, from what Leah could see, the only gruesome remnants that seemed to remain in the place of the vamptroll's two grotesque fleshly masses, once the doused spears and swords had been embedded in the hybrid's flesh, appeared to be two small pools of mucky water, the sight of which totally fascinated Leah because the creatures had looked so absolutely huge and so utterly unconquerable.

When it came to the issue of the third vamptroll, Leah swiftly noticed that the battle was nearly over in less than a minute because the three defenders that had leapt upon the hybrid, quickly plunged their swords and spears into his grisly, trolley, vampire flesh. Since the vamptroll had been hugely outnumbered, easily overpowered and actually cornered against one of the inn's exterior walls as the creature bared a huge set of scary fangs, Leah could see that the fangy threat didn't seem to scare any of the defenders as their relentless attacks continued because their battle with the hybrid had by that point, almost been won. Despite the injuries already inflicted however, the defenders relentlessly inflicted more wounds upon the vamptroll and as Leah watched them continue to battle the creature, she could understand why their attacks had not yet ceased because she had already been told that vamptrolls, if given the chance, would not only clobber human beings with their fists but also bite people and then drain their victim's blood in a matter of seconds.

Less than a minute or so later as the doused swords and spears fully penetrated the creature's flesh, Leah noticed that the repellent swiftly started to kick in as the third vamptroll began to evaporate and disintegrated into a small pool of mucky water. A huge sigh of relief escaped from Leah's lips as she observed the watery remnants of the vamptroll because that small mucky pool of dirty water looked far less scary than the actual simulated, hybrid creature had seemed whilst in a fully formed state.

Amazingly somehow, the vamptroll repellent from what Leah could see, would penetrate a vamptroll's flesh via a doused weapon after which point it would whip around their structure in destructive wisps and disintegrate their giant mass which meant, very little traces of the creature would remain afterwards. Although Leah knew deep down inside that the vamptrolls were actual simulations and that they weren't actually real, she still felt unsure that she could tackle such a large hybrid creature on her own or even beside anyone else because as Leah could quite easily predict, if a vamptroll tried to attack her, she would be unlikely to survive that attack.

"Now that was a very tough battle Lament." Leah concluded as she turned to face him and then shook her head. "And that was just three vamptrolls." She mentioned as she shuddered.

"Yes, and unfortunately Leah, our battle has only just begun. On our way to the palace there will be many, many more vamptrolls and we'll have to not only find them but we'll also have to totally destroy them." Prince Lament insisted as he gently held her arm. "We should join the others now." He encouraged as he began to lead her towards the rest of the group.

Once the seven had gathered in front of the inn and a few words of encouragement had been offered to the innkeeper by Prince Lament as the group prepared to move off again, Leah tried to muster up all the courage that she could find inside herself which at that point, wasn't really very much. The next battle with the vamptrolls as Leah already knew, would definitely occur shortly and as she also knew, she would be expected to join that battle but a deep undercurrent of fear chaotically surged through her simulated form because the vamptrolls were absolutely huge and they looked not only very powerful but also extremely savage. However, from what Leah could ascertain, no actual choice seemed to exist when it came to the issue of her participation in the vamptroll battles that lay ahead because if she wished to proceed in the emotional plane of surprise, she had to help Prince Lament who it seemed, was her current guide which also meant, she had to help him to not only save but also to regain control of his kingdom.

"We'd better get moving now Leah." Prince Lament urged as he turned to face her. "We not only have to clear this main street but also all of the back streets until we reach the palace. If we can clear the town's streets of vamptrolls then we're more likely to regain control of the palace because there won't be any easily accessible vamptroll reinforcements to call upon."

"What do you think will happen when we reach the palace?" Leah asked.

"I'm not sure yet. If it's totally infested then we will have to flush the vamptrolls out but hopefully, some of the other defenders will be around by that point to assist us." Prince Lament replied as he offered her an uncertain nod.

When the group were ready to proceed which was less than a minute later, the five defenders began to move off again with Prince Lament in the lead and as Leah started to follow the group, she noticed that the five defenders in her group visually scanned the town streets as they walked. The thoroughness of the defenders comforted Leah to some extent as she followed them and a few minutes later Leah actually began to enthusiastically join in the visual search herself as she started to visually scan the street as she walked as she searched for any signs of the grotesque vamptrolls.

Before very long and not even a hundred meters or so away from the first group of vamptrolls, Leah spotted the second group of hybrid creatures as they lurked around a residential doorway at the entrance to one of the town's backstreets and as the seven approached their position, it suddenly struck Leah that the hybrid creatures had probably infested the entire town. Although the vamptrolls appeared to be scattered quite sporadically across the interior of the town, from what Leah could see, the town's buildings had been infested by the hybrid creatures indiscriminately and that occupation it now rapidly transpired, was inclusive of not just commercial properties but also extended to actual residential homes. Some of the town's back streets it appeared had become an actual hang out zone for the vamptrolls, who Leah observed, were totally fearless, very aggressive and extremely bold as they occupied the streets of the town with a noisy air of savagery, entitlement and ownership but as she readied a spear and prepared for the second battle, Leah found a speck of comfort in the knowledge that at least, the first battle had actually been won.

Due to the vamptrolls frequent appearances and the subsequent battles that arose as Leah's group continued to make their way towards the palace, she rapidly began to lose count of just how many vamptrolls had been tackled, battled and then exterminated by the defenders. Initially, Leah had attempted to try and keep a quite precise tally but as that number had hit the twenty mark, she had totally surrendered and had actually given up because the vamptrolls' appearances had just been so frequent which had meant that all her efforts and focus had to be conserved for the battles with them as opposed to frequency and regularity of their appearances.

Despite Leah's lack of courage, she had tried to join the vamptroll battles with any spear strikes that she could as and when she had been able to but her contributions to victory had definitely lacked in comparison to the contributions from the defenders and those from Prince Lament. However, much to Leah's total relief, every vamptroll that had been met en route to the palace in the end, had been bravely exterminated as Prince Lament and the five defenders had fought the hybrid creatures boldly and without any fear and so as the seven neared the palace entrance, Leah released a very grateful sigh.

Although the entrance to the building itself was a welcome sight to Leah's eyes, what exactly lay inside the palace's walls remained for the meantime, absolutely unpredictable because she could not see through walls. Since a sight of hopeful relief had finally presented itself to Leah however, she tried to find some comfort in that sight for a few seconds as the group drew closer to the entrance before she began to consider the gruesome prospect of the next battlefield which would ultimately be the actual palace itself which was highly likely to be infested.

A quiet visual inspection of the palace entrance which had some gardens that quite delicately and rather sparsely surrounded it, was conducted as Leah considered that the grand structure might not actually be a safe zone in any capacity at all. In fact, it was highly likely that the structure had already been fully infiltrated by the vamptrolls since the palace would hold more abundant consumable supplies than the town houses, so Leah felt that it might be equally, if not even more infested than the town's streets had been. The exact extent of the vamptroll infestation inside the building was for the meantime however, rather hard for Leah to gauge from the structure's exterior, she rapidly concluded as she continued to visually peruse the perimeter walls, due to an absence of any external signs because no clear indicators seemed to exist that signaled anything much at all.

Another issue that worried Leah as her group neared the palace entrance was the fact that once the group were inside the structure, there might actually be very little chance to leave it because if the group were cornered inside the building by the vamptrolls, they would literally be trapped. Since there were no external indicators however, that gave Leah or anyone else in her group any kind of indications as to how populated the palace might be in terms of vamptroll occupation that lack of clarity immediately warned her that the group really had to be on full alert, once they stepped inside the palace's four walls.

In so many ways, Leah definitely feared what the group of seven might find once they entered the palace but since the full extent of the vamptroll infestation that lurked inside its interior really couldn't be figured out, until the group penetrated the building, Leah remained silent as she began to process the possible implications of that very uncertain threat. A large gathering of vamptrolls in Leah's mind, was a very scary notion indeed but a highly likely eventuality and so as she awaited further direction from Prince Lament, she tried to busy herself as she started to ready her weapons in an attempt to steady herself because fear had almost gripped every part of her interior which had caused her hands to tremble and shake.

"We should all wait here for a few minutes before we start to make our way inside." Prince Lament advised as he came to a sudden standstill and then turned to face the rest of the group. "We might spot some of the other groups and a few minutes rest will give us some extra time which we can utilize to prepare our weapons because before we enter the palace, we really should re-douse our spears and our swords with some more vamptroll repellent."

Some nods of compliance and agreement swiftly followed Prince Lament's suggestion, Leah observed as she too nodded her head in agreement, just before Prince Lament started to lead the group towards a nearby hedge that surrounded both the palace and the gardens. Since the hedge was actually quite low, Leah noticed that all the defenders had to crouch down as they hid behind it and so, she quickly followed suit because it was absolutely impossible to remain out of sight without doing so.

Fortunately for Leah, her group didn't have to wait for very long before some more defenders showed up as two more groups appeared just a minute or two apart from each other after which point, a signal was quickly given by Prince Lament to direct the new arrivals towards his group's hiding place. In some ways, the arrival of the two additional groups of defenders comforted Leah's mind slightly as she began to appreciate Prince Lament's efforts to boost their numbers before they even attempted to enter the palace because as Leah already knew, she certainly couldn't attack or tackle a vamptroll on her own.

One of the two additional groups included Foray, Leah swiftly realized as she began to count the defenders present which meant that the defenders' numbers had now risen to fifteen and also that their overall numbers had now increased to eighteen. The triple increase in the number of defenders present definitely comforted

Leah to some extent but as she watched Prince Lament, she noticed that he swiftly split the now much larger group of eighteen into two smaller groups of nine which did usher some more nervous worries back into the corners of Leah's mind.

Technically, Leah observed as she silently inspected each group, the two groups that Prince Lament had organized appeared to be equal in terms of headcount, since Foray had joined the second group of eight defenders which had brought their total number up to nine. However, as Leah already knew, the two groups would not actually be equal in terms of capacity because when it came to the actual issue of combat, her presence and her capabilities certainly weren't equal to any of the trained defenders in attendance and didn't even come remotely close to the capacity of the valiant, warrior Prince Lament himself. A shortfall in that respect definitely did seem to exist when it came to Leah's own group because she fell very short but since this particular challenge seemed to be a necessary part of her emotional journey that day, she silently began to humbly accept her rather limited capabilities as she prepared to persevere.

"What about the other group of defenders Prince Lament?" Foray suddenly asked as he turned to face him. "They could arrive at any moment, should we wait for them?"

"They might already be inside the palace Foray but whether they are or not, we really can't afford to wait out here any longer." Prince Lament replied as he shook his head. "We have to proceed with the next part of our plan now before the vamptrolls realize that they're under attack because if that happens then they might start to mobilize which would be a huge risk to us."

"True." Foray agreed. "Because reinforcements could arrive quite quickly and there could be lots of them."

"Yes exactly, so we'd not only be hugely outnumbered but also in a position of great weakness because our weapons are not infinite and they possess both fists and fangs which are of course, natural weapons." Prince Lament swiftly pointed out. "A large increase in the vamptroll's number could greatly enhance their capacity because it would bolster their ability to inflict more severe damage upon us at a far greater volume."

"Yes, I see what you mean." Foray concluded as he glanced at some of the defenders in his group and then nodded his head. "We'd be absolutely powerless and easily defeated."

Before the two groups started to move off, Leah listened attentively as some brief final instructions were quickly imparted to each group by Prince Lament which seemed to predominantly focus upon their method of entry into the palace and what the two groups should do, once inside the building. From what Leah could ascertain as she listened to Prince Lament speak, there were two side entrances to the palace that were situated on either side of the building which he instructed both groups to utilize. Since the two side entrances would be their points of entry, the large entrance at the front of the palace which was still visible from Leah's current position, would not actually be utilized at all it seemed in order to avoid detection which disappointed her slightly because the entrance to the palace looked so very grand but she could understand the need for their movements to be covert.

"We'll focus on the banqueting hall Foray." Prince Lament confirmed as he rounded off his instructions. "And your group can clear the main reception area, the ground floor lounge and the dining room which should flush out some of the vamptrolls and secure the ground floor. Once you've cleared out those three areas then you should come and join us in the banqueting hall because most of the vamptrolls that are inside the building will probably have congregated there which means, it'll be full of vamptroll activity."

"Right Prince Lament we'll do that." Foray swiftly agreed.

"I haven't had a chance to speak to any of the palace staff yet, so I'm hoping that the vamptrolls will just be on the ground floor but if not, we'll have to cross that bridge when we come to it." Prince Lament said as he shook his head.

"Well from what I've heard Prince Lament, from a few of the townspeople that usually work in the palace that I've spoken to, they've just taken over the ground floor so far." Foray rapidly confirmed. "But that was a couple of hours ago, so the situation might have changed since then."

Prince Lament nodded his head. "Which would make total sense since that is where all the edible consumables are usually stored." He mentioned.

"True. Well let's just hope that they stick to the ground floor." Foray replied.

"Yes indeed." Prince Lament agreed.

"And hopefully, I'll see you both again quite soon." Foray said optimistically as he offered Leah a polite, courteous nod and then prepared to move off.

"Yes, hopefully Foray." Prince Lament replied. "But just be careful in there, those vamptroll fangs can be deadly."

"I know that vamptroll repellent really has saved us many times today already." Foray humbly acknowledged. He turned to face his group and then gave the defenders a brave nod as he prepared to lead them into battle. "Right, we'd better get a move on."

"We'd better get a move on too Leah." Prince Lament advised as he turned to face her. "Before the vamptrolls realize that we're here because if that happens, they might send out a signal for reinforcements. Unfortunately, since vamptrolls can transform into clumpbats and clumpbats can fly, there's a huge risk that if they did manage to send out a signal successfully that those reinforcements would arrive in very large numbers and in a matter of minutes."

"Right." Leah immediately agreed.

Much to Leah's total relief, once again she had been allocated to Prince Lament's group for the second time that day and since their new group now consisted of nine members in total as they began to move off, Leah felt slightly comforted by that increase in size. Although the fourth group of defenders was still absent and as yet unaccounted for as Leah began to process the impact that their absence would have upon the battle that lay ahead, she started to appreciate the fact that at the very least, the seven defenders who were present that formed the majority of Leah's group and even Prince Lament himself, were all hardy, seasoned warriors.

When it came to the issue of Leah's safety there were no actual guarantees that she would be safe when the group entered into the palace but the defender's presence and that of Prince Lament did provide her with some gentle reassurances that she'd be slightly safer in their midst. Unfortunately, as Leah already knew, the nine would face an uncertain number of vamptrolls inside the building and so, the continuation of that protective comfort slightly buffered her fear which prior to that allocation had silently grown, accumulated and escalated inside her being.

Despite all Prince Lament's efforts to try and rid the town of the vamptrolls that day, Leah had noticed that so far, he had somehow managed to simultaneously keep an eye on her battles with the creatures as he had fought his own battles alongside her. In several instances in fact, en route to the palace, Prince Lament had already stepped in to assist Leah and he had delivered some very crucial blows to the vamptrolls which had been struck by his silver sword and as a result the vamptrolls that had threatened her simulated form at the time had quickly been extinguished. The continuation of Prince Lament's supportive presence therefore meant even more to Leah in terms of her safety than the actual increase in the number of defenders because he had so far conducted himself in a manner that had been very protective as he had shielded her from the vicious, savage nature of the gruesome, grisly hybrid creatures.

For the next few minutes, once the two groups had separated and had started to creep along the external walls of the palace in their respective directions, Leah noticed that there was total silence amongst her group and so she too kept her lips firmly closed. Although there seemed to be no vamptrolls present outside of the building, a strong undercurrent of fear still ran rampant through Leah's form which seemed almost relentless in nature which caused her to tremble and as she stuck to the rear of the group, she tried her best to comply with the group's covert movements.

The side entrance that the group were headed towards as Leah knew, would of course lead into Prince Lament's actual home and that notion intrigued her in some respects although it was of course, an artificial home, in an artificial nation that had been invaded by artificial creatures. Since the threat of a vamptroll appearance could occur at any given moment however, Leah still tried to remain in quite close proximity to Prince Lament himself even as she clung onto the rear edges of the group as she began to speculate as to just how many vamptrolls they might have to battle that evening.

An uncertain number of enemies definitely lay inside the external walls of the palace and so as Leah crept further along one of those walls, she fervently hoped that her pulse of bravery would remain strong enough for long enough to face not only the battles ahead but also to overcome the undercurrent of fear that ran through her interior. In terms of Leah's personal strengths, combat skills certainly weren't her forte or a zone of expertise that she felt comfortable to function or operate in which meant, in this instance confidence didn't brim from the interior of her being which felt more like a chaotic whirlpool of fear than a deep well of courage. Unfortunately, the emotional journey of surprise that Leah had embarked upon that day had really swept her away her with surprises and due to the nature of the challenges ahead which were unfamiliar territory in every way that they possibly could be, she felt more like a coward that wanted to run and hide than a bold, strong warrior with courage in their veins that was just about to head into battle.

Approximately ten minutes later, once Leah's group had crept into a side entrance of the palace and had walked along a quite long, narrow silverish hallway, the nine members of Leah's group arrived outside a side entrance to the banqueting hall which much to Leah's dismay, was a truly fearful sound and sight. The quiet approach of the group was totally shattered in just a matter of seconds by a loud sound burst of noises that clattered out of a narrow crack in the door to greet them and as Leah began to peek through that narrow crack in the side entrance, she almost froze in total shock.

Unfortunately, the narrow crack which kindly offered the group a flicker of visibility and a glimmer of access to the function room's interior without the commitment of making an actual entrance, did not actually render a kind sight to Leah's eyes which rapidly confirmed her current fears. Not only were the vamptrolls definitely present but they were also present in abundance and since they looked extremely comfortable in the room that they had decided to congregate in inside the building which they had of course, recently invaded, Leah felt it was highly unlikely that their numbers would reduce in the immediate future. In fact, from what Leah could see, the entire length of the function room was totally littered with vamptrolls which it seemed, they had decided to heavily populate, just as Prince Lament had accurately predicted they would.

Since the interior of the banqueting hall itself looked absolutely huge and besides the grisly vamptrolls and their gruesome mess, possessed definite traces of splendor, Leah was in total awe as she visually scanned the room and attempted to make a rough estimate as to how many vamptrolls were actually present. However, the vamptrolls didn't seem to have left much room for any other entities to be present at all and so, Leah struggled to arrive at an accurate figure or even a rough guess because her initial attempts to quantify the hybrid creatures seemed almost impossible. On a positive note however, from what Leah could see, most of the vamptrolls that had congregated inside the banqueting hall appeared to be quite deeply engrossed and rather noisily engaged in the consumption of an actual meal which looked almost as grotesque as their simulated forms.

Some large piles of bloody, raw meaty slabs, Leah observed as she watched the vamptrolls for a couple of minutes in silent disbelief, lay strewn across the tables that lined the room which were eagerly grabbed and then ripped to shreds by pairs of large, ugly, warty hands, the sight of which instantly struck chords of fear into Leah's heart and mind. Upon each table, at quite regular intervals, there also appeared to be large wooden jugs full of crimson red liquid which were frequently picked up and then the contents would be poured into tankards by the ugly hands as the vamptrolls enjoyed their feast which Leah noticed consisted of predominantly raw meat and some kind of animal blood. Despite all Leah's fears however, she somehow managed to keep the shrieks of horror inside her own form and remained completely silent as she watched the vamptrolls eat and drank to their grisly wart's content but shivers definitely ran down the back of her spine as the hybrid creatures enthusiastically indulged in their favorite consumable treats.

At quite regular intervals, Leah observed as she continued to peek through the narrow crack in the door, some cooks and kitchen staff that looked as if they manned the palace kitchens would dart in and out of the large function room doors with a continuous supply stream of vamptroll consumables. Most of the kitchen staff's hands, from what Leah could see, were either laden with trays that contained huge, raw, meaty slabs or large wooden jugs full of crimson fluid as they attended to the vamptrolls dietary requirements but as she could also see, along with the trays and jugs that the staff carried, their faces carried silent expressions of absolute fear and total terror upon them. Some of the kitchen staff, Leah noticed however, had no actual trays or jugs inside their hands as they rolled kegs of ale alongside them and as the gruesome feast of warts continued, totally uninterrupted, Leah shuddered as a large lump of disgust swiftly started to gather inside her throat which felt almost as large as one of the huge slabs of meat that sat upon one of the vamptrolls' tables.

Another silent attempt to make a rough estimate as to how many vamptrolls were actually present was speedily made as Leah continued to survey the large function room and since there definitely appeared to be at least fifty hybrid entities present, the members of Leah's group, were hugely outnumbered by at least five vamptrolls to one. However, as Leah turned her attention back towards her group and glanced around the palace hallway as she began to inspect the seven defenders' faces that were present, she noticed that not even one of them appeared to look worried or bothered in the slightest by the large presence of the vamptrolls because not even a shadow of fear ran across any of their faces. In fact, as Leah watched them fearlessly ready their weapons, there didn't appear to be even a second of nervous hesitation amongst them and their faces all bore determined expressions upon them that looked almost like shields of iron plastered to their simulated skin and so deep down inside, she definitely envied their abundance of courage which in this instance, she most certainly lacked.

Every inch of Leah's simulated form felt nervous as some low whispers were exchanged amongst the defenders as they prepared to launch an actual attack and as much as she admired their courage, she definitely feared what would happen when they actually entered into the banqueting hall and then tried to reclaim it. The vamptrolls were so huge and there were just so many of the hybrid creatures present which meant that the group were ultimately just about to charge into what was likely to be a very grisly end. Despite all Leah's fears and the mass of vamptrolls present inside the function room however, she tried to be brave and plaster a courageous expression across her face as another couple of minutes slipped by without any interruptions or any violent clashes as Prince Lament instructed the group as to how they should proceed.

Very admirably, Leah observed as she listened to Prince Lament speak, she couldn't sense even a flicker of nervousness from either his courageous whisper or his body language as he briefed those under his command in a hushed tone and he seemed to exhibit absolutely no fear at all. According to Prince Lament's instructions, to maximize the impact of the group's rather limited numbers, the group would have to enter the banqueting hall from several different angles which meant that most of the nine would now have to separate, a prospect which slightly worried Leah since she would be left with only Prince Lament by her side. Once in their respective attack positions, the defenders would then have to wait for Prince Lament's signal before they launched their attack but as the group started to separate and Leah began to the watch the seven defenders start to move off, the nervous lump of disgust inside her now parched throat seemed to become even larger.

A few more nervous minutes went by as Leah remained by the side door of the banqueting hall beside Prince Lament which as she could see through the narrow crack in the door, appeared to have at least ten entrances to its interior as the two waited for the defenders to creep into position. After another couple of minutes of silent stillness inside the hallway had gone by however, Leah noticed that Prince Lament suddenly took out a small horn from under his garments which he then proceeded to blow upon. Just a few seconds later as Leah watched in surprised astonishment, chaos then swiftly began to erupt inside the banqueting hall as the seven defenders started to storm the area and flooded into it from all sides of the large function room.

Much to Leah's sheer relief and surprise as two defenders jumped down from two chandeliers which hung from the ceiling straight onto the vamptrolls' heads, she noticed that more than just the seven defenders from her group actually seemed to be present and had entered into the actual banqueting hall. From what Leah could see, it appeared as if the five defenders from the group that had been missing, when the other three groups had arrived and then congregated outside the palace, had now turned up and had been met by their own group of defenders en route to their attack positions which had increased the defenders' numbers inside the banqueting hall to twelve. Although the vamptrolls still outnumbered the twelve defenders present, Leah could at least find a small glimmer of comfort in that slight increase in the defenders' number as she hoped that Foray's group would also join the battle inside the banqueting hall quite soon.

"Are you ready Leah?" Prince Lament suddenly asked as he turned to face her.

"As ready as I'll ever be I guess." Leah joked as she bravely held up her spear. "Is anyone ever really ready for a clash with tons of vicious vamptrolls?"

"Probably not." Prince Lament replied as he smiled, shook his head and then pulled the door open. "But let's give it our best attack mode anyway."

"I'll let you lead the way." Leah joked as she nodded. "You know your way around this place far better than I do."

Prince Lament grinned.

Due to Leah's nervous state, she kept quite close to Prince Lament's side as the two entered into the large function room and as she crept fearfully along beside him, Leah decided to focus her efforts upon the assistance of those already in battle with the vamptrolls, rather than an actual attempt to launch her own full-scale attack. For the next ten minutes, Leah ducked, slide and dove as she ventured around the interior of the banqueting hall mainly in a crouched position and as she did so, she wounded any vamptrolls that she could that crossed her path, the majority of whom were already locked in battle with some of the defenders present. From what Leah observed in the space of that ten chaotic minutes, the battle inside the large function room really was a battle of survival because it appeared as if the vamptrolls had risen to the defenders' challenge very quickly indeed and since the hybrid creatures were well equipped with easily accessible fangs and fists, both weapons were fully utilized by the vamptrolls as they not only defended their position but also eagerly attacked the town's defenders.

Unfortunately for Leah and her group, the vamptrolls had by that point definitely realized that an attempt to overthrow their dominion was underway and so, the hybrid conquerors had swiftly entered into full attack mode which included the delivery of some powerful knockout punches and some very sharp fangy bites. A few of the defenders were knocked across the room like ragdolls as Leah watched in total horror and started to tremble with fear but just as the battle seemed as it would be probably be lost quite quickly, some assistance suddenly arrived on the scene. Just in the nick of time, Foray's group reappeared which consisted of not just Foray but also eight defenders which meant that the number of defenders present rapidly rose to twenty again which Leah noticed very fortunately, had an immediate impact upon the battle against the vamptrolls as the new arrivals started to attack the hybrids with tenacity, strength and more doused weapons.

Fortunately, a flurry of powerful blows were struck against the vamptrolls in minutes and as Leah watched the new arrivals thrust the sharp edges of their spears and swords into any grisly vamptroll flesh that they could find, they inflicted blow upon blow upon the hybrid creatures present. Every inch of the banqueting hall seemed to be full of combat activity as the defenders' spears and swords clashed with the vamptroll flesh and as Leah watched the defenders leap upon the vamptrolls that remained from every possible direction and some of the vamptrolls evaporate into small puddles, the defenders seemed to successfully catch most of the hybrid creatures off guard.

Rather unexpectedly and just in time, reinforcements had arrived and it appeared as if the vamptrolls had been totally unprepared for that sudden increase in the defenders' collective capacity and so, the remainder were quickly overpowered. Not more than a few minutes later, the battle inside the banqueting hall swiftly came to an end as Leah watched the final few vamptrolls that remained be cornered then struck with doused weapons as the gruesome creatures were purged from the function room's interior. All that remained in the vamptrolls' place, once those last few hybrid creatures had been struck with doused spears and swords, were some small puddles of mucky water that much to Leah's relief had silently replaced their ugly, warty flesh and their sharp, scary fangs.

Once the scary hybrid creatures had been totally eradicated, Leah noticed that some of the palace kitchen staff suddenly rushed into the banqueting hall with smiles of relief upon their faces as they began to rejoice in the vamptrolls' defeat. In fact, expressions of total delight seemed to adorn each person's face, Leah observed as they made their way quickly towards the center of the large function room which is where Prince Lament, Foray and even Leah herself had gathered which indicated that the vamptrolls reign really had been a reign of fearful terror. Each person present, Leah noticed, gratefully began to express their delight at Prince Lament's return and eagerly welcomed him back as they neared and one of the male cooks at the rear of the group, a plumpish, bald man that wore a special kind of uniform which differed slightly from the other kitchen staff that surrounded him, seemed to take charge of the others as he approached.

The plumpish man who Leah instantly assumed was in charge of the palace kitchens because he seemed to possess an air of authority about him plus the difference in his uniform suggested that he might be, came to a standstill in front of Prince Lament, Foray and Leah as he prepared to address them. However, before the man began to speak, Leah noticed that he bowed down to greet the three and that once the man had delivered his gesture of royal courtesy, he then proceeded to address Prince Lament directly and as Leah listened to him speak, she smiled at his quite jovial comments.

"Prince Lament, it's so good to see you and may I just say that you're so much better to look at close up than those gruesome vamptrolls were." The male head chef boomed. "Thank goodness for your presence and for their absence. Really, I couldn't have kept up the food supplies for very much longer because the palace stores were starting to dwindle then goodness only knows what might have happened."

"I know Caspian, I hate to think because even my fighting spirit was starting to dwindle too." Prince Lament acknowledged. "Thank goodness those extra defenders showed up when they did."

"We should hold a feast this evening and a masquerade ball in honor of your return." Caspian swiftly suggested. "But we will need to find some more food supplies first because the palace kitchen cupboards are almost bare."

"I can help with that Prince Lament." Foray swiftly offered. "I have a huge store full of food at the back of the stables for emergencies."

"Right that sounds wonderful." Prince Lament agreed. "And will you attend this evening's festivities as my special honorary companion Leah?" He asked as he turned to face her.

Leah immediately smiled and nodded. "Definitely, I'd be honored to." She agreed.

"Truly, the honor really is all mine Leah." Prince Lament replied. He turned to face the other two men before he continued. "Gentlemen, this beautiful lady rescued me from the cruel clutches of Shamania the evil sorceress." He explained. "So, she's my hero and our hero. In fact, the whole kingdom of Fantoria is indebted to her, just as I am."

"That's settled then Prince Lament. We'll have a Grand Masquerade Ball and then a Feast of Heroes afterwards to celebrate not just your return but also to mark the brave deeds of the courageous heroine Lady Leah, since she saved the kingdom of Fantoria." Caspian acknowledged. "Because if you had not returned, we'd still be overrun by vamptrolls."

Just a second or two later a male palace attendant rushed over towards the four and as Leah watched, the man who appeared to be in his mid-fifties, approached Prince Lament with an air of familiarity.

"We're going to have a Grand Masquerade Ball and then a Feast of Heroes tonight Giles." Caspian swiftly mentioned. "So, you'll have to prepare Prince Lament and find a lady in waiting to attend to the heroic Lady Leah who will also grace us with her presence this evening."

"I'll do that straight away Caspian." Giles rapidly agreed. "And my wife Clarissa can of course, attend to Lady Leah."

"Thank you Giles, and thank you Caspian. I know I can trust you both to make all the necessary arrangements." Prince Lament replied.

"You certainly can Prince Lament, your evening and your night ahead is in very safe hands." Giles politely reassured him as he gave a certain nod and a polite courteous bow.

Less than a few seconds later, Leah watched in delighted amusement as Giles suddenly scurried off as he headed towards two large silver doors at one side of the banqueting hall which he then proceeded to pull open. Once the doors were open, Giles paused for a moment before he turned back to face Prince Lament and then Giles gave him a polite nod as he indicated that he was ready to proceed with the royal plans for the evening's special celebrations.

"We should really start to get ready now Leah." Prince Lament whispered to her as he gently held her arm. "We have a big night ahead of us."

Leah immediately nodded in cooperative agreement. "Sure." She replied as she allowed him to guide her towards the now open set of doors

After the two had stepped through the doors which much to Leah's surprise lead to a conveyor belt type escalator which seemed to go all the way to the top of the building, Giles followed the two out of the function room and then he pulled the grand doors swiftly shut behind the three of them. Since the conveyor belt escalator appeared to be the only form of transport to the next floor, Leah willingly, rapidly followed Prince Lament's lead as he stepped on to it.

"Since you've been gone Prince Lament, the entire kingdom has been thrown into total disarray, so we've really missed your guidance and your wisdom." Giles mentioned as he stepped onto the conveyor belt and then pressed a button.

"Well, I'm back now Giles." Prince Lament reassured him as he gave him a certain smile. "So, there's no need to worry anymore."

Giles smiled and nodded. "Yes, and thank goodness you are." He replied.

For the next few minutes as the conveyor belt type escalator made its ascent, Leah kept extremely quiet as she listened to the two men speak because the mode of transport to the next floor had surprised her since it had totally misaligned with her usual expectations. From what Leah could see as the conveyor belt moved upward at a steady, moderate pace, there appeared to be at least seven more floors above their heads and so the sheer sophistication of the building's interior absolutely stunned her. When the conveyor belt escalator arrived parallel to the first floor, approximately three or four minutes after its departure, Leah watched in fascinated silence as it came to a total standstill and as it did so, Prince Lament immediately stepped off it after which point, he politely offered Leah a hand of assistance.

"You can prepare for the feast and the ball in my living quarters Leah." Prince Lament offered.

"Thanks." Leah replied as she stepped off the conveyor belt and onto the first floor.

"Giles, can you ask Clarissa to bring Leah something appropriate to wear please?" Prince Lament asked as he turned to face him.

"Yes Prince Lament, once I've escorted you to your quarters, I'll do that straight away." Giles cooperatively confirmed.

Just a second or two later Leah began to follow Prince Lament and Giles as they started to walk along the silverish, grand hallway towards two large silver doors which were situated at the other end of it and as Leah walked, she quietly began to absorb and process some of the regal splendor that surrounded her. When Giles arrived in front of the two huge doors which Leah noticed, stretched all the way from the ground to the ceiling, she watched as he swiftly pulled them open and as he did so, Prince Lament started to enter into the large reception room that was swiftly revealed.

"These are my living quarters Leah." Prince Lament explained as he invited her to enter into his personal private space. "Please come in and make yourself as comfortable as you wish to."

Nothing but sheer luxury and absolute splendor greeted Leah's eyes as soon as she stepped into the room and the lavish nature of the reception room's interior, totally stunned her because it was as if she was now immersed in absolute luxury which almost looked too perfect and too immaculate to disturb. Once Giles had ushered the two inside Prince Lament's quarters, Leah watched as just a moment later, he departed and then closed the doors behind him and as he left the two alone, she released a grateful sigh because her fight with the vamptrolls for that day was now, definitely over.

"You know, I almost thought that you'd abandoned me completely Lament." Leah mentioned as she turned to face him and smiled. "When you disappeared in the Meadows of Surprise, I didn't actually think that you'd come back."

"Why would I abandon you Leah?" Prince Lament teased. "After all, you saved me, so I definitely had to return to say thank you."

"What do you usually do when you're not being captured by evil sorceresses?" Leah asked as she smiled.

"Well, I do have a kingdom to run." Prince Lament explained. "So, I usually have to attend to kingdom affairs and I have to govern the town."

"It must be a lot of hard work." Leah swiftly concluded. "If today was anything to go by."

"Yes, sometimes it does have tricky moments and today, was definitely one of those slightly trickier days." Prince Lament agreed. "It's not always so hectic though and I do have some advisors, ministers and governors to oversee certain matters, so they usually assist me with various tasks."

"How many people live in your kingdom?" Leah asked.

"Well, if you include all the townspeople and all the people that live in the surrounding land outside the walls of the town, about three thousand." Prince Lament replied. "And quite often, we trade with neighboring kingdoms, so I have to ensure that our relationships with those kingdoms stand in good stead at all times."

"My clothes are looking very grubby now, after all our clashes today with the vamptrolls." Leah solemnly mentioned as she glanced down at the clothes that adorned her form which now looked like mucky rags.

"Don't worry about that Leah." Prince Lament quickly reassured her as he smiled. "Giles, Clarissa and I will sort that out, this is my kingdom after all."

When Clarissa arrived just a few minutes later, the two women were swiftly introduced and then directed towards a luxurious guest bedroom which also had an en-suite bathroom so that Leah could prepare for the evening ahead. Everything that Leah could possibly want or need for her preparations, fortunately enough, appeared to be present and virtually at her fingertips as she started to visually inspect the large guest room and en-suite bathroom. The sunken bath inside the en-suite bathroom, Leah swiftly observed, was almost the size of a small swimming pool and a vast assortment of oils, skin creams and lotions sat neatly placed all around its edges which promised to cater to any skin type imaginable and so as Clarissa set the sunken bath, Leah prepared to cooperate in totality with the luxury that surrounded her in total willingness.

Approximately fifteen to twenty minutes slipped peacefully by as Leah lay, soaked, floated around and wallowed inside the sunken tub as she allowed the delicious, warm drops of water to fully penetrate her simulated pores. A thick layer of soft, silky, foamy bubbles gently popped and nestled against Leah's form and as that layer of luxury embraced her simulated skin, every part of her felt invigorated, fully restored and filled with a deep sense of gratitude. Since the drops of freshness inside the sunken bath, cooperatively sank into the grooves of Leah's simulated skin voluntarily, the water totally flushed out any mucky remnants that had been left behind from her earlier clashes with the vamptrolls that day and therefore very little effort was actually required on Leah's part.

About thirty minutes after Leah had entered into the bathroom, she finally reemerged and greeted Clarissa with a smile but now her simulated form was wrapped in a crisp white bathrobe that she'd found on a silvery hook beside the sunken bath. Since Leah now felt sufficiently cleansed and fully restored from the mucky vamptroll battles as she prepared to dress and to be pampered, she looked forward to the night ahead which promised to be the absolute height of luxury. An elegant evening definitely lay ahead of Leah which would be a very welcome change from the unexpected, rough, mucky vamptroll battles that she had endured earlier that day and so she couldn't wait to embrace the night and all it promised to deliver to her heart and mind. After all the surprising oddities of Leah's day up until that point, an elegant sip of sophistication was definitely more than welcome and this final surprise activity that had been sprung upon her, would certainly be far more up her street of personal enjoyment.

Upon Leah's face there was a smile as she headed towards the dress choices that had been laid out for her by Clarissa on top of the large four poster bed inside the guest bedroom and from what Leah could see at first glance, she simply couldn't fault Clarissa's attendance. A few minutes were spent in thoughtful silence as Leah began her visual inspection of the choices on offer but that silence wasn't a disappointed silence, rather a speechless one because the variety of available choices had definitely dazzled her simulated, artificial presence.

So far, Leah concluded as she touched some of soft, silky, satin material that dripped and slipped through her fingers with delightful elegance, Clarissa had attended to Leah's requirements impeccably and with absolute precision because each dress appealed to Leah so much that it really was hard to arrive at decision. Every dress on offer to Leah's simulated form looked not only extremely elegant but also the height of sophistication and some slipper like shoes had also been provided to match each outfit in a range of colors along with some jewelry sets and so there really was a wide range of elegant sophistication to choose from.

A few more silent minutes were spent in thoughtful consideration as Leah continued to peruse the material delights upon the bed, one of which she knew, she would definitely wear for the deep dive that she was just about to take into a sophisticated night of luxurious recreation until finally, she managed to arrive at a final decision. One of the outfit combinations seemed to stand out slightly more than the others and so that dress, finally won the battle of visual attraction as Leah picked up the deep, rich, satin burgundy and gold trimmed dress which had some beautiful golden cross over straps and some decorative jewels sprinkled across it. Since there was a pair of golden, jeweled slippers to match, Leah felt that both the outfit and the footwear looked elegant yet comfortable, stylish but unique and so as she fully committed to her choice, she prepared to slip the dress on.

"I think I'd like to wear this outfit Clarissa with these golden slippers." Leah said decisively as she turned to face her. "It was a very hard decision though because all of these outfits are absolutely gorgeous."

"Yes, I think that one will really suit you Lady Leah." Clarissa replied as she smiled. "Well, I didn't stitch a single one because all of these dresses were made for celebratory palace events by my seamstress. She's usually very good when it comes to occasional evening attire." She clarified. "But I'll pass on your compliments. Would you like me to help you put your dress on?"

"No don't worry Clarissa, I think I should be okay." Leah confirmed as she began to remove the bathrobe and then started to slip on the dress. "Will you be coming to the ball and the feast Clarissa?" She asked as she began to tie some of the dress's cross over straps around her form.

"I won't be at the Grand Masquerade Ball Lady Leah." Clarissa replied as she shook her head. "But I will be at the Feast of Heroes afterwards with Giles. We both have a few other things to attend to this evening, mainly palace duties but as soon as we finish with those tasks and then prepare ourselves, we'll come to the feast. If you'd like to sit down at the dressing table now, I'll attend to your makeup, hair and accessories before I leave." She offered.

Leah nodded. "Thanks." She replied as she walked towards the dressing table and then sat down in front of the huge mirror upon it. "You know Clarissa, I've noticed that Prince Lament's kingdom is very color coordinated, doesn't it look almost perfect?"

"Yes, but isn't perfection something that we all like to aspire to?" Clarissa teased as she walked towards the dressing table.

"True." Leah agreed as she thoughtfully considered her work on Spectrum and her own pursuit of scientific, technological, recreational perfection. "But it's not always something that we can reach as imperfect human beings."

"But at least tonight Lady Leah, your dress, shoes, mask and hair will all hit the very high heights of total perfection." Clarissa reassured her.

"Yes, and this will probably be as close as I'll ever come to actual perfection in my entire lifetime." Leah swiftly acknowledged. "Because perfection is such a hard place to find and an even harder destination to reach."

"Hopefully not Lady Leah." Clarissa replied. "Hopefully, you'll find perfection in some areas of life, or just enough perfection in enough areas of life to satisfy your own mind."

"Now that Clarissa is a very good point." Leah agreed as she nodded her head. "A very good point indeed."

Despite Leah's adventurous day and her very mucky afternoon, once her hair, makeup and jewelry had all been immaculately organized by Clarissa's gentle but precise hands and fingers, Leah almost felt like a princess as she admired the beautiful results in the mirror. Some stunning pieces of jewelry had been attached to Leah's simulated frame by Clarissa that now adorned her hair, neck and wrists in which matched her dress perfectly and with absolute precision. A very elaborate, elegant up style had also been created by Clarissa, Leah observed and some lines of jewelry had even been woven into her strands of hair which gave her whole head a very regal look. Every stroke of makeup had been applied meticulously and as Leah stared at her reflection, she noticed that the colors chosen by Clarissa matched her outfit and accessories immaculately and so as far as Leah was concerned, Clarissa's attentive efforts that evening, verged upon absolute perfection.

"Oh, before I forget Lady Leah, here's a mask to match your dress." Clarissa said as she walked towards the bed, picked up a golden bag and then slipped her hand inside it. "You can wear this to the Grand Masquerade Ball." She clarified as she returned to the dressing table. "Once the ball is over and the Feast of Heroes begins then everyone in attendance will unmask themselves but trying to guess who people are beforehand can be tremendous fun because it adds a bit of mystery to the evening."

"Thanks Clarissa for everything." Leah replied as she rose to her feet, accepted the jeweled mask offered to her and then held it up in front of her face. "A night incognito."

"You're welcome Lady Leah but we'd better go now because Prince Lament will be waiting for your return." Clarissa mentioned as she began to walk towards the door. "I should really return you to him now." She insisted as she placed her hand on the door handle. "And yes, for a night, you'll be a lady of mystery."

Every inch of the mask, Leah noticed as she began to inspect it as she started to follow Clarissa's lead and make her way towards the door, looked absolutely stunning from the deep burgundy surfaces to the delicate golden rims that decorated each of the edges along with the diamond jewels that had been sprinkled across it. Although Leah wasn't really accustomed to covering her face, since she felt eager to participate in the festivities that evening, she enthusiastically held the mask up in place as she arrived beside the door but because she still wished to see Prince Lament without the mask in place, Leah didn't actually clip the mask into position.

Fortunately for Leah, all the preparations for the evening and night ahead had gone exceptionally well and so as Clarissa opened the door and the two stepped through it, Leah felt extremely confident that at least she would be appropriately dressed for the occasion. Much to Leah's total delight, she noticed that as she walked, the satin material of her dress gently clung to her upper body and then cascaded down towards the ground into a fishtail style and as it fell, it softly lapped against her skin with her every movement as the gown seemed to embrace and accentuate every inch of her frame as it silently celebrated her femininity.

Everything around Leah currently felt absolutely realistic, totally heavenly and full of excitement which meant that all the long, continuous, stressful working hours down in the basement that had not just taken a toll upon Leah's relationship but even upon her own mind had finally paid off. For several years Leah had juggled moderate finances, scarce time and quite limited resources to achieve her professional goals but finally now it seemed, Leah's investment and professional efforts had been successfully achieved and almost fully realized because inside Spectrum, in recent times, she had found not only found fresh enthusiasm, a new zest for life but also some glamorous days that had been full of intrigue and topped up with an abundance of joyful delights. In some ways, Leah's experiences inside Spectrum had even motivated her to participate in her own real life a lot more enthusiastically and so in every sense imaginable, Leah definitely felt that Spectrum fulfilled its intended purpose which prompted a satisfied smile to cross her face as the two women left the guest bedroom and Clarissa pulled the door shut behind them both.

Much to Leah's surprise, as the two women re-entered the main reception area of Prince Lament's living quarters she found Prince Lament not only fully prepared for the evening ahead but also that Giles was now once again present. Since Prince Lament now looked utterly dashing and deliciously handsome, Leah couldn't help but smile as she stepped into the main reception area of Prince Lament's living quarters which was large enough to house two sofas inside it along with some armchairs and even a dining area.

From what Leah had observed so far, the four internal single doors in the main reception room led directly into two guest bedrooms, one library/study type room and the fourth door led directly into the master bedroom and so Prince Lament's living quarters were really quite large as well as very splendid. On one side of the room there were two large French window doors which a large patio sat politely directly outside but even the patio itself looked luxurious because it not only contained some silvery throne like chairs and a huge silver table which were generously scattered across it but it also housed a large sofa swing, all of which indicated that you could spend a whole afternoon out there, if you wished to do so. Since the town skewered out all around the palace which could clearly be seen from the patio, the patio offered a bird's eye view of the entire town and beyond from an extremely regal viewpoint which also meant that Prince Lament had a pretty good view of his kingdom whenever he actually needed one.

"Ah ladies, you're back." Prince Lament teased. "Just for a moment there, I'd almost thought that we'd lost you and Leah, can I just mention that you look absolutely stunning."

"Thank you, Prince Lament, and can I just say that you look very dashing yourself." Leah replied as she felt his eyes run over every inch of her body.

"You certainly can." Prince Lament replied as he smiled.

"I better be going now Prince Lament because I have a few tasks to complete and then I have to prepare Giles and myself for the feast." Clarissa suddenly mentioned as she began to excuse herself. She turned to face Giles for a few seconds before she continued. "And Giles, you'll definitely require a lot more effort than Lady Leah did because you are far less cooperative." Clarissa turned to face the two once again as she spoke to them both in a playfully loud whisper. "He absolutely hates waistcoats but they really do suit him."

"Right but thanks for all your assistance Clarissa." Prince Lament replied as he nodded appreciatively at her. "You've been a tremendous help."

"You're such a tease Clarissa. I just find waistcoats to be very awkward contraptions." Giles piped in as he grinned. "You know, you women are so lucky, you don't actually have to wear them so you should definitely consider that a plus."

"Well Giles and Clarissa, we'll see you both at the feast." Prince Lament said as he released the couple from service for the remainder of the evening. "Don't worry Giles, I'll take over from here because you both need some time to prepare yourselves. Perhaps you can choose what you would like to wear and then Clarissa can select what she wants you to wear and somewhere between the two, you might just find a compromise."

"Hopefully that will happen before the feast actually begins." Clarissa joked. "That could take a while though because our selections are usually miles and miles apart."

"Now that sounds like a tremendously regal plan Prince Lament and one that I fully support." Giles agreed as he nodded his head.

Some giggles managed to slip out of Leah's mouth as she watched Clarissa and Giles start to walk away as they both headed towards the large set of silver doors and began to make their departure but when they arrived in front of the doors, Giles paused for a moment before he turned back to face the two.

"I don't know Prince Lament, the things that make women happy, I'll never understand it." Giles concluded as he shook his head. "A waistcoat, a tight, stuffy material contraption that knots itself around the wearer's ribcage and ties up their every breath."

"Well Giles, since they do look extremely beautiful, I guess we just have to overlook the fact that we don't always understand them or what makes them happy." Prince Lament teased. "Do we always have to, can't we just love and appreciate them and sometimes, stick on the tight, stuffy, material contraptions?"

"You're a very wise man Prince Lament and I definitely think that you're right, it does make for a much more peaceful and a far easier life." Giles agreed as he pulled open the doors and grinned.

Once the two had departed and Giles had escorted his wife out into the hallway, Leah watched in amused silence as Prince Lament decisively strode across the room and then plucked a silvery, greyish wig from a wig mannequin which sat on top of a silver table that nestled politely in one of the large room's four corners. Rather delightfully, Leah noticed that Prince Lament removed his crown and then placed it upon the mannequin before he secured the wig to the top of his head which clearly indicated to her that he wanted to conceal his identity from the other ball attendees that evening as much as he possibly could which also meant that the two would be united in a delightfully warm, shared secrecy. When Prince Lament had finished with his hair, Leah noticed that he then turned his attention towards the mask that he would wear that evening as he picked up a silver jeweled mask that would mask his identity during their attendance at the Grand Masquerade Ball.

"Now Leah, absolutely no one in attendance at the Grand Masquerade Ball will know who I am, besides you of course." Prince Lament joked as he held the mask up in one of his hands and a mischievous smile crossed his face. "And that anonymity could actually be quite fun."

Upon Leah's face there was a delighted smile as she continued to watch Prince Lament as she visually scanned his appearance and attempted to absorb his now electrifyingly handsome state which was a far cry from their first encounter earlier that day and so much so that a pulse of passion surged through her simulated veins. The man that Leah had found chained up to the pet trader's Roundabout of Trickery had been a broken shadow of a man, a man without hope, a man without fight and a man who had lost all of his courage but now, Prince Lament looked absolutely immaculate in every way that he possibly could and deliciously so. In the space of that day and right before Leah's own eyes, Prince Lament had been restored to a courageous warrior, a righteous leader and a noble Prince and that transformation had been one of the most beautiful parts of Leah's emotional journey so far that day and the biggest surprise.

"Shall we go my lady?" Prince Lament asked as he swiftly clipped on the mask and then gently held her arm. "The Grand Masquerade Ball and the Feast of Heroes await us."

"Yes, I'm definitely ready." Leah confirmed as she too clipped on her mask.

Prince Lament nodded. "Right then let's start to make our way downstairs." He suggested as he began to lead her towards the door.

"Sure." Leah replied as she nodded her head. "And may I just say, before we vacate your living quarters that they are absolutely heavenly, so it was truly a joy to prepare myself here."

"You certainly can and before we get caught up in the hustle and bustle of the evening, I'd like to thank you Leah for everything that you did today." Prince Lament replied as he paused for a moment in front of the silvery doors. "Since we wish to remain incognito for the duration of the ball, we'll have to walk around the building via the palace grounds and then enter into the banqueting hall through the main palace entrance." He explained as he pulled the doors open. "Because if we enter through the same side entrance that we exited from earlier this evening, some people might guess who I am and that would spoil all the fun."

"Right." Leah speedily agreed as she stepped through the open doors and entered into the hallway.

The fact that no one else present at the ball would know who Prince Lament was besides Leah herself, held the promise of a pleasant, delicate secrecy that would exist that evening just between the two, a prospect that prompted Leah to smile in absolute delight. Once Prince Lament had followed Leah out into the hallway, the two began to make their way back towards the conveyor belt escalator as Leah silently considered that pleasant notion further which had definitely excited her since it would provide the two with something humorous to whisper and joke about as they confided in each other throughout the course of the evening. However, the most truly delightful part of that shared secrecy for Leah, would actually be the fact that for the first time that day the two would spend some time together that was a bit more their own because up until that point, their day together had predominantly revolved around Prince Lament's duties to his kingdom and so the night ahead promised to be full of flirtatious enjoyment.

"You know Prince Lament; the architecture and the interior design of this palace are truly amazing." Leah acknowledged as the two walked. "Were you involved?"

"Yes, I totally agree but no I wasn't. My parents had one of the best architects and the finest interior designer in the five kingdoms design this palace for them and for many years, this was their favorite residence." Prince Lament mentioned. "It is the smallest kingdom out the five however, so when I came of age it made more sense for them to allow me to govern this kingdom than any of the other four larger ones."

"It's absolutely breathtaking." Leah admitted. "I'd love to live somewhere like this."

Every place that Leah had visited so far within the palace's interior had possessed very high ceilings that arched way above simulated human heads and not only had Prince Lament's quarters been totally divine but in Leah's opinion, the hallway's interior was just as beautiful. Each side of the hallway had silver window ledges at frequent intervals where elegant, elaborate statues sat that looked to Leah as if they had been not only expertly crafted but also formed from some kind of precious materials and every simulated inch delighted Leah's eyes. In fact, the statues themselves were so beautiful that as far as Leah was concerned, each one could easily be a feature on display that one might expect to find inside any of the finest art exhibitions. Although Leah didn't actually remember her creation of the entire structure and every object it contained, she tried not to dwell on that mystery for too long as she accepted the beauty around her for what it was and attempted to focus upon the rest of her evening.

After the two had made their downward descent on the conveyor belt escalator, Leah was led down one side of the building and then out of an actual side door as per Prince Lament's plan which also held the promise of a grand entrance via the palace's grand entrance although that would of course be, in a masked state. Once the two had stepped outside, Leah was then led around the edge of the building as they headed towards the main entrance where Prince Lament had mentioned that they could blend in easily with some of the other Grand Masquerade Ball attendees and re-enter the palace's interior without being noticed. Since the actual Grand Masquerade Ball and Feast of Heroes were effectively being held in Leah and Prince Lament's honor, she felt a tremendous undercurrent of excitement ripple through her form as the two entered back into the main palace building once again through the actual main grand entrance at the rear of a group of ball attendees.

Inside the palace reception area, Leah instantly noticed that the large room literally surged with simulated people all of whom wore masks that covered their faces and as the two crossed it, they began to make their way towards the entrance of the huge banqueting hall. A beautiful melody flowed through the air and out of the entrance to the function room itself and as the two stepped into the large function room, Leah noticed that each beautiful note seemed to caress her ears as the delightful melody gently circled the room.

Since the function room now looked absolutely spectacular, Leah almost gasped in delight as she began to absorb the transformation that had taken place because it definitely differed vastly from the awful state that they two had left it in earlier that evening. Everything around Leah now looked ultra clean and utterly splendid as each ornament, every item of furniture and all the fixtures and fittings inside the large function room sparkled and shone, so it almost looked as if the vamptrolls had never really been there at all because there was now no traces or signs of them anywhere to be found.

In one corner of the large function room, Leah spotted a group of musicians that seemed to be responsible for the delightful melody that flowed across the room as the tune decorated the air inside the banqueting hall with delightful rhythms, wonderful chords and beautiful bars. Rather splendidly, in the very center of the room, Leah could now see that there was now a huge silvery, crystal dance floor which was semi-transparent and that just below the surface of that dance floor there appeared to be some silvery flowers and some silvery lights that sparkled and shone which made the entire room looked extremely elegant and very sophisticated.

Much to Leah's delight and surprise, the banqueting hall was now a far cry from the mangled function room that both she and Prince Lament had left behind earlier that evening before they had visited his living quarters which had possessed just some very vague traces of splendor. Some crystal, silvery chandeliers adorned the high ceiling and as Leah glanced at each one and absorbed their elegant beauty, she couldn't help but be in total awe because the elaborate chandeliers sparkled and shone brightly as each one lit up the room and performed their duty for the evening, silently but immaculately.

"Shall we dance Leah?" Prince Lament suddenly whispered in her ear as he turned to face her.

Leah immediately nodded her head in response. "Yes, I'd

absolutely love to." She replied. "I don't really know any of the songs or any of the dances though."

"Don't worry about it, just follow my lead. No one's an expert, especially not the first time around." Prince Lament swiftly reassured her in a hushed tone as he gently held onto her arm and then lead her towards the dancefloor. "It took me years to learn some of our national dances, so don't worry if you get a bit lost at times."

For the next hour or so, Leah plunged herself into the music, dance routines and laughter that filled the large function room which was definitely made far easier due to the fact that the she was masked because the mask seemed to offer her an anonymity that was extremely comfortable. In fact, due to the mask, Leah was able to totally cast her inhibitions aside because it seemed to allow her confidence to run on a full fuel tank and without any obstructions which was very unusual because so often she felt restricted in life by her own self-doubts.

On several occasions, when Leah did actually step in the wrong direction which resulted in an actual collision with Prince Lament, the two giggled and then teased each other as Leah silently rejoiced in the pleasantness of her evening which was a delightful treat after all the ugly battles and awful clashes with the gruesome vamptrolls. Sadly however, even though Leah hoped it would never end, the Grand Masquerade Ball finally ended as a huge drum roll sounded out across the room and the Master of Ceremonies made his way towards the center of the banqueting hall.

Unlike Sebastian however, Leah noticed that the Master of Ceremonies on this particular occasion was a serious looking man dressed in smart attire as he arrived at the center of the dancefloor with a small silver scroll inside one of his hands. A few giggles rippled through the sea of masks as Leah began to visually inspect the sea of simulated people around her but as the man clapped his hands together, the giggles swiftly faded and disintegrated into total silence as Leah watched everyone around her turn to face him.

"Ladies and gentlemen, you may now unmask yourselves." The man announced as he started to read out the contents of the scroll.

"And then the Feast of Heroes will commence."

An eruption of giggles, chatter and laughter suddenly joyously rumbled and echoed around the large spacious room, Leah observed as the simulacrums around her started to remove their masks and absolute hilarity was swiftly ushered in as the discovery of identities were fully made. Although it had been virtually impossible for Leah to recognize anyone with their masks in position, a flicker of recognition actually crossed her face as she glanced around the room and managed to spot some of the defenders that she had seen earlier that day and of course Foray, who was also in attendance.

Some beautifully dressed tables lined the four walls of the large function room and as some of the people on the dancefloor began to make their way towards them, Leah noticed that some servers started to rush in out of the room with silver trays full of delicacies inside their hands. Each table was quickly populated with an array of bite size canopies and as Leah was led by Prince Lament towards two throne like chairs and a large, grand table at the top of the room, it suddenly struck her that there had to be at least one hundred simulated people in attendance as more attendees suddenly started to arrive for the Feast of Heroes. The sea of predominantly strange faces, Leah noticed, politely parted in front of the two as they walked and some snippets of conversation could be overheard which mostly seemed to revolve around how grateful people were that Prince Lament had been rescued and that he had then returned to rescue the townspeople from the grisly vamptrolls.

Every table that Leah could see, was swiftly, generously adorned with large, silver platter trays laden with an assortment of meats, fish, pulses, breads and vegetables as the Feast of Heroes began and as Leah willingly participated, a buzz of conversation and laughter from the feast's attendees began to fill the room. Each of the four walls inside the banqueting hall were soon fully decorated in delicious aromas, joyful chitter chatter and jovial giggles of sheer delight as Leah started to heartily tuck in to some of the culinary wonders on offer to her simulated palate.

Much to Leah's delight, the Feast of Heroes continued at a

pleasant, joyful pace for the next hour and as she embraced the companionship of Prince Lament, she ate her fill as she enjoyed his discussions because he really was a great conversationalist as well as electrifyingly and dashingly handsome. Everyone in attendance seemed to enjoy the evening to their hearts content Leah observed as the hours of the evening scampered silently away, never to return and so as far as she was concerned, she wasn't in a rush to leave this particular Spectrum environment and certainly not in a hurry.

Since the Spectrum timer had initially been set after lunch for a full ten-hour adventure, Leah didn't feel any pressure to rush through any parts of her emotional journey that day because her adventure was due to end at about eleven that night and so she had enjoyed it at quite a relaxed pace. Although Leah's emotional journey that day would at almost midnight, it would not end on the wrong side of midnight, unlike some other instances when Leah had stumbled out of the basement in the early hours of the next morning. However, as the evening wore on and the night started to threaten to appear, Leah felt slightly saddened by the reality that her trip inside Spectrum that day, would soon be over because it truly had been extremely enjoyable.

Throughout the course of the feast, Leah had noticed that both Clarissa and Giles had been present, seated together at one of the long tables that lined the room and Leah had managed to exchange some polite smiles with them both as she'd admired their attire, presentation and overall appearance. Unlike earlier that day however, when Leah had first met the couple, the two were now dressed in satin robes and tailored apparel, all of which made them look extremely elegant and very dapper as the material clung to their simulated forms and their faces glowed. In accordance with Clarissa's preferences, Leah had also noticed that Giles now wore a waistcoat which had amused her as she had silently concluded that although Giles had braved the vamptrolls and had helped the kitchen staff earlier that day, he had definitely lost the battle of the waistcoats with Clarissa and had in the end it seemed, fully surrendered.

Approximately two hours after the ball had begun and once

Leah had eaten her fill, a suggestion full of sensual intrigue was delightfully whispered into her ear by Prince Lament that involved their potential departure from the festivities without anyone else's knowledge or involvement. Since Prince Lament's escape suggestion totally delighted Leah, she immediately prepared to comply because the two hadn't really spent much time together that day alone and so as he rose to his feet, Leah swiftly followed his lead as she prepared to vacate the large function room. Upon Prince Lament's face, Leah noticed that there was a mischievous grin as he started to lead her towards a nearby set of French windows which sat about ten meters or so away from their table and the throne like chairs at the very top of the room as if he wished to show her something outside.

Inside Leah a sensual current of excitement rapidly began to chaotically stir and swirl around as she walked as the passion that lingered on her lips provoked deeper internal questions within her as to the sensual delights that Prince Lament's seductive suggestion might contain. Since Leah had already spent a few hours in the companionship of Prince Lament, his subjects and friends, she now definitely wanted to spend some time in direct companionship with Prince Lament himself so that the two could embark upon an exploration of his private royal domain. A flag of passion could perhaps, Leah silently considered, be placed upon any sensual territory that the two discovered together in passionate unity but as she already knew, they certainly couldn't do that inside the banqueting hall and so a departure from it was therefore absolutely essential.

The large function room from Leah could see and hear, was still very much alive with eruptions of chitter chatter, rhythmic tones, rumbles of laughter and other joyful noises which flowed from every possible direction but that seemed to provide the two with enough of a distraction as they neared the French windows. A pair of long, silvery curtains hung down on either side of each window door and as Prince Lament led Leah towards one of the curtains, she began to speculate as to how a curtain could possibly help them to leave the large function room. For a moment, Leah wondered if perhaps they would have to exit through the window doors and then walk around the perimeter of the building again however, she fully cooperated and silently participated with Prince Lament's direction, despite her questions and despite the lack of any immediate answers.

After just a few seconds had gone by however, much to Leah's surprise, Prince Lament quickly pulled the curtain across one of the window doors which concealed both their forms before he walked towards the wall on the very right-hand side. Suddenly, Leah noticed that there was actually a small door on the right-hand side of the two window doors which was very discreetly positioned and as she watched in total fascination and amused silence, Prince Lament opened the small door up and then ducked down as he stepped through it.

Once Leah had joined Prince Lament, he then quickly shut the door behind them both as they left the banqueting hall behind and as the two made their actual escape from the hustle and bustle of the large, very populated function room, Leah started to giggle in delighted amusement. On the other side of the door, Leah swiftly discovered that there was a narrow passage which appeared to lead towards the rear of the palace and that at the end of the passage which wasn't very long, there appeared to be a wide glass tube that looked like some kind of lift shaft. When the two arrived at the end of the short, narrow passage and opposite the glass tube, Leah watched as Prince Lament pressed a button that was situated on the wall beside the glass door and as he did so, a circular, tube shaped glass lift suddenly began to descend until it was parallel to their position.

A cooperative, courteous invitation seemed to be swiftly offered to the two by the glassy contraption as Leah watched the glass door in front of them both, rapidly swish open and as the two were silently invited to enter into the glassy interior, a courteous lift was accepted by them both as they eagerly stepped into the glassy case. After the two had stepped inside the glass lift, Leah noticed that Prince Lament swiftly pressed a second button inside the lift itself that was situated on the right-hand side of the glass contraption and that as soon as he did so, the transparent door instantly swished shut just before the glass tubular lift actually started to move upwards.

Just a few seconds later the lift arrived at its intended destination and parallel to the first floor of the palace and once the door swished open for the second time, Leah followed Prince Lament's lead as he eagerly led her out of the glassy interior and into another narrow passage. At the end of the second narrow passage there was another small door which Prince Lament led Leah towards and once they arrived directly in front of it, he swiftly opened it up. The second door, much to Leah's total fascination, hopeful expectations and absolute delight, appeared to lead straight into the hallway just twenty meters or so away from the entrance to Prince Lament's actual living quarters which meant that no further deviations or complex routes would have to be followed in order to arrive at what Leah hoped would be a very sensual destination for them both.

"Ladies first." Prince Lament offered as he politely held the door open for her and flashed her a mischievous grin.

"Wow, those escape passages and that glass lift must really come in handy at times." Leah mentioned as she stepped through the door.

"Yes, that escape route is definitely very useful. I usually utilize it when formal occasions drag on for too long Leah." Prince Lament joked as he followed her into the hallway. "Some people seem to be overly attached to extra-long ceremonies full of very long speeches, so it can be a real blessing at times and provide me with an easy escape route from absolute boredom."

Leah laughed. "Do you think anyone will have noticed that we've left yet?" She asked.

"Probably not, well maybe one or two people but we did make a very quick, almost silent getaway, so it might take people a while to realize that we're no longer actually present." Prince Lament mentioned. "And since the wine and food are still flowing, I doubt that anyone will be particularly bothered by our departure."

Less than a minute later the two arrived outside Prince Lament's living quarters once again and as Prince Lament opened up one of the large doors and then held it open, Leah stepped back inside the large reception room. An air of sensual expectancy seemed to linger in the air all around the two as Leah entered the room and as Prince Lament followed her, she began to appreciate the privacy that was now on offer to them both which meant that a tender moment of appreciation could not only be enjoyed but also more fully explored.

"Right Leah, we need to do this properly." Prince Lament playfully and seductively suggested as he quickly shut the door behind them and then gently held her arm. "Because now, it's time for you and I to celebrate our victories today, privately and personally."

Much to Leah's total delight as she watched in excited anticipation, Prince Lament strode across the room towards a drinks cabinet which he then plucked a large ice bucket from and then eagerly filled. A bottle of champagne and two glasses were swiftly taken from the drinks cabinet as Leah continued to watch and as she did so, she couldn't help but feel bubbles of sensual passion ripples across the surface of her simulated skin.

"Where would you like to drink this my lady?" Prince Lament asked as he enthusiastically strode back across the room and drew closer to her. "In here, or perhaps somewhere else?" He asked playfully as a seductive smile crossed his face.

Deep down inside Leah already knew the answer to that question and it certainly wasn't the main reception room and as an air of sensual desire seemed to lace the air inside the room, an internal whirlpool of passion gushed through her simulated form. The current of absolute desire that surged through Leah's form urged her to provide an immediate answer to Prince Lament's question without any further delays and so as Leah prepared to respond, she welcomed the final surprise of her emotional journey that day which would of course be some time alone with Prince Lament himself.

"I think I'd like to drink the champagne somewhere else, somewhere a bit more comfortable perhaps." Leah replied as she smiled. "I feel like I've been on my feet all day." She explained.

"May I suggest the master bedroom?" Prince Lament whispered as he leant towards her. "It's very comfortable and you can definitely rest your feet there."

"Yes, I think that would be perfect." Leah swiftly agreed.

"Sorry about earlier today, the vamptrolls are a total nightmare. They've tried to invade my kingdom several times now but this time, since I was absent, they made themselves very comfortable." Prince Lament explained as he began to lead her towards the doors of the master bedroom.

"These things happen I guess, totally forgivable." Leah replied as she smiled.

When the two stepped into the master bedroom, Leah immediately noticed that there was a huge four poster bed that was adorned in silky, silvery voiles which hung down and across the large silver bedframe. For a few seconds and as Leah watched in silence, Prince Lament attended to the bottle of champagne as he placed the bottle, the two glasses and the ice bucket down upon a bedside cabinet next to the bed as she prepared to be swept of her feet by his masculine charm which oozed from every inch of his simulated being. Passion and sensual excitement seemed to linger on the tips of Leah's fingers and lips and as that wave of desire washed across the surface of her skin, the excitement seemed to flow through every part of her form as she waited for Prince Lament to return to her side.

Upon Prince Lament's face, Leah could see that there was now a seductive smile as he came to a standstill just inches away from her face and then stared into her eyes which made the sensual intensity between them both feel even more deeply passionate and almost electrifying. In a matter of just seconds however, the stillness between the two was broken as Prince Lament passionately pulled Leah closer to him and then swept her off her feet with a kiss from his soft lips which swiftly met and tantalized her own and as that delightful event occurred, she rapidly began to melt in his arms as she fully cooperated with their mutual desires.

Every inch of Leah's simulated skin seemed to tingle with absolute desire as she allowed Prince Lament to lead her towards the large king-size bed which sat in the center of the room almost expectantly as it waited patiently to accommodate their harmonious, celebration of passion which as Leah now knew, was definitely going to happen that very same night. The silky, silvery voiles that hung down from the large bedframe seemed to gently greet and caress Leah's simulated form as Prince Lament picked her up and then placed her softly down on top of it and each soft, silvery satin sheet that covered the surface of the bed seemed to float across the surface of Leah's skin as her simulated form nestled against them.

In a matter of just seconds Prince Lament leant down towards Leah and as he did so, their lips and bodies swiftly started to lock in a passionate embrace as Leah instantly welcomed and reciprocated his sensual, passionate expressions. Every inch of the material that adorned Leah's simulated frame was slipped silently off as Prince Lament began to explore her form with his tongue, lips and hands and every ounce of Leah's simulated form immediately responded favorably as her skin tingled with passionate excitement and sensual desire.

Some passionate strokes, soft touches and tender brushes swiftly occurred as Leah released some moans of pleasure because Prince Lament's touch felt absolutely heavenly and his expressions of sensual adoration surged through Leah's interior as his warm tongue, gentle hands and soft lips explored her naked flesh. The sexual exploration between the two quickly heightened and as Prince Lament penetrated Leah's interior just a few minutes later, she gasped in total delight as he entered inside her with a passionate urgency that almost took her breath away. Each sensual stroke of passion stirred the desires deep inside Leah's own being and as Prince Lament pushed himself further into her, Leah's back arched in total ecstasy as she welcomed him.

In a matter of just minutes every part of Leah swiftly became lost in passion as the couple made love from every angle and in every position imaginable as Leah allowed Prince Lament and herself to explore every inch of their sexual desires. Some gentle, tender sensual moments along with some more frantic, passionately hungry moments were fully explored, enjoyed and shared as the two celebrated their mutual appreciation for each other and Leah fully indulged in the sexual desires that swirled around inside every part of her simulated form. Nothing but passion and desire seemed to rule Leah's form and mind as she embraced Prince Lament and urged him to dive deeper inside of her and as he thrust himself more deeply into her interior, he began to quench the passionate hunger that lay inside Leah's form.

No ropes of restraint appeared to exist as the two made love over and over again and it almost seemed to Leah as if the passion inside of her was unlimited because it had somehow, provided her with an endless source of energy which had silently dissolved any tiredness that she had felt just moments before. Somehow, any fatigue that Leah had felt, had slipped from her now rejuvenated body which seemed to energetically burn with flames of desire and embers of passion as her veins surged with passionate excitement, her skin tingled with sensual delight and nothing but total pleasure swirled around inside of her. Time and time again, Leah climaxed in total ecstasy and as her heart raced with excitement, her own sensual desires conquered her form as passion gripped every inch of her being and it almost felt to Leah as if their own desires seemed to hold them both captive as they spared not even a single thought for anything or anyone else, except for each other and that particular moment in time.

Once Leah eventually tired and the two had both quenched their passionate desires multiple times, Prince Lament led Leah by the hand towards the en-suite bathroom where they showered together playfully as they both began to relax. Although the sexually charged, highly sensual passionate expressions had ceased between them both, some playful flirtatious interactions were still definitely present as Leah made the most of the luxury that surrounded her and enjoyed Prince Lament's companionship which was truly delightful and laced with absolute charm.

After the two had finished with their attendance to hygiene issues, they returned to the master bedroom and once Leah had lain back down upon Prince Lament's king-size bed, she nestled in his masculine arms as he began to affectionately and gently stroke her hair. Due to Leah's sheer tiredness by that point, her eyes rapidly started to close and as she began to drift off into the gentle arms of slumber, the master bedroom and Prince Lament began to melt silently away from sight.

Just a minute or so later, Leah suddenly reawakened and as she did so, she found herself back in her basement laboratory inside the transparent Spectrum capsule which prompted her to smile as she returned to her very real life and the very real basement. A few verbal commands were issued and the Spectrum capsule lid immediately started to rise and as it lifted, Leah quickly glanced up at the clock on the basement wall as she attempted to check the time just to ensure that her plans for the remainder of that night were still intact. However, much to Leah's surprise, the clock clearly illustrated that it was now actually almost midnight which meant that something had gone wrong with the timer inside Spectrum because she had definitely set it for a ten-hour experience which meant that she should have woken up at around eleven but from what Leah could see, it was now almost an hour after that since it was just a few minutes away from midnight.

Since Leah had exceeded her planned time expenditure that day with regards to Spectrum, she doubted that Zidane would still be awake and so as she rushed towards the basement steps, she instantly plastered an apologetic expression across her face. A wishful hope lay inside Leah's heart as she mounted the basement steps that an apologetic attitude might perhaps soothe Zidane, if he had not yet succumbed to sleep and since Leah did feel deeply regretful because she had spent more time in Spectrum than she had intended to that day, she hoped that her apologetic attitude would at the very least be interpreted as sincere.

Much to Leah's horror and surprise however, as soon as she stepped into the lounge she found it unoccupied and Zidane, quite strangely, was nowhere to be seen and so as she began to shake her head in total disbelief, her heart almost seemed to skip a beat, purely due to the shock of his absence. For a few seconds Leah froze as she processed her initial shock before she started to walk towards the bedroom because for the first time ever, since Leah had started her work on Spectrum, Zidane hadn't waited patiently and faithfully inside the lounge that night for Leah's companionship. Unlike Zidane's usual form where he would make the most of the sofa and patiently wait for Leah's return to the ground floor of their home, strangely that night, he had totally abandoned the lounge before she had returned to it and so as Leah walked towards the couple's bedroom, she began to fear that she might not even find him inside their bedroom either.

A sudden flurry of nervous doubts seemed to whirl around inside Leah's mind as she approached the couple's bedroom door which was almost closed and as she began to push it open, she fervently hoped that Zidane had just given up and then had made his way to bed without her. The thought of what Leah might do if Zidane wasn't present inside their bedroom was virtually unthinkable inside her mind but for the first time ever, Leah actually considered that possibility because such an eventuality, now felt actually possible. Such a negative discovery, as Leah was fully aware, would definitely shatter her heart and rock her world because Zidane had always been a very firm steadfast pillar of support, love and affection in every aspect of Leah's life and so it was almost unthinkable.

Inside Leah there definitely lurked a deep fear that Zidane might one day tire of her late working nights and then abandon their ship of love completely and for the first time ever in their entire relationship that thought almost capsized Leah's heart with worry as she stepped into the darkened bedroom. A quick visual scan of the bedroom's interior was performed as Leah began to visually seek out Zidane's familiar form which she hopefully expected would be nestled inside the couple's bed. Every part of Leah knew however, as she stared at the bed that the couple shared that in recent times, she had definitely taken Zidane for granted because she had totally ignored their relationship, his commitment to her and his absolute devotion to her heart.

Fortunately for Leah however, as she stared at the bed and her eyes grew more accustomed to the darkness, a glimmer of hope was found as she cast her eyes over Zidane's familiar body lumps which appeared to be snuggled safely under the duvet. A blanket of relief suddenly seemed to wash over Leah's body as she internally began to consider that Zidane really didn't have to tolerate Leah's later than usual arrival that night or any other night and so she prepared to apologize to him as she waited for a couple of minutes beside their bed, just to see if he would wake up. Since Zidane had always been such a dedicated romantic partner, Leah really couldn't fault him for being tired or for being human because she couldn't have asked or wished for anything more in a man than Zidane and so as she began to walk back towards the kitchen to heat up and then eat her evening meal alone, Leah began to silently rebuke herself as she walked.

Recently, Leah had definitely pushed the limits of acceptability because she had not only starved Zidane of the attention and affection that he so rightly deserved but she had also spent that time in her own frivolous sexual explorations with fictitious male creations that didn't even really exist. The artificial lifestyle that Leah had indulged in however, had now created a deep fear inside Leah's mind and heart that was absolutely riddled with guilt because she definitely feared that if she continued to live that way, Zidane would just not tolerate it anymore and that then he might leave her side forever. Although Leah doubted that Zidane would ever cheat on her, deep down inside she could not be certain that he would not get up and leave her side one day and actually dump her, if she continued to ignore his needs which were really quite minimal, very straightforward and amazingly simple.

When Leah had heated up the meal that she had been due to consume with Zidane that night, she walked back towards the lounge as she prepared to eat it as she accepted that unusually, on this occasion, she would eat alone even though Zidane was present. Some comfort was however found by Leah as she walked in the fact that at least, Zidane was still present and the reality that so far, he hadn't left her side or their bed to seek comfort elsewhere.

Quite strangely however, Leah found as she sat down and then began to consume her meal, the home-made Bolognese with pasta spirals actually tasted quite tasteless even though she had seasoned it with various spices and decorated it with grated cheese and it was almost as if her taste buds had gone on vacation. In fact, not even a mouthful of Leah's meal seemed to satisfy her palate in any way at all as she simply went through the motions and forced herself to consume it and it was as if her guilt had eaten up her appetite.

Approximately twenty minutes later and once Leah had eaten dinner as she walked back towards the bedroom that the couple shared, Leah reflectively appreciated Zidane's faithfulness which as she knew full well, right now, was definitely far superior to her own. Inside the bedroom everything was extremely still and very quiet as Leah walked towards Zidane's form and then prepared to snuggle up under the duvet beside him as she silently rejoiced in the fact that he was still present because his absence would have created a huge worry for Leah that wouldn't have been easy to remedy or resolve.

Every inch of Leah's body as she lay down felt almost completely worn out from the day's activities inside Spectrum because almost every minute had been action packed and full of surprises and so her fuel tank of excitement had run on a full load virtually all day. However, deep down inside, Leah also knew as she prepared to rest that even though she had satisfied every ounce of her being, she definitely hadn't satisfied Zidane that day in any capacity at all but as she began to drift off to sleep, she vowed to make it up to him and to deliver more appreciation, passion, romance and love to his heart in the near future.

Despite the fact that Zidane was fast asleep, his very presence seemed to soothe Leah's mind as sleep started to embrace her and as a sense of grateful appreciation settled deeply into her thoughts. In so many ways, Zidane's perseverance and his dedication towards Leah had always allowed her to sleep peacefully every single night because she had never once had to worry about where he was or what he was doing whilst she worked on Spectrum. However, Leah now accepted as she drifted off that perhaps, she had taken some of Zidane's admirable qualities for granted and that she really had to be mindful of that reality because the two were now so close to what they had worked so hard to achieve for years.

Since Leah had now completed Spectrum, she had stepped on the first stepping stone towards success and professional achievement and so, she hoped that once the walk-through tests were complete that would take her onto another financial stepping stone which would bring the couple closer to the realization of their future hopes and dreams. Luckily for Leah, so far Zidane had stood like a pillar of strength by her side and he was still very much the loving, dedicated partner that he had always been and that she had always loved, despite her various artificial indiscretions inside Spectrum and so as she entered into the world of slumber, she felt deeply grateful that so far, Zidane's love and support had not yet, actually wavered, faltered, changed or totally run out.

An Exploration of the Mysterious Bay of Wrath

For the remainder of the week as Leah faced her tasks and days an invisible gown of guilt seemed to adorn her person and so, she completely avoided the Spectrum capsule as she mulled over her seduction by the various fictitious characters that she'd met inside the artificial worlds that she had created. In some ways, Leah now realized that those fictitious wanders had created a distraction in her mind because they had disrupted her real life routine as fiction had spilled out into reality and then had saturated her evenings and nights with sensual exchanges which bore not even a whisper of anything real and that did not involve the one true love of Leah's very real life who had almost been completely ignored in the interim. Essentially, as Leah already knew, Zidane simply couldn't compete with any of the invisible challengers inside Spectrum or with the way that they made her feel and that meant, the competition that he was now deeply immersed in which was one that he wasn't even remotely aware off, was absolutely impossible for him to actually win due to the heightened sensual sensations on offer.

Some of the scandalous albeit fictional affairs that Leah had indulged in and enjoyed however, continued to haunt her mind as she tried to focus upon system tweaks and modifications throughout the remainder of that week but fortunately somehow, she managed to remain true to her own internal promises as she steered well clear of the interior of the capsule itself. Since Spectrum's final emotional journey still loomed upon the horizon of Leah's life, she knew deep down inside that it would be just be a matter of time before she would have to participate in Spectrum's offerings once again but for the first time ever, Leah hoped that she would not sway or stray as she began to consider her past participation with an ounce of regret. The reality was that the artificial temptations that Leah had faced inside Spectrum had chipped away at her usual solid rock of fidelity and that worried her slightly because it indicated that she was not a strong rock of faithfulness in the same way that Zidane was for her, since he had always treasured and honored her heart.

Fortunately for Leah however, when the new week arrived and as the mid-point approached, she started to feel slightly more comfortable about her Spectrum visits because the last emotional journey that she was due to embark upon that week would involve an emotional journey of wrath. Essentially as Leah already knew, wrath by its very nature was generally regarded as quite a negative emotion and so, she felt that her exploration of the final Spectrum environment was far less likely to present her with any sensual temptations but as she stepped into the basement on the Wednesday straight after lunch, she began to accept that once the Spectrum prototype had been sold, the damage that it had caused to her relationship would definitely have to be fixed.

Unfortunately for Leah, the fine tunes, repair work and tweaks to the couple's relationship would probably require even more from her than the creation of Spectrum itself had done and that emotional damage could not be fixed with a simple walk through test and a few changes. Nonetheless however, Leah continued to try and sow positive affirmations about Spectrum and the couple's future into her mind as she headed towards the capsule and prepared for her journey ahead. The issues that Leah's own recent simulated conduct had raised were quickly pushed to the back of her mind as she attempted to ignore them and to proceed with her final walk-through tests which that day, would bring her a step closer to the actual operational completion of the Spectrum prototype which would be an achievement that really excited her.

At one point during that past year as Leah had neared the brink of completion, she had considered the possibility that she should actually try to find someone else to perform the walk-through tests but that option as she already knew, may have presented other difficulties and might have slowed down her efforts. Third party opinions and conclusions as Leah had already decided, were ultimately far less reliable than her own and it would also have meant a more remote involvement for Leah herself because then she would have been totally reliant upon a third party's feedback which could either be inaccurate or might lack in some way. When it came to the actual issue of Leah's Spectrum workload, she definitely felt that a third party would have just resulted in more work for her in the long run because then she would have had to interpret and translate someone else's experiences in order to determine which observations were accurate and what corrections really needed to be made and since Zidane was usually far too tired to assist her, in the end she had waded through each emotional journey herself.

On the positive side of things, since the Spectrum prototype was now almost complete that essentially meant that the couple's relationship had so far survived Leah's simulated indiscretions but as she was fully aware, that situation could not continue indefinitely or even into the near future because the couple's future and their relationship were both definitely breakable. Time and time again Leah had inflicted way too many late nights upon Zidane's heart, body and mind and as a result, he had become extremely fed up and it had now become quite apparent from his actions that he was not going to tolerate that unromantic situation for very much longer.

Although Leah wanted to achieve professionally and to complete Spectrum so that it could be sold for a large sum, she did fear that she might jeopardize the real romantic relationship that the couple currently had in doing so, if she ignored Zidane's heart too much. An unromantic threat definitely lingered around Leah's days that was very real because if the couple's relationship was totally destroyed through her own lack of romantic action that would render all their sacrifices so far, not only worthless but also absolutely meaningless and it would break their future into a million tiny pieces of regretful heartbreak because the present's fictitious betrayals on Leah's part could ultimately, jeopardize and destroy the couple's potential future joys.

In every imaginable Leah absolutely hated what she had done to Zidane in recent times when it came to her dabbles in passionate simulated exchanges with fictitious male strangers but somehow, simultaneously and inexplicably, she had also felt absolutely powerless to stop herself. The shameful reality was that Leah's mind and body had never felt so invigorated, so alive or so sexually aroused before because some of the men that she had encountered inside Spectrum had invoked deep passions inside her during those highly sensual moments that had not only infiltrated but that had also penetrated and gripped all of her senses with a clamp of desire that had been hard to escape from. However, as Leah already fully appreciated, her sensual adventures during her sexual exploration of self, would not save the couple's relationship, if and when those intimate moments were actually discovered because their relationship was not just Leah's own to enjoy and destroy as she wished to with no consequences, since that relationship was a shared romantic commitment between two hearts not one.

Once Leah had mounted the Spectrum capsule and then had lain down inside its interior, she swiftly issued some verbal commands as she prepared to be transported to another place and another world and as the lid closed down over her head, she closed her eyes in preparation for her final new emotional journey in the Spectrum prototype. Since Leah's emotional journey of wrath that day would be her first visit to a new emotional plane which was ultimately, an essential task when it came to the actual completion of her walk-through tests, her next visit to Spectrum would be extremely significant because it would allow Leah to complete the final modifications and tweaks to the Spectrum system, so that the prototype could finally be sold. So in some ways, Leah actually felt quite hopeful as she waited for the sleeping gas to penetrate the interior of the capsule because the completion of the prototype would ultimately, ignite the couple's future plans which had lain dormant in the background of their lives for so long now that it almost felt as if each one was buried under a large pile of dust from the particles of stagnant inaction that had accumulated and settled in the interim with absolutely no interruptions or any disturbances.

Much as Leah expected, the sleeping gas rapidly began to circulate through the entire interior of the Spectrum capsule and as Leah's body started to quickly absorb the sedatory substance, sleep was silently and peacefully ushered in. Although a bright blue light did emanate from the capsule itself that shone out into the basement which was usual when it was active, the intense light didn't seem to detract from the effectiveness of the sleeping gas in any way, Leah noticed as she drifted off and so, sleep was hard to avoid, even though she had woken up quite late that morning and at around ten.

Just a minute or so later, when Leah woke back up inside the final new Spectrum environment, she suddenly found herself strewn across the ground on a dullish grey, dark brownish beach that appeared to be covered in small, shiny pebbles. The pebbles, Leah immediately noticed as she stood up, were a wide variety of shades and colors which seemed to range from dark charcoal black to light grey and as each hard-stony symbol of solid rebellion sat silently upon a bed of dark brownish sand, it almost looked as if each one was in direct opposition to the sandy, grainy, soft makeup of the sand and absolutely determined to cover every inch of it up.

From what Leah could see at first glance however, besides the sand and the pebbles, the solid parts of the bay looked really quite bland, uneventful and totally deserted because no simulated human forms or any other kind of simulated entities appeared to be present which meant, for now there would be no actual guide to guide her steps. Despite that absence and lack of clarity however, Leah began to hope that the watery parts of the bay might hold more promise as she turned her attention towards the water's edge and then started to visually inspect the shore as she sought out some kind of directional indication as to where she should go or what she should do next.

"The Bay of Wrath." Leah whispered to herself as she visually perused not only the watery edges that lapped against the pebbly beach but also the some of the rocky cliff faces around her that sat not too far away from the water's edge. "I wouldn't even dare to try and climb up any those cliffs." She swiftly admitted to herself as she shook her head and then glanced back out across the water.

A dark black broken skeleton of a ship which Leah rapidly spotted, seemed to jut out of the water which appeared to be quite close by but it looked as if it had been abandoned a very long time ago because the holes in the sides of the vessel clearly indicated that it was no longer fit for purpose and that it was totally unseaworthy. Since the shipwreck looked really quite ancient, Leah immediately assumed that it had probably been there for many years and perhaps even for decades and as she more fully inspected the watery edges of the shoreline, she observed that some jagged rocks jutted out of the water in a silent defiant protest which surrounded the entire base of the shipwreck itself.

Rather tragically it seemed, the spiky, jagged rocks that tightly surrounded the wreckage as the sea gently lapped against the carcass of the ship, silently indicated to Leah that their stony presence had somehow been responsible for and had actually caused the ship's actual demise. However, none of the treacherous rocky lumps from what Leah could see, showed any signs of regret or remorse nor did any stony one of them appear to want to take any responsibility and in fact, each one looked almost triumphant as the rocky surfaces proudly poked out from between the watery waves in a stony, outward display that glistened and shone as rays from the sun bounced off each one which almost looked like a silent celebration of their stony victory.

Despite the fact that the shipwreck was no longer seaworthy or capable of any kind of movement, since it was in such a delipidated state, Leah began to walk towards the edge of the water and the closest solid point to the vessel because its very presence seemed to silently urge her to explore it. Much like the dull beach as Leah glanced down at her outfit as she walked, she discovered that she was now clothed in rather simple, basic, dullish, grey attire that dripped with dreariness which seemed to match the beach perfectly but that also clearly indicated to her that this adventure was not going to glamorous in any way at all. However, since the dark grey almost black soft jeans, lighter grey top and black trainer shoes did feel quite comfortable, Leah wasn't particularly bothered by the simplicity of her outfit on this occasion although it definitely made her usual laboratory tunics seem a tad more elegant and so as she began to make her way towards the shipwreck, she started to process and accept the drab nature of her current environment which her attire seemed to blend into almost immaculately.

Some curious speculation swiftly began and then started to swirl around inside Leah's mind as she stepped out onto some of the jagged rocks and then started to make her way across the water as to what might actually be inside the shipwreck's rotten wooden remains. Although it was highly unlikely that the skeleton wreckage would contain any actual survivors, Leah quietly considered that possibility for a moment as she surveyed the shipwreck's ancient, crushed, mangled state and tiptoed cautiously across the rocks towards the broken vessel. A few of the jagged rocks seemed to be wrapped quite tightly around the shipwreck's nearest side which would at least provide Leah with easier access to the vessel's upper deck and so as she clambered onto one of the stony surfaces, she began to prepare for the climb upwards to reach the top deck which was still more than a rock and a few rocky climbs away.

After Leah had stabilized herself a bit, she enthusiastically began the upward climb as she made good use of the rocks around the carcass of the ship and maneuvered herself around the jagged, stony edges in an attempt to position herself as safely as she could because possible slippages at this point as she knew, would definitely be quite dangerous. Approximately ten minutes later Leah finally managed to clamber up onto the top, main deck of the shipwreck where much to her dismay, she found not just a main deck but also a very rotten deck which had lots of holes in it and some very large gaps. Unfortunately, the holes and gaps that gaped with nothing but a dark dreariness were littered sporadically but quite frequently across the main top deck's tired, worn out, broken surface which meant, it would not be that simple for Leah to walk across it as freely as she might have hoped to.

Another worry crossed Leah's mind as she began to inspect and then started to cross the deck and that was the fact that some of the wooden planks on the top deck of the wreckage looked absolutely rotten and as if they might collapse at any given moment. Some tired creaks and worn out groans came from the rotten planks as Leah tiptoed across some of their barely wooden, mouldy surfaces and as she went, she carefully tried to avoid any planks that looked too weak to carry her weight. However, as Leah walked, she noticed that every plank of wood, even the ones that seemed slightly stronger still sighed, creaked and groaned under her weight which definitely worried her because it almost felt as if they wanted to split into a million pieces.

An unusual, eerie, stagnant stillness seemed to surround Leah in every direction that she could face as she headed towards some wooden steps that appeared to led downwards because nothing on the ship itself seemed to move an inch. The lap of the waves against the shipwreck's sides and even the more aggressive watery crashes against the rocks that Leah had initially heard when she had drawn closer to the ship, could now no longer be heard Leah noticed as she approached the wooden steps and then prepared to make her descent. One final glance was cast over the top deck of the ship before Leah left the main deck but from what she could see, there didn't appear to be very much to be seen and there seemed to be absolutely nothing to do so, the wooden steps which looked extremely rickety, looked like the only possible route to explore where Leah would perhaps find something useful or something of interest that might yield some kind of adventure.

Much to Leah's absolute horror however, she quickly discovered that the wooden flight of steps was not very kind or at least not to her because when she stepped onto the fifth step, it suddenly snapped and then completely gave way whilst she was still situated upon it. On the positive side of that rather fearful discovery, only five steps actually remained and so Leah tried to find some comfort in that fact as she quickly started to creep down onto the next step and then took a deep breath.

Due to the condition of the rotten wooden steps, Leah tried to limit the amount of weight that she actually placed upon each one as she began to tiptoe gently and cautiously down the next four steps which she definitely feared might snap. A definite undercurrent of fear seemed to accompany Leah as she went that gushed, swirled and rushed around inside her interior because if the rotten, wooden steps did give way, she had absolutely no idea what she might actually fall down into or land upon and that fearful prospect definitely worried her.

When Leah arrived at the bottom of the steps as she stepped off the final one and onto the lower deck, she released a gentle sigh of relief as she swiftly concluded that the wooden steps were not just weak but also totally rotten which clearly indicated that she would have to tread very carefully indeed. Although the top deck of the shipwreck hadn't really contained anything of any real interest to Leah, she did still wish to have the ability to return to it when and if she wanted to and as she already knew, a potential return might be hampered or even made absolutely impossible, if too many of the wooden steps had been broken on the downward trip.

The lower deck of the shipwreck, Leah discovered, once she had stepped off the last rotten wooden step, felt very clammy, extremely musty and strangely eerie as she began to visually inspect her surroundings in silence and prepared to explore it further. From what Leah could see, the structure's lower interior seemed to be decorated in mold, caked in dust and blanketed in darkness, so for the next minute or two, simply due to a flurry of internal fears, Leah didn't move an inch as she stood completely still and absorbed the rotten wooden floor that surrounded her.

Rather eerily, Leah noticed that the thick blanket of mouldy dust that lay across the rotten lower deck looked extremely comfortable and so much so, that the dust seemed to have not only gathered but also happily accumulated on most of the ship's rickety interior which silently indicated to her that it hadn't been disturbed or touched for many years. Since a blanket of darkness also seemed to cover most of the lower deck along with the mouldy dust, it was hard for Leah to see very much besides the floor around her and the layer of dust at first but as her eyes grew more accustomed to that lack of light, she noticed that there appeared to be a large rectangular wooden table situated in one corner of the deck which poked silently out of the darkness that surrounded it.

Some prickles of nervous curiosity immediately propelled Leah to walk towards the wooden table so that she could visually inspect its rotten surface slightly more closely to see if anything useful was situated upon it but due to the darkness that seeped out from the edges of the deck which still slightly hampered Leah's visibility, each step towards the slab of rotten wood was taken carefully. Quite strangely and rather shockingly however, as Leah approached the corner that the wooden table was situated in and her eyes became more accustomed to the darkness, she discovered that much to her complete and utter horror all that seemed to be present was a skeleton which was even more fearful than either the rotten wood or the layer of mouldy dust.

Although the wooden structure that the skeleton was positioned next to, Leah noticed as she came to a standstill about six steps away, was totally rotten that didn't seem to bother the bony occupant at all who sat quite boldly at the other end of the rotten wooden table in an upright position. Despite the skeleton's proud, enthusiastic upright stance however, there appeared to be no actual clues present as to who the bones might have belonged to prior to that skeletal state and so, it was hard for Leah to draw any rapid conclusions but from what she could see, the bones did appear to have belonged to a male that still wore some kind of hat on top of his skeletal head.

Very sadly, Leah observed, the hat itself now looked pretty much like its owner, dusty and grey because barely even a thread of material seemed to exist anymore that was visible under all the layers of mouldy dust. In fact, much like the skeletal remains that the hat sat on top off which no longer possessed even an inch of flesh and whose bony remnants were also caked in musty, mouldy dust, from what Leah could see neither object had been moved an inch for years and maybe even for decades. However, Leah noticed that around some of the darker edges the hat did hold the possibility that at one time, it might have actually been black but its eroded state now clearly indicated to her that both the skeleton and the hat had rotted beyond redemption which also implied that both held very little promise of anything positive when it came to Leah's actual emotional journey that day.

Just a few seconds later Leah began to give the rest of the lower deck around the rotten, wooden table a quick visual scan but she could find no clues as to why the skeleton was there or what she was supposed to actually do next. Inside Leah there was a definite lack of answers that could not be satisfied by the abundant supply of mouldy dust that surrounded her which appeared to be the only major feature beside the skeleton and the rotten table that seemed to be consistently present at that point in time and so, Leah swiftly turned her attention back towards the skeleton as she attempted to seek out some more clues.

Another much more intricate visual inspection began as Leah peered at the skeleton's wide set shoulder bones which she immediately noticed, appeared to be bare apart from a grey dusty robe. Despite the lack of any visible encouragement however, Leah began to prepare herself to venture deeper into the dark corner that the skeleton occupied so that she could perform a closer visual inspection but as she did so, a nervous shiver ran down her simulated spine as she took her first nervous step towards the skeleton's current position.

Due to the presence of the quite creepy skeleton, Leah's interest in the shipwreck and her emotional state had been swiftly, totally transformed from that of curious intrigue and nervous anticipation to slight disgust which was now also coupled with an undercurrent of mild fear both of which definitely hampered her movements. Suddenly, Leah felt a very strong desire to return to the top deck of the shipwreck and to perhaps just inspect the rather bland, dullish bay instead but just as she was about to turn and walk away from the skeleton and the rotten wooden table however, she noticed that there appeared to be an ancient scroll on top of its rotten surface which drooped down from one of the bony hands that rested upon the rotten structure.

Although at least a hundred fears tumbled through Leah's mind and ran across every inch of the surface of her simulated flesh, the presence of the ancient scroll instantly provoked her curiosity and totally fascinated her and so, she thoughtfully began to consider whether or not she should try to pluck the scroll from the skeleton's bony hand. A definite temptation now existed that had not only interrupted Leah but that had also postponed her planned departure and return to the main upper deck however, the possibility that the ancient scroll could perhaps be a booby trap had also run through her mind too and so a bold dash towards it, was therefore deemed to be unwise.

For a few seconds Leah hesitated as a thoughtful glance was cast down towards the scroll as she mulled over her decision and she could feel a mild tug of war start within herself that mainly appeared to be between curiosity and fear both of which currently seemed to be in direct opposition to each other which unsettled her senses. After just a minute or so however, curiosity finally seemed to triumph in that internal battle as Leah's legs were suddenly propelled to move forward and to approach the skeleton's current, stagnant position.

The scroll, Leah swiftly concluded as she drew close to a corner of the rotten table, despite its silence which clearly indicated a lack of commitment to either a position of encouragement or dissuasion, definitely held a delicious mysterious secret full of intrigue which silently urged her to open it up. Since Leah hadn't yet unwrapped or unraveled that secret, she definitely felt as if she had to before she returned to the main upper deck of the ship because that secret might relate to her emotional adventures in the Bay of Wrath that day and play a very important part. However, Leah's decision as she already knew, also carried a certain element of risk and since her emotional journey on that particular occasion was actually due to be an emotional journey of wrath, an undercurrent of fear still occupied her body as she arrived beside the skeletal remains, came to a standstill and then cautiously, leant forward as she stretched her arm out towards the skeleton's bony hand.

Fortunately for Leah, as she leant nervously down towards the ancient scroll and the skeletal hand that it was clasped inside, she found that the document itself was actually quite easy to retrieve and that the bony fingers didn't seem to obstruct her in any way. Once Leah had the scroll in her possession, she then quickly stepped back as she prepared to open it up and read it, though the dull light of the lower deck as she was fully aware would perhaps make that task slightly more tricky but she persevered nonetheless, since her curiosity had definitely been pricked and fully aroused.

Inside the interior of the scroll, once Leah had fully opened it up, she found that some very strange words had been written upon it in jet black ink which seemed to form some kind of poetic riddle and she noticed that the largish letters appeared to have been written with a quill as opposed to a pen.

"My ship sailed and the cruel rocks prevailed, when anger gripped the seas but you can set me free." Leah said to herself as she read the words that had been written in black ink out loud and then glanced at the skeleton's face. "You may seek me here, you may seek me there but if you can find my warm heart somewhere around my ship and chair, then you can release my cold bones that do nothing now but sit alone and stare and scare."

Since absolutely no one else appeared to be anywhere nearby that meant that the bony skeleton, who it appeared had at one time been the ship's captain and the strange message were really all that Leah could act upon and so she silently began to prepare herself to search the rest of the shipwreck. The solitude of Leah's current position also swiftly confirmed to her that the message definitely related to the skeleton who was it appeared, the sole occupant of the broken, derelict vessel and that she had to solve that poetic riddle herself before she could actually proceed.

Unfortunately, since the sole, bony occupant of the shipwreck could not utter a single word or assist Leah in any capacity that meant that she would have to solve the riddle alone but the poetic riddle confused her slightly because the skeleton certainly didn't have a warm heart or any heart at all amongst his bones. In fact, all Leah could see was just an empty shell of a ribcage and so she definitely felt that it was highly likely that the skeletal remains of the ship's sole occupant that hadn't actually survived had probably been sat in their current position for quite some time.

Any internal organs or external fleshy remains that the skeleton had once possessed had clearly departed long ago through a process of natural erosion and decomposition, Leah observed which made the poetic riddle seem even more strange and far more mysterious. However, Leah still gave the skeleton one last quick but thorough visual inspection as she triple checked and then rechecked the bony ribcage several more times, just to make sure that she hadn't missed anything before she peered more deeply into the two corners of the lower deck nearest to her, inclusive of the one that the skeleton currently occupied but she could see absolutely no signs of anything that might help her to solve the riddle.

In order to proceed now as Leah knew, as she started to tiptoe back across the rotten planks of the lower deck towards the foot of the stairs, she might have to venture into all four dark corners of the lower deck in her search for some kind of answers which was far from a delightful prospect. The search itself, Leah suspected, would be a task that didn't really hold much hope and so such efforts on her part, she definitely felt, might not actually yield anything pleasant and were far more likely to yield something even more awful. However, Leah tried to remain hopeful as she headed towards the other end of the lower deck and the two dark corners that hadn't yet been approached that a closer inspection and something in the midst of all that eerie darkness, would perhaps hold the prospect of something slightly more positive.

Some particles of darkness seeped out from the edges of the two unexplored corners of the lower deck and so as Leah stepped into that darkness more fully and entered into the nearest of the two, those particles began to silently embrace and then fully engulfed her as she continued to tiptoe across the mangled, rotten planks that creaked and groaned under her feet. Despite all Leah's brave efforts however, she did actually feel slightly nervous and so her steps which were taken cautiously, fully reflected her nervousness as she held her breath in fearful but curious anticipation and readied herself to hunt for any mysterious clues that she could find. A huge question mark did cross and then lurk, linger and remain inside Leah's mind as she began to explore the first of the two dark corners as to the search itself because as yet, she had no actual clue what she was actually supposed to look for but despite all her doubts, she committed herself to the task at hand which was rather unfortunately, a full exploration of the lower deck's dark, dismal, dusty corners.

Approximately ten minutes later and once Leah had performed a far more extensive search of almost every single nook, cranny, inch and centimeter of the lower deck inclusive of three out of the four dark corners which she checked and rechecked several times,

Leah finally surrendered to total defeat. Unfortunately for Leah, the rotten planks that surrounded her and the three corners that she had inspected so far, hadn't seem to contain anything except mouldy, dusty planks coupled with rotten groans and creaks which frustrated her slightly because there seemed to be no actual way to proceed. Despite that rather large rotten setback however, Leah began to make her way back towards the skeleton and the final corner of the lower deck in thoughtful silence because as far as she was concerned, she had already checked that first dark corner, albeit it rather quickly, just before and right after she had plucked the scroll from the skeleton's hand.

Due to Leah's prior visit to the first corner which had borne no actual results, she began to feel not only very frustrated but also slightly dejected as she walked and with every step that she took, Leah found that her hopes seemed to sink silently, further down into the rotten planks below her feet. For a moment as Leah came to a total standstill just a few seconds later, once again at the edge of the first dark corner and the rotten table, it almost felt as if hope had not only set sail but as if it had now almost fully abandoned her mind's bay of curiosity because she felt that very little chance of success remained. However, Leah began to hopefully visually search the corner once again as she tried to clutch onto the last few thin, short straws of hope that still remained inside of her that it might actually contain something useful that related to the scroll which could perhaps help her to solve the poetic riddle inside it.

A few seconds of frustrated stillness went by as Leah just stood rooted to the spot as she fully gave up on the rest of the lower deck and focused solely upon her visual search of the dark corner for any signs of an entry or exit point which she felt almost certain did not actually exist in that particular corner of the lower deck. The possibility that Leah might have missed something however, did wander across and then lurk inside her mind as she conducted her visual inspection because the first time around, she definitely felt that she had been far less thorough which meant that she might have missed something really important.

Unlike the other three dark corners of the lower deck, much to

Leah's surprise as her eyes focused on and then grew accustomed to the darkness that lingered around the skeleton's remains, she actually discovered that there were in fact some wooden steps which led downwards that appeared to start directly underneath the rotten table itself. A second lower deck it now transpired definitely seemed to exist, albeit in an artificial, simulated capacity which also meant that Leah now had an actual choice to make in that she could either step down the second flight of wooden steps and make an attempt to solve the riddle or alternatively, she could just accept total defeat and flee from the shipwreck completely.

Quite strangely, the darkness seemed to intensify Leah noticed as she peered down into the hole and then stared at a few of the more visible rotten steps at the top of the downward flight before she began to try and search for the actual foot of the steps which was far harder to see. In fact, the base of the steps was barely even visible to Leah from her current position which gave absolutely no indications of what might actually be in store for her once she reached it and so there was an air of ambiguity as to what the second lower deck might actually contain.

Unfortunately, it now seemed to Leah as if the second lower deck would be far more eerie and even more of an ordeal than the first one had been which had already shocked her due to the skeletal remains that she had discovered within it which meant, a lot more courage would definitely be required to face that eerie darkness. However as Leah already knew, her bravery supplies were almost fully depleted because by that point, her internal brave-o-meter felt almost empty and so a trip down the second flight of rotten wooden steps wasn't particularly an activity that she really wanted to cooperate with or participate in.

Inside Leah a very strong temptation suddenly began to lurk that urged her to surrender to her own cowardly instincts because technically, she could just flee from the shipwreck in total defeat however, rather frustratingly, simultaneously there was also a strong urge which urged her to solve the riddle before she left the ship's interior. Since the curious urge to solve the riddle actually seemed to be just as strong, if not even stronger than the urge to flee, Leah began to accept and then fully resigned herself to the notion that for a while, she would definitely have to find a way to function in the midst of total discomfort because the second lower deck might hold an actual answer to the poetic riddle. The abandoned shipwreck had definitely contained a few surprises so far as Leah already knew but the riddle itself still remained unsolved which meant that it had to be solved before she left the mangled vessel otherwise that mystery would linger in her thoughts for the rest of her adventure because from what the poetic riddle had implied, the skeleton's heart was situated somewhere inside the shipwreck itself.

After a few more minutes of thoughtful but nervous consideration, Leah finally managed to arrive at a decision as she silently maneuvered herself into position and then began her downward descent as she placed her foot gently down upon the top wooden step and attempted to persevere. The second flight of rotten plank steps from what Leah could see as she headed downwards, seemed to lead towards the bottom of the actual shipwreck itself but the second lower deck looked much smaller than the first in terms of width though much deeper in terms of height because it appeared to narrow down in unison with the ship's exterior and it also looked more like a maintenance deck.

Along both sides of the main room, Leah discovered as she stepped off the final step and then began to visually inspect it, there were some long, rotten wooden benches which had several rotten oars strewn across each one which clearly indicated that the crew had at one time been very active in that lower part of the vessel. Some pieces of old-fashioned equipment that wore dusty, mouldy coats littered the main room of the second lower deck that Leah noticed as she started to saunter around its interior and a thick layer of mouldy dust covered not just the equipment but also the ship's walls and floor, the sight of which made a slight shiver run down her spine. A couple of narrow passageways seemed to lead off from the larger main room into several small dormitories and as the Leah arrived at the doorway to one, she peeked her head around it and found that it had six rotten, dusty, mouldy wooden bunk bed frames inside it which clearly hadn't been facilitated for a while because mouldy dust seemed to cling to every inch of each rotten frame.

Despite the bunk bed frames however, Leah didn't find much else inside the passageways and dormitories and so, she swiftly returned to the main room of the second lower deck to continue her search as she rapidly concluded that at one time, when the ship had been seaworthy and fully operational, the second lower deck probably would have been a hive of human activity. Much to Leah's satisfaction however, when she stepped back into the main room of the second lower deck, she noticed that there appeared to be an iron furnace at one end of it and so as Leah began to stride enthusiastically but cautiously across the rotten planks towards it, she hoped that it would hold the answer to the poetic riddle because furnaces as she already knew, could definitely be very warm since the iron contraptions were usually full of fiery flames.

Around the exterior of the small iron furnace, Leah observed as she neared, there really didn't seem to be much to see but once she arrived beside it and then opened it up, she began to hopefully inspect its interior as she sought out some further clues and perhaps something to light it with. A few useful items seemed to be present inside the furnace, Leah discovered as she silently inspected its interior, like some lumps of coal, some chunks of wood and there were even some crumpled sheets of paper all of which lay at the very bottom of the furnace which Leah definitely felt could help to create a warm blaze which she hoped would solve the skeleton's riddle.

On a shelf directly above the flammable useful items Leah found a small matchbox which indicated to her that she was supposed to actually use the matches to ignite the crumpled sheets of paper which would activate the furnace's internal blaze and power up the furnace. Due to the very dusty shelf inside the furnace however, Leah quickly concluded that the furnace, much like the rest of the shipwreck, hadn't been active for a very long time nonetheless, she tried to remain hopeful that a fire could actually be started and lit as she leant into the furnace and reached for the matchbox.

When Leah opened up the matchbox, much to her dismay, she

rapidly discovered that there were only five matches inside the small box which meant that her chances to start a blaze successfully, would be limited to just five attempts. The restriction of just five chances did make Leah feel slightly nervous but she ploughed on ahead anyway as she enthusiastically plucked the first match from the interior of the matchbox and then prepared to strike it against one of the matchbox's sandpaper edges. Rather unfortunately for Leah, despite all her enthusiasm, the first match when struck just gave off a small, cheery spark but no flame was actually generated and so, she shook her head in frustration as she prepared to make a second attempt and plucked a second matchstick from the box.

On Leah's second attempt she struck the matchstick against the sandpaper edge again but this time much more cautiously however, that only seemed to render a slightly larger spark than the first match but again no actual flame. Despite Leah's first two failed attempts, she didn't let those failures deter or dissuade her however, as she continued to try and strike another two matches and on the fourth attempt, a small flame actually appeared but then just a few seconds later, it quickly fizzled out which really frustrated her. Although Leah's chances of success had definitely greatly reduced and had by that point, almost completely vanished as she dipped her hand back inside the matchbox for the fifth time, Leah silently hoped for the best and feared for the worst as she pulled out of fifth and final match.

A gentle sigh of frustration was released from Leah's lips as she held the fifth match up in front of her face and a quick consultation began as she made an attempt to negotiate with the actual matchstick itself and urged the small wooden stick to cooperate with her plans. Since none of the five small matchsticks had actually been rotten, dusty or mouldy like the rest of the rotten ship's wooden interior, Leah definitely felt that her quest was a realistic and realizable goal and so she expressed this to the matchstick in the hope that the small wooden stick might participate and that a blaze would be successfully started on her fifth attempt.

"Now matchstick, I'm not usually so demanding but you really have got to grow into a huge flame, not a tiny spark, a huge flame."

Leah whispered as she stared at the fifth match and urged the tiny wooden stick to cooperate. "And this is not a wooden negotiation, it's an absolute dusty dust, sparky must."

Although by that point frustration had definitely begun to set in, Leah attempted to persevere, even though it almost felt as if that frustration had got the better of her as she inhaled deeply before she attempted to strike the fifth and final match because it was the only firestarter that remained. Since there didn't seem to be any other alternatives in close proximity to Leah's current position however, that meant that if her final attempt failed, she felt unsure what she would actually do beyond that fifth match. The chances of success as Leah already knew, were really quite low and pretty sparkless because she had failed four times already but one small hope did remain in that fifth and final match and so as Leah began to thoughtfully consider the actual strike of the match, she inspected the interior of the furnace to see if perhaps, she could direct her efforts more carefully on her fifth attempt and secure an actual fiery result.

An optimistic glance was cast hopefully towards the crumpled pieces of paper, lumps of coal and chunks of wood as a sudden potential solution struck Leah's mind and as she leant into the furnace for a second time, this time she leant towards the bottom of it as opposed to the shelf at the top. From what Leah could see the crumpled pieces of paper were scattered quite generously around the interior of the furnace both below and on top of the lumps of wood and chunks of coal which meant that if she managed to spark even just a small flame directly beside or under some of the sheets of paper that she could successfully start a small blaze. The chances were pretty slim as Leah already knew but she tried to remain hopeful as she prepared to strike the final match because the hope was that once she had lit the furnace, the actual blaze itself would solve the skeleton's riddle and that she would then be able to leave shipwreck without any curious questions because those unanswered questions would perhaps niggle away inside her mind for the remainder of her Spectrum visit.

One final nervous glance was cast towards the matchbox and

the final match as Leah inhaled deeply because unfortunately, the first four matches hadn't seemed very keen to participate with her plans and so, she felt uncertain that the fifth match would render an actual flame large enough to light up the furnace. So far, the first four matches had only rendered a few little sparks and one tiny flame that had fizzled out very quickly and so this time, Leah really could not afford to fail because from what she could see, no other alternative solution actually existed.

"An uncooperative solution is all I really have right now." Leah whispered to herself as she sighed, glanced at the crumpled sheets around the matchstick and then shook her head. "And I guess that has to be better than nothing."

Fortunately for Leah as soon as she struck the final match, much to her total relief some of the crumpled sheets of paper actually caught fire and then started to burn which satisfied her to some extent because it meant that now, the riddle had been actually solved. Once Leah felt satisfied that the fire was ablaze to a satisfactory degree, she then closed the furnace door as she prepared to depart because she wanted to return to the upper deck in order to leave the shipwreck but just as Leah started to make her way, she suddenly noticed that the walls and floor around her now looked slightly less dusty and mouldy.

The heart that Leah was supposed to warm, she now fully accepted, was the actual furnace itself which was the heart of the broken vessel and that heart obviously provided a heartbeat of energy and a warm lifeline that would reheat, revive and restore the vessel's interior once again. Since the skeleton had probably been the captain of the ship, Leah swiftly began to conclude that obviously meant that his heart was ultimately, the heart of the ship because before the ship's demise, his vessel had probably been his passion in life and quite possibly his whole life.

Rather intriguingly in the end, Leah considered thoughtfully as she walked back towards the rotten wooden steps and then began to make her way back up towards the first lower deck of the vessel, the heart that had been referred to in the riddle had really had absolutely nothing at all to do with the skeleton's bones. Despite that lack of direct correlation however, Leah now felt partially satisfied as she made her way back up the rotten wooden steps that at the very least, the riddle had now been solved which meant that she could now actually leave the musty shipwreck and the eerie skeleton peacefully behind her and start to explore the rest of the bay.

Just a few minutes later Leah arrived back on the first lower deck and as she did so, she immediately noticed that the wooden floor and walls on that deck also looked less mouldy and rotten, in comparison to her initial visit and that the eerie darkness had evaporated to some extent. Surprisingly however, as Leah returned to the wooden table, she could see that the skeleton was now actually absent as she glanced at the space where the pile of bones should have been seated and found absolutely nothing. Despite the oddness of the skeleton's departure which Leah realized must have occurred when she lit the furnace however, she politely placed the scroll back down upon the table because she didn't think that she should carry around for the remainder of her emotional journey that day since technically, the scroll did actually belong to the skeleton, absent or not.

Another oddity that Leah hadn't noticed at first, purely due to the surprise of the skeleton's absence, was the fact that the wooden table itself now actually looked quite respectable because the highly visible dark cherry surface almost shone and it now looked as if it had been polished not too long ago. The ship's wooden walls and floor, Leah observed as she began to make her way back towards the upper main deck of the ship and approached the first flight of wooden steps, now no longer seemed to accommodate the dust and mould that had once clung to and dripped from every splinter of the rotten wood and the first lower deck now also seemed far lighter because light seemed to seep in through every plank crack in the ceiling. In fact, the wooden planky walls and floor were now actually so bright and clear that Leah could even spot some wooden knots on the planky surfaces and that rapid transformation that had taken place inside the ship in just a matter of minutes, totally fascinated her as she began to make her ascent.

A slight sadness seemed to accompany Leah and wrap itself around her simulated form as she rushed back up the last few wooden steps and then arrived on the main upper deck of the ship once again because there had been absolutely no survivors on board the shipwreck at all although technically, the shipwreck itself Leah now felt, could no longer be described as a shipwreck anymore, since it no longer looked like one. Very sadly, although the rotten wooden planks that Leah had first met inside the ship had managed to survive the ship's rocky clash and had now almost been fully restored, the crew and captain certainly hadn't been so lucky and as she began to process and accept that rather cold, grim, simulated reality, she prepared to leave the vessel with nothing but the solitary, uncomfortable silence of her sad thoughts in tow.

In the end, despite all Leah's hopes, there had been no actual survivors and nor had there been any treasures to be found inside the skeletal rotten remains of the ship because the musty vessel's only real occupant had been death which had clung to every particle of air and splinter of wood inside its interior as the souls of those lost, had silently and invisibly hung over her head. Each deck that Leah had explored had felt haunted by those lost souls along with every rotten wooden plank that the unseaworthy vessel had initially contained and very sadly, all that she had found on the shipwreck itself had been the skeletal remains of a crew member that might possibly have been the captain of the ship at some point and even those bony remnants had later, rather mysteriously, totally disappeared.

Despite all those rather negative factors however, Leah tried to remain optimistically hopeful as she started to cross the top main deck of the ship and headed towards the side closest to the bay as she prepared to leave the vessel. Although Leah had rushed up the wooden steps on her return journey because by that point, the wooden surfaces had seemed far stronger and more intact plus any potential damage from her movements she had felt would matter far less on her return trip, suddenly her pace slowed back down again as she began to prepare for her climb back down towards the bay which she definitely accepted, would be far more hazardous.

Much to Leah's surprise however, as she arrived near the side of the ship and then glanced back across the main deck, she noticed that the shipwreck had been transformed even more and not just tidied up in that now, it looked like an actual ship that could perhaps even set sail because it had an actual captain's wheel which sat boldly upon the vessel's main deck. Since the ship no longer looked like the mouldy, mangled, run down, ruined shipwreck that had initially greeted Leah's eyes because it now sparkled, shone and glistened as rays of light bounced off the surfaces that cosmetic improvement comforted Leah to some extent, although the mystery of the skeleton's sudden absence did still linger in her mind. Fortunately, it now appeared that when Leah had lit the actual furnace and had solved the skeleton's riddle, her actions had set in motion the restoration of the shipwreck to its former ship worthy status and so a somewhat curious but visually pleasant transformation had actually occurred which for Leah, certainly felt a lot safer and definitely looked far more pleasant.

For the next couple of minutes Leah paused as she stood on the top deck and just admired the almost fully restored ship in all its glory as she attempted to catch her breath before she began to assess her return journey across the jagged rocks and a safe route back to the sandy, pebbly beach. A far more intricate inspection of the rocks that surrounded the ship was definitely necessary and required, Leah swiftly concluded as she started to turn her attention more fully towards the rocks and drew much closer to the side of the ship before she even made an attempt to depart. Unfortunately, as Leah already knew, the rocks had plenty of spiky, jagged edges that would not be kind to her if she slipped or misplaced a foot and so a couple of minutes in deep thought was absolutely essential in order to plan a safe route.

Once Leah had caught her breath and felt much calmer, she cautiously began her descent as she prepared to return to the pebbly beach once more and as she did so, she gave the shipwreck's main deck one last final thoughtful glance because the skeleton had not yet reappeared and that absence still puzzled her. However, that one final mystery, Leah started to accept, would probably linger in the background of her mind and dangle over her thoughts even after her departure because the skeleton as yet had not put in an actual second appearance and had it seemed, totally vanished into the wooden planks of the ship along with all the mouldy dust. Rather unfortunately for Leah, the same could not be said for the jagged rocks that surrounded the base of the ship which unlike the skeleton had remained fully intact and were definitely still present, and since those rocks did surround the whole length of the ship's two sides that meant that the rocks would be hard to avoid which also meant that she would actually have to face those hard stony surfaces alone.

The return journey, Leah noticed as she began to climb back down the rocky, jagged fixtures, seemed to be slightly more tricky on her return trip which she swiftly attributed to the fact that the visible parts of the rocky surfaces now appeared to be a bit wetter which made each rock a lot more slippery. Despite that rather hazardous complexity however, Leah persevered and clambered across a few more rocks as she fully committed herself to her chosen route and her return to the beach, irrespective of the potential perils.

Approximately fifteen few minutes later and much to Leah's total relief, she finally arrived back upon the sandy, pebbly beach and as she jumped off the last jagged rock and landed on the pebbles, she released a grateful sigh as she finally placed her feet back down on solid but artificially solid, simulated ground. A definite worrisome fear had pricked, needled away and had somersaulted through Leah's mind more than a few times whilst she had been situated inside the shipwreck that a return to the beach might become an absolute impossibility but fortunately, her fears had not materialized or held true which had meant that the beach had still been reachable, albeit with a bit of additional effort on her part.

In fact on several occasions, whilst Leah had been inside the rotten shipwreck, she had almost panicked at the thought of being stuck inside the musty, dusty, eerie vessel's walls where she would perhaps have been trapped alongside the skeletal remains for the remainder of her emotional journey that day and that fear had haunted her mind. Despite all Leah's fears however, somehow the skeleton's riddle had managed to hold her thoughts and curiosity captive inside that shipwreck, even though she had wanted to flee many times and even though at times, not even a small flicker of hope had existed as she had attempted to solve the riddle with nothing but planks of rotten wood and a pile of bones for company.

One final last glance was cast back towards the ship as Leah prepared to search for the next part of her emotional adventure that day which she hoped would not be inside a musty, mouldy, eerie, dark rotten location because the rotten shipwreck really had sent shivers down her spine. Suddenly however, just as Leah was about to turn away and proceed with her emotional journey, some very loud continuous noises emanated from the ship itself and so she continued to focus upon it as she began to visually search for the source of the loud noises which sounded like long grinds and creaks. However, much to Leah's surprise, she swiftly discovered that the once mangled, crumpled, crushed shipwreck now almost shone with glory because not only had all the wooden decks and exterior been fully transformed but now, all the sails had also been fully restored which was instantly noticeable because each one flapped and hung down from the ship's various masts and there were now several other essential bits of nautical equipment that appeared to be present, so it almost looked as if the ship was actually ready to sail away.

Just a second or two later Leah discovered what the actual source of the noise was due to the ship's sudden movement as it suddenly managed to free itself from the bed of jagged rocks that it had grated against and then began to move off. However, the ship's movement wasn't actually the final surprise that stunned Leah the most because as she began to flick her eyes across the ship's main top deck, she swiftly discovered that another huge surprise awaited her and that surprise which suddenly, silently greeted her eyes, related to the skeletal remains that she had discovered on the first lower deck which had it seemed, suddenly decided to reappear. Much to Leah's amusement and delight, the bony occupant of the ship that had been seated at the rotten table now appeared to be in actual command of the ship itself because he stood beside the captain's wheel as he steered, directed and supervised the ship's actual movements.

Since the skeletal remains now appeared to be in actual command of the ship, his boney position and actions clearly indicated to Leah that he was indeed definitely the captain, much as she had initially suspected and assumed and so for a few silent minutes of fascination she stood and watched him as he took full charge of his vessel. Less than a minute later as Leah continued to watch, the ship managed to fully clear the jagged, rocky bed of destruction completely after which point, the vessel started to glide across the waves as the skeleton captain directed his ship away from danger and towards the entrance of the bay.

A sudden hearty, bony salute was politely offered and given to Leah by the captain as she watched him suddenly turn back to face her and spot her watchful eyes but as he saluted, Leah noticed that his skeletal structure swiftly started to change as he began to morph into a male human form with fully fleshed limbs, surface skin and some clumps of human hair. The once bony presence and hand from what Leah could see, now no longer visibly comprised of any actual bones because every inch of bone had now been concealed by skin, flesh and even with some material cloth but a multitude of curious questions rapidly began to somersault through Leah's mind as she watched the captain's transformation occur which it appeared, was even more swift than the vessel's transformation.

Due to Leah's reluctance however, to brave the waters of the bay once again in the pursuit of any answers each question remained silently locked behind her lips because it had now become quite apparent that she had freed the skeletal captain and his ship from a bony, rotten eternity of perpetual decay. Although Leah's liberation of the captain and his ship didn't answer all of her questions, it did satisfy her mind to some extent since it had ultimately, now provided her with comprehensive answers to both the captain's riddle and the skeleton's absence and so she quietly fully accepted and processed his sudden reappearance which had actually been not only a surprise but really quite a delightful surprise.

Quite unexpectedly and much to Leah's satisfaction, somehow

she had managed to free both the ship and the captain from the angry seas, the wrath of the bay that had held the two captive, the jagged, treacherous bed of rocks and the stagnant stranded state that both had existed in and had been stuck in which really encouraged her. Both it appeared, had now been fully restored and as Leah might expect, the captain seemed eager to sail his ship as far away from the jagged rocks of destruction and the Bay of Wrath as he possibly could as quickly as he could but as his ship headed towards the entrance of the bay, Leah began to silently reflect upon how anger could hold people captive because the captain had mentioned in his riddle that he had angered the seas.

Inside Leah there was now a hopeful wish as she gave the captain a cheerful farewell wave in response that the ship would find a far more peaceful voyage to embark upon than the vessel's visit to the Bay of Wrath and as the next couple of minutes slipped by, Leah just stood and watched the ship in thoughtful silence. A huge transformation had definitely taken place not just to the ship but also to the skeletal captain himself which had totally surprised Leah but as she processed those changes, she felt really quite encouraged that at the very least now, the captain and the ship were both free to ride the waves once again.

Not more than a few more minutes went by before the ship approached the quite narrow entrance to the bay and then began to make its way out of the enclosed area but as the vessel glided across and cut through the waves, Leah continued to watch the ship's departure as she marveled at the complexity of her first random adventure that day which totally fascinated her. Somehow, not only had Leah finally managed to light the furnace but she had also found the skeleton's warm heart and she had released both the captain and his ship from the wrath of the bay which had taken not only his fleshy life but which had also held his ship captive for so very long that the rot, mold and dust on the wooden planks had become a permanent fixture.

Intriguingly for Leah that day, she had learnt how anger could capture someone, hold them hostage and keep them captive until their lives and being rotted away completely and unfortunately it appeared, the captain and his ship had been held captive by anger for so long that both had not only lost but also forgotten, due to decay, their once magnificent existence which had now been fully restored. Upon Leah's face there was a smile of satisfaction as she watched the ship slip through the entrance of the bay as she hoped that the captain's soul would sail across the seas until he found a much happier place of rest where both he and his ship could perhaps spend a far more pleasant, much more peaceful eternity because from what she could see, the angry waves that crashed against the jagged rocks in the Bay of Wrath, certainly weren't peaceful or pleasant.

The ship vanished from sight completely just a minute or so later and as it exited the bay, Leah swiftly turned her attention once more back to the sandy, pebbly beach as she prepared to seek out her next adventure or another directional indicator that could perhaps lead her to that adventure. Although Leah still felt quite fascinated and intrigued by the captain and his ship which now looked like a visual delight, she quickly shook off that fascination with the once battered, bruised shipwreck that had slept a rotten sleep upon a bed of jagged rocks that had ultimately, held it captive as she turned to face the rocky bay cliff faces that surrounded her and then prepared to move off again. Due to the restrictions upon Leah's time that day inside Spectrum, she definitely had to pursue her next emotional adventure within the Bay of Wrath straight away because the timer as she already knew, would continue to run regardless of whether she sought out her next adventure or not and as Leah also knew, time wouldn't stand still no matter how intrigued or fascinated she was.

Quite close to Leah's position there appeared to be a dark cave entrance that was eerily carved into the surface a rocky cliff as the darkness that it was made from silently burrowed its way into the stony surface which Leah rapidly noticed as she visually scanned the nearby cliff faces and searched amongst the rocky rough edges for some kind of route or entry point. Unfortunately however, the black hole seemed to hold no actual clues of what might lurk or lie behind that dark eerie stillness as it appeared to wait patiently and silently for Leah's attention and entrance and so as she began to walk towards it, she hoped that her next adventure in the Bay of Wrath would hold as much intrigue as the first.

Since the edges and almost the entire perimeter of the bay appeared to be formed from some very high rocky cliff faces which belonged to the mountains that surrounded it, there really wasn't much of a choice in terms of where Leah should head to next as far as she was concerned because she had absolutely no desire whatsoever to climb up a high rocky cliff face on her own without any equipment. The cave however, offered an acceptable compromise to Leah as it tunneled itself rather comfortably into one of those rocky cliff faces and committed itself to an actual exploration of the interior of that stony surface and since it would provide her with a means of progression that didn't involve any high jagged climbs or any potentially dangerous slippages, Leah nervously approached the entrance and the darkness that lived inside of it as she attempted to bravely swallow her fears.

Unlike most of the darkness that Leah had found inside the shipwreck which had been musty, dusty and mouldy and that had mainly lurked around the corners of the lower decks, Leah noticed as she drew closer to the cave that the darkness inside it was just a very intense pitch black. None of the dark particles, Leah observed, seemed to stir or move an inch as darkness oozed out of the cave's interior and covered the entire rocky entrance of the cave which worried her profusely because that dark unknown might be angry or contain lots of scary, savage simulated hybrid creatures.

Although the cave definitely lacked the extension of any kind, warm invitations as Leah peered cautiously into the still, eerie darkness, she definitely knew that she had to enter inside it and so a much closer inspection of that darkness swiftly began as Leah tried to search for some signs of simulated human life, or any other simulacrum life form. Unfortunately, however, the stagnant darkness, total stillness and absolute silence that lived inside the cave and that occupied the entrance to it, gave absolutely no indications that anything inside the cave was actually alive or to be found inside its interior as that dark, silent stillness neither committed to Leah's search for signs to proceed or offered any promises to her curiosity.

Despite the lack of encouragement from the rocky cave, Leah bravely braced herself as she started to enter into the dark blackness inside it and as she stepped into that eerie stillness, she suddenly heard a strange but quite regular noise which seemed to emanate from somewhere inside the cave itself that sounded almost like drops of water. For a few seconds Leah paused just inside the entrance to the cave where she stood completely still and then just listened to the drips which would plop into her ears now and again, every time a watery drop fell from the ceiling of the cave as each sporadic drip seemed to provide a polite but irregular rendition of watery comfort to the stony emptiness that each drop had managed to discover, drip into and find.

After Leah had listened to the watery drips for a minute or so more and once she felt convinced that those drippy noises posed no actual threat to her simulated person, several cautious steps were then taken as Leah resumed her exploration of the intensely dark cave. In order to proceed as Leah already knew, the dark, dismal, eerie cave definitely had to be explored further or her Spectrum experiences that day would just be limited to that of the shipwreck which had only been the first part of her emotional journey inside the emotional plane of wrath but as Leah's eyes started to adjust to the sudden change and lack of light fortunately, the cave's interior became slightly more visible to her and so, she began to visually inspect it.

Some jagged rocks appeared to litter the cave at frequent but irregular intervals from what Leah could see which she realized would slow down her progress and those stony obstructions also meant that her steps had to be taken quite carefully and planned in advance. The jagged rocks and their rocky existence however, did alert Leah to the fact that her actual exploration had to be conducted with care because the edges of those rocks did not look friendly at all and their appearance was so frequent that it would be hard not to bump into one with every few steps that she took. In fact in some ways, it almost appeared to Leah as she began to make her way through the cave as if the jagged rocks had deliberately been placed in their stony positions to guard and protect the cave's dark interior from any unwanted guests that might attempt to venture into its dark mysterious confines because there were quite a number of them which actually made their rocky edges hard to avoid.

A definite undercurrent of fear ran through Leah's mind as she walked through the cave that reminded her that she didn't actually know what she would find inside it but as Leah began to more fully explore the cave's interior, she managed to spot a tunnel entrance at the other end of it and then headed cautiously towards it. Some uncertain pricks of curiosity needled away inside Leah's thoughts that jiggled and somersaulted through her mind as she more fully explored the cave's stony confines and, in some ways, her impatience to find answers, almost made her feel like a small, impatient child that danced around on the spot to avoid a urinary accident whilst they waited an uncertain length of time for access to an occupied toilet. Unfortunately however, no immediate answers presented themselves to Leah's mind as she swiftly concluded that the amount of impatience that one felt and internally possessed, even if it rose and grew significantly, didn't seem to have a direct correlation to the length of an indefinite wait or have any actual impact upon the duration of it because any potential answers seemed to remain absolutely silent, completely motionless and totally indifferent to her far more impatient expectations.

No clues or indicators seemed to exist inside the actual cave itself that would provide Leah with any kind of answer as to what was supposed to happen next inside the rocky cliff face which meant, Leah would unfortunately, now have to step into the dark tunnel to secure the answers she sought. The second part of Leah's Spectrum adventure that day, she definitely felt, was hidden and concealed somewhere inside the rocky cave that she had just stepped into which had ultimately, led to that dark tunnel and so as Leah headed cautiously towards the entrance and then belong to walk along it, she hoped that the intensity of the darkness inside the tunnel wouldn't last for too long. Since at any given second as Leah already knew, the tunnel floor could give way after which point, she might be hurled towards an underground maze before she actually stumbled upon her next adventure or some kind of hybrid creature could perhaps even rush into the tunnel that would try to launch an attack upon her simulated person, she continued to air on the side of caution as she walked quite slowly along the tunnel's interior.

However, much to Leah's dismay, the tunnel was even darker than the first cave which initially restricted her visibility somewhat but as her eyes slowly adjusted and grew accustomed to the darker darkness that now surrounded her, the interior of the tunnel started to become slightly more visible as she walked on tiptoes along it and headed towards the unknown. Unlike the rocky cave, Leah could see that the tunnel had earthy, sandy circular walls and a sandy flat ground that could quite easily and comfortably be walked along and that it was almost free from any jagged rocks or any other kind of obstruction, although a couple of rocks did jut out of the ceiling in a couple of places.

Just to ensure that the tunnel was relatively safe to walk along as soon as Leah could visibly do so, she gave the interior of the tunnel ahead a quick visual scan as she walked in an attempt to reduce the fear that seemed to cling onto her every simulated pore which also seemed to haunt every inch of her simulated interior. Fortunately for Leah, her visual inspection rapidly confirmed that there were no dangerous hybrid creatures present which soothed her mind to some extent because it meant that an unexpected attack upon her person was far less likely to occur. Since no other entities were present however, Leah suddenly realized that there was also a slight drawback to that absence of simulacrums as she walked further along the tunnel's twists and turns because that absence also meant that there would be no human or any other guidance to steer her in any particular direction but Leah just hoped as she made her way along the tunnel that her next adventure wouldn't be too fearful or too angry.

At the other end of the twisted tunnel, just a few minutes later, Leah found the entrance to a second much larger cave which was far less dark where to her total delight, she swiftly spotted a humabear seated beside a small, cheery fire. Up until that point inside Spectrum, Leah's interactions and experiences with humabears had actually been quite positive, very amicable and even what one might consider pleasant, so the sight of the humabear who appeared to be busily engaged in the preparation of a some kind of meal, immediately put her mind at ease as she stepped more fully into the second cave.

Some metal skewers with chunks of food on each one, Leah observed as she began to walk towards the humabear and the small fire, appeared to be dotted around the edges of the fire that had either been leant up against it or wedged in-between some of the small rocks around it which made the humabear's immediate intentions very clear. Each metal skewer from what Leah could see had a long, chunky morsel of food wrapped around the end of it but what exactly those unrecognizable chunks were Leah had absolutely no idea, mainly due to their semi-toasted state. However, from Leah's past Spectrum experiences, she could quite easily conclude that those unidentifiable chunks would probably consist of undesirable edibles that would be totally unsuitable for human consumption and that it was safe to assume that those chunks wouldn't comprise of anything that she would want to have anywhere near her mouth, simulated or otherwise.

Although Leah had absolutely no interest whatsoever in the humabear's actual meal, she continued to make her way fearlessly towards the small fire because her last encounter with some humabears inside the Disgusting Dimension hadn't involved any actual scares which meant that there was no cause for any alarm. Once Leah arrived beside the fire, she sat down beside the rocks that surrounded it quite close to the humabear's position without even a second of hesitation because she actually felt quite comfortable inside the cave due to the humabear's presence and so she began to eagerly look forward to the potential provision of the hybrid's company as perhaps some kind of guide.

"Why are you here alone?" Leah asked politely as she turned to face the humabear and offered the hybrid creature a warm, friendly smile. "Don't humabears usually like to spend time with other humabears?"

"Well, my solitary humabear existence is slightly different from most." The male humabear started to explain as he enthusiastically plucked a skewer from in-between two small rocks and then paused for a moment as he began a quick visual inspection of his potential meal. "Because I was assigned to guard and protect the Bay of Wrath which can be a rather lonely existence." The humabear acknowledged as he released a sigh.

"Yes, the Bay of Wrath. Why do you have to guard and protect it?" Leah asked.

"Unfortunately, I was stationed here to warn anyone that might visit the bay about the wrath of the seas and the dangers that they may face, if they enter the caves and tunnels alone and then attempt to seek out the power of the bay to pursue their own evil ambitions and to serve their own power-hungry purposes." The humabear replied.

"What happened to the ship?" Leah asked. "Well, the shipwreck that was a ship that's now a ship again."

"Ah that's a pirate ship. Quite recklessly and very foolishly, the pirate ship came into the bay in pursuit of another ship which they then tried to destroy so that their crew could steal and loot any riches and gold that might be on board." The humabear explained as he gave the crispy object on the end of the skewer a swift prod. "But instead of gold and riches, the pirate ship ran into the jagged rocks of destruction which will trap or destroy any vessel that the seas bring to them."

"Really that's a pirate ship, I didn't realize?" Leah replied as a confused expression spread out across her face. "It didn't look like a pirate ship, I didn't see any black sails or anything."

"That's because the captain of that particular pirate ship disguised it so that if his ship ran into any other ships, those ships would not be forewarned or anticipate any potential attacks." The humabear said as he frowned. "Which is really quite clever when you think about it, in a very devious, underhand kind of way."

"What happened to the other ship?" Leah asked.

"Fortunately, the other ship actually managed to escape from the Bay of Wrath in one piece which has a lot more to do with the captains of the two ships and far less to do with the actual ships themselves." The humabear concluded as he shook his head. "Pirate ships aren't generally liked by the seas at the best of times and that particular pirate captain had done something very bad, so the seas in the Bay of Wrath gathered very strongly against his ship and the angry waves crushed it against the rocks to destroy not only the ship but also anyone that was on board the vessel at that time."

"What did he do?" Leah asked.

"His ship and his crew, both of which were fully under his command at the time, robbed a patrol ship that belonged to some of the creatures that live in the seas and then his pirate crew tortured some members of the patrol crew that were on board that patrol ship before they slaughtered them." The humabear explained. "It was a totally unprovoked attack and the talk of the waves at the time." He released a sad sigh before he continued. "You just don't rob sea creature patrol ships and especially not around the Bay of Wrath, not if you ever want to sail again, it was a very unwise and an extremely dangerous thing to do."

"Well, the pirate ship's gone now." Leah mentioned. "I set the ship and the captain free. How long had it been stuck on those rocks?"

"The ship crashed into the rocks of destruction a very long time ago, at least a decade ago now but the seas for some unknown reason, didn't actually crush it completely in the end or swallow the ship up whole which definitely surprised me because for that kind of sea crime, the waves usually tear ships to pieces." The humabear replied. "Sometimes I think it was just left there on that jagged bed of rocks to serve as a reminder to other sea voyagers and ships that might wish to enter the bay for the purposes of mischief that they too could easily meet their doom." He paused for a moment and then shook his head as he held up the skewer and prepared to consume the first part of his meal. "This bay isn't called the Bay of Wrath for nothing you know, the seas in this bay anger very easily and when those waves anger, you'd better ride the waves very quickly and find somewhere to dive into and hide."

"Have you lived in these caves long?" Leah asked as she

flashed him a nervous smile despite the fearful shiver that she felt slither down her spine.

A few seconds slipped crunchily by as Leah watched the hybrid creature in amused fascination as he bite into and then munched, chewed and crunched upon a part of the morsel of food from the end of the skewer which looked to Leah like some kind of large, crispy, barbecued insect before a response was offered.

"For as long as I can remember, definitely for more than a decade now." The humabear confirmed with a nod after which point, he bit into the toasted morsel on the end of the skewer again. He crunched and chewed on the crispy mouthful a few times and then swallowed it before he continued. "In fact, if I remember correctly, it's been almost two decades now."

"You must have seen a lot of ships in that time." Leah swiftly concluded.

"Yes, too many to count." The humabear agreed as he nodded and then paused thoughtfully for a moment. "Are you hungry?" He asked a few seconds later as he smiled apologetically. "You can have one of these toasted hopperworms if you like?"

"No thanks, I'm good but you go right ahead." Leah insisted politely as an amused grin spread out across her face which she then used to keep her lips shut tightly together as she tried to contain and mask some of the giggles which threatened to erupt and escape from her mouth.

Another few hungry, eager, loud crunches rapidly emanated from the humabear's mouth as Leah watched him resume the consumption of his meal which felt to Leah like an attempt to devour the remainder of the long, chunky crispy hopperworm in as few mouthfuls as possible. Although the humabear seemed harmless and pleasant enough, Leah couldn't help but feel some amused disgust as she waited for him to finish his meal because the crunchy morsels on offer which she now realized were actually another hybrid creation that she herself had created, namely grasshoppers and earth worms, really didn't appeal to her at all. The humabear's offer however, swiftly reminded Leah of her recent experiences with humabear delicacies inside the Disgusting Dimension where she had generously been offered a chunk of rat intestine cake which she had almost consumed but fortunately for her simulated organs, had actually been saved from.

"Are you absolutely sure you don't want to join me?" The humabear asked once he'd polished off the first hopperworm as he reached for another occupied skewer and smacked his lips together. He plucked the second skewer from its position and then paused thoughtfully for a second or two before he continued. "Would you like something else perhaps? I do have a mudrattysnake that I caught just yesterday, so I could always cook that up for you."

"I'm very sure." Leah quickly confirmed as she shook her head. "I ate lunch not long ago."

The thought of a mudrattysnake toasted to a crisp didn't even remotely align with Leah's very human perceptions of what a decent, nutritious, good meal should contain, fictional or otherwise because it absolutely repulsed her and so the humabear's offers were easy to decline. Not even one artificial hair on Leah's simulated head wished to consume dead insects, vermin or reptiles inside Spectrum or anywhere else but just for a moment, the humabear's meal and offer prompted Leah to consider and more deeply appreciate, the usual human edible provisions on offer to her in her very real own life that she usually just took for granted.

Although Leah had eaten some delicious meals and delicacies inside Spectrum, the meal on offer to her that day was situated a hundred miles away from her taste buds, palate and her usual dietary intake but the sight of the hopperworms had certainly put human culinary efforts and the usual grocery produce stocked inside fresh food outlets firmly into perspective. In fact, human produce, in direct comparison to the humabear's usual dietary intake, now almost looked to Leah like total luxuries because the hybrid's chosen edibles lacked any kind of appeal in Leah's sight and seemed really rather strange. Human beings as far as Leah was concerned, had definitely taken a step up from dead rats, snakes, grasshoppers and worms in terms of their dietary intake and so there was no way on earth, albeit a simulated form of earth that Leah was now going to take a step backwards.

For the next few seconds there was almost total silence inside the second cave apart from the noise of humabear's crunches as Leah watched the hybrid creature polish off the second crispy hopperworm in what seemed like no time at all. Just as the humabear started to reach for the third skewer and another crispy, toasted hopperworm however, Leah politely stretched out her arm towards the humabear as she offered him a friendly hand and prepared to shake hands and hand paws with him as she made her first attempt since she'd arrived in the second cave to formally introduce herself.

"What's your name please?" Leah enquired as she gave the humabear a warm, friendly smile.

"I'm called Bearciple." He replied as he stretched out his hand paw towards her and then shook her human hand.

"Nice to meet you Bearciple, I'm Leah. What do you do inside these caves all day alone?" Leah asked as she gave his furry but quite fleshy face a polite but curious glance. "Do you ever feel bored or lonely? Are there other humabears anywhere nearby and do they ever come to visit you?"

"Well Leah, I'm not always alone because sometimes visitors do come here to explore the Caves of Reflection but to be perfectly frank, not many humabears visit or spend that much time here because we tend to prefer to live in places where there are at least some trees though a nice freshwater lake or river can be quite nice." Bearciple explained. "Sandy pebbly beaches, rocky hard cliff faces and choppy salty waves aren't usually considered a great habitat, a nice home or even an ideal vacation spot for us." He acknowledged as he grinned. "But whenever visitors do pass by, I usually take them on a tour of the caves and guide them through the tunnels because like I said, the Bay of Wrath can at times be a very dangerous place. Sometimes though, I try to warn pirate ships not to enter the bay because I'm here to protect the Bay of Wrath from power seekers and troublemakers and since pirates frequently come here to do one of those two things, I try to scare them away." Bearciple paused for a moment, glanced longingly at the third skewer, smacked his lips together and then started to reach for it again. "Those are my main duties really but at times, when things are a bit quiet, I do try to do some other things but normally, I try not to venture too far away from these caves and I tend to stick to the bay at all times because troublemakers can pop up at any time."

"Do a lot of troublemakers come here?" Leah asked.

"The Bay of Wrath attracts many visitors for a variety of different reasons but a lot of power seekers are within that number because buried in the heart of the bay there is a great power source that can command and control the seas." Bearciple explained as he plucked the third skewer from its position and then held it inside one of his hand paws. "Unfortunately, since that power source lies in the Bay of Wrath's very core, some come here to seek out that power in order to utilize it for their own purposes and some of those purposes are very evil. In fact, to be perfectly honest, some of them will do anything just to get their hands or paws upon that power, even risk their own lives"

"Is the Bay of Wrath a very dangerous place?" Leah asked.

"It can be at times, especially if you come here to seek out that power because then you'll have to face the trials of the bay but you should be okay Leah as long as you're with me." Bearciple rapidly reassured her. He plucked the third crispy hopperworm from the top of third skewer before he placed the empty skewer down on the ground next to the fire and then stood up. "I can take you on a tour of the Caves of Reflection now if you like?"

"Sure Bearciple, a tour would be great." Leah replied as she enthusiastically nodded her head in response. "It's very kind of you to offer, I really appreciate it."

Some toasted crumbs were swiftly dashed from Bearciple's furry, hairy body as Leah watched him in amused fascination after which point, the third crispy hopperworm was eagerly popped into his mouth whole and then swiftly crunched upon. Just a few seconds later Leah heard a large gulp as Bearciple swallowed the chewed remnants of his meal which prompted her to smile as she accepted that whilst toasted insects, reptiles and vermin weren't exactly her idea of a great dinner or snack, those crispy, toasted chunks definitely seemed to satisfy Bearciple because he appeared to have enjoyed his meal immensely.

The next minute or so slipped busily by as Leah continued to watch Bearciple with an amused smile upon her face as some sand was enthusiastically gathered from the floor and then thrown over the flames of the small fire. Each flame quickly fizzled out as the grains of sand hit and then fully covered their fiery existence and once the small fire had been fully extinguished, Leah began to rise to her feet as she prepared to cooperate with Bearciple's friendly offer. Since Leah had actually wandered into Bearciple's cave, she now felt almost obliged to accept his kind offer as she swiftly began to conclude that it really wasn't the worst thing that could happen to her in the Bay of Wrath because from what Leah had already seen, the pirate ship had suffered a much worse fate and had endured a far tougher experience. In many ways, the humbear's polite invitation actually really suited Leah because she harbored absolutely no desires at all to potter around the Bay of Wrath on her own and since it seemed that the hybrid entity was to be her guide that day, for the meantime at least, it therefore made total sense to participate in his guided tour.

For the next couple of minutes Leah watched Bearciple bury the metal skewers that the crispy hopperworms had been roasted and toasted on, under a pile of sand quite close to the now fully extinguished fire as she prepared to be led on a tour of the tunnels and caves. Despite the fact that Bearciple had given Leah several reassurances, she still felt slightly nervous as she waited for his tour of the Caves of Reflection to begin but she hoped that the tour would at least be reasonably calm, despite the angry seas that surrounded the caves and despite the fact that wrath was generally considered to be a very fiery, extremely negative and really quite harsh emotion.

At the other end of the large cave, Leah suddenly noticed that there was an exit and what looked like the entrance to second sandy, earthy tunnel and as the two started to walk towards it as Leah followed Bearciple's lead, she attempted to strike up a conversation with him about what exactly his tour might entail and some of the potential sights that would perhaps be on offer. Rather curiously for Leah however, she noticed that Bearciple seemed to skirt around the questions that she asked with quite vague explanations which appeared to offer no real commitment or any comprehensive answers to her curiosity as he somehow, avoided a detailed in-depth discussion about what exactly she would be shown as he guided her around the Caves of Reflection. However, despite the lack of detailed descriptive input from Bearciple, Leah tried her best to remain as optimistic as the two neared the entrance of the tunnel as she hoped that if any surprises did present themselves to them both or even just to Leah herself that those surprises wouldn't be too angry or too chaotic.

Curious Reflections in the Crystal Mirror of Trials

When the two stepped into the second circular tunnel just a second or two later, Leah immediately noticed that it had a much higher arched ceiling than the first and that there appeared to be a large, silver square metal platform directly in front of both Bearciple and herself which instantly aroused and prodded her curiosity. A second thick, large, silver square block seemed to hover directly above the first large, square metal platform which was embedded into the ground, the presence of which instantly created a flurry of questions in Leah's mind as to its actual purpose. However, from sight alone, Leah had absolutely no idea what either of the strange, metal, square objects actually were or could be utilized for because no obvious indications or clues seemed to be present or immediately jumped out at her.

Since the second metal object hovered at least five inches above the first platform and at least ten inches above ground, despite its metal form, Leah observed as she stared at it and studied it for a moment with a blank expression upon her face, it seemed to defy gravity because it looked quite heavy but somehow, seemed to hover effortlessly above the ground. No matter how hard or intensely however, Leah stared at and visually inspected the two metal objects as she wished that one would respond with some answers that might satisfy her curiosity, no further clues seemed to emanate from either the square metal platform base or the square metal object that hovered directly above it. However, Leah did notice as she continued to stare at both objects that the square base was quite firmly embedded into the sandy, earthy ground which clearly indicated to her that it had lived comfortably in that position for quite a while which also implied that was highly unlikely that the metal base would move around or do anything at all.

Despite the lack of information and the probability that

Bearciple's answers might shed no further light upon either of the large square metal objects, Leah prepared to seek out an explanation as she enthusiastically turned to face him as to how the objects correlated with his tour. A doubt niggled away the back of Leah's mind as she stood and faced Bearciple however, because as she had just experienced and discovered, at times he could be like a wooden stick dam of vagueness that only allowed certain drips of information to squeeze through the gaps in its structure via some little spaces in-between a few roughly placed twigs and sticks which meant, the provision of details in some of his more selective discussions could be rather sparse. In fact, some of Bearciple's explanations from what Leah had heard so far, seemed to just skirt around the outlines of a topic much like a rough sketch as he paid absolutely no regard to the details that she might expect to fill the interior which meant that those details for the most part remained unfilled, blank, incomplete and unshaded, especially when it came to the issue of the tunnels and his tour.

Regardless of that possible lack of cooperation on Bearciple's part and Leah's uncertainty that he would actually provide a comprehensive response, she prepared to ask him some questions about the two metal objects anyway, since both objects had remained in a stationary position, were still motionless and had prodded her curiosity. The two large square items did occupy the tunnel that the two had stepped into and Leah noticed that one metal square definitely seemed to be ready to play an active part in Bearciple's tour as it hovered in silent limbo above the other and so, she suspected that the metal squares had some kind of purpose, albeit a rather ambiguous one.

A few seconds of thoughtful silence went by as Leah stared at Bearciple's humabear face before it suddenly struck her that for that day inside Spectrum and so far in the Bay of Wrath, he was actually her second guide and that the first had actually been the skeleton captain who technically, had been her first simulacrum guide. Unfortunately however, Leah's first guide the skeleton captain hadn't uttered a single word to her and so she definitely felt that Bearciple's partial explanations, no matter what each one lacked, were a definite improvement because his humabear presence and interactions somehow made her feel slightly less alone.

The possibility that a few strands of hopeful reassurance might be offered by Bearciple to appease Leah's mind after her earlier shipwreck experiences that day, offered Leah a small glimmer of hope and she definitely wanted some strands of hope to clutch and hold on to inside her mind that the two objects would not be harmful in any way. However, just as Leah opened her mouth to ask Bearciple for further information and some actual clarity, he suddenly interrupted her pre-question and then began to voluntarily offer her an actual explanation himself.

"This is my hovercart Leah." Bearciple proudly announced as he nodded his head enthusiastically. "You have to stand on it." He invited as he pointed towards the square metal object that hovered above the metal platform that was embedded into the ground. "It won't move a grain of sandy earth until you do."

"Really Bearciple?" Leah asked. "Are you sure I won't fall off?"

"No, try it and see. You won't fall off, not when I'm around." Bearciple insisted with a certain nod. "It's perfectly safe, I humabear promise you and I should know because I built it myself."

Although the hovercart appeared to have no sides which made Leah doubt that it could carry either of them anywhere, Bearciple's invitation did appeal to her a lot more than a potential hike and clamber through the sandy, earthy tunnels that would be visited on his tour. Since the tunnel that the two were situated in, from what Leah could see as she glanced further along it, had some large rocky obstructions that protruded from the tunnel's walls, ceiling and floor in silent but obstructive acts of defiance which seemed to be in direct opposition to their potential movements, she definitely felt that Bearciple's tour on foot would probably be far more strenuous and also that it would present many more potentially harmful hazards to them both.

Due to the jagged, rocky dangers that lurked in the tunnels ahead, Leah quickly decided to cooperate with Bearciple's suggestion even if just to humor him and so, a second or two later she decisively stepped onto the large metal block to see if anything would actually happen. From what Leah had seen and could see in the interior of the tunnel, if the hovercart did work, she began to speculate, it was far less likely to be hampered by the rocks so at the very least, that operational capacity held the possibility of a far smoother tunnel tour ride than a manual clamber through it.

Rather surprisingly however, once Leah stepped onto the metal block along with Bearciple who followed right behind her, any doubtful speculation about the limits of the hovercart that had erupted inside her mind, instantly fled and were swiftly dismissed from her thoughts as four silver, shiny hovercart walls suddenly, quickly sprouted from the metal base. Apart from the four silver hovercart walls that now surrounded the two, Leah instantly noticed that a metal bench also suddenly appeared which seemed to mold itself into shape very quickly as it grew from the square base until it reached a certain height where the bench then remained in a stagnant position as it lined one side of the hovercart's walls.

"Please take a seat Leah, it'll be much safer for you." Bearciple politely suggested and offered. "Because when the hovercart starts to speed up, it usually sways around quite a bit to avoid any rocks in its path." He advised. "I've built in some sensors that are installed in the hovercart's base and although it's a great functionality, I find that the rocks in the tunnels can at times make the ride a little unsteady."

"Sure. thanks." Leah replied as she immediately sat down on the metal bench and then glanced over the side wall of the hovercart nearest to her position. She smiled as she paused for a moment and just watched the hovercart hover above the sandy, earthy ground before she continued in a playful tone. "Well Bearciple, it certainly does hover and it definitely is a cart but can it actually take us anywhere?" Leah teased. "I sense a lack of cooperation on the part of your hovercart. Did you offend or upset your hovercart recently, because It doesn't seem to want to move?"

"Humabears never exaggerate Leah that's a very human trait and fortunately for our hybrid species, not one we evolved with." Bearciple joked as he deftly plucked a small remote control from his furry body and then nodded his head. "Now hold on tight because you are just about to experience some of the wonders of humabear technology."

Leah giggled.

Much to Leah's absolute delight and total amusement, the hovercraft suddenly gently shook as it started to move off after which point, it seemed to settle into a glidey slide through the air as their journey along the earthy, sandy tunnel began which created a slight breeze that softly brushed against Leah's simulated cheeks. In a matter of just seconds however, the gentle pace started to change as Leah noticed that the hovercart rapidly began to pick up speed and as it began to whizz around the twists and turns in the tunnel, she clutched onto one of the metal sides of the contraption as she made an effort to try and stabilize herself.

Just as Leah became used to the increase in speed and started to relax however, before she could even begin to enjoy the hovercart ride, she noticed that the tunnel took a very sudden, very steep, very sharp downward turn. Seconds later, the hovercart not only dipped downwards but then hurled itself towards the base of that steep downward slope as it followed the path of the tunnel and as a result of the sudden change in direction and speed, Leah almost gasped in surprise as she watched the walls of the tunnel whizz swiftly by.

Once the hovercart arrived at the base of the steep downward slope, the metal contraption slowed down significantly and as Leah watched, some sandy, earthy tunnels, platforms and paths rapidly started to appear from every direction imaginable as the space around the hovercart quickly filled up with potential entrances and exit points. From what Leah could see, the singular tunnel had suddenly been transformed into a sandy, earthy maze with a multitude of optional routes because now there were a vast number of accessible options available to the two passengers inside the hovercart which made Leah wonder how on earth Bearciple managed to find his own way around, let alone give anyone a tour of anything. In fact, as far as Leah was concerned, the earthy, sandy maze had so many entrance and exit points twisted around each other that it looked like a junction of jumbled, sandy, earthy confusion which she hoped Bearciple would be able to fully understand because she certainly had no clue on which path or tunnel to follow.

Each tunnel, path and raised sandy, earthy platform appeared to lead off in a different direction but much to Leah's horror as the hovercart slowed down even more, she quickly realized that there also appeared to be a definite downside to that sudden change which was the sudden appearance of a mass number of hybrid creatures. Rather unfortunately for Leah, it appeared that the appearance of the sandy, earthy maze routes had also ushered in the appearance of the hybrid creatures which mainly seemed to comprise of slimebattymice, mudrattysnakes, hopperworms, millipiders and a bunch of swampcattyrats, most of which either crawled, scurried or flapped around the scrambled sandy, earthy junction.

Since the hybrid creatures definitely looked a lot less friendly to Leah than Bearciple and much more scary as they speedily began to gravitate towards the hovercart which now moved at a far slower pace and then started to swarm across and flock around its exterior walls, Leah began to fear what actually might happen next. Due to the hybrids large number and their close proximity to Leah's current position because some of them were even in arm's reach, their presence definitely worried Leah immensely because it meant only one thing for the occupants of the hovercart and that was the possibility that a potential attack might occur shortly and perhaps even more than one.

Not a muscle was moved as Leah remained completely still and just watched the hybrid creatures as some swarmed over the sandy, earthy tunnel surfaces nearby, clambered across the metal hovercart's exterior walls or flapped chaotically around in the air just above her simulated head but despite her still exterior, total alarm swirled chaotically around inside her. Unfortunately, the creatures numbers were so great and the hybrid creatures were so very close that Leah doubted that the two inside the hovercart would be able to pass through the junction unscathed and those numbers along with the hybrid's proximity seemed to grow, intensify and increase with every second that went by. Upon Leah's face there was a frustrated, alarmed, fearful expression as panic surged through her simulated veins as she turned to face Bearciple with a sense of urgency because the pace of the hovercart had by that point, slowed down so much that it was now not only easy to reach but also very easy to attack.

"Can't we go any faster Bearciple?" Leah urged.

"No Leah, I'm afraid we can't not around the Junction of Mysteries." Bearciple explained. "I have to look for and find a particular exit and if I miss it, we could end up going round and round in tunnel loops for hours."

Quite predictably and fully in alignment with Leah's expectations as she turned back to the face the hybrid creatures, she noticed that some of the hybrids had begun to penetrate the interior of the hovercart as the creatures boldly drew closer to the two occupants inside it which sent a rumble of shivery earthquake like tremors of alarm down her spine. Some nervous screams threatened to erupt from Leah's lips from the volcano of fear that bubbled away just below the surface of her simulated skin but even more alarmingly for Leah, as the hovercart and the two passed by some of the creatures' positions that had not yet latched onto the hovercart, their proximity rapidly become closer as they too joined the hybrids that had already landed upon and infiltrated its exterior and interior. In many ways, it almost felt to Leah as if the hybrid's presence in and around the hovercart had signaled to any other creatures nearby that an attack on the hovercart was just about to occur and that they too should join in which those hybrid creatures definitely appeared to have responded to.

Just a few seconds later the attacks began and most, Leah observed as she started to flap her arms wildly around in response, came from either the interior and walls of the hovercart itself or from the air just above her head. However, a few leaps and claw attacks Leah noticed, did originate from some nearby walls, raised pathways and platforms from some of the mudrattysnakes and swampcattyrats that crawled across each one but despite all Leah's efforts as she flapped around chaotically and tried to scare some of the hybrid creatures away, at one point the attacks became so frequent and intense that she had to duck down inside the hovercart itself.

Unfortunately however, those actions on Leah's part didn't seem to actually deter or change the frequency of the relentless stream of attacks because the majority of the attacks, now actually emanated from the interior of the hovercart itself. Nothing that Leah did seemed to reduce the continuous stream of leapy pounces, clawy scratches or swipey flaps which continued at a rate that seemed to increase with every second that went by and since neither of the two hovercart passengers had any weapons, Leah doubted that those attacks would actually stop or reduce in quantity or frequency. Very uncomfortably for Leah, her attempts to defend herself didn't seem to shake the hybrid creatures off or scare them away in the slightest and so her efforts seemed to be almost pointless, due to the large number of hybrid creatures that appeared to be present which continued to swarm across or towards the hovercart from every direction imaginable in a constant animalistic hybrid stream.

Much to Leah's absolute disgust, more hybrid creatures had by that point landed inside the hovercart or had jumped into it whilst others had latched on to its metal sides which they now clung onto which meant that the hovercart's metal base and walls were hardly even visible anymore. Every single spare inch of Bearciple's hovercart was swiftly polluted, infested and contaminated by the hybrids as Leah watched in fearful silence as the creatures not only swarmed around outside it but also inside it like a relentless whirlpool stream of angry, wild aggression and a whirlwind swarm of animalistic rage and as the hovercart's interior become fuller, she cowered against a corner of it to try and avoid the increasingly bold avalanche of wild attacks. A couple of slimebattymice, a mudrattysnake and a few swampcattyrats did however, despite all Leah's efforts to try and avoid them, manage to grab parts of her clothing and her two legs which they then clung to and so a frantic struggle rapidly began as she repeatedly and desperately, tried to detach them from her simulated clothing and her simulated limbs.

"Please help me Bearciple." Leah pleadingly urged as she glanced at the humabear's face in alarmed frustration.

"Yes, they do seem to be quite unmanageable now." Bearciple

acknowledged as he nodded his head before he leant down, plucked a swampcattyrat from the interior of the hovercart and then speedily threw it out of the cart over one of the hovercart's silvery walls. "Don't worry Leah, I know exactly how to handle this." He swiftly reassured her.

Just a few seconds later, fortunately for Leah, the hovercart was steered by Bearciple towards a raised sandy, earthy path which the metal contraption then started to glide along in an upwards direction which appeared to be a far safer direction because as she instantly noticed, far less hybrid creatures were gathered around the outskirts of it. After a few more seconds had gone by, Leah watched in fearful silence as Bearciple touched the hovercart remote again but much to her astonishment, almost instantly, an electrical field of some kind seemed to be generated which emanated from the hovercart's walls that immediately shocked and stunned the hybrid creatures that either clung onto its exterior or remained inside its interior with a short, sharp blast.

The upwards route, the sudden change in direction and the electrical field, much to Leah's total relief, jointly appeared to do the trick as she gratefully watched most of the hybrid creatures that had latched onto the exterior of the hovercart, fall from the hovercart's walls and then land on the ground in a shocked, stunned and disgruntled state. Although some hybrid creatures did still remain inside the hovercart from what Leah could see, the creatures were in a stunned state and as she continued to watch Bearciple in appreciative silence, she noticed that he quickly threw the remainder of the unwanted passengers out with total ease which immediately appeased her mind and calmed her thoughts.

After all the hybrid creatures had been dealt with appropriately by Bearciple and totally eradicated from the interior and exterior hovercart, Leah noticed that he swiftly turned his attention more fully back towards their journey through the tunnels once more as he touched the hovercart remote once again and it suddenly began to speed up. Fortunately for Leah, their escape rapidly became even more certain and secure as the pace of the hovercart quickly accelerated and much to her absolute joy, the hybrid animalistic dangers that had just moments before literally surrounded them that had disrupted their peaceful slidey, hovercart glide ride, reduced significantly within just a matter of seconds. Another few seconds slipped by as Leah watched the appearances of the hybrid creatures dwindle even more in both frequency and number as the two travelled further along the new upward route at a much faster pace and as the mazey Junction of Mysteries was left firmly behind, both the hybrid creatures and the junction completely vanished from sight just a few seconds later.

Leah turned to face the male humabear as she released a sigh of relief and then began to relax a little. "Do many visitors come here Bearciple?" She asked.

"It depends really Leah, sometimes the Caves of Reflection can be very busy and at other times, the tunnels around the bay can be quite quiet, it just depends upon the seas. Sometimes the waves bring and carry many visitors here and sometimes, they don't bring any here for a while though some visitors do come of their own accord." Bearciple explained as he shook his head and sighed. "But I have to admit, most of the entities that do come here without the participation of the seas are usually troublemakers or power seekers, so I don't usually give any of those visitors a tour because they always try to avoid me." He scratched his head thoughtfully as he fell silent for a moment. "It's actually quite hard for me to try to estimate or predict how many visitors I'll have in any given month, any week or even on any single day because it can vary so much. For instance, sometimes I'll have no visitors for a month and then every day for a fortnight, I'll have as many as ten or fifteen a day."

"But Bearciple, how do all those visitors fit into your hovercart?" Leah teased as she grinned.

"Oh I just expand it Leah, like this." Bearciple replied with a certain nod as he touched the remote control and the hovercart suddenly grew in length. "I built this hovercart with the latest advancements in humabear technology and I do also perform regular upgrades, so I fine tune it quite often and although it might look very simplistic, it definitely has hidden potential and a far greater capacity than you might expect."

"Yes, I can see that now. Yes, you could easily fit at least fifteen people in here." Leah agreed as she inspected the hovercart's enlarged interior and then nodded her head in approval. "I'm impressed Bearciple, you must have put a lot of hard work and effort into this hovercart."

"Well fortunately, I was trained for a few years by a master humabear inventor before I was assigned to the Bay of Wrath." Bearciple mentioned. "And in fact, he was the only humabear inventor in the entire region that I lived in prior to my relocation, so I was really rather lucky and so that's why technological creations are one of my specialties." He announced triumphantly as he touched the remote control again to steer the hovercart down a sharp downward slope and to shrink the hovercart back to its usual size.

"How old are you Bearciple?" Leah asked as she glanced at his face.

"How old?" Bearciple replied with a quizzical expression. "What do you mean?"

"When were you born? How many humabear years have you lived? How many humabear birthdays have you had?" Leah teased playfully. "You do have humabear birthdays right?"

"What's a birthday?" Bearciple asked.

"It's a celebration to mark the day that you were born and to celebrate the fact that you've managed to successfully arrive at another milestone in your life in terms of the number of years that you have lived." Leah explained. "Most human beings usually celebrate their birthdays on the same date every single year."

"I think that particular celebration day must have slipped by our hybrid evolutionary process." Bearciple concluded as he shook his head. "Did we miss much?"

"Yes, I think you did Bearciple." Leah replied. "Birthday celebrations can be great fun because they are usually full of lovely gifts and lots of delicious treats." She paused thoughtfully for a moment before she continued. "Why do you refer to the seas at times as if they were a person? You mentioned that the seas bring or carry visitors and vessels here like the seas are capable of logical thought, emotional responses and subsequent actions. Aren't the seas just a mass of water?"

"The seas are very much alive Leah." Bearciple insisted as the hovercart suddenly approached a two tunnel fork and he touched the remote to steer the metal contraption towards the darker of the two tunnels and the entrance on the right-hand side. "The waves move, they act, they react and they respond to the various entities that travel through them in different ways." He explained as the hovercart entered into the darker tunnel and then began to glide along it.

"Now that is absolutely impossible and totally illogical." Leah swiftly concluded as she shook her head.

Although Bearciple's explanations seemed almost impossible to believe, for a moment Leah silently pondered over his words as she began to process the implications of his comments which implied that some of the elements inside Spectrum had perhaps taken on a life of their own and that those aspects of her invention had travelled well beyond her original creation. Some kind of evolutionary process had it now appeared, actually occurred that Leah herself had not input into and as she started to digest that notion which seemed not only slightly strange but also totally illogical and absolutely impossible, it simultaneously also felt like a delicious fascination of total intrigue. However, Leah suddenly began to realize that she had absolutely no actual control over that evolutionary process, even though she was currently situated inside Spectrum herself because she could not change what lay outside the scope of her own creational parameters.

Something else it appeared had definitely been set in motion through Leah's creation of Spectrum that could not now be controlled, modified or tweaked because her invention which she had given an actual life and form to had not just evolved but had also travelled along those evolutionary changes and uncertain routes in an unpredictable manner to a very unknown destination. Although Leah couldn't quite put her simulated fingers or mind on what exactly that something else was because it was something that she did not yet fully understand since it had not been foreseeable when she had initially designed and created the Spectrum prototype, the notion and implications of that uncertain evolutionary growth, captivated her thoughts for a few minutes as she remained silently fascinated and absolutely intrigued.

In some ways, Leah quietly contemplated as she watched the hovercart glide silently along the dark tunnel, she almost felt as if Spectrum had developed its own personality because it now looked as if each element within it seemed to organically grow and adapt within its own sphere of simulated existence every time it was accessed and she had experienced that herself since her very first visit. Quite strangely, the organic patterns that Leah had created to govern Spectrum's functionalities which allowed the system to respond to users and grow in various ways in order to provide them with much deeper and more varied experiences had responded to her own usage in an unpredictable manner which had really surprised her but also utterly captivated her. Despite the unpredictable nature of those evolutionary changes, Leah now felt intrigued by that random, sporadic capacity, although the technical issues that those evolutionary, random processes raised, did make her question how that organic growth might vary from user to user because those variable elements it appeared, could skew tremendously with steep trajectories of uncertainty and seemed to be able to generate an infinite number of totally random outcomes.

"Perhaps when we give life to something that we invent Bearciple, it can grow and travel far beyond our original creation." Leah concluded as she smiled.

"Yes, I totally agree Leah." Bearciple replied as he nodded. "When I initially started to work on my hovercart, I never planned that it would be expandable and then my creation just grew and grew, quite literally."

Leah giggled. "Do you plan to expand it even more Bearciple?" She teased. "I mean one day you could have a sudden rush and fifty visitors could come to visit the Caves of Reflection."

"Yes, that is true but I doubt it." Bearciple reassured her as he began to thoughtfully inspect the interior of his hovercart. "I never usually have more than twenty visitors on any particular day which is probably just due to the nature of the location because wrath isn't really a popular destination for most." He acknowledged. "It's usually a location that no one wants to see much, visit often or experience regularly."

"But I guess that's a good thing really or we'd probably have been eaten alive by now." Leah joked. "Because some creatures can be very angry, even when they're not in the Bay of Wrath."

"Another thing, most visitors that do come here never ever return." Bearciple admitted solemnly. "So I rarely have a rush on my hand paws, or a full hovercart."

"Really?" Leah asked. "You never have any repeat visitors?"

"No, the pirates and power seekers are usually too scared to return once the Bay of Wrath has dealt with them which usually comes in the form of stormy waves of anger that crash all over them until they flee." Bearciple replied as he shook his head. "That is unless they get crushed against the rocks then they usually sink straight away, so if that happens, they can't return at all because they are either lifeless or shipless. Other visitors, well they usually seem to be either brought here or come here for a specific reason and so once they fulfill that purpose, they leave and never come back."

"So the Bay of Wrath isn't a popular tourist spot." Leah teased.

"Definitely not." Bearciple remarked as he grinned. "In fact, from what I've heard, some visitors do say afterwards that they wish they'd never ever come here because the seas can be very unpredictable at times, especially towards troublemakers."

"Yes, I can imagine." Leah said as she glanced at his face and then shook her head. "But Bearciple, do you mind that everything around you is so unpredictable all the time, shouldn't most things in life be explainable and certain?" She asked. "Wouldn't that make you feel much safer and more secure?"

"Well Leah, I think that if everything was totally predictable, absolutely certain and fully explainable, life might lack variety." Bearciple concluded.

"True I guess." Leah agreed. "Oh well, we'd better hope that humanity and science never find a way to actually explain everything then or else human life, the human world and everything in it will become totally predictable and any evolutionary changes will be completely foreseeable which would probably be quite dull because then there would be no more evolutionary surprises at all."

"Yes because sometimes a surprise can be rather nice, especially if it's pleasant one." Bearciple admitted. "Like for instance, if someone offers you a chunk of humabear grand cake and some ginger earth tea." He smacked his lips together then grinned.

"Is that the cake made from the raw intestines of slimebattymice?" Leah asked.

"It is indeed Leah." Bearciple confirmed as he smiled. "Have you eaten a chunk of humabear grand cake before?"

"I can't say I have Bearciple." Leah replied as she giggled. "Well, I almost did once but I have to say, it was a rather lucky miss."

"According to humabear traditions we usually consume those two special treats on very special occasions like when we have important guests." Bearciple explained. "Sometimes I do try to make those delicious treats for myself but to be perfectly honest Leah, I rarely enjoy them that much because there's never anyone here to eat them with so that solitude seems to detract from the celebratory experience somehow and quite strangely, makes it feel slightly less enjoyable."

"Yes, I guess being alone can make life's experiences slightly less delicious although grand cake isn't exactly my cup of deliciousness and so it would never ever really be a delicious experience for me." Leah teased as she smiled. "Humbear ginger earth tea though, on the other hand, is actually quite pleasant because I did taste some the other day and I really quite liked it." She admitted as she glanced thoughtfully at the tunnel ahead and watched the hovercart glide along it for a few seconds. Leah grinned as she turned back to face the humabear. "Let's just agree to disagree on the issue of grand cake Bearciple because to the human palate, it does sit rather far away from an enjoyable edible destination or a culinary delight. When it comes to the issue of evolutionary surprises though, I do absolutely and wholeheartedly agree with you, I think some surprises are totally necessary to give human life and the human world some mysterious intrigue. I guess it just feels a bit strange to see some evolutionary surprises occur so rapidly."

"Don't worry Leah I understand, not everyone appreciates humabear grand cake." Bearciple teased. "Well evolutionary changes do happen every day everywhere, albeit rather gradually." He pointed out.

"Yes but usually, evolutionary processes take centuries or decades to manifest in the real human world and so, we human beings tend to look back at them through history because they are usually so slight that we can rarely even notice them in our lifetime or see them occur anywhere around us." Leah concluded. "I guess that's one of the drawbacks of a mortal human existence, whereas here those evolutionary changes seem to happen much more quickly."

The notion that Spectrum could evolve independently had caught Leah totally by surprise and as the hovercart glided down a deep slope she fell silent as she considered the implications of that notion further because it was not something that she had ever considered in any way during Spectrum's creation or even after the prototype's completion. However, since some of the manifestations of those changes had been really quite pleasant and had resulted in some delightfully unusual scenarios, those changes had not only fascinated Leah but had also thrilled her as each one had taken her on a simulated recreational flight of enjoyment beyond the limits of her own expectations. Although there were still no comprehensive answers in Leah's mind yet when it came to the actual mystery of how those evolutionary changes had actually happened, she somehow managed to push any curious thoughts firmly from her mind as the hovercart suddenly arrived at the bottom of the long downward slope and then came to a total standstill at the entrance to a huge open air expanse.

From what Leah could see at first glance as she began to visually scan the large open space, some crystal mountains appeared to be situated inside the expanse and it almost looked as if each one had been formed, sculpted and carved by hand because they had such precisely chiseled lines, edges and ledges. The crystal mountains, Leah observed, seemed to be scattered around the expanse at quite sporadic intervals but it was easy enough for her to see through each one of the crystal formations because the crystal mountainous structures were transparent enough to allow a great deal of visibility. Every single crystal mountain was a different color and Leah noticed that each one glistened and shone but before she could leave the hovercart and attempt to inspect the crystal mountains slightly more closely, the hovercart suddenly began to move off again but at a quite slow pace as Bearciple resumed his hovercart tour.

"What are these mountains made off Bearciple?" Leah asked as the hovercart started to gently glide around a crystal mountain base which she noticed was a beautiful pale aquamarine color that reminded her off a tranquil ocean. She turned to face the humabear as she admired the beauty that now surrounded her in total awe. "Are these mountains natural or were they made by someone or something?" Leah leant towards the nearest side wall of the hovercart as she continued. "I've never seen such beautiful crystals before and certainly not in such large formations or in such a vast range of colors and shades."

Due to Leah's curiosity which bubbled silently away just below her simulated pores, before Bearciple had managed to offer her a response she actually leant over the side of the hovercart and then tried to touch the nearby aquamarine crystal mountain face with one of her hands. For a moment, Leah noticed that Bearciple seemed to hesitate as he just stared at her and watched her movements before he started to respond which clearly indicated to Leah that something about those crystal mountain formations was perhaps slightly more complex than just an act nature or even the possibility of a carefully carved, meticulously sculpted, intricately calculated creation.

Bearciple released a sad sigh as he began to shake his head. "Quite sadly Leah, I'm afraid the Crystal Mountains of Lost Souls are natural but not in the way that you might expect because each mountain is actually formed from crystals that merge with the lost souls that the Bay of Wrath consumes." He explained. "So, I guess in some ways, the mountains are a unique blend of nature, evil and wrath. Unfortunately, although the mountains do look beautiful, inside each one they carry the stamp of wrath, the ores of wickedness and the remnants of death which means that the beauty you can see, is not virtuous in any capacity at all and nor does it represent anything pleasant."

"How awful." Leah replied as she quickly retracted her hand. "Why does the Bay of Wrath consume evil souls Bearciple?" She asked nervously as her initial admiration of the crystal mountains swiftly fled from her mind and totally abandoned her thoughts.

"Well, the Bay of Wrath only consumes the souls of those with a very impure mind or an evil heart from the lives that are lost here which are the lives that the seas claim for whatever reason because every death that occurs in the Bay of Wrath is actually intentional." Bearciple mentioned as he glanced at a shiny crystal surface nearby and shook his head again. "Once the Bay of Wrath captures and consumes a wicked soul, that soul then becomes an energy source that the bay utilizes to maintain and sustain its own lifeforce which is very much alive because at times, the bay needs to re-energize itself and who better to feed off than the wicked, evil, cruel and heartless? So essentially, the evil souls that are lost here become part of the source of power that some of them sought out and they then feed the Bay of Wrath's lifeforce with their own lives and souls, so what some initially sought after, they then become a slave to." He admitted. "It isn't pretty but then nothing about wrath is particularly attractive."

"Now that sounds really awful." Leah concluded as she winced with disgust and shivered with fear. "Have you ever seen it happen Bearciple?" She asked.

"Yes, a few times." Bearciple confirmed as he glanced at a crystal mountain on the other side of the expanse and then released a humabear grunt.

"What exactly happened?" Leah enquired.

"Well I've seen several and every situation was different, so different things happened to the individuals involved which I guess really depended upon how evil, wicked or cruel that entity had been during their lifetime." Bearciple replied as he glanced at a reddish gold crystal mountain and then pointed towards it. "But from what I can remember that reddish gold crystal mountain over there was probably one of the most scary, even for me and I don't scare easily, being that I'm a humabear." He continued as he proudly puffed up his chest.

"What happened Bearciple?" Leah asked.

"A hybrid pirate ship captain went on a spree, the main purpose of which was to loot any ship that sailed across his ship's path but his predominantly hybrid crew not only stole everything on board those ships but then also killed every person or creature that they came across along the way. At least one hundred and fifty crew members and passengers died on the seas in the space of just two days at the paws, claws and hands of his crew and nothing and nobody could stop him."

"What happened to him afterwards?" Leah asked. "What stopped him in the end?"

"The seas finally rose against him and the angry waves carried his ship straight into the path of the rocks of destruction where he met a watery grave, in that instance, extremely quickly." Bearciple explained. "Once the seas had risen against him, he was almost dead in a matter of minutes but just before he died, his wicked heart and evil soul were burnt in red golden flames of fire and that crystal mountain over there grew from his death as the Bay of Wrath took and claimed his soul for eternity."

"How horrible." Leah replied as she shivered with fear. "What a horrible way to die and what a horrible way to live."

"Don't worry though Leah, you should be okay. You haven't angered the seas or you wouldn't have even reached the Caves of Reflection if you had, so you can't be that impure or evil." Bearciple teased.

"I try not to be Bearciple." Leah joked as she grinned. "Do artificial actions count as impure, or just real actions, or is judgement based solely upon intentions?"

"It's hard to say really." Bearciple said as he shrugged. "Even I don't know the answer to that question. The Bay of Wrath doesn't usually provide any explanations, any instructions, a map or a user manual to any entities, man or hybrid, so some of its secrets, remain secrets forever." He paused for a moment and then touched the small remote as the hovercart suddenly arrived at a large fork that sat at the rear of two crystal mountains. "Now hold on tight Leah because we are just about to speed up a bit. We're quite close to the next location on my tour now, the Crystal Mirror of Trials, so we should be there in just a couple of minutes."

Leah nodded and immediately held onto the side of the hovercart. "Sure Bearciple." She said as she glanced thoughtfully at the beautiful crystal mountains and then shook her head.

Sadly and tragically, Leah concluded, the beautiful Crystal Mountains of Lost Souls were tainted because every single one had been created from a source of death and from the evil, wicked and cruel souls that had been taken to form each one's very existence and that simulated reality had no beautiful artificial edges to it. Although each crystal mountain surface shimmered and shone with splendor, glory and innocence as Leah now knew, their formation had originated from a truly ugly source but it still seemed slightly strange to her that such an ugly source had resulted in such beauty and such immaculate perfection because that beauty, despite its evil origins, was definitely, completely and utterly undeniable. However, the Crystal Mountains of Lost Souls did make Leah wonder for a moment, how such evil formations could embody so much wickedness and yet still look so splendidly magnificent with such total ease.

"Right, this is our exit Leah." Bearciple suddenly mentioned as the hovercart neared a tunnel entrance that sat at the rear of a crystal mountain as he touched the remote once again to steer it into the tunnel and away from the crystal formations.

In just a matter of seconds, the beautiful, tainted crystal mountains had almost vanished from sight completely as the hovercart entered into the tunnel and then speedily started to glide along it but as Leah glanced back and watched the crystal mountains disappear, she released a sad sigh as she shook her head. For the next few seconds Leah remained completely silent as she turned back to face the direction that the hovercart was headed in and waited for the Crystal Mirror of Trials that Bearciple had mentioned to appear but as Leah did so, she began to hope that the Crystal Mirror of Trials had not been sourced from an evil soul too because the death that the Mountains of Lost Souls had contained had already filled her with enough doom and gloom.

"Bearciple is the Crystal Mirror of Trials made from an evil lost soul too?" Leah suddenly asked.

"No Leah, the Crystal Mirror of Trials doesn't need any evil lost souls to exist or to sustain itself because it energizes itself from the reflective energy that comes from those who visit. it." Bearciple explained. "And since the Crystal Mountains of Lost Souls can be very hard to climb up, due to the evil souls and cruel nature that lurk and reside in the heart of each mountain, I decided that the Mirror of Trials will be the best place for our first stop off on our tour today."

"Okay, so are we actually going to stop off at the Crystal Mirror of Trials?" Leah enquired.

"Yes." Bearciple swiftly clarified. "And then after that I thought we could visit the Mountain of Perseverance and stop off at the Fountain of Sincere Wishes because these three areas are always very popular sights on my tours." He admitted. "The Crystal Mountains of Lost Souls is usually just a visit to view sight for most visitors really because very few want to try and climb up any of the mountains, especially after they find out what each one is made from. If you actually try to climb the mountains, it can be a treacherous climb at times and very slippery because some of the crystal mountains have hidden ravines that not only open up but that also expand as you try to move across those slippery crystal surfaces."

"Okay Bearciple." Leah replied as she nodded. "But will we stop off at the Mountain of Perseverance?" She asked thoughtfully. "Because if we do, I might not even get to see the Fountain of Sincere Wishes. I might run out of time."

"Probably not then, we can just hover around it." Bearciple replied. "The Fountain of Sincere Wishes Leah is definitely one of the most important stop off points on my entire tour because it's very beautiful and most visitors do say that if they ever came back to the Bay of Wrath, it's the one place that they'd want to visit." He continued. "Plus, you can't possibly miss out on having the opportunity to make a sincere wish."

"Yes, I can certainly understand why visitors would want to visit that fountain because wishes do come in handy at times." Leah agreed. "Especially if they come true."

"Well usually, after anger subsides there are things that people wish they hadn't said or done in some of their angrier moments and so, the Fountain of Sincere Wishes allows wish makers to correct and repair some of those angry mistakes." Bearciple mentioned. "It's actually one of the highlights of my tour and some people even visit the Bay of Wrath just to see it, especially if they've done something hugely regretful to someone else and that's usually where they make a repair wish to try to put things right."

"Now that sounds really nice Bearciple." Leah concluded. "Yes, I think we'd definitely better visit the fountain today because I actually have a sincere wish of my own that I really need to make."

"Don't worry Leah, you'll get a chance to make a sincere wish, once you've visited and faced the Crystal Mirror of Trials which will happen quite soon because we're almost there now." Bearciple swiftly reassured her as he guided the hovercart around a bend in the tunnel. "How have you found my hovercart ride so far, has it been smooth enough or a bit too rough and bumpy?"

"I think you've done an excellent job Bearciple, it's such a handy creation and from one technological scientist to another, I'd say it's pretty immaculate." Leah replied as she smiled. "Also it is a very unique form of transportation, so sturdy, so durable but very nimble in a metallic kind of way."

"Thank you Leah. I really appreciate all your kind words and the remote makes it very easy to maneuver the hovercart around the tunnels, so it can handle sharp corners, steep dips, sudden bends, high slopes and even complex twists and turns, so I did think about the location when I created it." Bearciple mentioned triumphantly as he touched the remote and the hovercart come to a sudden gentle stop close to the entrance to a cave. "I'm actually quite proud of myself really because it was my first big humabear invention." He paused for a moment as he touched the remote again and as he did so, the hovercart walls rapidly shrunk back into the metal base. "Right, we've finally arrived at our first stop off point." Bearciple mentioned as he pointed towards the entrance of the nearby cave. "So inside that cave over there, you'll find the Crystal Mirror of Trials." He politely clarified.

"Okay." Leah replied as she enthusiastically stood up.

For the next few seconds Leah just stood and stared at Bearciple as she remained in the same spot as she waited for him to join her but much to her total confusion, he didn't make any attempts to leave the hovercart at all as he simply continued to fiddle around with the remote control. Quite strangely it appeared as Leah continued to watch him in silence, Bearciple seemed to have absolutely no desire or any intentions to step off the hovercart's metal base, even though it was now in a stationary position and a motionless state. However, just a few seconds later Bearciple finally glanced up at Leah's face and she noticed that he instantly seemed to notice the expression of confusion that was now plastered across it and that he politely began to offer a response as he started to answer the silent unspoken question that sat behind Leah's lips.

"Oh, you have to go into the cave alone Leah." Bearciple clarified as he interpreted her confusion, translated her silence and processed her stillness. "The Crystal Mirror of Trials is a very personal challenge that you'll have to face without me."

"Okay, okay, of course." Leah replied as she nodded her head. "How silly of me, I should have realized." She glanced nervously at the cave's entrance which looked eerie, still and dark and as she prepared to leave the hovercart, nervous tension seemed to leap and bounce around inside her simulated frame.

Since Leah could progress no further it appeared on her emotional journey that day or on Bearciple's tour of the Caves of Reflection until she had faced the Crystal Mirror of Trials, she quickly stepped of the hovercart as she began to participate with Bearciple's instructions and then started to make her way towards the entrance of the dark, eerie cave in total silence. However, as Leah walked, she was well aware that her silence in this instance wasn't a comfortable or pleasant one and that it was one that seemed to lurk around and hang over the edge of a deep, bottomless, internal ravine of fear and so as she neared the cave's entrance, she paused for a moment then glanced back at the hovercart as she sought out some kind of final reassurances from Bearciple that her fears would not hold true or tip her straight into that dark, fearful, bottomless ravine.

Just a few seconds later a few nods of encouragement were politely and kindly offered to Leah from Bearciple which seemed enthusiastic enough to convince her that despite his reluctance to accompany her and the potential solitude that awaited her that everything would be fine. Since as Leah already knew, she could proceed no further until she had visited the cave she began to accept his silent reassurances as she turned to face the cave once again and then stepped into its dark confines. A deep breath was taken as Leah entered into the cave as she nervously prepared to face the Crystal Mirror of Trials alone because although Bearciple had mentioned the crystal mirror to her several times now, she still had absolutely no idea as yet what would happen inside the actual cave when she faced the Crystal Mirror of Trials because he had remained quite silent on the finer details of what that would actually entail.

Some jagged, spiky rocks were situated near the entrance to the rocky cave which Leah noticed seemed to obstruct her passage and so she quickly side stepped the rocky obstructions as she made her way towards a large cave wall at the other end of the cave that glistened and shone which she immediately assumed was the Crystal Mirror of Trials. Fortunately for Leah, the ground en route to the shiny cave wall seemed to be solid enough to walk upon but as she neared the mirrored wall, she couldn't help but stare at it because it fully reflected the entire interior of the cave across its shiny surface with total precision inclusive of Leah herself which fascinated her.

From what Leah could see at first glance, the mirror felt really quite usual in the sense that as she drew closer to it, she could see her reflection mimic her movements on its shiny surface but she still felt mesmerized by it, purely due to the sheer magnificence of the reflective inbuilt structure as it towered way above her head. A few curious seconds went by as Leah paused just a few steps away from the shiny reflective surface and then put her hands on her hips, just so she could observe her reflection's reaction and she instantly felt relieved to see that her reflection immediately mimicked everything that she did with absolute precision which not only comforted her mind to some extent but also encouraged her to draw even closer to the mirrored cave wall.

Not more than a few seconds later however, as Leah came to a standstill just an inch or so away from the mirrored wall, she noticed that it suddenly started to change and that a stormy sea scene began to form not just in directly front of her but also all around her as she was swiftly drawn into and somehow rapidly immersed in the mirror's imagery. Somehow it seemed, Leah's mind and viewpoint had been totally transported without any warning at all and it was almost as if her reflection had been combined with her actual simulated presence which was now positioned at the helm of an actual ship.

The mirrored wall, Leah noticed as she began to sway from side to side due to the stormy waters that surrounded the ship, had now totally disappeared and so too had the rest of the cave's interior and so, she started to visually scan the seas all around her as she began to prepare herself to face an actual storm. Around the ship there appeared to be not only some very stormy waves but also a scattered collection of jagged, hazardous rocks that appeared to litter the choppy waters that surrounded the ship and so in that respect, Leah felt that there was not just one dangerous hazard present but two and quite disturbingly, both felt equally dangerous.

Several crew members suddenly appeared and then began to rush towards Leah but as they crossed the top deck of the ship, she noticed that they too swayed from side to side in a slightly staggered progression as they headed towards her position. Due to the crew members slurred strides across the top deck however, their instability was far more noticeable unlike Leah's own but quite strangely, as she attempted to stabilize herself, she swiftly realized that her own movements were now not actually as straightforward as they usually were as it suddenly struck her that each one appeared to be a mirrored replication of her intended actions.

In fact, every time Leah tried to move one of her simulated limbs, she noticed that it now appeared to result in the opposite movement from her simulated form and her mind's intentions which actually felt extremely strange and even slightly uncomfortable. When it came to the actual issue of Leah's body movements, her neurological processes, her body's reactions and the coordination of both had never really been an issue that she had ever had to give much thought or any deeper consideration to up until that point in time because her coordination had always been very straight forward and had never been an issue before. Suddenly however, the interpretation of those internal messages from Leah's own mind and her external responses were totally out of sync which made any kind of coordinated movements feel almost absolutely impossible.

For the next few seconds Leah almost froze as total frustration gripped her interior because this new environment that she had rather suddenly been thrown into felt very strange and very out of sync. Unfortunately however, Leah didn't have very long to consider that strangeness much further or even any time to adapt to those huge differences because several crew members had already arrived beside her. The presence of the crew members and the alarmed expressions upon each of their faces implied a sense of urgency which meant that Leah had to act and as several more crew members drew closer to her and then also came to a standstill beside her, Leah tried desperately to get a silent grip on what adjustments she would have to make in order to coordinate her thoughts and movements effectively. Since the results of Leah's attempts to maneuver herself would definitely be mirrored that rather large adjustment which would have an impact upon every movement that she made, felt far less predictable and far more uncertain because from what Leah had already discovered, it would definitely result in far less accuracy, much more cumbersome reactions and a definite diminished precision on her part.

Some flickers of panic ran silently across the crew members' faces from what Leah could sense and see as she prepared to communicate with them and although some of crew tried their best to disguise those emotional flickers which could perhaps be perceived as a fearful weakness, fear flooded through their eyes which silently betrayed their external impressions of bravery. Due to the stormy situation and the ship's current position, Leah could totally relate to the crew's emotional state and the fear that flooded through their simulated forms as their eyes revealed their true internal state without the utterance of a single word which was clearly full of alarm, overrun with anguish and rampant with worry.

Unfortunately for Leah however, since she actually appeared to be situated directly behind the captain's wheel of the ship, her current position only added further to her worries because it implied that she was now in charge of the huge vessel. Since Leah had not once in her entire life up until that point in time so much as even sailed a yacht or a boat never mind a huge ship of that size, her current situation was almost like a nightmare for her because she now appeared to be the captain of an entire ship and the alarm and panic of the crew was not something that she could easily dismiss or hope to alleviate with any kind of confidence due to her own lack of nautical experience.

The dangerous predicament that not only Leah but also the entire ship's crew faced, deeply alarmed her as she just stood rooted to the spot, nodded her head and listened to three of the crew members speak as they imparted bits of information to her about the ship's current position, its operational status and what in their opinion had to be done next. Some of the words spoken by the crew members speedily confirmed and firmly reinforced the notion that Leah was indeed expected to act as the ship's captain because a couple of the crew members had even addressed her as such and from what Leah could glean and ascertain, after a few more minutes of attentive, thoughtful consideration, she had to direct and sail the ship through the stormy waters as the ship's captain. However, not only did Leah have to sail the ship through the choppy waves but she also somehow had to avoid the treacherous rocks that surrounded the vessel which were sporadically and haphazardously strewn across its watery path and so, the danger that lurked inside those dark, greyish blue waves filled Leah with absolute fear.

"Captain, you'll have to guide us through these jagged rocks and these choppy, stormy waters." One of the crewmen explained. "So, if you can take control of the captain's wheel and steer the ship as you do that we'll continue to row the ship down below, so that we clear the storm and the rocks more quickly."

Every part of Leah's simulated form inclusive of her nerves felt taut with tension and she noticed that her body suddenly began to tremble as she continued to listen to the crew members speak for a minute or so longer after which point, she stretched her arm out towards the captain's wheel and then rapidly clung onto it very tightly. Unfortunately for Leah, the vessel was absolutely huge and the waters that surrounded the ship appeared to be very angry and volatile and unlike Bearciple's hovercart which had seemed easy for the humabear to maneuver or Leah's own car back inside the real human world, this vessel was going to be far trickier to steer and much harder to control and so as she prepared to take command of the ship, every inch of her skin seemed to crawl with nervous fear.

Fortunately for Leah however, as she leant into the captain's wheel and made some attempts to try and coordinate her movements, her efforts to control and direct the ship seemed to be rewarded quite well as she leant from side to side in order to avoid some of the jagged rocks which jutted and poked out of the choppy waves in a hazardous fashion. However, as Leah guided the ship through some of the waves that crashed against the side of the vessel as it moved, the ship she noticed required a far more laborious effort on her part to steer than her car did which essentially meant that a huge amount of concentration and a consistent supply of simulated physical exertion was required from Leah herself and due to the dangers present that flow of energy could not possibly cease, not even for a split second.

Suddenly, some very spiky, large rocks that were in quite close proximity to not only the ship but also to each other appeared in stony comradery and friendly clusters and as each stony defiant obstruction loomed directly in front of Leah and the vessel's path, she began to struggle with her task. In a matter of just seconds, Leah had been presented with a huge challenge that she had not spotted and as she already knew, the rocks around the ship would not be friendly to anyone on board the vessel if she could not steer the ship around their edges, inclusive of herself.

Due to the rocky, treacherous dangers that lurked in the stormy, choppy waters around the ship, Leah's struggle continued for another few minutes and as her throat became dry and parched, it almost felt as if the fear of failure had robbed her airways of any lubrication as she leant in and continued to try and steer the ship. However, danger lurked in every breathe that Leah took and so she could taste the fear that clung on to the roof of her mouth and that lined her tongue because as she already knew, if she made one wrong miscalculation or failed to coordinate her mirrored movements correctly, everyone on board the vessel would perish. Just for a moment Leah's mind delved into the possibility that if she did make a mistake that the vessel under her command would then end up just like the shipwreck that she had explored earlier that afternoon and that perhaps she too would then become a skeleton captain who sat beside a rotten wooden table that would perhaps have to wait decades for chance and fate to rescue her from a perpetually rotten eternity.

A few minutes later and after a far more laborious effort on Leah's part which only delivered a very close shave of safety, the ship passed through a narrow gap between the groups of rocks that were closely bunched together, much to Leah's sheer relief. Quite strangely however, at that point, both the rocks and the ship suddenly vanished from sight but the interior of the cave did not reappear which confused Leah slightly as instead, she found that she suddenly dropped down into the actual water itself. In terms of the stormy waves, Leah noticed that the waters around her now seemed a little less stormy but still quite choppy and that there appeared to be several other people and some bits of wood around her, the latter of which floated upon the waves in a very inconsistent manner. From what Leah could see, unlike the people that seemed to far less enthusiastic about the waters that surrounded them, the pieces of wood bobbed merrily up and down rather indecisively but quite amicably as each one either drifted further away from her position or closer to it in accordance to the wishes of the choppy waves.

Rather curiously, it almost seemed to Leah as if the ship had not actually survived the stormy waves and jagged, treacherous rocks at all and as if somehow, she had missed the actual collision with the rocks and had started to sink along with the ship. Fortunately, unlike the ship, Leah's simulated form appeared to have survived and had somehow, managed to remain intact but from what she could see from the faces and actions of the survivors around her, survival was not guaranteed nor did it seem to possess even a shred of permanency as a few of them vanished below the surface and others thrashed around frantically, just to keep afloat.

Not more than a couple of minutes later, Leah's situation suddenly seemed to drastically worsen and deteriorate as her simulated form began to sink below the choppy waves which felt icy cold and as Leah felt herself slip deeper down into the watery depths, she started to splutter as her simulated airwaves rapidly filled up with watery liquid. Despite Leah's predicament however, she desperately and instantly sprang into action as she attempted to try and claw her way back up towards the surface where she noticed that a piece of wood floated just above her head which she quickly reached out to and then grabbed onto in an attempt to stabilize herself.

Once Leah had resurfaced, just a few seconds later, she then started to visually inspect the position of some of the people in the water around her, many of whom like herself clung onto chunks of wood just to keep themselves afloat. Not too far away from Leah's current position, she suddenly noticed a man that appeared to be in a similar predicament to her own just moments ago who sank below the waves as he battled the choppy, watery substance that surrounded him. Since Leah had now managed to resurface and she had also found a decent sized chunk of wood to hold onto, she felt slightly more stable but because the man's struggle was so near and so desperate, she felt compelled to assist him. Although the notion of a potential rescue attempt made Leah tremble with fear as she watched him fight to keep his head above the water that surrounded him, she felt urged to participate because she could not just float around and watch him perish.

Somehow, the man managed to resurface a few seconds later and as Leah watched him battle the waves, she noticed that he tried to grab onto a nearby piece of wood but the piece of wood it appeared, didn't seem to want to cooperate nor did it remain within his reach for very long as it quickly slipped back out of his hands and then floated away. Another few awful seconds slipped by as the man sank once again and as his head disappeared below the waves once more as Leah watched his situation deteriorate, she was suddenly spurred into action as she began to swim decisively towards his position and grabbed another quite large piece of wood en route which she then used to paddle her way more quickly through the waves towards him.

When Leah reached the man's position, she quickly dived below the waves in a heroic attempt to try and retrieve him and luckily, she managed to grab onto his dark, black, soggy jacket which she then utilized to pull him rapidly back up towards the surface once more. The spare piece of wood that Leah had brought along with her then came in very handy because it was quite large and so, she quickly pulled the man's body partially onto it and then utilized it almost as if it was some kind of small raft as efficiently as she could. Back inside the real world, Leah had never, ever rescued another human being before her first heroic moment that day and even though it was an artificial environment and a simulated response, it felt really quite special to her because it was still a heroic act on her part and so although she was deeply immersed in foreign waters and foreign deeds, a warm wave of satisfaction seemed to wash over her simulated form as she began to rejoice in her heroic achievement.

Much to Leah's relief the benefactor of her kind acts, a male that appeared to be in his late forties, seemed to cooperate with her objectives as he eagerly clung onto the piece of wood gratefully and then nodded his head thankfully at her in weak but thankful appreciation. Unlike the man that Leah had just rescued however, as she began to visually scan the waters nearby, it appeared that several other people were now also in a similar state, albeit slightly variable predicaments and that unfortunately, they had not been rescued yet by anyone. Some choppy waves seemed to grab some of the survivors and then toss them mercilessly around as the sea attempted to drag them below the surface and claim them as its own and as Leah turned her attention more fully towards their struggles, she was swiftly compelled to swim towards a second person nearby who appeared to be in distress as quickly as she could.

On Leah's way towards the woman she managed to grab two additional pieces of wood, one of which she utilized as a makeshift raft for her own body to keep herself afloat during her rescue attempt and the other two she used as paddles, so that she could paddle her way through the water more quickly. The water that surrounded Leah now felt icy cold again because the heroic warm feeling that had been present for just a few seconds, she noticed had rapidly deserted her as soon as the cold waves had started to more aggressively chop against her form, surge in and out of her pores and lash into her simulated skin all of which made her tremble and shiver. In fact, the harsh combination of coldness that Leah now felt, seemed to swim deeper and deeper into her simulated form with each paddley stroke as she swam and as it fully penetrated every part of her core from every direction and every possible angle, she longed to see the interior of the cave again, if only to experience the small glimmers and tiny flickers of warmth that it had contained just for another moment in time.

For approximately the next thirty minutes Leah diligently clasped onto the hope that she would be spared from the cold, watery depths quite soon as she focused more fully on her rescue attempts and attempted to push the harsh, watery, cold sensations from her mind. Throughout that thirty minutes and before a chilly numbness could set in which Leah definitely felt would happen if she remained in one spot, she managed to successfully rescue four more people which brought the total up to five inclusive of the first man that she had helped.

Whether Leah would be so brave in real life however, was an entirely different matter and as she completed her fifth rescue, she wrestled with the internal notion that quite possibly she wouldn't. Inside Leah's mind and heart as she already knew, there were definitely some cowardly instincts and so she felt that perhaps those cowardly instincts would conquer her brave, courageous aspirations which she had only really just discovered that day which definitely seemed to exist and hid somewhere deep inside her interior. Since the five rescue attempts had required so much discipline, bravery and determination, Leah swiftly concluded as she began to seek out a sixth person to assist that those watery, chilly rescues, no matter how chilly and unpleasant had definitely been the highlight of her emotional journey that day so far because each one had challenged her to step well outside her usual comfort zone in life.

Rather intriguingly for Leah however, just as she started to seek out a sixth person in need the water that surrounded her suddenly began to fade from sight and as the choppy waves started to vanish, she wondered for a moment if quite possibly the angry waves had simply tired of her presence. From what Leah had seen that day, anger could cause not only a tremendous amount of damage but could also take many hostages who then became potential victims that often had to powerlessly wait for whatever wrath had been unleashed to fully manifest itself in various forms of rage before they could even hope to escape anger's angry clutches. In this instance it appeared, the wrath of the seas had been provoked and disturbed and not even one person that had been present, Leah thoughtfully concluded, had been given any kind of exemptions as they had been equally and angrily tossed around by the watery, choppy, angry waves and had waited to be rescued from the anger of the seas.

Once again however, as Leah watched the external environment around her change, she noticed that she did not actually return to the interior of the cave and that instead of the rocky cave, she suddenly found herself surrounded by an actual graveyard. In some ways, the sight of the graveyard actually relieved Leah to some extent because the watery, choppy waves which had been extremely cold and very dangerous had at least now, totally evaporated from sight and hence no longer posed a dangerous threat to her simulated form.

Some cement grave stones were scattered around the graveyard, Leah noticed, at quite regular intervals in rough lines and rows that seemed to have some kind of order but from what she could see at first glance, overall the stony cemeterial symbols appeared to lack any real symmetry or full alignment. The lack of uniformity when it came to the actual gravestones appeared to be matched by the presence of some randomly dispersed simulated human entities who also seemed to be scattered across the graveyard as they stood by some of the gravestones either in small clusters or alone. Irrespective of what or who was or wasn't there however, Leah could see no obvious clues as to why she was there herself but the location intrigued her as she began to thoughtfully consider why she may have been transported to that particular location.

A few silent seconds slipped by as Leah stood rooted to the spot as she continued to visually scan the interior of the graveyard and as she flicked her eyes across each stony memorial, one grave stone in particular attracted her attention slightly more than others due to the large group of mourners that surrounded it. Most of the mourners present wore black garments that Leah noticed seemed to drip with grief along with the expressions that they wore upon each of their faces as they mourned the loss of their loved one but it still wasn't clear yet why Leah was there or what she was supposed to do next and so, she remained still and silent as she visually inspected the group of mourners slightly more thoroughly and searched for some kind of visual clues.

From what Leah could see a burial service appeared to be underway as she surveyed the scene from a distance because she noticed that a reverend stood next to the actual grave stone at the head of an open grave and that he read out some words from a book inside one of his hands as he spoke to the group of mourners. Due to Leah's curiosity, she began to saunter towards the group as she prepared to listen to the reverend speak, if only for a simulated moment in time or least until she could actually establish the reason behind her graveyard visit.

When Leah arrived on the outskirts of the group of human mourners who were quite closely bunched together but that also simultaneously stood in smaller clusters, she came to a total standstill and then just stood and listened to the reverend speak for a few minutes. Some tearful sobs, hearty nods and painful tears emanated from those nearby and around Leah's simulated form which immediately saddened her heart as she listened to the burial service in total silence and almost froze as she started to question her mind as to what exactly she should do next.

Due to the grief that trickled into Leah's senses from every direction, she suddenly began to feel like an intruder that had broken into other people's sadness which in this instance she felt, probably related to one of the people that had been inside the watery waves that quite possibly, she had not been able to rescue or reach on time. A sense of discomfort suddenly seemed to gather inside Leah's simulated form because her guilty discomfort was an extremely uncomfortable position to not only stand in but also be in and so, she swiftly began to survey the rest of the graveyard as she prepared to move off again as she attempted to interrupt and avoid her own feelings of guilty failure. Essentially that day, Leah had not only discovered her own potential heroic capacity but she had also uncovered and now had to fully accept her really quite dismal human limitations which had only lived up to quite limited heroic ambitions and results.

Suddenly, Leah noticed that at one end of the graveyard, there was a rectangular cement structure that looked a bit like a walk-in tomb which had probably always been there but that quite possibly, due to her need to find a meaningful distraction, now seemed to hold far more appeal, looked more mysterious and was much more noticeable. The stone structure was surrounded by a waist high metallic fence and since it held the promise of slightly more comfort for Leah than her present location because it was not surrounded by mourners and especially not mourners for a funeral service that had arisen due to her own lack of heroic delivery, she began to walk slowly but enthusiastically towards it as she prepared to inspect the structure's interior as if she had an actual legitimate reason to do so.

Upon arrival, Leah noticed that the external metal gate of the walk-in tomb opened easily enough as she pushed it open and as she walked towards the cement structure which lay inside the fence and gate, she surprisingly found that the door opened up without even so much as a squeak as she gently pushed it open. Due to the grand nature of the walk-in tomb which was certainly a lavish step up from the stony gravestones that surrounded it, Leah definitely felt as if the tomb had been made for someone important but as her curiosity provoked her to step inside and then start to inspect the structure's stony interior, she couldn't actually see any signs that clearly indicated who it belonged to.

Inside the walk-in tomb which it rapidly transpired wasn't really a tomb at all but just a small concrete room, Leah found some steps that lead downwards and so she quickly made her way towards the small flight of stony steps but her trainer shoes scuffed against the cement floor as she walked which appeared to be quite dusty, gritty and grainy which seemed to generate some slightly eerie echoes in the concrete room. At the bottom of the stone flight of steps Leah found another slightly larger subterranean concrete room which had a row of candles in it that sat upon a concrete ledge that gave off weak rays of light which were certainly not bright enough to provide Leah with a large degree of visibility but that managed to offer just enough light to allow her to see the interior of the underground concrete room.

Most of the candles were lit and had quite strong flames but one which appeared to have an object beside it, quickly flickered and then fizzled out just a few seconds after Leah's arrival which instantly drew her attention towards it as her curiosity provoked her to approach it. No simulacrum entities appeared to be present inside the stony structure, human or otherwise and so as Leah began to make her way towards the now dim candle, she started to visually inspect the strange but unique object that sat beside it which seemed to give the impression that perhaps it might hold some kind of mystery which she felt could perhaps relate to why she was actually there.

Since the small object looked harmless enough and like a piece of culinary equipment that one might find in the kitchen of someone's home and a bit like a nutcracker as Leah neared the object, she prepared to pick it up but as she did so, she did worry for a moment that the floor might suddenly give way under her feet. Despite all Leah's reservations however, just a few seconds later she arrived beside the ledge and the object with no unexpected interruptions or mishaps whatsoever but as she came to a standstill and froze for a second or two in slightly fearful hesitation, she noticed that there appeared to be a small note tucked neatly underneath the object, the presence of which instantly intrigued her. Fortunately for Leah on this occasion, her curiosity managed to conquer her prior reservations quite quickly and so just a few seconds later, she enthusiastically picked up the actual object after which point, she also collected the note from the concrete ledge which she then opened up and started to read.

"This gift of remembrance bids a secret farewell from beyond the grave, from one heart to another." Leah said in a low tone as she read the note out.

At first Leah was slightly unsure as to why the note was there or even why she was there but as she cast her mind back to the shipwreck and the note that she'd found in the skeleton's bony hand, it became apparent that she was supposed to solve the riddle clue that the note contained. Due to the strangeness of the note which appeared to be a second riddle, Leah was quite baffled but as she mulled the riddle over again and again inside her thoughts and then began to speculate as to what it could mean, she knew that the riddle would definitely have to be solved before she could proceed any further.

Somewhere in the graveyard, Leah thoughtfully considered, there would be someone that might want that object which had perhaps belonged to their deceased loved one which meant, her task was to find the correct simulacrum from the simulated human forms present that would remember and recognize the object and then give it to them. However, since there had been quite a few simulacrums present when Leah had entered into the concrete structure, she felt that her search was not going to be straightforward which also implied that the riddle itself would not be easy to solve.

"A farewell but a farewell to who?" Leah asked herself. "How will I know who this belongs to?"

Although the object didn't look particularly high tech or even that useful as Leah began to inspect it, she noticed that it was beautifully hand crafted in a skilled manner that was extremely unusual and so it held a certain appeal to its existence, despite its rather odd shape and design. No further clues however, seemed to be present upon either the note or the object and so as Leah prepared to depart and to embark upon her search to find that mysterious someone, she gave the interior of the subterranean concrete room one final glance as she attempted to seek out anything else that might assist her before she departed.

When Leah felt satisfied that there was absolutely nothing else to do or to be found inside the subterranean concrete room, she began to wander back towards the steps with both the object and note in her hands as she quietly considered who she should try to give the object to and if the simulacrums that she'd initially seen inside the graveyard, would still be present. One final quick visual inspection was indulged in as Leah paused for a moment by the foot of the steps and then glanced around the concrete room once more as she prepared to leave the stony structure but there didn't appear to be anything further to be found. Once again Leah found herself surrounded by a wall of silence because the first riddle note had been found in the same kind of circumstances with absolutely no further clues as to what it meant which again reinforced and implied that the answers she sought, clearly lay somewhere back inside the graveyard that she had just left.

A definite lack of clarity was all that met Leah however, as she exited the concrete structure and then began to saunter around the graveyard in a quite aimless manner because from what she could see, the mourners in attendance all looked pretty similar in that they were all simulated human forms dressed in dark clothes. No obvious signs or clear indications appeared to be present that differentiated one mourner from the next which really frustrated Leah because from appearance alone and the lack of any further clues, she could not establish that the object and note related to any of them.

Unfortunately, the lack of silent clues implied that Leah would have go on an actual tour of perhaps the whole graveyard which would quite possibly involve a stop off beside every group of mourners and perhaps every person present which held very little appeal due to the nature of their attendance and their grief. Another discomfort for Leah was the fact that not only would she had to stop at each group of mourners but also that she would have to approach some of them to ask some really quite awkward questions, if she wished to proceed. Since such actions on Leah's part felt highly inappropriate because to approach those in grief in such a crass manner was almost unthinkable, especially when they were in attendance at a funeral service or at a graveside to mourn lost loved ones but she really couldn't see or think of any alternative options.

Another issue that concerned Leah as she continued to saunter slowly around the graveyard, was that since she had visited the interior of the stony structure, several other funeral services it appeared had begun in her absence and the first burial service she noticed had now, actually ended. The addition of three more groups of mourners and the subtraction of one still increased the mourners numbers to two more groups of simulated human forms which meant, Leah would perhaps have to visit all three of the open graves if she wished to solve the riddle. Due to the increase in mourners that were now gathered around the three gravestones for the burial services that were currently underway, those changes as Leah already knew, would make her task far less simple and those increases also added even more to the uncertainty that she now faced. However, since Leah had no actual alternative options, her potential visit to at least one gravesite if not all three which would definitely involve some awkward conversations, appeared to be totally unavoidable.

Suddenly however, as Leah arrived at the other end of the graveyard, she noticed that there appeared to be a small church situated not too far away at the end of a narrow, stony, cobbled path which led off from the graveyard itself. The narrow path appeared to twist around in various directions as it wound its way silently through some bushes and meandered towards the church but as Leah visually followed it and began to consider a journey along it, she hoped that it might shed some light upon the second riddle that she'd found.

An open wooden gate appeared to lead directly into the path that was also connected to a wooden fence which wrapped itself around both the path and the small church and so once Leah had approached the gate and then had walked through it, she hopefully started to wander further along the cobbly path towards the church. Although Leah had no idea what might be inside the small church which looked run down and deserted, she did hope that she might find some clues or some useful information that could direct her steps towards the correct group of mourners or that might even lead her to the correct individual who would perhaps welcome the object which would effectively solve the second riddle in the note that she had found.

From what Leah observed however, as she arrived at the end of the path and neared the small church's entrance, there didn't seem to be anyone present around the vicinity of the stony structure and so the hope of a guide of some kind, seemed like a very remote possibility. Once Leah had stepped inside the building's interior, she found that the human absence from the exterior of the building continued because the interior not only looked but was also totally deserted and rather unfortunately, it appeared to be blanketed in nothing but an eerie silence. However at the back of the church and quite close to the entrance, Leah noticed that there was a sturdy pinewood table which had an open book on top of it that held the potential promise that a visit to the table might yield some revelations and quite possibly could furnish her with the provision of some actual clues and so she enthusiastically began to head towards it.

Much Leah's satisfaction, upon the table and handwritten on the displayed pages of the book, she found a church service schedule that appeared to list and correlate to the various funeral services that were due to be held that day along with some vague, minor details about each of the groups of mourners due to attend. For the next few seconds a quick visual scan was conducted of the handwritten entries as Leah skimmed through each one on the page until she found three entries next to each other that seemed to correspond to the three funeral services that were currently underway and the three groups of mourners that were now present in the graveyard outside for each of those burial services.

Each handwritten entry was visually inspected, cross checked and then given some thoughtful, careful, silent consideration as Leah remained completely still for a moment, channeled her concentration and focused her attention solely upon the task at hand. Essentially, since Leah had absolutely no prior knowledge of any of the parties involved that meant that she had to search for some kind of clue among the handwritten details but as she attempted to work out which deceased entity the object might relate to and which group of mourners could be connected to the object itself, it seemed almost impossible to tell.

One of the handwritten entries, Leah noticed, appeared to relate to a funeral service for a deceased male but the other two from the three entries appeared to relate to two females and so, she quickly decided that the hand crafted object had probably belonged to the man before his departure from life. Although it was a highly sexist assumption to make, Leah quickly accepted it without even a second of deliberation or any kind of internal rebuttals because that assumption did narrow down the three options to just one which meant, such an assumption might possibly save her some time, if it was indeed actually correct. Before Leah prepared to depart however, as she began to ready herself to embark upon her rather awkward task, she quickly gave the interior of the run down, deserted church one last visual inspection as she searched for any simulated human presence other than her own to verbally present some questions to but unfortunately, there was none to be found.

Due to Leah's lack of certainty, some more seconds were expended in deep concentration as she studied the church schedule entry once again because it suddenly struck her that she should memorize the name of the deceased male because that felt far politer than just a random, ignorant approach without so much as even a name to hand. Once Leah felt satisfied that she had sufficient knowledge to equip her for at least a semi-polite approach, she then left the interior of the church and started to make her way back along the cobbled path as she headed back towards the graveyard.

Just a few minutes later, when Leah arrived back inside the graveyard, she found that it was quite quiet despite the three funeral services which now appeared to be well underway which she swiftly concluded, was to be expected due to the nature of human grief and the sad, mournful purpose behind the graveyard's actual existence. The first of the three funeral services were not too far from the wooden gate and Leah's current position and so as she began to head towards the first open grave, she tried to keep the male name that she had memorized at the forefront of her mind however, that task in itself did feel quite tricky and slippery because it was a highly unusual and really quite complex masculine name.

In just a matter of minutes Leah had arrived on the outskirts of the first group of mourners and as she stood quietly at the rear, she attempted to peek around some of the human bodies to see if she could spot the name engraved into the gravestone which stood to attention and on guard at the head of the open grave. Since the first gravestone that Leah had chosen to inspect, she rapidly discovered, bore a female name upon it she quickly concluded that it probably wasn't the right one and so just a few seconds later, she edged away from the first group of mourners and then began to head towards the second open grave as she walked towards the second burial service.

When Leah arrived at the edge of the second group of mourners, she hung back on the outskirts once again as she came to a standstill in quite close proximity to a mature couple that looked to be in their late sixties. For the second time Leah attempted to discreetly peek at the name engraved into the second gravestone as again she tried to establish whether or not the deceased had actually been male or female. Unfortunately however, Leah quickly discovered that there was a female name etched into the second gravestone but just as she was about to turn and walk away so that she could head towards the third group of mourners, one of the mourners present, the female member from the mature couple, suddenly touched her arm and so, Leah paused for a moment as she politely turned to face the woman.

"Can I see that please?" The woman asked as she pointed towards the object. "If you don't mind."

"Sure." Leah replied as she handed her the object.

"Oh Katrina must have made that years ago, it certainly looks like one of her creations." The woman explained as a tearful smile and a flicker of recognition rapidly spread out across her face. "What do you think Ralph, it looks just like her handiwork doesn't it?" She asked as she turned to face the man beside her.

"Yes, it does Wendy." Ralph agreed as he smiled.

Since Leah's questions about who the object actually belonged to were effectively now answered, she leant towards the woman and then offered her the note which unlike the object was still in one of her hands as the mature couple started to discuss Katrina's life in slightly more detail.

"She was always so handy with her hands wasn't she Ralph and she was always making something?" Wendy mentioned as she graciously accepted the note and then began to read it. "All those creations she made, she called them Katrinations and sometimes they could be very useful." She mentioned as she inspected the culinary object with an affectionate smile and held it up in front of her face.

"And sometimes they weren't." Ralph whispered back in response as he released a soft chuckle.

"Well Ralph, I guess that just depends on how you define useful and what you consider useful to be." Wendy replied. She smiled softly as an obvious fondness for Katrina graced her face as she continued. "But anyway, let's not split hairs about it, not at a time like this. Perhaps we should give these to Chester, they were always so close."

"Yes, I think we should." Ralph swiftly agreed. "At least that's one thing we can agree on, though what it is exactly, is another highly debatable topic that might take hours to discuss and which might reach no actual conclusion." He mentioned as he pointed towards the object.

"Can't you tell Ralph?" Wendy asked.

"No, I can't Wendy." Ralph admitted as he shook his head. He paused for a moment before he continued. "Do you know what it is Miss?"

"Oh unfortunately I don't." Leah immediately confessed. "It does have a splash of intrigue about it though and it does look highly unusual."

"Yes, Katrina was a very unusual person." Wendy acknowledged as she smiled.

"But Wendy, unusual isn't always useful." Ralph quickly pointed out.

"It's very useful Ralph, it's a nutcracker, a very useful nutcracker but I think we should give it to Chester right now because he must be so devastated and so this, along with the note, might just comfort him a little." Wendy suggested thoughtfully as she glanced at a man in his mid-forties nearby. She shook her head and then paused for a moment before she continued. "Once Katrina returned from her trip at sea, our family were supposed to christen her cousin Chester's first child who arrived a few weeks earlier than expected and so, we all waited for her to return. They were always so close those two when they were young and Chester simply refused to go ahead with the celebration until Katrina came back." Wendy explained as she released a sad sob. "But now instead, we're here and in attendance at her funeral, it's so awfully sad."

Ralph nodded his head in agreement. "I know, I know Wendy." He swiftly reassured her as he placed his hand gently on her arm and then pulled her close to him as he offered her a supportive arm of comfort.

"I'm so sorry for your loss." Leah said in a soft apologetic tone as she prepared to depart.

"Thank you." Wendy replied as she nodded her head. "Katrina

was just like a daughter to me, she was my sister's daughter really but we didn't have any children of our own and when her mother passed away, I guess I was the only mother that she had left."

"Let me go and get Chester Wendy." Ralph insisted as he stood back and then released a sigh. "The service seems to be over now and he'll definitely want to see that note because it might actually be for him." He plucked a tissue from his jacket pocket which he then utilized to gently wipe some tears from her eyes. "Will you be okay, I'll just be gone a minute or two?"

"Sure Ralph, don't worry, I'll be fine." Wendy said as she attempted to smile and nodded her head through a few stifled sobs.

"Okay, I'll be right back." Ralph reassured her.

For the next couple of minutes as Leah stood by Wendy's side, she tried to comfort her in Ralph's absence as she placed her arm gently around Wendy's shoulders and waited for Ralph to return. Approximately fifteen other mourners stood around Katrina's open grave and as Leah watched Ralph, she noticed that he approached one of them and the man that Wendy had glanced at, who looked to be in his in mid-forties who she instantly assumed and concluded must be Chester, Katrina's cousin. Once the two men had held a brief discussion, Leah continued to wait as Ralph strode back towards the two women with Chester in tow, who came equipped with black rucksack and a polite nod but who also looked clothed in sadness which could clearly be seen from his downcast expression.

Another few minutes slipped by as Leah listened to Wendy, Ralph and Chester discuss the object in question along with her involvement prior to his arrival at which point, it became apparent that the object had been one of a pair of nutcrackers that Katrina had made for herself and Ralph in her younger years. From what Leah could establish from the conversation between the three, apparently the two youngsters had both liked to eat various kinds of nuts but they could rarely find a nutcracker strong enough to open certain varieties and so Katrina had created and made the two nutcrackers to ensure that they always had one with them whenever a strong nutcracker had been required. One of the two nutcrackers had actually been given to Chester by Katrina and as Leah listened to the discussion as it continued, she noticed that Chester opened up his rucksack and then pulled a second object out of its interior that looked very similar to the first with a sad smile upon his face.

"I still have mine." Chester mentioned as he nodded his head. "I never lost it or broke it."

"You do Chester and so now, you have two nutcrackers." Wendy replied as she handed him the second nutcracker. She turned to face her husband and smiled. "You see Ralph, two very useful items."

"Yes and these two nutcrackers are actually very special." Chester explained. "One of a kind, well two of a kind."

"Why?" Ralph asked. "Don't they just crack nuts open?"

"No, these nutcrackers both have a secret compartment in them where we would hide the keys to our treasure boxes." Chester confirmed as he touched a part of the nutcracker that he'd just been given and slid open a small secret compartment.

Upon Leah's face there was a surprised expression as she watched Chester pluck a small shiny silver key from the interior of the nutcracker and a small piece of paper that had also been wedged into that quite small space. For a minute or two a sheet of silence seemed to fall over the four as Leah waited for Chester to read the contents of the note that he'd found and as she watched him in total fascination, she began to wonder what Katrina might have planned to give to her loved ones after her departure from life. Once the note had been read as Leah watched in fascinated silence, Chester plucked a small golden box from his black rucksack which he then used the small silver shiny key to open up.

"Katrina left me her treasure box." Chester mentioned. "But I couldn't open it because I didn't have the key."

Inside the golden box Leah could see that there was a silver locket which Chester swiftly plucked from the interior and then opened up and inside the locket on either side, there were two photos with images of two children together which Leah noticed, prompted Chester to smile. Just a few seconds later Leah watched as Chester handed the locket to Wendy which she eagerly accepted and as a smile of recognition instantly crossed Wendy's face, she began to inspect the two photos that it contained which from the flickers of joyful recognition that were present, Leah could see she clearly, affectionately recognized.

"That's you Chester and that's Katrina." Wendy enthusiastically pointed out as she pointed towards one of the photos and smiled.

"Yes that's us. Just to see those photos brings back so many happy memories." Chester agreed as he smiled. "Wonderfully happy days."

The mourners around Katrina's grave suddenly began to disperse and as Leah watched some of them leave, she prepared to depart herself because since she had now solved the riddle and successfully somehow managed to deliver Katrina's gift to her cousin, it felt like it was time to depart.

"I'd better get a move on." Leah said as she smiled at the three.

"Yes and thank you. I'm just sorry that we couldn't have met in better circumstances." Wendy said as she smiled.

"Yes thank you very much, it was very nice of you to bother." Chester agreed.

A couple of minutes were spent in farewells as Wendy leant towards Leah and gave her an affectionate hug which Leah politely accepted after which point, Chester shook her hand but just before Leah departed, she noticed that Ralph, despite his slightly cold comments earlier in the conversation, offered her a warm smile along with a courteous nod. Just a second or two later Leah turned and then began to walk away and although she had no actual clue where she was actually supposed to go next or what she was supposed to do, she definitely felt as if it was time to depart because she felt a bit like an outsider to the family's grief.

Since nothing else inside the graveyard attracted Leah's attention or seemed to offer her any kind of direction, she decided to head back to the church where she felt, she might just find someone present, since most of the funeral services that had been scheduled for that day, now appeared to be over as she left the three to mourn. Grief, as Leah already knew from Zidane's experiences and her own real life experiences, was such a private despair and one that could rarely be alleviated or reduced by the presence of anyone else and especially not by the presence of a total stranger. An interruption to the family's grief had occurred that day, purely due to Leah's approach and presence and since she had absolutely no desire to interrupt the grief of the three that still stood around Katrina's grave for any longer than was absolutely necessary, she began to walk at a slightly brisker pace as she headed back towards the church.

Despite the emotional distance that had existed between the four, since Leah hadn't actually ever met or known Katrina, she felt a warm sense of comfort trickle across her pores as she walked because her rather awkward interruption and actions had it appeared, offered some kind of peace to the three mourners that she had interacted with. Fortunately, the object that Leah had found had sparked the remembrance of some happy memories in the minds of the grief stricken mourners which she felt, they could at least now dwell upon and remember in love but as Leah neared the church and the cobbled path once again and the air around her suddenly swiftly darkened, a shadow of guilt seemed to appear and cast itself over her simulated form.

Although Leah had managed to solve the riddle, it suddenly struck her as she walked through the open wooden gateway once again and stepped back onto the path that perhaps Katrina had been one of the survivors in the choppy waters earlier that day that had actually perished due to Leah's own failures. Another memory had been sparked in Leah's own mind which unfortunately, belonged to Leah herself as through her interactions with the three mourners, she was now reminded of her own inability to rescue more people than she had and that regretful discomfort now appeared to silently transform what had initially seemed like a heroic achievement into a truly horrible result which was far from pleasant. Very uncomfortably, Leah's inability to save more people now provoked her to question her own failures as the shadow of guilt that hung over her heart, lingered in the shadows of her conscience and clothed her thoughts in dark guilty discomfort, rapidly started to prickle her simulated pores and every inch of her simulated form.

Sadly and so tragically, Leah glumly concluded as she neared the entrance of the church once more, if she had been able to rescue more survivors that day, perhaps some of the four burial services that she'd seen occur might not have even taken place at all. Due to Leah's failures and the churchyard mourners' grief, a burden of guilt seemed to weigh heavily on her heart and mind as she walked through the entrance of the church once again and then started to seek out a human entity that might perhaps furnish her with some kind of explanation or perhaps some directions.

All the burial services that Leah had seen handwritten in the church's schedule, now appeared to be over for that day and so she hoped that someone would now be present and that she would be able to interact with that person. A part of Leah deep down inside, hoped that she would perhaps be provided with some kind of solace, peace or comfort since what she had encountered that day had been such a heavy load because anger from what she had observed, could result in so much heartbreak, such deep sadness and very steep levels of painful regret.

Fortunately for Leah however, her second visit to the church proved to be more fruitful because in one corner of the church and quite close to the table where she had discovered the church schedule on her first visit, she now noticed that there was a mature women clothed in religious attire which indicated that she was perhaps a church leader of some kind.

"Do you need something?" The woman asked. "I'm one of the church elders." She explained.

"I'm not sure." Leah replied.

"Yes, a lot of people do tend to come here when they're uncertain." The church elder replied. "Did you come here to attend a burial service today?" She asked.

"Oh no, I didn't but I met some people who did." Leah said as she shook her head. "I had to give them something."

"Really, what did you have to give them?" The female elder asked.

"It sounds silly really, just a nutcracker that I found in the graveyard." Leah replied. "But it was a very beautiful, hand crafted nutcracker and it even had a secret compartment built into it with a treasure box key inside it."

"Oh okay, then you must be a friend of Katrina's." She swiftly concluded as she smiled. "Her instructions were very precise, so I tried to follow them as accurately as I could."

"You did?" Leah asked.

"Yes, so I'm glad you found it." The female elder confirmed as she smiled. "Just before Katrina went on her trip which was a missionary trip, she came to me and she gave me the nutcracker and some instructions because although she expected to return from her trip, the seas had been quite stormy just before she left, so she was a bit worried about it. I agreed to keep it for her, just in case and she also asked me to put it somewhere where one of her family members would find it because she said, if she didn't return, they would know what to do with it."

"I'm so sorry." Leah said as she offered her an apologetic smile. "Sorry that she didn't return."

"Yes, me too but at least some comfort and peace has now been given from beyond the grave to some hearts in sadness." She replied.

"Yes but I still feel so awful. I just feel so guilty because I didn't reach Katrina on time." Leah admitted as she shook her head in sad frustration. "I'm should have seen her, I should have saved her but I didn't, so I failed."

"You can't save everyone." The woman advised as she stretched out an arm towards her.

"But why did I fail and why didn't I even notice that I'd failed?" Leah asked.

"Sometimes the comfort of what we manage to achieve and even the hope of what we can achieve in the future, can soothe and appease our feelings of inadequacy about what we don't have, what we can never achieve or what we fail to realize, it's just human nature." She mentioned. "But you really can't feel guilty about your own human limits, you are a human being and so this is not the first or the last time that you will fail, so you'd better learn to accept it, learn to cope with it and learn to live with it."

"To live with failure and guilt though to such a huge degree, how do you learn to accept those horrible things?" Leah probed.

"Guilt can be such a heavy weight upon the heart because it can live for so long and with time it can fester inside of you, decay every part of you and grow heavier and heavier. You can't possibly carry it around with you everywhere you go in life because you really won't make it that far, it will eat you up inside." The female church elder replied. "You should try to put it down somewhere really and if you like, you can even leave it here because fortunately, forgiveness in this establishment is a gift that will be given to you when you sincerely ask for it."

"I'll try to remember that." Leah replied appreciatively as she smiled.

"Yes, our door is always open." The female elder pointed out.

"Thanks." Leah turned as she prepared to depart and then began to walk towards the entrance of the church. She shook her head as she stepped back outside as it suddenly dawned upon her that she hadn't even asked the woman what she was supposed to do next. "How could I forget that?" Leah whispered to herself.

Just a few seconds later however, Leah's environment suddenly began to change as the cobbled path and the graveyard which sat not too far away from it, suddenly started to evaporate and then faded from sight and as the graveyard disappeared, Leah found herself back inside the interior of the cave once more. Since the huge mirrored wall that towered above Leah's head was now visible, just for a few seconds Leah moved around in front of it and as she did so, she glanced at it as she tried to watch her reflection mimic her movements.

Very surprisingly however, Leah found that there was no reflection to be seen in the mirror's reflective surface and since nothing else moved an inch inside the cave, not even a flicker of movement appeared to present as the mirrored surface just seemed to stare back at her with an eerie stillness. For a couple of minutes Leah clung onto that moment of stillness as she hopefully waited to see if anything would change but nothing did and so, she began to conclude that her trials in the Mirror of Trials for that day, were indeed over.

Once Leah felt satisfied that there was nothing else to be done inside the cave, she prepared to leave its interior as she turned to face the cave entrance and then began to walk towards it but part of Leah wondered as she walked why her reflection had not appeared in the mirrored cave wall upon her return and if Bearciple would still be present. Since Leah had spent quite a lot of time inside the cave because the trials that she had faced in the Mirror of Trials had taken quite a while, she quietly considered as she neared the cave's entrance, if he might perhaps have already deserted her and jetted off to somewhere else in his speedy hovercart.

When Leah stepped out of the cave's interior however, fortunately enough, she swiftly discovered that Bearciple was indeed still present and so she released a sigh of relief as she walked back towards the hovercart and the humabear. Unlike Leah's own reflection which she rapidly concluded had abandoned her at the very first sight of a trial inside the cave, the humabear it appeared had been far more faithful and had kept his promise to remain outside the cave until she returned and as she neared the hovercart once more, Leah offered the humabear an grateful smile as she silently appreciated his loyalty and honesty.

A few seconds later Leah arrived beside the edge of the metal hovercart square base once again, at which point she enthusiastically stepped back onto it because she had been promised a trip to the Fountain of Sincere Wishes which sounded a lot more hopeful and far more pleasant than her experiences inside the Mirror of Trials had been. The walls of the metal contraption swiftly began to rise and grow as Bearciple nodded his head in response and then touched the remote control and as Leah watched, she noticed that as the metal hovercart walls returned to their former state, the small bench also reappeared which prompted her to sit back down upon it.

For the next few seconds Leah watched Bearciple thoughtfully as he touched and fiddled around with the small remote control that controlled the hovercart's movements but as she did so, a few questions lingered in her mind about her experiences that day inside the Mirror of Trials. Essentially, Leah's experiences had lacked any kind of explanations and although a few parts she had been able to figure out or had managed to logically deduce herself as she'd gone along as she had tried to make some kind of sense out of all, she still had a question or two about what had just taken place inside the mysterious cave.

"What would have happened Bearciple, if I hadn't passed the trials?" Leah enquired since her curiosity had definitely been aroused by the mysterious events that she had just experienced. "Did I pass the trials?" She asked as a confused expression suddenly crossed her face. "I don't even know if I actually did."

"Oh I wouldn't worry about it too much Leah, the trials are just there to test your purity of spirit." Bearciple explained politely. "Did you see your reflection in the mirror?" He asked.

"Yes, I did at the beginning." Leah replied. "Not at the end though. In fact, I did notice that it was actually missing, is that a bad sign?"

"Oh." Bearciple said in a solemn voice. "Yes everybody's reflection shows up at first, not always at the end though."

"What does that mean though?" Leah replied. "Is a missing reflection a bad thing?"

"Well if you fail the trials, you can lose your reflection forever. The Bay of Wrath either keeps your reflection for a while and then returns it to you when you deserve it or just consumes it, it just depends on how impure, wicked or evil you are. Your reflection is the inner core of your soul after all." Bearciple explained.

Leah stared at him anxiously for a moment. "So, have I lost my reflection forever Bearciple?"

"I'm not sure, maybe just temporarily." Bearciple quickly reassured her in a diplomatic manner. He paused for a moment before he continued. "Don't worry though Leah, our next stop will be much nicer, the Fountain of Sincere Wishes is always a very popular stop off point."

"Should I wish to get my soul and my reflection back Bearciple?" Leah joked as her enthusiasm returned once more and then started to grow.

"It's really up to you Leah." Bearciple replied. "A wish is a very personal choice from deep within your own heart, so I can't really advise you on which wishes you should or shouldn't make."

An awkward silence seemed to blanket the hovercart as it started to move off again as Leah mulled over the implications of Bearciple's remarks as she began to question whether she would have entered into the cave at all, if she had known what had actually been at stake. The risk that Leah had artificially taken unknowingly, now felt absolutely huge because to lose your soul simply due to a few hours of recreational enjoyment seemed to be a rather harsh penalty to pay and artificial or not, Leah had just taken that risk and due to her recent simulated indiscretions, perhaps even lost that gamble.

Recently, when it came to the issue of conduct, Leah had definitely fallen far short of her usual moral standards, albeit it artificially, all of which she had self-justified but she couldn't sit comfortably with the notion that right now, her heart was in a totally pure state. Whether Leah's reflection would ever be returned to her was another issue entirely and not one that she could even attempt to answer with any degree of certainty but as the hovercart floated further along the tunnel and left the cave entrance far behind it, Leah hoped that her reflection would reappear when she returned to reality.

The journey along the interior of the tunnels continued and as Leah watched the Mirror of Trials cave vanish from sight, she tried to convince herself that judgement in this instance had perhaps just been attributable to her fearful hesitation on the ship. Since Leah had not taken control of the ship in the face of danger as quickly as she perhaps should have and she had also failed to assist more people in the choppy, angry seas than she perhaps could have, she definitely felt that those two factors might have had an impact upon the Bay of Wrath's judgement of her soul and perhaps even had resulted in the disappearance of her actual reflection.

Quite strangely it seemed, Leah concluded as she watched the hovercart enter into another tunnel and then glide gently along it, Spectrum seemed to have a moral scorecard inbuilt into this particular emotional experience and so her emotional journey that day had somehow, incorporated that ethical aspect into her experiences and her interactions within that environment. However, Leah now worried that her simulated acts of unfaithfulness and her fictional betrayal of Zidane might actually count as being impure in the moral scorecard that the Mirror of Trials applied and that perhaps Spectrum would consider that simulated aspect of morality as relevant and maybe, she began to conclude that was why her reflection had disappeared and had actually been lost.

Whatever had or hadn't been considered morally incorrect by Spectrum and the Bay of Wrath however, Leah still knew deep down inside herself that her recent simulated conduct and actions had definitely deviated far from the purity of the relationship that she and Zidane had once begun, shared, treasured and enjoyed. Although Leah had justified her own actions time and time again inside her own mind and thoughts, she definitely knew that she had strayed far from the love that the two supposedly shared but as Leah watched the hovercart enter into another tunnel, she hoped that when she returned to reality, she would at least find her real reflection again and that perhaps she would even somehow, be able to make it up to Zidane.

For the most part, Leah swiftly concluded, her Spectrum experiences that day would simply be utilized to make any required tweaks or modifications to the system prototype that she had created after which point, each important memory would be stored upon the memory shelves inside her mind which she might reflect upon at a later date. So in the larger scheme of things, as far as Leah was concerned, when it came to those memorable moments each one would merely be past moments of time that she had spent inside Spectrum but in terms of her own reality, none of those moments would have an actual real impact upon her real life and so neither would the artificial loss of her artificial reflection which in reality, she concluded, wouldn't mean very much.

After the two had travelled along a few more tunnels inside the hovercart they finally arrived at the entrance to a second large expanse, though this expanse Leah noticed, was much smaller than the first which had of course contained the Crystal Mountains of Lost Souls. A large, rocky, golden water fountain was situated in the middle of the expanse and as Leah watched Bearciple slow the hovercart down, just a few seconds later the hovercart came a gentle stop right beside it. Some golden rocks surrounded and formed the base of the fountain, Leah observed as she exited the hovercart along with the golden rocky central mouthpiece of the fountain itself and a constant stream of golden water gently cascaded down from that mouthpiece as each drop of water spilled out and then trickled back down towards the golden pool at the bottom of the fountain as each one searched for its watery comrades and returned peacefully home.

Every part of the fountain inclusive of the golden water that it contained looked beautiful, peaceful, serene and somehow even slightly magical to Leah as she neared the golden rocky base and watched the golden drops of water gurgle, bubble and swirl around its interior harmoniously without a care in the world. Just for a moment, Leah envied the simplicity of each golden watery drop's existence which seemed so pure, so peaceful, so tranquil and so simple but as she fully absorbed, processed and admired the beauty that now surrounded her, she suddenly remembered that she was actually supposed to make a wish which had been the main motivational reason behind her desire to visit the fountain in the first place.

"What are we supposed to do here Bearciple?" Leah asked as she sat down on one of the golden rocks and then gently ran her fingertips through some of the golden drops before she turned to face him. "Or rather, what am I supposed to do here? How do I make a wish?"

"First of all Leah, you have to step inside the water and then you can make a wish." Bearciple explained with a smile.

"Will this wish cost me anything Bearciple?" Leah enquired as she glanced at his face suspiciously as she thoughtfully reflected upon her recent experiences inside the cave of trials. "I mean, I've already lost my reflection today, so I really don't know if I can afford to lose anything else."

"Maybe." Bearciple replied. "Sometimes wishes do cost us something." He clarified. "But usually Leah, wishes only cost you something that you don't really want or need."

"What do you mean?" Leah asked as she questioned the vagueness of his response. "What could I possibly possess that I might not want or need?" She glanced up at the top of the golden rocky fountain mouthpiece as she considered some possible answers to her own question for a moment.

"It's just a universal law of nature Leah, when something is given, something is also usually, if not always, taken away in return." Bearciple mentioned. "But I don't make the rules, so I can't predict how those rules will apply to any individual." He acknowledged as he shrugged.

"Hmm, what could this wish cost me?" Leah considered thoughtfully as she began to deliberate over whether or not she could actually afford to make an actual wish. "What do you think Bearciple?"

"A wish might not cost you that much really, perhaps just a thought, a desire or something that you don't utilize in life or fully appreciate the presence of and perhaps never will." Bearciple replied. "Because someone else will perhaps be wishing for the things that you don't want or need and the things that you don't appreciate or use." He continued. "It's a highly logical, very diplomatic system really. Something that you don't need, want, desire or appreciate, someone else will."

"I guess that makes some kind of sense, though it does seem to be a very tough wish system." Leah concluded. "From what I've always read and heard, wishes are supposed to be free to the wish maker."

"Nothing in life or nature is ever really free Leah." Bearciple teased as he grinned. "Even your own usage of time will cost you any other opportunity that could occur in the minutes and hours that you expend upon a particular task, achievement or life experience which you could perhaps have spent on something else. Every choice in life that you make costs you something because you forgo any other alternatives that are accessible to you."

In some ways, the explanations provided by Bearciple seemed to make sense which satisfied Leah to some extent because he had managed to convince her that at the very least, she wouldn't lose out or pay too much for her wish and so as she flashed the humabear a smile, she enthusiastically began to remove her trainer shoes. Since Leah had already arrived at the conclusion that nothing inside Spectrum was actually real which meant that whatever fictitious wish she made inside it wouldn't be real either that also implied that neither would the fictional price that she was required to pay for her fictitious wish being granted be real, so as far as she was concerned, the fictional price would never actually ever be expended, or so she hoped.

Once Leah had lain the black trainer shoes that had been on her feet in a dry spot by the side of the rocky fountain, she then stepped into the water as she prepared to participate in the wish exchange as she chalked her participation down to something that she was doing purely for the fun of it. The positive side of that frivolous cooperation meant that there would be no huge expectations on Leah's part, if her wish didn't actually materialize in reality though she still hoped that at some point or when she did return to reality that her reflection would at least reappear.

Some golden ripples and drops of water gently lapped around Leah's ankles and calves as she stood inside the water in the base of the fountain and just enjoyed the warm, delightful refreshment on offer which seemed absolutely delicious and appeared to revitalize her inner core. A warm glow seemed to emanate from the water itself as Leah began to paddle around inside the golden drops which quickly embraced and then infiltrated her form and as it started to flow in an upwards direction across her skin, the pleasant sensation that she felt as a result, seemed to make her simulated interior feel extremely relaxed and very comfortable. Although the golden fountain might not really grant real wishes, Leah could at least find comfort in the pleasantness of its simulated existence which was a far cry from the cold, rough, choppy waters that she had been stuck in earlier that day but as she did so, she turned to face Bearciple and then extended an invitation towards him to join her as she encouraged the humabear to join her paddle around the fountain.

"You should join me Bearciple. The water is warm and

amazingly delicious." Leah teased. "Or do humabears fear water?"

Bearciple shook his head. "What would I wish for? I have everything that I could possibly need or want as a humabear." He replied as he smiled. "A dry cave to lay my head in, some responsibilities that make the most of my time, a food supply that is easy to catch whenever I hunger and some spare time to make inventions when the Bay of Wrath is quiet."

"Better food, a female humabear companion or perhaps even a luxury cave to live, eat and sleep in." Leah suggested as she shrugged. "Just a few suggestions."

"I think I already eat the best food that a humabear could possibly eat, so that's not really a problem because I can catch whatever I want to eat every single day. You have to remember Leah, there's a constant food supply in the tunnels that run through the mountains, so I never ever go hungry." Bearciple acknowledged. "Plus, I have a cave full of useful things inclusive of a comfortable bed to rest in, so that's not an issue for me either." He paused thoughtfully for a moment. "Maybe a female humabear companion would be nice though but I won't make that wish today, perhaps I'll come back and make that a wish another day. I'll have to think about it a bit more, female companions can be very demanding at times. Today we should just focus your wish."

Leah laughed. "Now that point I totally agree with Bearciple, some female companions can be very demanding. You know, you're a very wise humabear." She teased. "Right, so how do I actually make a wish? Do I say it or do I just think it? What exactly should I do?"

"You just close your eyes and then think it inside your mind." Bearciple explained.

"Okay, okay here goes." Leah replied as she giggled and closed her eyes. "One big, brave, sincere wish is being made right now Bearciple."

Another couple of minutes slipped by as Leah thought about and then decided upon her wish which was almost completely filled with quietness except from the gentle gurgle that emanated from the golden fountain itself. In terms of the actual wish itself, it really wasn't a difficult wish for Leah to make as she wished that Spectrum would have lots of potential bidders and that she would be offered a large sum of money, so that she could live the rest of her life in financial comfort. Although it was a simple wish, Leah wholeheartedly yearned that it would be more than fiction and that it would actually come true because then the couple could start to raise a family which was something that they had both planned, wished and hoped to do for at least the past couple of years.

When Leah reopened her eyes, she noticed as she glanced down at herself that her simulated form was now almost totally golden and that somehow, she seemed to have absorbed more of the golden water which shone, glimmered and sparkled all around her. Fortunately, Leah observed as she cast a glance towards the humabear, Bearciple had once again remained steadfast and had not deserted her and as she watched him for a few seconds as she began to head back towards the edge of the fountain, she noticed that he plucked a very large handkerchief from under his furry, hair skin which he then politely handed to her.

"I always keep a handkerchief handy." Bearciple explained. "I guess that's the human part of my humabear existence but you can use that handkerchief to dry your feet." He politely offered.

"Thank you Bearciple." Leah replied as she graciously accepted his kind offer and then sat back down upon the rocky outer edge of the fountain as she prepared to dry her feet. She smiled as she started to dry her feet then paused for a moment as she glanced up at his face. "How will I actually know what the Fountain of Sincere Wishes took in return for my wish?"

"You might never know or ever find out." Bearciple replied. "If something is taken in return, it won't be something that you need or really appreciate the existence off, so perhaps you won't ever notice that it's absent."

"Okay. I guess I can live with that." Leah joked as she grinned.

Rather intriguingly, Leah suddenly noticed that her skin had now returned to its normal tone but she didn't have long to dwell upon the golden fountain or the wish she had made because as she slipped her trainer shoes back on, she noticed that Bearciple eagerly returned to his hovercart where he appeared to wait for her to join him.

"Would you like to visit the Mountain of Perseverance now Leah or perhaps I can take you somewhere else?" Bearciple called out.

"Sure, I guess we could hover around the base of the mountain, probably not for long though because my trip for today is almost over now." Leah agreed as she stood up and then began to walk back towards the hovercart. "I guess time just isn't on my side which is a shame really because I'd have loved to spend more time with you Bearciple and your hovercart, it's been truly delightful." She smiled before she continued. "Oh except the part where you weren't around and I had to swim through the freezing cold seas."

Bearciple grinned as he touched the hovercart remote. "Yes, the Mirror of Trials can be quite tricky." He admitted. "Even for the bravest of hearts."

The timer that Leah had set for Spectrum that day as far as she knew, would by that point have almost run out and if anything, would probably have less than an hour left but since she hadn't counted every second, she couldn't be entirely sure. A visit to another location to indulge in another complex activity as Leah already appreciated, would therefore be totally out of the question that day but as she sat back down inside the hovercart and glanced at Bearciple's face, she hoped that one day she would perhaps return and that then she might be able to participate in his tour once again.

Interestingly, Leah observed as the hovercart started to move off, on this occasion the humabear guide had presented Leah with an actual choice which hadn't always been her experience on some of her prior visits to Spectrum and some of the other emotional planes that she had visited. More often than not, Leah considered thoughtfully, she had simply been thrown headlong into challenges and activities with absolutely no warnings at all and quite often those challenges had not only come as a total surprise but had also been very unexpected and the fact that in this instance, her humabear guide had consulted her, really encouraged her because it had felt so personal and so individual.

For the next fifteen minutes as Leah watched Bearciple direct his hovercart through the tunnels and caves as he politely continued to usher her through her the remainder of her emotional journey, Leah swiftly concluded that the humabear really had been one of the politest and most considerate non-human guides that she had met inside Spectrum. A worrisome question did remain and linger inside Leah's mind however, as she was whisked through the tunnels and caves which related to her actual reflection and what might happen in reality, if it never returned which she continued to think about.

The issue of the couple and any photographs that they might wish to take did cross Leah's mind just for a moment as she indulged in how that could perhaps impact upon her in reality because if she had no mirrored, reflectionary image, she doubted that she would show up in any photos that the couple might want to take together. When most human beings walked past any window or glanced in a mirror anywhere, Leah thoughtfully considered, they would always seek out their reflection and always expected to find it and so, it would feel very strange, if she returned from Spectrum that day and her reflection remained absent and lost. Although a reflection wasn't an essential to human life and was usually just something that most human beings took for granted, Leah definitely felt as if she would be lost somehow without it because it was something that she had always had but on the other side of that strange notion, the ethical aspect of the day's events had totally intrigued her, despite her reflectionary losses.

Several elements inside Spectrum definitely appeared to have deviated immensely from Leah's original programming inputs which had followed her own original specifications to the dot and that had not only intrigued Leah but it had also surprised her. Somehow, it was almost as some of the fictitious, artificial variables inside Spectrum had taken on a life of their own and there was just no way that Leah could explain those deviations or even attempt to rationalize a single one. Absolutely none of the evolutionary deviations could be attributed by Leah to possible fluctuations in the random settings that she had created because they had been so vastly different in terms of structure, complexity and had seemed very precisely engineered which puzzled her slightly but since in many ways that day, Spectrum had not only surpassed but had also flown far above and beyond Leah's original expectations, she tried to accept those unusual deviations which she felt overall, had resulted in mainly positive, pleasant experiences.

Approximately thirty minutes later and once the hovercart had hovered around the Mountain of Perseverance, the hovercart arrived back inside the tunnel close to Bearciple's cave once again and as Leah prepared to depart, she focused upon Bearciple's tour and her departure. In almost every way possible that day besides a couple of instances of vagueness, Leah felt that Bearciple had been a wonderful host and the perfect guide and because she felt unsure that she would ever come across the humabear ever again, she really wanted to thank him for his attentiveness and assistance.

"You've been a great guide Bearciple." Leah said appreciatively as she watched the walls of the hovercart shrink back down into the base and then stood up.

"Thank you Leah but I am just a guide to the Bay of Wrath, so I can't control anything that happens here." Bearciple quickly pointed out. "Which sometimes, can actually result in more than just a touch of frustration."

"Well, you're more than that you are a protector and a guide but I understand what you mean because in some ways, you're like a powerless spectator to this powerful force and to the things that happen around you." Leah acknowledged. "Sometimes that must be rather exciting but I guess at times, it might be rather restrictive. Still Bearciple, you were a great companion, so you should definitely make that wish soon because some cute female humabear is probably missing out on some great male humabear companionship." She teased.

"Thanks Leah." Bearciple said as a bashful smile crossed his face. "I hope you come back to visit me again one day." He mentioned.

"Who knows, it might be possible one day and I'd definitely love to be your first return visitor." Leah teased as she stepped off the hovercart.

The two began to walk back towards Bearciple's cave as Leah

started to prepare herself for her return to the real world which definitely would not be anything like the Bay of Wrath with its choppy, cold seas, skeleton captains and its treacherous Crystal Mountains of Souls. Soon as Leah already knew, her emotional journey for that day would be over at which point, both Bearciple and the Bay of Wrath would disappear and whatever she'd experienced inside Spectrum that day, would simply remain there but the Bay of Wrath had really intrigued her and so some of the more memorable moments and the deep, curious considerations that had been provoked in her mind, would definitely remain with her and inside her thoughts. Very interestingly for Leah however, throughout her experiences inside Spectrum she had discovered the deep depths of the full human emotional spectrum and how both positive and negative emotions could invoke deep emotional responses and reactions from others where there was an emotional correlation or any kind of close emotional proximity to an event, outcome or experience that triggered or created deep wells of emotion.

Once the two arrived back inside Bearciple's cave, Leah hugged the humabear affectionately as she prepared to leave but as she bade him farewell, she noticed that his furry, fleshy skin felt warm, soft and really quite human, almost like her own.

"Until next time Bearciple, take care of your humabear self." Leah said softly as she glanced into his eyes sadly.

Bearciple nodded and smiled. "Well, I'm always here Leah. So you can come back to see me anytime." He replied. "I'd love to have a return visitor and especially one that is a fellow technological scientist like myself."

"I'll definitely try to and you never know by the time I return, you might have made that wish." Leah teased as she gently released him. "And so by then there might even be a bunch of baby humabears living in your cave."

"You never know, one day I might just take the wish plunge." Bearciple joked. "Sometimes, a change can be pleasant."

"Yes and that change probably would be." Leah concluded as she glanced around the cave's interior. "Certainly beats staring at cave walls all day alone and you'd also have someone to eat humabear grand cake with."

"Now that Leah is an excellent point." Bearciple agreed. "Yes, I think you've managed to convince me because that kind of wish would definitely be favorable to my humabear existence.

"Good luck Bearciple and good wishes." Leah said as she turned and then began to walk back towards the entrance of the cave.

Sadly, Leah concluded as she walked, she would probably never ever return to the Bay of Wrath or artificially meet Bearciple ever again because as she already knew, if she did seek out another adventure in that particular emotional plane, due to the random nature of Spectrum, it was highly unlikely that she would return or that the two would cross paths again. A functionality did exist in Spectrum that allowed users to revisit a past adventure but since that would simply return Leah to the original point in time that she had entered into the Bay of Wrath, so that she could replay and re-experience that emotional journey but did not actually extend it, utilization of that functionality meant that Bearciple's wish would still remain unwished and that she would still be a first time visitor to the bay. However, since Bearciple had been so truly delightful, Leah definitely felt that perhaps that functionality should be tweaked and extended.

Somewhere, deep inside Leah's heart and mind an emotional bond had definitely been formed with Bearciple which felt deeper than any other that Leah had experienced with any other guide in Spectrum so far because he had been courteous, helpful and so likable which meant that as a guide, he did not need or require any modifications or tweaks at all. In terms of the environment, the Bay of Wrath had definitely been by far the most unusual of Leah's emotional journeys among her visits to Spectrum because it had challenged her in many different ways and had given her so much to think about. From what Leah had understood and had realized from her experiences that day, anger could create so many hostages of pain and so many casualties of despair because quite often anger could be a response to grave wrongs that had been suffered, huge injustices that had been experienced or deep hurts that had been inflicted which meant that actions in anger often bore not only the remnants but also the backlash of tremendous hurts entrenched in the devastation of heartbroken shock.

Although Leah did consider for a moment what might happen when she returned to the pebbly, sandy beach as she neared the entrance of the first cave and then prepared to step back through it, she never actually had a chance to find out. Once Leah stepped through the cave's entrance, she once more found herself back inside her basement laboratory and as she prepared to return to the real world and her very real life as she slipped out of the Spectrum capsule, just for a moment her mind returned to Bearciple, his hovercart and his tour of the Bay of Wrath which had not only deeply engaged her but that had also been so finely tuned to her own individual aspirations in life.

When Bearciple had discussed the creation of his hovercart, the technical build of his contraption and how aspects of it such as the ability to expand its interior had surprised him and had surpassed his original expectations, Leah had not only understood his frustrations, been able to identify with his achievements but she had also related to his struggles. Since that day some of Leah's experiences within Spectrum had intrigued her above and beyond her initial expectations and some of the things that she had created and then encountered, she simply did not possess technical explanations for even though she had created Spectrum herself. Various elements inside Spectrum had combined in such a unique way and seemed to contain elements of unpredictability and how each of those various elements had been tailored towards her own very personal, individual journey inside each emotional plane had absolutely surpassed her initial hopes.

A deep sense of personal satisfaction accompanied Leah as she arrived at the foot of the basement steps and then gave the subterranean room one final glance because that day, Leah had fully experienced the full capacity of the recreational system that she had built herself and it had been absolutely phenomenal because the creation of Spectrum had at times seemed, almost impossible to achieve. Fortunately for Leah, the clock on the basement wall which suddenly caught her eye confirmed that it wasn't yet very late and so as she instructed Fink to shut everything inside the basement down, she stepped onto the first step as she began to make her way towards Zidane who she hoped would not yet have fallen asleep on the couch.

The wish that Leah had made that day in the Fountain of Sincere Wishes quickly sprung to the forefront of her mind once again as Leah bounced enthusiastically up the basement steps as she quietly considered the possibility that perhaps her fictitious wish might actually come true. Although it was a very remote possibility but definitely a hopeful one, Leah concluded as she arrived at the top of the basement stairs, the fulfilment of her fictional wish if it did manifest itself in reality, would result in a real fairytale future for the couple and a future that she believed, they truly deserved.

Upon Leah's face there was a hopeful smile as she began to walk towards the lounge of the couple's home as she formulated a plan about how she would spend the remainder of that day, tucked up in Zidane's warm arms and engulfed in as much passion and affection as the two could muster. For once no shadows of guilt accompanied Leah as she walked along the hallway and then stepped into the lounge because that day, her heart and mind had stayed firmly tied and rooted to her Spectrum tasks and had fully honored Zidane's heart.

Due to Leah's walk-through tests, a large chunk of the couple's potential evening together had already vanished and the Bay of Wrath had stolen some of their possible shared moments that day but at the very least, Leah hoped that they could both still make the most of the night that remained. Some tender affection, devoted attention and passionate adoration, Leah felt, were definitely overdue and owed to Zidane's heart because he had not only remained but also sustained and maintained such a consistent supply of supportive love to her own heart even though it had required huge sacrifices from him and it had cost the couple years in terms of her work on Spectrum, through his acts of extremely selfless and tireless devotion.

Not a whisper could be heard as Leah hopefully glanced at

Zidane's face but found him fast asleep on the sofa which didn't totally surprise her because as she already knew, he did wake up very early each morning and work very hard all day. Just Zidane's presence however, comforted Leah's heart tremendously as she reflected upon her experiences inside Spectrum that day and the disappearance of her own reflection which had challenged Leah to consider not only her own conduct but also her own temporal existence along with the couple's limited, physical existence.

Life as Leah knew, could be very uncertain, no matter how much the couple planned or how hard they worked but Zidane was the one person and most stable factor in Leah's world that had not just been a solid emotional anchor to her heart and mind but that had also been the strongest mast on board her ship of life. Although Spectrum had consumed much of the couple's time over the past few years and Leah's own, she hoped, wished and prayed as she glanced at Zidane's face that her Spectrum wish would actually materialize because then they could enjoy the life they had always dreamed off.

Perhaps, Leah considered, a slice of Spectrum and a hopeful, fictional wish could come true because prior to her graduation, she had never even imagined that she could build a prototype like Spectrum and she had managed to which meant, some wishes definitely did come true. Perhaps, some small real part of Leah's fictitious, artificial journey inside Spectrum that day would actually result in the occurrence of a real miracle which would provide the two with the real future together that they had always wished for but as Leah knew, there were no guarantees. Perhaps, Leah hoped as she leant down towards Zidane and prepared to wake him so that they could eat dinner together, her artificial wish would provide the couple with real financial stability which would then allow them to have the real family together that they had waited years to birth and to give life to and perhaps just perhaps, a wish was worth the cost of something that she didn't want or need, just to have a future that she could commit to, believe in, participate in and fully love in.

Fragments of Betrayal, Reflections of Justice & Broken Destinies

The next few weeks for Leah went by like a whirlwind of total delight as she fine-tuned Spectrum and then started to prepare for the potential sale which loomed upon the not too distant horizon of her future which she hoped would be amazingly lucrative. Much to Leah's surprise, once she advertised the actual sale of the Spectrum prototype and system on various technological and scientific trade sites, multiple bids started to pour in from speculative buyers as if from nowhere and Leah had absolutely no idea how news of Spectrum had circulated so widely because she really hadn't advertised that much. Although Leah could have attended exhibitions to showcase the Spectrum prototype to potential buyers which might have generated a huge response, she hadn't actually done so and the commercial interest in Spectrum now greatly exceeded her initial expectations because buyers seemed to have been enticed by Spectrum's full recreational capacity and extensive range of emotional adventures.

In fact, some of the offers had been so large that Leah had been slightly seduced by the numbers and sums on offer because she could not have predicted that Spectrum and the prototype that she had designed, created and made would command such high levels of commercial interest. Since the offers had practically flown in throughout that fortnight, due to Leah's excitement, she had let Zidane know each day about every single one as they were offered to her but once the offers reached about thirty in number, she started to feel slightly unsure about which one to accept because there were just so many. Some of the offers, Leah noticed, appeared to be laced with some questionable intentions that indicated that perhaps Spectrum might be utilized for other purposes which might not be as innocent as Leah's original intentions had been when she had created the Spectrum system and so she definitely felt that she should consult Zidane before she made a final decision because that decision would ultimately affect, both their futures.

Once the sale offer process had ended which was about three weeks after it had begun at the close of business on that Friday evening, Leah began to whittle down the offers from potential buyers to a list of about ten which she felt would be in the couple's best interests. However, since the weekend was just about to step into the couple's lives, Leah decided to consult Zidane that weekend about each one of the final ten offers because it really was such a huge choice to make and since that choice would have an impact upon their shared future, she definitely wanted Zidane's input into that decision before she made it. In terms of the couple's shared years together as Leah was well aware, Zidane had always financially and emotionally supported her and his positive contributions along with his devotion to her heart had been a fundamental pillar of supportive care that had led to Spectrum's actual completion and realization and so she trusted his opinion along with his judgement which she valued very highly.

On the Saturday afternoon as the two sat on the sofa inside the lounge, Leah began to show Zidane the final ten offers that she had received and as each one flashed up on the large screen on the lounge wall, she made comments about each one and answered any questions that he asked. For at least twenty minutes their discussion focused upon the final ten buyers and the potential pros and cons of each one as Leah pointed out various aspects of each offer to him and as the couple began to embrace their moment of triumph, there was a huge smile upon Leah's face as she reveled in her moment of achievement that at one point, she had doubted that she would ever reach.

Although Zidane didn't seem to be as tremendously excited about the offers on the table or infused with the same sense of achievement that Leah felt which was obvious from the expression of quite mild excitement upon his face, in some ways Leah could understand the absence of any vigorous enthusiasm. Essentially, for the past three years Zidane had almost been like a third wheel in their relationship because of Spectrum and so Leah knew that for Zidane, the most jubilant expression on his part would probably be felt, occur and be expressed when Spectrum had finally been sold and once the capsule had been carted out of the couple's basement.

Since the financial rewards from Spectrum's sale did loom on the couple's not too distant financial horizon however, Leah hoped that Zidane would at least be able to find some comfort in those rewards and benefits because he had definitely sacrificed and worked hard enough to enjoy them along with Leah herself. This moment for Leah was essentially, the couple's moment of triumph and their moment of glory because all the sacrifices that they had made were just about to pay off, just about to materialize in reality and were just about to lubricate and furnish the couple's future with a step up from the daily hard slog that they had diligently endured for the past few years. In terms of Zidane's cautious attitude as Leah listened to his observations as they discussed each offer in more depth, she couldn't help but appreciate his sensible approach because she could see that he really had Leah's own and their best interests at heart which as usual, were his primary concern and top priority.

"Well, I guess the good news is that once you sell Spectrum Leah, it won't steal your time from me anymore." Zidane concluded as he glanced at an offer on the screen and nodded his head in thoughtful approval.

"Aren't you excited Zidane?" Leah asked. "Some of these offers are absolutely huge?"

"I'll wait until one of those buyers seals the deal with monetary funds." Zidane replied. "Then I can get excited about it."

"We'll be able to buy a bigger house now Zidane and we can have some children because we won't be under so much financial pressure." Leah gushed as she giggled and panted with excitement. "Just think, we might even be able to work a regular work week like other couples do, won't that be great?" She flicked through a couple of the offers again, displayed them side by side upon the screen and then pointed towards each one. "I mean these offers are absolutely a million light years away from our current lifestyle which means that

Spectrum is our ticket to financial freedom, so we won't be living in the cargo baggage area anymore on this flight of life." Leah pointed out triumphantly.

"We could certainly have a bigger wedding." Zidane replied as he glanced at the offers and nodded his head. "I've just about saved enough up our wedding now, so that it'll be the way we want it to be. I wanted to give you the wedding that you've always dreamed off. I was going to put some of that money down as a deposit for a bigger house but since you have all these huge offers, perhaps we could spend all the money that I've saved on our wedding instead and you can sort out the deposit for the new house, since you will be a lot richer than I am."

"Yes, that's a good idea but Zidane, this money is our money and it's for our future, so I won't be richer, we'll be richer." Leah insisted. "We did this together, this is what we sacrificed for and this is what we worked hard for, so this is what we achieved together."

"Okay." Zidane agreed.

"At long last now, we'll finally be able to move out of the dusty, grimy city and we'll be able to buy a nice house with a large garden on the outskirts in a nice peaceful area just like we planned to." Leah said as she smiled. "Now Zidane, all of our dreams really can come true."

"But are you sure some of these companies are legit?" Zidane asked. "Some of them seem to be offering such huge sums of money, do you want me to check them out a bit, I could do some corporate background checks and things?" He offered.

"Yeah that's probably a good idea." Leah agreed. "I'm not that clued up when it comes to corporate dodginess, so you probably know far more about such things than I do, since you are a technician and you have been immersed in corporate entities far more than I have for the past few years, so I'll leave that with you."

"Okay. Yes, I think you will have to be really careful Leah, the Spectrum software, framework and capsule are such a powerful combination and if that powerful tool was given to the wrong corporate hands, I can see how disastrous that might be. Some companies might utilize Spectrum for something really negative or something really destructive, so you need to consider and think about that before you make a final decision."

"You're totally right Zidane and that could definitely happen." Leah concluded. "Do you think I need to hire a lawyer about all these contractual offers and things? I'm not a legal expert, so it is a bit beyond my usual area of expertise."

Zidane nodded. "You definitely need to but don't worry, I can sort that out." He offered. "There are some really good lawyers in the legal department at Stantons and they should be able to handle this quite easily. I'll just give one of them a bit of money and ask them to give each offer a read through, after all the last thing you need is some unscrupulous company taking everything from you after all your hard work."

"True. Yes, that would be a wise thing to do." Leah agreed as she nodded her head in response. "You know, I just feel so excited Zidane, it feels like the air around me is made from happiness and as if every time I breathe in, each breath lifts my heart and mind higher up into the air. Now, after all that frustration I endured in the basement, it feels like achievement is just hanging around in the air all around me like a piece of ripe fruit that's ready to be plucked, devoured, savored, tasted and enjoyed. I remember how frustrated I could be at times but now, it's like success has stopped avoiding me, has come to visit me and has even knocked upon my front door.

"Yeah but you'd better come back down to Earth Leah." Zidane teased as he pulled her towards him affectionately. "You haven't actually sold Spectrum yet, so you'll just have to keep both your feet on the ground until you do."

"I'll try." Leah promised.

"Look, let's go out somewhere nice for dinner, you can celebrate the final completion of Spectrum and I can celebrate the return of my fiancée." Zidane teased as he stood up and then offered her his hand.

"Sure Zidane." Leah agreed as she accepted his hand and stood up.

For the remainder of that day and well into the night, Leah allowed thoughts of Spectrum and the Spectrum sale to vacate her mind as for once, she focused solely upon the couple's relationship and their time together because time for the couple had been in such short supply in recent years. Somehow, Zidane had trekked through the deserts of solitude and he had coped with the lack of attention and the usual focused devotion that Leah usually offered to his heart and she simply couldn't fault him for his loyal, faithful, tireless dedication which had been admirable because he had continued to remain steadfastly joined to her side with ribbons of love that had been stretched, knocked around, torn apart and trodden into the ground for several years.

Unlike other lovers that would perhaps have abandoned Leah at the first sign of hard work, concentrated effort and prolonged sacrifice since the couple's relationship had been quite young at the time of their graduation, Zidane had rolled up his sleeves, put his hand on the plough of effort and then had not only planted seeds of supportive care but had also tended to each one meticulously. Deep down inside Leah definitely knew, as the couple enjoyed their meal and discussed the restaurant's menu, sophisticated decor and prime city location that Zidane's sincere heart was extremely unique because the levels of love, patience, adoration, tolerance, devotion and commitment that had been offered, supplied and given to Leah's heart by his own, she had never ever felt before. Such high levels of appreciation from one heart to another could only really be felt when one heart looked at another through a lens of sincere, genuine, deeply supportive love and Leah could see that Zidane's heart definitely offered that deep depth of sincerity to her own and that he saw her through a lens of true love because joy danced through his eyes every time they whispered, spoke, laughed and touched.

Never before in Leah's entire life had she ever felt so certain about anyone else's commitment and devotion to her heart than in Zidane's arms and it was the first time that anything outside Leah's own being, except of course scientific principles, models and formula, had ever given her that stability of absolute certainty which was a huge comfort in the mass jungle of life's fluctuations. Life as Leah already knew, usually offered very little certainty and extremely risky potential returns of happiness that were not often guaranteed or ever truly realized but Zidane was ultimately, the one reliable supplier that was focused solely upon her heart that wanted to ensure that it would be full of as much happiness and love as it was possible for one person to provide.

True to Zidane's word, in the week that followed, Leah noticed that he swiftly consulted some of the lawyers at work and that by the midpoint of the week, she had not only been provided with several recommendations but also some cautious impartations of legal advice about the potential risks that a few of the offers might present. Due to the potential riches that loomed upon the horizon of Leah's life that would follow once the sale of Spectrum had been finalized and had been honored with monetary satisfaction, not just professional but also commercial achievement had hung in the air above Leah's head throughout the start of that week and so, she found it hard to contain her excitement as she participated in the sale process, analyzed the legal advice and then narrowed the final ten offers down to five. A multitude of sacrifices had been made by the couple to arrive at that point and they were now as Leah knew, on the verge of success and so she wanted to savor and enjoy every single delicious minute of that success because all their devotion, discipline, hard work and efforts would finally reward them both with not just the wedding day that they'd dreamed about and planned but also a beautiful home to live in and a luxurious financial safety net.

Once Leah had chosen the final five buyers from the list of ten that had remained, on the Wednesday evening and when Zidane returned from work, she proudly displayed them to Zidane after which point, the couple took a trip down to the basement as she encouraged Zidane to help her prepare for the actual sale itself. Since the basement had been Leah's second home for so long, it almost felt strange to Leah as the couple walked down the steps that she now no longer spent every single second that she could inside it and that huge change as she now knew, wasn't something that was going to be reversed in the near future because Spectrum was already on its way to an actual departure from the couple's lives and home. Every part of the couple's lives would change but for Leah that impact would definitely be felt the most in her own life because once she had sold Spectrum, there would a professional absence in Leah's life that would no longer be filled with the countless hours of hard work and the tireless professional dedication that she had invested into her invention and creation all of which had definitely been required to arrive at the port of success.

Upon Leah's face there was a slightly sad expression however, as she crossed the basement and walked towards the Spectrum capsule as she began to not only process the impact of those changes but also considered what might perhaps happen to her empty days once Spectrum had vacated her daily work hours in her basement lab. In some ways for Leah, it almost felt as Spectrum had motivated her to get up each day, had encouraged her to participate in life and had compelled her to work hard towards her goal but without that sense of purpose, Leah wondered for a moment if perhaps she would become lost in all the empty hours of each day.

"Do you think I would be bored with being just a housewife and mother Zidane?" Leah suddenly asked as she glanced at his face. "I mean, if I don't do anything else."

Zidane smiled. "Just a housewife and mother, those are actually two very difficult jobs and not many people male or female get either of them right. Well, if you feel there's a lack of intellectual stimulation in your life, you could always start working on another project, just a smaller project perhaps, maybe something slightly less stressful and something less brain intensive. You could perhaps do something part time for a few years, so that way you would still have something to do each day that would stimulate your mind intellectually." He suggested. "But you definitely need a rest and at least a year where you just have a break from any mental pressure and any professional stress, so I wouldn't rush into your next project but perhaps you could take that year to plan something."

"I think you could be right Zidane, a little less stress for a while might be nice." Leah agreed as she considered the couple's future thoughtfully. "I guess life will really change for us both now but we could always do different things with our time, things we have more control over, so that should be much more interesting."

"Yes, and I could perhaps even start my own consultation business which would allow me to work more flexible hours once we move." Zidane suggested as he watched her run her fingertips across the capsule. "We don't have to stop living just because we have a bit more money and if you find something else to work on that will ensure that your professional skills are kept up to date, so that you don't get scientifically rusty." He teased. "Do you think you'll miss Spectrum Leah?"

"I think I will." Leah admitted as she turned to face him. "But I know the sale of Spectrum is for the best, the best for us, the best for our future and the wisest thing to do. The alternative options would just be impractical because to maintain Spectrum ourselves would cost us millions and millions that we don't have, so I always knew that I would have to say goodbye to Spectrum one day but I guess I just thought that day would take years and years to arrive, since it was so complex to create and build Spectrum in the first place."

"Yes, unfortunately, millions in our bank account and Spectrum still living inside our basement are not mutually achievable goals and are definitely mutually exclusive results." Zidane agreed as he glanced at the capsule. "And I just have to say Spectrum, no offence but I definitely won't miss you." He admitted as he touched the capsule and grinned. "In fact, I'll even carry you out of the house myself to help you on your way and start you off on your journey to another home."

Leah released a soft giggle as she lovingly stroked the capsule once again. "Sadly Spectrum, you are worth much more to us if we sell you to someone else." She admitted. "And I'm so sorry but I just have to be practical about things, after all that is why I created you in the first place."

"Never mind Leah, I'll comfort you." Zidane reassured her as he pulled her close. "Oh, and don't worry I can fill up your evenings quite easily with lots of interesting things to do, so that you won't miss Spectrum too much."

Deep down inside, Leah knew that Spectrum's sale was the

wisest thing to do in the long term and that even though the couple had both made some huge sacrifices to realize that achievement, she could now see that Spectrum itself was the ultimate sacrifice that she would have to make, especially if she wished to salvage her relationship from the brink of a delicate breakup that now just sat a few disappointments away. In order to keep Spectrum now, Leah knew that it would simply burden the couple with a very heavy financial load in terms of the vast financial assets and finances that would be required to maintain Spectrum and to provide Spectrum's services to a market of consumers which would be a far harder load to carry and so she fully accepted that it was not a viable outcome to Spectrum's completion or even something that she should actually consider or try to aspire to.

Ultimately, the sale of Spectrum would provide the couple with the happy ending that they had worked so hard to achieve and as Leah now fully appreciated, fairy tale endings certainly weren't cheap or even easy to secure because at times her work on Spectrum had verged upon the impossible and had tied her mind up in knots of mental frustration. However, Leah had diligently climbed up that mountain of achievement and had finally managed to reach the glorious top with the supportive financial safety harnesses that Zidane had generously provided, so to try to climb up another even bigger mountain of achievement didn't really make much sense, not if she wanted to start a family with Zidane in the near future because such actions and decisions, would only place the couple under tremendous financial pressure.

"How will I know who to sell Spectrum to Zidane, I mean there are five buyers and offers left on my list but which one do you think should I choose?" Leah asked as she glanced into his eyes.

"If you want me to I can get the guys at work do some final checks over the legal documents and I'll get them to run some background checks on the businesses and people that made you those five offers before you decide and I'll even check some of them out myself." Zidane gently reassured her. "So that you don't have to worry about anything."

"Okay but I do only have about two and a half weeks left now to finalize a sale agreement." Leah mentioned. "Will that be long enough?"

"That'll have to be long enough." Zidane replied. "Don't worry, I'll make some calls tomorrow and get the ball rolling but right now, we should get ready to go out for dinner."

Leah nodded. "Thanks for all your encouragement and support Zidane." She replied as she gave the Spectrum capsule a final glance. "I really couldn't have done all this without you."

"Sure, you could have, I just helped out where I could." Zidane said as he smiled. "You are capable of great things Leah, so I just helped you find that greatness that was always inside of you."

"Still your supportive arms and loving words definitely encouraged me." Leah acknowledged.

"Let's go and get ready to eat." Zidane insisted as he took her hand.

Leah nodded.

A blanket of silence fell across the basement as the couple started to walk towards the basement steps and as Leah followed Zidane, she quietly considered just how much he had contributed towards Spectrum's creation because she felt unsure that she could have actually achieved such a huge professional goal on her own. Financially, Zidane had always supported Leah and he had made sure over the past few years that she had never suffered from the severe pains of hardship or poverty that so many of her colleagues in the scientific industry usually bore as they sought to pursue their lifetime ambitions and the actual physical manifestation of their research as they aimed to reach for the creation and completion of their inventions. Unlike the start of the couple's relationship where Leah had rescued Zidane from the brink of despair, for the past few years he had through his consistent efforts and tireless dedication, provided a crutch of loyal love that had supported Leah through some of her more dismal moments inside the basement throughout Spectrum's creation as she had wrestled with frustrations and tackled problematic situations that at times had seemed fathoms deep and so she doubted her own ability to reach that port of completion without his loyal support.

In some ways, Leah felt as the couple arrived at the foot of the basement steps and she reflected upon Zidane's commitment and devotion to their relationship that his dedication to her had almost been like the provision of a human savior in more ways than one. Not only had Leah managed to achieve some of her lifetime ambitions but she had also had a peaceful, romantic, pleasant relationship to accompany her along the way and as she glanced at Zidane's face, she quickly began to conclude that he was definitely the perfect life companion for her because his heart was definitely full of sincerity. Since Zidane had held onto Leah's hand in life, their walk-through life together had been a total joy and full off as much happy companionship, devoted affection and sincere love as she had wanted or needed as their romantic partnership and his companionship, affection and sincere love towards her had adorned their mutual attraction to each other with absolutely tons of heavenly devotion.

For a split-second Leah paused before she began to mount the steps and glanced back at the Spectrum capsule as she cast her mind back over some of the artificial, fictitious affairs that she had indulged in while inside Spectrum but as she did so, she silently vowed never to participate in such betrayals ever again. An imaginary affair could keep Leah's mind occupied for a moment but such casual flings could never replace what the couple had in reality and as far as she was concerned, had just existed in that moment in time, albeit in an artificial capacity because there had only ever been one real man in Leah's life in the romantic sense and that was definitely the very real, the very committed and the very handsome Zidane.

"Come on Leah, let's go." Zidane urged as he held her hand and then began to lead her up the steps.

"Sure." Leah agreed as she began to follow him.

Although part of Leah wondered as the couple left the basement behind how Zidane might react to her indiscretions inside the basement in his absence if he knew, she felt slightly unsure about how such discoveries would affect him because it was such a grey area of infidelity. The brief moments of experimentation that Leah had engaged in inside Spectrum, she had now simply locked away inside her heart as she'd cast each memory aside within her mind all of which she had attributed to, simply something that she had participated in purely to satisfy the walk-through test requirements of the Spectrum system.

Every single act of fictitious betrayal had been buried deep inside Leah's thoughts and in the remotest possible corners of her mind so any disclosures to Zidane had not even been considered for a single second because she had convinced herself that each simulated action had purely just occurred to ensure that Spectrum was actually ready for consumers and the market. However, as the couple stepped out into the hallway and then began to walk along it as Leah glanced at Zidane's face, she knew that if her moments of fictional passion came to light, Zidane might feel deeply hurt by her simulated actions and her total disregard for his heart.

The lounge was silent as the couple stepped into the room and as Leah cast a nervous glance up at the display screen which still displayed the final five offers upon it as she began to process the hugeness of each one, she began to wonder if perhaps a slither of artificial reality had slipped into the real world and her very real life. A wish had been made at the Fountain of Sincere Wishes by Leah and a bundle of generous offers for Spectrum had flooded in and since she hadn't given any presentations or any demonstrations of the prototype to anyone, she felt as if perhaps her magical wish that had been made in the waters of the magical fountain had perhaps been granted.

"Right, let's go and change." Zidane eagerly urged as he picked up the remote and then switched off the visual display screen. "We can worry about those final five buyers and their potential dodginess later."

"True." Leah agreed as she began to walk back towards the lounge door.

"For tonight Leah, let's just spend some quality time with us." Zidane joked. "We definitely deserve it."

"Yes, we really do." Leah agreed.

Once the rest of the week and the weekend that followed had

sprinted by and ended, almost too quickly for Leah as the next week arrived and the Monday stepped into the couple's lives, she noticed that true to his word, Zidane had already actioned his plan to assist her which seemed to be well underway. On the Monday evening, when Zidane returned from work, Leah listened to him speak as they sat in the lounge and ate dinner together and she noticed that he mentioned a legal advisor that he worked with called Neil who seemed to be eager to help. Since the legal advisor specialized in Intellectual Property, Leah definitely felt that Zidane had approached the right person because his expertise would really come in handy when it came to the issue of Spectrum's actual sale. Another positive aspect Leah felt as she listened to Zidane speak as he related his conversation with Neil to her over dinner was the fact that the legal advisor's field of expertise was well established and so Zidane felt that he would be a good person to assist.

"Oh, Neil said that aside from the buyer recommendations, background checks and legal advice that he'll have to come around on Friday to check the parameters of Spectrum and that he would help us to make sure that everything is ready for the sale." Zidane mentioned.

"Oh okay." Leah agreed. "No problem, I'll make sure I prep Spectrum by then."

When the Friday evening arrived, just as Zidane had promised Leah, he arrived home from work with Neil in tow and as the two men stepped into the couple's home with a bunch of pizza boxes and Zidane introduced Neil to Leah, Leah greeted them both with a polite nod and smile as she stepped out of the lounge.

"Come this way Neil." Zidane explained as he began to lead him along the hallway. "We keep Spectrum in the basement."

"Ah the basement." Neil joked with a grin. "The place where all great inventions are usually birthed and then kept for years in darkness and dust until the light rays of ingenuity finally strike and illuminate their fully glory."

"Well, I do try to dust my basement laboratory at least once a week Neil." Leah mentioned as she smiled and began to follow the two men along the hallway. "So hopefully, it won't be too dusty down there."

"Yes, Leah does keep her basement laboratory very clean and immaculately organized, so we should be quite safe to eat the pizza down there." Zidane agreed as he nodded.

"Well, hopefully my legal compliance checks shouldn't take too long but I do need to make sure that when Spectrum leaves your home and basement that it is in the state agreed to with these buyers." Neil advised. "It's nothing major to worry about really, I just need to iron out some of the contractual details of the sale and advise you on prep protocols to ensure that you don't breach any sale prerequisites."

"Sure." Leah agreed as she arrived at the top of the basement steps.

Approximately an hour went by as Leah showed Neil around the Spectrum prototype, capsule and system and as she gave him a tour of Spectrum, she listened to his legal advice and opinions on the five final offers as the three ate dinner and emptied the pizza boxes which were full of pizza, chicken wings and garlic bread. Most of Neil's recommendations, Leah noticed as she listened to each point that he made and enthusiastically jotted some notes down to ensure that she didn't miss anything out, seemed to predominantly revolve around system back up files, packaging and delivery of the capsule prototype and there were also some other files that had to be supplied to the buyer.

Since Leah had never sold anything to anyone before in her entire life besides some homemade fairy cakes which she had sold at a bring and buy sale once in her childhood years, she paid attention to every single word spoken by Neil as she clung onto every word and planned how she would comply with every recommendation that he made. Essentially, Spectrum's sale would be absolutely huge in terms of the monetary sums involved and so Leah definitely didn't want to screw it up because that would perhaps undo all her hard work and render the sale invalid which would then also jeopardize all the couple's plans.

Later that night and once Neil had left the couple's home, the couple discussed his visit as they prepared to rest and as they did so, Leah felt extremely grateful that Zidane had taken such a wise approach because she would never have even thought of things like background checks. When it came to legal or corporate matters, Leah was by her own admission, no expert and since she had never worked in a brisk corporate environment where such things usually mattered or happened often because she had worked predominantly in research posts, the technical legalities and those processes just hadn't been something that she had ever had to think about or participate in.

The whole visit that day from Neil however, set Leah's mind at rest throughout the remainder of that night and as the rest of the weekend slipped by, she began to relax in the knowledge that Zidane had ensured that the sale of Spectrum would be as straightforward for her as it possibly could be. In the lead up to Spectrum's sale and upon receipt of the offers from the actual interested buyers, Leah had worried at times that she might become bogged down in all the legal details which made very little sense to her and that she might possibly have swum way out of her depth but Zidane had stepped in and had supported her efforts with some professional input and that at least had saved her some nights full of stressful worries and disturbed rest.

On the Monday morning Leah decided to treat herself to an appointment at her local hair salon and so once her household chores for the day had been done, since the hairdresser that she normally saw had a vacant slot an hour before noon, she eagerly prepared to leave the house before lunch in order to attend. Since the salon wasn't situated too far away, Leah debated as she stepped out of the house whether or not to drive there because her car, a small black salon was parked just outside the house in the couple's small driveway which would offer a more comfortable alternative than the soles of her feet. Usually, Leah's car lived in the garage and the small driveway was normally occupied by Zidane's vehicle when he was at home or it would be empty when he wasn't because Leah rarely ventured out that far or very often during the week. However, since Leah had much more free time now and had popped out to one of the local stores earlier that morning, she had left her car in the driveway, a choice which now offered her the convenience of an easy ride to her appointment with minimal fuss.

Due to Leah's celebratory mood and the potential sale of Spectrum, she began to take her car keys out of her handbag as she headed towards the vehicle as just for the day, she decided to ignore the environmental concerns that she usually adhered to and kept at the forefront of her mind. A slightly lazy but totally justifiable indulgence as far as Leah was about to be enjoyed as she opened up the car door and then sat down in the driver's seat which meant that the potential pollution that her short trip would create, was an issue that just had to be momentarily pushed to one side. Sometimes, Leah did wonder when a scientist or a technological scientist would invent a mode of transport that was equally as convenient as cars but that would create less environmental damage but despite all man's strides technology wise that important invention did not seem to have happened successfully so far and for some inexplicable reason, humanity seemed to be stuck with just modern interpretations and adaptations of older forms of transport, some of which were slightly more environmentally friendly but that quite often cost an absolute fortune to run and maintain.

"In the absence of any modern convenient and affordable alternatives, I'm afraid you will just have to do." Leah whispered to herself as she started the engine.

A hand was run through Leah's hair as she began to consider how much the hairdresser would have to cut off because she hadn't been to the salon for a while and due to that lack of attention, her hair now felt like a bunch of twigs and branches that had simply been plonked on top of her head or a garden bed of flowers that was overgrown with knotty weeds. The car's engine started to purr as Leah drove it slowly out of the driveway but since she was quite early and her appointment wasn't for at least another thirty minutes, she decided to head towards and stop off at the Malley's grocery store en route which was a store run by a mature couple in their late sixties that she often visited because it stocked a huge range of groceries and quite often items that were hard to buy anywhere else or that could rarely be found on supermarket shelves.

Upon Leah's arrival at the grocery store, the owner of the store Mr. Malley who was positioned behind the cash counter, welcomed her politely as usual and his wife quickly followed suit as she walked towards the front of the store and Leah's position with a warm smile upon her face. From what Leah knew, from the couple had told her, they had owned the store since they had been in their twenties and so it was seasoned with their years of experience and retail ownership and since Mrs. Malley often baked and baked far too much for Mr. Malley's stomach to handle, sometimes Leah would even be offered some sample chunks of breads or cakes full of fruits, marzipan or vanilla essences as she shopped. Some freshly baked cakes and loaves of bread would also be on offer, positioned on stands on top of the cash counter for sale and so Leah often picked up a freshly baked cake or loaf of bread when she visited.

Although Mr. Malley seemed to be in charge because he often sat behind the cash counter and beside the cash register, Mrs. Malley definitely seemed to be the one in control which was often a source of amusement for Leah when she visited. Quite often, Leah had observed on many occasions, Mrs. Malley would often ask her husband to perform certain tasks which he never seemed to perform to her satisfaction which often result in frustrated head shakes and disappointed comments. From what Leah had sensed, he certainly he wasn't the most organized man on the face of the planet but as she watched him suddenly stand up and then flick a fly squatter at a fly which appeared to be present, she smiled as he continued to flap around armed with the fly squatter for a few more seconds which clearly indicated that he had missed the fly and was still hotly in pursuit of his buzzy target.

The aisles inside the store were slightly narrow and as Leah began to browse and walk along one of them, she noticed that as usual each shelf seemed to be packed to the brim and at times, it definitely felt as if there were too many items upon each shelf. However, Leah noticed that the shelves didn't seem to mind and seemed to stand in place without any creaks of complaint as each one participated in the couple's ambitions and displayed as much stock as it was possible to carry. Essentially, that was one of the things that Leah absolutely loved about the Malley's Mart 'O' Mart that you could walk in, browse the aisles and then leave with all kinds of items that you had never have even thought about when you'd initially planned to visit the store and so quite often, she would return home from a visit with lots of useful but even some rather strange and unusual purchases.

Once Leah's arms and basket were laden with goods which consisted of some things that she definitely needed along with some things she didn't need at all, she approached the cash register and then smiled at the couple as she placed her basket down on the ground beside her and waited to be served because by that point, there was another customer in front of her. Due to the couple's often quite comical interactions as they served customers, Leah grinned as Mr. Malley served the lady in her late fifties directly in front of her who also had a basket packed to the brim as his wife stood by the counter and micro managed his customer interactions and service provisions.

In many ways, Leah deeply admired the couple's dedication and commitment to not only each other but also to the business that they had built over the years from scratch because their harmonious unity and dedication really encouraged her. Deep down inside, Leah hoped as she continued to watch the couple that one day, she and Zidane would manage to mature together as gracefully as the Malley couple had and that they would also still be as strongly and harmoniously united in their romantic partnership as the couple seemed to be because that for Leah would definitely be a real achievement, although it would be a romantic achievement not a professional one.

Not only had the mature couple's relationship stood the test of time, Leah observed but it had weathered the many storms of life which they had survived not only as individuals but also as united allies in their union of love and that harmonious achievement, although it lacked any professional capacity, somehow seemed equally important in Leah's mind to the business that they had managed to sustain and maintain throughout those years. The couple's professional dedication to their business was also admirable in Leah's sight, although the fruits of their labor were quite simple and humble but the couple had somehow, managed to survive the many years of pressure from large corporate competitors and had managed to accommodate impulse buyers with unique and unusual product ranges and a delightful range of freshly baked cakes and breads. Somehow, Leah concluded as she waited to be served, the couple had found a way to operate and function in a highly competitive retail environment and their business which had stood strong, now crowned their union and their relationship almost like a crown of triumphant glory as it stood as a testament to their years of hard work and commitment to each other.

Just as Leah prepared to move forward however, once the other customer had paid up and left, she noticed that a sudden loud noise emanated from one of the nearby aisles which as Leah turned to face the source of that noise, appeared to originate from a woman in her mid-forties who had a small child in tow. The loud noise itself, Leah swiftly discovered had originated from the toddler and there appeared to be some kind of dispute underway which involved a desirable item that had been spotted upon one of the shelves by the child which had it seemed led to some disagreement between the two as the female toddler had attempted to negotiate and toddle her way around a parental refusal to cooperate with her wishes.

Since the cash desk was now free however, Leah quickly turned her attention back towards it as she picked up her basket and then placed it down on top of the counter as she smiled at Mr. Malley and waited to be served. Unfortunately, though as Leah waited, she noticed that as the woman strolled through the aisles and away from the desired object which remained on the shelf, the child's temper outburst rapidly started to accelerate and worsen as a full-scale temper tantrum quickly erupted. In a matter of just seconds as Leah watched, the woman swiftly became fully occupied with her struggle and the toddler's demands as the child started to rant and flounce around the shopping aisle without any reservations or any restraint at all. A much angrier negotiation from what Leah could see and hear, now appeared to be underway about what the toddler felt she was entitled to and wanted and as Leah listened to the two in silence, she began to conclude that sometimes the joys of parenthood didn't really appear to be joyful at all which was definitely something that she and Zidane would need to be prepared for and probably have to face.

"I want that." The child angrily demanded as she pointed towards the bag of candy on the shelf that she had spotted and wanted. "I want that tweetie."

"No Lauren you can't have that you've just had some sweets and too many sweets in one day isn't good for you." The frustrated mother insisted in response.

"I want that tweetie." Lauren continued to demand as she suddenly threw herself onto the floor and then started to scream.

"You can have this nutrition bar instead, it's much healthier." Her mother pleaded as she picked up a nutrition bar from a shelf nearby.

Apparently however, it rapidly transpired that the female toddler didn't want to compromise, negotiate or accept her mother's decision in any capacity at all and as Leah watched in silence, the temper outburst and toddler's demands continued to escalate into an even more rowdy temper tantrum with multiple loud screams and even some kicks in the air. The screams unfortunately grew louder and louder as Leah continued to watch the scene in frustration and she noticed that the woman's face went bright red with embarrassment as she finally reached down to the floor and the toddler's position and then attempted to moderate the toddler's reaction and actions.

Suddenly however, a sharp, short, loud slap emanated from behind the cash desk as Mr. Malley crushed the fly with the fly squatter which instantly attracted Leah's attention and as she noticed that he finally managed to exterminate the fly, an amused smile crossed her face. Rather amusingly, Leah observed, the stroppy toddler in response to the loud, sharp noise suddenly stopped mid scream and then sat up because it had been very loud and so from what Leah could see, it seemed to have penetrated the child's ears. For a few seconds, Leah noticed that the whole store virtually came to a standstill and that nothing but silence filled the aisles as the mother stared at the toddler's face and waited for the voice of reason to appear.

"Do you want the nutrition bar Lauren?" Her mother asked. "Or you can just go without anything and wait until we get home and eat lunch." She insisted as she verbally put her foot down.

"Okay." Lauren replied with a sullen nod.

Quite amusingly, Leah concluded as she watched the mother smile with relief, the screams had been silenced and the tantrum had ended due to the actions of Mr. Malley which had appeared to be quite unintentional. However, as Leah paid for her groceries and glanced at Mr. Malley's face, she couldn't help but wonder, if he had perhaps somehow, intervened when he had voluntarily delivered a short, sharp shock to the toddler's ear drums. The defeated sullen tone from the toddler had prompted Leah to smile but as she watched Mr. Malley pack up her shopping, the entire incident made her start to appreciate that children could be quite a handful and definitely required a lot of work, patience and a tremendous amount of effort.

In fact, Leah now doubted as she picked up her purchases from the counter that she would have been able to complete Spectrum in just a few years, if the couple had started to have children straight after their graduation because her work hours definitely would have been impacted by such a huge responsibility. The hours that Leah had spent in the basement would definitely have been much harder to squeeze in because children required a lot of time, devotion, attention and care which would have been very hard to balance with the full working days that Spectrum's creation and completion had actually required.

Since Leah's hair appointment was due to commence in the next five minutes, once she had collected her purchases which on this occasion included some walnuts, fresh mint leaves, a freshly baked loaf of bread and a bottle of vanilla essence, she quickly vacated the store. Most of the items had been purchased for a couple of recipes that Leah had discovered that she wanted to experiment with that weekend but an unneeded but much wanted snack bar had also been purchased just to consume before lunch simply because it looked delightful.

On Leah's way out of the store as she walked, she began to unwrap the snack bar and eat it as she nervously touched her hair which definitely looked as if it had been totally polluted and contaminated by split ends and as she stepped out of the venue, she began to head towards the hair salon which was quite close by. Unfortunately, as Leah already knew, her hair had missed out on any special treatment for at least the past nine months as she had labored to finish Spectrum and squeezed as many basement hours into each day as she possibly could and so each lock of hair now felt and looked, limp and lifeless. A hopeful wish did occupy Leah's heart and mind however, as she drew closer to the salon that the hairdresser would be able to breathe some life back into her roots which might revive some of the strands and at least make it look semi-presentable.

Another issue for Leah was her current wardrobe which now lacked any kind of appeal since it was full of items that no longer even saw a glimmer, flicker or shred of daylight due to their worn-out undesirable state. However, unlike Leah's hair renovation which she knew, would cost but not cost too much, her wardrobe interior would require much more in terms of financial input to refurbish and renovate the contents and so, she felt that such expenditure would be better indulged in, once she had sold the Spectrum prototype. Some of Leah's clothes that lived inside that wardrobe, she definitely felt now verged upon being classified as rags because she had expended all of her available resources in recent years on Spectrum to ensure that it would be complete as soon and as quickly as possible. Although that lack of expenditure on Leah's wardrobe had required some sacrifices and lots of self-discipline, she definitely felt that it had been a worthwhile one to make because Spectrum's completion as she already knew, had an impact on the couple's future and impacted upon how quickly their future dreams could be kickstarted into actual actions which would lead to the accomplishment of now realizable goals.

Once Leah had entered the salon and had been greeted and seated with a hot cup of coffee and some magazines, she prepared to spend the rest of her morning in gift of indulgence to herself which

Leah felt, from the state of her hair was long overdue and well deserved. Since the proceeds from the Spectrum prototype sale were on their way to Leah's bank account and would be there in a matter of a few week's or a month's time, she felt really quite comfortable as she waited patiently to be attended to by her usual stylist who on this occasion, she would ask to give her hair not just a trim and tidy up but also a complete hair makeover and total style renovation.

For the next hour or so Leah was pruned and tended to by the delicate hands of Slick Rick, a trendy stylist with the meanest scissors but gentlest hands that Leah had ever let near her head or hair and as she watched him work his way around her split end hair strands, she marveled at his ability to sculpture strands of perfection from total split end chaos. When Leah once again looked presentable and her hair had been washed, conditioned, treated, trimmed and cut to absolute perfection, she then left the salon and began to head home with a spring of excitement in her step because her hairstyle was so delightful that she felt that Zidane would absolutely love it.

Approximately twenty minutes later Leah arrived home but much to her surprise as she stepped through the front door and into the hallway, she could hear some male voices that appeared to emanate from the basement which confused her slightly and surprised her. An undercurrent of curiosity ran speedily through Leah's mind and veins which drove her towards the basement steps because the male voices, one of which she felt certain belonged to Zidane, clearly indicated that he was at home in the middle of a weekday and that not only was he at home but that he had also brought someone else along with him.

Just a minute or so later Leah arrived in the basement but as she stepped off the final basement step, she noticed that Zidane and Neil who were both present didn't turn to face her which confused her for a moment as she began to walk towards them. Since the basement was ultimately, Leah's laboratory territory and more of her comfort zone in the couple's home than Zidane's usual place of comfort which tended to be the sofa in the lounge, she didn't really understand why they were both present or why they appeared to be totally transfixed with the screen that clung to one of the basement walls which they both stared at and seemed to be focused fully upon.

Upon Zidane's face Leah could see that there was a stressed, uncomfortable, tense, shocked expression and as she turned to face the screen, much to her absolute horror, she suddenly realized why because she was the star of the show upon it but this particular show was more like a soft porn show than a clean-living sitcom and so she could fully understand his facial expressions. Some awful, silent seconds went by as Leah watched some seconds of offensive passionate footage on the screen as a wave of total embarrassment and shame flooded over her body and a sudden wrench of guilty vomit seemed to turn over inside her stomach due to her unfaithful antics inside Spectrum which were now on full display. Nothing but absolute shock and horror seemed to adorn Zidane's face as Leah stood completely still for a few seconds in total silence and then turned to face him as it become absolutely clear that not only had Zidane discovered Leah's simulated acts of betrayal but also prior to her return, he had actually watched some of those acts in person.

Suddenly, Zidane turned to face Leah as he seemed to notice her arrival and as he did so, she immediately began to shake her head apologetically as total dismay not only engulfed her but also penetrated her every pore because his discovery had not been expected or anticipated in any capacity at all.

"Zidane, I can explain." Leah immediately pleaded.

"Explain what Leah?" Zidane asked. "What you did when I wasn't present, why would you want or need to explain that it's perfectly obvious to everyone here?" He shook his head in disgust before he continued. "You know, we just came down here because Neil missed a checkpoint the other day that he felt was pretty important then when the system switched on, these images immediately popped up on the screen and I have to be honest, I'm glad that they did. What I've seen today has really opened my eyes to our relationship and what you really do when I'm not around."

"I'm so sorry Zidane." Leah whispered.

"I'd better go." Neil said as he stood up.

The discomfort inside the basement seemed to ooze out of every corner and then flood over Leah's being as she stood rooted to the spot and stared at Zidane as the tension between them both seemed to grow into an invisible mountain of tense hurt. In so many ways as Leah already knew, Spectrum had been Zidane's rival in that it had siphoned her love and drained her attention away from him as her invention had starved Zidane off her time but that wasn't the only issue now, because now he also knew, that Spectrum had also stolen her fidelity to his heart which was the one thing that had held them together through the past few years of hard daily slogs. Although Leah should have spent more time wrapped up in Zidane's arms, some of her evenings inside the basement she had spent not only wrapped up in her invention Spectrum but also wrapped up in the arms of fictitious strangers as he had waited patiently for her attention to return to his heart and unfortunately, Zidane had now discovered her very real, artificial betrayals which had no pleasant edges just ugly, tainted, rotten decor tinged with mould and drenched in the stench of betrayal.

"Do you need me to see you out Neil?" Zidane asked politely as he watched him walk towards the basement steps.

"No, don't worry about it Zidane, I'll be fine." Neil swiftly reassured him as he paused, faced him and then shook his head. "And everything seems to be in order now, so you should have no problems with the sale. I'll send you my final recommendations and findings by Wednesday morning, just to ensure that everything goes as smoothly as possible."

"Thanks Neil." Zidane replied as he nodded. "Yes, the deal has to be finalized by Friday, so Wednesday morning should fine."

An awkward, uncomfortable, unbreakable heavy silence suddenly seemed to rapidly fill the basement to the brim as Neil walked up the steps and then vanished from sight and as that heavy silence hung over the couple's heads for a few seconds, Leah waited for Zidane's anger to erupt. Rather uncomfortably however, Leah noticed that Zidane did not utter a single word as he remained completely silent as her heart began to internally grieve because from the expression of total heartbreak on Zidane's face, Leah doubted that her indiscretions would be forgiven. The silence between the couple on this occasion was not like the couple's usual silences in moments of sensual admiration or joyful appreciation and Leah definitely felt the ugliness of it because this silence was the ugly silence of Leah's betrayal and the awful silence of Zidane's discovery and a very bitter silence that could not deny or avoid the acknowledgement of the truth which now hung over their lives, heads, home and future like a huge, dirty, very dark black cloud.

For a few minutes more, Leah remained totally still as that bitter silence continued to linger in the air like a mouldy piece of fruit that no one wanted to pick or touch to avoid any bacteria or contamination but in some ways she almost felt relieved that the silence was there and she definitely felt scared to breach the emptiness. Somehow, the quiet stillness felt to Leah as if it protected them both from the unspoken, angry words that Zidane might perhaps say in response to her simulated actions full of heartbreak and any angry ugly insults that could be returned to her heart because of what she had done.

Just a minute or so later however, the silence was suddenly broken as Zidane shook his head and then started to pace the underground room but much to Leah's relief, no angry displays appeared as he simply released a heavy, hurt, disappointed sigh

"You know Leah, I used to feel quite envious of Spectrum and the time that you devoted to it, even though I knew, Spectrum wasn't a human being and that it could never steal you away from me." Zidane paused as he turned to face her. "But somehow now, it really feels as if it has." He admitted. "I thought that once Spectrum vacated our basement, the time and love that I'd been robbed off for the past few years would be returned to my heart but now, I don't even think that I want that time and love anymore."

"Zidane it was just a simulation, just some artificial, fictional actions, none of it was real." Leah pleaded as she shook her head. "There was no real love or any real attraction involved."

"I have to go back to work now Leah." Zidane replied as he shook his head. "This is technically my lunch break and lunch breaks don't last forever."

"I'm so sorry Zidane." Leah insisted apologetically.

"But it was more than one simulated indiscretion Leah, I saw all the images, you betrayed me more than once." Zidane mentioned. "Where did you go this morning, I told Neil you were out shopping and at a hair appointment but now can I even be sure of that anymore, was that just fiction too?"

"No, I would never Zidane." Leah tried to reassure him.

"Look Leah, once the images appeared I interrogated the core program files of Spectrum's system and I found loads of these scenes in the user memory log files, so that means that you actively and willingly participated in those simulated activities many times." Zidane explained. "When I arrived today, I mentioned to Neil that you had gone shopping and he joked that women and retail outlets were practically a marriage made in consumer heaven and that you'd be gone for a while, so he probably wouldn't see you today but now, can I even be sure that you were out doing what you said? I mean do you have other fictitious affairs that you indulge in with real individuals? When does an affair or infidelity become real to you?"

"I'm so sorry Zidane." Leah said in a hushed, apologetic tone. "I don't know how to make this right." She admitted.

"I don't think you can Leah." Zidane replied as he glanced back up at the screen and stared at it for a few seconds before he continued. "Neil said that any user memory logs had to be removed from the Spectrum system presale in a certain way to avoid any traces being left inside the system and that he'd forgotten to mention it to you the other day. So, I suggested that he should come around this lunchtime to show me where the files were and what had to be done, so that when I returned from work later this evening, I could then show you what to do with those files but instead, all I found was your betrayal of our relationship."

"This really wasn't supposed to happen." Leah whispered.

"So, what was supposed to happen Leah?" Zidane asked as he paused for a moment and faced her. "There was me thinking that we were working towards our future while you were destroying our relationship with fictional affairs. I was absolutely horrified when I saw those scenes, it just made me want to vomit and then for someone I work with to see my wife to be in that naked state with another man and more than one man, it was a huge embarrassment."

"What can I do Zidane?" Leah pleaded. "To make things right between us again?"

"I just don't know if you can Leah." Zidane explained. "A thunderbolt of reality struck me today because those scenes and your betrayals were so visual and so real. This is a very hard blow for my heart because I have always been faithful to you in every possible way that I could be and to know that the trust I placed in your hands was trashed so casually, so many times, absolutely disgusts me."

Another raunchy scene filled the screen and as Leah turned to face it then glanced at Zidane's face she could see him wince in total disgust as he watched her engage in a sexual embrace with Lament, another man and another male guide inside Spectrum. Not even a drop of comfort seemed to exist for Leah as just a few seconds later she watched Zidane shake his head and then instruct Fink to switch off the Spectrum system as he prepared to depart.

"Please Zidane." Leah pleaded as she began to follow him towards the basement steps and tried to hold onto his arm. "Please forgive me."

"Right now Leah, I really need some space because all I can feel in my stomach is the vomit from your betrayal which is churning and turning over and over at about a hundred miles an hour." Zidane said as he paused for a few seconds and pulled his arm away. "You've crushed my heart and smashed it into a thousand tiny pieces like a demolition bulldozer and that just can't be forgiven and forgotten and certainly not in a few regretful minutes. Every act of betrayal was like a blow to my heart and mind because you were so willing, how can I just forgive that? Seedy humiliation after humiliation and so many times, how can I just forget those?" He shook his head in disgust. "I can't even think about this right now, it absolutely repulses me."

Leah nodded her head. "Okay, okay you need some time, I

understand." She replied. "Just please try to forgive me Zidane, if you can find the love in your heart to do so because I do really love you." She pleaded.

"I can't make any promises to you Leah. My heart can't promise you anything right now and especially not things that I know, I really can't do. My heart can't lie to you and so I can't pretend to forgive you." Zidane admitted. "Then we would just be living another lie but this time it would be a lie from my own heart." He shook his head. "There's just no disguises or illusions in this is there? I mean, it was right in front of my face and you did these things in our home, in our basement, so it will be very hard now to get those images out of my mind."

Leah nodded.

"And to think that the person that I'd brought here to help you, became a spectator and audience to your destruction of our relationship that's another very deep hurt to carry and something else that I'll have to come to terms with." Zidane admitted. "Today I've had to swallow a very bitter pill of infidelity and it feels like a rock of pain inside my stomach, I mean I even helped to pay for Spectrum's creation and I supported you financially which means, those same supportive efforts, you basically trashed and smashed to bits. So, I can hardly even breathe right now because I feel like the air in here is suffocating me."

"What should I do Zidane?" Leah asked

"I think you need to give me some space right now Leah." Zidane insisted as he started to walk up the basement steps. "I need to escape from this painful suffocation and those bitter betrayals, so I need to be somewhere else right now, alone. I need to time to think and I need time to make the right decision."

"Okay." Leah agreed as she watched him walk up the basement steps.

"I have to go back to work in this state of brokenness." Zidane mentioned as he paused for a second at the top of the steps. "My body feels broken, it feels engulfed, immersed and weighed down by all this heartbreak, so I need some space and time to recover from what I saw today, my heart and mind need time to recover."

"I know." Leah replied as she nodded her head in sadness. "I understand."

A guilty residue seemed to line and burn the insides of Leah's heart and lungs with each breath that she took as she watched Zidane depart and the snack bar that she had eaten earlier that morning seemed to churn around inside her stomach as the scenes that she'd watched in Zidane's presence, flashed through her thoughts and the graphic imagery ran through her mind. Although Zidane had left alone, Leah felt as if a shadow of disappointment had followed him out of their basement which he had left clothed in an invisible robe of hurt, weighed down by the heavy weight of heartbreak that she had ultimately created and caused, all of which had hung from his broken frame but she felt powerless to change anything because ultimately, his broken state had arisen due to her own heartless actions.

For the remainder of that day, Leah walked around the couple's home in a state of numbness as a bundle of worried deliberations scurried through her mind as to what Zidane would do as she wondered whether the couple actually had a future at all anymore. Every part of Leah knew as she tried to remain calm and attended to the couple's evening meal which she felt unsure would actually be consumed by either party, that she had really screwed up because she had orchestrated and participated in fantasy affairs that now threatened to destroy the couple's whole relationship.

The remainder of that afternoon crawled by very slowly for Leah and it almost felt as if every second and minute wanted to torture her mind as her thoughts repeatedly wandered through her mistakes and almost drowned her mind in tearful regrets. When the evening finally arrived, Leah tried to find some comfort in the fact that she had prepared one of Zidane's favorite meals for him as his usual expected arrival time approached which was usually between seven and eight each weekday evening but as Leah waited patiently for him inside the lounge and kept her eye on the front door, Zidane did not appear or return to the couple's home.

Finally, at around ten that night, Zidane returned and as Leah watched him enter into their home and then start to walk along the hallway towards the couple's bedroom, she could see that he struggled to be in close proximity to her or anywhere near her and that there was now an aloof, hazy remoteness between them both. A grunt was offered however, as Zidane passed by the lounge door where Leah was seated on the sofa as he made his way towards their bedroom but no verbal explanations were given or offered at all and none were asked for or expected by Leah with regards to his late return from work.

Just a few minutes later Leah watched in silence as Zidane stepped into the lounge with a large holdall in his hands which was filled to the brim with his clothes and she began to process and absorb the silent implications of the holdall in his hands, his actions swiftly confirmed that his absence from the couple's home would be more permanent than just a a few hours of lateness. Due to Zidane's actions and from what Leah could sense as she continued to watch him in horrified shock, she started to accept that forgiveness would definitely not be on the menu that night and that nor would it be consumed by her heart any time soon.

"I've booked a hotel." Zidane said in a solemn voice. "I'm going to stay there for a while until I make a decision."

"Okay Zidane." Leah replied as she processed the actual implications of his words which really disappointed her. "But I did make some barbeque steak with fried mushrooms and some fresh new potatoes for dinner, can't you at least eat dinner first?" She asked as she tried to convince him to stay.

"No Leah, I think it's better that I leave now." Zidane insisted as he slung the full holdall over his left shoulder. "We can talk later, on the phone."

Deep down inside Leah knew that very much like the marinated steak that she had prepared earlier that day, Zidane's words were marinated in falsehood and simply uttered to appease her because it was highly unlikely that they would speak to each other again that day and so his promise meant very little, due to his obvious lack of desire or any willful intentions to honor it. Each word uttered by Zidane, Leah felt had simply been spoken to lubricate and usher in his escape from the couple's home which contained Leah's betrayals inside its walls, down in their basement and those betrayals which had broken his heart so much, from what she could sense, he could not face, accept or deal with in any capacity at all.

"Okay." Leah agreed as she watched him turn and walk away. "I'll call you later."

An hour later as Leah tried to consume her evening meal alone it was almost as if every lump of food stuck in her throat as she reflected upon Zidane's avoidance of her like she was a plague and although she knew she definitely wasn't, her hurtful actions seemed to have had the same affect and had killed their relationship in one foul swoop. Over the years the couple had faced many obstacles as Leah already knew but for the first time ever her own actions and fictitious betrayals had been the obstacle in their relationship and whereas usually, they had jumped over each life hurdle together, this time was very different because this obstacle had created deep divisions between their two hearts. This obstacle which Leah had created herself had created a deep divide between them both that she could not even hope to cross or attempt to build a bridge across and so all that remained were her own tearful regrets because Zidane had already walked out of her life and she felt that it was highly unlikely that he would ever return.

Soon as Leah knew, the fictional male guides that she had enjoyed inside Spectrum would depart from her life but so too had Zidane and that very high price that her heart would now have to pay, felt extremely bitter because there were no remnants of comfort or glimmers of hope inside that despair or on offer to her heart. Every part of Leah regretted what she had done because Zidane had always been such a faithful man and so very honest and his expectations of her had always been realistic and simple, yet she had failed to honor his heart and to meet the most important one. A simple expectation of fidelity as Leah knew, wasn't a hard thing to live up to but she had crashed straight through that wall of decency and not just once, several times and Zidane couldn't live with or accept her painful mistakes or her blatant disregard for his heart.

Due to Zidane's departure Leah couldn't even eat half the food on her plate and as she stood up and then carried the half empty plate towards the kitchen, her mind continued to fill up with regrets as she reminisced on all Zidane's tireless efforts and his commitment to their future. Every month Zidane had balanced the finances from his own labor and he had not just paid the household bills but had also supported most of Leah's upkeep and on top of that he had also contributed to her work on Spectrum and had even squeezed, skimmed off and saved up any additional money that he could for their wedding.

In terms of Zidane's own personal expenditure upon himself, Leah had seen with her own eyes how every transaction had been basic as he had kept his own life minimalistic and had avoided any lavish extravagances, from his basic second-hand car to his wardrobe of simple clothes that were usually purchased from the cheaper high street stores. When it came to the actual issue of what Zidane actually earnt as Leah knew, he earnt a decent amount which meant, he could certainly afford to spend much more on himself but he had been very disciplined and totally committed to Leah's heart with not just his heart and mind but also with his wallet.

Despite all Zidane's efforts however, Leah had insulted him through her own simulated actions in the least expected way and that insult had been too heavy for him to carry or to forgive, so now all she was left to stew in was Spectrum and a basement full of regrets, the very same things that she had ultimately utilized to betray Zidane's heart in the first place. Every part of Leah felt empty and totally defeated as she walked back towards the lounge and then collapsed on the sofa because she now felt that all that lay ahead for her without Zidane's devotion, was an empty future that had been vacated by hope and abandoned by love.

A romantic partnership like the one that Zidane had provided to Leah's heart as she already appreciated, was almost impossible to find and offers of romance weren't usually that sincere at the best of times and at the worst could be a total nightmare and so Leah had taken a very unromantic step backwards in life. In terms of Leah's personal love goals and life goals, she had wanted to marry Zidane and to raise a family with him but that final romantic achievement that had lain just outside the couple's romantic grasp and reach, just before it had been realized, had now been reversed and the couple's steps towards it totally erased which meant that her romantic achievements in life were now, completely null and void.

The rest of that night seemed to crawl by as only Leah's tears kept her company because although she had attempted to call Zidane a few times, he had not accepted a single call from her phone and so Leah had remained uncomfortably wrapped up in an icy cold solitude made from nothing but guilty, self-inflicted heartbreak. Later that night and once Leah had cried some more tears because she had tried to call Zidane again but he had actually switched off his phone by that point as she made her way towards the bathroom with her phone inside her hand, she tried to comfort herself as she prepared to rest but it was extremely hard and nothing seemed to quench or rebut her worries because Zidane's attitude towards her and his heart had definitely hardened and he was now, like a rock wall of total refusal.

For the first time ever that evening, Zidane had lied to Leah's face when he had said they would talk on the phone later that day but as she processed that reality, she really couldn't blame him because the imagery that he had seen in the basement had been so shockingly awful. Even if Zidane forgave Leah, she knew deep down inside herself as she stepped into the bathroom that their relationship would never be the same again because those images that he had seen of her infidelity, albeit simulated indiscretions, would stand between them like a deep crevice of hurt. Each image of betrayal would remain in Zidane's mind every time he looked at Leah's face at which point, everyone would replay inside his mind and continue to haunt his thoughts but despite that very likely negative reality, Leah still couldn't surrender to her own self defeat and yearned to try again.

Inside the bathroom it was cold, silent and dark as Leah stepped into the room and then turned on the light before she made her way towards the sink and all that seemed to be present were some lonely, scuffley echoes of solitude that accompanied her as the soles of her feet stepped onto and crossed the cold bathroom tiles. Unfortunately, the light that Leah had switched on although it made the interior of bathroom more visible, didn't seem to change much in that not even an ounce of warmth was provided to her heart as she began to process how alone she now actually was and wished for Zidane's forgiveness and return.

Suddenly however, a text message was received as Zidane finally broke his silence at almost two in the morning and as Leah neared the sink with her phone inside her hand, she paused for a moment and glanced down at it with a hopeful expression on her face as she wished for some positive words and news from Zidane's heart. Sometimes as Leah knew, a relationship could survive a physical act of infidelity but usually, such betrayals had never been visually witnessed by the person that had been betrayed and so the straws of hope that she now clutched onto inside her heart, were very short and very weak because forgiveness was such a remote possibility. The impact of the footage from Spectrum's memory log files had hit Zidane's mind like an fiery arrow of heartbreak and pierced his eyes like darts of icy betrayal and as Leah knew, those memories were irreversible and could not be tweaked, repaired or deleted from any system files but as she prepared for the worst and hoped for the best, Leah took a deep, brave breath as she glanced down at the screen of her phone.

'I'm so sorry Leah, I just can't move beyond this. The mistrust between us now would just be too much for your heart and mine and it would just tear us apart. I'll send someone round to pick up the rest of my things in a few days' time.' Zidane explained.

Upon Leah's face there was nothing but shattered heartbreak as she glanced at the words on the screen of her phone and processed the permanency of Zidane's departure as their wedding plans and future instantly flew out of her heart and out of the couple's once shared bathroom and home. Although Leah tried to disguise her disappointment because just for a moment, she had hoped, wished and even believed that perhaps the couple might spend some time apart and that after a while, Zidane would return home because he loved and missed her, his text message had swiftly confirmed that definitely that remote possibility was never going to actually happen.

In some ways, deep down inside although it broke Leah's heart, a strand of her own fabric and being appreciated Zidane's honesty because he had at least spared her from any bitter hurt that he might have felt that would perhaps have made her suffer, if he had returned to their relationship. If Zidane had said that he could forgive Leah and their relationship was resuscitated and revived, she knew that there was a huge risk that it may just be laced with a trim of pretense and some threads of false affection which he would then pretentiously have had to try and hold together in order to function within it. The fact that Zidane had not erupted in anger when he had left, had filled Leah with even more regret as she had seen nothing but hurt devastated disappointment in his eyes and although their separation had been very amicable, it still tore Leah's heart apart that forgiveness had lain a million miles away from her heart's reach.

Nothing but absolute disappointment seemed to wrap its clammy arms around Leah's body as she stood beside the bathroom sink and prepared to wash her cheeks which now stung due to the all the salty tears that she had shed. The fresh warm water however, didn't seem to help because as Leah splashed some water onto her face, she noticed that the disappointment that oozed from her pores seemed to antagonize every drop and prickle the pores of her skin which made her face sting even more. In some strange way, it almost felt to Leah as if fate and life were against her because she had worked so hard on Spectrum and Zidane had been totally devoted to their relationship and it now felt so cruel that their combined efforts had resulted in nothing but hardship and punishment to both their hearts.

Sadly, in the end, Leah had been the one that had failed Zidane's heart but in so many ways, she could not understand even for a second how that could have happened because due to her long hours in the basement if anything, she would have expected it to be more likely that Zidane would have let her down but he hadn't. The hotel room that Zidane had sought refuge in that night as Leah knew, had really been an escape for him from her side because she had seen his face before he'd left their home which had been decorated with nothing but total disgust. Even though Zidane had smiled at Leah for a split second when he had promised that they would speak on the phone later that night the pretentious, fake smile he had given had simply masked not only his disgust but also his absolute rejection which had lain unflinchingly just under the surface of his skin and inside his mind because she had seen the reality from the disgust that had dripped from his eyes.

Very devastatingly for Leah, for the first time since the couple had laid eyes on each other, Zidane could no longer stand Leah's company for a single second and she honestly couldn't blame him because she felt almost saturated in her own self-disgust. Despite that hurtful desertion just as Leah thought her day couldn't get any worse, as she glanced up at the mirror inside the bathroom, she suddenly noticed something else in that her reflection appeared to be present for just a second before it began to swiftly fade from sight then vanished from view completely which added to her worries even more.

Due to what would now be the more certain permanent absence of Zidane in Leah's life and the departure of her reflection, for the next few seconds Leah froze as she tried to process the disappearance of both because each one had slipped out of her grasp and she had felt absolutely powerless to stop the departure of either. The sudden, abrupt disappearance of Leah's reflection had definitely caught her by surprise but due to her guilty discomfort over Zidane's departure, she could hardly even focus upon it because it somehow, in the midst of her heartbreak, just didn't seem to matter.

In fact, everything that had seemed to matter that morning to Leah's mind, now seemed to have totally deserted her because the happiness from the potential sale of Spectrum had fled from her being earlier that day, due to her jaded simulated indiscretions which had now been fully exposed, uncovered and discovered. Instead of the expected Spectrum departure from Leah's life in the coming week, another very unexpected departure had interrupted that joyful moment and had instantly preceded it and replaced it with total heartbreak. Due to the raw self-inflicted wounds that now lay inside Leah's heart and mind, no self-forgiveness was on offer yet or available to her heart, nor was it a gift or a luxury that she could give to her own mind because the heartbreak still beat hard inside her heart as it pounded against her ribcage and nothing but absolute guilt seemed to flush through her veins.

A minute or so later Leah began to make her way along the hallway towards the basement as she decisively decided to delete the offensive user log memory files that had torn the couple's future into shreds of nothing in just a matter of minutes but as she walked, she began to wonder if perhaps she should have tried to defend her position. Since Zidane's discovery, Leah had not even made one single attempt to offer any kind of explanations nor had she tried to provide him with any kind of justifications for her simulated conduct and so now, she questioned herself and her own efforts as she started to walk down the basement steps.

Rather frustratingly, it now almost felt to Leah as stepped off the final basement step as if she had allowed her relationship to slip from her hands and heart because she had not even tried to fight for Zidane's heart as she had just accepted her wrongs and had allowed him to walk away from their home, their life and their future. Just for a few seconds Leah began to question her lack of action because she had not even tried to verbally fight to save the relationship that the couple had sacrificed so much for and against all odds, had tried to keep alive and deep down inside part of her began to question her own commitment to Zidane. Ultimately, the couple's relationship had collapsed due to Leah's betrayals of Zidane's heart and the fact that she had done nothing to try and save it, now filled her with even more guilty discomfort as she silently probed her own mind for answers.

Every part of Leah as she walked towards a work bench at one side of the basement, now felt weakened by her own guilty discomfort and her own failures because not only had she failed Zidane romantically but she hadn't even made any attempts to explain her wrongs as she had merely accepted his decision, his departure and then had watched him walk away. Although part of Leah wondered if her explanations would have made any difference at all to Zidane's heart or mind, a huge part of her felt that nothing she could have said would have probably changed anything because he had seemed extremely upset and his lack of interest in forgiveness had seemed absolutely unnegotiable.

From what Leah could sense, when Zidane had left that night, his decision had already been made which meant that the fate of their future had virtually been written off and sealed earlier that day and that decision had probably happened the very second that he had seen the offensive footage. Throughout the remainder of that day as Leah had wished for Zidane's forgiveness, she now realized that he had probably just spent his day in deliberations over decisions about his departure and it was unlikely that he had even considered an actual reconciliation with Leah at all which saddened her heart.

Sadly, Leah concluded as she verbally instructed Fink to activate Spectrum, she would never be given another chance to convince Zidane to stay and that path of destruction that she had walked so willingly along had not only tarnished and spoilt their relationship but it had also completely ruined the love between them both that had once been so innocent, pure and so deeply sincere. No remnants of comfort however, were now available to Leah's heart or could be found anywhere inside her mind because all that seemed to exist now, was just guilty discomfort wrapped up in total self-defeat and Zidane's text had made that heavy burden of shameful guilt even heavier because he had made it clear that a hand of forgiveness would not be offered, extended or given by his own heart.

Once Spectrum had been activated Leah began to search the memory logs for the files that she required but as she did so, she analyzed Zidane's actual departure because for the first time ever, when Zidane had left earlier that night, he had not kissed Leah's cheek or touched her hand once, not even for a split second. The split second when Zidane had offered Leah a pretentious smile that she had noticed which had crossed his face just for an instant had been full of tension, heartbreak and hurt and he had rushed out of the house straight afterwards like he could barely stand the sight of her. Not even a remote ounce of affectionate care had been offered to Leah as Zidane had distanced himself from her as quickly as he possibly could and no matter how hard she had worked on Spectrum, it now seemed absolutely meaningless because she had ultimately, lost Zidane's heart and love in the process.

Some of the offensive memory log files suddenly appeared on the large screen that clung to one of the basement walls and as Leah prepared to delete the records that had revealed her acts of betrayal, she started to accept that her walk through tests on Spectrum could have been performed just as effectively, without any of the simulated passionate interactions. In many ways, Leah appreciated Zidane's self-restraint because he so easily could have insulted her because of what she had unjustly done to his heart due to his years of sacrifice but he had retained his self-respect and his composure and had just walked away.

"I guess you're all that I have left of Zidane now Fink." Leah whispered.

Strangely and for some reason although Fink had obeyed Leah's voice commands throughout that evening and night, Leah suddenly noticed that the voice system had gone completely silent and that not a word had been uttered by the program since Zidane's final departure.

"That's of course, if you are still here." She mentioned.

For a moment Leah wondered if perhaps Zidane had deactivated the voice system in a last act of final total rejection to ensure that he would not remain in her life in any capacity at all but she felt almost certain that he hadn't because he hadn't really had time to do so that evening. In fact, on both occasions that day, even when Zidane had been down in the basement that lunchtime, Leah had been present, albeit towards the end of his basement visit and so she felt sure that she would have noticed any such actions on Zidane's part yet rather strangely, Fink's voice now definitely seemed to be absent.

"Are you still there Fink?" Leah asked as she directly questioned the lack of vocal response from the computerized system.

No vocal response however, was offered or given by Fink and as Leah began to shake her head, she quickly pushed her own question to one side as she swiftly concluded that it really didn't matter because essentially, Zidane had now left her side and so an attempt to try and hold onto the last remnants of his voice whilst it might provide a grain of comfort, wouldn't actually bring him back. The remnants of Zidane's presence in Leah's life which was what Fink now represented, would perhaps just become an ugly residue and an awful stain of pain upon Leah's heart that would painfully remind her each day of her guilty participation in Zidane's departure and so unusually for once, she decided not to fix the vocal programmable output which appeared to have suffered some kind of malfunction.

"At least we didn't lie to each other." Leah concluded as she attempted to console her sad, disappointed heart and started to delete some of the offensive memory files. "Zidane could have pretended that things were okay between us and then he might have even cheated on me at a later date to get revenge. I guess that's a small consolation and comfort really but at least, it's something."

Upon Leah's face there was a painful expression as she continued to delete the files from Spectrum's memory logs as she considered the whole issue of Fink once again much more thoughtfully because it didn't seem to make any sense to retain Zidane's voice on the program, since he would no longer be around.

"Since my relationship with Zidane has been terminated and he's been released back into the wild, single world now Fink, I should probably deactivate his voice." Leah swiftly concluded. "There's just no need for him to speak to me every day now in his absence because he won't ever return."

The guilty robe of discomfort that Leah now wore, weighed her down as she attended to Spectrum because she had definitely gone on a detour of wrong that she would never be able to correct or ever put right and she squirmed under that weight as she tried and tried to avoid her own internal discomfort. Nothing however, that Leah thought or said to herself seemed to shake off the heavy chains of pain which now hung invisibly around her neck and shoulders due to the emotional injuries and scars that she herself had caused and inflicted upon the one person that she loved so dearly. A promise to be faithful and true had been made by both members of their romantic partnership and Leah had always stuck to that promise and had fully honored it with her mind, body and heart and she had never regarded it as an obligation that she had no desire to pay, it was a price of their love that she had always paid very willingly but somehow, recently, she had strayed far from her own love and far from Zidane's heart.

Nothing but a shadow of disappointed hurt with dark edges of guilty discomfort seemed to linger all around Leah as she finished with the Spectrum files and then stood up as she prepared to leave the basement because she had become so comfortable with her life inside her wrongs that she had almost forgotten that her simulated betrayals had even happened or existed. Sadly, for Leah on this occasion however, the truth could not be avoided because Zidane had already made his position absolutely clear through his refusal to return to Leah's side and his permanent departure from their home which would definitely be permanent because he had clearly stated that even his possessions that still remained inside their home would be collected in the next few days.

"I don't think Zidane will ever come back Fink." Leah acknowledged as she glanced at the screen that clung to the basement wall and addressed the programmable voice directly but also her own inner thoughts. "He's gone forever. Very stupidly, I traded my future and our tomorrow in for a more exciting today and so now, I've lost everything and the one person in this world that really mattered the most." She mourned.

Somehow, Leah had soldiered through the night since Zidane's departure but she had been shocked by his actions and the fact that he had made hotel reservations without her and then had left their home alone, like a single person with no attachment to her heart at all. Not even an ounce of deceit had been offered to Leah or her heart which meant that Zidane had harbored absolutely no wishes or desires to play 'happy couples' in a pretentious display which might perhaps delay their separation slightly or by even a few minutes. An immediate, abrupt termination of their romantic relationship had occurred that day and as Leah walked towards the basement steps and commanded Fink to shut the Spectrum system down, she silently accepted that Zidane had at least spared her from any emotional fallout.

Just before Leah started to walk up the basement steps a final glance was cast around the underground room which was essentially Leah's makeshift laboratory and as she glanced at its interior, she began to reminisce upon some of the happy times that the couple had shared when they had first moved into their home. Every inch of the basement had been cleared out, painted and cleaned from top to bottom by the couple and Zidane had helped Leah to prepare the underground area for her work on Spectrum with a tremendous amount of supportive efforts as he had spent every minute of his weekends and evenings upon the renovations required until her laboratory had been ready to work in.

A heavy sigh managed to escape from Leah's lips as she began to walk up the steps and as she left the basement, she reflected even further back to the start of the couple's relationship when Leah had almost been like a human savior to Zidane's heart and had provided him with a consistent supply of both comfort and joy. In a strange turn of events and harsh twist of fate however, Leah had now become the root cause of Zidane's pain not the main source of joy to his heart that she had once been and instead of love, Leah now represented heartbreak, instead of hope, she was now a symbol of despair and instead of a beautiful future, now all the two had was an ugly recent history tarnished by Leah's own hands, actions, mind and creation.

Some of the painful debris from Leah's simulated actions and Zidane's subsequent departure, Leah knew as stepped back into the hallway, would remain inside her heart and mind for a very long time which had stemmed from her own simulated acts of unfaithfulness and the betrayal of Zidane's heart because he would never ever forgive her. Honesty had always been one Zidane's strengths and it was one of his personal attributes that Leah absolutely loved but, in this instance, that honesty it now appeared had become a shield to his own heart that sought to protect him from Leah's betrayals and her false pretention which had inflicted severe damage upon his heart and there would be no return from that dark, dismal, cold, lonely place of hurt for either of them. From what Leah had seen from Zidane's actions and the emotions written across his face that evening, her presence now created intense discomfort inside him, instead of the joy that she had once invoked and there appeared to be not even a tiny remnant of love for her left inside Zidane's heart, or even a drop of forgiveness.

The lounge felt bare and cold as Leah stepped inside the room and it no longer seemed to offer her even a glimmer of comfort because Zidane's usual spot on the sofa remained empty and vacant and as she walked towards the sofa her heart mourned its empty state. In a sad, awful turn of events a hotel had now become a refuge for Zidane instead of the couple's own home and a place to hide from Leah's painful arrows of betrayal which deeply saddened her heart because Zidane really had been her first real love and her only true love so far in life. For Leah there had never been a 'Plan B' just a 'Plan Zidane' but his departure that day as she already knew, although it had just lasted for a few minutes, would haunt her for years with guilty shadows of self-blame, none of which would be pleasant or comfortable to live with.

Once Leah arrived in front of the sofa as she sat down upon it, she began to consider whether she should actually move home since Zidane would never return and every single room inside it, now just reminded her of his departure and her betrayals. In terms of the house that the couple had shared which would now become Leah's sole financial responsibility, it was rather expensive for Leah to pay for alone and since she felt uncertain as to when the money from the sale of Spectrum would actually land in her pockets, purse and bank account, it seemed to be the most logical thing to do. However, as Leah sat back and glanced up at the large, wafer thin screen of the entertainment center which clung to one of the lounge walls, her thoughts and mind were suddenly interrupted as she noticed that one of the sexual, sensual, passionately offensive scenes appeared to be displayed upon it which didn't seem to make any logical sense because she had just erased all the offensive memory files.

For the next few seconds Leah absolutely froze as she watched the sensual, sexual scene play out on the screen and as it did so, she wondered how that was even possible because she had deleted every single file of the sensual kind from the memory logs of Spectrum before she had left the basement. Not one single offensive file from what Leah could recall had been left on the Spectrum system when she had left the basement and no files had been left open or in play mode yet somehow, now some of those offensive scenes filled the whole screen along with some of the sensual, seductive interactions that had shattered Zidane's heart into a thousand little pieces in the first place.

Another couple of shocked minutes went by as Leah continued to watch the scene in horrified silence before she stood up as she prepared to head back down to the basement so that she could switch off the scenes and delete any files that still remained inside the Spectrum system. Although Leah had been very thorough, she swiftly assumed that she must have missed some of the memory log files that contained those scenes and that perhaps she had left something on play mode accidentally when she had left the basement and since her mind had been distracted by Zidane's departure most of that day, it did seem like a remote but plausible possibility.

"Zidane's gone, my reflection's gone but these files are still here." Leah whispered to herself in frustration as she stared at the screen for a few seconds and then shook her head. "How can that be?"

No answers appeared however, as all that greeted Leah was a few muffled noises from the scene on the screen and as she fully resigned herself to the fact that none would be offered, she began to make her way back towards the basement. Just a couple of minutes later Leah arrived back inside the basement and as she prepared to command Fink to reactivate the Spectrum system, she noticed that it was already on and that the images that had filled the screen inside the lounge also now appeared to fill the screen inside the basement. Despite that rather strange occurrence however, Leah fully committed herself to the removal of all of the offensive files as she sat down on a chair beside one of her work benches and then began to check the memory log folders once again.

"This time I have to be even more thorough." Leah admitted to herself as she began to browse the system files. "So, this time, I'll delete all the memory log files just to make sure."

Quite strangely however, no matter how hard Leah searched and interrogated the Spectrum system as she deleted some of the memory log files, she could not find the offensive file in question which definitely frustrated her as she watched the intimate scene between Ravid and herself play out on the screen. For approximately the next whole hour, Leah continued to search high and low inside the system architecture of the Spectrum system which she had created herself because the appearance of the footage had definitely disturbed her mind but unfortunately, the file was nowhere to be seen. At the end of that hour of absolute frustration, Leah finally surrendered to total defeat as she accepted that due to the dramatic events of the day which had worn her out and the time because it was now actually very late and almost four in the morning, she was really far too tired to find anything.

Just a second or two later Leah stood up and then began to walk back towards the basement steps and as she commanded Fink to shut the Spectrum system down, the basement suddenly went very dark and totally silent however, once again there was no actual vocal response from Fink. Due to the silence that now filled the basement, the late hour and because Leah was totally alone inside the house, she suddenly began to feel quite uncomfortable and so, she rushed up the steps that led to the hallway as quickly as she could after which point, she started to rush along it.

When Leah arrived outside the open bathroom door however, she paused for a moment and then stepped inside the room so that she could prepare herself for the remainder of the night ahead which didn't hold the promise of much sleep due to the chaotic events of that day but since it was late as Leah knew, it seemed like a sensible thing to do. Once again as Leah walked towards the sink however, she noticed that her reflection was absent and was still nowhere to be seen which definitely worried and disturbed her because it reminded her of Zidane's absence because both permanent vacancies would not be restored to their rightful places and owners from what Leah could sense, anytime in the near future. Due to Leah's upset and the absence of her reflection, she quickly surrendered to total defeat as she turned and then rushed out of the bathroom just a few seconds later as a fresh set of tears started to stream down her cheeks and wet her skin with the guilty, salty remnants of her own sexually offensive conduct.

Less than a minute later Leah arrived inside what had once been the couple's bedroom but it felt like a far less glorious room now, since it could no longer actually boast of that admirable title because it would never be occupied by both members of Leah's now past romantic partnership ever again. Instead, in the space of that single day, the couple's bedroom had simply become Leah's own bedroom and as she sank down onto bed full of regretful shame, she began to shake her head in total dismay because that painful reality contained no simulated joys, polite pleasantries or any real happiness.

While Leah had been fully occupied and focused upon building the couple's future and Spectrum downstairs in the basement, her relationship with Zidane on the ground floor of the couple's home had literally crumbled and was now it appeared, absolutely beyond repair. Although Leah had loved and even still loved Zidane from the deepest depths of her heart, unfortunately and sadly that love had not provided her with an exemption from her own errors or an exclusion clause from her own human nature which had definitely failed her and so, she suddenly began to question how shallow her own emotional depths of love for Zidane's heart had really been.

In the space of just one day the mask of betrayal that Leah had worn as she had dabbled in sensual, passionate, artificial adventures had now been fully stripped away and her mistakes had cost her absolutely everything that she truly cared about because now, the couple's future no longer actually existed. The sincere intentions that Leah had always tried to sustain throughout her relationship with Zidane had not immunized or exempted her from her own fallible, imperfect human tendencies which definitely seemed to be insufficient and that was something that Leah knew, she was totally responsible for herself which made it even more bitter and painful to accept.

"I just don't know how this could have happened." Leah whispered to herself as she sobbed and shook her head. "How could I have betrayed Zidane that way? How could I have become so lost in Spectrum that I betrayed my own heart?" She mourned as she glanced down at her hands and continued to sob. "How could I do that to myself? I destroyed our future with my own two hands."

Every part of Leah knew as she glanced around the empty bedroom and at the empty bed that she was still seated upon that Zidane and their romantic partnership had been the one luxury in life that her heart had been able to easily afford because Zidane had given his own heart to her so sincerely, so willingly and so generously. In every possible area of the couple's romantic partnership as Leah knew, there had been an abundance of romantic riches and the wealthy joys from their romantic companionship which had stemmed from their mutual appreciation of each other's hearts had grown from their mutual respect for each other and those wealthy romantic joys had regularly overflowed as they had meandered through each day of life together. However, in the end, Leah had actually been the one that had unromantically failed them both not Zidane and it had been nothing to do with her professional successes or failures but rather due to her own personal infidelity and a lack of respect for Zidane's heart and emotions.

Although Leah's hands were empty as she glanced down at her palms, each one felt heavy from the shame, blame and guilty discomfort that now seemed to line every inch of her skin. The future that Leah had wanted, sought after and had worked so hard to build had been totally destroyed by her own two imperfect, human hands and the weight of blame which now bore down upon her heart and shoulders, felt almost too heavy for her to stand up with and absolutely impossible to carry around because the chains of her own guilt would not and could not set her free. An abundance of time now sat in the palm of Leah's hands that Zidane had often pleaded for which she still wanted to lavish upon his mind, body and heart but heartbreakingly for Leah, he no longer even wanted a second of her love, affection, attention, passion or time.

"In just one short day, the future ran out on me and when it disappeared, it took Zidane with it." Leah acknowledged as she picked up a small circular mirror from the top of a bedside cabinet beside the bed and then stood up. She sobbed a few more times and then began to walk back towards the bathroom as she carried the small mirror inside one of her hands. "And I don't even have my own reflection anymore, so the future probably took that with it too when it left."

Once Leah arrived inside the bathroom, she swiftly instructed Fink to switch on the lights which once again happened almost instantly and as soon as her verbal commands had been spoken, yet once again no verbal response was returned from Fink as that event occurred. For the next few seconds Leah just stood in front of the mirror and stared at it even though her reflection was still absent as she began to process and accept that she had ruined her whole relationship and that it was doubtful that she would ever find anyone again to spend the rest of her life with that would love her as much as Zidane had. No matter how hard however, Leah analyzed what had happened that day every part of the awful truth felt extremely uncomfortable for her to now live and reside in as her skin crawled with absolute self-disgust because in every way, her own conduct now seemed totally illogical and extremely self-destructive because Zidane had always been good to her heart and good for her life in every way that he possibly could have been.

In one sharp downward turn of reality that day, Leah's life had totally deviated from the almost formulaic romantic bliss and happiness that Zidane and she had both totally subscribed and fully committed their hearts to and her departure from that romantic bliss didn't make even a scrap of sense because she had ruined their relationship herself. The commitment and the sacrifices that the couple had diligently both made so consistently as Leah knew, should have resulted in a beautiful home, a pleasant marriage and a wonderful family not a deep plunge into an immersive closeup relationship with the deep waves of heartbreak, pain and hurt that she had taken a hard dive into, some remnants of which might not ever actually leave her heart due to her own self-inflicted loss.

Upon Leah's face there was a sad expression of dismay as she pulled some tissue paper from the roll by the toilet, tore it off and then sat down on the edge of the bath and began to cry again because that day, she had practically lost her whole world. No matter how many tears Leah cried however, nothing seemed to make her feel any better or less guilty about her own involvement in the collapse and destruction of her romantic partnership with Zidane. For a few seconds Leah tried to nurse her own heart and to retrieve it from its broken state but as she brushed the tissue against her cheeks, the small mirror slipped from her hands and then smashed against the tiled bathroom floor where it shattered into a multitude of tiny pieces.

A few nervous seconds went by as Leah glanced down at the broken shards of mirrored glass and her bare feet which suddenly presented her with a hazard and an element of danger because if one of those shards damaged one of her bare feet and got stuck in her skin that would definitely make a horrible day even more miserable and much more painful. Despite Leah's broken state however, she began to pick up some of the pieces as she fully committed herself to an immediate cleanup of the mess that she had ultimately created and tried to avoid any unnecessary movements which might jeopardize the safety of her feet. Another few minutes slipped by as Leah diligently picked up each large broken fragment from the ground and as she glanced at some of the broken mirror pieces as she retrieved each sizable and easily reachable piece, she could see that her reflection was still absent and nowhere to be seen.

After Leah had retrieved a handful of broken mirrored fragments, she leant towards the bin that sat under the sink and then tipped the broken pieces of the mirror into it but as she did so, she somehow cut her hand on one of the shards which immediately created a small gash on one side of her hand. Due to the sudden outpour of blood which instantly began to flow from the fresh wound, Leah quickly stood up and then reached for some more tissue paper which she then utilized as a kind of makeshift bandage as she wrapped it quite tightly around her hand and attempted to stop the flow of blood.

Just a second or two later Leah heard some noises that seemed to originate from the basement and as she listened carefully to those noises in silence, her curiosity urged her to leave the bathroom to investigate where those sounds actually originated from. However, as Leah began to make her way out of the bathroom, she resigned herself to the reality that sleep was still a destination that she would not be able to reach for at least another hour that night. Although Leah was now alone inside the house, she tried to dig deep within herself to find some remnants of courage because usually, if anything strange happened late at night, Zidane would be around and he would always definitely assist, yet for the first time ever Leah now had to face a strange occurrence alone which definitely made her feel slightly nervous.

Very strangely that day, a few unusual incidents had occurred which Leah suddenly started to question as she began to make her way to the basement like the sudden appearance of the sensual scene on the screen inside the lounge, the offensive footage that Zidane had mentioned had just opened up and then started to play and the disappearance of her reflection but as yet she had absolutely no explanations for any of it. Upon Leah's face there was a puzzled expression as a few minutes later she stepped off the last basement step and then crossed the room because the screen once again had a scene upon it but this scene, Leah noticed as she drew closer to it, did appear to be far less sensual in nature.

Much to Leah's surprise as she neared the screen and then stood totally still, from what she could see the footage in this instance appeared to be from her visit to the Fountain of Sincere Wishes because the golden rocky fountain, Bearciple and herself, albeit a simulated version of herself, were clearly displayed upon the screen directly in front of her. Since Leah's emotional trip to the Bay of Wrath inside Spectrum had been her last emotional journey and visit beside some tweak checks which rarely involved more than a few seconds of interaction with the Spectrum system, she definitely remembered every aspect of it as she began to watch and listen to the footage which was certainly far less offensive in nature than any of the previous scenes she seen that day.

The rocky, golden water fountain gurgled away in the background as Leah's simulated figure sat on the rocky edges of it and as she watched herself run her fingers through the golden drops, Leah smiled a tense smile as she instantly remembered how deliciously fresh the golden drops had felt. For a couple of minutes, the two simulated figures held a discussion as Leah's simulated form asked Bearciple some questions about her wish and as Leah watched herself on the screen, she stood completely still as she listened to her discussion with the humabear and searched every question, word and answer for any possible relevance or any deeper significance.

"Will this wish cost me anything Bearciple?" Leah's simulated image asked him as she glanced at his face suspiciously. "I mean, I've already lost my reflection today, so I really don't know if I can afford to lose anything else."

"Maybe." Bearciple then replied. "Sometimes wishes do cost us something." He clarified once again. "But usually Leah, wishes only cost you something that you don't really want or need."

"What do you mean?" Leah's simulation asked. "What could I possibly possess that I might not want or need?"

"It's just a universal law of nature Leah, when something is given, something is also usually, if not always, taken away in return." Bearciple mentioned. "But I don't make the rules, so I can't predict how those rules will apply to any individual." He acknowledged as he shrugged.

"Hmm, what could this wish cost me?" Leah considered thoughtfully. "What do you think Bearciple?"

"A wish might not cost you that much really, perhaps just a thought, a desire or something that you don't utilize in life or fully appreciate the presence off and perhaps never will." Bearciple replied. "Because someone else will perhaps be wishing for the things that you don't want or need and the things that you don't appreciate or use." He continued. "It's a highly logical, very diplomatic system really. Something that you don't need, want, desire or appreciate, someone else will."

Suddenly, a landslide of guilty realization seemed to land upon Leah's head and jump into her thoughts as she began to process the scene that she had just watched and Bearciple's comments which had ultimately, been generated by a product of her own creation which now pierced her heart like a very sharp dart full of painful truths. The price of Leah's wish it now appeared had been Zidane, the person in her life that she had not fully appreciated and perhaps never would that someone else would definitely want and treasure and though it tore Leah's heart in two, she could not actually dispute it because that truth was totally undeniable and absolutely unavoidable.

When Leah had made her wish at the Fountain of Sincere Wishes, deep down inside herself, she had known at the time that it should have been a repair wish that sought forgiveness for her wrongs against Zidane's heart. Once again however, Zidane's heart had been pushed to one side and taken for granted as Leah had placed material possessions above their romantic partnership and the wish that she should have made about the things that she had done wrong to him behind his back hadn't been made which any sincere wisher and sincere hearted person would definitely have done. Ultimately, Leah had been left that day with her own wish and the material possession that she had invested most of her time, attention and care into and her wish had determined what she had cared most about in the world and that certainly hadn't been Zidane.

Somehow, it now appeared that Leah's own creation had judged her heart and then Spectrum had taken something away from her life that it felt, she did not fully appreciate or never would and that painful reality was definitely not a simulation because it was now, Leah's very real reality. From deep inside Leah's being she mourned as she commanded Fink to shut the Spectrum system down and as she began to process and accept that now, she would have to cope with and find a way to live with what had happened to her, due to her own human failures, a residue of bitterness seemed to line Leah's tongue and turn her stomach inside out. Not only had

Zidane had to swallow a bitter pill that day when he had discovered Leah's betrayals but now Leah also had to swallow huge stone of regretful guilt herself which seemed to stick in her throat as she silently accepted that her own creation had in the end, become her whole life and squeezed Zidane out of it. Nothing had been given to Zidane's heart that should have been when Leah had made her wish and it had instead been given to Spectrum and her creation had not only devoured and swallowed up her relationship with Zidane but he had also been left behind and out in the cold.

Unlike Leah, Zidane had always kept his professional aspirations fully aligned with their relationship and his heart tied to Leah's side every step of the way and he had always given Leah precedence over everything else around them both but her failure to do so, had now resulted in a severe loss to her heart. In a regretful twist of fate Leah's own simulated actions which stemmed from her mind and heart, it transpired had been judged by her own creation and that judgement had now spilled out into reality and ultimately, cost her everything in life that she had ever wanted, cared about and wished for because her own actions had failed the tests of sincerity inside Spectrum that she had created herself.

The next morning at about noon, when Leah finally tumbled out of bed after a restless night as she made her way towards the basement, she prepared to say goodbye to her invention which she still had to prep for the sale which now loomed upon the near horizon of her life. Every step that Leah took however, felt heavy and uncomfortable as her mind and body felt weighed down with guilty hurt and sadness because in her mind, Zidane had been the only man that she had ever felt that she would spend the entire remainder of her human life with and since the couple's plans now lay in the garbage can of falsehood which had been filled to the brim with the trash made from Leah's own unfaithful simulated actions and her betrayals, she couldn't help but mourn.

A basic breakfast of cereal was slowly prepared as Leah began to mull thoughtfully over the years that it had taken her to actually create and build Spectrum which truly had been a labor of love and an act of intense devotion to both Zidane's heart and her own.

Since Leah had started her work on Spectrum inside the basement, she had faithfully honored Zidane's financial contributions, his hard work and his tireless support as she had looked after their home and had cooked him a delicious meal each day in an attempt to relieve his tiredness when he returned from work but now a dirty spillage of unfaithful pollution had contaminated her once honorable intentions and their relationship. Regretfully and sadly, Leah's deception and betrayals which had now been fully exposed to Zidane by her own creation, had definitely been deemed an unacceptable accompaniment to his usual dietary intake which had sought only a basic menu of love, care, honesty and fidelity without any nasty, bitter side portions of heartbreak.

Despite the gloomy mood that emanated from Leah's heart and mind that seemed to saturate the air inside the kitchen, Leah hoped that at least the sale of Spectrum would be straightforward as she started to consume a mouthful of the cereal but struggled to eat anything due to her lack of appetite. The cereal bowl was quickly placed inside the sink and then swiftly abandoned as Leah prepared to head down towards the basement, so that she could make the final preparations for Spectrum's sale and departure which irrespective of Zidane's departure from Leah's life the previous day, as she already knew, still definitely had to be made but as she walked along the hallway, she considered her final choice as she hoped that Spectrum's sale would at least be straightforward because now, she actually wanted Spectrum out of her home.

In the end Leah had chosen a huge corporate tech giant called Deeper Immersion Inc. as the buyer for Spectrum because after all the legal advice that she had been given, the company had seemed to be the most closely aligned to Spectrum's main objectives and purpose, since it offered technological recreational provisions to consumers. From what Leah had read on the documents that they had sent to her which had contained their generous offer, it appeared that the corporate entity's main intentions were to replicate Spectrum's various components like the capsule and that they would also provide core program features centrally via technological programs and software connections which would allow Spectrum to operate and function in order to serve the needs of a mass consumer market. Although there had been several buyers that had appealed to Leah commercially, her final choice had been made in the end due to the fact that the company specialized in the provision of deeper virtual experiences for consumers and their services promised to enhance consumer leisure time in a way that was beneficial to them and so Leah felt that Spectrum would not only fully align with their objectives but also fully deliver on those corporate promises and that Spectrum would fit into their brand extremely well.

Unfortunately however, as Leah glanced at the Spectrum capsule and sadly shook her head, Zidane would not be around to share or participate in Leah's moment of glory which would now be tainted by her own dark deeds and decorated with her guilt but as she stepped off the final basement step and then began to walk towards the capsule, Leah couldn't help but wonder why her own creation had now seemingly turned against her. Deep within Leah's heart and mind, she wanted some kind of answers and as she glanced at the Spectrum capsule, she felt that the only way she would ever get those answers would perhaps be if she was brave enough to venture into the Spectrum capsule again before Spectrum left the basement and her now solitary home because then those answers could never be sought ever again. Inside Leah's throat there was a nervous lump as she neared the Spectrum capsule and then came to a standstill beside it because her invention had already destroyed her relationship with Zidane and had already cost her so much.

"Even though Zidane is fully entitled to my guilt, he doesn't seem to want it, or me." Leah mourned as she ran her finger across the smooth, transparent capsule surface. "We were so close to having the perfect life together but now, we don't even have a life together."

A definite temptation lingered in Leah's mind as she stared thoughtfully at the Spectrum capsule for a few minutes and then instructed Fink to open it up because although she understood the moral judgement that had taken place, she did not understand why it had happened in the first place since Spectrum operated from programs that she had essentially, written herself. Everything that Leah had ever wanted Spectrum to be, it indeed was because every desired feature was present in the finished prototype which she ultimately controlled and that complex system architecture had been created by her own mind and fingertips yet something it seemed inside Spectrum, she concluded as she watched the capsule silently open up, had taken on a life of its own. Something, had deviated from Leah's expectations and had functioned in a manner that was highly unusual and although it wasn't yet clear to her mind or thoughts what that something was because it seemed highly strange, Spectrum was now capable of its own logic thought and subsequent actions.

Although Spectrum had cost Leah almost everything in life that she held dear, she glanced at the now open capsule and then released a sad sigh as she began to mount the steps and slipped into the capsule's interior because she just couldn't leave that uncomfortable issue to rest or accept its current state which in her mind, was beyond belief because it felt so hard, so cold and so hostile towards her own life. Some of Leah's artificial, fictitious actions had somehow, slipped into reality and her own creation had ultimately betrayed her just like she had betrayed Zidane's heart and that outcome just felt so unacceptable and inexplicable to her that she just needed some kind of answer or explanation as to why that had occurred. Another worry however, occupied Leah's mind as she lay down inside the capsule and that was exactly how that judgement would now impact upon her life in terms of the future and if that judgement over her life, heart and mind would continue because she now feared any future reoccurrences.

No answers however, greeted Leah's mind and so as she commanded Fink to close the Spectrum capsule, she decided to activate the random emotional journey option because in this instance, she wanted to see if Spectrum would reveal more to her mind about the events that had taken place. The sleeping gas began to circulate inside the capsule and as Leah closed her eyes and began to drift off, she just hoped that this trip to Spectrum would not cost her anything else although as Leah already knew, now that she had lost Zidane there really wasn't much else of any real value to her life, mind of heart to take.

When Leah reawoke she found herself strewn across the ground inside the Fearful Forest once again and as she stood up, brushed herself off and then began to walk cautiously and carefully through the foliage, she glanced up at the nearby tree branches as she walked, just in case any hybrid creatures decided to put in an unexpected appearance. Just a few seconds later and quite unexpectedly, the ground caved in under Leah's feet as she walked and as it did so, she slipped down into the ground but this time, quite strangely, she landed in the same sea that she had visited in her last emotional adventure during her visit to the Bay of Wrath when she had faced the Mirror of Trials. The second visit to the sea felt, seemed and looked very different for Leah however, in that there were no other people around and there appeared to be no debris from the ship that had sunk and so she felt slightly nervous as she attempted to keep herself afloat and tried to tread water.

Suddenly, the Mirror of Trials appeared around the seas and above the surface of the icy cold water and as Leah glanced around her, she could see that the mirrored, reflective surface grew and grew until it surrounded her in every direction that she could face and then started to close in on her until it was almost like a circular dome shaped cave that surrounded her position. Some tender moments from the couple's relationship rapidly started to appear on the reflective surfaces all around Leah and as she watched each scene play and listened to each conversation that occurred, she began to reminisce on some of the happier times that the couple had shared.

One scene in particular made Leah smile which had occurred one night after the couple had eaten dinner inside the lounge, when she had teased Zidane both seductively and playfully as she had encouraged him to participate in a night of passion. Sadly, in recent times, as Leah had become more and more involved with Spectrum those days and nights which had been full of romantic efforts had long vanished and she definitely knew, there was no one else to really blame but herself.

"Let's go to bed Zidane." Leah's image said as she seductively tugged on his arm and encouraged him to join her. "I bought some special purchases today and I wanted you to give them a quality control inspection to see if my software aligns with your hardware components."

Upon Zidane's face there was a tired but delighted grin as Leah watched him stand up and instantly comply with her request and she shook her head as she shivered in the icy coldness of the waves because the dark shadow of betrayal that now hung over her heart and their once pure love haunted and tormented her thoughts. A second or two later as Leah watched the couple walk towards the door of the lounge, the scene started to fade from sight and another scene rapidly replaced it but she swiftly noticed that this scene was very different because in this scene there was something important absent and that important something or someone was Leah herself.

From what Leah could see, it appeared to be the previous night and around the time that Zidane had returned to the couple's home, packed his belongings and then had left because he was in the couple's bedroom all alone with his holdall inside his hands. For a few seconds Leah held her breath as she watched Zidane pick up a photo in a silver photo frame which contained a photo of the couple that usually sat upon one of the beside cabinets beside their bed and then stared at it with a heartbroken expression upon his face as he ran his finger across it. Just a few seconds later Leah watched Zidane put the photo back down as he released a heartbroken sad sigh.

"A sentimental token that now, is nothing but a symbol of total and utter heartbreak." Zidane whispered to himself. "Just a painful reminder of the sad truths that I cannot avoid or ignore. All I have left now Leah, are just some beautiful worthless memories that have lost all their value and meaning because they can no longer be treasured. Each one is marred by the ugly remnants of a relationship that I can no longer believe in or participate in because we were just a love that meant nothing to your heart, wrapped up in betrayal and lies. You stamped on my heart, crushed it and then ground it into the ground and I can't find it anymore because you buried it so deeply in all that horrible dirt."

The holdall was picked up from the bed before Zidane strode towards the wardrobe as he prepared to fill it with his clothes and as Leah watched Zidane, she began to cry because he looked so totally alone in his private heartbreak and she couldn't even comfort him since ultimately, she had caused every ounce of pain that he had felt.

"It feels like acid has been dripped all over my body Leah and the worst part is that you did this to me yourself, you, not someone else, just you." Zidane whispered to himself as he packed some items into the holdall and then shook his head. He filled the holdall before he closed it and then he walked back towards the photo and just stared at it. "How do you expect me to live in a house Leah that you paid for from your betrayals of my heart?"

Some tears trickled down Leah's face and then dropped into the water that surrounded her and as she glanced at the waves inside the mirrored enclosure, she shook her head as her salty tears mingled with the icy cold waves and instantly vanished from sight. No comfort seemed to exist however, as Leah glanced back up at the mirrored circular wall that surrounded her and then continued to watch Zidane because all that surrounded her simulated form, was just cold, empty drops of water that saturated the pores of her body with their icy cold sadness but as each chilly wave lapped against her neck, she tried to keep herself afloat as she regretfully absorbed the pain that she had inflicted upon Zidane's heart. Nothing seemed to be present in Zidane's eyes but a cold, sad emptiness Leah noticed as she glanced at his face and tried to search for the usual glimmers of love that were normally present whenever he was around her person and inside the couple's home but no signs of any affection could be found.

"I really screwed up Zidane." Leah admitted to herself as she continued to cry. "And now another woman will be given a chance to enjoy the love that I've lost and that we should have shared for the rest of our lives, another person will be given a chance to appreciate you and they will be given a chance to love you because

I failed to love you properly. I had it all and I lost it all, you, me, us and our future. My wish definitely had a price and my wish cost me what I did not include in it because my wish didn't include you. Maybe you do deserve someone better than me Zidane and maybe, I don't really deserve you because you didn't betray me, I betrayed you and you, you would have included me in any wish that you had made about our future and that I definitely know."

The look on Zidane's face as Leah watched him walk out of their bedroom broke her heart because their relationship had ended and their future had become obsolete in one short, ugly paragraph of life, not even a chapter but just a few short horrible sentences full of hurt, strung together with nothing but a few scribbly notes of heartbreak and written in letters with fonts of pain. Although Leah wanted to be strong and wanted to keep herself afloat as she watched Zidane walk out of the room and the couple's bedroom vanished from sight, the waves around her suddenly started to become much choppier and it almost felt as if her heart had stopped completely as she struggled to keep herself above the watery surface as weakness suddenly seemed to sweep across and through her simulated form. In one painful day and night, Leah's whole world had been stripped from her in a single gut punch and that hurt would and could never be fixed, tweaked or corrected because the irreversible damage had already been done and Zidane had already left their relationship.

Sadly, Leah concluded as she gasped for air as she slipped below the water's choppy surface unable to hold herself against the waves for any longer, the very creation that was supposed to lubricate, enhance and usher in the couple's future had destroyed it because it had brought out the worst in Leah herself. Inside Spectrum, where Leah controlled her own environment and her own world much like a God, she had hidden her darkest desires and those desires, she now felt as she churned the events of the previous day around inside her mind had probably lain dormant inside her all along and when Zidane had discovered her deepest, darkest secrets, he had simply walked away in horror from her heart, her life and their future. Although the words that had been spoken directly to Leah by Zidane the previous night as he had departed had been sparse, the distance between the couple had been absolutely huge as he'd skirted around Leah's presence with minimal conversation and no physical or intimate interactions but from the scene that Leah had just watched, she could tell that his heart had suffered some very harsh injuries and that those wounds now ran very deep because his mind had seemed soaked and saturated in heartbreak which had ultimately, originated from the most unexpected source.

Unlike Leah's previous visits to Spectrum, she suddenly noticed that on this occasion, she could not see an exit menu and as she slipped further down into the watery depths, she could not see the bottom of the sea either as her airways and lungs quickly filled up with icy cold water which caused a flurry of panic to rush through her simulated form. For a few seconds panic, alarm and total confusion seemed to completely engulf Leah and fully gripped her senses as she struggled and attempted to thrash around inside the watery depths which she hoped might take her in an upwards direction but no matter how hard she tried, nothing seemed to change her predicament. Suddenly Leah's alarm started to heighten as she slipped more rapidly further and further down into the watery depths and as she sank, she began to frantically wonder, if she would actually be able to leave Spectrum that day because the provision of an exit now seemed like a very remote possibility which meant, Leah's chances of survival inside Spectrum itself felt extremely bleak.

An uneasy flurry of confusion, tension, alarm and panic continued to swirl around inside Leah's simulated form as each icy cold minute went by which seemed to last an eternity as she sank deeper and deeper into the water and frantically searched and searched for an exit point that did not appear. Just as Leah felt as if she might pass out however, she suddenly noticed that there was now an edge to the watery depths in the form of a smooth surface and although she had very little energy, she quickly swam weakly towards it. When Leah arrived beside the smooth surface which was a transparent aqua marine color, she eagerly stretched her hand out to touch it and then drew closer to it as she peered through the transparent surface but much to Leah's absolute horror as she tried to search for a way out, she swiftly realized that she was now stuck inside a crystal mountain inside the Bay of Wrath. In fact, the aqua marine crystal mountain, from Leah could see, was definitely a Crystal Mountain of Lost Souls because she could now see some of the other crystal mountains that surrounded it through the smooth transparent surface and not only that but it was in fact, the very same mountain that she had admired during her tour with Bearciple when he had shown her around the crystal mountains inside the large expanse.

Some tears of sorrow ran down Leah's face as she began to claw the shiny surface in a desperate attempt to escape the watery depths but as she did so, she began to slip in and out of consciousness and the water around her suddenly felt heavier and heavier and as if it was made from all her regretful tears. Sadly for Leah, she had definitely steered her own heart and mind in the wrong direction inside Spectrum and there was now it appeared, no escape from that very harsh truth as she began to accept that the detour of wrong that she had taken had cost her Zidane's heart which she had now lost through her own actions. Not only had Leah lost Zidane's heart however, it suddenly struck her as she struggled to breathe that she had lost something else even more important because inside Spectrum Leah had also lost herself, her own principles and her own moral values that had always guided her through life and steered her away from wrong and Leah regretted every single second of that departure and that harmful diversion that had now destroyed her life. In this particular instance, Leah now knew that there would be no return from the detour of wrong that she had taken because a route to forgiveness from Zidane's heart would not be provided and so as the crystal mountain surface became less visible and hazier and hazier, her eyes finally closed and then remained shut as Leah fully surrendered to absolute, guilty, shameful heartbreak and total defeat.

Printed in Great Britain
by Amazon

17215151R00447